58MS02: This is an engro___ ___ ___ ___ ___ ___
finish it later, as I had time to review it. However, ___ ___ ___
hours later, I had finished it, amazed at its effect. The story
captures you quickly, and won't let you go until you finish it.
That's good, and the author tells a great tale that is honest,
believable, and interesting from Chapter One through the end.
If you like historical fiction, you will surely like this volume.

49HL01: It held my interest, I didn't want to put it down. Just
when I thought I had some insight into one of the characters,
something would happen and I had to re-think my original
impression. I enjoyed it very much and anticipate sitting down
with it again.

47HL00: In the Brief Eternal Silence has some wonderful
passages, with great twists. The story-line is intriguing. . . .

37MS01: I liked the constant suspense. I also liked the
characters and story line. I found it hard to put down. This was
a great book packed with plenty of action and suspense.

You, too, can impact our publishing decisions!

Go to **doubleedgepress.com** and click on Public Library.
There, you will find manuscripts submitted to *Cutting Edge
Literary Services* by writers who are looking for publication.
Make a choice, read your selection, and then fill out a report.
It's free!

As we see manuscripts that grab readers' imaginations as this
title did, we'll publish them.

In the Brief Eternal Silence

Rebecca Melvin

Double Edge Press ™

Double Edge Press

ISBN 0-9774452-1-6

Printed in the United States of America

For Jesus Christ

Acknowledgments:

I wish I had a long list of people that helped me in my endeavor, but I really don't. I have the obvious, but incredibly important: my family.

To my mother and Tom, thank you for the encouragement.
To my brothers, Mike, Andy and Jerry, same goes.
To my children, Garrett, Austin, Coleman and Shelby, thank you for your patience, your love, and for not minding having dinner late so many nights. Thank you for being mine.
To my husband, Neal, thank you for being you. Without you, it couldn't have happened.

My greatest acknowledgment goes to Christ. He was there when that long list of people wasn't. Without You, Lord, I am nothing. Without You, my words would only be so many splatters on the page. Thank You for the words to write, the patience to endure, and for two important lessons (among many others):

I judge myself and find myself unworthy,
    but in the eyes of the Lord, I am perfect,
        for I am cleansed with the Blood of the Lamb.

And:

I am a woman of great blessing,
    for I am a woman of great faith,
        and the greatest blessing of all is faith.

Thank You for covering my imperfections. Thank You for blessing me with faith. Thank You for saving me, not just once, but every day I exist.

It's been a long, hard road.

In Christ,
Rebecca Melvin
November 14. 2005

Between the striking of the Lightning
and the rolling of the Thunder
There is a brief, eternal Silence

Between the firing of a Bullet
and the crack of the Shot
There is a brief, eternal Silence

And between actions taken
and consequences paid
There is a brief, eternal Silence

PROLOGUE
December, 1839

The ten year old boy sat in the finely upholstered seat of the coach. He was wrapped in an expensive coat of navy blue, tailored to fit his small shoulders and a matching blue silk scarf was wrapped about his neck and tucked neatly into the collar of the coat. He idly twirled at one of the many gold buttons down the front of the coat as he waited, his oddly colored hazel eyes glinting nearly as gold as the buttons in the dim light of the coach.

The door was opened from the outside, letting in more light from one of the torches that was lit, and the soft rustle of skirts told him that it was his mother just outside the door. "Is his Grace nearly ready, then?" he heard his mother asking the coachman. "Tell him that we await him in the coach and to try not to be long," and then she was climbing into the coach to sit next to him, her cheeks colored from the cold night air. She settled in, straightening her skirts and turned to him.

"Dante, darling. Does mummy look pretty tonight?" she asked.

"Yes, mummy," he agreed readily. "You look beautiful tonight." His ten year old face shone with adoration, which inspired her to pinch his small cheek.

"And you, son, shall be the terror of all the ladies in another year or two," she said with pride. Then, "Why, what's the matter? You look as though you are about to choke on something," for his eyes had lost their adoration and showed an inner, preoccupied look and his face turned a blotchy red.

For answer, he began to cough; two small wheezes followed by a great wrenching bark. He was aware enough of his mother to see her expression change from good natured indulgence to quick annoyance, but all he could do was wrench out a stream of coughs that sounded as though he were a dog, and which tore at his throat in painful intensity.

"Oh, heaven," his mother said with irritation. "The croup. Dante, you can not possibly have the croup. You haven't had that for ages." She paused, as though expecting him to admit to some joke on his part. But he only looked at her helplessly, his little hands at his throat, and coughed again.

With that, his mother rapped upon the window of the coach door, her knuckles pounding out a demanding tattoo. The door was immediately opened. "Take my son back into the house," she told the coachman dismissingly. "And have Mrs. Herriot attend to him. He has the croup."

"What is this?" Dante heard his father from outside ask. He peered into the open door. "Are you not well, son?"

Dante attempted to speak, "Just a cough—" and he wrenched out another bark, "father. I'm sure it will pass in a moment."

But his father was shaking his head. "Alas, no, son. We can not take any risk that your mother should catch it in her condition," and he said the last words with a tender pride. "Come now, up into the house as your mother has bid. You do not wish your new baby brother or sister to become sick before they are even born, do you?"

Dante could not argue with that. He had been in a perfect transport of joy at the news that he would soon become a brother when it had been announced at the family dinner table just three nights ago. He climbed from the coach. His mother followed.

"I shall just speak to the Dowager," she explained to her husband, "so that she shall know that Dante is to return to London with her at the end of her holiday."

"You should stay also," he urged.

"La—no," she answered. "I can not take another day, here, William, I swear I can not. Between your mother and our new sister-in-law, Lydia," and she shook her head. "I will be much happier in Town."

"But in your condition and traveling at night. I do not like it. It is not necessary, you know. You should stay and come up with my mother when she returns."

"Now we have been all through this already," she admonished. "We had planned on trying to be more of a family, and because Dante can no longer go does not mean that I cannot. Now, allow me to speak with your mother so that we may leave. You have pressing business, remember?"

Dante heard no more, for he went through the manor door, miserable that he would not be travelling with his father and mother. He was miserable as Mrs. Herriott was called for and he was shooed up into bed by that indomitable housekeeper. By the time his father came into the room, there was a bedwarmer beneath the blankets at his feet and a poultice wrapped about his throat.

"There you are, snug and warm," his father said as he came to his side.

"I'm much better, now, father. Mayn't I go?"

"No. The cold night air would only set you off again, I should fear. You remain here, where your grandmother may send for a doctor should the coughing return and be worse."

"It is just that I have hardly spent any time with you at all. Or mother," Dante sighed.

"I know, son," his father said and rumpled his hair. "I know that it is hard on you, but some day when you are older, you shall understand. There are things that must be done that are bigger than ourselves and even our loved ones. The Queen is counting on me and there are many lives at stake. I must advise her to the best of my ability so that she has good, accurate information to make her decisions on. And she must be very close to making a decision for her to have called me so abruptly over this holiday time. We would not get to spend much time together, other than the journey, at any rate, I fear. You shall be much better off remaining out your holiday here with your grandmother."

Dante only nodded, his eyes clenching shut in order to squeeze back any unmanly tears. "I understand, father" he coughed.

His father nodded, looking relieved. "Now, I must gather my briefcase and go. You shall look after your grandmother, shall you?"

"Yes, father, if you shall look after mother."

"I will do that," his father told him seriously. "Better than I have before. Of that, I promise you."

And although Dante did not know what that meant, it was enough for him to close his eyes without trouble as his father quietly left the room.

It was not until nearly noon the next morning that he was fetched from his room by Mrs. Herriott at the bidding of his grandmother. He had eaten breakfast from a tray and been allowed to move about quietly, but he had not been allowed far from his bed. Now the housekeeper knocked lightly and then opened the door. "Young master," she choked, her face blotchy and her eyes red, which alarmed the boy. "The Dowager asks for your presence in the study."

The study! Dante was over-awed at the thought of going through those doors into a room that was reserved strictly for adults and the conducting of adult business. But he was distracted by the agitated movements of the housekeeper, and her face which looked as though it had been weeping, and at the same time, bravely trying to staunch it. "Whatever is the matter, Mrs. Herriott?" he asked in his small, boy's voice as he went to the door which she held open.

"Your grandmother must speak with you," she whispered, and would say no more.

He left the room. The halls that were so familiar to him now seemed echoing. The huge clock at the head of the steps seemed to tick all the louder in the hush of the house. The pattern of the rug of the stairs, deep red with gold triangles, was impressed forever on his memory, so that when he thought about that day, years hence, he would see that pattern over and over in his head, the endless walk down those stairs, when he knew not what was coming, but was certain in his little boy's heart that something had happened that would change his life forever. Finally, along the main hall of the first floor, to the double doors of the study, which were opened for him by the butler of the house. "Your Grace," the butler said as he passed through that portal. *Your Grace*. He was never referred to as Your Grace. That was the title reserved for his father, the Duke of St. James.

"Dante," his grandmother bade from where she sat in a large wing-backed chair. Her voice trembled as she spoke. "Come and sit down, here, next to me. And try to be very brave."

Twenty-three years later
November, 1863

Chapter One
Sunday Afternoon

Miss Sara Elizabeth Murdock stroked the wet neck of the horse she was astride. It was a dun color that even the grey of the day could not mute. It shifted in eagerness but Miss Murdock's father at its head held it with expertise and it settled into walking again. "Do you think she'll be bothered by the slop?" Lizzie asked. "We've never had her on the track in the rain before."

The training track was just ahead of them, a level area not far from the stables that Lizzie's grandfather had cleared many years ago.

Her father seemed to consider his answer before saying, "I can't rightly say. Be cautious, but don't hold her in too much, Lizzie, love." He turned to look at her. "We need a good showing in this."

Lizzie nodded. "I understand. I had so hoped to race her before she became brood stock, though."

"Aye. I know it. But you know as well as I that we could use the brass. And if these gentlemen that are coming today are impressed. . . well, could be a right good turn to our fortunes."

"Or lack of them," Lizzie smiled. "Don't worry, father, it'll all come out right. I only hope she has at least a modicum of sense today. What is this man's name again? The one you met yesterday?"

"Tempton. From over Lincolnshire way." Her father looked over his shoulder at her again. The rain was running down the heavy, over-indulgent lines of his face and dampened the thick gray of his hair. He was portly, and the walk was making him huff. "But t'won't be him that'll be interested. A friend of his is supposed to be joining him and his brother. That's the one we want to impress. Tempton said this other fellow owns Behemoth."

"Behemoth," Lizzie breathed. "That certainly shows he knows his way around horseflesh. Unless," she frowned, "he's one of these in name only owners that leaves all the work to his grooms."

They arrived at the beginning of the oval, but there was no one else in sight. "Do you think they won't come because of the weather?" she asked.

"I don't know. We'll give them a minute, any rate." Her father stopped her mount and turned to come to her knee. "Get yourself settled in, Liz, and try not to be nervous. I know this isn't what you had in mind when you picked out this little filly, but at least we can maybe cut a deal where we can keep her."

"I know," she returned and fingered her hair more fully up beneath her riding cap. She was in breeches tucked into her boots, and the short jacket she wore was large on her. "But what use will she be once she's foaled is what I ask myself. Unless she has a really outstanding colt, she'll not be in demand as a broodmare either and I still can't help wishing we could have given her a shot at the track."

Her father chuckled. "And you would like to see if your training has been any good, I'd lief bet. Never mind, Lizzie. At least we can mayhaps get enough to see that you have a real dowry instead of a four-legged one."

"As if I have need of one at all," Lizzie countered but she grinned. "You'll not be rid of me as easily as that, father, even if you have a thousand pounds with which to entice the local gentry, instead of an untried filly."

But he didn't respond to her teasing, only said, "They're here."

"Oh," Lizzie said and turned in her saddle. A trio of men were moving up the lane, evidently leaving their mode of transportation, whether mounts or carriages, back at the stables. Two were tall, with wavy red hair, although one, the older looking one, was much stouter than the other. The brothers, Miss Murdock surmised. The third one was slender and not as tall. His hair was a dark shade of brown that, with the rain upon it and in contrast to the paleness of his face, appeared nearly black.

His coat was a heavy navy blue, with many capes, and it came down to the tops of his high riding boots. It was November and the rain falling was cold and Lizzie had a sudden wish that she were half as warm as he appeared to be. The stout brother was in a bright, nearly overpowering yellow coat. There was nothing significant about the tall, rawboned younger brother's attire except for a fine, shining gold watch chain that dangled in an extravagant loop from his pocket.

Lizzie's father took two steps forward to meet them. "Lord Tempton," he said, and pumped yellow coat's hand. "Happy to see the weather didn't keep you."

"No, indeed, Squire Murdock." He turned to pocket watch. "This is my brother, Ryan Tempton," and then indicating the other man, "and my friend, St. James."

Squire Murdock shook Ryan Tempton's hand as Lord Tempton was making the introductions, but he halted for a second, his hand half out-stretched, as the other man was named. "St. James?"

"Yes. The owner of Behemoth," Lord Tempton prompted.

The man designated as St. James extended his hand to the half-held out one of Squire Murdock. "Squire," he said. "Forgive us for being late but I fear I'm a bit hung-over and have a lethal headache. I didn't re-ceive word from Bertie of your filly until this morning and so did not have this meeting in mind last night."

"Well," the Squire answered. "I'm the last fellow to hold that against a man. Now, if you wish to take a look at our girl, here, go on and do so, and then when you're ready, we'll give her a run."

The two Tempton's remained back, but St. James went forward after thanking the Squire. The Squire went again to the head of the filly.

"Her name?" asked St. James as he ran his hand down the filly's chest and front legs.

"Leaf," the Squire answered.

St. James' hands moved back along the horse's barrel and he glanced up at the rider. Lizzie looked down and was met with a pair of startling eyes, an odd color that bordered between hazel and gold. They flashed for a second as she met his glance and his eyebrow lifted. "Rather unusual," he said.

And for some unaccountable reason, Lizzie felt herself blush.

"Aye. T'is indeed. But my, uh, daughter, um, named her. She's visiting right now, my daughter is. Not at home."

Lizzie tried not to start, and when she looked to her father, all too aware of the man that had passed behind her now and was feeling down her mount's hocks, her father only risked a slight shake of his head.

"I see," St. James said. Then he stood back from the horse. "Have your groom trot her about in a circle there, and then let her loose on the track, shall you."

"Yes, milord," The Squire said and turned to do as he had been asked. Lizzie, relieved to be doing something, had no time to wonder why the man called St. James had suddenly been elevated to 'milord' by her father. She was only concentrating on getting Leaf to go as smoothly as possible through her paces.

"What do you think, St. James?" She heard the yellow coat--Lord Tempton ask.

St. James ran a hand through his wet hair, raking it back from his eyes. "I think she should do, if the circumstances are right."

"It was only a cursory look at best," his friend muttered. "You have no idea what you may be saddling yourself with."

"And I said that if the circumstances were right that I did not bloody care. Really Bertie. You were the one that brought her to my attention."

Then Lizzie heard no more, for her father, with a glance at St. James, who nodded, called for her to walk the filly to the head of the track.

She settled into earnest business now, and despite herself, she could not help a surging thrill. No, it was not a race, and she was fairly certain her father would have drawn the line at her jockeying in one at any rate, but it was nearly as exciting to have spectators to what she had achieved with her training. Maybe they would be so impressed, she thought with giddy guilt at her fancies, that they would entrust her with some of their stock from their stables. But it all depended on Leaf, and Leaf could be woefully undependable.

Then the man, St. James, was there at her mount's head. He looked up at her for a moment and she still could not determine if he had realized she was a female rather than the boy she must appear. "Don't push her too hard in this slop," he advised. "I'm not looking for speed. If she impresses me enough with her action, I'll make a point of returning to see how fast she can go on a better day for it. Maintain control and keep her in hand. If she seems to be doing well with her footing then you may extend her on the last quarter. Understand?"

Lizzie, mindful of her father's inexplicable lie, only nodded. Then the man released Leaf's head. Lizzie gathered herself, could feel Leaf responding to her rider's intense focusing. They remained still for a second playing off each other through reins, legs and body movement, and then Lizzie loosed the reins and tightened her knees, bent her body forward and the horse hurled out into the middle of the track.

Lizzie controlled her, kept her steady as her feet slid around in the mud with her great effort to find her stride. Then she had it and her legs were extending and sailing about the track, and Lizzie half laughed with the wind stinging her eyes and the mud flying into her face. Her father and the other three men were forgotten. She only saw the faded grey of the rail as it flashed by, the overgrown infield of the track. Leaf was pulling hard at the reins and Lizzie's arms ached from the effort of holding her to a less reckless pace. The filly's feet hit the slop with more and more confidence and Lizzie relented and allowed more rein.

They swept around the first turn and in to the back stretch. The last quarter was coming up and Lizzie settled down tighter in the saddle. Now her concentration was total as she gauged every flying step of the filly. She was holding in the mud well now, but would she in the final turn? But the final quarter, which included part of the final turn, was where the man, St. James had allowed she could extend her. It was banked, Lizzie reminded herself, but it hadn't been graded for years. Still, she knew this track well, had spent innumerable hours out here with her father, and the filly knew it well also. There should be no problem.

She loosened the reins more, concentrating, wanting the filly up to her utmost speed as she entered the last quarter. They were half through the turn and the filly was still going easily through the heavy slop. Lizzie felt a burst of pride at how well her horse was doing. "Easy now, I'm going to let you out a little more." The track showed pristine in front of them, the mud unchurned and untouched. There was a puddle in their line but Lizzie could not think it was any more than surface water and should not be any deeper than the surrounding mud.

Leaf came up on the puddle, fully extended, running with grace and power. Her sudden spook to the side caught Lizzie unawares.

In mid-stride the horse attempted a sudden shy away from the water. The jump was awkward and bone-jarring and when her feet landed, they no longer were placed surely but skittered out from beneath her. Lizzie had kept the filly hugging the rail to make the best time and with a piercing shriek of panic, the horse slid into the fence.

The old boards splintered and broke. Lizzie flew from her mount and landed in the infield. Leaf went down into the midst of the broken fence and wallowed in an agony of confusion, her legs scrabbling as she tried to roll to her feet but was hemmed in on all sides with broken boards.

Lizzie was jarred hard in her landing. Her cap was half knocked from her head and the straps that were meant to hold it in place dug into the flesh beneath her chin. She rolled to her back, the mud seeping through her jacket and breeches to freeze her skin, and swiped at her eyes in an attempt to clear them of the mud that was ruining her vision.

She made an effort to get to her feet but her body refused to do more than allow her to sit up and that with a great deal of regret. Lizzie gathered herself, tried again and wasn't sure if all the pain she was feeling were coming from injuries or simply from the freezing mud that enveloped her.

"Lizzie! Are you all right?"

It was her father, running as quickly toward her as his stout figure would manage. With him, in front of him, was the man, St. James, and between he and her father were the two Tempton brothers, the younger one, Ryan, and then Bertie.

"Leaf," Lizzie called. "Get her before she does anything further to herself." And she was amazed to hear her voice so close to tears. She wasn't crying, was she? But with all the mud in her eyes, she couldn't tell.

"Ryan, get the bloody horse," St. James said. "You," he said as he came to her. "Stay still. I'm sure the horse will be all right and you needn't risk your neck trying to get to her when there are others that can take care of it." He crouched down beside her, and as she was still struggling to try and get her feet beneath her he placed both hands on her shoulders. "Stay still, you little fool. I knew I should have yanked you down from that damned horse as soon as I saw you were a female. If I had known you also couldn't control your mount, I most certainly would have."

"It was the mud puddle," she said, the freezing mud making her gasp. "I can control my mount." But he had turned his head, his hands still on her shoulders to check to see that Ryan had gone to the horse. Ryan had and Bertie as well and only her father was coming the last few panting strides over to the infield and them.

"Is she to be all right?" Lizzie asked.

"I don't know, but I will find out for you in a moment. Forgive me if I'm more inclined to be worried about her wretched rider for the moment."

"I'm surprised," Lizzie was still gasping, "that you are not more concerned about your wretched headache."

"This has certainly not done it any good. Now, are you hurt?"

"I'm not sure. All this mud is freezing and I can not tell if I am hurt or only suffering from the cold. Oh, please do tell them to be careful with her. I am sure they are only frightening her more."

"Try moving your arms. Pain? No? Your legs. Yes? Where?"

"My knee. I may have twisted it, I think."

"This one?" and he moved his hand to her right knee.

She flushed, was thankful for the mud on her face that hid it. "Yes. But really, I'm sure that if you can just give me a hand up that I shall be quite fine--"

"Please, milord, I must ask you to unhand my daughter," the Squire broke in as he arrived next to them.

St. James turned with a raised brow. "But, sir, this could not possibly be your daughter, for she has gone visiting, you know."

"Be that as it may," the Squire continued with a darkening expression, "I know who ye are and I'll not stand for any of your shenanigans with any of mine."

"Indeed?" St. James said. "My reputation precedes me, I surmise."

"Father?" Lizzie faltered.

"Never you mind, Lizzie, love. Are you able to get up?"

"Yes, of course. I only need a moment, as I was saying. . . . It's just all this blasted mud."

"Miss Murdock," St. James said, "as I now gather is your name, if you deem your father a reasonable substitute, I shall go and see about your horse."

"Yes. Indeed. Thank you," she answered.

He arose and her father stooped to take his place and Lizzie watched as St. James strode to where Ryan and Bertie had managed to calm her horse. He moved lithely and his voice was compelling and yet he was slender and did not seem powerfully built.

"Who is he, father?" she asked.

But he did not answer her question, only said, "I'd not have him here at all if it were not business." He gave her a glance. "Stay away from him, Lizzie."

She gave a short laugh. "I'm sure you have no worry upon that head. It is only the mud covering me that made me palatable in the least for if he saw me as I really am, he would have saved his concern for the horse."

"Aye. Well I daresay his tastes be a little more exotic. All the same, Liz. . . . But here," he added before she could interrupt, "try to get to your feet now, if you feel able." And he held out his arm to her.

Lizzie took it and between the two of them, they got her standing. "Let's get you to the house, lass, before you freeze."

"Leaf, first," she said.

He sighed, but moved them in the direction of the horse. Ryan was still at her head and Bertie seemed to be heatedly protesting St. James' suggestion that he help with removing the boards. "Nonsense," Lizzie heard him saying. "I'm sure there are grooms who will be out momentarily to help. I can't see mucking about in all this mud."

"Save your vanity, Bertie," St. James responded. "There is no one here to see you, save young Miss Murdock, and I am sure she will be happy to overlook any marring of your attire considering she is dressed as a man and disgustingly filthy."

"Thank you," Miss Murdock interjected.

He turned, startled, at her voice. "Miss Murdock, I apologize," he said. "It's just that Bertie is being difficult."

"What?" she asked, and then waved an irritated hand. "No. I meant thank you for helping."

His gold gaze arrested upon her for a thoughtful moment. "I see."

Then he turned back to consider Bertie. That man stood with his hands upon his hips, studying the scene of broken boards and downed horse with a grim shake of his head. "Bertie," St. James said, "allow me to relieve you of the cause of your reluctance."

"Now, St. James. No. No, please, don't do that."

But St. James stooped down and fisted a great handful of the mud that surrounded them and, straightening again, gave it a calculated fling onto the front of Bertie's yellow coat.

"Damn you, St. James," Bertie said, looking down at his sopping coat. "I utterly loathe you when you are this way. It was I that brought you here, you might remember."

"And, indeed, I am grateful."

"Oh, bloody hell take you. I'm sending you the bill for a new one."

"And I shall pay for it. Now grab a bloody board if you please." St. James stooped to his own work and Bertie moved to the other side of the horse and began pulling the broken boards from around it.

Miss Murdock, with the aid of her father, moved to where Ryan Tempton knelt at her horse's head. She managed to crouch down beside him, her limbs protesting and her body shivering. "There now, Leaf," she told the filly, "all will be well. I've a warm blanket waiting for you and we will get you out of this silliness soon enough." The horse made a small snuffle of resignation. Its neck muscles relaxed from the straining they had been exerting. Her ears pricked forward as Lizzie continued to croon soothing nonsense to it.

"Squire," St. James said as he worked at clearing the boards, "you'd best get your daughter to the house before she dies of the pneumonia."

"She'll be fine, milord," the Squire returned. "I've seen her take worse spills, and she's been colder. T'is not your concern."

But St. James turned with sudden ferocity at the Squire's answer. He grabbed the older man by the collar of his wool coat. "Let me make this very clear," he said. "I am not impressed with your daughter's inability to ride and the fact that between the two of you, you may have ruined a promising horse. Be that as it may, I am even less impressed with your lack of consideration for your daughter's safety or health. You show an exaggerated concern in regards to me possibly sullying her in some manner, but you have no care at all if her neck should be broken or if she should die from the freezing cold--"

"You can take your damned hands from me and keep your mind on the horse, miduke--" The Squire made an effort to remove St. James' hands from his collar. St. James, although he was in fact several inches shorter than the other man and a good deal lighter, held him fast and shook him.

"I should throttle you," St. James said, his voice savage. "When a perfect stranger such as I seems to have more care for both your daughter's and your horse's necks than you do, you need throttling."

"Here, here, St. James. You really can't be murdering the chap, you know," Bertie Tempton tried to soothe.

"And give me one reason why I should not, for I am looking at two reasons why I should."

Lizzie broke in, making an effort to remain calm. "Would you please kill him some where else if you must, for you are upsetting Leaf. Mister Tempton?" she said to the tall one with red hair. "Can you, at least, endeavor to help me in getting this poor horse out of this mess instead of throwing a tantrum and making everything worse? Thank you. I could see that at least you had a modicum of sense to you, however much everyone *else* seems to be lacking it."

St. James dropped his hands from her father's coat. He and the Squire squared off for a tense moment, and then St. James said, "Squire, be so kind as to start pulling boards from that side away from the animal. I'll take this side. Ryan, stay with Miss Murdock, for I can not believe she is in any condition to control that horse if it should panic again."

The Squire turned and walked stiff-legged to the boards indicated. Miss Murdock turned her attention back to Leaf and Ryan returned to his original position with her. Bertie muttered, "This all could have been avoided if only the damned grooms had come out to help as they should have."

"There *are* no grooms," Lizzie jerked out. "Just old Kennedy and he's in no condition to be doing any of this." And she wondered why she felt like crying again.

Then St. James was there, holding a handkerchief down to her. "Use it, Miss Murdock. If you insist upon remaining out here, you should at least clear the mud from your face. It's packed about your nose, you know, and I can not see how you are even able to breathe."

Lizzie took it less than graciously.

Chapter Two

Lizzie wiped her face with the handkerchief and returned her attention to keeping her downed mount calm. We need a good showing in this, her father had said. Well, they had not had a good showing. She wasn't even certain if Leaf were all right. There were no obvious fractures, but they wouldn't know until they attempted to get her to her feet.

She turned to the raw-boned young man at her side. "It is Mister Tempton, isn't it?"

"I beg pardon," the youth replied. He stuck an awkward hand out to her from his crouched position by her side. "Yes. I am Mister Ryan Tempton. That is Lord Bertram Tempton, my brother, and the other is Milord Duke of St. James."

"Mr. Tempton," Lizzie acknowledged. "I won't muddy your hand. I am Elizabeth Murdock and, as I am sure you have gathered, that is my father, Squire Edward Murdock." She peered with frank curiosity around to the man designated as the Duke of St. James. "So that is the infamous Duke," she commented to her companion. "He is hardly as threatening looking as I would have expected from all that I have heard of him. More like a spoiled bully."

"I rather like him myself," Ryan confessed. "And normally he does not throw such a fit, but he had been drinking rather indulgently last night, so I fear he is a bit short of patience today. But his reputation, I fear, is rather daunting. If I had not come to know him through my brother, I would probably have steered clear of him as so many of the peerage do."

Miss Murdock turned her attention back to the red-haired young man at her side. "It is true then that he owns Behemoth?"

"Yes. That is why he was naturally interested in seeing your filly. He wishes to turn Behemoth to stud soon and he is looking for quality mares to purchase."

"I see," Lizzie said, but she frowned. "Although we had hoped to keep Leaf and allow him only the foal. If the duke is interested in her, which I can barely credit after the performance we gave."

"Leaf?" Ryan Tempton inquired.

"Gold-Leaf-Lying-in-the-Sun," Miss Murdock elaborated. "A tad long-winded, but it was the only name that could adequately describe her beautiful coloring. Strangely, it suits her disposition also. She's always ready to be blown by whatever prevailing wind comes along, and lacks any real stability. In short," Miss Murdock laughed, "I fear she is a complete featherbrain."

"She also travels like the wind," Ryan offered.

Lizzie smiled and patted the filly's wet neck. "Yes, she does. And usually without running amuck into a fence. But she is not used to a muddy track and she was startled by her own reflection in a mud puddle. Not that that is any excuse," she clarified self-consciously, "for a rider should always be prepared, and I am afraid she caught me quite flat-footed. I should have realized she would react so foolishly."

Ryan paused and then asked, "May I ask what you were doing up on her on the track? It just seems a little. . . unusual."

Lizzie ducked her head, but before she could make known her reasons, St. James' voice broke in. "Yes. I was wondering the same. I take it you have no suitable groom, but there must surely be someone more qualified for this type of work available to your father. Someone, perhaps, more used to wearing breeches," he ended on a dry note.

Lizzie's cheeks were burning beneath the smears of mud that remained. "I understand, milord, that you are quite used to, I am certain, a deal of scraping and bowing, but please do not think that every one you meet is eagerly awaiting for you to order their lives for them. Leaf is my horse. I have trained her. I ride her. I am sorry if this does not suit your overzealous sensibilities. Indeed, I am a little surprised, I admit, to find the infamous Duke of St. James lecturing anyone on proper decorum."

"Are you quite finished, Miss Murdock?"

"Indeed, I am most decidedly finished."

"Then allow me only to say that perhaps as I have more knowledge than most of what costs there are to pay for a damaged reputation, I am better suited than most to lecture, Miss Murdock."

Lizzie met his eyes for another moment, her own brown ones rather large in her muddy face, then she turned back to tending her mount, unable to find any words that would help her to come back from that oh-so-casual set down. Her knee was aching, the cold had her teeth nearly chattering, and she had managed to not only have a Bad Showing with her horse but had managed to outright offend the man they had hoped to impress.

Ryan gave her a slight, sympathetic smile. Then the duke was crouched there between them. His coat spread, revealing his riding pants and polished black boots, now splattered with mud. Miss Murdock kept her attention carefully away from the muscles that showed beneath the tight material of his clothing. It was unlike her to be self-conscious, but she became very aware that she was wet and muddy and not in a proper dress. Her hair had come partially undone from the tight bun it had been in and the tendrils that hung down were as muddy as the rest of her.

"Shall we try to get her on her feet now, Miss Murdock?" St. James asked, and she was relieved to have his question interrupt her thoughts. She gave herself a sharp reminder that even if she had been dressed appropriately and cleaned of all mud, that she would not have warranted a second look from this man, or any man. Never had and probably never would. If she wasn't exactly resigned to being a spinster, she was certainly not going to be entertaining foolish thoughts about an uncommonly handsome man, that despite his reputation, she would wager, had enough females throwing themselves at him, without adding her plain, muddy self to the list. So when she replied, her voice was a little short, and her words were a little testy. "Certainly, milord. If you and Mister Tempton would kindly leave me room, I shall have her up in short order."

He raised his brows at her tone, but she was only grateful that he and Ryan Tempton did as she asked. Miss Murdock pulled on the bridle and coaxed the animal until the filly stood trembling, legs splayed apart. Then she took a minute to pat her, speak softly to her, and congratulate her on her success.

"Well done," she heard the duke behind her say. Miss Murdock felt an unexpected burst of pleasure that she had performed well and made up for at least some of her poor horsemanship of before.

She took one last measure of his lordship, his dark, soaking wet hair, his gold eyes, which met hers with a reflective glance before shifting to inspect her mount, raindrops clinging to their lashes. Now that he was standing, only his boots showed from beneath his coat, and although his figure was slender, she remembered the muscles in his legs and thought of him now as so much coiled and finely tempered steel, ready to spring without warning.

Miss Murdock smiled at her thoughts, telling herself that at least she could claim acquaintance with the notorious duke whose exploits, all unsavory, were bandied about even in this far off region of the realm, and that she had survived the encounter with at least a small success at the end of her unfortunate afternoon.

Old Kennedy, their only groom, had at last made appearance, and with some relief she handed him the reins. All the same, when he began to lead the horse slowly toward the stables, she followed, gimping, after him, her concentration on the filly's stride, watching carefully for any sign of limp or lameness.

"Goodbye, Miss Murdock," Ryan Tempton called.

She turned and waved a brief salute. Then she continued up the track, her shoulders hunched against the still drizzling rain.

Rather than letting up, the rain that had been coming down all day had intensified by the time St. James and his party made the five mile trek to the crossroads inn.

It was becoming dark, the horses they had hired out for their excursion (as they had all left their conveyances and teams at the inn's stable) were roundly disgruntled, and Squire Murdock, who had joined them, was less than enthusiastic with his choice of accepting the unexpected invitation to join St. James and the two Tempton brothers.

It was the filly, he supposed. Perhaps all was not lost after all.

His gout was acting up with the wet, and although a meal at the inn would be quite pleasant, he still missed being home in front of the fire, his foot propped up, with a glass of adequate if not exceptional rum to help him forget his discomfort.

But when a lord of high ranking, such as the Duke of St. James, requested one's presence, one did not lightly put him off, despite his reputation. Or possibly, even more so because of his reputation. So the Squire, sopping wet and miserable, found himself pulling his horse up in front of the inn and dismounting in the company of the duke, and Lord and Mister Temptons.

The private salon they were shown to helped bolster his spirits. The fire was built up and snapping. The table was set for three, but a chambermaid quickly added an extra plate, and the innkeeper assured the duke that food would be brought in shortwith. St. James, only dispensing of his riding gloves, but before taking off his great coat, poured into four glasses from a bottle of brandy. Yes, the Squire thought as he shrugged with difficulty from his own worn coat, things were definitely looking up. St. James offered around the glasses and the Squire accepted with gratitude. He settled himself in a seat at the table, feeling the steam rise from him as he began, at last, to dry out and warm up.

"Here's to a filly with promise," St. James said, lifting his glass. Then added, "If not ruined by the unfortunate episode I witnessed today."

The Squire raised his glass to meet the salute.

Lord Bertram Tempton, his red hair plastered to his head, but his yellow coat dispensed of and revealing him in all his brightly clothed glory, said, "I say, St. James. Told you was a good filly!"

"You did," St. James replied. "But forgive me if I have rather small faith in your eye for horseflesh." He set his glass aside, took off the caped coat he wore to reveal tanned riding breeches and a rather plain white shirt, its only adornment being lace at the cravat and cuffs. As his long fingers wrapped again around his goblet, the lace fell back to reveal the delicate whiteness of his skin. He was not tall, the Squire noted, nor was he powerfully built, but there was an air of intenseness about him, a feeling that the mind behind his dark locked brow was churning away at endless and complicated thoughts, that made his presence a little overwhelming. And intimidating.

The Squire, who viewed himself as a crusty old soul who made up for his rather slow intelligence with a bulldog temerity, found himself annoyed to be somewhat ill-at-ease in the younger man's presence. He wasn't used to rubbing elbows with the very *crème de la crème* of his society, true, but such things had never much mattered to him. He was an excellent shot and had a good seat on a hunt, and those two things, along with the fact that he was always willing to play a good hand of cards, and bet a good deal more than he owned, had always made him welcome company in the circles he chose to move in. But he found this circle to be a little above his comfort zone, and the only other in the room he felt any kinship to was young Mister Ryan Tempton, he of the tall, lanky, raw-boned build and hair a more shocking red shade than even his older brother's.

Bertie swallowed from his glass. "Well, much as I would like to say I discovered her on my own, I have to give credit to Ryan. He was the one that first brought my attention to her, and suggested that you may be interested likewise."

"Indeed?" St. James asked, turning to the young man that flushed a little under his gaze. "Very promising for someone fresh out of University. I shall have to take you with me on some of my scouting trips, young Ryan. You may be useful, if I can get to you before Bertie, here, does too much damage to your natural eye with his ill-conceived ideas of what to look for in a horse."

"Still say you can't go wrong with looking at color, St. James," Bertie replied. "Everyone knows a black can't run. And never have seen an all white horse do anything good over seven furlongs. Stands to reason you must start with at least something in between."

"And I beg to differ," St. James countered. "Behemoth is totally coal black, and has never been beat at a mile and above."

"Yes," Lord Tempton nodded, but wagged a finger. "But anything below that and he almost always loses. Why the hired nag I rode today could beat him."

"He's a distance runner. That is why I wish to breed him to a sprinter. See if we cannot get more early speed as well as stamina." The duke turned to the Squire. "Which brings us to your filly, Squire. Her times were impressive, considering the condition of the track. And the ill-advised rider up on her."

"Ah, Lizzie does well enough," the Squire defended. "Better than most. The filly is rather short on sense and long on spooking."

"Anyone could have ridden her into the rail today. That did not take much skill," St. James returned.

"I thought she handled the whole rather admirably," young Ryan broke in. "Anyone could see that the filly had the bit in her teeth and was not to be controlled."

St. James gave a small dismissive shrug, turned back to the Squire. "No apparent harm done, but I would like to see her again in the morning, make sure that she is sound, and, of course, any offer I make for her will be dependent on that."

There was a brief silence as the Squire opened his mouth, closed it again, and ran a hand through his heavy, damp, gray hair. "Uh, milord, I appreciate your interest, indeed, I find it very flattering that you should take such an interest in my horse. But--"

There was a tapping on the door, and then it opened and two chambermaids brought in several steaming platters of food. "Shall we dine?" St. James asked. "We can iron out any difficulties afterward."

With relief, the Squire pulled his chair in to the table and the other three men joined him. There was a well cooked leg of lamb, a side of filling with apple, boiled red potatoes, hare stew in a rich brown gravy, Yorkshire pudding, a dish of mixed vegetables and lemon cake. None of the four wasted time on conversation as they filled their plates. After being in the raw weather for most of the day, their appetites were mighty and the Squire spent a pleasant hour enjoying his meal, drinking further, and successfully pushing from his mind the fact that he was going to have to disappoint the duke and he was not looking forward to it.

They were just satisfying the final twinges of hunger with the lemon cake when St. James returned to the conversation of the Squire's filly. "You have other plans for the filly besides selling her, Squire?" he asked. He had pushed himself back from the table and, unlike the others, a great deal of the food remained upon his plate. He refilled his glass, for the fourth time, the Squire counted, and now sipped from it steadily.

A boozy bloke, for all his elegance, the Squire thought. Not that he could hold that against the fellow, being a rather boozy bloke himself. "Well, miduke. It's Lizzie that I'm concerned for. She doesn't wish to sell the horse."

The duke raised his brows. "Was I mistaken in believing the point of my visit today was to be, if I were satisfied, the acquirement of this horse? Bertie, is that not what you understood after speaking to this man last night?"

Bertie lowered his glass. "I told you all I knew, St. James."

The Squire drew himself up in his chair. "If that be true," he pronounced, "he would have told you of it being an iffy proposition, miduke." He took a hearty bite of lemon cake and when he spoke again, several crumbs sprayed out and down his immense stomach. "That horse is the only means I have of securing my daughter's future."

St. James was half slouched in his chair. His glass made a steady journey from table to mouth. "Indeed, that is what Bertie conveyed to me. What is your daughter's desired outcome for this horse, may I ask."

The Squire lost some of his stiffness and his hand again found his own glass. He had every appearance of a poker player settling in for the real play that may well take him into the wee hours of the morning. "She wishes to rent the filly out to you, so to speak. You breed her to your stud and receive the foal, but she keeps the filly. For a fee, of course."

"Of course. And your desired outcome? Does it differ from your daughter's?"

The Squire took a heavy swig that emptied his glass. "Indeed, miduke. It does."

St. James rose from the table, refilled the Squire's glass and his own. Bertie and Ryan demurred. Then the duke returned to his seat and his attention back to the Squire. And his gold eyes were now half-hooded as though already in deep thought. "You may begin, Squire. Tell me your concerns for your daughter and I will endeavor to come up with a solution that you may live with."

The Squire took a moment to look at the faces about him. Young Ryan, a slight frown of perplexity upon his face as he followed all of the conversation. Bertie, whose blue eyes met his with impassive reassurance. And St. James, whose half hooded eyes revealed nothing, who lazed in the chair, his legs stretched and crossed in luxurious languidness. And the Squire hunched a little defensively in his seat, his only seeming comfort the regularly refilled glass in front of him. With a feeble gathering of courage, he said to St. James, "I don't much like you. I've heard enough about you even in this far-flung region of the realm to know that you are more devil than saint you are titled."

"Indeed, I have never denied it," St. James returned.

"I did not know it were you I would be dealing with. Your man, friend, whatever he is, failed to include that bit of information."

"Indeed, if you have other takers you prefer, I do not see them here before you." St. James lost his air of languidness as he sat abruptly forward. "Come, Squire. Need I sum up what I have surmised and which you are now so reluctant to put into words? It is your daughter's future you are concerned for, yes, as you had said. But I daresay your own nest could use some feathering also."

"Do not damn me with that tongue of yours," the Squire said. "If I am simply more aware than Lizzie that our circumstances can not be adequately improved by the mere renting out of the horse as she supposes, it is hardly something for which I may be condemned for."

"I do not understand," Ryan broke in. "I mean, I understand, of course, that you do not wish to upset your daughter and that she has become attached to the animal. But as her father, surely you have the final say in what happens to it?"

"Indeed, I do not," the Squire admitted. "The horse was bought with money set aside by her mother for Lizzie's dowry. I can not in all decency do whatever I like with it."

"Decency?" interrupted Lord Tempton. "It is hardly decent to spend the girl's dowry on a horse, Squire, in case that escaped your notice."

"Aye. Well it is done now," Squire Murdock replied. "There was no arguing with her reasoning. She is my daughter and all, but even I was forced to admit that her having a suitor is unlikely and with each year that goes past is more unlikely still. She wanted the horse, saw it when it was just a foal, and said that in the doubtful event she ever did get a suitor, well then the horse could be her dowry.

"Aye! Scoff if you want," he added as Bertie snorted. "But the child has nothing else to occupy herself with, and that money sitting there for her dowry was bringing her no happiness. But now I fear the small bit I had put back has been run through and with no prospects for Lizzie. . . ."

"Surely she must have some suitor," Ryan interjected. "She seemed like quite a likable lass to me. Whatever could be wrong with her?"

"Yes. What is wrong with her?" Bertie asked, dabbing his mouth with a napkin as he spoke. "Couldn't see more than two eyes in her head, she was so covered with mud, but she was not over-large. She was neither humped-backed nor broken-toothed. Surely, she can not be as homely as all that?"

"No, no. Of course not," the Squire hurried to say. "I am her father, but I tell you quite honestly that she is nothing worse than plain. Nothing really wrong, just nothing really *right* if you know what I mean. Brown hair, brown eyes, skin too brown from being outside in the sun over-much. If her mother were still alive, well, perhaps she could have done something for her. Kept her indoors, did her hair more attractively, sewed her the proper dresses and taught her how to be more lady-like. But I fear that she's run wild for the past seven years, and I can do nothing with her, even if I knew what it was I was supposed to do.

"And to make matters all the more bad, she will not even consider going to London for her coming out, and now that she has had her twentieth birthday this past spring, I fear it is nearly too late for her."

"She won't have her coming out?" Bertie asked. "I thought all girls lived and died for that nonsense."

"Well, if she were the normal sort, I guess that would be true, but she says she can think of nothing more appalling than trying to be something she is not and perhaps actually duping some poor fool into marrying her, and then after the wedding he would find out what he had actually married, and then wouldn't she be to blame for deceiving him to begin with?"

This brought a startled laugh from St. James and an answering guffaw from Lord Tempton. Ryan merely looked a good deal puzzled.

"Good God!" Bertie exclaimed. "A right odd one. Never thought any of those women had any feeling for the poor groom other than how deep his purse was and how they can go about spending it. I told you, St. James, how my cousin's new bride set about redecorating their London home and is insisting on an entire new wing being added to their country estate! T'is no wonder he is always at White's trying to get a little entertainment for his money before she manages to run through it all. And hardly married a year!"

"You act as though I should be shocked to hear it, Bertie, when you well know my feelings on the matrimonial state. Merely a business proposition, and there will always be one in the party left feeling that he or she did not get quite the bargain they deceived themselves into thinking they were getting," the duke replied. "No, Squire, if I were you I would disabuse your daughter of such foolish notions, for no doubt, she would be getting a great deal less than what she thought also, and hence, they would be even."

"By God!" Ryan interjected, sounding exasperated. "Whatever has happened to love?"

The other three in the salon turned to look at him, a great deal surprised. "Love?" Bertie asked. "Why, what in the world does that have to do with marriage?"

"Pshaw!" the Squire added. "Well and good for a young man fresh out of University to dream of such, but we're talking marriage, my boy. No place for it there, if a man is a wise man! Why, it's difficult enough to keep the wife in line without being besotted by her in the bargain."

"They are quite right, young Ryan," St. James added. "Love is best kept for those little indiscretions on the side. Much easier to be rid of the object of your passion once the passion has waned and you realize you really can not bear to look at the girl another moment. Can you imagine waking up feeling that way one morning and realizing she is your *wife*?" His slight frame shuddered at the thought. "No. Much better to go into marriage with someone pleasing enough that you can do your duty as a husband and procure heirs, but not in the least under illusions of love. Makes, I imagine, for a much better union than otherwise."

"Listen to St. James, my brother," Bertie waved a glass in the direction of the duke, who at the end of his words, had gotten up from his seat to open yet another bottle of brandy. "For he has escaped the clutches of anxious mama's and besotted young beauties for many years now."

"But," Ryan began, looking somewhat chastised, "I always believed it was because you had not found one yet that you truly loved."

That brought a rude bark of laughter from St. James, one that made him spill onto his wrist some of the drink he was pouring. He put the bottle down, switched his glass to his other hand and raised his wrist to his mouth and licked the brandy from it before turning to Ryan. His eyes were dancing, or possibly it was just the fire from the grate reflecting in the gold of them. "You credit me with more feeling than I possess, I assure you, young Tempton. When I marry it will be for no other reason than that I have come to a point that I deem it desirable to do so. Any available baggage at hand will fit the bill then. I will not care what she looks like or behaves like, as long as she has enough intelligence to be a mother to my children." He gave a deep frown before continuing. "Actually, I would require that she have rather more intelligence than usually found in our fairer sex, for it is quite possible, likely even, that she would have to watch over my estates and affairs until my heir was old enough to take care of what was his."

There was silence after this remark. The Squire, of course being not at all familiar with the duke and his odd takings, could only believe that the amount of liquor he had been consuming had put him in some dark mood. As if in agreement with his thought, Lord Tempton said, "Don't get gloomy on us, St. James. T'is only too much drink, you know."

For answer, St. James downed the contents of his glass, which he had just finished pouring. "Not enough is my take on the situation, Bertie, old boy. Care for another while I am pouring?"

"No. For if you are going to be in for a taking again tonight, then it is my duty to stay sober and keep you out of the trouble you are always wont to get into. Blast you, St. James!" he said. "You sore wear my patience. Just for once, I should be allowed to drink myself silly, and you should have to stay sober and keep an eye out for me."

"Why, Bertie, I do believe you resent me, and I have no idea why. Have I not always been ready to stand by you through thick or thin? And even when I am drunk, have I ever failed in my duty to you?"

"No. Too damned quick to fulfill it is the problem when you're drunk. You see slights where there are none, and insults where there are only slights."

St. James grinned. "Perhaps my perceptions are merely more acute, rather than askew. But leave it as you would like to believe, I would not let it stop you from drinking tonight, for what trouble can I possibly get myself into? I am here among my friends, have no place to go and nothing pressing to do. So you see, we are all quite safe and you can imbibe to your heart's content knowing I am safely under wraps."

For answer, Bertie pushed his glass forward. "Fill it then, and damn you while you're at it. There will be trouble and you know it better than I."

"Posh! We shall now find out," St. James said.

Bertie took his glass without further comment and drank from it.

"I was thinking, Squire," St. James turned to that man. "Your daughter shall keep her horse and you shall secure her future. And I shall get what I am in need of also."

"Here we go," Bertie said. "You have as much subtlety as an axe, St. James."

"Hush, Bertie. This appears to be promising. Squire, do you wish me to continue?"

The Squire felt a little quiver go up his back. His mouth was dry, despite his drinking, and he suddenly felt the amount of alcohol he had been consuming was too much. "Aye, miduke. You may continue."

St. James seated himself. His voice, when he again spoke, was low and pointed and the glimmer of the gold of his eyes seemed ominous and forbidding. "First, tell me of your daughter. Is she intelligent? And you will tell me the truth of this."

The Squire gave a shiver. He wanted to ask why it mattered, and if he were really the one to measure the intelligence of another, being not the sharpest knife in the drawer himself, and where was this question to lead at any rate? Instead, he knotted his brows, looked to the ceiling, finding himself unable to meet that shuttered, elusive, golden gaze, and said, "Well, miduke, she took over the accounts when she was fourteen, the year after her mother died. Wasn't much good at them myself, I admit," he added.

"That is a start," the duke agreed. "Go on."

"And she knows her way around horseflesh. I saw no promise in that filly at all, if you must know the truth, but Lizzie, she said, that's the one, and she's turned into a right runner, she has."

"Can not be but an asset in my eyes. Continue."

The Squire scratched the top of his head. "Don't know what else. She's a good housekeeper, but she can't sew worth a lick. She can shoot well enough for a girl, better than most, but I've never seen her hunt. She can cook well enough, but not without getting soot smeared all over her. She can muck out a stall as fast as pretty near any man I've ever seen," he ended on a slightly triumphant note.

The duke stared at him for a long moment. "Lovely," he said at last. "You have just described your daughter as a glorified scullery maid with a little stable groom mixed in. But what any of that has to do with her intelligence, I can not fathom."

The Squire flushed. "She's smart enough to know how to make a month's worth of coal last all winter, and a single joint last all week, if you must know. She's smart enough to know how to make roast one day, take the leftovers and make stew the next, take the leftovers from that and add a little pastry and make potpie the next and take the leftovers from *that* and make vegetable soup the next. And if that doesn't give you an idea of how poorly our situation truly is, I can tell you that she was smart enough to tear out her mother's flower garden and plant vegetables instead and she's bullied our one remaining groom, old Kennedy, to raise chickens and hogs in the back sheds.

"So, milord," and his lip curled as he finished, feeling the bite of his humiliation at the extent that he had exposed his poverty to these men in their fine clothes with their fine estates and fine London homes, "she may not have the book-learning you were asking after, but she's intelligent enough to keep a roof over our heads and food on our table with my limited income, and for me, that is good enough."

St. James made no answer, just raised the lids of his eyes for a brief second giving the Squire the full impact of his piercing gaze, then he turned with considerable nonchalance and poured himself another brandy, and in turn refilled the Squire's glass, Ryan's glass, and then Bertie's glass.

"There you go, St. James," Bertie said when the pouring was finished. "So now you may put an end to this before it goes any further."

"An end? No, Bertie. It just begins." St. James raised his glass in salute. "I say, she'll do."

Chapter Three

Bertie let out a groan. "Egads, St. James! Can I not convince you the whole scheme is foolhardy? And you have done nothing but drink since we arrived here. It is already past midnight. Go to bed, I say, and sleep it off. If it is still what you wish to do, you can be at it tomorrow. But I guarantee you, you will be glad you left it all unspoken tonight."

"What? Left what unspoken?" Ryan asked. Through much of the preceding conversation, he had sat slumped to one side of the table, stifling his yawns, but now, feeling he had obviously missed something, he sat up and asked again, "Whatever are you two talking about now?"

"We are talking about the same thing we were talking about earlier, young Ryan," St. James told him. "Marriage."

"Marriage?" Ryan echoed.

"Marriage?" the Squire asked also in a surprised voice.

"Marriage," Bertie sighed.

"Yes. Marriage," St. James repeated. "Squire, I'll ask for your daughter's hand in marriage and take the horse as her dowry."

"By God, I think you mean it! You want the horse that bloody badly?"

"Do I want the horse that badly?" St. James mused to himself. He looked into his glass to see if the answer were there. "Yes. I think it amuses me to say I want the horse badly enough that I would offer for the daughter of a Squire. Plain, scullery-groom girl that she is."

"You can not be serious, St. James!" Ryan exclaimed. "You are jesting us, surely. Even you can not want a horse badly enough to marry someone you have only seen once, and then she was covered with mud!"

"Why not, young Ryan? You yourself professed her a likable lass."

Ryan flushed, looked at his brother as a weatherman looks at a barometer. Bertie shrugged. "Have another drink, St. James. Perhaps you'll fall flat on your face before this goes any further."

St. James did take another drink, a long one. Where his movements of before had seemed slow, they were now sharp and agitated. He was very drunk, as Bertie had observed, drinking perhaps three drinks to every one of theirs, only the Squire keeping up with him. That he was still standing seemed unnatural, an abomination even. What man could put that much poison into his body and still be upright, alert, talking coherently? Pouring yet another?

"You have no objections, Squire?" the duke asked after a moment.

"What?" Squire Murdock asked with obvious befuddlement. "Marriage? You mean my Lizzie to *you*?"

"Why, yes, of course. I thought I made it clear, but perhaps I did not. I offer for your daughter, as I said."

"My Lizzie marry *you*?" the Squire asked again, with seeming growing disbelief instead of lessening.

"Yes. Yes. Your Lizzie to me. Come. Do not say that you had no hope of such in mind."

"Indeed, I did not," the Squire answered with florid face. "Not bloody likely with *you* at any rate!"

St. James let out a brief chuckle.

Becoming aware of Ryan's look of shock, the Squire hastened to explain. "It was possible, I thought, that Lizzie could be attractive to someone with a common interest." He paused and then continued in impatience. "They would've been thrown together a good deal. Stranger things have happened. And she *is* likable. A regular wit and sensible as the day is long."

The Squire halted as he took in their silent faces. Then to St. James he said, "Marriage, damn you. I'll have nothing less for her and my circumstances can be hanged."

"I assure you, Squire, it will be marriage."

"And whatever filth you're into, you are to keep well away from her!"

That brought a tight-lipped smile from St. James. "Indeed, there is a great deal of filth. I have no intention of allowing her to know of any of it."

The Squire gave him a hard stare, then he dropped his head to rest in one hand, his gray hair glinting in the lamp light.

St. James appeared unmoved at this pitiful sight. "Squire," he insisted. "Do I have your permission to wed your daughter?"

The Squire did not lift his head, but murmured, "Proper amount of time. . . . Proper placing of banns. . . . Several months down the road. . . ."

"No. No, no. That will not do at all," St. James mused. "Tonight, I think. The border is not all that far from here. If I start out now, we should make it by tomorrow eve."

The Squire hunched further in his chair and let out a small groan.

"St. James!" Ryan gasped. "You can not be serious! Think of the girl involved if you can not think of anything else. You can not go and haul her from bed in the middle of the night and take her to Gretna Green with you. She has no chaperone for one, and, and, Well! It is just not done. It is not civilized!"

"By tomorrow night it will not matter if we are chaperoned or not," St. James replied and he pulled the brandy bottle up to his mouth, drank deeply from the mouth of it, as though to show just how uncivilized he could be.

"Why?" young Ryan asked incredulously when the older man replaced the bottle, the level of its contents quite a bit depleted. "Can you just tell us why, for God's sake, you have taken this notion into your head?"

"Of course, young Ryan. I like the horse. Very much," he added with a tight smile. "That's reason enough, don't you think?"

Ryan could only shake his head, feeling quite a bit disillusioned. "I always thought. . . ." he trailed off.

More gently, the duke asked, "What, Ryan? What have you always thought?"

With defiance, Ryan raised his head. "That the tales about you were exaggerated, that you were not. . . were not as bad as all that--"

His words were cut off by a great laugh from St. James. "Oh, but they are true!" he said, wiping his eyes with his sleeve. "They are all true. I am that bad and much, much worse, young Ryan. So, enjoy my company, but never forget the entertainment I provide is usually the shocking sort. I'm bad enough to take a young girl from her bed in the middle of the night and haul her unchaperoned to Scotland at my whim." He reached an arm out for the Squire. "Come, Squire Murdock. T'is time for me to collect your daughter, and I would rather you were there to smooth the way."

Ryan turned to Bertie. "Aren't you going to stop him?" he asked a little desperately.

"No," Bertie replied, refilling his glass. "For I have never been able to stop St. James once he has taken a notion into his head. And if it is not her tonight, it will just be another on another night. Let him be, Ryan. This is what he wishes to do."

"And you agree with him?" Ryan asked, incredulous.

"Agree with him? No. Not at all. But I know from experience there will be no changing his mind."

The Squire rose to his feet. He was drunk and more than a little confused. But, by God, Lizzie would have a husband. He may not be all that he should be, but at least he was well-set for blunt. And if Lizzie could not stomach him, she could come home again, and bring his damned money with her.

St. James eyed his large, swaying form. "Well, I shall certainly have suitable company, in any event," he commented. He walked to the door, opened it, barked out a single call into the dark of the inn's hallway. "Tyler! Damn it, Tyler. I have need of you. Now!"

A door was heard opening, and then closing, further down the hall, and then a large man loomed in the doorway, dwarfing his employer.

"Aye, milord," he said, rubbing the sleep from his square, craggy face. "What's your pleasure?" and his voice sounded of resignation, as though he had been summoned from his sleep many times before at the request of the duke.

"I'll need my curricle brought around, if you please."

The groom tugged on his cap and without any further answer retreated back down the hallway to make his way to the stables.

There was a brief silence in the room as they waited. St. James picked up the Squire's coat, threw it to him. Then he put on his own, lurching a bit at the task and the booze awash inside of him. Still, he stood straight, and if his face was haggard and paler than usual beneath his dark hair, it only served to make his eyes seem all the more poignant in his dissipated face.

It seemed a very short period of time before the groom came back, announcing that all was ready, and the duke took the Squire's thick arm into his hand. Just before they passed through the door, he turned to look at young Ryan, whose worried eyes were following his every move. "Don't forget, either, young Ryan, that I have my reasons," St. James told him, and then the door was closed behind them.

Ryan turned to his brother. "What reason could he possibly have for this?" he asked, feeling very much indeed, young and wet behind the ears.

For answer, Bertie pushed the remaining bottle of brandy toward his brother. "I fear I know what his reasons are. I pray to God I am wrong," he said. Then he let out a long stream of curses that was very much at odds with his usual boisterous banter and finished with, "God help him."

"God help her, you mean," Ryan said.

"No," Bertie replied. "Whatever else happens, she'll be taken well care of, lucky lass. No. God help him."

"Milord," Tyler began. "Slow down, or t'bloody fool you've carted a-long will be splattered all over t'road!" He was perched on the back of the curricle as was the norm, but instead of holding onto the frame with both hands, he was trying to hold the drunken Squire in the vehicle.

"Good God, Tyler, complaining again, are you?" St. James asked. He slowed the horses to a hard trot and out of the gallop they had been in. As there was only a half moon to light the road before them, Tyler was relieved for more than the Squire's sake. "Out cold, is he?" St. James asked.

Tyler gave the Squire a shake, got only a half-snore, half-grunt as response. "Aye. Right out of it, he is, milord. Nearly made me swallow me chaw when I saw him listing half-way out of t'curricle on that last turn. Grabbed him in just a nick of time."

"Well, would never do to kill my future father-in-law before the nuptials even take place."

Tyler made a gagging noise and began to cough. When he gained his breath and his composure, he said, "Now, I *have* swallowed it, thanks t'you! Are you trying t'kill me?"

St. James threw him a look, half laughing, half concerned. "I apologize, Tyler. Didn't mean to shock you like that. But you should know it's the only logical next move. I've tried everything else to no avail, and lately, I have come to think this is the only way to flush the bastard, whoever he is, out."

Tyler thought hard on this for a moment, and then said quietly, but with enough force to be heard over the horses' hooves, "I hope you're wrong, milord. T'is possible, you know, that t'fiend is dead, and that is why everything you have tried t'learn his identity has come t'naught."

"It is possible," his lordship said, "that he is dead. It *has* been twenty-three years. But I can't believe that after all I have done, that I would not find some trace of him. No, Tyler. I think whoever I seek is alive and well and continues to make sure that I find no clue to his identity."

"But, to marry. Forgive me, milord, but that implies. . . ."

"I know what it implies. I've always been reluctant to look in that direction, but I have hit so many dead ends that I am left with no option, God help me. I pray that I hit another dead end with this, but God help whoever it is if I do not."

They drove on in silence for another mile, only the Squire's snoring interrupting them, before Tyler broke the quiet by saying, "Your grandmother will be happy, I dare say, milord. If you are serious."

"I'm serious. And I expect you're right. She will be happy. But she can't know the reason for this marriage, Tyler. Not that I couldn't trust her to play the game to perfection if I were to ask her to do so, but for obvious reasons, it would hurt her too much if she knew what I was really about. No. She must think I came down here, met this Miss Murdock, and fell madly in love with her. And if there is a guilty party among those I hold closest to us, they must believe the same. Only if they believe it is a natural and unplanned occurrence will they mayhaps slip off their guard and, hopefully, make a rash move."

"They may very well make an attempt on your life, milord."

A single glance from drunken gold eyes. "I certainly hope they shall, otherwise this is all so much waste." He turned back to his driving. "Now, we shall collect my future wife, and we shall see if this last ploy puts the proper pressure on the proper person." St. James shook off a sudden weariness that came across him. "Damn me to hell for drinking so much," he muttered. "I am so foggy I am not the least bit sure how to go about this. I would have done myself a good deal better if I had allowed myself to retain a clear head."

"Aye, milord. Expect no sympathy from me. I've told you many a time before that no one need make a move on you for they merely need to sit back and wait for you to do yourself in. If not from the drinking, then from the dueling. And if not from the dueling, then from the womanizing. You'll get a pox one of these days, of that I am certain. And if not from that, then from your trips to the sorry side of town. I know you have your reasons, but you must have a care, milord."

"There will be no care in me until I have put an end to this. I dare not even try to live until I am assured that he is dead, and by my hand! And you, of all people, should know that every stunt I've ever pulled was in the pursuit of finding that knave. So let me hear no more of care and caution from you. For if I do stir them from their hiding place with this marriage, then the last thing I need to be feeling is some fear for my life, for if I am afraid, he has won already, for it will keep me from doing what musts be done with the single determination that I have always pursued it."

"That, I suppose, is why you have chosen a lass you do not know and do not care for?"

"Precisely, Tyler. I can not go into marriage believing I am building something for the future, for it may very well be a future that I will never see. And I don't wish to leave a grieving widow in my wake, in any event. Someone with a good head on her shoulders, who can care for my estates and my child, if we are lucky enough for her to conceive before I am killed."

"And if you are not killed, but succeed?"

"Then I will make do with whatever pathetic lot I have saddled myself with, and count myself fortunate." He pulled up on the horses, and they skidded to a halt so quickly that the Squire would have been thrown from the curricle if it had not been for Tyler holding him. "Was that a lane there, Tyler, on your right?"

Tyler peered into the dark. "Aye. And a sorry looking, overgrown one t'is, too."

"That's the one we want," St. James nodded. He backed the horses, chirped them around, and then started at nearly the same ill-advised speed that he had traversed the main road.

Chapter Four
Monday Morning

Lizzie was roused from her sleep by a determined knocking on the front door. She peered, confused, from between the heavy, closed drapes of her bed, noticing first the still solid darkness beyond her window. It was not dawn, looked to be several hours from it, at least.

The knocking came again, proving it had not been a dream. As she was alone in the house, it was up to her to fling back the bed-drapes, wrap herself in her robe, thrust her feet into her heavy wool slippers, and go below to answer the pounding summons on the door, which was still repeating itself after every few seconds.

She hurried from her room and down the long hallway to the top of the stairs that pitched rather sharply down to the front of the house and ended a few yards from the front entrance. In the dark, for she carried neither lamp nor candle, they seemed more prone to awkwardness than even what they normally did, and she caught herself once against the wall peeling of paint. Miss Murdock paused at the bottom stair, then turned and went into the parlor, pulled the drape back from the window to allow her to see who was demanding entrance in the wee small hours of the morning.

A high curricle stood in the drive, looking skeletal in the wan moonlight of the night. The team of horses at its front were lathered and blowing, showing they had been driven hard. A tall figure was to its side, his cap indicating him to be a groom, and a portly silhouette of a man was pitched far to one side on the seat, the groom attempting to help him down. Lizzie recognized this indisposed man as her father, even in the darkness, and with a little groan of exasperation, she delayed no longer but went again to the hallway and to the front door, of which the pounding had returned with a vigor.

She pulled her robe belt tighter, ran a hand through her loose hair, in some attempt to make semblance of it, and flung the door open. A deep flush took hold of her features as she recognized the man in front of her. There was no mistaking the dark, unruly hair, the laconic dissipation of his face, or the glimmering brightness of his gold eyes. "Milord," she said, feeling both shock and resentment that he should forever be seeing her when either muddy or mussed. She was also certain that whatever difficulty her father found himself in that this man was directly responsible. "What has happened to my father?"

"A bit of drink, Miss Murdock. You are indeed Miss Murdock?" he asked, and when she nodded, he gave a mocking bow in her direction. "I apologize, but you were quite unrecognizable upon our first meeting. But as I was saying of your father, a tad too much drink. If we can endeavor to get him inside and in bed, he will be better in the morning, although in all probability, well and truly hungover."

Miss Murdock, smelling a strong stench of booze coming from her informer also, said, "I will fetch a lamp then, and be with you," which she did, getting one from the parlor and lighting it. When she returned to the door, the duke was beside his curricle, and between he and the groom, they managed to alight her father upon his feet between them.

She hurried to light their way, and with the Squire's arms slung around their shoulders, an awkward picture, as the groom was taller than the Squire and the duke was shorter, they stumbled toward the front steps and the house.

Miss Murdock said nothing as they made slow progress, merely listened to a long string of whispered cursing from the duke, and an answering admonishment from the groom that if his lordship were not so drunk himself, the task would have been all the easier.

"And if the man did not weigh close to twenty stone, it would be a good deal easier also," the duke returned in an aggravated voice.

"Perhaps I should rouse Kennedy from the stables," Miss Murdock suggested as they all stopped before the stairs. There were only six flagstone steps up to the front door, but they suddenly seemed very long to her and she knew from prior experience that they seemed impossible to the two men that were supporting the considerable weight of her father.

"No, Miss Murdock," the duke replied. "We will manage, I believe." He moved one of his hands from supporting the Squire and made a quick swipe at his face with the sleeve of his coat, wiping it clean of the sweat that was upon his brow. Then his gold eyes beaconed at her. "I apologize, Miss Murdock, for the condition of your father. But I assure you, although I did the pouring, he did the drinking."

"As did you, I should hazard to say," Miss Murdock returned tartly. "But do not blame yourself too much," she relented, seeing his quick frown, "for I allow that it is not the first time he has come home in such a condition, nor, probably, will it be his last. I must confess myself grateful that at least you and your man are here to shoulder the burden instead of myself and old Kennedy, as it normally is."

He gave a slight, amused smile at that. "Well then, Miss Murdock, if you and an elderly groom can manage, then it seems that we must, for it would never do to have it said that we can not even take on a task that an old man and a wisp of a girl can do."

She didn't return his smile, her face remaining solemn as she answered. "Yes, milord. But we are not usually drunk when we are attempting it."

"All the more is the pity. Come, Tyler. Let us get him up and in, for I'm afraid my shoulders are becoming quite numb from the supporting of him."

"Any time you're done jawing, milord," the groom returned. "T'was not I, I remind you, that needed a rest."

The duke grunted, and then with Miss Murdock again going before them, they started up the steps. Again the only sound was muttered oaths, and an occasional, "Watch it, damn it, Tyler, or we'll all be flat on our faces!"

They managed at last to get the Squire to the top and in the front door, which Miss Murdock closed behind them, relieved to be out of the cold, for if the duke and his groom were sweating from their exertion, she was freezing with only her robe and sleeping gown on. "His bedroom is above stairs," she couldn't resist saying as she saw his lordship eyeing the steep, long stairs with every appearance of loathing.

"Very funny, Miss Murdock. You will not convince me even in my present condition that you and your groom manage to get him up those stairs and tucked neatly into bed!"

She couldn't help but smile as she shook her head. "Indeed, we do not, nor would we be silly enough to try. If you will just bring him into the parlor, he will be quite comfortable on the sofa. He normally sleeps there at any rate, for when his gout is acting up, he does not go up the stairs even when he is sober."

"You have my eternal gratitude."

It took some comic maneuvering to get her father through the parlor door, as it was narrower than the main entrance, but at last they succeeded and with twin groans of relief, the duke and his groom settled her father onto the sofa.

Miss Murdock set down the lamp, kneeled by her father and unbuttoned his coat, despaired of getting it off him. He opened his eyes once, looked unseeingly at her, and then closed them to begin snoring now in hard earnest. She gave a little resigned sigh, settled with loosening his collar and cravat, and rose once again, now wondering what she was to do with the two men that stood in her parlor in the middle of the night.

The Duke of St. James unbuttoned his great coat. "Tyler, if you will see to the horses?"

Miss Murdock divined, less than happily, that he intended to stay. She would have to make up a spare room, she supposed, and none of them had been used in several years. "Call for our groom, his name is Kennedy, as I said, when you reach the stable, Tyler is it?"

The lordship's groom nodded. "Yes, miss. Pleasure to meet you, miss."

"And you, I'm sure, Tyler. Kennedy sleeps above the stables, and he can direct you where to put the horses and where the feed and hay is kept. He'll also make you comfortable afterward." She turned to St. James. "And I can make up a spare room for you, milord, but as that will take a few minutes, can I interest you in something to eat or drink?" He shrugged with an effort from his coat, and she took it from him. She dropped her gaze to the rich blue, heavy cloth of it, suddenly finding it easier to stare at than to meet his bemused gold eyes.

"Coffee, I think, Miss Murdock. If it is not too much trouble."

"Not at all. I would deem myself a poor hostess indeed if I could not even boil water. Would you like to come along with me to the kitchen? Or I can make you comfortable in here, although my father does tend to snore loudly." She put a hand to her forehead in thought. "Or the dining room, but it is under dust cloths and hasn't been used in years."

He raised a dark brow. "The kitchen will be more than adequate, I think, Miss Murdock. It is not my intention to put you out at half-past two in the morning entertaining me." He turned to Tyler. "I'll call for you when I am ready, Tyler."

"Milord," the groom returned with a small pull on his cap, and then he left to go to the stables, and Miss Murdock had the sudden realization that she was alone with the Duke of St. James, he of the sordid reputation, with only a drunken, passed-out father for protection.

His eyes did not reassure her, for he had focused all of his considerable attention upon her, an attention she felt she neither warranted nor welcomed, and she flushed lightly, imagining how she must look, in her worn sleeping costume and thread-bare, colorless robe, her hair down her back and tangled and her face not even washed of sleep. A more pitiful specimen of the fairer sex he had probably never encountered, and she could not blame him if his silence were one of shock and dismay.

But be that as it may, she could do nothing to rectify the situation at this moment, and so turned on her slippered heel and said, "If you will follow me, milord?" of which he did.

Her first assessment that he was in no better shape than her father became apparent as he stumbled through the door to the hallway with her, and then immediately leaned one shoulder against the wall of the hall, and proceeded down it, halting often, using the wall to support himself. She slowed her own steps to match his, knew not whether to be disgusted with his behavior, or to laugh at the utter ludicrousness of it.

"You are a sorry sight, milord," she could not resist commenting when once he reeled away from the wall and then found it again with a painful bump of his shoulder.

He stopped, threw her a crooked grin that made her stomach do a sudden, unexpected lurch, and made her smile freeze foolishly on her face. "As are you, Miss Murdock," he returned. "But I should wager that in the morning, we shall both be looking a good deal more fit."

It was a long trek to the kitchen, for although the house was old and dilapidated, it was quite large, and with the duke's slow and laborious moving, it was another minute or two before she directed him into the kitchen, and taking her lamp, set it upon the large, square, wooden table and indicated a seat for him to take.

He settled himself into it with every appearance of relief. Without comment, he cupped his forehead in his hands in brooding silence.

Miss Murdock left him be. She lit another few lamps to see by, stoked the still glowing embers of the fire in the stove and added fuel to set it again snapping. She got a streak of soot across her face in the process, gave it a brief wipe with a rag, then pulled out a bag of ground coffee and the coffee pot. She filled the pot with water, added the grounds, and put it on the stove. They were all tasks that she had performed many times, and she fell into them without thought and with a serene rhythm.

St. James closed his eyes, the quiet lulling him and easing the pounding that was already enveloping his head. Miss Murdock did not chatter, and he was thankful for that. He was not a man given to doubts, not because he never had them but because he refused to entertain them. They had their place to insure proper reasoning, but if one let them grow, one would find oneself paralyzed and incapable of any decision and any action.

Now, as he listened to the brief, soothing sounds of the fire being stoked, the coffee being put on, and cups being retrieved and set down, he allowed himself to review his doubts, and then discarded them. His actions appeared rash, but they were well thought out in advance. He had settled on marriage as being his last ploy to flush out an enemy unseen, and although he had not foreseen how he was to go about procuring a wife without wooing, pursuing, and otherwise deceiving a young miss into that role, he had certainly recognized the perfect opportunity when it had been presented to him.

He removed his hands from his brow, slouched back in his chair, and concentrated on the female before him. She was plain, as her father had said, but not displeasing. She had an ordinary face, with ordinary features, and perhaps if just one of those features had been out of the ordinary, had been remarkable, then she could have been quite breathtaking. But every feature *was* ordinary. From the average brown of her hair to the solemn brown of her eyes. And her skin was certainly too brown, far beyond the realm of fashionable and more in the area of commonness.

Her form, petite and rather delicate, as suited her small stature, was not voluptuous in the least, and induced thoughts of efficiency rather than romance. Her hands were small, but the nails of her fingers were cut short, showing she viewed them more as tools to be used than a point of vanity. Even now, after giving him an appraising look, she took out a side of pork and cut off strips with a large knife and settled them into a cast iron pan to fry. To this, she added eggs, and then using a bread knife, cut off slices from a loaf, placed them in a toasting iron and opening the door to the stove fire, propped it just above the flames. She took out a large mound of churned butter from the pantry and set it on the table.

All of her actions, St. James observed, were done with practiced economy and efficiency, relaxed concentration on her nondescript face, and he was suddenly moved by the thought of a hummingbird hovering in mid-air as it gathered nectar from a morning-glory. And if Miss Murdock were not as flashy as that hummingbird, she was certainly as riveting in her effortless complacency as she went about her tasks.

He could well believe that no one had ever found her exciting, but as St. James watched her move about in the dark of early morning, with her hair undone and down her back, and a faint streak of soot still upon one cheek, and her robe fluttering open to reveal her thin gown that was moved by her slender legs, it occurred to him that he had more excitement than most in his thirty and three years, and that it was very pleasant indeed to allow her silent serenity to wash over him, like a balm on an itchy patch of skin.

And if her solemn eyes met his from time to time, taking his measure with a quiet and somewhat timid curiosity, he did not blink, but met her questioning with a sudden sureness that he would not have guessed at. For he was quite certain that Miss Murdock was precisely what he needed for his plans, and for the first time, he thought it may just be possible that he not only complete his endeavor, but survive the completing of it.

The coffee was ready and Miss Murdock filled his cup, placed it in front of him. He declined her offers of cream and sugar, and instead took it black. She watched his long fingers as they wrapped about the cup with a simple and elegant grace. He raised the cup to his lips, paused a moment as his gold eyes focused on her. Nonplused, she turned, took a cloth and removed the hot skillet from the stove. She fixed him a plate of side, eggs and toast. She put out some homemade peach preserves, and then when she saw that he had all he needed, she poured herself a cup of coffee and sat at the table, its wide, wooden expanse separating them, leaving her at one end and he at the other.

He viewed the plate of food, which he had not asked for, for a moment, and then without comment, picked up his fork and began eating. Lizzie sipped her coffee. She watched the slight trembling in his hands wane, and his foray into his meal became more sure. His eating was sporadic. He would take several bites and then pause for long moments at a time to sit and drink his coffee and look at her, eyes unblinking, mouth unspeaking.

His lips, she noticed, were tight, compressed and rarely moving in either smile or frown. His face was pale, certainly much paler than her own, and in contrast made his dark hair seem nearly black. His brows were arched, even in rest, and when by chance he arched one higher in a quizzical look at her and her glances, it gave him a satirical look. There was a harshness about him, an unforgiving, unyielding aura that was at a disparity with his casual, indifferent demeanor, his disheveled appearance, and the lazy languidness of his movements.

Only his eyes sealed the two seemingly divergent parts of his character, shifting constantly not from motion, for they were always quite steady, but from emotion and mood, looking at one moment morose and in another flickering with excitement, and then he would hood them with his lids, making the little sparks of gold that were still discernible all the more tantalizing to her. For some reason, she felt she would give quite a bit to step into his head and view his thoughts for a single moment.

At long last, he pushed his plate away, much of the food left uneaten, and Miss Murdock got up from her chair and refilled his cup with coffee. She rinsed her own cup and placed it on the sideboard, then turned to him. "I can make that room up for you now, if you wish, milord."

As she was standing but a foot or so from him, he reached out and caught her hand, making her start in surprise. She did not try for release, only stood steady, her heart giving an uneven beat in her chest and looked at him, wary of his next move.

"What is this, Miss Murdock?" he asked, his voice teasing. "Are you nervous that the disreputable Duke of St. James is about to take advantage of you in your kitchen?"

As she did not answer, only tugged at her hand and stared at him with her solemn eyes, his own eyes narrowed as he continued. "Well, at one time, and if you were a woman of a different caliber, I may have."

Lizzie flushed, could not decide if she should feel relieved or insulted, or disappointed. "I have no doubt, milord, that you are capable if you so wished," she answered. "But I am sure that I would be poor sport for a man of your tastes and so you would do better to merely release my hand and allow me to make up your room."

He did not release her hand, instead tightened his grip and leaned back in his chair, forcing her to take an awkward step forward. St. James looked up into her face, her just shy of panicking eyes. "How am I to go about this?" he asked. "I have been pondering just this question for over an hour now, and I still have no clue."

"I am sure I do not understand you," Miss Murdock replied. "I am also sure that what you need now after being fed is sleep, and that whatever answer you are looking for will be there for you in the morning."

"No, Miss Murdock," he shook his head. "I will not be here in the morning and you need not make up a bed for me. So you can quit worrying your head about that task. I feel I have put you out quite enough for one night at any rate. Although I am afraid I am going to have to put you out quite a bit more."

"I--It was no hardship," she said. Her voice was breathless and she blamed it on the fact that he had begun to rub her hand with his thumb, the soft, hypnotic reassurance of a mother rubbing a baby's back. And as a baby is lulled into sleep, she felt as though she were being lulled into a spell that consisted of nothing but that single moving thumb and those two golden eyes. She gave a sharp pull on her hand, gaining abrupt release and losing her balance. She reached behind to steady herself and her palm came down on the still hot stove. "Ouch!" she squeaked, and her injured hand flew to her mouth.

St. James rose, banging his knee in his haste. "Damn it, Miss Murdock. What did you think I was going to do to make you burn yourself getting away?" He grabbed her wrist, pulling her hand from her mouth.

Miss Murdock, finding his question unanswerable, her hand smarting, and herself feeling a good deal foolish, lashed out in return. "What any young female would think when a drunken scoundrel takes their hand and there is no proper chaperone! I should slap you if it were not hurting so badly!"

"You may slap me with the other hand, if it should make you feel better," he informed her. He studied her injury. "I imagine it is quite painful."

"As if I needed you to determine that. Simply allow me my hand back, and I will draw some water and soak it."

"No, Miss Murdock. You must use butter. My grandmother has always said so."

"Then you may go fetch your grandmother's butter, for I shan't waste any of mine."

He raised his head, and his gold eyes met her angry brown ones. "Ah, the first challenge. Your way or mine? I think you should learn now that it shall be mine." He stepped to the table, her wrist tight in his grasp, forcing her to step with him. He moved the plate with the great pat of butter upon it to the edge of the table and forced her hand into it. He pushed it down so that she was unable to keep even her fingers from it, and when he pulled her hand up, her hand print was imbedded in the butter.

"You simply could not resist ruining the all of it, could you?" she asked, furious.

"Oh, but, Miss Murdock, when a lovely hand such as your own is at stake, what is a mere pat of butter?"

He released her wrist and she wrapped her injury in a dishcloth. She wished to wash the butter from it, just to spite him, but she could not see the sense in it, as it was on there now and was soothing to some degree. Still turned from him, she told him in a muted little voice. "You need more coffee, sir, for if you see my hand as lovely, you are obviously still drunk."

Which caused him to laugh, a full, rich laugh that surprised her out of her crossness and had her looking at him with stark curiosity, for she would have never dreamed from her short acquaintance with him that he could be capable of such laughter, free of sarcasm or rancor or jadedness.

"I see," he said at length, "that I shall have my way, but that you shall always endeavor to have the last word."

"Yes, milord. I can see how that is so, since you are leaving, and I must ask to be excused now, and there will be no further conversation between us, then I have managed to have the last word," she told him and turned to leave the kitchen.

Her uninjured hand was at the door frame and with one more step she would have been into the hallway when he spoke. "You are mistaken if you think there will be no further conversation between us."

She hesitated for just an instant, but it was an instant too long, for his next words had her turning to stare at him. "For we became betrothed at approximately one hour after midnight." He raised the lids of his eyes, giving her the full impact of their golden stare at her look of shocked disbelief. "So you see, Miss Murdock, when I leave here shortly, you shall be accompanying me."

Chapter Five

"You expect me to take you seriously?" Miss Murdock asked.

"I can not, at this point, expect any thing from you, Miss Murdock."

"Indeed, I am glad we are in agreement on that," she returned. She paused another thoughtful second in the door and then with a little sigh, went back to stand before him. "Milord, you are drunk. It is nearing dawn. I will make up a room for you and you shall sleep and tomorrow you will have forgotten your foolish statement, as I will have. Surely, you see the sense in that?"

"I am no longer drunk, Miss Murdock, but nearly sober, to my regret, after two cups of coffee and the meal you placed before me. Sober enough to know I am not displeased with the alliance I have made." He pulled a chair out. "Come, Miss Murdock, and be seated. I am sure you have questions."

"No, milord," she shook her head. "I am too tired to humor your odd fancies."

"Ah. But your father was in a more agreeable mood."

"My father tends to agree to a great many things when he is drinking," she returned with a rueful grin. With her eyes twinkling, she added, "as I daresay, do you."

"You refuse to take me seriously for even a moment, Miss Murdock."

She made a sudden weary gesture. "Indeed, sir, please do go on, for I see that you are quite set upon it. It will only needs cleaning up in the morning if I do not attend to it now any rate."

He raised a brow. "I applaud your indulgence, Miss Murdock." He sat himself, his fingers drumming on the table before him in light contemplation. "I asked your father for your hand. He has agreed."

"I am sure I am quite flattered." She gave a little laugh. "It is not often that I receive proposals at dawn, even from drunken suitors. Indeed, I do thank you, even as I must decline. Regretfully, of course. Is it possible for me to return to my bed now?"

"You are being difficult, Miss Murdock," he observed.

"Indeed, I think I am showing remarkable restraint." Her amusement waned. "Please do not pursue this ridiculous conversation any further."

"Miss Murdock, I realize this must be difficult for you," he took pains to explain, "but it is important that you accept that I am serious. Can you at least entertain that assumption for the purposes of this conversation so that we may discuss your concerns at this circumstance?"

"I am to assume," she said with a wry twist to her mouth, "allow me, please, to state this correctly, that a duke, moneyed and privileged and despite a certain sordid reputation, still a desirable match in marriage, by those far more suitable than myself, has settled upon my being his wife after, of course, only one meeting, where I was covered with mud and running a horse into a fence." Half smiling, she awaited his answer, but he gave none, only waited for her to continue. She made an impatient gesture with her hand. "The whole idea is ludicrous. What could possibly motivate you?"

"My motives are no concern of yours, Miss Murdock. I would rather you consider your own concerns, as I had asked."

"You believe that after I give your suit the consideration I am sure you believe it deserves that I will leap upon the obvious advantages to me and agree?" she asked, her tone somewhere between disbelieving and offended.

He gave an impatient little sigh and rose from his seat. He turned from her and strode the room. He paced back to stand before her. "Must I list them, Miss Murdock? For I find it distasteful to have to enumerate my 'desirable' qualities." His lip curled in an unsuspected ugly wrath that had Miss Murdock sobering from her prior glibness. "List them, Miss Murdock. Let me hear you say the words so that I know you understand completely what you are to gain. If one, indeed, looks upon it as gain."

"I can assure you, that I am one that does not, milord," she said in sudden icy anger. "But I will list them as you ask as the sooner this interview is complete, the sooner I may return to my own business, and you may return to yours."

He made no answer, only stood, waiting, for her to continue.

She drew in a breath, calming herself. "Your title, I suppose."

He nodded. "Go on."

"And it is purported that you are quite. . . well off."

"On the mark again, Miss Murdock."

"Your family's standing in society," she added. She glanced at him, hoping he would be satisfied, but he closed his eyes for one brief instance and when he opened them again, he raised a brow to her at her hesitation to continue.

"Anything else, Miss Murdock?" he asked, his voice mocking. "Any other reason why most any female in society would view me as a desirable match in marriage?"

"Maybe I should begin listing your *un*-desirable qualities, milord," she retorted. "Your ego, your reputation--"

"But we are still on the desirable list, Miss Murdock. I am sure if you merely search about your mind but another moment you should be well able to come up with one more reason."

"Oh, very well," she said, exasperated, but pushing on precariously. "You are not displeasing to look at. Is that what you wished to hear, milord? Does that flatter you and satisfy you? Tell me, do you often go through this charade so that you may gain glory for your vainness from some naive country bumpkin when I am sure you have had enough simpering females throwing themselves at you for years now?"

But he leaned forward, placing his hands upon the arms of her chair and spoke down to her, his face near hers. "I merely wished to hear you say it so that I am sure you are aware of it," he told her, his gold eyes glinting. "I do not know you, Miss Murdock. I do not know what is important to you, what you find desirable. I merely wish you to realize, that if your young heart fancies romance, it shall be available to you, no questions asked and with nothing withheld."

"Jesus, Mary and Joseph," she exhaled. "Are you mad? You speak of a marriage of convenience where you have no feeling for me or I for you and you speak of this matter as though it were another bargaining chip upon the table--"

He released the chair arms, paced away from her. "The 'catch of the decade' I was called ten years ago, Miss Murdock." He turned back to face her. "Now--well, that decade has passed, has it not? My reputation has grown, and although not many would care to dismiss my suit out of hand, the doors of those families that have no need of further wealth have been closed to me. The peers I have with daughters of marrying age are content to settle for a marquis or an earl, the fellow of course being a little more, how shall we say it, commendable in his morals."

He paused and when he continued, his words were quieter but much more pointed. "But for the daughter of a Squire to be so squeamish, Miss Murdock, well, it nearly boggles my mind."

"Does it?" Miss Murdock asked with sudden icy rage. "It is true that I find your reputation distasteful--"

"I am so shocked to hear it."

"--But what I find more distasteful is your thinking that you may stroll in here and offer me your ridiculous proposal and have me leaping for it as some starving dog at a piece of meat." She rose from her seat, beside herself with rage. "Allow me to, for a moment, fulfill your expectations: Oh, thank you, milord, for choosing me! I have been made complete now that you have humbled yourself and sought my hand. My life, I am sure, will be naught but a fairy tale, where I may wear fine gowns, and ride in a fine carriage with fine horses. And I shall spend all of my allowance on fancy hats, and luxurious furs, and eat sweetmeats all day while I have a dozen or more servants to fetch me whatever I care for." She drew herself up, her worn gown and falling hair taking nothing from her disdain. "Is that what you expected to hear, milord? For if it is, you are wildly mistaken. If you think that I am flattered by your choosing me to fulfill some cold motive on your part, you are most decidedly wrong. When and if I am ever chosen as a wife it will not be for some calculated reason, I should hope, and I will certainly not agree to a marriage based on a proposition that, among other things, offers your *body* as something to be gained for my amusement." Her face was flaming with embarrassment but her outrage was such that she was not even aware of it.

"If you prefer the illusion of a romantic wooing, Miss Murdock," he countered, "then I am afraid I can not accommodate you. For I can not and will not go into this marriage with you believing there is a feeling there which can not be. Neither do I wish for that feeling from you. It is precisely these restrictions that have made me, yes, *choose* you!"

His words hit her like a slap in the face. Oh, she had always been plain, had accepted it long before, but to be told outright that the very reason, now, that her hand was being sought in marriage was because her unlikely suitor had determined that she would never be a threat to his heart or his libido, and for some unknown reason sought that sad state of affairs, was going just a tad too far. "Then I suggest you travel on down the lane, milord St. James, for although I am above calling any person ugly, there is a lady just above a mile from here that would shock even you."

Her words took him by surprise. "I am not sure that I follow you, Miss Murdock."

"No? Well, it little matters. If you are loathe to point out your own 'desirable' qualities, I am equally as loathe to point out my own 'less than desirable' ones. I am going to bed now, milord, for I have had quite enough of this ill-advised conversation. Where you sleep, or how you spend your time before your leaving, I really do not care."

With those words, she left the room, half-afraid that he would make some retort that would stop her once again in her tracks, so she turned a deaf ear when he called out after her. Once in the hall, she moved quicker still, holding her hurt hand in front of her and feeling a stinging in her eyes that she tried hard to convince herself was from tiredness and her injury, and she hurried up the stairs, and once she made her room, she closed the door behind her and slumped against it. She blinked back any tears that had the temerity to even think about falling, swiped her hair from her face, when and how it had fallen there she was not certain, and when she at last glanced out the window, she saw that dawn had come after all, or was well on its way, for the horizon was just beginning to lighten.

She could have cried then with frustration and fatigue, for instead of being able to throw herself on her bed, sleep away the headache that odious man had given her, she would only have time to bathe and dress, and then she would have to start her day's work. Well, she certainly intended to dawdle, for her father would not be up for hours yet at any rate, and she wanted to give the duke plenty of time to clear out before she was forced to once again go downstairs.

With that thought, she removed her robe and sleeping costume, bathed herself in the cold water she poured from her pitcher and into her basin. She welcomed the iciness of it, even in the chill of her room, feeling as though she were cleaning off the filth that man had somehow heaped into her mind.

She gave a slight shiver, toweled off more quickly than she had bathed. As if she didn't have enough to worry about, she thought with exasperation, without some fool of a fop coming in and upsetting her for half the night. She wished she had taken that iron skillet to his skull rather than cook him eggs in it.

No wonder he had thought that she would swallow his outrageous tale. He had only had to look around and see the drudgery that was her life. He must have deemed her very ripe indeed for what she could see now as nothing more than some cruel jest, designed to tease a naive country maiden with few prospects.

Curious that, that he had not once asked, where is your maid? Where is your cook? Where is your butler? Why do you eat in the kitchen? Why are you the one preparing the food? One would think that a man such as he could barely fathom a life without servants.

She pulled on a dress, it was her best, just in case he had not left before she was forced to go down, and she was not going to give him another opportunity to mock her for being dirty or disheveled. Not that there was much difference between her worst and her best. They were all out-moded and faded, and as they had been her mother's, too large, for she hadn't the time nor the skill to take them in.

But she needn't have worried, for as she was buttoning the last pesky buttons up the back of it, she heard sounds from below in front of the house, and moving to the window, she saw that the duke's curricle had been brought around by his groom, the same team of horses at its front and an additional horse tied by a lead to the back.

She gave a single nod of satisfaction, thinking goodbye and good riddance, when something made her remember that she did not recall seeing a spare horse when he had arrived. She drew back the sheer from the window, enabling her to see the tied horse more clearly and with a gasp of dismay, feeling as though the air had been beat from her chest, she cried, "Leaf!" and turned and ran from the room.

She reached the bottom of the steps and flung open the front entrance door. "What are you doing?" she demanded. "That is my horse, milord Duke, and I do not take kindly to having it removed from its stall and tied to the back of your curricle!"

St. James turned to her. He had on his great coat, buttoned to the top, and Lizzie had a moment's thought that once again she was out in the cold with no proper protection and he was again warm and comfortable. "Ah, there you are, Miss Murdock. I have been awaiting you."

She went past him, deigning him with only a glare from her brown eyes, and went to the back of the curricle, where she gave the quick release knot a single, angry yank, freeing her horse from the vehicle. Then she turned on the duke, holding the lead in her uninjured hand. "I do not know what bargain you think you struck with my father last night after getting him drunk, but he was not at liberty to sell this horse, for she is, in essence, mine!"

"So he told me, Miss Murdock," he said. "He explained quite poignantly that she is, in fact, your dowry."

His words came at her like a board to her head. Her cheeks paled from the flush that had been staining them, and her eyes looked at the man in front of her unseeingly for a long moment. At last she said the words, words she knew to be true, but could hardly believe them long enough to even speak them. "It was the filly then," she choked. She looked at him accusingly. "You wanted my *horse.*"

He sucked in a deep breath, but his eyes did not flinch from her face. "Yes, Miss Murdock," he told her. "I wanted your horse."

A spasm went through her, making her rigid. "You--you are more despicable and disgusting than anyone I could ever imagine."

"You are probably correct on both points, Miss Murdock," he said in cool agreement.

"My father was drunk. He would have never agreed to this otherwise."

"Your father should be sobering by now. Ask him if you wish. See if he still is willing to stand by his agreement."

She clutched the lead, undecided, and he prompted her, taking the lead from her hand and beckoning to his groom. "Come, Miss Murdock. I don't wish there to be any doubts in your mind, any thinking on your part that I am abducting you against your father's wishes. Tyler will hold your horse, will not steal her off from you while we go inside. Shall we?" he asked, and his voice was soothing to her ears, as though he regretted very much the tactics he had taken.

"You have no heart," she said. "For I can see in your eyes that you know exactly what you are doing and do it all the same."

"Yes. I know exactly what I am doing. Never doubt that, either, Miss Murdock."

Tyler took the lead, and St. James took her elbow. He wore his driving gloves, and the leather of them dug through the thin material of her sleeve. They went in silence up the steps together, the groom behind them spitting a long stream of tobacco with a loud *pththttt.* Then they were through the door that she had left standing open in her urgency, and went again to the parlor off the hall.

"Father," Miss Murdock called when they came within a few feet of the sofa and the duke dropped his hand from her arm. Her father stirred. The sun, now peeking above the horizon, shone a beam in and upon his eyes, making him blink when he at last opened them in his drink swollen face.

He looked with incomprehension at the two of them standing there, then sat up, groaning. He ran a hand through his thick, gray hair. "Aye, Lizzie, I'll be needing your special coffee this morning, luv, for I surely indulged myself a bit too much last night."

"Oh, whenever did you not?" she asked. "Father. . . there is something I must ask you." But she could not frame the words, afraid that her father had done as the duke suggested and agreed to a marriage designed for his lordship to obtain a horse.

At her hesitancy, St. James stepped forward. "Squire?"

Her father focused on his lordship. His expression changed from lazy waking to full cumbersome alertness. "Ah, yes. That business. Is it time?" He looked at his daughter's face, the wide open, pleading eyes, the shadows beneath them, and the paleness of her normally dark skin. "Ahhhh," he said. He turned to the duke. "I was to pave the way, you know."

Lizzie dropped her chin to her chest. "Oh, God, father, do not tell me it is true?"

"And why would you say it like that, lass?" he asked in sudden anger, as though she had accused him of an unspeakable crime. "I have made you a brilliant match, with no help from you. You should be well-pleased, instead of standing there looking as though the fireplace is smoking again."

"Oh, father! How could you?" She brought her chin up and held her hands out before her in supplication. "You have bartered me off as part of a horse bargain!"

"That horse is your dowry, and don't you forget it! No one says anything if a man marries to gain his new wife's cash or lands or jewels, but if it's a horse, suddenly there's something evil in it?" Her father pointed his finger, his face turning red which indicated that he would be impossible to deal with. "T'is a duke, you know! You could have never done better."

She turned once to look at the object of their conversation. "T'is *St. James*!"

"Oh, ho," her father exclaimed, "and of course you have a dozen more duke's lined up at the door and can afford to be choosy."

"I'd rather not marry at all than marry him!"

"Well, you hit that nail right on the head, missy, for that's the only choice I see that you have. Either him or no one, for you're twenty summers old and haven't had a suitor yet!"

She opened her mouth to berate him, but he waved a hand at her, shutting her off. "Oh, do not start, I'm not blaming you, by any means. Lord knows I have failed in my duty up to this point in getting you up to snuff and out the starting gate," he told her. "So do not get on your high horse. The offer was there, I fully apprised him of your short-comings and he was not put off. Who is to blame me for snagging him while I could?"

"Fully apprised him--! Oh, God, I wish the floor would open up and swallow me! I want no husband through trickery. I'd rather have no husband at all."

"Do you feel tricked, miduke?" the Squire asked.

"Not in the least. If I had not wished to offer for your daughter, I would not have done so. Believe me, I have been under rather more pressure in the past," and his lips twitched, "and you can see that I came out unscathed."

The Squire nodded. "There you go, Lizzie. The man wished for a wife and he offered for you. You have no complaint."

"I have no complaint?" she asked. "You are both out of your heads!"

"Please do not shriek, Lizzie, dear," the Squire implored, holding his head. "For you are making me sick with it."

"You made yourself sick with the drink you took last night, and now I am the one that must bear the foolishness of it," she told him. "Oh, you have done folly before, father, but never as bad as this! You've gambled off the money for the winter's coal, and lost every decent mount I had besides Leaf. You bring home your cronies for pot-luck when there isn't much luck in the pot to begin with. You've scared off every maid we've ever retained that was under fifty with your groping ways, and agitated every one older than fifty with your ill-temper until they have left in a huff. You leave me the accounts to juggle when there is more money going out than coming in, and then gaily set down your bills for jewelry and perfume for payment to those women who would not have anything to do with your gouty, portly, black-toothed self if not otherwise, as though they were just another feed bill.

"Through it all, I've neither complained nor upbraided, but now you have gone too far! I swear, I could choke you where you sit," she finished.

"Yes, yes, Lizzie. You are a saint and I am the first to say it," her father returned. "But, now, go on. At the very least you shall not have to put up with me and my weaknesses, and even the dreaded Duke of St. James could be no worse, I wager."

Miss Murdock, at her wit's end, placed a hand on her forehead, winced when she realized that it was the burnt one, which she had quite forgotten in all of her agitation. "Oh, damn this bloody hand," she murmured, jerking it back down again. She turned on St. James. "Of which I have *you* to thank for, so you could look a little contrite instead of standing there smirking!"

St. James was, indeed, looking quite diverted as he witnessed the exchange between father and daughter, but at her words, he sobered enough to say, "Most certainly, I am contrite, Miss Murdock. I would be much too frightened not to be in your presence." Of which he received a glare that was clearly meant to leave him dead.

St. James asked, "Have you any further doubts, Miss Murdock?"

Miss Murdock turned again to the Squire. "Father? I'm asking you once more. Can this be what you truly want?"

"Aye, lass. T'is for the best. Every woman should be married and have children to keep her occupied, instead of dreaming of training race horses and spending time caring for a rather unfit father."

She kneeled in front of him, her anger gone and only worry in her voice. "But, father, whoever shall look after you?"

He chuckled, patted her head. "Oh, I shall be fine on my own, missy. I shall do what I have been longing to do but which I haven't been able to because of care for you. I shall drink myself silly and ride to hounds 'til I break my neck like all old widower's do. You need not worry about me."

"Oh, father," she moaned, "I love you dearly, even if you are an old fool."

He gave her head a final pat. "Now get on with you, lass. Leave an old man to peace and quiet. You were always much too active and it has tired me to watch you work so hard for the last seven years."

She was reluctant to leave him, and when she looked about, her eyes were tinged with tears and frantic. She was being sent away, her father obviously convinced that it was for the best. And although she could fight the duke to the end, she would not fight her father.

Then St. James was there, pulling her gently to her feet. He handed her a handkerchief from his coat pocket, and she stood staring at it dumbly for a moment.

He took it and wiped her eyes and it was only then that she realized she was crying. "Go now, Miss Murdock, and pack a valise. You shan't need much, for if your dress is any indication, you will need new in any event. Gather a warm cloak. I will be waiting for you in the hall."

Miss Murdock, clutching the handkerchief he had returned to her hand, went to do as he bid, her mind numb so that she wondered if he had not told her what to do if she could have realized it herself. He followed her to the foot of the stairs, told her before she ascended, "It is for the best, Miss Murdock, I assure you."

She turned to look at him, the gold eyes, the lithe figure, the impossible perfection of his face. "I cannot see how it could be for the best, milord, either for you or for me," and she went up the stairs.

When she again reached her room, she dug a battered valise from her closet, unclasped it and opened its mouth wide. But something about its yawning emptiness, which she had been assigned to fill, defeated her, and she sat down on her bed beside the empty traveling case.

She wasn't certain how long she sat there motionless, only her mind racing, but it was enough time to pass for the duke to evidently become impatient, for there was a light tapping on her door. Miss Murdock had not closed it, and now as she glanced up, not startled, more just dismayed, she saw St. James hesitating in the opening. "Miss Murdock? Is there anything I can assist you with?"

She took a moment to answer, and when she did, she spoke with a calmness that she in no way felt. "No. I'm sorry, but I just needed a moment to sit and think and allow myself to catch up with everything that is going on." She gave him a baleful look. "Do you always move so quickly, milord, and expect others to merely follow your lead without question or delay?"

He rubbed his upper lip with his gloved finger, a habit, she was beginning to notice, that he did whenever he did not have his usual immediate and flip response handy. "I expect that, yes, I normally do."

He added a little more sharply, "I am not your father, Miss Murdock. I do not need looking after or a firm guiding hand."

"So why take me from him when you can see that I am clearly needed here?"

He clasped his hands behind his back, still speaking from the door-frame. "There are many good reasons that I could list why it is better for you to go with me, Miss Murdock, than remain here. But as I in all honesty did not care two pins if this circumstance benefited you at the time I offered for your hand, I will not now attempt to make you believe that I had your best interests at heart from the beginning."

Miss Murdock rose from where she had been sitting, opened her wardrobe. "I appreciate your candor, milord Duke," she said. "I hope that if nothing else, this indicates that I can expect honesty from you, however unpleasant it may be." She took down one of her four remaining dresses, inspected it, folded it and placed it in the traveling bag.

St. James moved through the doorway then, a restriction of propriety that he crossed with no evident regard to it. He walked over to her and Miss Murdock paused in her packing. "I did not expect this to be pleasant, Miss Murdock," he told her. "And although many other crimes have been laid at my door, real and imagined, no one has ever dared call me a liar. That, Miss Murdock, is because I *will* tell you the truth. If you find it unpleasant, I do not apologize."

She raised her brown eyes to his. Her words were soft but dripped with distaste. "And the truth is you wanted my horse and as there was no other way to attain it as it is my dowry, you offered for me."

He gave a small sigh before saying, "In part, that is true. Do not ask for the rest of it, Miss Murdock, for it will only interrupt your peace of mind."

She let out a little, bitter laugh at the end of his words. "I'm afraid my peace of mind has been well interrupted already."

"I imagine that is so, which I do regret, Miss Murdock. But I would wager that in a very short time after our wedding you will be counting yourself a lucky lass indeed."

"You have a very high opinion of yourself, sir," she was stung into retorting.

"Not at all, Miss Murdock. I simply believe there is a very good possibility that you shall become a widow at an extremely young age." He paused letting his words sink in, then continued, "So you see, if you can merely bear my presence for a short while, you shall in the end be a duchess and very rich, and free to choose another. If nothing else, I can guarantee that you will have no end of suitors then, plain little mouse or no."

He did not wait for her to respond, but turned on his booted heel and went to the door. Miss Murdock, whose hand had been reaching for her toiletry items on her vanity and had stilled at his pronouncement, listened to his retreating steps. She was not surprised when they paused at the door, and he told her over his shoulder in a self-mocking voice. "So be a sport, Miss Murdock. I can not guarantee that I shall die, and you will forgive me if I try mightily not to, but if I were laying odds, I would have to put them against me. Now doesn't that make the prospect of marrying me much more pleasant?"

Lizzie listened to his footsteps as he moved again, echoing down the hallway and fading. "No. It doesn't." She shoved her hair brush, comb and mirror into the bag.

"Well, milord," Tyler asked when his employer came once again down the flagstone steps alone. "Is she coming?"

St. James came up beside him. He took the filly's lead from his groom and led it to the back of the curricle. "Damned if I know! I'll give her exactly ten minutes before I go up and throw her over my shoulder and carry her down!"

Tyler could not resist a wide grin which he did not even attempt to hide. "Aye, milord, she's got you a tad riled, I see!"

At which the duke gave him a sharp glance from his gold eyes. He tied Miss Murdock's horse to the rear of the curricle once again, ran a gloved hand through his disarrayed hair, and said, "It is only that I am devilishly tired, and hung-over on top of it. I can at least say that she spared me the hysterics and did not faint. Of which I should be forever grateful. But she has a damned shrewish tongue and is not hesitant to use it in the least. Now, Tyler, if you will wipe that grin from your face and remain here for another few moments, I'll return shortly. If Miss Murdock arrives out before I do, please endeavor to make her comfortable, and tie her to the seat if she seems inclined to be difficult."

"Aye, milord," Tyler answered, and although he was happy to follow the duke's instruction of remaining, he could not obey in removing his smile.

"Bugger you, Tyler! I should knock that grin from you if I were not feeling so damnedably out of sorts." But even as St. James turned to make his way up, once more, to the entrance of the house, a smile flashed across his face, lightening his features for that brief instance, and then all the groom saw was his back.

Tyler had a few minutes to consider all the strange goings-on of that morning before the door opened again, and a diminutive Miss in a very plain brown cloak came down the steps toward him. Her bonnet was the same lamentable brown, and as she drew closer, he saw that her face was a good deal brown, and her eyes, although finely shaped and rather solemnly large, were brown also, of no particularly remarkable shade, so that one could not say that they were chocolate brown or cider brown or nutmeg brown, but where one could only say: they were brown. And her brows above them were brown, indicating that the hair done up beneath her bonnet was also brown.

And although Tyler recognized her from when they arrived, and then her brief rescuing of her horse, he had to admit that any attractiveness he remembered about her must have been washed out by the morning's sun, for when she set down her valise and extended her hand to make a formal acknowledgment of his presence, rather unusual as he was only a groom, he answered by saying, "Pleased to meet you again, Miss Brown, *ahem*, I mean Murdock."

"And I am pleased to renew your acquaintance, Mr. Tobacco, oh dear me, I do mean, Tyler!" she returned.

Tyler made a startled little noise in his throat, and then seeing her eyes twinkling, began to laugh, of which she joined him. "You're having me on a bit, are you, miss?"

"Oh, do forgive me, but I was," she said. "But I have often thought it would be so much easier to remember names if we could only call people by their most distinguishing feature. Take Mr. Ryan Tempton that I met yesterday. Would it not be so much easier if his name were Mr. Red?"

"Aye, Miss! I wouldn't argue with you," Tyler agreed. "And his brother, Lord Tempton, I should think t'would be easier if his name were Lord Peacock."

Of which Miss Murdock gave a helpless laugh, knowing it was most unseemly, but finding it most gratifying to be entertained by the likable groom rather than think another moment about the predicament she was in. "And my father, he should be Squire Indulges, for he overindulges on everything."

"And the Duke, miss, he should be called Lord--"

"Habitual Ill-Humor."

And they were both laughing, much to his lordship's puzzlement when he came up beside them, and instead of acknowledging his presence, the two of them set off into fresh gales of mirth, Miss Murdock putting a hand on Tyler's arm to steady herself.

"Tyler, if you can leave off whatever entertainment yourself and Miss Murdock have managed to manufacture in my brief absence, you may fetch a saddle from the stables and tack up Miss Murdock's filly."

Miss Murdock released Tyler's arm, said to neither of them in particular, "Good God, but he can wipe the smile off anyone's face with a single sentence! What is this, milord? I thought the filly would be traveling with us to London?"

"London? No, Miss Murdock, we are not traveling to London as of yet." He turned from her as though he did not care to spend the time nor the energy with debating over yet another point. Miss Murdock stood a little huffily behind him, feeling helpless to stop whatever plans he was putting into action now. Really! The man was exhausting her, and she had only known him but a scarce few hours.

"Tyler, I have two letters here," St. James was saying and Miss Murdock could see that while she and the groom had been busy giggling he must have been busy penning them, for they were in his hand, sealed and addressed, and he was going over them with Tyler as he spoke. "This one is to my grandmother, deliver it first. Then, you will go to my solicitor to deliver the second. Then you will hire a conveyance, a carriage, not too flashy, and hire a team also, again not too flashy, and you will meet us in Gretna Greene as early as is possible. Do you have all that?"

Tyler tugged his cap. "Aye, milord. And if your grandmother asks where you are?"

"Tell her I am about procuring a horse. Nothing more." His lordship handed him the letters, unbuttoned his greatcoat and reached beneath it into an inner pocket. "And here, this will finance the journey and all your needs," he said, and handed a purse over to his groom.

Tyler took it, pocketed it. He glanced once at Miss Murdock, his earlier humor gone from his now serious face. "And t'miss, milord?"

"She goes with me as planned, to where I have already stated, and you shall find her and myself in good order there awaiting you. So please do not tarry. I do not expect you to kill yourself with a superhuman effort, but I want all of this done in as short a time possible."

Tyler nodded. "As you say," and without further 'aye's' or 'yes, milords' or 'you can count on me, milord', he turned and with a single glance at Lizzie, told her, "You'll be okay with his lordship, Miss, don't worry."

Miss Murdock, wondering that her concern had been that apparent on her face, only gave a brief nod, more to reassure the groom than that she believed it herself, and she watched him untie Leaf, and with the filly beside him, stride to the stables to procure a saddle as ordered.

"Now, Miss Murdock, I shall assist you in mounting, if you please," said St. James, and he took her valise, flung it up onto the floor boards of the curricle. Then he took her arm at the elbow, gave her a moment to gather her skirts, find a foothold and a handhold, and then Miss Murdock clambered up the tall skeletal frame of the curricle and found herself high above in the seat. The horses moved from the activity and St. James soothed them with his voice as he reached up and gathered the lines. Then, holding the lines in one hand, he swiftly climbed up and joined her. He settled himself, gave her a moment to rearrange her skirts, straighten her bonnet, and then he chirruped to the horses and the team moved out into a matched trot, their bay heads bobbing in unison.

Miss Murdock turned once to look back toward her home, but her father was not in sight, and the house stood silent, impassive to her leaving.

Chapter Six

As the curricle traveled at a smart trot to the end of the lane from Miss Murdock's home, the sun was revealed above the further hill, and although the air was still cold, the sun's warm beams were a welcome respite from the raw rain of the last several days. Miss Murdock turned her face up to it, allowing its warmth full access to her face beneath the rim of her bonnet.

With a little sigh, she closed her eyes, clasped her hands together in her lap, and tried to be oblivious to the man next to her, whose thigh, out of necessity on the narrow curricle's seat, was pressed against hers through their clothing.

It was in her mind to once again reiterate that he was being foolish, his plans of marrying her ill-conceived, and that it would be best if he turned the curricle now, before they were too many miles from her home and it became a greater inconvenience. But she advised herself to be patient, for she was certain as the dawn came more fully upon them, and the light of day made its way more completely into his mind, that he would begin to rethink his position. From his attitude thus far, she believed that any idea that he could not claim his own was dismissed out of hand, and so it would behoove her to allow him to make the first opening remark that would allow him to admit that, just perhaps, he had made a mistake after all.

Surely, it could not take over long.

So Miss Murdock sat quietly, tried to focus her thoughts on the strengthening sun, and the enjoyable sensation of the wind snapping past her face, and resigned herself to waiting with fortitude for the dawning of reason in the duke's mind.

It was only when they were some mile and a half from her home and she felt his lordship fumbling about his person in an annoying manner that she opened her eyes and glanced at him in an irritated way for interrupting her quiet reveries. He was unbuttoning his coat with one gloved hand while retaining the ribbons with the other, and as she watched, he dug inside some mysterious inner pocket of his coat and brought out at last, a small, silver flask. He uncapped it with a practiced proficiency that showed he had done this particular task many times before, and then took a deep drink from it.

Miss Murdock's nose twitched as the strong odor of whiskey wafted over to her. "Jesus, Mary and Joseph," she swore in exasperation, her visions of his regaining his senses evaporating with alarming swiftness. "Do not tell me you are going to continue to imbibe in that horrid stuff? Have you not done enough damage already because of your fondness for the drink?"

At which point he turned to her. "Really, Miss Murdock. You can not just go about swearing like a sailor. You will shock every female in society once we finally reach London. I really must ask you to be more conservative."

"I find that a rich jest, milord. Whoever would have guessed that beneath your rakish exterior you were so strait-laced! Now kindly cap your flask and place it away," she returned. "Better yet, you had better give it to me, so that you shall not be again tempted." And she took her hand from the small warmth she had found in her lap and extended it palm up so that he could place the flask in it.

He chuckled and did replace the cap, but rather than hand it to her, he deposited it once again in his coat pocket, to her dismay. Then he put one gloved finger between his teeth, pulled upon it and removed his glove. Then, dropping it in her still outstretched hand, surprising her, he switched the reins to his now bare hand and repeated the procedure with his other glove, depositing it also in her hand, to join its mate.

"Put them on, Miss Murdock. Your hands must be cold."

For some peculiar reason, which she could not explain, she felt like boxing his ears. His careless concern for her welfare, and his equally careless disregard to her wishes was somehow infuriating, and where she had tried being patient before, her tongue now loosened. "I don't want your gloves, milord. I want you to turn this curricle around and take me home where I belong."

St. James gave a long, weary sigh, and when he again turned his head to look at her, she saw how exhausted he was. His gold eyes were dulled and his face was haggard as he contemplated her. "I shall make you a deal, Miss Murdock," he told her at last. Miss Murdock clutched the gloves in her hand, feeling a large bubble of hope swell in her chest. "I am very tired, and as I still have to stop at the inn to settle my account from last night, we will remain there for a few hours. I shall get some rest, and then, after we have dined, for although I ate this morning, thanks to you, you did not, then we will go through this whole arrangement one final time, and I promise that I will listen to every complaint that you have, and answer them satisfactorily. Will that do for you, Miss Murdock?"

Miss Murdock flushed at the condescension in his voice. "And if I am not satisfied, as you promise?"

"Then we will come up with a mutually satisfying alternative."

"That is not the same as saying I may return home."

"No. It is not. But I promise that we shall hash all of this through in a mere few hours, so if you could restrain yourself until then?"

Miss Murdock flounced in her seat. "I can hardly see how you will be more capable of seeing reason if you have that whiskey flask at your disposal, milord!"

With barely controlled impatience, he unbuttoned his coat once again, with more ease this time as his hands were bare of gloves, and taking out the flask, thrust it at her rather rudely. "Take it, then, Miss Murdock, if it will make you quit your incessant nagging."

Miss Murdock took it with triumph, and rather than place it in her reticule or her valise as she had first intended, impulsively flung it out onto the side of the road, where it landed with a soggy splat in the ditch. St. James reined in the horses, looked back at the now mud splattered flask, gave her a single hateful glare from his expressive gold eyes, and then slapped the reins on his horses' haunches. His team took off into a hard canter that had the curricle jerking forward with such suddenness that Miss Murdock was knocked hard against the duke's side. She righted herself, straightened her bonnet once again, and then with an air of calmness, put on his lordship's gloves that had remained in her lap. Once she had her fingers snug in their enveloping warmth, she said, "Thank you, milord. I feel much better now."

"I am certainly glad one of us may say so," St. James replied, and he ran a delicate fingertip over his upper lip.

Perhaps it had been that last drink he had consumed before Miss Murdock disposed of his flask, which being of a good grade of silver, was certain to make some passing local extremely happy, or perhaps it was the fact that the duke had been awake now for some twenty-six hours, or perhaps it was because he found his new fiancé to be excessively wearying, or perhaps it was a combination of all of these, but St. James found himself unable to hold his eyes open for what seemed a moment longer.

He struggled with them, reminded himself he had a bare two miles to go before they would reach the inn and he could have rest. To keep himself awake, he asked his companion, "Have you ever been out of the county before?"

She answered in her soothing, solemn voice. "No. I am shockingly rural, never having been further than the local villages. But Froeburgh has a surprisingly well-stocked library, which I try to visit regularly, and the market at Blytown every second Saturday of the month is a sight to behold. I scarce credit even London has a larger display of goods for sale. And Sherrington is quite famous for its carnivals, which they have in the fall. . ." she continued, but St. James was having difficulty following even this simple conversation. He did have sense to pull the horses back, first into a trot, and then as even that were becoming difficult for him to handle them, into a walk.

Miss Murdock left off talking, which he really did not notice, and then as he fought his ever heavier growing eyelids, he felt Miss Murdock's gloved hands over both of his, taking the ribbons from him. "I can manage," he mumbled.

But she only tsked. "Certainly you can, milord. But I shall take them just for a moment, and then you may have them once again."

St. James nodded, closed his weary eyes, and his head lulled back and jounced as there was no support for it. "Make for the inn, Miss Murdock. I'll not have you turning the horses about and heading home."

"I am satisfied with the inn for now, milord." She paused for a moment, then added, "Here. You may rest your head on my shoulder, for you will get a cramp in your neck having it bouncing about like that."

Without thought, he did move, found her shoulder with his eyes still closed. Thought once that for such a small shoulder, it remained quite steady with the added weight of him against it, and then he abandoned himself to the sleep that called with insistence out to him.

He awoke at the noise of the inn's yard: the snorting of other horses, the rattle of their conveyances' wheels, the different sound his team's hooves made as they went from dirt road to the cobblestone of the yard. Voices were heard, the heavy country accent of grooms, the more cultured voices of patrons, and one voice in particular, "By Gad, there he is now! Told you, Ryan, if we waited but an hour or two, he would surely come past here, for there is no road out of this part of the county that does not come past this inn."

St. James sat up with a jerk, was shocked nearly senseless by the fact that Miss Murdock was driving his most prized team, and with not even a hair out of place beneath her ugly bonnet. "The devil take it!" he said, reaching and taking the ribbons from her. "I did not allow you to drive my bays?"

"You were hardly in any condition to argue with me, milord, as I could have told you would happen since you insisted on having that last drink from your flask. Anyone could see that you were barely fit to drive before that, let alone after."

"I've driven while worse, you wretched lass. I would have managed."

"Be that as it may, I've contrived to get us here without any unfortunate incident, so you may quit glaring at me like that." She rubbed her shoulder as she spoke, and it occurred to him what a sight they must have made pulling into the yard, she handling the ribbons, while he passed out and leaning upon her small shoulder.

He glanced about the yard, his thoughts bringing him back to the familiar voice that shocked him into wakefulness. Seeing the source of that voice, he directed the team further into the yard and arrived to a halt a few feet from Lord Bertram Tempton and his younger brother Ryan. They were both in black riding breeches and bright red coats, lacy white cravats showing at their necks, and high black hats upon their heads. Beside them were two hunting horses, tacked and waiting, and they each held a quirt, Ryan tapping his against his high black boot.

"St. James," Bertie said as the curricle halted. "That's a bloody fine show to be putting on, leaning insensible against a young chit of a girl and making her drive your bloody monsters. Where, by the by, is Tyler? Surely he could have driven if you felt the need to pass out while on the road!"

"Tyler had an errand to run. He will be meeting up with us later."

"Bloody soon, I hope! Needn't tell you, bad enough to ride about with a girl with only a groom as chaperone, but to have no chaperone at all!

There will be no end to the scandal if someone else were to see you," his friend advised him.

"I am well aware of it, Bertie. Thank you for your concern." St. James summoned one of the inn's grooms over to take the reins. "Can you handle them, boy?" he asked, as the groom was quite young.

"Pardon me, milord, but if t'miss there can drive 'em, then I'm coiton I can hold 'em," the groom said with a grin.

St. James scowled, murmured under his breath, "My team's celebrity will never live this down, if word should get out." He handed the reins to the boy, jumped down from the curricle in sharp contrast to his prior obliviousness of just moments before. Then he turned, reached up a hand to Miss Murdock, who placed her gloved one into it, and allowed him to assist her down.

St. James gave her a critical scan then turned to Lord and Mister Tempton. "Allow me to properly introduce Miss Sara Elizabeth Murdock, whom you met yesterday under even less seemly circumstances."

"Ah, yes," Bertie replied, taking her hand. "And you look much more . . . clean today, my dear. I am Lord Bertram Tempton, Earl of Edison."

Miss Murdock flushed slightly. "Pleased to make your acquaintance again, milord."

"And, of course, my younger brother, Mister Ryan Tempton."

"Mister Tempton," Miss Murdock acknowledged.

"Miss Murdock. I hope that we do not find you in any difficulty today," Ryan said.

His words were more intense than a casual greeting and Lizzie was a little taken aback at his concern. "I am well, thank you," she stammered and could not help glancing at the duke who was frowning.

"As I can see we are delaying you from your hunt, we shall bid you goodbye for now, as I have promised Miss Murdock breakfast here at the inn," St. James interrupted.

"Ah, yes," Bertie returned. "We were, I confess, delaying our leaving on the chance that you may turn up here, as there could be no other logical way for you to go but past the inn. But, as I see you have all well in hand, we will be going now. Good day, Miss Murdock. Good luck, St. James."

"Thank you, Bertie. I appreciate the sentiment."

Lord Tempton turned to his brother. "Ryan? Are we ready?"

"I--just a moment." He turned to Lizzie. "Miss Murdock, I am not being presumptuous, I hope, but if you would care for a chaperone, I would be happy to remain with you and his lordship until his groom is able to arrive back."

Miss Murdock flushed at his words. "I, indeed! Thank you for the offer, Mister Tempton, but I really cannot see any harm if you go ahead with your hunt and not interrupt your pleasure on my account."

"It is just," and Ryan glanced at the duke, who remained silent, before continuing, "I would understand if you were apprehensive of perhaps the wrong connotation being construed upon being in his lordship's company alone, and would wish to avoid any unpleasantness. . . ."

Feeling more equal to the task, Miss Murdock replied in a much surer voice, "Oh, I can not think that we would run into any one here that would matter, that is, assuming of course, that we can trust your and Lord Tempton's discretion to not go about blabbing some ludicrous tale of his lordship and I having a *carte blanche* or some other such unlikely silliness! For I can tell you that nothing could be further from the truth, as any one with two eyes in their head looking at me could see for themselves. I am confident that Tyler will return in good time and that we will be, if not entirely appropriate, at least passably respectable from that point, and that neither I nor my reputation will come to any irreparable harm."

At the end of her speech, Ryan gave a grave nod, said, "If you are certain. Of course, you *can* trust my and Lord Tempton's discretion, but I must add, Miss Murdock, that I really can't see it, what you were saying about anyone looking at you being able to see out of hand that such a tale would be ridiculous." He looked more awkward than usual, and his ears reddened until they nearly matched the redness of his hair, but he turned with dignity then to the duke and added, "Milord St. James, I trust that you will behave appropriately in this situation?"

To which St. James replied with matching seriousness, "You can have my hand upon it if you wish, young Ryan." Ryan murmured that of course the duke's word was more than adequate for him.

With that off his chest, Ryan mounted his horse, waited while a groom assisted his brother in mounting his. Then with a last penetrating stare at Miss Murdock from his young, earnest eyes, he tipped his hat to her and said, "Miss Murdock, milord Duke." Bertie echoed his sentiments, and then they were off, trotting from the yard and into the chill of the morning.

Miss Murdock turned to find St. James' eyes assessing her, which made her color heighten.

"Well, Miss Murdock, as you can see, I am honor bound to behave myself, for I do not wish to have young Ryan calling me out in a duel if I were to perhaps sully you in any way."

"And I am sure, milord, that it was no hardship for you to promise such, so please do not make yourself sound in any way self-sacrificing."

He did not say anything for a long moment, but the gold of his eyes flared up, and he said, "Ah, it must be a comfort for you to believe that, Miss Murdock, so I shall not disabuse you of that idea. Not now at any rate." He took her arm, made to escort her in to the inn, then hesitated. Instead, he added, and his words were husky as he spoke softly into her ear, "Do not forget that just a few hours past, I saw you when your hair was down and your eyes had the soft glow of the lamps' reflections in them, and you moved with surety and grace in your worn night gown and robe. And if there was nothing in your actions that was overtly seductive, there was still enough in your appearance to cause any man to have thoughts that are common at that time of the night." His hand tightened on her arm, and his breath brushed off her bonnet and found a crevice between her cloak and neck. "Enough said, Miss Murdock?"

And she nodded, mute, feeling her heart pound uncomfortably. In an abrupt tone, he added, "Come, for I am tired. And I do not wish to frighten you when I am not totally in control of what I say. If you are very hungry, you may dine privately, or if you wish to wait, I can join you for a meal in a little above an hour. It is up to you, Miss Murdock."

He moved with her to the door of the inn, and Miss Murdock fell into stride beside him, his hand still at her arm, and they entered the darkness of the inn's interior. "I shall wait with no hardship," was all she could think to say and he nodded. He spoke with the innkeeper, advising him that he should like to retain his rooms from the night before for another few hours, and also a private salon for Miss Murdock, with tea, and any buns or other light snacks that she may wish.

The innkeeper appeared happy to fulfill his lordship's wishes and St. James accompanied her to her salon door, apologized for the inconvenience to her of being left to her own devices, and then seeing her settled, excused himself to go to his room of before next door. "If any one disturbs you, Miss Murdock, you need only summon me. So please do not be afraid."

Miss Murdock, who was not in the least afraid, for she could not likely credit anyone bursting into her salon and offering to do her harm when she was but five miles from her own home and had spent a good deal of time alone there without incident, merely said, "Of course, milord." Then he was gone. A chambermaid brought her in an assortment of buns, cakes, breads, biscuits, a steaming cup of tea, and a London newspaper on the side, a day old, but what matter, as it was all new to Miss Murdock, and she settled in to a comfortable respite from the duke and his disturbing presence and, she admitted to herself, his even more disturbing words.

It was little more than an hour later when he returned. He was shaved, his dark locks tied back in a brief ponytail and he had on fresh clothing from his bag, which had evidently remained at the inn. Miss Murdock wished she looked half as fresh, for she had, to her chagrin, ended dozing on the settee, finding herself tired after being up at half past two that morning, and now she felt a good deal crumpled. She was in the act of re-pinning her hair into its severe bun at the nape of her neck when he knocked and then entered. With his appearance, she found her fingers clumsy, and when she wished to be done with the task with the most possible speed, she instead was fumbling beneath his gold eyes.

He closed the door behind him, strode over to where she sat, still dealing with her rebellious hair, and he told her, "Turn slightly, Miss Murdock, and I will endeavor to help you. For frankly, you are making a mess of it. If we walk out of here with you looking like that, there will be no end to the ruination of your reputation."

"Oh, bother!" she said and allowed him to help.

"Have you a brush?" She had taken a small one from her reticule when beginning her own efforts, and now she handed it to him, feeling foolish.

He took the brush and showed a good deal of finesse in brushing out the long strands of her hair and then twisted them tight, wrapped them around and pinned them into place. She did not ask where he had attained his skill, guessing sourly that it was not the first time that it had been imperative that a young miss walk from a room appearing unmussed in his presence.

There was a knock on the door, and he called enter and rose from where he had placed one knee on the settee as he had assisted her. The door opened and two men brought in a small table, set with two places, and a chambermaid followed with a tray holding several covered platters of food. The men put down the table, drew up two chairs to it from one side of the room, and the chambermaid placed the platters on the center of it. She asked milord if there would be anything else to which he replied that all looked well, and the three left without any further comment.

St. James pulled out a chair for Miss Murdock, settled her at the table and then took his own place.

Miss Murdock, who had eaten rather more of the buns and cakes than she had first expected, ate little, and St. James ate hardly more, causing her to wonder that he survived adequately, for she was far more used to her father's incessant appetite.

In short order they were finished, and lingered only over their cups of tea, which she had been surprised to see him settle for, as there was an ample supply of brandy, whiskey, claret, sherry, and assorted schnapps on a sideboard in the room.

"Now, Miss Murdock, we will have that promised conversation if you wish."

"Yes. I am glad to see you have not forgotten."

He raised a brow, took a sip from his cup, set it down and waited for her to go on.

Miss Murdock gathered her thoughts, wanting to approach the subject with firm diplomacy. "Milord," she began. "As it is apparent that you entered this foolhardy agreement with the aim of acquiring my horse, perhaps that is where we should begin." She waited for his comment but there was none, so she continued. "I admit it would cost me personally a good deal, for I prize Leaf highly, but I have come to the conclusion that the only way for me to be out of this predicament is to give her to you."

He gave a thin smile. "That desperate, Miss Murdock?"

"No, milord. Merely that filled with misgivings. As surely you must be by now."

"I have been filled with misgivings from the start, Miss Murdock."

"Well! I am only surprised because you have not shown it. But now, with your admission, I am hopeful that you will take what I am offering you and leave this situation feeling completely satisfied, that in the end, you have attained your objective after all, and with a good deal less pain than what could have been otherwise."

"But I have not obtained my entire objective, Miss Murdock," he countered.

"Be that as it may, any further objective you may have, can not be, I regret but truthfully say, any concern of mine."

"But it does concern you, Miss Murdock. For my further objective is to marry you."

No, milord!" she returned, more heat in her voice than she thought was advisable, but unable to help herself. "If you are truly bent on marrying, your objective clearly can not be dependent upon my being your wife. I have come to the conclusion from what little I have been able to gather of your unfathomable motives, that you merely think you require *a* wife, not a *particular* wife. If I am correct and that is the case being, may I suggest, humbly but sincerely suggest, that you find *another* wife. Someone perhaps that is actively seeking a husband, and not myself, who is *not* actively seeking a husband."

His eyes narrowed, not from anger or even irritation she suspected, but more from his thoughts. "Let us leave my motives for seeking a wife be for a moment, Miss Murdock. Let us rather discuss why it is you are not seeking a husband. Can you elaborate on that please?"

"I hardly see that it could make any difference to you, milord."

"You are curious of my motives, are you not?"

And as much as Miss Murdock wished to say she wasn't, she couldn't in truth reply in that manner, so she did admit, "I have wondered, yes, what would impel a duke, moneyed and privileged and, despite being of a certain disreputable renown, and rather disagreeable, I might add, but still extremely favored as a husband by most any female, to feel that he must obtain a wife in a highly unorthodox manner."

"So you are allowed to be curious of my motives, but I am not allow-ed to be curious of your own?"

"Mayhaps I am curious, but I do not see you *satisfying* my curiosity, milord."

"Satisfy mine, Miss Murdock," and he gave a delicate pause, a wicked little grin turning up the corners of his mouth, "and I shall satisfy yours."

Miss Murdock bowed her head, sipping from her tea cup in a shaking hand effort to hide her fluster. How could he know that she could be, in fact, curious about that, when she herself had not acknowledged it to herself? Or had he in his great egotism merely assumed that every wo-man he encountered under the age of eighty must have that thought flit through her mind at some point in his presence? And had probably had enough cloying attention to prove him right?

"Miss Murdock," he began, and his brief suggestive look was not evident in his voice, reassuring her, "let me suggest that you mayhaps envisioned yourself remaining on with your father well into his dotage, until at some unfortunate time in the future when he died. And that after that, assuming that he lived for a goodly amount of years and you were perhaps by then in your forties or mayhaps even fifties, you had envisioned yourself having a small bit put back, through diligence and economy, and bethought that you would perhaps sell the estate, your father having, I am guessing, no apparent heirs, for whatever sum it would get, and buying yourself a small cottage, and living the remainder of your life doing whatever small tasks you found pleasure in. Perhaps gardening, or reading, or being of some use nursing others in need."

"Vetting," she said, her voice small. "I'm good with all animals, not just horses, and have learned quite a bit from our old groom, Kennedy, about poultices and herbs and drenching. I've nursed numerous hares and birds, pigs and calves, as well as horses. He says I have the knack for it."

There was silence, and she was reluctant to meet his eyes, for now that she had spoken the words aloud, there could be nothing but condolence in his eyes, for it all sounded pitiful and hopeless even to herself, and she snuffled, afraid she would cry, and wondered why on earth she should find anything to cry over, for it was as good a life as many had and better than a good deal many more.

"I thought as much," he said. "Although I did not foresee the vetting. Of which I should have, for it is apparent that it is very important to you to care for others, be it your father or those that can not even voice their needs."

She nodded, feeling miserably exposed, to criticism or laughter or pity.

"I admire your plans, Miss Murdock," he told her, his voice grave. "For you to think of nothing but the comfort of others and to intend to devote your life to it, and finding pleasure and, I dare say, fulfillment in it, is breathtakingly fresh from what I have been exposed to."

"Then perhaps," she sniffled, "you should find a more worthy crowd to run with, milord, besides gamblers and the like."

He smiled as she glanced at him. "I admit that what I have been exposed to, I have sought out, but I have had a reason for keeping the company I keep and spending time in the most unsavory of places. To find a snake, one must seek where they are apt to be found, and perhaps become a bit of a snake himself, in order to slither in their midst."

He shook his head as she stared at him, took a ruminative sip of his tea. Then he glanced at her, his eyes like a pointed finger. "Let me sketch another future for you, Miss Murdock, and please do not dismiss it out of hand. Your father taken care of, either in our home or his, whichever he prefers. And perhaps his life lengthened somewhat by the joy of a grandchild to dandle on his knee. And what could be more satisfying to a caring heart than to have a tiny babe to look after, to nurture and love, spoil and discipline? To have the time and the means to travel with that child, to educate him, and to show him all those caring skills you already possess. To be free, perhaps, to live your life any way you choose, whether it be a cottage, after all, where you can grow many flowers instead of vegetables from necessity, or a great manor, if your taste runs for it, or a townhouse in London, if you enjoy the opera and the playhouse and the amusing social circles. In short, Miss Murdock, I am offering you the freedom of choice, to live as you please, where you please, or to change residences and activities as you see fit. Mayhaps you would be constrained in having me as a husband, but as you admit that you were not hoping to fulfill some ideal of love, would it really matter? And there is always the possibility that you would be free to marry again, should I die prematurely, and even that constraint would be gone from you. Am I really doing you such a disservice, Miss Murdock? For I assure you, should I live, I would make every effort to accommodate you and your wishes, would not stand in the way of your finding fulfillment in any way you wished, even if it meant a lover that you found yourself attracted to, as long as I had an heir already, and you were properly discreet."

She nearly dropped her teacup at his final words, could not keep herself from gaping at him.

"Do not look so shocked, Miss Murdock. It is often done so, I assure you."

"I find that appalling," she gasped at last. "I am not sure which is more appalling: that you fully intend for this marriage to be--to be--so *complete* as for you to have an heir, or that you would so casually turn a blind eye if I were to carry on an indiscretion after you had obtained an heir!"

"Ah, you have very provincial notions about marriage, indeed, Miss Murdock. I vouch that, as I have described, it is very common and accepted. No one would think the lesser of either you or I."

"I should think that *I* would think a great deal less of myself," she squeaked. "I can only credit your belief that this behavior is acceptable to the company that you keep. For if you associated with a more decent class of people, I am certain you would find that their views match mine."

"Enough, Miss Murdock," he said. "You are moving beyond expressing your views and into lecturing them."

"Be that as it may, milord, I have to decline your offer, finding it both distasteful and smacking of immoral. To enter into a marriage with every expectation of being adulterous within it can not, I believe, be advisable."

"I am sorry you feel that way, Miss Murdock. Would you rather that I woo, pursue and court you, profess feelings I do not have, elicit these same feelings from you, maneuver you into marrying me, and then perhaps leave you a grieving widow in short order? Or bearing in mind that I survive, have you shocked and hurt when I conduct affairs on the side, to which you in your belief that I truly loved you, would be hurt, humiliated, and possibly heartbroken?"

"You are a cad! The options you present are equally objectionable to me, as they must be to anyone with even a shred of decency, of which you are obviously *lacking*. I can not prevent you from offering this atrocious proposal to another female, but I can, myself, refuse it, of which I am doing now. I would wish you better luck elsewhere, but I would be lying, for I certainly hope that no other female out there is so anxious to be titled and rich that she would sell any other chance at happiness she may one day have to attain those much over-touted commodities."

St. James stood up from his chair at the end of her words, placed one fist on the table top and leaned upon it. "Is there any thing you wish to add to your diatribe, Miss Murdock? Or are we finally at the end of your reprimand?"

She stood herself, furious, for he seemed totally unaffected by her speech, except for a small tic beneath one eye. "Oh, there is plenty that I could add, milord, but I fear that I would be merely covering much of the same ground, and as a result, beating a dead horse! For if the words I have already spoken do not shame you into seeing sense, I fear that nothing on this earth could."

"Good," he ground out. "Now, if you can possibly keep your outrage under wraps for a brief few minutes, I will endeavor to think of a satisfying compromise to this situation."

"I have already offered you one," Miss Murdock reminded him through clenched teeth. "You take my horse and walk away and I return to my home."

"Unacceptable, Miss Murdock," the duke returned in short order. "Now if you will be quiet and allow me to think for a moment!"

Miss Murdock stood fuming, biting her lip, but when St. James turned from her and began pacing back and forth the width of the room, one finger rubbing at his upper lip, she realized that he was, in fact, concentrating, and felt a small hope that he *would* heed her words, *would* give consideration to her utter reluctance to enter into alliance with him, no matter how much it seemed to be upsetting all of his carefully set plans.

She had a sudden wish that she could understand why it was so important to him, not that it would change her mind, she reassured herself, for it most certainly wouldn't! But for any man to be so bent on marrying a woman he had not met until yesterday, and who professed no infatuation or other romantic feeling for said woman was a mystifying puzzle to her, and she would have been less than human if she were not the slightest bit intrigued.

He turned on her, his pacing halted. "I shall have to change my plans slightly, damn it. And the bit of insurance I hoped to have will be gone."

"I am sorry if I am inconveniencing you, milord," Miss Murdock said with bitterness.

He threw her a quick grin, obviously distracted as he had been speaking more to himself than to her. "Are you, Miss Murdock? I doubt it!" Then he was off pacing again, his finger rubbing, rubbing at his lip. "There is no way around it, that I can see," he muttered. "I had planned on your going to London and having your coming out, as you had not had it yet. I shall have to simply go forward with this immediately instead of delaying until after we had gone to Gretna Green."

Miss Murdock, making every effort to follow this dialogue his lordship was having with himself, said, "I can not see, if that were your intention all along that I should have my season, how forgoing a trip to Gretna Green would be so very bad."

His dark head came up and his gold eyes focused on her with intensity. "But it is, Miss Murdock, for now I can hardly send you to London with, had God been willing, my child in your womb, if I have not taken you to Gretna Green and married you first."

Chapter Seven

Miss Murdock collapsed onto her chair. She placed her head in her hands, and from between her fingers said, "I really, really wish to go home now."

"I'm sorry. I have shocked you," St. James told her. He ran an agitated hand through his hair. "Blast this whole situation. I have cursed it many times, but I have never had to see it so completely bleed over onto another as it is today."

In response to his words, his savage voice, Miss Murdock dropped her hands from her face and regarded him in silence. He spun away from her on his booted heel, walked the length of the room with jarring strides. Then he spun back around, walked back toward her. "I am trying very hard to accommodate your wishes, Miss Murdock, so you needn't look at me like that."

Miss Murdock, who could not have named what expression she had on her face, for it felt so foreign to her, merely said, "I am sorry, milord," and she gave a little grievous laugh. "I must apologize, I suppose, for interrupting your so very thorough plans for my own person."

"Come, Miss Murdock. I said marriage, I said it would be as soon as possible. I spoke of heirs. I assumed you would naturally realize what marriage would entail. Immediately."

"Frankly, milord, I had given it no thought at all, since, as you had made clear, this was to be a bloodless marriage made out of convenience and not feeling."

He sighed at that, a single sound of displeasure and exasperation. "Now that you know exactly the extent of my intentions, you would not see your way clear to changing your mind, would you, Miss Murdock?" he asked her cheekily.

"No!" Miss Murdock returned. He had shocked her to such a degree that even this further reference to unmentionable matters could shock her no further. Or his suggestion that she would welcome them.

"Quite." He paced again.

Miss Murdock sat back in her chair, struggling with the undisciplined, shadowy images that his words had brought to mind. Because her thoughts were getting a bit out of control, she said more sharply than she intended, "Since I am being so *unfairly* uncooperative, perhaps you would do better to abandon any further plans you have for me, milord, and find another a little more eager to accommodate you."

St. James glanced at her, a frown drawing his brows together, but when he spoke, his voice was flip, "No, Miss Murdock. I have already spent a good deal of my time merely convincing you to leave your home. I do not look forward to starting anew with some other female. So please, bear with me, and I am sure if I cannot make you happy, I can at least make you somewhat less unhappy."

"You think I am being totally unreasonable, I see, in wanting to control my own life," Miss Murdock observed. "To me, it is not only reasonable, but a basic desire, and yet all you do is mock me, as though I were some sort of oddity."

"You *are* an oddity, Miss Murdock," he returned. "But you misunderstand if you think I mock you, for I mock only myself. Your desires are reasonable, and what I ask of you is totally unreasonable, and yet I find that I am even willing to do this with barely a qualm." His next words were murmured to himself more than to her. "I have walked so long with the dead, have practiced their ways for so long, that even should I have the chance to live, I doubt if I will know how to go about it."

Giving a puzzled frown, Miss Murdock said in impatience, "I do not understand you, milord. You give every appearance of regretting what you do even before you have done it, and yet you insist on doing it."

"If I were as insistent as you say, we would not be having this conversation now, but would instead be on our way to fulfill the plans I had made previously."

A bright spot of color invaded each of Miss Murdock's cheeks. "You shall hold that threat over my head, now, I see, in order to keep me in line. You are something of a bully, sir."

"I am not used to this incessant questioning of my motives and my decisions, you stubborn lass," he returned. "I realize that your acquaintance with me is short, but if there were another here that knew me, they would tell you that you have already pushed me far further than I normally allow."

"And you seem to think that no one but you is capable of making any decision, even if it is about their own future happiness," she countered. "I can not believe that whatever motivates you is so compelling as to make these actions you take right or even acceptable."

His jaw tightened, and he did not look at her for a long moment, but placed a fisted hand on the table and bowed his head. "You are right, Miss Murdock, and I can hardly blame you for pointing it out to me. No motive, however compelling can make this right. But what you do not understand, and what I will endeavor to explain to you for the final time, is: I do not care." He lifted his head and his gold eyes were like twin icons in his face, cold and hard and metallic. He went on, his voice chillingly reasonable, "You are of the proper age, a little young for me perhaps, but better than being thirteen years older. You are no beauty, but neither are you so displeasing as to make one stop and wonder why I should marry you. Your father is, I regret to say, rather poor protection and you have no other relatives to interfere in whatever decisions I make regarding you and our life together. You have no other suitors for me to deal with and nothing in your life that I am taking you from that I should feel I am doing you any real disservice. In short, Miss Murdock, you are available and convenient. And I need you very badly. So if you must rail against something, rail against fate for bringing you to my attention. For now that I have turned my attention to you, you may fight the good fight all you wish, you may even scream and kick and slap, but it will not deter me, for I have devoted my life to accomplishing what I must accomplish. If it means turning your life upside down, I regret it, but I shall still meet my eyes in the mirror every morning without flinching. You may curse this day for the rest of your life. You may curse me, if you so wish. But in the end, you will walk down the aisle with me and if it will not be tonight, do not doubt that it will be tomorrow or the next day."

Miss Murdock blinked once, solemnly, like an owl. Her blood was beating in her head. "Why?" she asked, her voice colorless. "Why do you do this?"

St. James' eyes half closed, shuttering his expression. "It would make no difference to you, would it, Miss Murdock? For I am just a fiend, bent on my own will, and no explanation could make it seem less so to you."

Miss Murdock said with thoughtfulness, "I just wish to know for what I am being sacrificed."

His head snapped back, as though she had slapped him. "Sacrificed?" he asked wonderingly. "Now there is a word that I would not have expected." He considered for a moment, his eyes narrowing. "It does not concern you," he said finally. "As I said before, I shall either die rather abruptly, leaving you a very merry widow, or I shall live and spend all of my incredible will trying to atone to you. There is no more you need to know."

"Mayhaps not, milord. I guess that I, in all my apparent dim-wittedness, have no need to understand you or your reasoning. But you did promise, milord, to satisfy my curiosity if I satisfied yours."

His mouth twitched in some wry amusement known only to himself. He pulled out his chair at the table, seated himself with innate elegance into it, and rubbed his upper lip with one finger, brooding. Even as she watched him, knew as soon as his finger went to his lip that he would honor what he had said and tell her, as she had asked, she saw his eyes darkening as if two dark clouds had passed over the sunshine brightness of them. "I was ten years old, Miss Murdock," he began.

I was rather wild at that age, as I am sure you can believe.

Yes, milord. At this point I would believe you if you told me you were born with two horns and a tail.

If you wish to hear the story, Miss Murdock, you must indulge me just a little bit. I spent a lot of time alone, having no brothers or sisters, and at that point no cousins either. Bertie, Lord Tempton, lived on the neighboring estate in Lincolnshire, but as we were only there for holidays and summer, we did not, as of yet, see much of each other.

My father, William Desmond Larrimer, then Duke of St. James, was a close confidant of the then young Queen Victoria, as he had been to King William the fourth before her. He was very involved in sensitive work for the crown and was rarely at home for more than a few days at a time.

Larrimer. I did not even know your family's name. Or your Christian one, for that matter.

I apologize, Miss Murdock. It is Dante. No one uses it, except for my grandmother. I have been called merely St. James for many years.

My mother was very social. Big season, little season, Bath in the off-season. I never really saw her except for the summer month and Christmas at the manor. So you see, I was left mostly to my own devices and being rather naturally headstrong, I was well on my way to being out of control even before that Christmas of my tenth year.

We had gathered at Morningside, our country estate, as we had every year since I had been born. My grandmother was there, but my grandfather, the prior Duke of St. James, had already been dead since before I was born. He was much older than my grandmother when they married, and he did not marry her until he was nearly forty. It's said that I get much of my temperament from him, for he caused his share of scandals in his day also. He had eyes similar to mine. I know my grandmother still receives a shock every time she looks at me. I gather she loved him very much.

My father's younger brother was in residence for the holidays, and his new bride, my aunt Lydia. You shall meet her eventually, for she has been residing with my grandmother since my uncle's death last winter. Miss Murdock, I would not be lying if I told you that this is perhaps one of the best memories of my life. My father was there, my mother was there, and they were uncommonly happy. They were going to have a-nother child you see, after ten long years of trying. And I was very glad, for I thought, of course, that perhaps then I would not be so alone. I was very excited, for they had just confirmed she was expecting and it was all very new to me and to the others when they announced it at Christmas Dinner. I was filled with thoughts and plans, already eager to show my younger brother, for in my youthful mind it could not be but a brother, all of my secret hiding places, and the best places to scale the walls to sneak off into the surrounding woods, of which I had been strongly warned against wandering in. And I imagined being with him when he was first learning to ride, and that I would allow him my prized pony to learn upon, as I was growing too big for him at any rate, and on and on and on. I can not tell you how utterly exulted I was. I did not realize of course, that had he lived, there would have been that span of years between us, and that in reality, we would not have had as much in common as I imagined.

He did not live?

No, Miss Murdock. He was not even born.

It had been planned that we remain at Morningside until after the new year, but mid-week between Christmas and New Year's Eve, my father received a summons from the Queen. I never have been able to ascertain what it was about, as my father evidently destroyed all correspondence from the crown and kept no notes on what he was doing. All those secrets he held in his head died with him. I have often wondered how the last two decades of our history would have played out had he lived. What projects had he been working on that were to be left forever incomplete?

My mother was not particularly unhappy about the change in plans. Despite being with child and all the annoyances that I am sure a woman goes through in that condition, she was feeling quite stifled at Morningside. So she refused my grandmother's offer to stay on and to allow my father to go on ahead alone. Instead, she made ready for the trip, which, as the summons had only been received late that afternoon, would have to be made during the night. She ordered that only the essentials be packed for us, and that the rest of the luggage could be brought up the following day at a more leisurely pace. I was dressed and ready, looking forward to the trip as I considered it an adventure. For I normally traveled with my grandmother, and every journey with her was as big as a caravan and as slowly moving. She has grown even worse over the years, by the by.

However, I was no more than settled into the coach when I began to cough. It had been the cold night air, I suppose, and then the sudden closeness of the coach. And it was not just coughing, but great, loud barkings. I remember feeling my throat constricting just as quickly as you please, and wrenching out those barking coughs. It was the croup, my mother told me, and she was rather annoyed, I remember, for I hadn't had that malady since being a very young lad. There was no way she could expect me to travel in that condition. I tried to argue, for as I had said, it appealed very much to me to be out on the road at night, traveling lightly and quickly with none of the constraints of my grandmother's great expeditions. It still does, to this day, appeal to me.

At any rate, I was quickly hustled off back into the house. I no longer had a nanny, of course, but the housekeeper, Mrs. Herriot, tsked and sighed over me and hurried me up into bed, where she quickly heated and shoved in bed warmers below my feet and prepared a poultice for my throat. And all the while, I was perfectly miserable, because I knew that my time with my parents was once again at an end.

Of course, I was right. My mother spoke to my grandmother, and it was arranged that I would remain on at Morningside until after the New Year and return to London with her. My mother would go on ahead with my father, where she would manage, in all probability, to keep herself entertained in Town while my father went on about his important business.

But my father never finished that business, Miss Murdock, and my mother was never again entertained, for they were not above two miles from our home when they were set upon on that dark road and murdered. My father, my mother, and her unborn child.

It was Tyler that found them, strangely enough, for one of the horses at last managed to break free of its harness and made straight back to the stables, wild-eyed and spooked by the smell of blood in its nostrils. Tyler recognized it immediately and he and my uncle set out to find what the trouble may be, assuming at first there must have been an accident. It was well into the following morning by then. What they found was no accident. Both coachmen were dead on the ground, having been, apparently, ordered at gunpoint from their stations.

My father was still in the coach, huddled partially over my mother's form. They had killed him, and Tyler told me it looked as if they had then kicked him aside in order to, yes, kill my mother.

He should not have told you such a thing! It is too horrible!

But he did, Miss Murdock. For I have questioned him to the degree that every detail of that scene that he still sees in his mind, I see in mine.

Suddenly the salon, which had faded away from her, reeled back in upon Miss Murdock as the Duke of St. James before her uttered these last words. She blinked several times, trying to orient herself.

She was shaking, she realized, and when she spoke again, she could only choke, "I'm sorry."

The gold eyes razed her. "I did promise to satisfy your curiosity."

He pushed back his chair, got up abruptly, almost as though they had conversed of nothing of more consequence than the weather. He went to the sideboard and picked up a bottle of brandy. He hefted it in his hand several times, as if contemplating its exact weight before opening it, tilting it, and filling his glass. Then he turned to her. "As I said before, Miss Murdock, even this tragic story does not make what I do right. I would rather you go into this alliance with your eyes firmly on what you are to gain and upon nothing else. I would not wish you to get some misguided notion in your head of cooperating out of pity for me. I would much prefer you continue to hate me and argue with me than that."

"There is a large difference between pity and sympathy, milord," she attempted, but as his eyes only brooded at her, she added, "But I assure you, I will not suddenly become compliant because I still cannot fathom how your marrying in this hap-hazard manner is to further whatever cause you have set for yourself."

"You can not realize my objective?" he asked. He took a long sip of brandy and considered her over his glass rim. "You think, perhaps, that my reputation as a skilled shot is merely some fluke of nature? You don't think that I spent more time practicing with a pistol than most people spend on their knees at prayer, even the most devout?"

Miss Murdock blanched, feeling her stomach knot.

St. James nodded. "I see you understand me now, Miss Murdock. Vengeance is the word you are thinking," and he smiled.

"But marriage," she stuttered.

And he put his glass down with an abrupt thump. "Enough, Miss Murdock. I deem it necessary, and that shall have to be enough for you for one day. Do you never get weary of picking at my mind? What do you think you will find if you pick long enough? For I can assure you, you will find nothing to your liking. If my best memory is punctuated at the end by the death of my parents, what do you think all my worst memories are punctuated with? No, Miss Murdock. Do not prize at me any further than you already have, and although I am to be your husband, you would do well to keep your distance."

"I hardly find that possible when you have every intention of, of--"

"Making love to you, Miss Murdock?" he finished for her. "Well, that shall certainly be a challenge."

Whereas milord seemed to have had no qualms in traveling to Gretna Green with no proper chaperone, he seemed rather more concerned about doing the same on a journey to London. He summoned a messenger to their room, directed him to seek out Lord Tempton, Earl of Edison, at the local gentry's hunt that morning, and entrusted him with the message that the Duke of St. James would be in need of his and Mister Tempton's services after all.

Then he sat back to wait, and as he did not take kindly to cooling his heels in any one place for any length of time, he made a steady inroad into the opened bottle of brandy and presently started another.

Miss Murdock, not much happier to be stuck in the inn's salon, watching his lordship's drinking erode away the few, very few, commendable qualities she had been able to find in him, merely picked up the London newspaper that had been left with her earlier, took a seat away from St. James and near a window and began to pass the time by reading.

The only noise in the room to disturb her was the occasional clink of bottle on glass.

Some two hours had gone by, and as once again she heard him pouring, and the clinking was rather more pronounced and more jarring than it had been before, she turned in her seat and gave him an accusing glare.

He met her brown eyes, the gold of his own ominous in their warning. "Do not start, Miss Murdock, for I am beyond the recall now, and I have been known to get surly on these occasions."

To which Miss Murdock with a mumble beneath her breath for once heeded him, for the expression of his face was too forbidding for her to doubt his words. She turned back to her newspaper, wondering however she was to deal with him on a long journey to London.

Having been half-consciously waiting for relief in the form of the Tempton brothers, she caught sight of them immediately out of her window when they rode up to the yard some time later. She let the paper, which she had now perused several times in search of those articles she may have missed on her prior reading, drop in her lap as she watched them dismount. "They are here, milord," she broke the heavy silence. When she got no response, Miss Murdock turned to him.

His change of clothing, which had made him look so fresh a few hours ago, were now wrinkled and crumpled as he sprawled in his chair. He had loosened his cravat, the first few buttons on his shirt were undone, revealing the white column of his throat and a pale glimpse of upper chest. His hair had escaped the neat ponytail he had put it in before and now skewered about his dissipated face. His booted legs were stretched slothfully before him, and two empty bottles of liquor and a freshly opened bottle on the table beside him confirmed her fears that he had drank with silent, determined moodiness for the past hours.

His eyes were slits in his pale face, his dark brows drawn into a knot above them, and even as she watched, he moved his hand from the table, balancing a goblet in his fingers and brought it to his mouth.

Miss Murdock gave a sigh and moved toward him. She removed the glass from his hand, with some difficulty as he seemed reluctant to give it up, and set it with distaste on the table. She was forced to move it back further when he again reached for it. "I think you have had quite enough, milord," she told him.

He gave a soft curse. "What are you doing, Miss Murdock?"

"Buttoning your shirt and your cravat, milord, if you can endeavor to hold still for a moment. The Temptons are here, and it will not do for them to see you as such."

He brought his hands to both of hers, pinning them to his chest, where she felt his heart thumping beneath her palms, and she raised her large eyes to his drink clouded ones. "I can manage, Miss Murdock," he told her. "I wished to acquire a wife, not a nanny."

And Miss Murdock, despite feeling her face coloring, told him, "Then you should act as a man and not a child, milord."

He drew a deep breath, one that made her hands go up and then down with the movement of his chest. She became aware that she was leaning over him, that his boots were stretched out to either side of her skirts, and that he was making no sign of moving to sit up straighter nor to release her hands so that she may again stand erect. Instead, his eyelids drew up, like the hoods on a snake's eyes drawing back when something has roused it, and she found herself lost in the deep golden depths of them, aware that his nostrils were flaring and that her own chest were hurting as she held her breath.

There was a soft tapping on the door, and then it was flung open with no further ceremony and Lord and Mister Tempton strode in, panting, as they had evidently made haste upon receiving their summons. Miss Murdock tore her eyes from St. James' stare at their entrance, her face flaming with embarrassment, and tried frantically for the release of her hands from his lordship's chest.

He released them with a brief chuckle, which set her hackles up all the more, and with a little squeak, she straightened, turned in a flurry of skirts, and hid herself by going to the far corner of the room. She remained there under the pretense of searching for something in her reticule, which to her chagrin, she managed to spill in her fluster.

"Up to your old tricks, again, I see, St. James," she heard Bertie say as she dived to the floor and scrambled after her belongings. "Lucky we arrived when we did."

St. James buttoned his shirt, straightened his cravat. "I dare say it is," he agreed in a lazy voice. "For Miss Murdock has rather more charms than I initially gave her credit for."

Ryan Tempton strode over to Miss Murdock who rose to her feet, snapping closed her reticule. "I say, Miss Murdock, are you all right?"

"I am--I am fine, Mister Tempton," she managed. "It was not at all what I am sure it looked to be. He is very drunk, you know, and I was merely attempting to button his shirt and redo his cravat so that he could look more presentable." Somehow this explanation only seemed to make the situation worse, for she supposed that Mister Tempton's mind would quite naturally wonder why his lordship's cravat and shirt were undone to begin with.

But Mister Tempton placed a gentle hand on her arm, and she looked up the tall length of him and into his concerned face. "I am certain that it was all innocent on your part, Miss Murdock, but I can not doubt that Lord St. James, *being* St. James, took it in another spirit altogether."

"Oh my!" she said, his words giving her a new and unpleasant perspective. "You mean to say that he may have thought that I was--I was *initiating*. . . ?"

"I'm afraid that is very likely what he thought."

Miss Murdock, feeling quite horrified, said in a small voice, "Oh. I see. I must be more careful in the future."

"Do not blame yourself, Miss Murdock, for I am sure you could not have known! I am equally certain that had St. James not been so drunk he would not have presumed, well, what he presumed. In all likelihood, he will not remember it when he sobers, so you need not feel embarrassed or the need to explain to him."

"Yes. Of course, I am sure you are right, Mister Tempton. But I do admit I feel very foolish, indeed."

"You must realize, Miss Murdock, that St. James has not had much cause to associate with decent young ladies in his life."

"So I have come to understand," she acknowledged.

"I am glad that you shall not hold it against him, for he really is a dependable fellow, if perhaps at times a bit difficult. And I am glad that we have been summoned to chaperone you, for I must admit that I was feeling quite a bit of concern for you, not that St. James would offer to harm you," he hurried to say, "but simply because of his lamentable reputation."

Miss Murdock smiled up at him. "And I am grateful that you and Lord Tempton could see your way clear to assist us, for I must admit, I was somewhat worried that this. . . arrangement milord has in mind shall be difficult enough without a lot of gossiping to accompany it."

Ryan asked her, "It is true, then, that St. James has plans to offer for you?"

"In fact, Mister Tempton, he already has, much to my astonishment and, I confess, my dismay." She paused for a moment, then continued on in an even lower voice, "I take it that you were there, when the duke and my father were discussing. . . my future?"

Ryan made a sympathetic noise in his throat. "I am reluctant to admit that I was, Miss Murdock, only because it shows badly upon me that I did not do more to stop their shameful behavior. I advised milord quite strongly against it, and was quite scandalized when he made it known that he meant to carry out his plans immediately. I thought at the time that it could not be anything short of terrifying for you, but nothing I could say, nor Bertie even, would dissuade him. I am only grateful that he has indeed offered you marriage and has not toyed with you in any way."

"He has in fact been most adamant about marriage," Miss Murdock responded. "And although I have become aware of some of his reasoning, I still cannot think that this shall alleviate his problems in any way, but shall in fact, add to them. But no, Mister Tempton," she added, "you can at least rest easy in your mind that I was not terrified in the least, for it was all rather comical, as my father was passed out cold and the duke hardly in better shape. Watching him and his groom carry my father into my home in the middle of the night, with milord, of course, cursing roundly and abusing his groom in the most unsavory manner, was worth a lot of entertainment to me. And the poor duke was most shocked, I daresay, at my appearance, for I was in the most dilapidated sleeping costume, and when I went to make him breakfast and coffee, I sooted my cheek and burned my hand. And all this time, we are arguing, and he is quite furious, both that I should be so uncooperative and at the fact, I am sure, that he had saddled himself with such a plain bite, when although he claims to have no care what his future wife looks like, I am sure he was hoping for an *incomparable*, for wouldn't any man?

"So you see, Mister Tempton, it was not terrifying in the least, but all merely very funny and odd. And as I have convinced him to allow me a season in London instead of eloping off to Gretna Green, I can not find it in my heart to feel sorry for myself, for I am sure it is the grandest adventure I shall ever have. And I am not worried in the least, for after the duke has fully sobered and had a few days to think about it, I am sure he will cry off in a most undignified manner, and I shall return home with exciting stories to tell of my sojourn in London and my encounters with the wicked Duke of St. James."

Ryan was laughing, all the concern now washed from his face as she had intended, stretching the good points and squelching any doubts in her voice. Now he told her, "By Gad, but you are a good little trooper, Miss Murdock. If any one is able to come out of this the better off, I am sure it shall be you. Why having your season could be the making of you, and I for one, will look forward to seeing you. You shall certainly lighten the mood of what has become, I'm afraid, a bit of a bore."

He took her arm in his. "Now, we should probably assist my brother in helping St. James to his feet and readying him to go. How ever he shall drive his curricle, I do not know, and I for one, am not about to attempt driving those wild beasts of his that he calls horses."

"Oh, they are really not so bad," Miss Murdock said with just a little pride in her voice that she had managed them well enough earlier that morning, when apparently they were well-known for their hard to handle temperaments. They turned then to assist with his lordship, found to their surprise that he was already upon his feet, coat on and buttoned and although he was conferring with Bertie, he interrupted his conversation with that man at the sight of the two of them returning from the far corner of the room. He gave them both a quizzical look and then raised one silky eyebrow at Miss Murdock. "Discretion, Miss Murdock. I only require discretion. And an heir that I can confidently claim as my own, first, if you please."

Ryan dropped her arm, his face flushing, and he stammered, "I say, St. James! That was entirely uncalled for."

To which his lordship bowed. "Perhaps," he admitted. "And if I have put the wrong connotation upon your little *tête-à-tête*, I apologize."

"I would not interfere in your business, milord, even if I do not agree with it," Ryan hasted to say.

"You misunderstand me, young Ryan," St. James told him in a smooth if somewhat drunken voice. "You may interfere with my business all you wish. It is the interfering with my betrothed that I would look so unfavorably upon."

Ryan appeared to take offense at this glib response, but Bertie stepped between them. "No harm done, St. James. Ryan is aware of his responsibility, that he must look higher than Miss Murdock if he is to secure his own future. Very well for you, milord, do not get me wrong. You have money you see! But for Ryan, t'would not do at all, as well he knows it, so there is no call blustering at the boy when I am certain he was merely showing a courteous concern for Miss Murdock's welfare."

St. James nodded. "Ah, yes. The old 'slights where there are none, and insults where there are only slights' speech. I remember. Well, can not hurt to let him be warned, but I will not badger him further."

Miss Murdock, who had been somewhat taken aback by the little scene being played out in front of her, realized now that Lord Tempton seemed to have his lordship well in hand, so she turned to gather her cloak, tie on her bonnet and again pick up her reticule. Her valise had remained with the curricle, so she did not have to concern herself with it.

They left the salon, waited as St. James settled his account, asked that his bag be brought down, and called for his curricle to be brought around. Then they left the inn and went out into the welcoming sunshine, although there was still a good deal of chill in the air, to await St. James' conveyance. Bertie had evidently already spoken with his groom, who had remained at the inn while he and Ryan had gone on their hunt, for a barouche with the Edison crest was already drawn up and waiting.

"Are you well enough to drive, St. James?" Ryan asked, being of good nature and more inclined to let the small unpleasantness of before die in peace. "For as I was telling Miss Murdock, I would as lief not try to drive your bays."

"I will manage, young Ryan, do not fear. But I have been thinking that it may be rather better for Miss Murdock to travel with you and Bertie in your barouche rather than have her arrive in London in my company. It will be after dark when we arrive as it is, and even with a chaperone, I fear it will draw attention to her before I really wish it."

"That makes good sense," Bertie agreed. "And I needn't fear for Miss Murdock's safety if you drive yourself into the ditch in your condition, either."

"I've never driven into a ditch yet, Bertie, as you very well know it. But all the same, I am sure Miss Murdock will be more comfortable with you. I shall ride ahead and attempt to intercept my groom, who I will in all probability meet somewhere upon the road. You may deposit Miss Murdock at my grandmother's home, as I have already written her a letter telling her of a coming visitor. I shall be there before you to let her know that she will be arriving a little sooner than I had anticipated, and will see you there."

Miss Murdock, feeling like a package being passed from one hand to another to be finally *deposited* at her designated destination only bowed her head as these instructions were being made known and had the vague thought that she would miss riding with his lordship, for surely the trip would have gone much faster if she only had someone to argue with.

To her surprise, St. James stepped forward, lifted her down turned chin with one slender finger and told her in a teasing voice, "Goodbye, Miss Murdock. I shall see you in London. And as we have thoroughly exhausted each other, I am sure you shall welcome the opportunity to recover without my presence."

Bertie gave a little harrumph and Ryan gagged a cough, and Miss Murdock came to realize that quite a bit could be read into his lordship's statement. She colored up furiously and it did not help when milord added before releasing his finger from her chin, "You have very fine eyes, Miss Murdock, especially when you are blushing."

Then he turned and sauntered away, unsteadily mounted his curricle which had made its appearance in the interim, and took the reins from the groom who had been leading his team.

Chapter Eight

Lady Lenora Larrimer, Dowager Duchess of St. James, unsealed the letter that her aging butler, Ashton, had brought in to her. She had just finished her evening meal, eating at the hour of eight o'clock, and had settled herself in her most favored chair in the drawing room. Her daughter-in-law, Lydia, joined her, doing petit point, her blonde head with the few strands of white through it bent over her work and reflecting the light of the fire from the fireplace.

"Thank you, Ashton," Lady Lenora said, and then, as she scanned the signature at the bottom of the short missive, added, "It is from Dante."

"Yes, milady. His groom, Tyler, delivered it just a few moments ago."

Lady Lenora read the short missive, one of her silver brows raising higher as she read each succinct sentence. She reached the end, turned the letter over in her fragile, arthritic hands in futile attempt to find further information. "What is this, Ashton?" she asked her butler, who, of course having no knowledge of the contents of the letter, was unable to answer. "Is Tyler still here?"

"Yes, milady. The cook was giving him a plate in the kitchen. He looked rather done in as well as hungry."

"Well, you had better show him in, Ashton, for this letter is only mystifying me rather than enlightening me. Hardly unusual for my grandson," she added on a dry note.

Ashton left to procure Tyler and Lady Lenora once again skipped from sentence to sentence in the letter, her faded eyes bright with interest. *A charming young lady from Chestershire. . . daughter of a Squire.* A Squire. Lord help her, Lady Lenora thought. Still, for Dante to show an interest in any young lady, in a respectable way at least, was quite re-markable. Quite remarkable.

As she is already in her twentieth year and has never had her coming out, and knowing, dear grandmother, how you are always looking for some activity to lighten your boredom, I shall be sending her to you in a few days. I trust that between you and Aunt Lydia, you will make her welcome to stay for the season and help her with any little adjustments that may need made in her wardrobe.

I shall finance her, of course.

Until I see you again
Your loving grandson
Always
St. J.

It was the last sentence that seemed to be the crowning touch on the whole disturbing letter. Finance her? St. James could not be so blind as to think that if this were made known, there could be any chance of the girl making a proper alliance with anyone else. Not that the Dowager would not enjoy spending his money, but it would have to be kept carefully under wraps. Which meant that the Dowager would have to find some reason for this--this Miss Murdock having been invited to her home for the season that had nothing to do with her grandson.

Surely he must know this. Knowing her grandson, he knew it very well, and had been laughing to himself as he penned that line, already foreseeing the ancient wheels of his grandmother's mind starting to spin. He knew her too well, that one did, and he knew very well she would enjoy the touch of intrigue that wafted from the letter like a faint perfume.

And whatever was possessing her grandson to take an interest in this young lady? Quite, *quite* unlike St. James to expend any time or energy in trying to assist some one else. Not unless he were after something himself.

Ashton tapped on the door, causing Lady Lenora to fold up the letter even as she bade him to again come in. Her daughter-in-law, Lydia, was still sewing, but she saw her blue eyes glance up, curious of whatever was progressing without her knowledge, but reluctant to show it. Oh, she was a dull one was Lydia. Lady Lenora would never fathom what her younger son had seen in her, other than that she had been extremely beautiful those twenty-three years ago when they had first married. Twenty-four, actually, as it was November.

God help her, although she would love to see St. James married, she hoped he had not fallen for an empty, pretty face. Like Lydia.

"Milady?" Tyler asked, coming awkwardly within a few feet of her chair. He could not be anything but confident and in-control when outside or in the stables, but bring the man into the house and he was all thumbs and elbows. He shifted some object in his mouth from one guilty cheek to the other and Lady Lenora, not knowing whether to be amused or exasperated, told him, "You may spit your tobacco into the fire, Tyler, and try to remember not to chew again when you are in my house."

He did as she asked, wiped an indelicate arm across his mouth. "Sorry, milady."

"That's quite all right, Tyler. Though why you insist on that filthy habit, I do not know. Probably from dealing every day with my grandson, I suppose, for one must surely have some vice to keep themselves sane when being constantly in his presence."

"Aye, milady. You've hit the nail on the head there, milady," he told her with certainty, which made the many papery lines about her mouth crease into a smile.

"Now, Tyler, you will tell me what it is my grandson is up to. Who is this Miss Murdock? When did he meet her and why is he sending her to my home for her coming out?"

Tyler rubbed one hand along his grizzled jaw. "Well, milady, she is the daughter of a Squire in Chestershire. He met her yesterday afternoon when he went to look at a horse of the Squire's. I gather she has no relatives or acquaintances in town for her to stay with for her coming out, and St. James, seeing her plight, was moved to help her."

"*Humph!*" Lady Lenora said. "St. James has never been moved to help any one in any plight." She paused a moment, her fingers tapping a delicate tattoo on the gold head of her cane that rested by her side. "Is she enough to turn his head, Tyler? For I have seen St. James pass by some uncommonly beautiful women, or if he became involved with them, drop them without a qualm when whatever business he had with them was at an end. She must be very beautiful indeed, if he has been moved to this."

"Beautiful?" Tyler asked with an unreadable expression on his face. "No, milady, t'is not the tag I, for one, would put upon her."

Lady Lenora eyed him with some annoyance, feeling she was getting no where quickly, and getting the suspicion that Tyler had distinct orders to make sure that she did not. "Well, what 'tag' would you put upon her?" she asked the groom.

Tyler considered a moment standing stocky-legged, his shoulders still broad despite being now some fifty years of age. His hand went to his pocket for his pouch of tobacco before he remembered himself and let it be. "Brown," he answered, causing the Duchess to leave off fingering her cane and to instead grasp it and bang it on the floor.

"Brown?" she demanded. "That is all you can say about the girl is that she is brown?"

"Very much so, milady. Very brown."

And Lady Lenora responded by saying tetchily, "Be away with you, Tyler, you cheeky bugger, for I can see my grandson holds all of your loyalties, as usual."

"Yes, milady," he said, hiding a smile.

"Well, you heard me, be off, before I take this cane to your back."

"Yes, milady," he said again, not in the least intimidated, which caused her to give a reluctant smile. "I will add, milady, that I think you shall like her."

"Indeed?" the duchess grinned, finding some satisfaction, at last, in this assessment. "Well, I shall look forward to seeing what St. James has selected to keep me entertained for the coming months. For I can see no reason for this behavior other than his ill-conceived notion that I have nothing better to do with my time but follow his vagaries."

And Tyler could not resist saying before he turned to leave, "I think you will find the coming months very entertaining, milady, and a good deal at St. James' expense."

This caused the Duchess to laugh, and she muttered to herself as she watched the groom move to the door that Ashton held open for him. "Cheeky as always. Cheeky as always. Well, Ashton," she continued when her butler returned to her side, his back rather bowed and what was left of the hair on his balding dome very white. "What do you make of this?"

"I learned many years ago, Lady Lenora, that where your grandson is concerned, one should always hesitate in making any deductions, for he is certain to confound whatever conclusions one makes."

"You are so right, Ashton," she returned. "As always."

"Well," Lydia spoke up from where she had sat in silence through all, "I think he is up to his usual disgraceful conduct. Expecting you to take on this girl without ever having made her acquaintance."

And Lady Lenora banged her cane once for effect. "If she is good e-nough for St. James to take even the slightest interest in, she shall be good enough for me, Lydia. And for you, also."

Lydia pulled her thread through her cloth with more than her usual force. "Of course, Lady Lenora."

The door opened then, and a young man with dark hair and blue eyes strode into the room. His face was rather petulant, although un-commonly handsome, and Lydia dropped her sewing, saying, "There you are, Andrew. If you insist on missing your evening meal, you should send word around, as I have told you many times."

"Yes, mother," he said with impatience. "Was that St. James' man I saw leaving?"

"Yes. It was," Lydia returned. "But you needn't get excited, for St. James has not, to my knowledge, returned to town. His groom was merely delivering a missive to your grandmother."

"Oh," the young man said, seeming quite a bit deflated. "That is all very well, then, it is just that I thought he may have returned early. Frightfully boring in this town without him around."

"Pleasantly peaceful, I should say," his mother returned. "I have told you before that although he is your cousin, I would not wish for you to put too fine a point upon his behavior, as more times than not it is disgraceful."

At which point, Lady Lenora interrupted. "And I have told you before, Lydia, please do not run St. James down in my hearing. Your opinion of him is your own and I can not change it, neither, I admit, has St. James ever done anything to ease your mind in regards to his character, but I will not tolerate hearing his own family speak ill of him."

Lady Lydia gave a tight smile. "I apologize, Lady Lenora. It is, of course, inexcusable of me. I only wish that when Andrew is around that St. James would be a little more considerate of the fact that he is still quite impressionable and is wont to romanticize his lordship's behavior rather than see it as the handicap it actually is. I have often thought that he has not married because his reputation is nearly impossible for those worthy families among our peerage to ignore, rather than that he were merely so choosy. If he has taken an interest in a Squire's daughter, I daresay it is from necessity rather then any thing else."

"Nonsense!" Lady Lenora replied with force. "He is a Larrimer, I need not remind you. If he were to merely bow in any baggage's direction they would immediately favor his company over all others, no matter what his reputation. And her father and mother would be quickly, and somewhat joyfully, I dare say, mollified by his worth and his title!"

"Yes, milady. I dare say you are right. But I only say this and I will say nothing more: he is lucky to be a duke, for if he did not have that protection, every respectable door would have closed to him long ago."

"You may be quiet now, Lydia," the duchess said, ending the conversation.

Andrew, who had been striding about the room while his mother and grandmother bickered, broke in to say, "Really, mother, he is merely going about the business of finding the murderer of his parents. There is bound to be some fallout from that sort of activity, but you can not simply expect him to stop because it has put a few mars on his reputation."

His mother gave a little gasp, her needlepoint forgotten. "Who told you that?"

"Why, no one," Andrew said with a vague wave of his hand. "I know it is only what I should do if I were in the same situation. I admit, I admire him for it."

"See!" Lydia turned to the Duchess, quite beside herself. "He breaks every rule of society with seemingly no regard for it, and my son *admires* him for it."

Lady Lenora's faded eyes narrowed, and her head shook a little as she responded, "There are some things, Lydia, that are bigger than social standing and who gets vouchers to Almacks. I for one, do not think it will harm Andrew to find this out now."

"Well, I for one," Lydia returned, picking up her petit point and jabbing her needle through it with viciousness, "would never be able to hold my head up again if my son were denied vouchers to Almacks. And I happen to know that St. James has not been sent vouchers for that establishment in years!"

Andrew said, "Oh, Almacks is a bloody bore, mother. I should be happy if I were to be taken off their precious list."

"Do not curse, Andrew, in the presence of ladies. And you would do yourself better to attend Almacks more often instead of hanging about Whites or Boodles and those other unsavory places."

"St. James hangs about a good deal more unsavory hells than that, and he has come out all right."

"Enough!" the Duchess cried before her daughter-in-law could respond, and hence the argument should go further. "Lydia, you keep your son on much too short a string. He shall turn out even worse than St. James if you continue to nag him to death. He is twenty-three years old. You can not expect him to hang about dancing attendance on your every smothering whim. And as for Almacks, I merely need to say the word and I could have vouchers for St. James tomorrow, if I so wish. And I guarantee that rather than reluctance, the committee ladies would fall all over themselves with eagerness to provide them. For if they quit sending them to him, it is only because he has never stepped foot in that place once in all his years and they had given up on luring him in." At the end of her words, she banged her cane for her butler, who had left the room some time ago, as was his custom. "Ashton!" When he opened the door, she told him a good deal out of humor, "You may assist me up the stairs now, for I am ready to call it a day!"

Andrew came over to her even before the butler with his aged strides could reach her. He kissed her wrinkled cheek, which she turned up for him to do so, and he whispered, "I am sorry if we have upset you, grandmother."

"Not at all," she returned, but when her daughter-in-law bid her good night, her head once again bent over her sewing, the duchess merely said, "And good night to you, also, Lydia," and allowed Ashton to help her from her seat.

It was well past eleven and although she was now comfortable in her bed, the lamp still burning beside her, a novel held in her fragile hands, and a plate of wafers at her side, she could not concentrate on reading, and she knew herself also to be unable to sleep if she tried, although she was quite tired.

She had her concerns. Oh, indeed, she had her concerns.

It was not often that she allowed Lydia to upset her with her strait-laced views. For she knew her daughter-in-law to be such a slave to the conventions as to be blind to any other consideration in life. But her accusations of St. James' very public and unrepentant behavior coupled with Andrew's off-hand summary of why he behaved as he did had disturbed the Duchess greatly.

She had realized for years what St. James was about, although she could not approve of his methods. And as much as she would like to see the perpetrator of the crime that had robbed her of so much, had indeed been the greatest grief in her life, brought to justice, she was reluctant to see her most doted upon grandson continue in what was beginning to seem to her a futile quest. He was nearly beyond the recall of all civilized boundaries of society, as Lydia had so spitefully pointed out, and she had a sudden fear that she would see him go beyond the recall of even herself.

St. James had always heeded her to a degree, more to indulge her, she had the suspicion, than because he truly took her advice to heart. But if she were to see him make any sort of life for himself beyond this unholy mission he had set for himself, she was going to have to make a valiant effort to take him in hand, a final time, and convince him that all he had done these many years was enough, and that it was time for him to move beyond. If the murderer of those many years ago had been findable, surely St. James would have found him by now!

It was time for him to stop, before he spiraled further down a path that would result, she was now sure, only in his own self-destruction.

Somehow, this sudden involvement of a mysterious Squire's daughter did not bring her any comfort but more of a feeling of foreboding. She could not credit that even an *incomparable* could manage to halt Dante long enough in his tracks to have him for an instant take anything or anyone else into consideration, not when he was so bent on vengeance. From what Tyler had told her, this Miss Murdock was not an *incomparable*.

This Miss Murdock was merely brown.

There was no rhyme nor reason to any of it, and she felt that there was something spinning in St. James' unfathomable mind that was going beyond even his usual tactics. And his usual tactics were quite deplorable enough.

There was a tap on her bed chamber door, and rather than being annoyed to be interrupted at this late hour, she rather welcomed it, for it at least stopped her mind from the endless circles it had been moving in. "Yes. I am awake, you may come in," she bade, and moved her thin-fleshed arms to aid herself in sitting up further.

It was Soren, her lady's maid, as bowed with age, nearly, as her employer. "I am sorry to interrupt you so late, milady, but I thought you would wish to know that your grandson, milord Duke of St. James, has just arrived."

"Here?" her ladyship asked, surprised. "If he has blown back into town, I can hardly see why he would come here instead of his own townhouse. Has he asked for me?"

"No. He did not wish to disturb you, but. . ." and Soren paused for a delicate moment, "he has asked that a guest room be made up for a young lady that will be arriving. He says that he has already notified you of her visit, but that it has been pushed unforeseeably up and he expects her here within the hour."

"My God," Lady Lenora exclaimed. She glanced at her clock. "It is past midnight now!"

"Yes, milady. It is highly irregular, milady, and I thought you would wish to know."

"You are indeed correct, Soren. You had better help me into my dressing gown so that I may go below and find out from him just what is the meaning of all this. He had told me in his letter it would be several days before she arrived, and he said nothing of returning himself to London."

Her lady's maid fetched the required garment, helped the Dowager to sit on the edge of the bed and assisted her into it. Then she removed her sleeping cap for her, ran a comb through the still considerable length of her thin, white hair and then pinned it up, the Dowager's pink scalp showing through beneath it.

Then the dowager, muttering with exertion and annoyance, struggled to her feet with the aid of her maid, procured her cane which had leaned against the bedside table, and then as she stood on her flimsy, shaking legs, she began the trek below stairs on Soren's arm, banging the cane beside her.

Her grandson was in the salon. Evidently he had heard her coming, as she had wished, for he was standing awaiting her when she struggled into the room. "Grandmother," he said, and came to her. He took her aged hand in his, kissed the back of it, and then retaining his hold on it, said with quiet concern in his voice, "I did not wish you to be disturbed."

The dowager dismissed her maid before turning her faded eyes to her grandson. She took in his appearance, going over his face detail by detail and at last settling on his eyes. "You look like hell!" she said, her voice harsh. "When is the last time you slept? You ate? And you have been drinking again, I have no doubt, for there is the smell of now stale booze upon you."

He chuckled, his eyes glinting and there was a suppressed excitement in them that worried her, for that look could only be associated with when he was enjoying himself, and enjoyment for Dante usually meant something bordering on outrageous. Or dangerous. "I slept for an hour this morning. I ate immediately afterwards, and yes, I have been drinking, but that has been some hours ago now."

Her faded eyes went over him in critical assessment. "Well, whatever damage you have done yourself, I can see that you are in good spirits."

He suppressed a smile, and she could almost feel the secrets he was suppressing along with it. "Fair spirits, yes, grandmother. Fair."

"*Humph!*" she snorted. "You may help me to a seat, you young rascal, and then you can explain what trouble you are about now."

"Trouble, grandmother?" he asked as he helped her into her seat. "Why ever would you think I were about some sort of trouble?"

"Because your eyes are glinting in that way they have when you are feeling particularly pleased with yourself. Although," she added as she settled back into her seat, "you are not normally wont to go on a binge when you are occupied by something that you find promising. So, really, I do not know what to think, Dante. But whenever have I known when it comes to you," she ended with tartness.

He smiled but his voice was sober. "Well, I shall not lie to you, for I have been on quite a tear, I regret. Nearly two solid days, but as you know, the mood comes upon me from time to time and there is nothing for it but to ride into that blackness until I ride out of it again."

"Hmm," she ruminated, her eyes missing nothing about his demeanor or expression. "And this Miss Murdock that I understand is to arrive rather prematurely within the hour. Is she connected to this latest lapse?"

"Somewhat," he told her, and his eyelids which had been up and unguarded, came half down, cutting her very much off from him.

She sighed. "I see you shall be as stubborn as your groom was. Curse you, Dante. What is it that your are taking such pains to hide from me?"

He was silent, and to her regret, he moved to the sideboard where several decanters of excellent liquor remained out. He searched through the crystal bottles, settled at last on a light sherry, which mollified her to some degree. He poured into a slender glass, turned to her. "Would you care for one, grandmother?"

She waved a hand, indicating that he should pour, which he did, and then he came back to her, a glass in either hand and offered one to her. For another minute, they each drank in silence, and the Duchess felt again that vague foreboding that she had felt earlier in her bed chamber. At last she said, "You do not mean to tell me, do you, Dante?"

"No, grandmother," he replied. "I know that you would do anything that I ask, but in this case, all I ask of you is that you make Miss Murdock welcome when she arrives. She has had quite a trying time, of which I am, I am sorry to say, directly responsible for."

His grandmother choked a little on her drink. "Egad, St. James! Do not tell me that in some drunken state you have compromised the girl!"

To which to her puzzlement, he laughed with very real amusement and said, "No, grandmother. Nothing quite that drastic, for she is as pure as the driven snow, I dare say, if rather somewhat browner."

"Brown!" the Dowager said, irritated. "All I can gather from you or your groom is that the young lady in question is somewhat brown. Whatever do you mean?"

"I mean that her eyes are as softly brown as a hart's and that her hair is as velvety brown as cattails in summer, and that her skin is as freshly brown as creamy tea. And as a guinea hen hides in the bushes she hides in her brownness and thinks herself undetected. But she is as steady and riveting as a hummingbird in motionless flight as she flits nearly silently about, never realizing that her very brownness and her very solemnity draws the very attention she thinks she is so adroitly avoiding," he told his grandmother. And he took a long, debating swallow from his glass as she watched him, and when he met her eyes there was an expression of regret in them, as though in finding something, it were somehow eluding him.

"Well," she said, her voice faint. "I am certainly looking forward to meeting this Miss Murdock."

St. James thumped his drink down upon the sideboard, still half full. "She shall need a lady's maid, grandmother, for she has none."

His grandmother gave a sharp twist to her head as she turned to him. "Who is escorting her here, then?"

"I have enlisted Bertie, and his younger brother Ryan, to bring her up in their barouche. And of course, Bertie's groom is along with them."

"Still hardly respectable, Dante."

"Rather more so than if she had ridden up alone with me in my curricle," he returned. And the Duchess had to accede that point.

"If she is to be here for the season, as you indicated in your letter," she told him, "it will still not do for it to be made known that she arrived in London in the middle of the night with only the Tempton brothers to chaperone each other." Without waiting for any response from him, she added on the heel of her words, "Ashton!"

Her butler came in, his clothing as perfectly pressed as though it were the beginning of the day, instead of well into the next one. "Yes, milady."

"I shall need you to procure a lady's maid for our guest that is arriving. Have her here by morning, before the house is awakened. It will be said she arrived with this Miss Murdock tonight so that the servants should not gossip."

"Yes, milady," her butler replied, seeing, evidently, nothing at all amiss with having to acquire a lady's maid to start immediately at nearly one a.m in the morning. He withdrew as stoically as he had arrived.

St. James told his grandmother, "Very good, grandmother. That is one point I should have covered had I not been so damnedably tired."

"You should go home, now, Dante. Get some sleep. I am capable of making Miss Murdock comfortable when she arrives."

"I am certain that you are," he agreed. "But I am also certain that you are capable of prying a good deal of information from Bertie and Ryan when they arrive with her, and I would lief stay around and make sure that they remember themselves."

"And what of your Miss Murdock?" the Duchess asked somewhat piqued, for it had been very much in her mind to grill the two Temptons without mercy when they arrived. "Is she so unaware of whatever plans you have that you need not worry about me gaining information from her?"

"No, blast it," he said with sudden vehemence. "For she managed to get a great deal more of my motives out of me than I was readily willing to give! And she may, in fact, tell you the all that she knows." He ran a finger along his upper lip before adding, "I do not think she shall though. At any rate, there is nothing I can do about it if she does, and as I say, there is a possibility that she will not. Whereas the Temptons on the other hand I know to not be equal to the task of evading your questions."

The Dowager could not resist a slight smile, for it satisfied her old heart to know that she was still quite capable of being terrifying when she wished it. But she did have to admit, as much as it galled her: "Tyler, on the other hand, is quite impervious to my attempts."

St. James smiled. "Yes, grandmother. That is the only reason I entrusted him with those letters rather than going to the bother of hiring a messenger."

"Letters?" she picked up, causing him to grimace and again reach for his glass to sip from it. "There was more than one letter? To whom did another letter go?"

"My solicitor," he admitted. "But thanks to Miss Murdock, it was quite unnecessary. For now. All the same, I shall leave it as it now stands in his hands, for I should only have to make the proper arrangements again soon, at any rate. Mayhaps, I should visit him tomorrow, to ensure that he understands precisely what I wished him to do," he added to himself.

The Dowager's fingers found the gold head of her cane and rubbed there as she fully prepared herself to dog this subject until she had as many details as she could win from him, but there was a slight tap on the door and Ashton put his head in to announce, "Lord and Mister Temptons, and Miss Murdock, milady."

"Ah, yes," the old Duchess said. She could not keep the eagerness from her voice as she responded, "You may show them in, Ashton."

She had enough wit to her to observe her grandson, for he had turned at Ashton's words and was engrossed upon watching the threesome come in the door of the salon. His face was tight, concentrating, a question within himself waiting to be answered. And when the Temptons and Miss Murdock entered the room, came close to where St. James stood by the sideboard and his grandmother sat a few yards away in her chair, the Duchess still did not turn her head to observe the newcomers, although curiosity was eating at her, for she was much too intent upon watching her grandson's face with him unaware of it.

She watched as his eyes sought out and settled on the Squire's daughter, and as he gave her rapid appraisal, the questioning went out of his face and there was an odd look of contentment in his eyes for the brief second she had to observe it. Then his eyelids came half down, hooding any expression in them at all, and his face took on the unreadable quality he was capable of when he most wished to keep his thoughts to himself.

Only then did the Dowager turn her head the slight degree that was needed to observe Miss Murdock, and if her delayed reaction in greeting that young Miss made her seem very haughty and untouchable indeed, she was quite unaware of it.

Adding to her aloofness, she still did not acknowledge the new arrivals, but scanned Miss Murdock from head to foot, ignoring the two Temptons that stood to either side of her. Unfortunately, their presence as twin footmen, so to speak, made Miss Murdock appear all the shorter, as they were both quite tall, and their fine red hunting jackets and snowy white cravats, well shined boots and silky black breeches made her brown, worn cloak and brown, somewhat battered bonnet appear all the more shabby. Ashton took these items from her and the dress beneath was as brown and shabby as the rest.

Brown, indeed, was the first word that came to the Duchess's mind. And where her grandson's description had led her to believe that although this Miss Murdock was not an incomparable, that she would at least be uncommonly pleasing, if perhaps in a way contrary to what was fashionable, what the old Duchess saw now quite dismayed her. For besides being exceedingly brown, the miss in front of her looked exceedingly *plain*.

There was not, as far as the Dowager could see, a single laudatory feature about the girl in front of her. Brown hair, brown eyes, and much too brown skin. Adding to that a short stature (which as the Duchess was rather short herself she could not truly find fault with) and when one thought of the fair, voluptuous beauties that one normally associated with St. James, she could only find it very perplexing, indeed! Her eyes, when one took time to look, were rather fine, but as for expression, the Duchess could find nothing but tiredness and a certain wary bewilderment, as though the miss could not credit that she were here in this room being beneath the scrutiny of the Dowager Duchess of St. James. And did not in particular care for it either.

St. James stepped forward and said in a diverted voice, "Grandmother, may I be allowed to introduce Miss Sara Elizabeth Murdock, daughter of Squire Edward Murdock of Chestershire, my betrothed, if I can, in fact, induce her to accept my proposal."

The Dowager let all the air out of her chest in a single shocked exhaling and she watched in quiet amazement as the young miss before her whirled on her grandson, her tiredness and perplexity leaving her in a sudden call to arms, and glared at him.

"That has not in the least been settled, milord!" Miss Murdock told St. James, and as he only chuckled to himself, she turned to his grandmother, her worn, threadbare, poverty revealing skirts twirling with her. "I am sorry, milady, and I should not carry you such tales, but he has been drinking quite lamentably, and such being, anything he says to you this night must be disregarded out of hand!"

The Duchess, recovering from her shock, managed to smile, for with the sudden animation in Miss Murdock's face, much of her prior assessment of her being plain took a sudden reversal. She would never be a beauty, but there was something. . . . "Please do not upset yourself, Miss Murdock, for I can see that you are all but done in. It is just like my grandson to say something shocking when one is most incapable of dealing with it."

"As I have come to understand, ma'am," Miss Murdock returned, still quite angry, the duchess could see. "And as you know him much better than I would even *want* to, then I am sure that I can count on you to see that he is merely being ridiculous."

The Dowager could not answer that, for as shocked as she was, she had never known St. James to be less than serious when making one of his outrageous statements. So instead of agreeing with or disabusing Miss Murdock of her idea that St. James was being ridiculous, she merely bade Miss Murdock to have a seat, and the Temptons must make themselves comfortable also of course, and she directed Ashton to please bring in tea and cakes, as the poor child and her escorts must be famished.

"Thank you, milady," Miss Murdock said as she settled herself and heard these requests made. "For I fear I am tired and hungry and very out of sorts. And it is not at all the way I would have wished to be upon making your acquaintance, so I do apologize."

"No apology needed, my dear, for I can see that my grandson has had you dragged around in quite a deplorable fashion, and I daresay I would be much out of sorts if he were to do the same to me."

"You are very kind, ma'am," Miss Murdock replied with a tired smile that still did much to light up her plain face.

"Kind is not normally the assessment that is placed upon me, Miss Murdock, so please do not bandy it about to any degree, for it shall quite ruin the reign of terror I have managed to sway over for the past fifty years."

To which Miss Murdock bowed her head and replied, "Then of course I shall not interfere with that perception after you have tried for so many years to maintain it."

The duchess smiled at this solemn answer, but when she spoke again her voice was a bark, causing the two Tempton brothers to jump in their chairs. "And what call have you two gentlemen to be aiding and abetting my grandson and fagging this poor child half to death with his antics?"

To which Bertie replied, fumbling, "Why look at the time, Ryan! Had no idea it was so late. Dowager, St. James, Miss Murdock," he bowed in each direction after bouncing from his seat. "Must really beg pardon but fear we must be going now."

"It is as well!" the Duchess cried. "For I am too tired to upbraid you properly now. And St. James, you may leave now also, and the next time I see you, you had better not be looking as hellish as you do this night. You may call upon Miss Murdock tomorrow, but not until the evening, mind you, for I will not have you here disturbing her rest after exhausting her all of today."

And with these regal orders, the Temptons hastened to take their leave, only Ryan pausing long enough to say to Lizzie, "Miss Murdock, it has been a pleasure, and if I can be of any further assistance, you know you need only call upon me!"

And as Miss Murdock began to acknowledge this statement, feeling very moved at his concern, the duchess overrode her, saying, "Yes, yes, Mister Tempton, that is all very well and good but you may get out now."

St. James took his grandmother's hand in his own, kissed the back of it. "I see you have everything well in hand, grandmother, so I shall take my leave." He turned to Miss Murdock who sat with her face downturned on the settee, her hands held clutched together in her lap and waited for her to raise her eyes to look at him, her expression still very baleful, before saying in a voice that showed he was enjoying himself very much, "Until tomorrow, Miss Murdock."

She gave a sudden, exasperated sigh. "Yes, milord. As you say, milord." But her tone was anything but compliant.

The Duchess surprised herself by giving a merry chuckle.

Chapter Nine
Tuesday Morning

Ashton came back in the salon door with a tray of hot tea and cakes, and if he was surprised that the number of people he had been sent to serve had dwindled with alarming quickness, he made no show of it. He set the tray down within easy reach of the Duchess, asked if he could be of any further service, to which the Dowager only replied to make sure he saw about the lady's maid. He assured her he already had some promising leads on that endeavor and then bowed himself out the door once again.

"You may pour, Miss Murdock, if you are not too tired," the Duchess informed her.

Miss Murdock did as she had been asked, and that serene efficiency that St. James had noticed nearly twenty-four hours prior was evident to the Duchess. One would think that a poverty stricken, exhausted, rural Squire's daughter would be clumsy with tiredness and nerves, but Miss Murdock completed the task with such preoccupied ease and grace that the Dowager had a small moment's admiration for such a feat, inconsequential as it may seem.

"So, Miss Murdock," she said as she took the tea cup and saucer that Miss Murdock held out to her. "Perhaps you can explain to me what is going on in my grandson's mind."

"Indeed, ma'am, I wish I could. For I have spent all of the past round the clock trying to deduce it myself." She glanced at the Duchess from her solemn brown eyes. "I fear, milady, and I do not wish to shock you, but it is perhaps best that you understand the full absurdity of this situation, that St. James offered for me, while very drunk I may add, because my father, who was also very drunk I may add, informed him that the horse he wished to purchase from my father was in fact my dowry."

"Your dowry!" the duchess choked. For of all the things she imagined that could be the cause of St. James' current escapade and Miss Murdock's being there, she would never have imagined it was a dowry, most especially not in the form of a horse.

"Yes, I know it is shocking. And perhaps tomorrow after I have rested, I will regret very much telling you for it is also quite humiliating."

"Never, my dear," the Duchess told her, her mind racing over this information. "For I can not believe that St. James would offer for you merely to gain your horse. You met him before this offer was made, perhaps?" she asked. "Perhaps he developed an unexpected *tendress* for you?"

Miss Murdock let out a small peal of laughter. "Oh, ma'am, I am sorry, but yes, he did meet me briefly before this. But if you could have been there, you would realize that no! an unexpected *tendress* was most impossible. For I was in men's breeches, you see. Yes," she nodded in earnestness at the Dowager's diverted look. "For I was riding the horse in question on the track. Which I may add, when his lordship realized I was a female, he was most outraged, which knowing his reputation, I could scarce credit. Oh, sorry, ma'am. Did not mean to mention that, his reputation, I mean."

"I'm well aware of it," the Duchess returned in a dry voice. "Do, please, go on."

"Well," Miss Murdock set her cup down so as not to upset it as she expanded. "Not only could I not credit it because of as I mentioned, but I could not believe he could be so dense. For, I ask you, am I to ride on a race track in a ladylike sidesaddle?" and her brown eyes were very wide as she asked this. "Or perhaps astride, but with my skirt up about my knees? So you see, ma'am, I could not see how the perfect *sense* of the breeches so utterly escaped him."

"Indeed," the Duchess returned trying very hard to hide her grin. "I have never known St. James to be so stupid."

"Oh, but the senselessness grows, ma'am. And although I do not mean to offend you, there is no *reasoning* with the man on any point, whether large or small."

"Tut, child. I know exactly what you mean."

"Do you, ma'am? I am relieved. But I get ahead of myself. If my being in men's breeches were not enough to discourage him, I am afraid that I rode quite shabbily, allowing Leaf, that is my horse, to get out of control and run into the fence. Your grandson was, of course, furious. And although he showed concern for me, I daresay he was more worried that Leaf had been ruined."

"Indeed?" the Duchess replied. "If I found it unlikely that he merely wished to gain your horse before, I find it even more unlikely now after hearing that the horse is lame."

Miss Murdock took a defensive swallow of tea. "I can not see, ma'am, where it could be anything else. Leaf luckily appears to be sound and I daresay it added to his determination to have her for he certainly would not wish for me to have further chance to maim her. He was cursing quite frightfully throughout the entire episode. That is how I know that he was most irate at me even though he was kind enough to make sure I had not broken my neck."

Which Miss Murdock's saying caused the Dowager to laugh. "That is his standard demeanor, my dear, and does not mean a thing."

And Miss Murdock replied with wide eyed solemnity, "So I have discovered. I am so glad that you understand just how unmovable he can be for then mayhaps you will understand, I hope, and not think badly of me, for being here. I swear I tried every argument I could muster to have him cry off immediately, all to no avail. I held out the hope all through this that once he sobered he would see the extreme error of his ways, but he was quite determined to continue *drinking*," and she looked very put out as she said these words. "How is he to see any sense in anything when he is forever keeping himself in that condition?"

Before the Duchess could answer, and she was a little glad of that, for Miss Murdock's question was, really, quite unanswerable, Miss Murdock twisted her hands in her lap and continued. "Oh, I should not be laying all this at your door, ma'am, for you are doing me a kindness in even taking me in when we have never even been acquainted before, and all I have done is run down your grandson. I am dreadfully tired, and still quite irritated, for his proclamation to you tonight was simply unforgivable, and done for no other reason but to provoke me, I am certain, but at your expense also, I dare say. For I can only think that if you took him seriously for even a moment, you must have found yourself very shocked indeed.

"And why," she went on as though unable to stop herself, and since she had not had a female to lament her troubles to, the Duchess could not blame her, "he insists upon continuously provoking me, I can not tell you, for I have done my best to not provoke him," and Miss Murdock's face suddenly flushed a very red color indeed, causing the Dowager to wonder what had brought that on! But instead of revealing anything that may account for her blush, Miss Murdock only added, "Except I did throw his whiskey flask into the ditch. I suppose that could be considered provoking, if one were wont to drink whiskey, which he is."

"And I say that it did him no harm whatsoever, and that you are obviously nearly overwrought, Miss Murdock," the Duchess told her.

"I confess, I feel nearly overwrought, which I have never felt until this day, except of course when my mother died." She looked again at the Duchess and much of the animation had left her eyes as her anger had abated with the telling of her tale, leaving only tiredness. She added, "That is pretty much the story, milady, except for a good deal of pointless arguing throughout."

"Then I shall not keep you up longer, child," the Dowager replied and she called for Ashton to have Miss Murdock shown to her room. "I shall see you in the morning, and I daresay that we shall have a good deal of shopping to do if what you are wearing is any indication of your wardrobe."

"We shall have to discuss that, milady, no disrespect meant, but I will not have you going to expense on my account when surely St. James will soon see his mistake and I will be returning home again."

The Duchess could only say, "Well, we shall see," and she remained for a while in her seat after Miss Murdock had been led off to her guest chamber, considering all that had been said and, she was certain, all that had not been said.

St. James made his way to his curricle, which had remained with Tyler at the front of his grandmother's home. He had intercepted that good man only an hour outside of London with no great difficulty, and now he strode up to the groom who was half-dozing on his feet and told him, "Very well, Tyler. I shall take them. I ask that you remain here on my grandmother's premises until I give you further word. See to it that Miss Murdock does not stray, will you, and as you have already delivered that letter to my solicitor, there is a slim possibility that word of our proposed premature 'nuptials' may have already leaked and cause some stirring from whomever we seek."

"Aye, milord, thought of that meself when I was asked to deliver to your solicitor. You informed him that you were to be wed this night?"

"I did. At the time it seemed a good calculated risk, for I would be ensuring that my new wife were well taken care of if I ran into any difficulty. Now, with no wedding, I fear it may hurry my difficulty and take care of her not at all. So, please keep a sharp eye out, Tyler, and let me know of any strange activity immediately."

For once his groom hesitated at his orders. He shook his head, told his lordship, "I understand your reasoning, milord, but I can't like it. They will do her no harm, I don't think, but your driving home alone, and as poor a shape as you're in, they couldn't ask for an easier target."

St. James took the reins, swung himself rather less than surely onto the curricle. "What is this, Tyler?" he asked as he settled himself into his seat. His eyes were tired but they glinted, still, with amusement. "I have not had my wishes questioned enough this day so that now you musts question them further?" He gave a quick laugh as Tyler gave him a reproachful look and finished, "Just do as I say. I know the risks and I'm still at the ready, tired as I am. Whereas Miss Murdock is a reluctant participant and it must be made certain that she has no further regrets than she has already. And I really do not trust her to stay where she is placed, not after she has had a good night's rest at any rate." Without further words or waiting for Tyler's response, he whistled to his horses who, being in London and familiar with the sights and sounds knew themselves to be very close to home indeed, took off with a more enthusiastic trot than they had shown when coming in above an hour before. Tyler watched the curricle out of sight with considerable misgivings and then turned with a sigh to find himself accommodations above the Dowager's stables with her grooms.

St. James, who doubted that his old family solicitor could not be trusted, still remained, as he had said, at the ready, both his dueling pistols retrieved from their padded box on the floorboards of the curricle and loaded and lying on the seat next to him, but as he had thought, he was not molested on the few blocks to his own townhouse, other than a single drunk that reeled out into the street nearly in his path and almost got shot for his troubles.

At this incident, St. James rubbed a hand over his face when he continued and confirmed to himself that he was very tired indeed, and hence a little more dangerous than usual, for his first instinct, without thought to temper it, would always be to kill first and ask questions later.

If his father had honed that instinct, which was more learned than natural, his father may have still been alive. But there were a million 'ifs' and probably always would be and sometimes St. James had to ask himself if part of his quest for vengeance was not just so he could know *why* it had been so important to someone that his parents be dead.

Killing, when the time came, could not be good enough. He had to have some answers.

His horses came onto the cobblestone half circle drive of his London home, all four stories of it, and a lesser groom came out of the shadows where he had been dozing and took their heads. "All right, then," St. James said, stowing his pistols beneath his coat and flipping the reins over to the groom for him to drive the horses along the mew beside the house and back to the stables. Then St. James climbed the four wide steps to his home with uneven strides, was let in as he reached the door, not by his butler, as he was not expected, but by Effington, his valet.

"Good God!" St. James exclaimed, very much surprised to see that tall, thin, straight man. "What ever are you still doing awake?"

"I was merely down for a cup of tea, being unable to sleep, when I heard your curricle on the stones, milord," Effington answered, and indeed, he was in a dressing gown and a night cap upon his oh-so-proper head. "Seeing as how we were not expecting you and the lateness of the hour, I perceived I may be needed to help you above stairs."

"No. I'm not drunk tonight, Effington. Not now at any rate," St. James ended with ruefulness. "Just damnedably tired."

"I can see that, milord. If you are hungry, I can procure something from the kitchens for you."

St. James considered this for a moment, glanced at the cup of tea in his valet's hand. "No, I don't think that will be necessary," he said, reaching out and taking the cup from the saucer. "A spot of tea will be adequate, thank you, Effington." And drinking from the cup, he turned to make his way above stairs.

Effington gave the slightest of beleaguered sighs as he glanced at his now naked saucer and turned to go back to the kitchens to brew himself another cup of tea. St. James called over his shoulder, "Let it steep just a tad longer this time, Effington. This cup is a little weak."

"Perhaps milordship should try adding a dollop of brandy to it if it is not up to your usual potency," his valet returned with just a tinge of spitefulness in his voice.

St. James let out a single guffaw, and then he made the turn in the staircase and was out of his valet's sight. "By God," St. James said to himself, "one would think from what all those about me say that I have a problem with the drink." He considered this for a brief moment, then shook his head with a small grin on his face. "No, I'm sure Effington was merely trying to be helpful." He entered his rooms, went to the sideboard next to the fireplace and uncapped a decanter of brandy, added a healthy bit to his cup, tasted it, and found his tea much improved.

He removed first his pistols, lay them aside with care, then his coat, flung it with little regard across one chair, collapsed on the chaise lounge and sprawled back. It felt very good to rest for a moment, and a moment was all he had, for he was certain that Effington would be up to offer assistance, and it amused the duke to be forever finished with his ablutions and leaving his valet with very little to do. If Effington were not otherwise occupied when St. James was dressing or undressing, then the duke would find some task that musts need done immediately, effectively removing Effington from the duties that he had been hired for. And St. James could not have really told anyone, had they asked, why he insisted on doing this, other than that he knew it annoyed his valet quite completely. The man was forever lamenting that he would quit his employ for St. James' careless appearance was a black mark on Effington's reputation, and if milord could not have a care how he looked, he could at least have a care how he made his valet feel to see his employer walking around quite disheveled and knowing that everyone must be blaming Effington's skills.

But for tonight, St. James was moving slow indeed, for when Effington returned with his fresh cup of tea, his lordship still was sprawled upon the chaise lounge, his boots not even removed and Effington, seeing his chance and seizing it with as much glee that St. James normally took in denying him his duty, quickly set down his cup and bent to the task of removing the tall black boots from his employer's feet.

St. James opened one eye. "You've caught me, Effington, damn it."

"Yes, milord. For once I shall feel that I am earning a little of the salary you pay me."

St. James thought about this for a moment, then closed his eye again, leaving his valet to his rightful tasks. "I should take comfort in the fact that you are merely readying me for bed. It will be a terrible day when you get your hands on me to fit me for going out."

"I, on the other hand, milord, am very much looking forward to that day. And I must warn you that the longer you delay, the more elaborate I shall have to dress you, so that I may recoup my reputation all at once, for I may never have another chance."

"If you rig me out to that deplorable degree, you may be sure it will be your only chance," St. James confirmed. But he did have to admit to himself that the simple task of readying for sleep would have been beyond him this night. He wondered how Miss Murdock was getting along, for if she were half as tired as he, she had his sympathies. Not to mention that his grandmother had probably taken advantage of the situation and grilled the poor girl while she was at her most defenseless.

Which thought made him grin, for Miss Murdock even at her most defenseless was a force to be reckoned with, he concluded. For some unaccountable reason, that trait in her pleased him very much. He could settle with having a less than beautiful wife, and as it was necessary to merely have a wife as conveniently as possible, he could not afford to be choosy, but it would have galled him to be married to a namby-pamby, and if nothing else, that could not be laid at Miss Murdock's door.

All in all, he was convinced that she would do better than he had dared hope, for if this did not all come out right, she would need some fortitude to deal with what was left. She would manage it, he wagered. Had in reality, already wagered quite a bit on it.

If he could only get her down the marriage aisle, then all would be set, mayhaps not as neatly as he had planned, but that could not be helped. It had not occurred to him that a Squire's daughter would find his suit objectionable.

"Up, milord," Effington interrupted his musings, after tugging off his shirt and maneuvering him to remove his breeches also, "and I will put this over your head and help you into bed."

St. James opened his eyes again, his thoughts evaporating as he saw a long bed gown in his valet's hands. "Oh, no, Effington!" he said. "Lamentable enough that I need your services tonight when I am not even drunk, but you will not prevail upon me to put that on. I can not imagine where you even found it, for it was not in my wardrobe, I am certain."

"Indeed, it was, sir," Effington answered, "for I took the liberty of buying you several when I first started as I was quite frankly appalled to find that you normally slept nearly without any clothing at all."

"And so I shall sleep again tonight."

"It is not seemly, milord," Effington argued, "for a man of your station to sleep like the veriest common of the common."

"Bah!" St. James returned. "And who is to know it, other than you? And if I offend your sensibilities, I can not find it in myself to care over much. Good night, Effington. I can make my own way into bed. Pour me a glass of brandy on your way out."

Effington, feeling a good deal of disapproval at the duke's lack of cooperation in the area of his night attire, drew himself upright in indignation at this last request. He returned the rejected garment to its wardrobe and then went with meekness to the sideboard, where he did pour a brandy. Then he turned to his employer. "There you go, milord, poured as requested," and leaving the glass on the sideboard left without further comment from the rooms.

He heard St. James' outburst of laughter behind him as he closed the door, knew not whether to go to his rooms and write up his resignation papers, a task he contemplated on a daily basis, or to try again to adjust to the many eccentricities of his employer, a goal that had so far eluded him. He was well-paid, he reminded himself, but the thought of putting up with such indignities for many years to come nearly was enough to make him weep. "If I were only allowed to dress him appropriately just *once*," he consoled himself as he made his way up to his room on the third floor, "then I would be satisfied. But if the chance does not come soon, I will have no other choice but to find a position in another household where my considerable talents at hiding the negative and playing up the positive can be used and appreciated."

With that half-formed decision made in his mind, he turned into his own rooms, realized he had forgotten his tea cup in milord's chamber, and did not doubt that the duke had somehow orchestrated that little lapse in his memory also, as merely another way to bedevil him.

His lordship, unaware of his valet's ire, had forgone the poured brandy as too much work in retrieving it from the sideboard, and had closed his eyes as he remained on the chaise lounge in nothing but the most intimate of his under apparel. His naked chest gleamed in the moonlight that shone through his window, and his dark hair fell into his face and he slept.

Effington, upon finding him in this disgraceful manner the following morning, marked it down as yet another grievance to be aired for when he would finally have had enough and did compose his letter of resignation.

Miss Murdock, on the other hand, woke up quite refreshed when a young lady who let it be known that her name was Jeannie and that she would be Miss's lady's maid, brought in Miss Murdock a steaming cup of chocolate, fluffed and propped up her pillows so that she could enjoy her cup in bed, and then whipped back the curtains across the windows in Miss Murdock's room allowing in a glorious morning sun.

Miss Murdock blinked in bewilderment at all of this activity, had to, for a moment, remind herself of where she was and all the events that had brought her here, and allowed herself to sit back in this newfound luxury and enjoy the first day in many years that she had not had to spring out of bed, bathe in the cold water of her bedroom basin, quickly dress and go below stairs of her home to stoke up the kitchen fire and begin procuring breakfast for her father and herself, and like as not, Kennedy the groom also.

"I am to inform you that the Dowager Duchess plans to take you shopping immediately after breakfast, Miss," Jeannie told her. She had deep red hair and interesting green eyes and an aura of maturity about her, although Lizzie could not believe she was more than a year or two older than herself. "So I shall set out your dress and your shoes," Jeannie continued as she opened the wardrobe, "and then when you are--Oh, my," she ended on a disapproving note. "Whatever has happened to all your luggage?"

Miss Murdock choked a little on her hot chocolate, said, "Oh, why, I hadn't the time to pack it and bring it with me, you see." Which saying made her feel a little better, for she was not outright lying.

"I see," said Jeannie. She pulled the single change of dress, that the very nice Soren, the Duchess' own lady's maid, had hung up the night before, out of the wardrobe. "Oh, dear," she said.

Miss Murdock sighed, said with total frankness, "The others I left behind were worse, I assure you."

"Well," Jeannie said, "I can see why the Duchess wishes to take you shopping post-haste then, for I must tell you to go shopping so early in the morning is quite remarkable."

"And quite pointless," Miss Murdock added. "For I do not at all wish to have a new wardrobe as I do not intend to be here above a day or two and do not see myself having any callers or going to any events that would necessitate the expense. But I shall have to take that up with the Dowager, of course."

Jeannie looked taken aback by this confiding, but she did give the dress a good brushing and made no further comments on it, much to Miss Murdock's relief. She finished her chocolate, allowed Jeannie to help her dress, an uncomfortable feeling, as she had never thought herself so helpless as to be unable to dress herself before, and presently found herself ready to go below stairs and join her hostess for breakfast.

Ashton showed Miss Murdock into the morning room. Lady Lenora was already there, and Lizzie was introduced to her daughter-in-law, Lydia.

"Very pleased to meet you, ma'am," Miss Murdock responded.

Lydia set down her fork and gave deliberate appraisal to the new arrival. Looking less than approving, she said, "And very *surprised* to meet you, Miss Murdock. I could scarce credit it when my mother-in-law informed me that St. James had foisted your presence upon her in the middle of last night."

Miss Murdock blushed but was saved of a response by the Duchess saying, "Enough, Lydia. I will not tolerate such a poor welcome from you to Miss Murdock. It is hardly her fault if St. James has seen fit to have her dragged about the countryside in the night."

Lydia sniffed, retrieved her fork, took a dainty bite from the plate in front of her. "Of course, she is welcome, as it is your home and you may welcome whom you may."

"Thank you so much for recalling that," the Duchess returned. Her tone was a good deal warmer when she turned to Miss Murdock and bade her to be seated. "I trust you slept well last night, Miss Murdock?"

Lizzie smiled at her benefactress. "Indeed, I did, ma'am. Thank you."

"Good," the Duchess continued, "for I have quite a busy day planned for us, as your lady's maid should have informed you."

"Oh, she did, ma'am, but I was hoping to discuss this with you before leaving. I really do not think it would be wise under the circumstances. . . ."

"Poppycock!" the Duchess replied. "We shall go shopping if for no other reason then that I will enjoy it and you should indulge me. So let me hear no more of what is wise and unwise."

"Of course, ma'am. I did not mean that I would not enjoy the outing with you. I just have some concern. . . . ."

"Well, concern yourself no longer, dear. It will amuse me to spend a day outfitting you as you should be and I will not take no for an answer so you may as well enjoy your breakfast and place yourself in my hands to get the job done as it should be."

"Yes, ma'am," Miss Murdock replied, her misgivings not at all lulled but seeing from the old lady's face that she would make no headway and that if she persisted she would be forced to reveal more of the circumstances of her being there to Lydia, whom she had understandably taken a dislike to.

Lydia said now in a helpful voice, "Really, Lady Lenora, I should be happy to escort Miss Murdock around to the shops and make the proper purchases. You should not allow yourself to be put out at your age."

"I shall not be in the least put out," the Duchess replied. "But am looking forward to it, as I have said. And I do not mean to insult you, Lydia, but my taste has never matched yours and I would much prefer to do this myself."

"Of course," Lydia replied with exaggerated sweetness. "I admit that you would have more experience in choosing clothing for someone of such short stature. And I must admit that I would not know what to do with her coloring," she stared at Miss Murdock, "which I do not mean to offend but she is so dark. And that hair, it is so extremely brown, and her eyes are so perfectly bland. I'm sorry, Miss Murdock," she confided. "It is just so uncommon for St. James to be moved into doing anything out of *kindness*. . . ." She shook her head in despair. "I had rather hoped when I heard the news that you were to come and visit us that St. James had at last formed a serious attachment. . ." and she sighed.

Miss Murdock, not knowing in the least how to defend herself after these remarks, merely answered, "Indeed, ma'am, I am sorry to disappoint you," and with an air of serenity that she did not quite feel, took up her fork and stabbed a bit of fluffy egg from the plate that had been set before her.

"If you are quite through, Lydia," the Dowager cut in, "then I have several letters in my study that need sent around by messenger. Please see to it that Ashton takes care of this immediately."

"Of course," Lydia replied, recognizing the dismissing tone in the Duchess's voice. "Very nice to have you here, Miss Murdock," she added and pushed back from the table, her still enviable figure moving to the door.

"Please forgive Lydia," the Dowager told Miss Murdock once that lady had left. "She can be quite insufferable, but I hardly think she has the wit to know better."

"She was merely speaking the truth in this matter, milady, so it is impossible for me to take affront," Miss Murdock replied. "It is obvious to everyone just how disparate this match is except to his lordship himself. Once he realizes that he is not fooling anyone, then this will all, thankfully, be at an end."

"And whom is it he wishes to fool, Miss Murdock?" the Dowager asked in a casual voice.

Miss Murdock looked at her rather startled, said with guilty evasiveness, "Oh, I could not say, ma'am, if that is even his intention. For I have no idea what goes on in his head. It is merely the horse, ma'am, that he wished to procure, and he will see that it is not worth all of this, I am sure."

The Duchess replied, "I think you do know what is going on in his head, on this matter at least. And that in itself is rather significant, Miss Murdock, for I have never known him to confide in another." Seeing that her words were making her protégée uncomfortable, she added, "But be that as it may, I shall not pry, for I am certain St. James will tell me what he wishes me to know when he wishes me to know it."

With relief (which she would not have felt if she had but known the duchess better), Miss Murdock agreed, "I am sure that is so, ma'am, and as I have no doubt that this is all a bust at any rate, it would not do for you to become enmeshed in it only to have it all come to naught in the end."

"Tut. We shall see child. Now, if you have finished your breakfast, then I will call for the coach to be brought around so that we may begin getting you into something a little more the thing, my dear."

"Yes, ma'am. I only beg that you keep the expense modest and that we only buy one or two things so that once this is all over I may repay you."

"Do not think of it, Miss Murdock. You should have a new wardrobe for no other reason than putting up with my grandson's shameful conduct. I dare say, you have earned it, and I mean that in the most respectable way."

So Miss Murdock found herself only a short time later in the unmerciful hands of the owner of the *Mystique Boutique*. The equally unmerciful Duchess sat in a padded chair in the private salon directing all that went on with an iron will. "No, no, Dora, those colors are not at all what I had in mind. Apple green, I should think, and powder blue, and dare I say buttermilk yellow? Yes. I think buttermilk yellow would be just the thing. A ball gown from it, I believe."

Dora turned her stout figure with shocking quickness to the Duchess, the violet material she held in her hands drooping. "But, milady, those colors will make her seem even darker than she already is, I assure you. And she is already much too dark. I despair that even a thousand cucumbers will induce her skin to become the shade she was born with."

But the Duchess only nodded in approval. "Exactly, Dora! We can not make her into something she is not, so change the rules, I say. Make them compete on her turf. She has no remarkable features to speak of so we will make that dark complexion her calling card."

Dora opened her eyes very wide. "I see," she said and paused, her face taking on a calculating expression as she turned back to Miss Murdock, who was standing on a low stool in only her chemise and feeling very uncomfortable with her lack of clothing and the ruthless way the two older women were assessing her. "Yes," Dora was now saying. "The very thing. I can not believe I did not see it." She turned to an assistant. "You heard the Duchess, what are you waiting for? Take these and come back with what milady suggested and may I also suggest," she asked the Duchess, her face questioning, "a red velvet for her riding habit?"

The Duchess chuckled. "Oh, very daring, and she shall carry it off splendidly. Now you have the idea, Dora."

"Indeed, I do, milady."

"Pardon me, ma'am," Miss Murdock interrupted as Dora's assistant scurried out of the room. "I thought we had agreed to keep the purchases modest."

"Nonsense!" the Duchess replied. "I don't remember agreeing to any such thing. Besides, it is St. James' money I am spending, so whatever do I care? Do you hear that, Dora?" she turned to her old friend and dressmaker. "The bills go to my grandson."

If Dora showed any surprise at this news, she made no indication of it, merely made a note on her pad. Then she was busy sketching, appraising Miss Murdock as she did so. "I have some very good ideas already, milady," she said, tearing off a top sheet and starting on a new sketch on the next one. Miss Murdock could see that at the top of each page with its, to her anyway, bewildering lines, was her name, neatly written, and the Duchess's address and then in large letters: Bill to Duke of St. James.

That single line of letters seemed to wrap about her rib cage and nearly suffocate her. The implications were damning.

The assistant came back in, a flurry of fluttering cloths as she carried an assortment of bolts of differing colors. She was quite red in the face from her efforts, but stood patiently as Dora selected each in turn, holding it up to Miss Murdock's form for effect, draping it this way and that. The entire time, she and the Duchess kept up a steady chatter, much of it gossip as well as critiquing.

As Miss Murdock could see that the Duchess was enjoying herself, she kept her doubts to herself over the selections made and the expense being incurred. Mayhaps she was caught up just the tiniest bit in the excitement of it, for she had never imagined how pleasing it could be to see so very many colors and materials and all of them being draped across her. Surely it could not harm anything to allow such a vast selection to be presented when she would narrow it down to only one or two?

"And of course all new under garments, and the proper accessories, which I will trust to you, Dora," the Duchess was still talking several hours later, "as I can see you know exactly what I want at this point."

"You can trust me, milady," Dora reassured, jotting still further notes into her pad.

"And I would like the first of these to be delivered tomorrow morning. I can not have this child wearing those clothes she brought another moment longer if I can help it."

"Oh, milady, that will be very expensive!" Dora warned. "It will mean taking girls from other projects and bringing in extra ones and sewing, sewing, sewing. . . ."

To which the Duchess cackled. "Good! I hope St. James has the apoplexy when he gets the bill. It should be quite entertaining."

"Ma'am," Miss Murdock moaned. "It is too much. I have told you it is too much. Walking dresses, afternoon dresses, riding habits, ball gowns, tea gowns, morning dresses, and all the slippers and bows and hats and gloves, not to mention the unmentionables!"

"Hush, child. Why we've only just begun. There will be several more shopping trips before we have you precisely the way I want you. But nevermind," she added as she saw the frightened look on Miss Murdock's face, "for we will save that for another day. I am quite exhausted, I admit, but in a totally pleasant way, so do not look at me like that. I think when we go home, I shall take a little nap, and then this evening, we shall see what we can do with your hair. That bun, quite simply, has to go."

"Oh, dear," Miss Murdock said, feeling utterly out of control. "Not my hair also."

"Indeed, yes, Miss Murdock," the Duchess replied in a voice that brooked no argument. "It may not be of any compelling color, but there is quite a bit of it, and thick also. We shall contrive something more attractive to you than all that, that *primness.*"

"Oh, certainly, Miss," Dora added. "And may I also suggest," and her voice lowered to a conspiratory whisper as she leaned to the Duchess, "that you put just the faintest, *faintest* spot of rouge on either cheek, milady? I know it is quite unacceptable, but everyone is doing it. Discreetly, of course, but still, there it is."

"Yes," the Dowager murmured back, making the two seem like secret agents on some horribly important mission for the crown. "I had already thought the same, and I admit, only to you, Dora, mind you, that I have, on occasion, indulged myself." And she nodded. "Yes. Even at my age."

Dora giggled. "Oh, I would have never guessed, milady. I always said you were very sly." She went on, her whisper becoming even more furtive. "And milady, I do not mean to pry, but the fact that St. James is to be billed for her coming out, does that mean that there will be congratulations in order?"

The Dowager smiled rather thinly. "Of course, I can not say, Dora, not even to you, after all these years. But it is the first lass he has ever taken a respectable interest in, and so I intend to build most strongly upon that."

Dora fanned herself in her excitement. "Oh, ma'am, I am so happy for you, and to think that I will have my part in this!" She turned to look at the object of their conversation, who was fidgeting at this further delay in her being able to be dressed. "I would never have thought your grandson to have such. . . unusual taste," she added in an undertone. Then she brightened. "But she really does have potential. There's more there than first meets the eye, so perhaps St. James is wiser than most men after all. Here, Miss Murdock! Do not dare put that dress back on that you wore in here. Isabelle!" she called again for an overworked assistant. "Take that garment from Miss there and burn it. Get something from in the back for her. I think the Bevington girl returned several things yesterday that she decided were not what she wished after all that should fit. That will have to do for you, Miss Murdock, until we have whipped up some of your own."

Miss Murdock sighed, dispirited, as the ruthless assistant snatched her worn dress from her hands. "Yes, I see. Thank you, Mrs. Dimple."

"Thank you, Dora. It is so much nicer to see immediately that we are making progress. And of course, this girl has not *worn* this clothing anywhere?"

"No, no!" Dora exclaimed, horrified. "Whatever do you think I am, milady, after all these years! No, I assure you, she received them just the day before yesterday, and yesterday she returned them, saying the cut wasn't quite right." Dora sniffed, offended at just the memory of this comment. "As if *my* measurements or design have ever been off! More likely she has been indulging herself a little overmuch in the week since her last fitting, I say. But of course, you could never convince young Miss of that!"

"Of course not, Dora. I merely wanted to be sure that there would be no one chance to see Miss Murdock and recognize the dress, and as I know the Bevingtons live in the opposite direction from which we will be going, I find it doubtful that we should run into her. But of course if we do, I shall tell her that Miss Murdock has owned her dress for three whole months. That will really set her off to think that you had given her something from last season's fashions!"

"Oh, you would not do that, milady!" Dora cried. "Why it would ruin me!"

"Better you than Miss Murdock," the Duchess replied, totally unmoved. "But if it makes you feel better, I shall tell her we got it from that inferior shop from down the street."

"That is nearly as bad," Dora argued. "For if it were thought that you were patronizing it, then everyone else would be flying off down there, and I would still be ruined."

"Tsk," the duchess replied. "I am sure it is all a non-issue, for Miss Murdock will be only wearing it this day and we are only going straight home."

Miss Murdock, during all this long discussion, had been busy putting on the new dress with the help of the assistant, a red and white striped concoction that, if it did not fit her like a glove, fit her with adequate elegance and as the two ladies at last turned to her almost in unison, they stopped their mild bickering and stared at her in silence.

Miss Murdock, anxious at the expressions on their faces, asked, "What? Oh, do not say that it looks that bad! It cannot be worse than what I came in. Can it?" she asked.

Dora said with quiet near rapture, "Oh, Miss, you look so. . . so *bright*," and she dabbed at her eyes.

Miss Murdock stared in question at the Duchess, for if she did not quite disbelieve the shop's owner (for she seemed to be easily moved by her own creations) she still needed reassurance from that crusty old lady.

The Duchess studied her from her faded eyes and at last gave a single, deep, satisfied nod. "Yes, Miss Murdock. Without that baggy brown dress making you seem so very dowdy, I find that you are very bright indeed. You look warm and healthy and bursting with energy, and the color positively makes you bloom. Why I do not think we shall even need rouge on your cheeks for they are quite highly colored already. Who would have thought it, Dora?"

"Who would have, indeed? Milady, I must take my hat off to your grandson, for obviously he has seen it all from the beginning."

Miss Murdock, released from her somewhat stunned trance at those words, broke into a prolonged fit of the giggles that had the shop owner and the Dowager looking at her quite dismayed, but she could only lean against the work table and laugh until she was gasping. It might suit these two older ladies' romantic fancies to think that St. James had somehow deduced that she were not so very plain after all, and she had not the heart to tell them differently, but she certainly *knew* differently and that is what she found so very funny.

Chapter Ten

Dante Larrimer, Duke of St. James, stared at the parchment he held in his hands. He had not opened it yet, so it was not the contents that held his intent attention. It was his grandmother's seal upon the back of it, indicating it was from her, but the handwriting of the address upon the front of it was not her own. Had her arthritis become so bad of late that she was now dictating her missives?

He was frowning when he opened it, wondering at this development in his grandmother's health, but the letter itself added to his puzzlement for it was quite clearly his grandmother's own handwriting, as he had always known it. He began reading.

Well, Dante, was the missive's abrupt beginning, *I have had the whole of the tale from Miss Murdock last night, and as usual, you have been behaving abominably! I have no need to tell you, I hope, that your actions have been inexcusable! You can not go about such activities as you have partaken over the past forty-eight hours and not do the girl's reputation irreparable harm. I will expect you after dinner tonight so that we can discuss this, but you should already know what solution I am recommending, and I expect you to do what is right by the girl with no attempt to shuffle off your responsibilities. In this matter, at least, you shall behave as your station demands you. 9 o'clock sharp!*

Your Loving Grandmother

The frown St. James had begun reading with became more pronounced. "Bugger take it," he whispered beneath his breath. "I should not have left her alone with that wily old lady, and if she really knows the truth of it now. . . ." Without going through the rest of his mail upon his desk, he turned and left the room, going to order his horse saddled.

Miss Murdock had nearly dozed off in the carriage as she and a tired Duchess returned just after noon from the dressmaker's shop. So it was that she was in no mood to fight with St. James when she came through the salon door and saw him standing with his back to her before the fireplace.

"Oh, God help me!" Miss Murdock exclaimed. "But I am in no mood for you and your obstinacy. Unless you have come to tell me that upon reflection, you have seen the error of your ways and are now, at last, willing to call this whole absurd affair off, then I swear I will turn and walk directly out of this room I have just entered."

At these words, the man at the fireplace did turn, to reveal not St. James, but a very similar younger version of him. The eyes were a pale blue rather than gold, and the face was perhaps more round instead of angling in sharp planes around cheeks and chin, but the resemblance was very pronounced all the same, and Miss Murdock gasped as much from surprise as from embarrassment. "Oh, my," she said with sudden weakness. "But you are not--! Well, never mind who you are not. May I ask who you *are*?"

The blue eyes twinkled with mischief. "I am not St. James, who is my cousin, by-the-by. You are not the first to make that mistake, and as usual, the person making the mistake is angry with him, so I am forced to take the brunt of the abuse that is intended for the duke. I am Earl Andrew Larrimer, at your service, ma'am," and he bowed and clicked his heels. "And may I have the honor of *your* name?"

Miss Murdock clasped at the neck of her new red and white striped afternoon gown. "I'm sorry! Of course! I am Miss Sara Elizabeth Murdock and of course you must be here to visit your grandmother, and here I am demanding your name when I am but a guest."

He came forward, and she noticed that he was in fact, taller than the Duke of St. James, and that he was bulkier, but the hair was the same dark shade of brown that bordered on blackness. "Please do not apologize, Miss Murdock. As I have said, it happens often."

"Then you have my condolences," Miss Murdock answered without thought. "For I am sure it has been very miserable listening to the many tirades that were intended for your cousin's head."

Earl Larrimer laughed at that. "Indeed, it has been. But very interesting also. So tell me, Miss Murdock, what has my cousin done to get your lovely face so flushed?"

Miss Murdock backed toward the door. "Oh, he has just been as he usually is, I suspect. For I have not known him above two days."

"And he has you so angry already?" Earl Larrimer asked. "And that time frame does seem rather short for an 'affair'," he added with a teasing note to his voice. "But my cousin has been known to move quickly when he sees something he wants, and you, Miss Murdock, if not quite in his usual way, are extremely. . . interesting."

"I assure you, I am not," Miss Murdock replied, feeling a good deal of disgust at herself for being intimidated by a boy but a few years older than herself, and thinking to herself that she must be rid of this dress for when she had worn her own clothing, she had never been subject to anyone's interest whatsoever and that this experience was very disconcerting. "And I used the word 'affair' in the sense of situation, not--not as you would *unwisely* imply."

"I see," he said, stopping in the center of the room much to Lizzie's relief. "I apologize if I misunderstood. I lief to admit I would find it unlikely for St. James to park one of his females at his own grandmother's home."

"Yes. It would be very ridiculous, indeed," Miss Murdock agreed.

"What precisely are your dealings with my cousin, Miss Murdock, if I may ask?"

Miss Murdock searched about in her mind for a suitable answer but could find none readily available. "Why, he, uh, has prevailed upon his grandmother to take me in for a short stay as I have not been to London before," she answered at last, sounding less than certain of it herself.

Andrew raised his eyebrows. "Oh. Your coming out, is that it? Though I thought you to be a little older than that, no offense meant, of course."

"Of course," Miss Murdock replied. "Indeed, I am twenty years old, so I really do not like to refer to it as my 'coming out'. In fact, I do not expect at all to go to any of the events that are normally associated with that phrase, as I am not hanging out for a husband at all. I am merely here for, as I said, a short stay. Nothing more, I assure you."

"Pity, that, Miss Murdock. I would rather look forward to going to those beastly evenings at Almacks if I thought I might meet someone there as glowing as you."

"Your compliments only serve to make me think you are somewhat less than perfectly honest, sir," Miss Murdock returned. "But I expect that flattering tongue of yours will have enough females fluttering about you to keep you entertained even in my absence."

Earl Larrimer laughed. Then he said with refreshing candor, "I go it too brown, then, you think, Miss Murdock? I confess, my cousin has often advised me not to be *too* gushing and I must admit that although his approach seems rather astringent, it has the most damnedable results."

"I am sure it does," Miss Murdock returned in a dry voice. "But I beg you to not become too like him, for he does go a little to the extremes, I think, in being inscrutable and unfeeling."

"Those are harsh words, Miss Murdock, even for my cousin. I can see he has you very angry indeed. Are you sure you will not tell me what he has done to get you so, for I may be able to help, you know."

Miss Murdock, deducing that Earl Larrimer was in fact, fairly harmless, relaxed enough to move to the settee and seat herself on it. "No. Oh, no. I assure you, he has done nothing very dastardly after all, for I managed to reason him out of the worst of it. I am afraid it is just his high-handed manner that sets badly with me."

"Ah, yes," Andrew returned, settling himself in turn in the wing-backed chair that his grandmother normally sat in when she was in the room. "My mother is always enraged with his behavior and I think that really it is more the unrepentant attitude he takes than the actual actions themselves."

"That would be Lady Lydia?" Miss Murdock asked.

"Yes. You've met her?"

"Just this morning at breakfast. She does seem very proper."

"Too proper!" Andrew sighed. "I've been out of University for a year now, and she still insists on knowing my every move. I would like to reopen my father's townhouse here in London and reside there. You must understand, it is rather hard to be, well, as a man should be, when you are sharing an establishment with your mother and your elderly grand-mother."

Miss Murdock let out a small giggle. "I understand," she said. "My father was quite eager to take St. James up on his offer to--to let me visit here, for I fear he was in the same predicament, having a daughter about the place, I mean. The very sensible routines I prescribed to keep him healthy and whole seemed to irk him considerably. He would much rather eat at odd hours and drink late into the night over a hand of cards with his cronies than worry about his daughter alone in the house with naught for protection but an old groom."

"Oh," Earl Larrimer exclaimed as he laughed. "That *is* sorry. I can see that even my cousin would be moved to kindness over that state of affairs."

"You see!" Miss Murdock pointed out. "You have just used that word and you meant nothing disreputable by it! And strangely enough, your mother said much the same thing, only I am afraid it was because of my *appearance* rather than any knowledge of my wayward, widower father. I very much fear that St. James more than likely took pity on my father, being unable to do as he wished, than on me at any rate."

They were both laughing at these sayings when Andrew sobered and said, "But, Miss Murdock, there is nothing at all wrong with your appearance. You *are* interesting and glowing."

"Pshaw," Miss Murdock said, not at all intimidated now as she had been before. "And I assure you it is only an illusion created by a good dressmaker, for if I were as I normally am, you would not think so."

"Well, neither are half the other chits that are in society then, I assure you," he countered. "And you do not see them putting a disclaimer upon themselves that once you marry one of them and get them home that mayhaps they are not all you thought they were. Neither are the gentlemen, for that matter, and I should not tell you our secrets, but you really are the most easy girl to talk to I have ever met," and he nodded at her look of disbelief. "No, Miss Murdock, I am not going brown, I assure you, but am merely being honest, for they mostly wish to talk about the most insipid things. If they were only interested in something worth being interested in, like dueling or race horsing--"

"Oh, but I *am* interested in race horsing," Miss Murdock broke in, rather proud of herself. "In fact that is how I met your cousin, for he took an interest in *my* horse, Gold-Leaf-Lying-in-the-Sun. And as I am given to understand that he owns Behemoth, I am very flattered indeed, for that shows he has a good eye for horseflesh."

"Indeed he *does*, Miss Murdock, for that is his only other passion other than seeking the murderer of his parents." He stopped abruptly. "Oh, should not have mentioned that, I am sure. Not common knowledge, I don't believe." And he looked very guilty indeed.

Miss Murdock was quiet for a moment, all the laughter going out of her, which was rather sad when she had been having such a splendid time with her new friend. "I have already come to understand that," she said, because she could not bear to see him so obviously silently berating himself. "So please do not feel that you have betrayed your cousin in any way."

"Well," he said, his head hanging in dejection. "I am glad that I have not told you anything you did not know or at least suspected, but it was still damned careless of me, for I am sure he has tried very hard to be circumspect as it would not do to tip off the person he seeks, especially if St. James should ever get a good lead onto him." He raised his head and the bantering young man that had been before her a moment ago was quite gone, and he reminded her suddenly most painfully of his cousin. "That is why I most wish to reside independently from my mother and grandmother," he told Miss Murdock in a sudden outpouring of confidence. "I would so much wish to help St. James in his task, and I can not feel as though I can do it from here for I am afraid of putting my mother and the Duchess in any danger."

"Oh, you can not!" Miss Murdock sprang from her seat in her shocked dismay. She entreated the young man in front of her. "Can you not see how utterly consumed your cousin has become with this quest? And from what I understand, it may very well all be futile! He would not wish you to sacrifice any chance at happiness as he has, I can assure you of that!"

"You do not understand!" he returned with sudden, young savagery. "For a man to go through life knowing that there is an enemy out there that has harmed members of his family and goes yet unpunished! Why it can only be that you are a woman that you would dream a man could just forget about that and go on. It is the responsibility of every Larrimer from now until the end of time to seek vengeance!"

"That is obscene," Miss Murdock broke in, wide-eyed. "Why the murderer could possibly be already dead. What then? Do you seek out his children and punish them?"

"If what they have is a direct result of my uncle's dying, then yes! We should at least deny them of what was gained if we can not kill the actual perpetrator of the deed! They can not be allowed to profit in any way from it."

Miss Murdock felt a wave of dizziness come over her and she sank back down onto the settee. If she had allowed St. James to elope with her last night, had allowed him to get her, as he said, God willing, with child, would her own son if it had been a son, been raised on this same vengeful wrath? And my God, what had she been thinking if these thoughts should upset her to such a degree? She could not believe that she had been becoming complacent, pliable, *open* to his suggestion of marriage!

Andrew was on his knees in front of her and he patted her hand to induce her to open her eyes. "Miss Murdock. Sara. I am so sorry. I do not know what came over me to make me speak in such a manner to you. It is quite unforgivable of me. I totally lost all sense of decorum, for I know perfectly well that this subject is not at all suitable for a female. I pray that you are all right! I beg that you forgive me!"

Miss Murdock sucked in a deep, calming breath. "Lizzie," she said.

"I beg your pardon," Andrew said. "What?"

"Lizzie," Miss Murdock gave a weak smile. "My friends call me Lizzie, so you must also. And yes, of course, I forgive you. I am not usually so fainthearted, it just. . . disturbs me very much to hear you talk so. I beg you to, if nothing else, speak to your cousin of all this before you do anything on your own. Will you promise me that, Earl Larrimer?"

"Andrew. If I am to call you Lizzie, you must call me Andrew. And of course I will promise you that if you will forgive me."

"It is done. Think nothing more of it," Lizzie replied. "And I must really go up to my rooms, for I must still be very tired to be behaving so missishly."

"Do you wish me to escort you up the stairs?" Andrew asked as he got up from his knees and held an anxious hand on her arm to help her up.

"No. That is not necessary although I thank you for the offer. I have enjoyed meeting you very much, Andrew."

"And I you, Lizzie."

She left the room, a swirl of red and white stripes, and mounted the stairs with no indication of weakness now. But she felt rather cold, for although she had not wished to aid the duke in his plans before she had not felt as though she were going to betray those plans either, but she now realized that it would have to be one or the other, and that she had no stomach for what he offered. If she had allowed herself in some deep recess of her mind to believe that there was some hope of miracles happening and happiness somehow, someway waiting, she understood now that she had been deluding herself quite completely, if only very briefly. An old Duchess and an old dressmaker's romantic dreams had been just a little contagious and she had caught them. But now, Miss Murdock assured herself, she was quite, quite cured.

In her room, upon reflection, she realized that deciding to leave and setting out were two different things. Besides a few pence in her reticule, she had no funds. The only horse she owned was, she assumed, at the residence of St. James himself, and she would not pay back the Duchess's kindness by stealing a horse on top of her desertion. Which thoughts led her back to where they always began. She would have to convince St. James for once and for all. It had been he that had taken her from her home, and it would have to be he that sent her back.

With this thought, Miss Murdock kicked off her slippers and lay back on her bed to think of what arguments she could use. And she prayed that he would not be drinking this time.

St. James rode into the stables of his grandmother's house and dismounted. "Tyler, you scraggly old scoundrel, where are you?"

An insolent splat of tobacco landing near the high-glossed shine of his boots was his first indication that his groom was on hand. "Aye, milord, right where you left me, and damned unhappy about it, too."

"Bah, Tyler. Spend a couple of nights away from your own comfy bed and you are crying like a woman. You are getting old and soft."

"Soft in the head to be listening to the likes of you, I agree," Tyler returned with an impudent smile. "What's in t'works now, milord? Mayhaps I can return to my rightful position instead of spending my days saddle-soaping leather that does not even belong in my care?"

"No. Sorry, Tyler. See anything unusual this morning or last night?"

Tyler shook his head, spat another stream of tobacco from his mouth, this time into the drainage ditch to the side. "Not that I can say."

"Any visitors to the house?"

"None that I've seen."

St. James rubbed his upper lip with his gloved finger, his gold eyes looking up into the face of his groom before him. "Odd. Very odd. I am nearly certain that a letter my grandmother sent by messenger to my home had been intercepted. But it had her undisturbed seal on the back of it, which convinced me that if it were intercepted it had to be by someone who had access to her seal."

"Mayhaps some one has made a copy of the seal, milord."

"Mayhaps so, but who would go to the trouble before hand? For it is not something that someone could whip up on a moment's notice."

"Perhaps they have had it on hand from needing it in times past."

"Exactly what I was thinking," St. James agreed with dark expression. "Every staff member in this house has been with my grandmother for years, and I have long since been able to ascertain that there was none among them that would have done my family harm."

Tyler scratched his head. "There is the new lady's maid that arrived in the wee hours of the morning, milord," he said.

"Yes. I had thought of that. I already have someone working on her background. She is much too young, I gather, to have been involved in a crime of twenty-three years ago, but it is possible that someone has approached her, induced her to gather information. But. . . ." St. James pondered for a moment, and he snapped his quirt against his boot, causing his horse behind him to jerk its head up. He gathered the reins a little tighter in his hand, then said to Tyler, "Who ever intercepted this has a very good fist. Ask Ashton if he has any thing from this new lady's maid that shows her handwriting. A letter of application for employment, anything. I want to see it as soon as possible."

"I'll take care of it, milord," Tyler agreed. "But you sound as if you are not hopeful in that direction."

"No. I'm not. Something about it just does not feel right. For someone to be able to orchestrate her being here under such bizarre circumstances as we arrived is either impossible or, more ominous, shows that we have been watched quite closely and our moves had already been anticipated. Which would put me very much at a disadvantage." He gave a sudden curse. "Damn, Tyler. Either I am up against someone that is truly genius, or I am being blind on some point that I can not fathom. Which I can not comprehend, for I have gone slowly and thoroughly and there can be nothing I have missed. *Nothing.*"

Tyler moved uncomfortably. "Here, milord. I know it. But take heart, for if your suspicion is correct about the letter, then obviously you have moved someone t'begin taking action, which is more than we have seen since you began searching."

St. James brightened at this observation. "Yes. You are right, Tyler. What began as only a hunch on my part, a last desperate measure, is suddenly appearing to be promising. But I needn't tell you that it raises all the more questions in my mind."

"Such as why it should matter if you marry?"

"Precisely. It would seem to point toward someone whose inheritance is at stake, but that is impossible in this situation." He paused, thought for a moment, then shook his head. "No. Utterly impossible. I have gone over this time and time again. Andrew who is to inherit if I die without issue was not even born at the time of my parents' deaths. And my uncle, who would have inherited at the time, I had to mark off because of the strength of his character and morals. In fact, it was he that first set me to looking, and he had been searching all the years prior to my reaching my majority. And now, if there had been any doubt, which I had felt none, he is dead. So if he had been the purveyor of these schemes it would be quite impossible for this present action to be taking place. Endless circles," he sighed at the end of his words. "Always, if only I could deduce what had been to gain by their deaths, and presumably my own, for I was supposed to have been in that coach as well, then I would know, I am sure, who was behind the all of it."

"I know, milord," Tyler said. "But we will know, I am sure of that. I only hope that we know in time to keep you safe."

"And Miss Murdock. For I begin to fear. . . ." He turned, mounted his horse. "Talk to Ashton immediately, Tyler. If this lady's maid is some sort of threat, the last thing I want is for her to be attending to Miss Murdock alone in her bedchamber."

"Aye, milord," Tyler said. "But I can not believe that Miss Murdock would be very accommodating of any schemes t'have harm befall her."

To which St. James was forced to chuckle. "I am certain you are correct on that point, Tyler, but Miss Murdock does not have the advantage of being wary, so we must help her out a bit." He turned his horse, ducking his head to avoid a heavy supporting beam above him, then stopped to add over his shoulder, "I shall be back this evening for an appointment with my grandmother, as she has quite imperiously demanded my presence. I fear from her note that Miss Murdock has let rather more out of the bag than I thought she would, but I can not really blame her for I well know how much pressure my grandmother can bring to bear. At any rate, I shall be here, to salvage what I can.

"You may inform me of your findings then, unless it is something urgent, in which case you may find me at my solicitor's for now. I'll leave word at my house where to find me if the need should arise after that."

"Aye, milord. Until tonight."

"Until tonight." St. James rode out into the bright sunshine of the afternoon, but he did not even notice it, he was so intent upon his thoughts.

A half hour later he handed his reins to a young boy of perhaps thirteen who volunteered to watch his lordship's horse for tuppence if milordship would not be above an hour, that is. Which St. James, smiling at such audacity, flipped him the coins in agreement and strode into the busy office of C. Edmund Bickerstaff, Barrister of Law.

He was shown into that old gentleman's office, where the gray haired, rather emaciated man rose from behind his large desk and leaned over to shake hands. "Milord. I am nearly as surprised to see you today as I was to get your message of last night! Surprised and also somewhat relieved. Are congratulations indeed in order, or have I been the victim of some preposterous joke? Although I must tell you, it was your man himself that delivered it!"

"And have you begun the paperwork I indicated?" St. James asked as he let go of his solicitor's hand and, flipping his coat tails up, seated himself in one of the slatted back chairs.

Barrister Bickerstaff harrumphed, said, "Well, milord, I have begun to carefully research any and all changes that will need to be made and to get the proper paper work in order. Of course, I will need your signature upon everything. And a copy of the marriage certificate."

St. James crossed one leg over the other. "There will be a slight, very slight delay on that document," he told the man across from him. "At this point, I wish you to continue getting everything in order just as I instructed. I would like to have it ready for my signature on a moment's notice, so I would appreciate it if you made this an item of some priority."

"I can do that, milord," the Barrister said, sounding relieved at this delay. "And you are aware that your marriage will enlarge upon your responsibilities somewhat significantly?"

St. James cocked his head. "No. I am not. Please enlighten me, Charles."

The Barrister straightened the stack of papers in front of him. "I would not have known it myself except that I had made it my business to review all of the provisions of your will, your father's will at the time of his death, and as I saw that we unexpectedly had a copy of your uncle's will, his also."

"Very thorough," St. James agreed.

"Everything was as I had expected, until I got to your uncle's will. I had not handled his affairs, you know, and so I was rather surprised to see that we had a copy of his will in our files. It had been sent to us by his solicitor, a," and he paused a moment, picking up his spectacles and holding them briefly in front of his eyes as he read from the documents in front of him, "Barrister Collins of Bedford Street, here in London."

"Yes. I'm familiar with whom my uncle used as his solicitor. Go on."

"As I was saying, it was sent to us by Barrister Collins as there are certain provisions in there that concern you. Upon your marriage, you are to take control of all of his affairs concerning, and I shall read it to you, . . . *his widow if still living, and his son, Andrew Harold Larrimer, if not yet married. Upon Andrew's marriage, these holdings will revert to him, as sole heir, and all affairs, holdings, properties, and otherwise that were previously beneath the control of said widow, Lady Lydia Francis Taylor Larrimer, will also revert to control of said son. Until the date of son's marriage, and after date of Duke of St. James, Dante William Larrimer's marriage, all these assets will be in the possession and control of said Duke, and will be retained by said Duke in the event of premature death of son, Andrew.* The Barrister looked up from the paper, dropping his spectacles and meeting the eyes of St. James.

St. James settled a little deeper into his chair, and his gold eyes moved to over one shoulder of Bickerstaff. "If Andrew were to die prematurely and his mother were to live, would not everything be returned to her?" he pondered. "Why, indeed, would they be stripped from her to begin with on the event of my marriage?"

Bickerstaff shrugged. "It is all rather odd, milord. But there is no mention in the will of Lady Lydia receiving anything upon her son's demise, if it were to happen. As I read, all of the inheritance that would go to your cousin Andrew is to instead remain in your hands and your future descendents' hands. Including, and I do not know if it were made clear here, but believe me, upon reviewing the will in entirety it is clear, are several major holdings, assets, properties and accounts that were brought to the marriage *by* Lady Lydia."

St. James eyes snapped back to the Barrister at this pronouncement and his eyebrows made a deep furrow in his forehead. "That is preposterous. Archaic. It is still law that a woman's holdings become those of her husband's, but it is normally practiced that such holdings are held independent from the husband's, and are returned to the wife if the husband precedes her in death, am I correct on this? Regardless even of a male heir?"

"That is the standard practice, milord, but, as you can see in this case, still entirely dependent upon the discretion of the husband involved."

"Interesting," St. James reflected. "Tell me, was my uncle's will always set up in such a manner, or had it been changed, perhaps shortly before his death?"

Bickerstaff shook his head. "I wouldn't know that, milord. All we have is the most recent copy, which," and he flipped through many pages until he reached the end of the will, "by-the-by! Is dated just two months before he died!!"

St. James raised a brow. "I wonder what the one prior to this one read. Very well, Bickerstaff. To recap: if I marry, I will have the added responsibility of overseeing my cousin's inheritance in its entirety until he himself marries?"

"Yes, milord. And I do not mean to be in poor taste but if something were to happen to your cousin, well, you can see that it would benefit you."

"My uncle must have had a great deal of faith in my integrity," St. James mused.

"Well, milord," Bickerstaff interrupted, shuffling that pile of papers to the side and replacing it with another pile, "which brings us back to your own will. As you can see, I need to know what provisions I should put in here concerning your cousin if you should die and he is not yet married. Do you not think it would be more prudent to hand control back over to his mother until his marriage? Surely you do not wish to burden your new wife with this responsibility in addition to all that she will shoulder as it is? In fact, I would heartily recommend that you place some trust-worthy male in charge of everything, and simply give her life's use of your homes, unless of course she marries again, and a monthly allowance. It is how it is done, you know."

"Normally, yes." St. James hesitated for just the briefest of seconds, then said, "But I wish it to be as I had written in my letter. Miss Murdock will have sole control and ownership of my estates, to be dealt with as she sees fit in the event that I have no heir, and to act as custodian over them, if I do have an heir, until such time that she feels he is capable of taking over that responsibility."

"Milord," Bickerstaff gasped, making his thin chest rise and fall in a-larm, "you realize what you are saying? Why she could squander every penny you own! And God only knows, *if* there is anything to pass on when she dies, whom she will *leave* it to."

St. James gave an infuriating grin. "Well, I shall not care at any rate, as I shall be dead. But there, Bickerstaff, I do not mean to send you into an apoplexy. Look at it this way. Perhaps you will be able to woo her and wed her yourself, and then you may keep a tight rein on all that I own for yourself instead of for an unappreciative bugger like me."

Bickerstaff could not quite see the humor in his client's words. He drew himself up with indignation in his seat. "I did business with your father for nearly twenty years before his death, and I have done business for all these years since his death with you, milord. If you do not know my character by now, then I can only say that I am a great deal affronted."

"Then you must accept my apologies," St. James said. "For I in no way wish to call into question your principles or your honor."

"Thank you, milord," Bickerstaff said with great dignity. "That means a great deal to me."

"And it means a great deal to me to not be forced to meet you at dawn when you called me out for besmirching your name," St. James added, deflating his solicitor's dignity.

That man said, "Well, uh, yes. Quite, milord," and his old hand shook for a second as he fussed with the papers in front of him. Then with a defiant look from his old eyes, he said, "You are very lucky, indeed, that I have such a forgiving nature."

"Indeed," St. James agreed, "for then it would be known that I am a coward when I was forced to flee the country rather than meet my nemeses and possibly die. I do thank you, Bickerstaff."

"Bah," the old man said. "You are as insolent as you were when you visited my office still on your father's knee. Now if you are through badgering an old and, I might add, busy man, you may leave this in my hands. But about your cousin's inheritance, milord. . . ?"

"That, as I had no prior knowledge upon it, I shall have to think about. I will stop around tomorrow or the following day to let you know. Is it possible for you to continue with the rest as I have indicated?"

"Yes. Reluctantly, but yes," Bickerstaff agreed.

"Good. And there is one other small matter. I should like to set up an allowance for Squire Edward Murdock of Chestershire. A hundred pounds a month I should think. This will go toward procuring him a proper staff for his house, the maintenance of his household, and add any sum that is needed in order to procure immediate repairs on his home. Should this cover everything adequately and yet give him a respectable sum in order for him to keep himself entertained?"

"I *should* say so, milord," Bickerstaff said as he jotted down these notes.

"These arrangements are to start immediately. If you write it up quickly just as I said, I will sign it now."

"Yes, milord. That will get us started. Of course, I shall have to draw up something more legal for you to sign on your return, including event of your death, or if, as I take it you have not yet had that happy occasion you anticipated having last night with Miss Murdock, there is some reason why this marriage does not come off, the cancellation of this allowance."

"There will be no cancellation, Barrister. It is as I have said until the date of his death. In fact, you can add that if for some reason I do not marry Miss Murdock, which I find extremely unlikely that I do not, but in that event, the allowance will be transferred to her until her death."

"What if she marries another, milord?" Bickerstaff persisted, pausing in his writing.

"It does not matter, man," St. James replied in impatience. "She is to get the money with no exclusions. Really, Charles, you act as though the money were coming out of your pocket instead of my own. Which, by-the-by, reminds me. You will be receiving bills from dressmakers and the such in her name. You are to pay them, and anything else that is billed in her name. Oh, and a bill for a new coat, I imagine, will be coming in from Lord Tempton. Pay it also, please."

"Anything else, milord?" Bickerstaff sighed.

"No. I think that should cover it. For now. Unless you have any further questions, I will leave now and be around in a day or two."

"Sign here, milord," Bickerstaff advised, finishing his writing for the Squire's pension with a flourish. St. James scrawled his signature.

"Very well," he said. "Good day, Barrister."

"Good day, milord," Bickerstaff said, and then muttered to himself as the door closed behind the duke and he glanced over the two pages of notes he had taken in the past hour, "I pray you know what you are doing. Ten to one all this work will be for nothing for you will come in tomorrow and reverse everything." He glanced at the words he had written with a large question mark after them. "Very odd, though, about his uncle's will."

St. James came out onto the street, tipped the lad who had held his horse an extra hapenny, and mounted the skittish stallion. Then glancing down at the boy who had held his horse, he said, "I'll give you a crown, lad, if you run a message for me."

"Aye, gov'ner," the boy said. "I'll run me legs off for a crown. Clear across London if you wish."

"No," the duke smiled, "t'is not that far. Can you read an address if I jot it down?"

"Aye, and I know's me way all right. Gov'ner," he added as a quick after thought and tugged at his hair in respect.

"Good," St. James said and pulled a small pad of paper from one of his many pockets and a small lead pencil. On it he wrote: *Tyler, will be at Barrister Collins' office on Bedford street. By the by, have the kitchens give this boy something to eat, and as I can see we are going to be sending a lot of messages, see if he would like a permanent post as my messenger boy, assuming of course, that you receive this in good order. St. J.*

He folded the paper, printed the address on the back of it so that the boy could read it easily. "Read it back to me, lad, so I know that you understand," he said, handing the note to the boy.

"Aye, gov'ner." He squinted but his reading was clear if somewhat slow. "15 Heffington Drive, home of the Dowager Duchess of St. James. The stables. Groom Tyler, man of Duke of St. James." The boy looked up at the end of this and said, "Are you him, m'lord? The Duke, I mean?"

"Aye," St. James said in somber reply, mimicking the boy's oft said response. "T'is I."

"Coo, m'lord," the boy said, tugging at his bangs. "Coo. I'll run quick, I will. For me mother says you're an evil one you are, and that you'll come for me in the night if I don't do as she says!"

"Be off with you then, lad," St. James said with a laugh. "And here, do not forget your crown!"

The boy bobbed again. "Thank you, m'lord. You may think of t'as already there, m'lord." With that he was off, darting across the street and causing St. James a moment of true terror as he dove between on-coming wagons, causing several drivers to curse at the imp running loose amongst them and startling their horses. Then he was across the street, and as he was headed in the right direction, St. James shook his head as he watched the slight, dirty figure disappear, and then turned his horse toward Bedford street.

Chapter Eleven

By tea time, Miss Murdock was feeling composed, if just a little flattened by the depressing strength of her now sorted out convictions. She was preoccupied as she entered the salon, finding the Duchess, Lady Lydia, and Andrew already in presence, by the problem of how to, in fact, beg audience with St. James in order to put forth her carefully thought out arguments.

"Miss Murdock," Andrew said, rising upon her arrival. He came forward, took her hand in his own and bowed over it. "I am so very glad to see you feeling better."

"What is this?" the Dowager asked as Miss Murdock thanked Earl Larrimer and agreed that she was, indeed, feeling better. "Have you not been well, Miss Murdock?"

"I had the headache earlier, but I am feeling much better now, thank you," Miss Murdock answered the old lady with as much brightness as she could muster. "It was really a small thing and a quiet time in my room was all that I needed. And I must confess, I dozed, for I was still frightfully tired." She paused there, wanting to ask if the old Dowager knew when St. James was expected to be seen again, but hesitating as she was certain that the request would be construed in the wrong way.

Lady Lydia, however, interrupted the brief silent spot by saying as she put aside her petit point and Ashton brought in the tea tray, "Well, Miss Murdock, I must say that you certainly look much more presentable than this morning. I am afraid, however," she said in her prim, disapproving manner, "that my mother-in-law has chosen less wisely than I should have, for those red and white stripes merely intensify how very *unfashionably* dark you are."

"Do you think so?" the Dowager asked. "We have been hugely successful then. Thank you so much, Lydia."

Lydia, frowning in confusion at the obvious satisfaction the old Dowager had gotten from her remark, went on to observe, "I do hope that Lady Lenora has something in mind for your hair. That bun is much too provincial. Really, Miss Murdock," she went on without pause, "after reflection, I have come to the conclusion that since St. James has not developed any sort of attachment for you, then his motivation must have been for you to come to London in the hopes that some lesser person would find you attractive. It would only be prudent for you to make the best of what little you have to offer."

As Miss Murdock's cheeks burned at these remarks, Andrew turned on his mother and exclaimed, "Mother! That is the most indiscreet, unkind thing to say, and quite inaccurate. I assure you, Miss Murdock is extremely attractive in her way, and I see no reason why you would want to make her feel as though she will go begging for a suitor." And he glared at Lady Lydia from his pale blue eyes.

"Well!" Lady Lydia said. "I am certain I did not mean to give that impression at all! And I must say that I had not realized fashion had changed so much from when I was a girl." She patted her gray streaked blonde hair and settled her admirable figure into a better posture upon the settee. "Come sit with me, Miss Murdock, and we shall see, at least, if you are capable of pouring the tea in the proper manner." She twitched her crinolined skirts into a somewhat smaller pool about her to enable Miss Murdock room to sit.

Miss Murdock glanced at the Dowager, as it was, in fact, her place to designate who would pour the tea, but she merely nodded to her and said, "That will be fine, Miss Murdock."

So Miss Murdock seated herself with her normal serenity beside Lady Lydia, who, she thought with small satisfaction, at least could not say that she was graceless as well as unattractive, and went through the rather fussy, ceremonial procedure without flaw and unruffled.

"Well!" Lady Lydia said, sounding surprised, as the cups and plates were handed out and everyone settled back to sip, nibble and converse. Andrew took the chair to one side of his grandmother's large, regal, wing-backed one as his mother continued, "At least you can not be faulted on your tea-pouring skills."

"Yes, thank you," Miss Murdock replied. Some imp inside of her made her add, "But I do have the deplorable habit of getting sooty when I am cooking at the stove." To which Lady Lydia choked on her tea.

"Well done," Andrew encouraged.

Lady Lydia said, "Most improper, Miss Murdock!"

"But I think starving would be much more improper, would it not, Lady Lydia?" Miss Murdock replied with wide-eyed surprise.

"Indeed, it would, child," the Dowager agreed, much to Lady Lydia's disgust. "For one could not hold the tea-cup properly if emaciated to such a degree of weakness."

"And that is another thing," Lady Lydia broke in, seeing an opportunity and seizing it. "I have noticed, Miss Murdock, that your arms are a little. . . less soft than is desirable. You must make an active effort to not be lifting anything of consequence for no husband will want a wife that does not appear to be properly helpless and weak."

"Nonsense, mother!" Andrew broke in, his eyes twinkling. "However shall she ride to hounds if she is not able to properly control her mount?"

"*Ride* to hounds?!" his mother asked in a scandalized voice. "Oh, no, Miss Murdock," she turned on that young visitor, her voice pleading as though she thought Miss Murdock's very soul were in danger. "I know that there are a few, very few, women of the peerage that partake in that activity, but I must tell you, they are in danger of doing their reputations irreparable harm! It is quite unseemly, and I dare say that none of them partook in such an activity before they were married, and had their husbands been aware of it before they were married--well, my dear! I shouldn't even need to tell you that they would not have made the match they made."

"Indeed, I do not ride to hounds, Lady Lydia," Miss Murdock told her with perfect honesty. "And it was unkind of Andrew--Earl Larrimer to say such a thing," and she shot that laughing young man a rebuking look. "No, I am much more happy to ride on the track than to chase some poor fox around."

"*Ride on the track?*" Lady Lydia pronounced in utter disbelief. "You can not mean to tell me that you *race?*!"

"Oh, no, ma'am!" Miss Murdock hastened to say. "Even I am aware that is beyond the recall. No, no. I merely train."

"Merely. . . train," Lady Lydia said, her outrage so complete that she was nearly in shock with it. "Oh, my, what ever shall we do with her?" she moaned to her mother-in-law.

"Do?" Lady Lenora asked, nibbling at a cake. "Why should we do anything? The girl is quite all right, I say. Better than these namby-pamby's that go about nowadays, fluttering and swooning. In *my* day, a man wanted a woman with some backbone to her, not a near invalid afraid to even go out in the sun."

"Oh, my. Oh, my," Lady Lydia moaned. "It is all going to be quite hopeless. Quite hopeless."

"Oh, fear not, mother," Andrew told her. "I for one think she will be smashingly popular this season. I dare say every other man my age is dreadfully bored with the women that are pranced before us with each year's coming out. Dull as ditchwater, all of them, with more hair than wit. Why, when I stand up with one to dance, I am always left to feel as though I am dancing with someone who does not even speak my language, so difficult it is to converse with them. At least with Miss Murdock, I can say what I please without fear of sending her into a faint. Well," he amended, "almost anything."

Miss Murdock was moved by this unexpected seal of approval from her new-found friend and looked over at him, her eyes shining, and said, "Thank you, Earl Larrimer. I am quite touched that you at least feel I shall not be a total flop. However," she continued in a stronger voice and her eyes searched out the Duchess who was making another careful selection from the tray of cakes and sweets, "it really all is a moot point, for I have determined that I can not continue to take advantage of your hospitality, Lady Lenora. I hope you will forgive me, but I believe I should make arrangements as soon as possible to return home."

"No!" Andrew said before the Duchess could even reply. "Say you do not mean it, Miss Murdock, for I am sure the entire season will be contemptibly flat without you here to share it with."

"Indeed," the Dowager agreed. "I have been so much looking forward to having someone to launch! Do not say that you will deprive me of that pleasure, Miss Murdock, for I simply will not hear of it."

Miss Murdock, with a blotch of color on each cheek, replied, "I am sorry, but I have determined that I must speak to your grandson as soon as possible as it was he that issued this invitation and it is only correct that I tell him personally that I can no longer accept his. . . his hospitality," she ended on a weak note.

The Duchess's faded eyes studied her with concern, but she seemed disconcertingly calm. "Well, I shall leave it to you and St. James, then, Miss Murdock, as I am sure that he will be able to overcome whatever has you disturbed. He will be here this evening, at any rate, so you may take up the matter with him then."

"This evening," Miss Murdock echoed, finding that just a little sooner than she had expected. But, she had decided the sooner she left the better, so she should not turn squeamish at having her wish to speak to him as soon as possible granted. "Well, that will be fine then. Thank you, ma'am. I hope that after speaking with him I will be able to give you a more understandable explanation rather than this somewhat vague announcement. It is really just so. . . complicated."

"Nonsense!" Lady Lydia interrupted. "It is just nerves, my dear, at your coming out. I really can not blame you, as you are rather old for such an activity, and must feel that you are at a distinct disadvantage. But I assure you, that with the Dowager and myself working on you, you will do well enough."

"That is very kind of you, Lady Lydia," Miss Murdock returned. "And I must say, very unexpected. But I really am not in the market for a husband, so you see how misguided all of these *efforts* are! I think it would be much more prudent for me to return home now before I become more of an expense and feel bound to walk down the aisle with. . . someone. . . just to justify those same expenses."

"Tut, child," the Duchess broke in. "Do not upset yourself. You know very well that I do not count the expense at all. Why I could not be more oblivious to it than if I did not have to pay out a single pence!" she added with a wicked little gleam in her eye. Miss Murdock blushed and set down her tea cup with a less than graceful clang onto her saucer.

"All the same, ma'am," Miss Murdock returned. "I can not accept such generosity when I can see no *acceptable* way to repay it." Before the Dowager, or anyone else had a chance to comment, she went on in a disturbed voice. "Forgive me, ma'am. I did not mean to go into this now and I think I very much understand your feelings of disappointment, and, indeed, I care very much if you are. . . are hurt. But you must understand my position as well, or at least I hope you can understand."

"I do, child. So do not fret," the Duchess hastened to say. "And I am sure it will all come out right in the end, whatever you decide. But, here, let us talk about something else. There is a ball at Almacks' tomorrow, the first of the Season. Surely, even if you decide you must leave, you will indulge me by at least attending *one* ball?"

Miss Murdock twisted her hands in her lap. "I--I can not say for sure, ma'am. . . ."

"But certainly you will go to one, Miss Murdock?" Andrew encouraged. "Why, if you are going to go home, you must be able to say you went to Almacks! And I should so like to take you to some of the other sites here in London for who can say when you will next be here? It would be a shame for you to only go home saying that you saw nothing but the Duchess's home and the dress maker's!"

"Oh, yes, Miss Murdock," Lady Lydia added. "One must visit the hat maker's also. And no visit would be complete if you did not go at least once to the park in the morning to take the air. And if your stay is to be so short, we should have at least a dinner party in your honor before you go. Do you not think so, Lady Lenora? It has been so long since we had a party here," and the longing in her voice was unmistakable. "It has been nearly a year since Morty died, and we have not had a party since his death."

"Yes. You are right, Lydia," the Duchess replied, for once in perfect agreement with her daughter-in-law. "Just because the Queen seems determined to be in mourning for ever over Prince Albert does not mean that the rest of us should be so gloomy. Miss Murdock," she commanded. "You will remain out the week, no matter what you and my grandson decide."

And Miss Murdock, seeing how churlish she appeared to be by wanting to return home immediately, agreed with reluctance that she would go to Almacks and allow a dinner party in her honor, though the thought of both fairly terrified her. Andrew expressed his relief, and the Duchess nodded in approval. Lady Lydia expressed her pleasure, "Very good, Miss Murdock. I shall make a point of inviting a great many eligible bachelors so that you may at least see what is being offered this season."

To which Miss Murdock rolled her eyes in exasperation and met Andrew's amused look. "Yes, Miss Murdock," he agreed. "You should at least see what is being offered this season." And his blue eyes seemed very warm as they looked into her own.

St. James was in a thoughtful mood as he mounted his horse after spending an hour with his deceased uncle's solicitor. The will that had been sent over to his own Barrister's office had been correct and St. James had been unable to find explanation for the strange arrangements that his Uncle Mortimer had made just two months before his death.

Barrister Collins had been of the opinion (observing with dryness that St. James' aunt was, in fact, rather ill-suited to be in charge of such a large estate, or even, in fact, *any* estate) that his Uncle had wanted a more capable hand at the reins of control. That could very well be true, St. James conceded, but it did not explain why St. James had not then been put in charge of the estate immediately, instead of upon his marrying. Or why, once put in charge of said estate, if his cousin Andrew were to die, the estate would not return to Lydia but remain under the control, and in fact, ownership, of St. James himself.

It seemed very odd, indeed.

St. James had asked if Collins thought Lady Lydia were even aware of this wrinkle in her husband's will, and Collins had been of the opinion that although he could not know for certain, that she was not, as she had taken no real interest in any of it and had left the decisions to be made by the managers who had always taken care of the various properties and accounts and who reported to him. When Earl Mortimer Larrimer had been alive, Collins had passed on all this information to him to be decided according to his wishes, but since his death, Lady Lydia had not moved herself to make any decisions on the estate and had left it in his hands. Of which, he assured St. James, he had been very profitably able to do.

All this information, which really was not much at all, left St. James with the strange feeling that his uncle had felt him even less capable of handling the estate than his feather-brained widow. Not a heartening thought, nor one that he could endorse as the true reason, for he had worked with his uncle for many years, and his uncle had seemed to trust him a great deal, and to rely on his abilities.

"M'lord," a young voice piped up, interrupting his musings. St. James, who had settled himself in the saddle but had not yet turned his horse into the street, looked down to where the voice had issued from, saw the same bedraggled youth that he had charged with carrying his message to Tyler earlier.

"You, laddie," he said. "Do not tell me you could not find the address?"

"Oh, no, m'lord. Found it just as I said I would. And your groom Tyler, too. He guv me somethin' to eat, m'lord. I hope you don't mind," and he rubbed his raggedy shirt covered stomach to give proof to his words.

St. James gave a faint smile. "No, laddie. I don't mind. Did my man tell you I have a position for you if you want it?"

"Coo, m'lord. He did. He told's me to comes find you here in case I was needed by you."

"Did he send a message?" St. James asked. He leaned down from the saddle, his gold eyes dark with interest.

"Nothing written, m'lord," the boy replied. "Only that he had what you had asked for this morning and that you should look at it this evening when you arrive as planned. He bade me tell you that," and he frowned as he said this, his dirty face concentrating as the words had no meaning to him and he wanted to repeat them correctly in case they had meaning for his lordship, "he has a better fist than t'maid has."

St. James laughed at this. "Well, that is not saying much," he commented. "But it is as I expected." He looked down at the boy, debating for a moment, then said, "Have you ever been up, lad?"

"On a horse, you mean, sir?"

"Yes. On a horse, I mean. Can you ride?"

"Coo, never been on a horse, m'lord. But I guess I can hold on as well as the next boy can."

"I expect you can," St. James agreed. "You look like a scrappy young fellow." He removed his boot from the stirrup and put a gloved hand down to the boy. "Put your foot in there and I'll lift you up behind. No, your other foot, otherwise you'll end up seeing where we've been rather than where we're going."

The boy put in the proper foot and St. James grabbed his hand and hoisted his light figure up behind him. "I only ask you hang onto the saddle as best you may," he instructed, "for you shall get my coat filthy otherwise."

"Aye, m'lord." The boy was shaking with excitement. "But I be the king of the world from up here, m'lord. This is a grand way to be!" Then he was silent for St. James kicked his stallion into as fast a pace as he could go in amongst the traffic of the street and the boy was too intent upon hanging on to say anything further.

"By-the-by, boy, does your mother know where you are?" the duke asked when they had reached a less congested part of the street.

"Aye, sir. I took's me crown to her on me way back here. But the tuppence and ha-penny, I kept for meself," the boy replied in short, breathless bursts. "She wasn't happy about me working for you, m'lord, but she were happy about the crown. That's what decided it, m'lord."

"It usually does, lad," St. James replied, and as the street was clear for a straight section, he put his heels to his horse and it went into a canter.

And so, my lord, Effington summed up at the bottom of his letter, *it is with great regret, but with, I deem, necessity, that I resign my position as your valet. If you wish, I can recommend someone for replacing me, but as you do not seem to require the services of a valet to the degree that a valet is trained for, indeed, spends a good many years studying for, I can not in all conscience recommend any one that I admire as a friend, for I fear that they would never forgive me for doing them such a grievous disservice.*

I only hope that my resigning will at last shock you into realization that you owe your station more in respects to your attire and appearance than you have so far been wont to show, and that you will take this into consideration upon hiring another valet, and allow that employee more leeway in doing his duty.

Yours regretfully but sincerely,

Effing--
"Effington!"

His name being shouted from one floor below startled that proper valet to such a degree that he put an unsightly blotch where the end of his name should have been, and he fussed over it, wondering if he should in fact rewrite the whole letter. As there were some three pages of it, he decided that of course he should only rewrite the final page and at the same time he got up from his desk with a guilty start and hurried from his room. "Yes, milord," he asked with as much serenity as he could manage as he saw his employer standing not in his rooms, as he had expected, but at the bottom of the stairs. His coat was filthy, Effington noticed with disapproval, with what looked to be, but surely could *not* be, some young urchin's hand prints.

"When was this missive delivered?" St. James asked, holding out a rather plain envelope with the seal now broken. "I have asked Applegate, but he said you were below stairs and took delivery of it."

"Yes, milord. Half past two, I believe, milord." Effington paused for a moment, his eyes straining to see what looked to be a royal seal on the paper held in his lordship's other hand. "Is it something important, milord?" he asked, unable to hide the eagerness in his voice. "I took no particular notice to it as it was delivered in only a plain envelope."

St. James looked more irritated than eager. "Yes, damn it." He glanced at the short, one paged missive that he raised from his side and Effington was now certain that it *was* a royal emblem at the top of it. "And I have already had a rather commanding summons from my grandmother to be at her home this evening, and now I shall in no way make that. Effington, you will finally get your wish for you had better outfit me in whatever is deemed appropriate for a visit to Buckingham."

Effington had to hold on to the newel post to keep his hand from shaking at the sudden fervor that went through him. "Yes, milord. Certainly, milord. It will be my pleasure, milord. Is that to be for this evening, milord?"

"Yes, blast you, Effington, and you needn't look so bloody eager."

"Is it to be an audience with the Queen, milord?" Effington asked in a near reverential whisper.

"I am not at liberty to say, Effington, but you may outfit me to whatever degree your imagination deems necessary. And a God-awful miserable evening it shall be," St. James muttered. "I will be below in my study as I will have to write a very unwelcome note to my grandmother expressing my regrets. Of which, I may add, I am sure I will be paying for for some time and I will not even be at liberty to tell her what 'pressing matter' has come up to make me beg off. Although, I doubt in her mind that even the Queen herself would be a suitable engagement to keep me from coming to her when she has so brusquely commanded my presence." He turned to Effington before descending further down the stairs. "Not a word of this to anyone, Effington, you understand," and the gold eyes were very piercing indeed, making Effington draw himself up in defense.

"No, of course not, milord. I have never had lack of discretion laid at my door, I need not remind *you.*"

St. James relaxed enough to grin. "Much to my benefit, you would probably like to add. But of course, you are much too *discreet* to say so."

"Indeed, I am, milord," Effington replied.

St. James only waved a dismissing hand. "Go about the business of dreaming up how you shall shame me tonight with your notions of fashion, Effington." He continued on down the stairs and so did not see that man rub his hands together in glee, already envisioning what he would attire his lordship in. Royalty deserved something bright, he decided, but not too bright, for the Queen herself still remained in mourning. Perhaps conservative black with a colorful cravat, waistband and boots? he wondered. No, he shook his head. Black boots. Black waistband and black cravat. That would show a proper degree of respect for her majesty's mourning and at the same time allow him the liberty of dressing his lordship in more colorful pantaloons and shirt. And his jacket could be something colorful also. A turquoise jacket, Effington thought, yellow pantaloons and shirt. Yes, that would be fashionable and with the black counterpoints, properly respecting the Queen's sensibilities. If, indeed, it were the Queen his employer had been summoned to see. It must be, Effington thought, for he doubted anyone lesser than the Queen could induce the Duke to allow his valet full control of his wardrobe for the evening.

But of course, before he could do any of this, he had to return above stairs and rip the letter he had been writing to shreds.

"Applegate," St. James said to his butler upon reaching the ground floor of his house. "I have a new messenger boy. He's in the kitchens now, I believe. See to it that he has the proper clothing."

"Yes, milord. Will you be dining in this evening, milord?"

"Yes. But then I will be going out after. I do not know how late I shall be so please do not remain up. By-the-by, when you speak to this messenger boy I have retained, send him round my study in a bit for I shall have several notes for him to deliver."

"Very well, milord."

St. James continued into his study to compose first a note to Tyler, short and easily written, and then a somewhat more difficult note to his grandmother.

In between them, he paused, stared at the fire for a brief moment wondering why ever the Queen should have the sudden desire to summon him to Buckingham Palace. It was an annoyance at best and could be a distraction at worst, and at the moment he didn't need any further distractions, for he already had one in the form of Miss Murdock residing at his grandmother's home.

With this thought in mind, he began the composition of his letter, and it came more easily than he had expected:

Dearest Grandmother,

I received your warm regards earlier today and had every intention, of course, of coming around your house at the appointed hour. I am sorry to say that I have become aware of a pressing and unavoidable obligation. Please know that only something of the most supreme importance could keep me from you when you have asked for my audience. Or from Miss Murdock, for that matter. Please express this to her. I am sure she will find it comforting to know that my attention has not strayed from her in the hours I have been gone from her presence.
Until I can be there,
Your loving grandson,
Dante

St. James laughed to himself as he put his signature to the letter. His grandmother would be most enraged to find him thwarting her wishes but he would wager Miss Murdock would be even angrier when she was conveyed his warm sentiments.

The damnedable part of it was she *had* been on his mind for all of the day. This was understandable, he reminded himself, as she was a most important part of his plan. What was not understandable to him was the way he remembered her: her accusing glare as she turned from reading her newspaper in the inn's parlor to find him partaking with a-bandon of the available brandy. And the degree of shocked discovery in her eyes when he had held her hands to his chest a good many drinks later.

Perhaps a look of discovery that had mirrored his own.

A discovery, at any rate, that he had no time for, nor wish for, and that he had no desire for Miss Murdock to feel either. But it did so amuse him, he conceded, to provoke her just a little more in his letter, and to sit, now idle, at his desk, and spend a brief moment imagining her cheeks flushing in her plain face and her solemn eyes trying very hard to hide in their brownness as though she could become invisible to him. And his attention.

For if nothing else, Miss Murdock did have his attention.

St. James reread the final line of his letter. If it did not disquiet her so for him to fluster her, would he take such a perverse pleasure in doing so? No. He thought not. But it amused him, and inspired some strange sympathy in him as well. A sympathy for what, he really could not name, other than, perhaps, it had to do with the way she was forced to re-examine how she thought about herself. And that was nearly a shame, for she had seemed to have it all sorted out quite neatly and now he was forcing her to reevaluate who she was and where her place was in the world. Although he was of the opinion that her place in the world would be better as a result of his interference than what she had, was it really for him to say what it was she sought for and would be happy with?

If she were happy being as she had been: a near spinster caring for her father in lamentable circumstances, did he have any right, whatever his motives, to take that from her?

St. James shook his head, and a ruthless part of his mind overrode this bit of rare second-guessing, for he understood only too well what having things taken from you was all about. If Miss Murdock were to mourn what she had before, he could only try to assuage that grief as best he could, but he would not be able to wipe it away entirely, however this turned out. This he would regret. But this he would live with as he had so many regrets before this.

He rose from behind his desk, found the boy he had employed waiting in the doorway. "There you are, laddie. You may take these to the same address as before. This one is for Tyler, whom you have met. This one you are to deliver to the butler of the house."

"Aye, m'lord," the boy said. He was cleaner now, his face scrubbed, his hair slicked back and he had on some clothing which did not fit him well but which were at least clean and decent. "I'm to get new clothes, m'lord, they tell me," he confided, looking uncertain whether to be happy or disgusted.

"T'is a great shame, I know," St. James said with uncharacteristic gentleness. "But if you wish to work here, you can not look like a street urchin."

The boy nodded. "Aye, m'lord. I ken that. It's just--you shan't have someone beat me should I gets them dirty, should you?"

St. James shook his head. "No. You shall have several sets of clothes, and you shall change them every day and the maids will clean the dirty set while you wear the clean set."

"Every day, m'lord?" the boy asked. "And will I have to wash every day, too?"

"It is generally recommended, yes."

"Coo, m'lord! Lucky you're payin' me 'n' all, for I wouldn't take a bath that often elsewise, I wouldn't."

"Yes, it is a great bother, isn't it? Now, lad, you may return home to your mother each night if you wish, or if she wishes, or you may have a room here and see her on your days off. You will let Applegate know which you choose, shall you?"

"Aye. I will, m'lord. A room all to meself, m'lord?"

St. James thought about the disruption of staff hierarchy for a moment, then allowed, "Yes. A small one, mind you. But it will have your own bed and your own dresser for your things. Will that be suitable for you?"

The boy nodded. "T'is all a boy could ask for in the world, m'lord. Me mother will be very happy."

"Good. That will be all, lad."

The boy took the envelopes before leaving the room. St. James nearly stopped him, deciding that maybe he should at least know the boy's name. But he let the boy go on. He needn't a name. St. James already knew enough names. He went to the sideboard and bypassing the gentler liquors, reached for the decanter of whiskey in the back and poured himself a very stiff one.

In the silence of the study, he made a toast that only he heard. "To vengeance and death. Whether another's or my own." Then he drank in a single, continuous swallowing, feeling the alcohol burn down his throat and into his stomach. Then in a rare, out of control movement, he slammed the small, elegant glass into the fireplace, shattering it with finality.

Chapter Twelve

Miss Murdock sat with fortitude as the hairdresser drew his brush through her hair and exclaimed something in muttered French.

The Duchess was seated in Miss Murdock's dressing room with them, her old, frail hands crossed and resting on the head of her cane in a picture of perfect patience. Lady Lydia was there also, but she flounced in her place upon the chaise lounge, and was bent upon giving the Duchess's hairdresser frequent and contradictory instructions on how to go about his business. Miss Murdock had the impression that his muttering was as much directed at that Lady as at her troublesome hair. Her new lady's maid, Jeannie, was also in attendance, standing to one side and providing pins, ribbons, combs and the hot iron when asked for them, and picking them from the floor in silence when the frustrated hairdresser threw them down in exasperation.

Andrew, quite comically and unpredictably, had stationed himself outside of her bedchambers and paced the hallway as he waited for the grand undertaking of trying to turn Miss Murdock into, if not quite an incomparable, then at least someone memorable.

And Miss Murdock, seated with apparent meekness, was in turns despairing at the pointlessness of it and amused to such a degree that intermittent giggles escaped her.

"That will not do, Alphonse," the Duchess commented over Lady Lydia's unhelpful directions. "That is nearly as prim as the bun she wore."

Miss Murdock bore the hard pulls on her hair as he ripped out all the combs and pins he had just spent the previous half the hour putting in. They rained down like a shower onto the floor and Jeannie again bent to retrieve and order them. Miss Murdock gurgled another laugh, trying to stifle her amusement into her hands. For her troubles she received a glare in the mirror from the hairdresser. "She does not have the proper respect for what I am trying to do!" he exclaimed in his thick accent to the Duchess. "How am I to work miracles when she only sneers and laughs at my efforts?"

"Forgive me!" Miss Murdock begged him, even as she tried to control her amusement at the pained expression on his face. "I am not sneering. It is just that--it is so very hopeless, you know!" and she covered her face with her hands and gave herself over to the silent shaking of it.

"What do you want from me?!" Alphonse demanded of the Duchess. "This style too prim! That style too elaborate! Bah! I have gone through every mode that is currently in fashion and you like none of them!" He threw his hands out in a mixture of defeat and disdain. "*Mon Dui*, but it is too much to ask of *any* man."

"Something fashionable," Lady Lydia exclaimed. "As I have been saying all this time."

The hairdresser spared her a murderous look.

"Something simple," the Duchess countered. "Look at her, please, Alphonse, and tell me what you see."

"Certainly, madam," Alphonse said with simmering dignity. He turned to look at Miss Murdock who uncovered her face and returned his gaze with her solemn eyes, only a corner of her small mouth twitching.

Alphonse obviously had begun his study of his project only to humor the duchess but his frustrated features lightened and he made a thoughtful noise and put one finger beneath his chin. "Ah," he said at last. "Yes. Simple. Straightforward. A little severe, I think, but as you said, not prim. Nothing on her forehead, I think, for we do not wish to take any attention away from her eyes. You know, of course, madam, that she is much too, how do you say it, sun browned?"

"Yes, Alphonse. I know," the Duchess returned, her initial enjoyment at this frequent observation fast turning into tedium. "But you begin to see, I hope, that anything currently in fashion is not going to suit Miss Murdock?" Her words turned more acerbic, "For if it would suit her, we would not need you, then, would we, Alphonse? Any other hairdresser in town is quite capable of turning out what every one else is wearing."

He gave her an injured look, but said, "Of course, you are right, madam. This is an assignment that *only* Alphonse can do." He held out his hand to Jeannie. "Brush!" He brushed Miss Murdock's hair back from her forehead and high onto the crown of her head. "Combs!" he commanded, holding the thick length of her hair there and passing his other hand over for Jeannie to fill. He fitted the combs so tightly that Miss Murdock felt that he were jamming them into her very skull. Then he removed his hold. Her hair was pulled back from her face to a point just above and beyond her ears, from where it flowed in a heavy cascade down her back. Alphonse nodded in determination. "Hot iron!"

He curled innumerable ringlets down her back, until her hair was a mass of shining, dancing curls. The effect, when he at last called finish with a flourish, sweat standing out on his brow, and Miss Murdock was allowed to turn and see herself in the mirror, was such a subtle and yet such a total transformation that she could only stare at herself.

The solemnity of her eyes was still evident, but the curls added such a mischievous aura about her that her eyes seemed to twinkle with it, like a well-hidden joke that only she was privy to and found enjoyment in. Her features were small and delicate, as they had always been, but now they were immediately, and somewhat entrancingly, she dared add to herself, noticeable. Her arched brows were exposed so that her every thought, nearly, was expressed in their slight raising or lowering. The high collar of her red and white dress (which as she was not to be delivered of any other until the following morning, she was still wearing) seemed an enchanting and appropriate setting for the sudden flirtatiousness of her new look, and for many moments, Miss Murdock could only stand and, in truth, look at herself in wonder.

She had the sudden vision of half-hooded gold eyes opening from some lazy, languid, drunken half-slumber, and nostrils quivering at her unexpected nearness.

"Turn, child, so we may see the full effect," the Dowager commanded her. Miss Murdock did so, her hands trembling a little and a flush warming her face. The Duchess appraised her, her faded eyes studying her with ever growing satisfaction. "Yes," she said at last. "*That* is how it should be. I am sure Dante will be very surprised when he arrives tonight."

Jeannie said, "You look very well, miss. It is a stunning success, if I may say so."

Alphonse drew himself up to his full, not very impressive height with each of these praisings. "It shall be," he announced, "all the rage in a fortnight, I have no doubt."

Lady Lydia at last spoke, having been, for once, struck silent. "I am sure it will be," she said, and if there was a sudden dryness to her voice, Miss Murdock really did not pay attention to it, too intent, still, on the Duchess's words of St. James to be there that night. She had not forgotten that he would come, but somehow it seemed his arrival was now very immediate and the strange giddiness that was coming over her, and the painful shyness, had her feeling more confused with each passing moment.

The Duchess glanced at the time, said in her autocratic manner, "Well, enough of this. It took long enough is all I have to say. But it is near dining time now, shall we go below? Well done, Alphonse."

"Thank you, madam," and he clicked his heels as he bowed.

In the hallway, Andrew turned to them when he heard the door open. "Devil take it, but you have been long enough in there! I had nearly decided to go to White's rather than sit about here any--" He stopped at sight of Miss Murdock. Then he strode over, took one of her hands and stared down at her. "Miss Murdock," he said at last, "you are lovely."

"I--why thank you," Miss Murdock stammered. "But really, Earl Larrimer, it *is* only my hair," she could not help adding for there was a certain disgruntlement to be felt with discovering that something she had always disdained as rather silly and wasteful of time could in fact be, apparently, so important.

"But what lovely hair it is. And its effect is to make you positively charming," he returned with boyish admiration.

"I think," Miss Murdock said as she looked at him, "that a new hair style only has the effect of making a female more susceptible to the flattery she would have dismissed out of hand prior to it."

To which Andrew burst out laughing. "You may be right, Miss Murdock," he agreed and returned to the warm friendship they had begun cultivating earlier that day. "But isn't it delicious?" he asked with an impish grin. He held out his arm to her to escort her to dinner and took his grandmother's hand onto his other arm, leaving Lady Lydia to follow behind.

"I believe it is," Miss Murdock agreed, her eyes twinkling and feeling at last more herself with his easy bantering. "If for no other reason then to see young, silver-tongued rogues such as yourself stretching the limits of credibility even further than I would have first supposed."

They were laughing as they descended. The duchess snorted at their comments, bade them to go on, as she was slowing them down, and as Ashton came up the stairs to assist her, they relented and did as she bid. Andrew escorted Lizzie into the drawing room where he proclaimed they should first have a glass of sherry before dinner. He poured their glasses and then toasted her, "To the new Miss Murdock, who looks as enchanting and shining as I already knew her to be."

Miss Murdock gave a wistful smile. "Thank you, Andrew. I shall need practice deflecting such comments as these, if I am to suppose every other young man in town has the deplorable habit of being so flip with his praise, and it is good of you to help prepare me."

He had just begun to protest when the Duchess came in the room with Ashton and the sudden ill-humor of her mood was immediately noticeable to them. "Blast him!" she was exclaiming to no one in particular. In her hands was a short missive, which she had apparently already read through once and was now perusing again. "I have never known him to be so impertinent. Not to me at least! He has never before dared," she fumed.

"Grandmother?" Andrew asked, his gaiety leaving him. "Whatever is the trouble?"

Miss Murdock took one look at the wrathful, disappointed countenance of the Duchess, who was standing leaning on her cane despite Ashton indicating her large chair in readiness for her. "Is it St. James, Lady Lenora?" she asked, somehow knowing only he could inspire such anger and hurt in the old lady.

The Dowager turned her eyes to her, and there was such a frown between the faded silver brows that Miss Murdock was at once alarmed and also reminded of St. James' similar habit of glaring doom when crossed. "There is a part in here for you, Miss Murdock," the Dowager told her, her rage so biting that she did not even soften her tone as she normally did when speaking to her young protégée. "You may as well read it and draw whatever conclusions from it you like. Though I would say his very *absence. . .*" and she trailed off, at last seating herself in a sad and, for her, rare, defeated manner, "is in itself *damnedable.*"

Miss Murdock took the missive that Ashton held out to her, scanned the lines, *. . .comforting to know that my attention has not strayed. . .* and in a sudden spasm of extreme rage and, even more upsetting, disappointment that he was in fact, *not* coming, crumpled the letter in her hand.

"What ever is it?" Andrew asked.

Miss Murdock did not even glance at him. "It is nothing!" she said, her voice a little desperate. "Nothing."

"Well, it certainly seems to be something," Andrew pressed.

She looked at him then, said with a little more control, "I expressly wished to speak with him this evening, as I think I had made clear earlier, about my returning home. And he has. . . begged off."

"But he could not possibly know that this meeting with him held some importance to you, could he?" Andrew defended his cousin, his voice confused. "I mean, he could not know that you suddenly wished to leave."

"Certainly he could know," Miss Murdock returned. "In fact, I would not put it past him to have known and deliberately not be coming this evening because of that suspicion."

"Why," Andrew replied, taken aback by her cold fury, "that is hardly reasonable to assume--"

"Well, he is hardly reasonable, is he, Earl Larrimer?" Miss Murdock returned with more scorn in her voice than she had intended. She turned to the Duchess, who had been watching her with a renewed interest. "Do you have further need of this, ma'am?" she asked, holding the crumpled letter in her hand.

"No. Not at all." The Dowager's sniff told her feelings on the subject and the writer of the letter.

Miss Murdock, without further ado, tossed the letter into the fireplace where it caught flame, said to everyone and no one, "Forgive me, I should not let my--my disappointment at being unable to make my arrangements with any degree of firmness tonight as I had planned disrupt our evening."

"Of course, Miss Murdock. We quite understand," Andrew told her.

"Indeed, we do," Lady Lydia, who had come in just a moment behind the Duchess and had caught the most part of Miss Murdock's small scene agreed. "St. James is in no way ever to be relied upon, and *I* can quite sympathize with how you are feeling, having felt equally as frustrated myself in the past with him. He utterly refuses to take into account any one but himself!"

"I still am certain--" Andrew began but Miss Murdock cut him off.

"I--I don't wish to speak any more about it now," she pronounced. "Please, can we just go in to dinner, I really must be more tired than I thought to be reacting in such a--such a foolish manner."

"Yes, I'm sure you are still tired," the Duchess agreed. "Ashton, if all is in readiness?"

He bowed, his face impassive, and yet still managing to convey a warm sympathy, "Yes, milady."

The Dowager made a motion to get up and Andrew helped her from her seat and they went in to dinner. Miss Murdock ate as well as she had ever eaten, but somehow despite Andrew's occasional admiring look, she felt extremely silly with her new hair style and her new dress, and where before she had wanted to go home to escape greater difficulty with the duke, now she found herself positively longing for home, her weak, comical father, and her oh-so brown, unassuming dresses.

St. James had ordered a closed carriage to be hired, plain and black, with a pair of black horses to match. The Queen's secretary had asked him to use discretion and the commonplace envelope that his summons had been delivered in showed that they had evidently been following their own advice. So now, as the carriage was drawn up to the front of his house with one of his own grooms at the reins, St. James stepped out of the door and down the wide granite steps to alight into the carriage.

It was not his usual mode of transportation, himself much preferring to drive the racing curricle, as he had the day before, despite however good or bad the weather may be, or riding astride. But as he was outfitted in the outlandish attire that Effington had deemed appropriate for his visit, it was perhaps best that he was not concerned with any detail other than trying to keep from wrinkling his turquoise coat. He looked down at himself with disgust as the carriage door was closed behind him. Yellow pantaloons and shirt! God help him, at least Tyler was not here to see him, for there was no way, he would wager, that man could have restrained from laughing outright.

St. James had rained a great deal of insults upon Effington's head as that man had fulfilled his duty in dressing milord, but for once, he could not provoke Effington in the least. He had gone about his purpose in an unflappable manner and had answered St. James' ongoing abuse with, "Yes, milord. No, milord. You have my *deepest* sympathies, milord."

To which St. James had answered, "Yes, I can see that I have, Effington," and had at last said no more, merely gritted his teeth and endured as best he could being dressed in a manner he despised as being unmanfully vain and damningly restrictive in any natural movement. How was he to even bloody walk in boots that had heels nearly as high as any woman's slipper? He asked this of Effington, half begging to at least be allowed a more practical choice of footwear, but the valet, face shining with pride in the result of his efforts, said with certainty, "But you carry it off so well, milord! And I must say, your only lacking in attributes is your height, and you see now how easily that has been remedied?"

"I have never been so short that I could not thoroughly thrash someone who has annoyed me, Effington," St. James returned. "And I put you on notice that *you* are annoying me!"

Effington, who had appeared to be taking as much pleasure from his lordship's discomfort as from the effect he had created, only smiled with smugness and replied, "And when have I not, milord? Now mind that you do not muddy your boots for I have taken an hour to shine them this afternoon."

"Bloody nurse maid," St. James muttered beneath his breath, but now as he sat in the carriage, he did glance down at them to be sure that they were not sullied in any way. Then a movement from outside his window caught his eye as the carriage jolted into motion, and he banged his cane, a before now useless accessory that Effington had insisted upon, on the roof of the carriage, commanding it to stop.

"You, lad," he opened the door to call to the messenger boy he had hired that day, for it had been he that St. James had caught sight of, watching the duke's preparation to leave with a look of longing from the mew to the side of the house. "Care to be a footman tonight?"

The boy came forward eagerly, gray eyes shining in anticipation. "You mean it, m'lord?" he asked. "What am I need do?"

"Just ride on the back there, you'll see the platform and the holds, and when I arrive at our destination, you're to jump down smartly and open the door for me, and see that I in all my feebleness do not trip and land upon my face when I alight from the carriage," St. James told him.

"Coo, I can do that, m'lord!" the lad said, and without waiting for further instruction, he went to where St. James had indicated. The coach dropped down a small bit as his gangly figure climbed to stand up behind. St. James tapped the roof again, and the carriage resumed moving. He sat back, and oddly, instead of studying upon his strange summons to Buckingham, he wondered what Miss Murdock's reaction had been to his not coming this evening. He imagined her with her hair pulled back in its prim bun, the soft loops of it coming down like an arrow from her forehead to cover her ears, and her plain brown dress that whispered with reticence when she walked. For all of her unobtrusiveness she had somehow managed to become a focal point to him for the past near forty-eight hours. The lingering of hummingbird wings, perhaps, that quietly and efficiently held one captivated at their delicate strength of rhythm, moving so quickly that one could barely discern them and yet one was keenly aware of them all the same.

Yes, St. James thought, there was an essence to Miss Murdock that was barely discernible, but that was engagingly evident. He wondered if Miss Murdock were even aware of it? Or if the very charm of it was that she was not and dismissed the notion of it out of hand as having no place in her practical outlook on life.

If one wished someone to quit drinking, one threw that person's flask away.

If only it were that easy, St. James pondered.

If one wanted to live, one made the decision to live.

An option not open to him.

If there was a heretonow not evident bitterness in this thought, he did not entertain it. It was only that he had the suspicion that he was at last stirring his foe, and hence he now felt that the past many years of his quest had been only so much exercise. In possibly a very short time, he would engage in the true conflict. He had always been aware that his opponent had very much the advantage on him and that there may in fact be little that he could do before he became enough of a threat to receive his own speedy dispatch. It was part of the puzzle that this person had apparently never sought to dispatch him in the years since his parents' murders, but with St. James resolutely digging about, whatever had stayed the murderer would no doubt stay him no longer.

But it was oh so satisfying to find that he had finally found the proper means of disturbing his enemy, and to know that even at this moment, said enemy must be feeling, for once, hunted himself.

In the midst of these dark, nearly unconscious thoughts, the carriage entered the gates at Buckingham Palace, where it was stopped by two beefeaters as the occupant's business was made known and acknowledged as expected. Then it moved forward up the long drive, but instead of going to the circle in front of the main entrance, took another road on around the long, overpowering length of the building, then down one side of it to a smaller, but still impressive entrance. There it stopped, being met by yet another beefeater, whose only recognition of their presence was to stand from parade rest to full attention at their arrival. The messenger boy did not disappoint St. James, but perceiving they were at their final destination, jumped down as before instructed and opened the carriage door for him. St. James alighted out by the small step of the carriage, his yellow shirt and pantaloons glowing in the jealous light of the moon and twin torches that lit the entrance way. His turquoise coat was shadowed to inky purple and his highly polished boots reflected like deep, dark mirrors. The boy bowed in inspired respectfulness, and as he rose from it, he looked up at the duke and said, "Thank you, m'lord!"

"I thought you may enjoy this," St. James returned. "Now mind you stay with the carriage and the groom. I don't think they take kindly to street urchins running willy-nilly about the grounds."

Then he stepped forward and the tall doors were opened to him by a butler that made his own Applegate seem like some clumsy oaf in comparison. He was led but a short way down the long hallway, shown into a rather intimate small chamber where a fire was built up in the fireplace. It was an elegant room, but it had neither the opulence nor style of the social rooms he had prior seen of the palace when being there for the occasional function years earlier. The butler directed him further into the room to a chair by the fire. There was one other chair there, well-upholstered but not otherwise remarkable and it was occupied by a woman of no great beauty. Her nose was rather long, her jowls rather fleshy, and her hair was dark brown streaked with gray and worn in a bun, remarkably, not unlike the one Miss Murdock wore. She was in her mid forties and she made no apparent artifice in concealing it. There was a matronly, comfortable look to her, and an air of one who speaks plainly and expects the same in return.

St. James sketched a deep and humble bow. "Your Majesty," he intoned.

"St. James," the Queen acknowledged. "I am glad that you were available. Will you be seated?"

St. James took the proffered seat, which was close enough to Queen Victoria that they could converse without effort. The butler offered him a cup of tea, which he accepted and the Queen joined him. They sat in silence for a moment, each sipping their tea and the fireplace snapping when the mood suited it.

"I had heard from my intimates," the Queen began, "that you were in the habit of dressing extremely plainly, much to their disappointment. I must count myself honored, I suppose, that you have put some effort into your apparel this night."

St. James smiled. "It only goes to show, Your Highness, that I am willing to sacrifice even my dignity for the crown's sake."

She did not laugh, but she did smile at this light sally. "Or," she went on, "perhaps you have taken to dressing appropriately to better impress your new fiancé."

St. James did not quite choke on his tea, although he felt very close to it. Instead, he paused with the cup to his lips for a long, deliberate moment and then took a small sip before replacing the cup on his saucer. His eyelids half-hooded over his gold eyes and when he at last answered, his words were measured and thoughtful. "I pity those who believe that you have become such a recluse that you are not properly aware of the activities of the realm, Your Majesty, for I can see that they are grossly mistaken."

"Yes," she said, her eyes penetrating. "They are mistaken. I could tell them that since Prince Albert's death I have been more devoted than ever before to seeing that things are done in a proper and *respectable* manner. It is the mistake my uncle made before me, you know. He did not realize that the only way we now have of leading is to earn the respect of the people, lords and commons alike. If the people are behind the throne, the prime minister dare not wander too far from our edicts. If they are not behind the throne, then the prime minister can and will go counter to the crown's policies."

St. James nodded once but he did not speak. The Queen hardly needed his stamp of approval on her thoughts.

"But I digress. You did not directly acknowledge that you are engaged."

"I am not officially engaged, if that is what you mean, Your Highness."

"But you are engaged all the same?"

St. James paused for a moment, and his face must have shown how unsettled he was with this conversation, and the possible reasons behind it, for the Queen raised a brow before he could answer. "I am being rather blunt, I am afraid. And prying, you may believe."

St. James raised a brow in return. "I admit that I am. . . shocked at your knowledge."

That did bring a laugh from her, a very short one. "Do not doubt that if it is possible that I know then it is possible that there may be others that know. Prepare yourself well, St. James."

He did not answer, and if his silence was taken as impertinent he could not help it for he could not think of anything to say that would not further reveal his position.

Of an impulse, Queen Victoria reached out her hand and touched his arm. "I had great respect for your father, St. James. If it is true that you are to marry, there is work that he had started that needs to be carried on. We recently had a great victory in China that allows us to send in Christian Missionaries, but I fear that the complete legalization of the opium trade there can be looked upon as nothing but a defeat, despite our monopoly upon it and the profits it brings to our country."

St. James was mystified, for he had no idea what work his father had done for the crown. He only sipped again from his tea, and kept his face unreadable.

"I have hesitated to approach you," the Queen continued, "for, candidly, I was not sure if you could leave go the trail of vengeance you had set for yourself so many years ago in order to give the tasks I have for you your full attention. I wish to know if it is true that you are to marry this daughter of a Squire," and she smiled as though this amused her very much. "I wish to know if at last the trail is too cold for even you to pursue."

St. James answered with care, "I am going to marry this daughter of a Squire. But I beg Your Highness for just a short time longer before asking for my assistance on the matters you have referred to. If you can grant me that short time, I will deem it an honor to perform any task you hand me, especially any that my father may have left. . . unfinished."

She sat back in her seat a degree. This time it was she that took a long moment to answer, and when she did she spoke with as much care, her words as veiled as his own had been. "Then it shall be as you ask. However, in preparation for your impending duties, I will have certain documents made available to you, so that you may review them, and gain some idea as to what your father had worked on before you."

For just a second, St. James' eyes flickered to meet hers squarely, flaming up like twin candles. "I would be very interested to know how my father served the crown before me, Your Highness, and how I will function in serving the crown in his stead."

"I believe you shall be. Perhaps. . . these documents will be useful to you as well."

"And if they are useful to me. . . ?"

The Queen gave a grim smile. "Then I am sure that your conclusions will be useful to the crown also. We will speak again, St. James. It has been a pleasure seeing you again."

St. James placed his now empty tea cup and saucer aside, rose from the chair. He bowed again before the Queen. "And it has been an honor and a pleasure seeing you also, Your Highness."

Then the butler was there once again, seeming to come from the darkness like a shadow to escort him, and St. James was at the door when Queen Victoria said, "St. James?"

He turned. "Your Highness?"

"You may give Miss Murdock my congratulations, as I extend them to you also."

St. James gave a single taut smile. "I will, Your Highness. Thank you."

Then he walked from the room, his mind turning and stretching in all sorts of new directions. Two things took precedence in his mind: Her unexplained knowledge of his coming marriage. And the promise of his father's files.

When he reached the coach, the lad opened the door for him as smartly as if he had been doing it all his life. St. James held the door. "Lad, tell the driver that we will be going to my grandmother's house."

"Aye, m'lord!"

"And what is your bloody name?"

A single look of startled gray eyes. "Steven, sir. Me name is Steven."

"Very well, Steven. Carry on." St. James pulled out his pocket watch, glanced at it. It was nigh on midnight and he cursed the lateness of the hour, but as usual, he was not to be denied.

Chapter Thirteen
Wednesday Morning

Miss Murdock awakened in the wee small hours of the morning and she was not sure why. The room flummoxed her for a moment and then it took on the vague familiarity of the room she had spent the night before in. She was at the Dowager Duchess of St. James' home. With this realization, she let out a long sigh, turned in her bed to face the windows where a gentle beam of light came in between the drawn curtains: a combination of silver moon from above and gold street lamp flame from below. An unnatural shadow moved beyond the small opening and Miss Murdock sat up with the sharpness of one drenched with cold water. A little involuntary gasp left her lips.

She sat for a moment in the midst of her bed, her heart pounding, and she studied the window. The shadow moved again and there was the slightest of tappings on the pane. The very gentleness of the tapping was somehow as reassuring as it was terrifying. She did not light a lamp but instead fumbled for her robe on the chair beside her bed in the dark, struggled into it and climbed from beneath her covers. She tiptoed to the window, went not to the revealing middle gap in the curtains but to one side of it and cautiously pulled the curtain back a miniscule amount.

A boy was outside her window, causing her heart to do a quick flutter. He was perched precariously on the slight ledge that separated the first and second floor and even as she watched with apprehension, he tightened his grip on the outside of her sill with one hand and made a motion of questioning with his other to someone below.

As he was looking away from her hiding spot, Miss Murdock drew the curtain back a small amount further, pressed her face to the glass to look below her. The sight that met her eyes there caused her to suppress a little surprised laugh. A dandy dressed in a turquoise coat, and God help her, yellow shirt and pantaloons stood on the pavement of the mew beneath her window. He held a cane in one hand and as Miss Murdock watched, he signaled up to the boy at her window with it, holding it in mid-air and miming taps. The boy outside her window gave a disgruntled shrug and turned back to do as he was bid.

But Miss Murdock did not draw back and conceal herself in the curtain, for something about the man below had made her draw a quick breath of recognition. His eyes had glinted gold in the darkness.

As if to confirm her suspicion, another man moved into her view, and the very height of him next to the dandy, the very powerfulness of him next to that other slight, lithe figure, told her it was none other but Tyler. And that foppish dandy could be none other than St. James!

She moved now with quickness and drew back the curtain so that she could unlock the window and draw up the sash of it, nearly surprising the young boy off the ledge. "Am I to come down?" she whispered to that startled lad.

"Aye, miss, if you please," he answered in a short breathless burst.

Miss Murdock nodded once. "Typical," she said with cryptic crispness. Then she drew the window up further. "You may as well come in and go down with me. I wouldn't be risking my neck further for *him* if I were you."

The boy climbed through the window with a good deal of finesse which Miss Murdock had to admire. "Risked me neck for a lot less honur'bul reas'ns, Miss."

"'If you judge waking a poor girl in her bedchamber in the middle of the night and scaring her half from her wits as being more honorable than what you've been about before, then you are in very sad shape, indeed," Miss Murdock replied in a tart, hushed voice. "But here, I do not mean to abuse you, for I well know who has put you up to this stunt," she added in the cause of fairness. "Just allow me to put these slippers on and then we will go down."

"Yes, miss," the boy said, not in the least chastised at any rate. "Coo, miss, this is a grand room!" he whispered in admiration.

"So it is," she agreed and taking him by the shoulder she opened the door to the hallway, looked quickly up and down it and then shoved him without ceremony out into it. "And you may wait for me out here for you have no call to be in a lady's bedchambers," she whispered back. Then she shut the door, ran to her closet, dug out the same cloak she had worn on her journey to London and put it on over her robe. She buttoned it up quickly, as quickly as she could, for to her surprise, her hands were shaking, and then she paused a moment to look in the mirror, and wished she hadn't, for of course the beautiful hairstyle she had worn earlier that evening was quite gone except for a mass of tangled, ratty curls.

"Oh, why in God's name do I have to look like a perfect shrew each and every time I see that man?" she asked herself in exasperation, and then gave a little sigh and a laugh. It did not matter. It could not matter.

She opened the door, found the boy in the hallway, looking rather subdued at being left alone by himself in the luxurious expanse of it. "I am Miss Murdock," Lizzie whispered. "And I had better get your name, I suppose."

"It is Steven, miss. I'm pleased to meet you, miss."

"All right, Steven, this way."

They snuck along the hallway and down the staircase, Miss Murdock having a moment's doubt about what she should say if they were caught, but the house with the most of its servants being nearly as elderly as their employer remained quiet. Miss Murdock realized it would have been more expedient to go out a different entrance than the front, but as she was unfamiliar with anything but the main front rooms, she did not want to be stumbling about any more than she had to. So she carefully unlocked the large front doors, opened one enough for she and the boy who was nearly as tall as she at any rate to slip through, and then clicked it closed again, seeing to it that it remained unlocked.

Then Steven was skipping ahead of her, laughing in the night. "You're a right cool one, Miss. I was made sure that you would scream when I came to your window, but his lordship, he said he thought not, and so he was right. Was you expecting him then?"

"No," Miss Murdock replied a little crossly. "I am certainly not in the habit of slipping out of the house at night to meet gentlemen, so you can disregard that notion out of hand! I would not be down here now, but would have sent his lordship packing except that I have something I expressly need to talk with him about."

"Oh," Steven said, much of his pleasure taken out of the escapade as she had managed to make it all seem very reasonable and respectable. But then they rounded the corner and Miss Murdock sighted St. James and was impaled by the gold gleam of his eyes. She drew up for a second, having forgotten just how overpowering his gaze could be, then she continued to walk and her pace was slower, as if she were measuring him with every step she took.

He came toward her, using the cane as elegantly as it was useless to him. He stopped in front of her and Steven went ahead to where the carriage, the driver and Tyler were, leaving them in semi-privacy beneath the moon and the street lamp at the corner of the house. "Miss Murdock," he said with a wicked little flickering of an eyebrow, "you are looking very well tonight."

To Miss Murdock's disgust, she felt her face heat into a blush. "I know very well how I look! And I fear it is not half as well as you, milord," she managed to say. "Your sudden pressing engagement must needs you to look very fine, indeed."

"Ah, yes," St. James returned and gave a self-deprecating glance down at his clothing as though he had forgotten it until her reminder. "Ludicrous is it not? You suspect I did not put on this peacock attire to come and visit you?" he asked.

"You would hardly need to put on boots with a heel to be higher than me, milord," Miss Murdock returned with dryness. "Evidently whoever you have spent the evening calling upon is taller than I."

"Let us just say of a loftier stature than either of us, Miss Murdock, and leave it at that, shall we?" His tone was light and bantering, but he seemed very preoccupied all the same, and she fell silent despite wanting to press her own concerns on him and be allowed to go home.

He turned, so that he was at her side, and of mutual accord they began to stroll toward the carriage. "By the by, how is your hand, Miss Murdock?"

"My hand?" she asked. "Oh, the burn. Of course it does not pain me any longer."

"I am relieved to hear it," and as he said so, he took her hand in his and raised the back of it to his lips. "Shall we go for a drive, Miss Murdock?"

She did not answer for that swift, careless gesture he had made toward her had her quite speechless. They were still several feet from the coach and he stopped, waiting for her answer. "I--I'm not properly dressed for a drive, milord," she managed.

His answer was gentle, "Neither are you properly dressed to be standing here with me for anyone passing by to see, Miss Murdock. Which is my fault, as usual, you may point out, but I had a wish, a need, to talk with you tonight."

Of course he was right. The fact that she had been slow in realizing the possible consequences of remaining in the mew with him for anyone to see, she could only account for as the result of her hand's tingling where he had kissed the back of it, and the unexpected rushing of blood to her head. She had the sudden certainty that if she allowed him to draw her forward and into the coach, that he meant to seduce her. Which was a ridiculous thought, for if she had been feeling somewhat attractive earlier that night, she was in no way attractive now, she reminded herself.

That sobering reflection brought her more to her senses instead of standing in the light of the moon feeling a little moon struck herself, and she nodded. "It is rather chilly out here."

"Good lass," he told her, and they crossed the few feet to the coach.

Tyler was there, standing next to the conveyance, and he nodded and pulled his cap, said around his ever present wad of chewing tobacco, "Evening, Miss," as though it were not at all uncommon to see a young lady of quality in her night clothes with only a robe and cloak to make her closer to (but still a far cry from) decent.

"And to you, Tyler," she returned, the very normalcy of it comforting her and making any remaining thought of seduction fade away.

The boy, Steven, hurried to open the door for them and sketched a half nod, half bow while pulling his forelock in a confusion of motion. Tyler clambered up to join the groom that was already above minding the horses. St. James climbed into the conveyance after her and Steven shut the door and ran around to the back.

St. James unfolded one of the rugs stored beneath the seats and spread it over her lap. "Warm enough?" he asked her from his half kneeling position, his gold eyes disquieting in their nearness.

"Indeed, yes. Thank you," Miss Murdock replied, a little breathless. He settled into the seat opposite her. The carriage began moving at a lazy pace and in the dim interior, he was silent.

It occurred to Miss Murdock as she watched the Duchess' house slip from her view and other houses take its place outside the carriage window that it was somehow very peaceful. Not a word she would have thought to associate with her companion. But tonight his preoccupation with his thoughts did not disturb her, but rather as a person observes a dog when it has caught the scent of something, and raises its head to more closely examine this scent, she merely observed him and wondered what conclusions he was coming to, knowing she would be alerted if said conclusions were anything to alarm her.

"You are very quiet tonight, Miss Murdock," he said at last.

"It is just very peaceful and I am loathe to interrupt it. Or you in your musings."

"You've interrupted them quite regularly today."

"Oh," she said, and then, feeling a little foolish, "I'm so sorry."

His lips quirked but he did not go so far as to laugh at her. "I did need to see you tonight, Miss Murdock, and I very much regret being unable to keep my earlier appointment."

"Your grandmother was very disappointed, you know. She has gotten the wild notion in her head, I believe, that we should suit. Of course, you are to blame for that, because of your ill-advised announcement upon my arrival last night. No," she shook her head in warning, "I have not forgotten that, nor forgiven you."

He did chuckle at that. "Ah, the Airing of Grievances. Have you a scorecard, Miss Murdock?"

"No, I do not. But I am fast believing that I shall need one, for before I can voice my displeasure at one of your antics, you are already set upon another, usually worse one. And," she continued, "your grandmother spends all of her considerable energy defending you, when I can not see in the least where you deserve it."

Although she was doing no more than lightly upbraiding him, he frowned as though her words had reminded him of something. "My grandmother, yes. Tell me, Miss Murdock, how much did she pry from you of my motives?" She hesitated and he added, "Come now, you may tell me for I will not blame you. I know how wily she can be when she has a mind, and you were not up to your best the night of our arrival."

Despite his reassurance, Miss Murdock felt as though she were being called on the carpet. "In retrospect, milord, I am sure I could have been more discreet, but as she was pressing quite determinedly for an explanation, I am afraid that I told her. . ." and she ducked her head down in a guilty little motion of confession, "that you had offered for me in order to obtain my horse."

To which he laughed, a very relieved note in his voice.

"Well, it is not a lie, is it?" Miss Murdock asked. "And I had to come up with some kind of explanation for your ridiculous behavior. I apologize that you did not come out looking well, but it hardly made me seem any better. Quite pitiful, I think, it made me."

"No, no, Miss Murdock. You did precisely right, I assure you," he protested. "I feared much worse, believe me, for the missive I got from her this morning demanding my audience led me to believe that you had spilled the whole to her, promptly and completely."

"Well, that would have hardly been wise, would it?" Miss Murdock returned. "For despite her great energy and will, she is quite old and, I think, rather soft-hearted. *I* am certainly not going to tell her the extent of your foolishness and send her into some sort of apoplectic attack." And she flounced a little in her seat, very much annoyed that he should think she could be so dense.

"Of course not," he agreed, and it charmed her somehow, to see that she could make his voice shake with laughter. "I should have realized that you would not. It would have saved me at least one worry all of today."

Miss Murdock sobered. "But she is very upset with you for not coming this evening."

St. James grimaced. "I knew she would be, but I could not avoid it." His gold eyes pierced over to her in the dimness of the carriage. "And you, Miss Murdock? Were you upset that I did not come earlier?"

Miss Murdock drew in a steadying breath. "Indeed, I was, milord! I had something I most expressly wished to speak with you about."

He leaned forward and the beam of the moon from the carriage window found the pale plains of his cheeks and his high pale brow. "Go on. You have in essence answered one of my concerns."

She was suddenly loathe to continue. How pleasant it could be to just let him carry her along to where he would. But she had such a dread in her heart of the final outcome that she *could not* merely sit back and allow it. "You, of course, will not be surprised to learn that I have not changed my views on this arrangement?"

His cheek ticked. "No. That does not come as a surprise to me."

"And I fear now that your grandmother has become involved that the longer I delay in returning home, the more she will be. . . disappointed in the end."

"So do not disappoint her," he told her, still sitting forward in his seat. "Do not disappoint *me.*"

"Surely you see that I must?" Miss Murdock nearly wailed. "I had not wanted to--to actively go contrary to your plans, but after reflection, I can see no other way. My mere presence in your grandmother's home gives her a false sense of hope that we are to be," and she blushed, which she did not think helped her cause at all, "married."

"But we *are* to be married, Miss Murdock," he told her with quiet conviction. "If I had not acquiesced to your wishes we would be married already. I have spent much of my day doing a great deal of maneuvering and it all hinges on my marrying you." He paused for the briefest of seconds, whether for effect or because he deliberated telling her something further, she could not determine, but when he continued, he only finished by saying, "I can only reassure you that you will be well taken care of, whatever the outcome of my endeavor."

"Reassure me?" she asked in a querulous voice. "You think I could be *reassured* by the knowledge that I will be well taken care of in the likely event of your *death*?" She made a motion with her hands, as though shoving his suggestion and, in essence, him also, from her.

As if in accordance to her unspoken wish, he sat back abruptly, frowning, as usual.

She felt brief dismay that there was no longer laughter in his voice when he spoke. "Damn it, Miss Murdock! What do you want from me?"

"Nothing," she cried. "I want nothing but to go home. I can not deter you from this path you have chosen, but I do not have to be here to see it."

"You innocent child," he said, and his tone was so close to pity that it made her cringe. "You merely need to set aside your *illusions* of what marriage is, and you will find that I ask no great hardship of you."

"You are the one suffering illusions, milord," she returned. "The illusion that you can control anyone you wish to serve your own purposes. Then you feel profoundly *dis*-illusioned when they do not fall neatly in with your plans."

"If you would but serve my purposes, I assure you, I would serve yours to a degree of fulfillment that I doubt you can even imagine," he suggested, his voice low and dangerous.

"Forgive me, milord, if I feel more threatened by that statement then titillated," she said between her clenched teeth. She was shaking and her hands clutched in her lap. "I think I can say with certainty that you have absolutely no concept what I seek in the way of fulfillment."

"And I say," he countered, "that you underestimate me most profoundly."

"Be that as it may, milord," she choked, close to tears and wanting very much to be done with this interview. "I am not asking your *permission* to return home. I am merely informing you out of courtesy so that you may adjust your plans accordingly."

"How very thoughtful of you," he returned. "And when, may I ask, do you plan to return?"

More steadily, Miss Murdock answered, "The end of the week. I had not intended as long as that, but I fear your grandmother was quite adamant that I go to Almacks tomorrow as it is the first ball of the season, and your aunt is planning a dinner party, and Andrew--Earl Larrimer has expressed a wish to show me a few sights in Town before I leave. Between the three of them, and in light of the expense of the clothing procured for me. . . ." She trailed off, because the man across from her was bearing that expense, and she dug her nails into her palms and called herself a fool and vowed that in some manner, she would repay him every cent, but of course, to say so now would only be so many words.

He gave a long and profound sigh. "You are exhausting me again, Miss Murdock," he warned her.

"I am sorry, but I see no way to avoid it."

"We could avoid it if you would merely stop being so aggravating, you wretched lass." He scrutinized her as though she were a perplexing problem to be solved. "Oh, Miss Murdock, what am I to do with you?"

Rather than answer his question, Miss Murdock merely made her point all the more clear by saying, "I think, of course, that any further contact between us before I leave is unwise."

He lifted a dark brow, observed, "We seem to be at cross purposes, Miss Murdock. I wonder which one of us shall prevail?"

"It is not a question of prevailing," she returned, "but more a question of--Nevermind! I see no reason to explain to you any further than I already have," she amended, flustered, her own unfinished thought unnerving her. "For if you have no understanding of my reluctance, further explanation will not enlighten you I am sure." She closed her eyes in despair at her own lame answer.

When she dared to open her eyes, he was frowning, his gaze on her, deep and probing. But all he said was, "Very well, Miss Murdock. I stand on notice of your planned departure."

"And you agree that you will not interfere and that we will have no further contact?"

"I did not say that, Miss Murdock," he told her, and then with a suddenness that startled her, he banged his cane upon the roof of the carriage, and as the horses slowed and then did a careful turn in the road, Miss Murdock was given to understand that it had been his command to return to the Duchess's home.

She settled back in her seat, hoping that her face was enough in shadow that he would not notice how dismayed and unhappy she was.

Self-preservation. That had been the word she had nearly said before catching herself. Not a question of prevailing but of self-preservation.

He seemed to be as engrossed in his own thoughts, his lids hooded over his eyes making him very distant from her. Where before it had been peaceful to her to leave him alone in his ruminations, now it made her afraid.

"Your cousin, Earl Larrimer, has spoken of trying to assist you on your trail of vengeance," she said into the silence between them.

The full painful gold of his eyes fixed upon her. "Indeed? He has said this to you himself?"

"Yes," she said with defiance. "He voiced the thought that as long as there were a Larrimer alive that it was their duty to see this through to the end. How many shall die on this futile quest of revenge, milord, I wonder, before someone has the sense to call an end to it?" His brows narrowed into an angry, frustrated knot upon his forehead in warning, but she continued unheeding. "If you by some miracle find a woman that will trust herself to your scheme, and you procure an heir before you die, is your son to be brought up to continue in this? Is that what you want? To see your own son sacrificed, and perhaps his son after him? When and where does it end, milord? Have you asked yourself that or have you been too blinded by the taste of blood in your throat?"

He came across the narrow space between them like that suddenly released spring that she had sensed in him upon their very first meeting. He grabbed her arms and pressed his face close to her alarmed one. "It ends with *ME*, Miss Murdock," he told her, his voice savage. "For if I do not do all I can to flush this enemy out, how am I to know that any son of mine will even survive? Or Andrew for that matter?"

She blinked, sorry now that she had pushed him to the very edge with her scathing contempt of what she considered folly and he considered holy. He was clutching her with such intensity that she hardly dared breath and she was afraid that her eyes were very wide. His hands unclenched from her arm a degree, but he did not release her. He was crouched in front of her, his face on a level with her own and she could see the erratic beating of his pulse in his temple. She was aware of his body, taut and struggling for control.

"Do not push me, Miss Murdock," he said, his voice strained. "I understand your reluctance and have some sympathy for it. But if you continue to insist on going contrary to what your father and I have agreed upon, you will find that I have more weapons at my disposal to convince you than perhaps you had originally counted upon. I assure you, I will not hesitate to use them."

"Which should not surprise me in the least, milord," she gasped. "For I should have guessed that threats were not at all beneath you!"

"See to it that I shall not find it necessary to place *you* beneath me, Miss Murdock," he told her with rough impatience. "For I swear if you continue to provoke me, I shall resort to it with or without a marriage license." He raised a brow at her stunned look. "Many weapons at my disposal, Miss Murdock," he reminded her. "And I can not think of any that would please me more to use."

"Release me," she cried. "I would not have come with you tonight if I had not--!" and she bit her tongue rather than go on.

"Trusted me?" he asked, and his eyes glimmered with sudden, damning sureness. "Oh, you can trust me with your life, Miss Murdock. I just would not be so certain of trusting me with your virtue." He did release her arms, and she drew in a ragged breath of relief that was short lived, for he sat back on one heel, took one of her agitated hands and raised it to his mouth, a movement as delicate now as though he were about to partake of a very fine and rare wine. Just before his lips, he murmured, "Perhaps you are in need of an appetizer, Miss Murdock, so that you can fully appreciate how well prepared the meal will be. I know that *I* am in need of just a small taste, for you build a tension in me--" He turned her hand palm up and settled his mouth on the pounding pulse of her wrist. His eyes burned at her as he studied her reaction to his tongue tracing the blue vein of it, and he raised a brow when he must have felt the sudden jolt of her blood rushing through it and her other hand fluttered somewhat helplessly to her breast.

He pushed her sleeve up, traced his lips and tongue up her arm to the soft inside of her elbow, and Miss Murdock gave a little defenseless murmur, a sighing acquiescence. He pulled his head back, moved her hand so that he kissed only her fingers, his breath heavy on their tips. "Make no mistake, Miss Murdock, you are as dangerous to me as I am to you."

The coach stopped and Miss Murdock blinked her brown eyes, feeling as confused as if the earth had suddenly quit turning. A voice came to her from outside in the sudden stillness: "But his lordship said t'was my job tonight!" Young, boyish. Miss Murdock remembered that it must be Steven, he who had tapped for entrance upon her window.

She started up, frantic. "Would you leave go of my hand?" she asked in hushed urgency.

"Tsk, Miss Murdock," St. James replied more evenly as he released her hand in lazy gesture. "I am sure even a lad of Steven's age has seen hand-holding and wrist-kissing."

She blushed furiously at his easy summation of what they had been doing, and his words made it seem a good deal less significant than it had been, for her at any rate. The thought that it could be, in fact, of so little significance to him mortified her, but the ease in which he had accomplished it seemed to confirm this conclusion.

As these thoughts whirled in her brain, she heard Tyler saying to Steven outside, "I'll attend to the door, lad, I'm sure his lordship would prefer it."

That Tyler should have so clear an inkling of what had been progressing in the coach, and seemed to be quite at home with the discretion it called for from him (evidenced by his not throwing open the door as would have been customary and as Steven, no doubt, had been about to do, but by tapping with diffidence upon it) brought her scattered emotions together in such a fury, that before she knew what she was about, she whirled on St. James and slapped him with force across his cheek.

His head whipped back at the impact, and she saw her handprint, a white branding, on his cheek. She burst into very unladylike tears.

"Take a walk, Tyler!" St. James ordered less than graciously.

The implications the groom must be arriving at by this announcement upset her all the more. "Damn you!" she said through her crying. "That was entirely beyond all bounds of fairness."

"So is slapping, Miss Murdock, but you do not see me bewailing the sudden lack of rules."

"You deserved it."

"I did."

"I should box your ears also."

"If it will make you stop crying, you may do so."

"Oh, you are a bloody fiend."

He dug in his pocket and held out a handkerchief to her. "I have never denied it."

She took his handkerchief, a delicate affair, dabbed her eyes with it, and then, rather defiantly, blew her nose into it with less than ladylike restraint.

St. James took the abused garment back when she handed it to him, stared at it for a thoughtful second, and then unlatched the door and threw it out into the gutter.

Despite herself, Miss Murdock gave a snuffling giggle. "Sorry," she said.

"Miss Murdock, I assure you I have a dozen, and for no other reason than that distressed young ladies may blow their dainty noses in them with great bellowing honks." He gave a twisted smile and she saw with dismay that her hand print was already welting on his cheek in flamboyant color.

"Oh, dear," she said. "I am not apologizing, mind you, but I do rather wish I had not slapped you quite so hard."

"It is but a small matter, Miss Murdock. I am sure society will merely mark up my injury as another tasty *on dit* to add to my rakish reputation." He ran a finger along his cheek as he spoke and then gave a nearly imperceptible shrug. "If you are feeling better now?" he asked.

She nodded, feeling crushed at how badly everything had turned out. He kicked the door that was still ajar from his disposing of his handkerchief further open and called out softly into the night, "Tyler?"

That man appeared out of the shadows not far from them. St. James nodded. "Thought you would have not gone far."

"Aye, milord. Wouldn't think it prudent for several reasons." He squinted for a closer look at his lordship's countenance. "By gaw, worry for Miss Murdock didn't need t'be one of them, I see!" he exclaimed with more pleasure in his voice than Miss Murdock could readily find reason for.

"I fear I needed more protection than she," St. James admitted stepping down from the carriage. He turned then and Lizzie took his hand as he helped her out.

"Just so the point is well taken, milord!" she told him.

He retained her hand for a thoughtful moment. "But one has to weigh the pleasure against the consequence to decide if the action was worth it, does one not?"

She blushed and dropped her gaze but Tyler came to her rescue by saying, "That will be enough, milord! I shan't have you frightening her more than you have already and having to put up with your foul mood for weeks to come when she refuses to have anything to do with you," and he spat tobacco at the end of his words as if to punctuate them.

"See her to the door, would you, Tyler," St. James directed. "And where, by the by, has the lad gone to?"

"I sent him to make sure the front door was still unlocked. Didn't want anything unseemly spilling out of the coach in front of his young eyes." He tugged his cap in Miss Murdock's direction. "Pardon me for saying so, Miss, no reflection on you, of course. It's just I know how the lordship can be."

"So I have already gathered, Tyler, so no offense taken," she answered, her voice bleak.

St. James frowned at his groom. "If you are finished disparaging my character now, Tyler?"

"I won't send a lamb off with a wolf and tell her it's her dear, sweet grandmother, milord, if that is what you are getting at," the groom returned unperturbed. "If you are ready, Miss?"

"I am!"

She took his arm and Tyler led her around to the front of the house where Steven waited for them. The door was indeed unlocked, and as Miss Murdock bid them quiet good night and slipped through it, she was overcome with such profound relief that she could have wept.

Her room when she reached it was as she had left it, even to the window that still remained open, like an accusation of her ill-advised activities. It had brought quite a chill to her room and she went to close it and again draw the curtains even before taking off her cloak. She must have been in a state indeed to forget that simple task, and she had to wonder at herself, for it was something so automatic to her that she could scarce *credit* that she had forgotten it.

But the window was open, so she must have.

She disrobed back down to her sleeping gown, and when she crawled into bed, she lay awake for a long time, although she was very tired, and consoled herself that she need only avoid him for the remainder of the week before she returned home.

Which did not quite answer the question of how she would return home, but she was certain that she would procure the funds somewhere. In the midst of these comforting and distracting thoughts, she dozed off, and slipped finally, into deep sleep.

In the morning she was awakened by Jeannie, who handed her a cup of hot chocolate and opened the curtains to let the morning light pour into the room. She was chattering as she did so, most of her words and their meaning going quite past Miss Murdock as she was too engrossed upon trying to decide if all that had happened the night before had been real or merely a very compelling dream.

However, when Jeannie threw open the door to Miss Murdock's bed-chamber and began directing two maids (of the housekeeping variety) to bring in the parcels, Miss Murdock perceived that Jeannie's happy chatter had been that the first of Miss's new clothing had arrived that morning. Jeannie seemed to be in perfect ecstasy as she began opening the many boxes that were piled onto the foot of the bed with little ceremony. "Oh,

Miss," she exclaimed as she pulled out the first dress, a ball gown of buttermilk yellow, "I have been in an agony wondering what had been procured for you. And so quickly!" Her green eyes met Miss Murdock's now attending ones. "You will look so beautiful in this and when your hair is redone. And to think, I shall be the one getting you ready this evening."

Miss Murdock choked. "This evening?"

"Why, yes, Miss! Almacks' first ball of the season is tonight and I had word from the Duchess that you are attending, along with herself and Lady Lydia and Earl Larrimer also. Do you think, Miss," she asked in a whisper, "that they may be matchmaking the two of you?"

Miss Murdock, regaining her equilibrium, said rather shortly, "No."

"Oh," Jeannie sighed, apparently very much disappointed. "It is just that he is so handsome and an Earl."

"And a mere boy only out of University less than a year ago," Miss Murdock pointed out, totally ignoring the fact that this made him three years older than herself.

"Oh, but that is nothing to look upon as a deficiency, miss," Jeannie returned, "for I believe it is better to get them when they are still young before they become old and dissipated like his cousin the Duke of St. James." She busied herself hanging up the ball gown, but she put it on the door of the wardrobe so that it would be within easy reach for later that day. "Do you know," she asked Miss Murdock as she turned to open the next box, "that I have heard that the Duke cannot even get vouchers for Almacks? Have you ever heard of such a thing, miss? A *Duke* unwelcome at Almacks?"

"Indeed, I have never heard such a thing," Miss Murdock replied. She sat up more fully in bed, and tried to decide whether she was relieved or disappointed that the possibility of seeing St. James that night at Almacks was clearly out of the question. If nothing else, she conceded, it would all probably be a little flat without him.

"Ah, all the proper undergarments, miss," Jeannie was saying as she laid out countless silk intimates. "I ask your pardon, but I was quite worried about that, you know. Not proper for a miss such as yourself to be wearing cotton underthings. And the fact that you had no crinoline--!" She shook her head at her remembered dismay at discovering her new charge had lacked that essential.

For the first time, Miss Murdock paid attention to the amount of clothing that was being laid out on her bed below her feet that Jeannie was carefully sorting, refolding or hanging. Not only were there countless chemises and intimates and stockings and no less than three crinolines, but as Jeannie opened the next box, an assortment of hats, reticules and gloves spilled out of it, and the next box contained no less than a dozen pair of shoes: slippers with heels, walking slippers, dancing slippers. . . .

"Good Lord!" Miss Murdock interrupted the ongoing inventory. "I do not remember ordering any of this. Or even looking at the half of it!"

"Oh, but miss," Jeannie hurried to say. "You must realize that for every dress you ordered the proper shoes and reticule and hat and gloves had to be ordered also? And as they have only delivered the very beginning of your order, there will be many more coming tomorrow, and the next day also, I expect. And once you go to Almacks tonight and see what every one else is wearing, I am sure that the Duchess will have you down at the shops again tomorrow to order any of those things that are the *rage* and that you simply *must* have."

Miss Murdock was left quite speechless and could only put her cup a-side and put a hand to her forehead as she watched the countless items being so efficiently unpacked, appreciated, sorted and stowed. The room she was in was fast taking on the quality of a resident's room rather than a visitor's, and Miss Murdock watched it all with a sick feeling in her stomach.

The amount of *money* that was being spent upon all of this. And she to be here only to the end of the *week*! If St. James had received the bill for this yesterday, he more than likely would have strangled her last night instead of--Nevermind! she told herself sharply.

Oh, God help her, how was she to repay all of this? How could she ever! Even if she had some sort of employment, there was probably over a year's salary sitting in her room at this moment, and as Jeannie had pointed out, there would be more coming. And it was too late to cancel, for although she was not certain how these things worked, common sense told her that once the cloth had been cut to fit her, they could not simply use it for someone else. Payment would be demanded and if the intended wearer of the outfits disappeared, it was not the shopkeeper's problem.

Jeannie interrupted her quiet, sick dismay. "Oh, miss, this apple green morning gown will be just the thing for this morning, do you not think so? If you are ready, I will help you dress now."

Miss Murdock threw back the blankets that still covered her legs and said with rather less enthusiasm than Jeannie was obviously expecting. "I suppose so, Jeannie."

Jeannie helped her to bathe and dress. The green gown was becoming on her, Miss Murdock noticed. It had a high collar and many buttons down the front of it that matched the material and the crinoline fluffed it out from her small waist to fall in a graceful, subdued bell of material that, when Miss Murdock slipped into the matching slippers, fell to just above the floor.

Jeannie, after a quick search through the boxes that she had not yet unpacked, made an exclamation of satisfaction upon finding a matching green ribbon, and she tied Miss Murdock's hair up into a graceful, thick knot on top of the back of her head. It was not as elegant as the hair-style of the night before, Jeannie pointed out, but it was appropriate for morning wear, and she was sure Alphonse would be back this evening to do miss's hair again for going to Almack's and Jeannie would no doubt be instructed on how to do it properly from then on.

"Oh, dear," Miss Murdock said, wondering just what Jeannie was to do when she returned home, for she could not afford to take her with her, and here the lady's maid was taking so many pains to learn how to do everything in the way Miss Murdock needed it done.

"Is there a problem, miss?" Jeannie asked.

"Yes, many, but nothing you have done, Jeannie, I assure you," Miss Murdock hurried to reassure her. "I look quite splendid if I do say so myself, and it is all because of you, and the Duchess of course, and . . ." but she trailed off for she could not mention the duke as being party to this. Oh, how was she to walk out on him after this expense, and indeed, how was she to *not*?

She turned to go out and downstairs, leaving Jeannie to her efficient sorting and stowing. Ashton met her at the bottom of the stairs, informed her that the Duchess had not yet come below but that Earl Larrimer was in the drawing room if she wished to join him and that Ashton would inform them when breakfast was being served. "And may I add, Miss, that you are looking very bright indeed this morning," he added in his sober way.

"Why, thank you, Ashton," she was surprised into saying. She looked down at her new dress as she added, "I feel like such an imposter."

"Tsk, miss, you look exactly as you are. A young lady, bright and healthy and vivid. Now where is there any sham in that?"

She smiled, something inside of her relaxing with his words. "Thank you, Ashton. You always know precisely the right thing to say." He moved to open the door to the drawing room for her and she moved on into the room. Ashton spared an extra moment to watch her go before once again closing the door behind her and withdrawing to his post of overseeing all that went on in his domain.

Andrew was there, as Ashton had said, and he looked up from his cup of coffee at Miss Murdock's entrance. As they were alone, he said with quiet pleasure, "Lizzie, I am so glad to see you up and well this morning."

"And you also, Andrew," she smiled in return. "Has your mother not come down yet?"

"No. She has a deplorable habit of being late each morning. I think that it takes her a little longer each year to achieve the degree of lacing that makes her figure still fashionable at her age."

Miss Murdock giggled. "That is quite indelicate of you, Andrew," she admonished. "And I for one, can only hope to look half as beautiful as your mother when I am at her age, or indeed, even at my age."

"She would be happy to hear you say so, for she is still quite vain you know."

"So I have come to understand, but as it is really quite harmless, she deserves our indulgence, does she not? Am I to understand you will be at Almacks tonight?"

"Indeed, yes," he replied. "And for once I am not positively dreading it for I think it shall be very amusing to see you launched this evening."

"Launched and sunk, I fear," Miss Murdock returned and settled herself onto the sofa.

"Nonsense! I think you shall do splendidly. You may not be the most beautiful, but I wager you will be the most memorable. It will not go unnoticed."

"I would much rather go unnoticed entirely," she bemoaned. "You can not know how much I am truly dreading this. The only bright point, and you must forgive me for saying this as I know you admire him very much, is that your cousin can not possibly be there for I have had it on the good word of my maid that he is barred from Almacks."

"Indeed, he is. But I have always thought it was rather because they were tired of his snubbing them and thought it was more seemly to thus snub him back."

"Oh," Miss Murdock replied.

"Yes. He has never set foot in the place to my knowledge, and the ladies in charge did not take kindly to that. A voucher, Miss Murdock, is not much unlike a royal summons. It is all right to miss one or two e-vents of the season, but to bypass the entire season, and year after year, well it is quite unforgivable. Especially if they suspect that your only pressing business is to sit at a table in a gaming hell, gambling your inheritance away instead of going about the proper business of courting and marrying beneath their helpful eyes in preparation to passing your inheritance along as is accepted."

"But I thought St. James spent all of his time. . . on that matter we previously discussed," she protested.

"Oh, do not get me wrong, the fact that he spent so much time in unsavory places I am sure was a means to an end, but you can hardly expect the ladies of society to know of that. To their way of understand-ing, he is a rake, through and through, of the most unrepentant sort. And although I think all ladies secretly love a rake, there are still limits which even they will not put up with being crossed, and I am afraid St. James has passed well beyond all those limits in one manner or another. Not that he has ever much cared."

"Well, then, Andrew," she replied with a twinkle in her eye, "it is up to you to save the Larrimer name from utter ruin and toe the line."

He shook his head in mock despair. "It is, I have come to realize. I could strangle him for that." And they both laughed.

The door opened then, and the banging of a cane announced to them that it was the Duchess even before she struggled through on the arm of Ashton. "Here, you two," she said, her voice tart. "Must I forever find you both closeted together and sharing in some unseemly mirth? Go on, the both of you," she said with more indulgence, "do not let the presence of an old lady interrupt what ever amusement you have dreamed up."

"We are merely discussing your other grandson, grandmother," Andrew enlightened her, "and it is an extremely difficult task to find much to be amused about there."

"Indeed," she returned and settled herself in her customary chair. "Thank you, Ashton. I, however, have had a missive from him already this morning, and I have found very much cause to be amused in it," she confided, her eyes merry. "*Very* much!"

Miss Murdock felt the blood drain from her face and was thankful that Andrew was quick to respond, saving her the necessity of doing so. "From how lightened your spirits are, I would say that must be true," Andrew observed. "Do you care to share?"

"No. I think I shall not," the old lady replied. "For you will find out yourselves in due time and I think it adds to my pleasure to wait for that moment. Ah, I think it shall be a grand day. Miss Murdock, may I say that you are looking very fine indeed this morning?"

"Thank you, ma'am. As are you, I must say," Miss Murdock returned, distracted. "I am glad to see that St. James has somehow found a way to wheedle his way back into your good graces."

"Oh, he has," the Duchess replied. "Quite a feat when his missive contained but two short lines, would you not say? And what is all the more pleasant to me is knowing that he did not send it because he thought it would make me happy, but because, for once, he had no one else to turn to that could help him on this matter. And I will see to it! Oh, yes, I shall see to it quite enthusiastically."

Ashton tapped on the door at the end of these words, and then putting his head in, bowed and said, "Breakfast, milady."

"Thank you, Ashton. Andrew, would you be so kind?"

Andrew jumped up to assist her. "Of course," he told her.

"And where is your mother?" the Duchess asked before starting the task of getting up from her chair.

"She is late again, as usual," her grandson replied.

"Probably has broken a lace again," the Duchess observed.

The three of them went in to breakfast and although she tried to relax, Miss Murdock was, she admitted to herself, a bundle of nerves. But she ate with good appetite, all the same, finding oddly enough, that being roused by St. James in the middle of the night to drive around in his carriage had made her quite hungry.

Chapter Fourteen

Somewhat earlier that morning, St. James was awake, and lay in bed, the sheet covering his naked chest, his gold eyes studying the soft wavering of the sheers at his window. He liked the window open a crack, even on the coldest of nights, and he liked his curtains left drawn back, for he did not like his room in tomb darkness.

He ordered his thoughts, much easier when one was not hung over, he was discovering, and decided that he had three things to pursue that day. Two of which he was not even certain how to begin to pursue. The third, he concluded, had a clear course of action, which in an unexpected way appealed to him very much.

It was always good to be unpredictable, and this course of action he was settling upon was quite unforeseeable to anyone who may be in the position of caring to try and guess his next move. Yes, it had the advantage of being out of character, and of giving the appearance that St. James' mind was quite taken up with a different endeavor than the one of trying to find the murderer of his parents. In reality, it may bring him closer to that discovery than pursuit of his other two more puzzling, but at first glance, more promising leads.

After all, his unexpected interest in Miss Murdock and marriage had brought him the other two leads already, and as he had only been at this endeavor for three days now, it would be very foolish, indeed, to drop it.

It was with this thought in mind that he was interrupted by Effington arriving in his bedchamber and voicing with some surprise that his lordship was already awake. His critical eye took in first the dropped clothing his lordship had worn the night before, as St. James had come in so late that even Effington had dozed at his post. He clucked in disapproval, began to pick up the splendid attire of the night before.

"Leave that for now, Effington," St. James requested, causing the valet to drop the clothing with disgruntlement into a chair, "and fetch me some paper and a pen from my writing table."

"Certainly, milord," Effington responded as St. James stretched in the bed.

"And pour me a drink, and *bring* it to me," St. James could not resist adding.

"It is not yet even nine the clock in the morning, milord," Effington advised even as he poured the drink in a short, disapproving motion. He brought it all the same, guessing that his lordship would not heed his words. Then he stopped in mid-stride, his eyebrows going up in a rare revelation of surprise as he stared at the duke. The duke's face, to be precise.

"Is there something the matter, Effington?" St. James asked.

"Er, no, milord," Effington replied. "It is just, you must have had some sort of accident last night, for your face is quite red and welted."

Thus saying, he handed the drink to his lordship, who sat up in bed, the sheet falling to the loosened laces of his under attire.

St. James took the drink, sipped from it, a sherry, the lightest drink that the valet could find that could still be classified as a 'drink', and he smiled at this little bit of attempted censorship.

Effington was studying his lordship's face with interest from this closer vantage. "Funny thing, milord," he commented in his most reproachful voice, "this injury seems to be in the exact shape of a hand. Almost as if you had been slapped."

To which St. James said, "How very interesting. By the by, Effington, I am awaiting on that paper and pen."

"Of course, milord," Effington said, unhappy to have to be reminded. Still quite distracted by his lordship's odd injury, he retrieved a bottle of ink from the desk, several pieces of paper, and a sharpened quill.

St. James took these items, said in an exasperated voice, "And something to write upon, Effington, unless you care to kneel on the floor and let me use your back."

"I do not find that funny, milord," Effington returned with an irritated frown. He returned to the secretary to pick up a large book, a racing annual put out the year before, and handed it to his employer.

St. James, oblivious to the curiosity that was eating his valet alive, put aside his drink, settled the paper on the book, uncapped the ink bottle and paused before writing.

Has it really come to this? he asked himself. And then, with an unexpected grin, began to write:

Dearest Grandmother,
I need your help. I wish to attend Almacks tonight and shall need vouchers.
Your loving grandson,
St. J

He folded it and let it lay for a moment, on the off chance that he should decide that this unexpected turn of events was not to his liking, but as he only felt a great deal of titillation to think of the expression on Miss Murdock's face when he arrived, he decided that no, this was precisely what he wished to do. Effington handed him an envelope. St. James scrawled an address, put the missive inside and sealed the envelope with a drop of red wax that Effington lit and held out for him. St. James placed his signet into the wax, marking it as his.

"Have the messenger boy I hired run this around immediately, Effington," he bade.

"Yes, milord." He paused for an expectant moment, obviously waiting for some sort of explanation of his lordship's strange injury, but St. James only looked at him with negligent gold eyes. Effington gave a very slight sigh, drew himself up and said with more authority than he would have dared yesterday (but of course, yesterday, the duke could not have been aware of Effington's true worth, but after the splendid outfit Effington had prepared for him last night, now he undoubtedly was), "You rest there, milord, and I shall help you dress upon my return, which will only be above a minute," he warned.

St. James watched him go, laughing to himself. The race was on, for he had no doubt that Effington would go as quickly as was dignified about his task. St. James threw back the covers, pulled plain tanned breeches from his drawer and a white cotton shirt with lace at cuffs and cravat, one of many that he owned. He was into both, although he had left his shirt open, riding boots upon his feet, and was setting out his razor by a fresh bowl of water from his pitcher to shave when Effington returned. "Milord!" he exclaimed, aggrieved. Then he held out his hand. "Hand me that razor!"

"And have you slit my throat, Effington? I think not," St. James said as he put his chin up and, staring into the looking glass, the red hand-print on his cheek obscenely noticeable, ran the first stroke up the column of his throat.

"I swear I shall wrestle you for it, milord," Effington threatened, at the very end of his patience. "It is my rightful duty, as is dressing you, and you utterly refuse to do as is expected of you! Now give me that razor, or I shall resign *immediately*."

St. James glanced at him from the mirror, his gold eyes dancing. "Oh, you can not do that, Effington. However shall I dress properly for Almacks tonight?"

"Almacks?" Effington whispered in uncertain hope. "Buckingham Palace last night and Almacks tonight?"

St. James turned, handed him the razor. "Quite, Effington. A rare boon for you, and one I would have wagered would never happen. Now if you promise not to slit my throat over my misconduct of dressing myself as every other able man, I shall allow you to shave me."

Effington sniffed. "You are only frightened that I shall best you in the wrestling, milord," he paused before adding in a snide tone, "as you so evidently lost last night."

St. James chuckled. "You had better hand over my drink, Effington, for I was bested by a female last night and am threatened by my valet this morning. It is a sorry state, indeed, for me to be in."

Effington positioned his lordship's head before beginning and observed, "You seem uncommonly happy about it, if I dare say so, milord."

"Do I?" his lordship asked, staying Effington's hand that was poised with the razor and meeting his valet's eyes in the mirror. "That is the damnedest thing I have ever heard you say." He released Effington's hand. "Get on with it, Effington, and some silence would be appreciated. Can't take this incessant chitchat of yours so early in the morning."

"Yes, milord," Effington replied, feeling as usual that just when he was beginning to finally understand his employer, he said or did something that made him understand him even less. But his movements were sprightly, all the same, as he shaved the duke, humming and dabbing with a towel at any water or shaving soap that dribbled from his lordship's neck to his narrow, steel cage chest. In his mind danced a single word: Almacks.

When the duke was at last presentable, he bypassed breakfast and went instead to the stables to order a mount. Then he rode out alone with quite another matter than Almacks on his mind altogether.

He arrived some fifteen minutes later at the London home of Lord Tempton, and upon dismounting, bade the groom that came out to hold the horse in readiness there, as he should not be long, and asked the butler upon his entrance if young Ryan Tempton was yet in residence.

"Indeed he is, milord Duke," the butler eyed the duke's red hand-printed countenance with disapproval, "but I do not know if he has come below stairs yet."

"Well, rouse him if you must. I would like his opinion on something to day."

The butler showed St. James into a receiving room. He returned a few minutes later, saying that young Mister Tempton would be happy to accommodate his lordship if he could but wait a few minutes, and then he inquired if there were anything he could bring him.

"A cup of coffee would do nicely," St. James told him, and was sipping it with satisfaction when Ryan half bounded into the room.

"I say, St. James! Hardly have known you to be up and about so early," he exclaimed with pleased surprise. St. James turned to him at his entrance, and Ryan gave a little fumble in his eager walk. "Good God! Are you aware that you have the most blatant hand print I have ever seen upon your face?"

St. James smile rather thinly. "As I was there when I received it, yes, I am very much aware of it."

Ryan seemed diverted by this happenstance and stared at the mark, grinning. "I only hope you got something worth the slapping!"

"Let us just say I would take my chances again."

Ryan shook his head. "You stir up more trouble in three days than most people do their entire lives," he commented, but he seemed quite taken with the idea of the intimidating Duke of St. James evidently having trouble with some uncooperative female.

"I have a matter to take care of to day, Ryan," St. James began, growing bored with the stir his besmirched cheek was causing with everyone he had so far encountered. "I thought you may wish to help me with it as you have made known your good instincts on horse flesh."

"I should be happy to do so! Are you in the market for something for your racing stable?" Ryan asked with eagerness.

"No. Rather a lady's mount. Something suitable for riding in the park and such, but that would be equally suitable for country riding as well. I find to my dismay that I have taken Miss Murdock's only mount and as I have already had it taken to Morningside, I wish to acquire her a replacement."

"Oh, jolly good!" Ryan said. "And how is Miss Murdock? I daresay your attention has swayed rather quickly, but I am hardly surprised. You were very drunk you know. Do you mean to still keep her horse then?"

St. James' eyes widened at this stream of artless questions. "Well, certainly I shall keep her horse. I still intend to marry her."

Ryan seemed taken aback at this pronouncement. "Well, Bloody Hell, St. James, you can't blame me for assuming otherwise with that--that *mark* upon your cheek!" He put his hands upon his narrow hips as he continued in indignation. "Rather in poor taste I should think, to bring your fiancé to town one night and earn that the very next from Lord Knows What Female. I certainly hope you will at least let it *fade* before taking her down the marriage aisle."

St. James rubbed a finger over his upper lip. "Do you think so?" he asked with perfect puzzlement. "Hadn't thought of it, I confess."

Ryan, perceiving that the duke was deriving a great deal of amusement from his outrage, accused, "You are having me on, milord. You do not mean to marry Miss Murdock after all and it only amuses you to let me believe it."

"No, young Ryan. I am quite serious."

"The devil you are!"

St. James gave an elegant shrug. "I have determined to go to Almack's tonight in pursuit of that lady if that means anything."

The door opened to admit the stout figure of Lord Bertram Tempton. "Here, St. James, thought that was your mount I saw from my window above stairs," he said in way of greeting. He was still in his brocade dressing gown, and it swayed around him as he walked across the room, making not for St. James or his brother, but the tray of coffee and cups set on the low table between them. "What ever has gotten you up and about at this time in the morning?"

"I've come to ask Ryan to help me in finding a proper lady's mount, as I was quite impressed with his previous selection on my behalf," St. James told him.

"Oh, I'm sure between the two--" Bertie finished pouring his coffee and his gaze fell fully upon St. James' face, and although he looked a little startled, he merely interrupted himself by saying, "Oh, ho, St. James! Your true colors are showing!"

"It is really that goddamned obvious?" St. James pronounced more than asked, his patience wearing thin at this final comment on his injury.

Bertie, looking very much entertained at his old friend's discomfort, only said, "I can count all four fingers and the thumb. What ever did you do to earn that!"

To which St. James gave him a single aggravated look from his expressive gold eyes and returned, "Not nearly enough."

"Oh, ho!" Bertie repeated. "Someone has not fallen for the lethal Larrimer charm. I must meet this young lady."

Somewhat pushed past the point of discretion, St. James replied with dryness, "You already have."

Bertie and Ryan each stared at each other for a moment, perhaps wanting confirmation that they were each thinking the same thing, and then in quiet unison they said in wondering disbelief, "Miss Murdock?"

St. James shot them an inscrutable look and took another sip of his coffee.

"Hardly up to your speed, St. James. I'm surprised at you," Bertie said.

"You as much as promised that you would not sully her in any way," Ryan pointed out with growing anger.

"And as you can see, I did not get the chance to," St. James returned. As Ryan did not seem in the least mollified, he added with ill-disguised impatience, "She is to be my wife, you know, young Ryan. It is not as if I were dallying with her merely for my amusement."

"You have others," Ryan pointed out.

St. James' jaw clenched but with self-control, he only answered, "When it was necessary."

"If I find that you have hurt one hair upon her head--!"

"Enough, Ryan!" Bertie broke in. "You know nothing of what you talk about, either of the past or the present. It is none of your business, you know. St. James has said he will marry her and that is all that needs concern you."

But St. James set down his coffee cup as Bertie spoke and took two strides over to stand in front of Ryan, looking up into the youth's face. "No, let him finish, Bertie. You will what?"

"Well, I--" Ryan fumbled. "I should have to call you out. I suppose."

St. James gave a tight smile but his gold eyes were snapping. "Call a man out for courting his own fiancé? That seems a little extreme, Ryan. Unless, of course, you have some interest in that Miss yourself?"

"Egads, St. James. I only met her the once. Twice actually. But she seemed a most, well, innocent thing, and I just do not wish to see you hurt her in any way," Ryan blushed.

But St. James, rather than being mollified by Ryan's expressed concern for Miss Murdock's welfare, was more annoyed. "Let me tell you something very plainly, young Ryan. Do not ever *suggest* that you may call a man out. For many view the mere suggestion as damning enough to then call you out. And you may take it to your grave that I am normally one of those. Do you understand?"

"I--I think so."

"Secondly, the fastest way to get yourself into a duel is to interfere with another man's wife. Miss Murdock is to be my wife. Do you understand this, young Ryan?"

"I do."

"Thirdly, and I do not need to tell your brother this, but it appears that I have rather overestimated your good common sense, so perhaps I should tell you, if you speak of how Miss Murdock and I met or the means in which our marriage was brought about, or, for that matter, how I got this palm print upon my cheek and from whom I received it, I *will* call you out. Friendship or no friendship."

"Of course, St. James," Bertie interrupted before Ryan could answer. "You have no need to remind him of that. Even Ryan, young as he is, would certainly be aware of this."

"I am merely making it clear. Ryan seems to have the belief that I mean Miss Murdock some dreadful harm, when for the past two days I have expended a great deal of energy seeing to it that whatever becomes of me, that she will be very comfortable indeed for the rest of her life. And if he could not gather this from the fact that I am wasting precious time today procuring her a horse when I have other pressing matters, then I have misjudged him. Have I, Ryan?"

Ryan shook his head. "No, St. James. It is rather I who have misjudged you."

"Jolly good," St. James replied in nearly a snarl. "By God, I need a drink."

"Help yourself," Bertie said, seeming in no way shaken by the duke's unexpected display of temper.

St. James turned and walked over to the sideboard, selected a fine whiskey and poured into a glass, leaving a rather stunned Ryan standing alone in the middle of the room. St. James glanced at him, said in a much more normal voice, "Care for one, Ryan, while I am pouring?"

"If--if you don't mind," Ryan swallowed.

"I do not mind in the least," St. James replied, and after pouring the second glass, he poured a third for Bertie. Then the duke turned, carried Ryan's glass over to him, told him, "Do not look so chastised, Ryan, these are merely a few things you must understand, you know, if you are to get on properly."

Ryan took the drink but before sipping from it, he asked, "Is it really as you say, that if someone says they should call you out, that it is as much as a challenge?"

"Indeed, it is," St. James returned. "You must remember that, for if someone ever says such to you, you can not hesitate, but must immediately draw your glove and issue the challenge that was insinuated."

"Have any of your duels begun. . . in such a way?" he asked as though someone still trying to follow a difficult lesson.

"Yes."

"And you did as you said, pulled your glove and issued the challenge because of the insinuation?"

"I have." St. James looked at him for a studying moment. "The threat is only the beginning. If you leave the threat go, the action will follow. No matter how much you may try to appease. Do you follow me, Ryan?"

Bertie was standing patiently following this bit of unorthodox tutelage.

"I'm not sure," Ryan said.

St. James sighed. "I should hit you."

Ryan stiffened, his face reddening in confused anger. "What?"

"I said," St. James repeated, "I should hit you."

Ryan balled his fist and if Bertie had not stepped in hastily, he would have smashed it into St. James' face, who had not moved or even blinked. But Bertie grabbed his arm, and Ryan stood still, furious, and said through clenched teeth, "Let go my arm, Bertie."

St. James raised a brow and asked with lethal softness, "Now do you understand, Ryan?" and as Ryan did not respond, he continued. "It is very hard to explain. If someone threatens to hit you, it is the same as hitting you. If someone threatens to shoot you, it is the same as shooting you."

"I understand," Ryan said abruptly. He shook his arm free from Bertie and repeated, "Damn it. I understand, I say."

"I expect you do," St. James replied, looking up at him. "Don't ever threaten to call someone out again, Ryan. If you feel that strongly about something, just remove your glove and commence."

"I will," Ryan answered. He looked thoughtful for a moment as he stood there, his drink spilled and his feet still spread in belligerence. Then straightening himself, he said, "Thank you."

And St. James, with a little sigh, said, "You are welcome." Then looking at Bertie, he told him, "You really should be teaching him this, you know."

"I've taught him all I can. He's graduated to your class, now, St. James," Bertie answered.

In a much surer voice, Ryan asked, "Are we ready to leave, St. James?"

St. James threw him a warm, true smile, downed the remainder of his drink and said, "Yes. Bertie, care to join us? We'll wait if you do."

"No, St. James. For if I heard correctly upon my entrance that you intend to be at Almack's tonight, I have a few wagers to lay. Just do not kill my brother, is all I ask."

"Tsk, at the rate he is learning, it will be more likely that he kills me."

And Ryan, following milord duke out the door, had to reflect that for all St. James' roughness, he taught a very good lesson. But then, he guessed, his lordship had not had a kind teacher himself.

Miss Murdock looked with disappointment at the patently uneven stitches on the small doily she had been working on. Not only was the work tedious, but not surprisingly, she showed no skill at it. And the back of her neck hurt.

She glanced at Lady Lydia, who had made her belated appearance at breakfast, apologizing rather vaguely of not feeling well, and then had gone on to pick at her food. Now, she was bent over a piece of petit point, as seemed to be her sole occupation if she were not shopping, receiving callers or calling upon others. Andrew had left after breakfast to meet with a friend of his from his 'University Days' which he pronounced in such a way as to make the listener feel that he had been out for decades instead of not even a year. The duchess, as was her custom, had gone above stairs for a nap.

Lady Lydia glanced up at Miss Murdock's sudden inactivity and said, "It takes time, my dear. Surely your mother should have taught you all this years ago."

"Indeed, I'm sure she would have if she had lived," Miss Murdock responded absently, her mind more preoccupied with restless thoughts of the night before and the dreaded evening she had to look forward to.

"Oh, I am so sorry," Lady Lydia exclaimed. "I had no idea that your mother was not living."

"And how could you?" Miss Murdock replied. In a sudden yielding to defeat, she placed the doily away from her onto the arm of the chair. "For I do not recall mentioning it before to you, and it is not as if you have known me long."

Lady Lydia continued her sewing even as she spoke. "Somehow I feel as though I have known you longer." She pulled the thread further through. "I had my reservations about you, Miss Murdock, as I am sure you are not surprised to hear, but looking at you now, only two short days since you arrived, I must pronounce myself pleasantly surprised."

"Why, thank you," Miss Murdock said, very much surprised herself.

"You get along quite well with my son the Earl, do you not?" Lady Lydia asked while continuing to sew.

"Oh," Miss Murdock said. "He is the most pleasant sort, I agree."

Lady Lydia glanced at her again, but Miss Murdock had turned her face toward the window. "It is such a beautiful day," she continued.

"It is," Lady Lydia agreed.

"Do you think that the Duchess has any mounts?"

"I expect not," Lady Lydia said frowning, "as she has not ridden for many years and I myself have never ridden." She gave a slight shudder at the thought. "Of course Andrew rides, but I can not recommend your riding his horse as he is quite temperamental even if he did not have it out presently. I have often told him he should get something easier to control, for I positively live in dread of his spilling and being seriously hurt."

"He is not a child any more. I am sure that he shall manage," Miss Murdock responded, uncertain herself whether she meant to be comforting or critical.

"As he has often told me himself," said Lady Lydia, and picked up her small gold sewing scissors and snipped through the thread with ferocity. "It just goes to show that he does not fully appreciate how important it is that he does not do himself harm or take unnecessary chances, despite how often I have tried to tell him so."

Miss Murdock turned her head to study Lady Lydia. "No young man, I expect, ever takes the thought of his mortality seriously," she said, sensing that lady's very real concern for her son. "I am sure he will come around in just another year or two."

"If another year or two is not too late. But it is not your concern, is it, Miss Murdock, and so I do not mean to burden you with my motherly misgivings. Let me only say I am glad that the two of you seem to be such chums."

"Chums. Yes," Miss Murdock agreed. "Or a brother. I think he feels it is his responsibility to get me up to snuff for Almacks tonight, which I think is very dear of him."

Lady Lydia smiled with a radiance that showed in detail the remnants of the *incomparable* she had once been. "It is dear of him, isn't it?" she asked. "When ever I begin to positively despair, then he does something like that which reassures me that. . . well, nevermind. It is just so hard, Miss Murdock, when so often he seems determined to follow in the footsteps of his cousin. And as you have had your own experience with that man, I need not tell you how much I object to Andrew turning out the same."

"I can quite understand," Miss Murdock said with sympathy, thinking of the conversation she had in this room with Andrew yesterday afternoon.

"You know, I saw the most odd thing last night," Lady Lydia continued. "A carriage leaving here, perfectly black and plain, I almost think it must have been hired. It was after two, I believe, and I'm certain it must have dropped someone at the door, for I saw a groom coming back around from the front of the house before it left out of our mew." She glanced in question at Miss Murdock, but Miss Murdock had decided she might have a fresh try at her embroidery after all. She picked it up and bowed her head over it in devoted concentration.

"I asked Andrew this morning if he had someone drop him off, for I know that he was out quite late, and do you know, he acted most perfectly surprised and said he could not guess who it could have been or what it could have been about. Do you think he may have been lying to me?"

Miss Murdock bowed her head further over her work in a frenzy of endeavor. "Oh, I do not think he would lie to you, Lady Lydia. I am quite certain he would not."

Lydia made a little noise of astonishment. "Well, I am puzzled then, for if it were not him, whyever would a strange coach be at our house in the midst of the night?"

"I am certain it is most odd," Miss Murdock agreed. She winced as she bloodied her finger with the needle. "Ouch!"

"Oh, dear!" Lydia said. "Did you hurt it very badly?"

Miss Murdock pulled it from her mouth where she had placed it, stared at it for a critical moment, and although it was not at all hurt badly, said, "I think perhaps I should go and get some brown paper on it, after all." Seeing good her escape, she set aside her doily once again and left the room, begging Lady Lydia's pardon.

She did get brown paper on it in the kitchens, on the off chance that Lady Lydia should remember and inquire after it later, and then as a means to escape more permanently until she was certain Lydia's subject of conversation had quite left her mind, decided it would do no harm to visit the stables on the off chance that the Duchess did have a decent mount, for she missed riding very much, and wondered quite often how Leaf was doing in his lordship's stable.

With this decided, she went to the hall and front foyer, accepted a wrap from Ashton who appeared silently and promptly. "Will you be needing your maid, miss?" he asked.

"No. Thank you, Ashton. I'm merely going to visit the stables and shan't be gone long." She smiled up at him, thinking that he really had the most calming effect on people even when he only spoke a few words.

"As you wish, miss," Ashton agreed and held open the door for her.

Lizzie stepped out into the sun, enjoying the warmth of it on her face as she blew frosty air out into a mist in front of her. It was a glorious day, as the view from the window had promised, and she was glad she had stepped out into it. She followed the walk around the imposing town house and marched along the mew that she had met St. James in the night before, but now with the sunlight slanting down, it all seemed very far away and even unimportant. In the stables, all was quiet except for the rhythmic munching of horses on their hay, and the warm odor of their bodies tinged her welcoming nostrils.

It was the closest to being home that Miss Murdock had found, and she allowed herself a brief moment of examining the underlying worries she had of how her father was getting along. He may have been lamentable in her upbringing, but she did miss him and his takings dearly. After a moment, she reminded herself that she had come out of the house to leave her troubles behind, not study upon them, and she went along the center aisle, stopping at each stall in turn. Those horses that came forward, she patted and spoke to, eyeing each as a mount. None added up to what she was looking for, and she sighed, having expected to find nothing adequate to begin with. The Dowager did go to the park a few mornings a week, but she was driven in her crested carriage. Not surprising the only decent mount in residence should be Andrew's, and of course, he was gone for now at any rate.

Voices reached her from the tack room, and she wandered over to stand in the door, loathe to return back to the house and idleness just yet. She wiped her nose on a hanky, which had begun running after being outside and then in again, and peered through the door that stood open. Tyler glanced up at her shadow, surprising her, and a brief look of consternation flitted across his face. Then he grinned. "Why if it isn't the little Miss that slapped t'duke's face," he said with more warmth than she would have thought she warranted. "And not a bad wallop you gave him."

Miss Murdock flushed a very deep red at his words and glanced at the older groom beside him, who quit his saddle-soaping at Tyler's words. "It was just a misunderstanding," Miss Murdock stammered, wishing the floor would swallow her where she stood.

But Tyler didn't seem to think she should be embarrassed in the least. He spat out a stream of tobacco into the corner and told her, "No need t'downplay it, Miss, for I'm sure I've felt like boxing his ears on many occasion. I've never in me life met anyone as difficult as he, even when he was just a lad. Took t'his behind with a switch when he was young more than once, of which t'old Duke, he wouldn't have appreciated, but he drove me t'the point where I didn't care. Wish I could take a switch after him now, at times."

"St. James you be talkin' about?" the other groom asked in astonishment. "You slapped St. James, miss?"

"She did," Tyler told him when Miss Murdock did not seem inclined to answer but only shook her head in exasperation. "I dare say he'll carry t'mark for at least a day or two," he laughed. "And won't that set t'tongues t'waggin'."

"That may very well be, Tyler," Miss Murdock interrupted, "but I see no reason why it need be known that I was the one that put it there."

"I wish I'd seen it," the older groom said with a great deal of longing in his voice.

"Oh, you've no call t'worry about old Bedrow here," Tyler reassured her. "He'll not carry t'tale any further. And I won't tell another soul for although I know St. James would skin me for it, I can see by t'look in your eye you would be none too happy either, and I think I'm rather more scared of you than him now at any rate," and he guffawed at his own joke.

"I don't find that amusing, Tyler," Miss Murdock said.

"Oh, I'm sure you don't," Tyler agreed. "But after you've known his lordship longer, you'll find it a great deal funnier then."

She was silent for a moment, having no answer for that, and as Tyler's amusement seemed to have run its course and the other groom, with only a shake of his head went back to his cleaning and did not seem inclined to pursue the topic further, she asked, "But, Tyler, I was wondering, I thought you were employed by St. James, not the duchess."

He looked at her for a moment, his face unreadable. "So I am, Miss. Just visitin' me uncle here on me time off."

"Oh. I see," Miss Murdock said, wondering how she had missed Tyler introducing the other groom, whom she had gathered was named Bedrow, as his uncle before this. "I didn't mean to pry for of course it isn't my business. I just came down to see if there were anything worthy of mounting, but alas, I could find nothing," she explained. For just a moment, the thought had occurred to her that St. James had sicced his groom on her to make sure of her where abouts. Of course, that was silly, as she had told him she would be here until the end of the week, and surely he must realize that she would not go back on her word.

Tyler said, "Now, Miss, I know that milord St. James would see to a mount for you if you merely tell him you wish t'ride."

"Oh, no," Miss Murdock shook her head, even backing away a step. To add to the expense that had already been spent on her was just too terrifying. "That just would not do, Tyler. That just wouldn't do at all."

He gave her a puzzled look, spat more tobacco juice. The uncle and nephew exchanged glances. "Well, now, Miss," the older groom began, "I know the Dowager Duchess can be rather daunting, but she would be more than pleased to procure you a mount during your stay with her."

But Miss Murdock only shook her head again with a wistful smile. "Thank you for trying to help, but it really is such a small matter. I'll not bother her with it. I don't intend to be here so long that anyone should go to all that trouble."

"Why, miss, t'season's just beginning!" Tyler exclaimed. "You'll have a long, enjoyable winter, and from how nicely and ladylike you're dressed, you'll be fighting off t'beau's. Nothin' could be more fun for you than t'have a mount t'ride in the park each mornin' and lead those young swains on a foolish chase."

She laughed at the picture he presented. "Thank you, Tyler." She smiled, but added with frankness, "I can't think of anything that would distress me more, however unlikely." She sighed, leaned against the tack room door jamb, unmindful of getting dust on her fine new wrap that had only been delivered just that morning. "I truly wish for a ride in the country anyway. The park, I think, would just be a poor substitute in any event. Swains or no swains."

They laughed with her and she felt some of her home sickness slip away. "Would I be making you too uncomfortable if I just sat and listened to you both talk for awhile?" she asked. "I do so miss being in the stables."

"Miss," the older groom said, "we would be honored." Proving his uncle's words, Tyler got up, laid his coat across a tack trunk and offered her this seat.

Miss Murdock smiled at him, unbuttoned her wrap in the relative warmth of the room and sat down. "Please, just begin where you left off. I shan't interrupt," she encouraged.

They did, and drew her out with their nonsense until she was laughing and quite forgetful that she had seen Tyler just last night under the most unseemly circumstances and had never clapped eyes on his uncle until today. The hours flew by, and it was with shock that she finally looked at her watch. "Oh, my! I am sure they are looking for me, for it is past tea time!" she exclaimed. "I really must go right away."

She stood, buttoned her wrap in hurried movements. "Thank you so much," she said. "I don't know when I've spent a better afternoon."

Tyler said. "Nor we, I dare say, Miss. Now hurry and come back anytime."

She gave them one last grateful smile, and hurried out of the tack room. For the first time that long afternoon, she thought of the ordeal that awaited her that night and sighed. Well, she had managed to push it back these past hours. At least she had that. And the assurance that by being at Almacks she was out of reach of St. James, who could not get vouchers!

And if he showed up with Steven knocking on her window tonight, Miss Murdock vowed, she would not go down to him again.

It now seemed, as she hurried up the mew, that it was possible she really did have everything well in control, and that instead of cursing the social schedule that the dowager and Lady Lydia had planned for her she should be thankful for it, for the very respectability of it would keep her out of St. James' reach.

If St. James were even still in pursuit. If he had taken her words seriously, would he not be better serving himself by finding another to fill the role she so wished to avoid? And this thought brought her up short, for there was something most troubling in it.

"Think!" she commanded herself with impatience, for she was standing stock-still in the mew and she was already extremely late. She tried to push past the conflicting emotions that, now freed, seem to batter her without mercy. Of course, she was infatuated with him, she could not deny that. But why should she not be? she argued with herself. Every female in England who had ever clapped eyes on him was probably infatuated with him to one degree or another.

It was not that, she decided. It was something beyond emotion and squeamishness on her part. It was something. . . logical. "Damn it!" she cried to herself. "Think of it the way *he* would. Cut all the blood from it. . . what is it that I see that makes perfect sense that he has not seen in all his--"

But just then the sound of horse's hooves nearly overtaking her caused her to look up, her thoughts torn away. It was Andrew returning with speed from his excursion. He reined in his horse just in front of her. "Lizzie," he panted. "Whatever are you doing out here in the mew? We are late for tea you know, and although I knew I would be in for a lecture, I never dreamed you would be also!"

"I was just on my way in," she said as he hurried to dismount. "For I was in the stables and I lost track of the time."

"As did I," he said more quietly now that he was on level with her. "Wait a spare second for me to get a groom, and we shall go in together. A united front!" and he grinned, as though very much taken with the idea of the two of them being dressed down together.

"Of course," she said. But something inside of her mind that was still plucking away at that problem, which was not even *her* problem but St. James' problem, thought maybe it's not logical at all. Maybe it's *intuitive*.

Even as she was thinking this, Andrew turned to lead his horse on into the stables. Miss Murdock was aware of Tyler coming out to take his horse, which she couldn't help thinking was very good of him as it was his day off and he was only visiting. At the same time, Andrew knelt down and grasped something in his hand that he found in the gutter alongside the mew with a little exclamation of surprise. "Miss Murdock!" he exclaimed with boyish triumph as he held the item up. "You have lost your handkerchief."

Over Andrew's head, she saw Tyler's face take on a very strange expression, and she met his eyes for the briefest of seconds. On instinct she began moving forward. "Why, yes, I must have. Thank you--"

"But this is not your handkerchief at all!" Andrew said, looking at the garment in wonder. "For there is St. James' crest upon it, just as bold as you please." And his eyes came up to meet hers, stopping her in her thanks.

Before she could answer, a voice behind her, *very* near behind her, said, "It is tea time, Andrew, as I was just coming out to tell Miss Murdock. I saw her from the window while I was sewing."

Chapter Fifteen

"Oh, dear!" Miss Murdock said beneath her breath. Tyler was looking at her with a great deal of concern on his face, and she was afraid that her expression appeared much the same to him.

As if to confirm this fear, Andrew rose to his feet and said, "Are you quite all right, Miss Murdock? You suddenly look very disturbed."

She forced a smile. "Not at all, Andrew, I assure you." Whether she was assuring him that she was quite all right or quite disturbed, she left rather unclear. Then she turned to meet the eyes of Lady Lydia with a distinct lump of dread in her stomach.

She could not have been more correct than to feel that lump, either, she saw at once. For Lady Lydia's mouth was clamped together in a most intimidating manner, and she drew her breath in and said in an undertone for Miss Murdock's ears alone, "Well! I suppose that explains a great deal, does it not, Miss Murdock!"

With desperation, Miss Murdock said, "I'm afraid I don't follow you, Lady Lydia."

"Well, we *shall* discuss this later. As I have said, right now, you are late for tea. As well as Andrew. Andrew!"

"Coming, mother," he told her. Tyler was taking his horse, and as Miss Murdock turned, she saw Tyler also take the handkerchief from Andrew, who was distracted enough by his mother's wrath (whom, he must have been thinking, seemed even more upset than usual for his merely being late for tea again) that he really did not notice.

Tyler met Miss Murdock's eyes, nodded once in reassurance, as though he knew of some way to help her in this predicament, and then turned without saying anything to lead the horse into the stables.

"Come along, Miss Murdock," Lady Lydia commanded in a tone full of righteous indignation and, holding her skirts up the required inch, marched Miss Murdock and her tardy son into the house.

And Miss Murdock, as she followed that Lady's back, could only conclude that Lady Lydia was not nearly as dense as everyone thought she was.

"I can not tell you," Lady Lydia began as soon as the sitting room door of Lizzie's bed chambers was closed behind her, "how shocked and disappointed in you I am, Miss Murdock!"

"Indeed, I think you are rather over-reacting over a wayward handkerchief, Lady Lydia," Miss Murdock replied from where she sat. She had been gnawing her fingernail just the moment before in dread of this interview, but she saw no reason why Lady Lydia should know this.

"Oh, do not try to be coy with me, Miss Murdock. I was young once, also, you know. And although I am sure I felt myself quite daring, I would have never done as you have done last night."

"And what ever is it you think I have done?" Miss Murdock asked. Lady Lydia seated herself on the chaise lounge, and Lizzie could have sworn she heard the lacings of Lydia's stays creak as she did so.

"Oh, very sly, Miss Murdock. Gain from me how much I know and in that manner avoid telling me anything I may not already be aware of. Well, I am aware of a great deal, so we may as well speak plainly."

"Forgive me, ma'am, but I wish you would."

Lady Lydia nodded. "Then I shall. You rode with St. James last night, *unchaperoned* in his coach. Is that speaking plainly enough for you, Miss Murdock?"

Miss Murdock cringed on the inside but she maintained a brave front. "And you have come to this conclusion merely from a found handkerchief in the gutter, Lady Lydia? Why, it is a fantastic supposition!"

"Not when you add that I saw a coach last night from my bedroom window. Not when I am certain that I saw a groom returning from escorting someone to the door, and a man, Miss Murdock, would certainly not need to be escorted. I had my suspicions already, Miss Murdock, but I could not believe with your only being here in London but *one full day* that you had managed to procure an admirer so quickly. I know the term *fast* indicates just what it means, but even I could not credit anyone being that *fast!*" She fanned herself with her hand as though the very thought of it made her faint. "So of course I tried very strongly to withhold any judgments. But when it was *St. James'* handkerchief found in the mew just now, it all came together with *shocking* clarity! And I, of all people, should not be surprised that he has had the audacity of parking one of his lightskirts in his own *grandmother's* home!"

Miss Murdock colored at the end of these pronouncements. "I do not view myself as a *lightskirt*, ma'am, and I shall try very hard to overlook that insult as I understand you to be beside yourself."

"Indeed, I am! I can not think what you were thinking to repay the Duchess' hospitality to you in such a way! And after all the expense she has gone to to launch you properly in society! If I did not think it would kill her, I would march in there now and tell her what a viper she has taken to her bosom, and indeed it was my first instinct to do so. But of course, I do not wish to do that, no matter how angry I may be, but let me assure you, Miss Murdock, you will be leaving here on the morrow, or I will do as I should, and the results will be on your and St. James' heads and not on mine!"

"You will do no such thing," Miss Murdock exclaimed, her simmering anger getting the better of her. "For if you were to do that, you would be doing it for no other reason than to spite her! Oh, do not look at me as though I have lost my mind! I know perfectly well that you bypass no chance to rundown St. James to her, and granted he has given you many opportunity, but you take a great deal of pleasure in throwing his escapades up into her face.

"If you recall correctly, I had every wish to leave *today*, but it was at the insistence of *yourself* as well as the Duchess and Andrew--Earl Larrimer, that I stayed. If I am having an *affair* with milord Duke, which even you should be able to see is utterly ridiculous, then perhaps you can explain why I would be so anxious to return home?"

"Oh, dear, you are right," Lady Lydia gasped. "I *have* misjudged you shockingly! It is all so clear now. You are trying to save yourself from him," she said with a great deal of drama. "Oh, my dear!"

Miss Murdock, thrown quite a bit off stride, said, "What?"

"Yes," Lady Lydia nodded, evidently finding this line of thinking more obvious and correct with each passing moment. "Oh, I can see it all now, and it is all so perfectly understandable! He offered to send you to his grandmother's in London, as a *kindness*, he told you. And you, of course not knowing his true character, took him up on it, having no idea. . . ! And only once you got here did you realize what he *truly* had in mind! Oh, my dear, I could weep for you," she finished, looking as though she would weep. "And to think I have been in here dressing you down. But of course, Miss Murdock, you must know that you can never, *never* ride with a gentleman without chaperone, not even in the daylight, let alone in the *middle* of the *night*!" She shook her head as though to clue Miss Murdock in as to her proper response.

Miss Murdock, feeling a great deal mystified at this reversal in Lady Lydia's attitude, found herself shaking her head.

"And no matter what he says to lure you down in the *middle* of the *night*, you must never, *never* go!" More head shaking by Lady Lydia and responding head shaking from Miss Murdock.

"Normally, I would not be so understanding, but, of course, your mother has been dead for some years and there is no way that you could *know* what every other young lady of quality has had positively *drilled* into her head." And she dabbed at her eye as though most overcome by this sad, sad state of affairs. "Oh, my poor, dear child," she whispered.

Then she sat forward. "You must tell me, Miss Murdock," she advised in a hushed, sympathetic voice, "Did he *compromise* you in any way?"

And Miss Murdock, feeling off-balance, shook her head and said, "No, of course he did not."

And Lady Lydia patted her hand. "Then you got off very lucky, indeed, my dear. But I don't have to tell you, that if it ever came out that you had even met with him, you would be quite, quite ruined. But you needn't fear, for I shall not breath a word of it to anyone."

There was a tapping on the door, and Miss Murdock called for entrance with a great deal of enthusiasm.

Jeannie's red head stuck in upon the door's opening, and her green eyes took in the presence of Lady Lydia closeted with Miss Murdock in her sitting room off bed chamber with a degree of suppressed interest, but she only said, "Miss, the Duchess has asked that you come below, for she has a caller and wishes you to meet her. And Lady Lydia, I am sure she would wish you to know also."

"Oh," Lady Lydia smiled, always anxious to receive callers, which in the year after her husband's death had dwindled in respect for the household's mourning. "Who is it?"

"Lady Frobisher, ma'am," Jeannie replied.

"Oh, very important," she said. "Go on, Miss Murdock, for you would not wish to snub her in *any* way. I'll follow you down in just a moment, I just need to quickly refresh myself in my room." She took Miss Murdock's hand in hers and patted it in a reassuring fashion. "And about this other matter, Miss Murdock, I have quite a bit of advice to give you, for I can see now that if any one is at fault, it is I for not seeing more clearly my duty by you, as the Duchess is just not fully up to it any more. And of course she has a blind spot where her grandson is concerned large enough to drive a dray through--but nevermind! We will take this up where we left off later, shall we?"

But she did not even leave time for Miss Murdock to answer as she rose from her chair as she spoke and the tail end of her words came just before she passed Jeannie and went out the door.

"Do you wish to freshen up, miss?" Jeannie asked Miss Murdock.

Miss Murdock, who had risen from her seat also, paused in her strides to the door. "Do I look badly?" she asked, uncertain.

"No, Miss. You look quite well."

"Well, then, I think I shall just escape before she changes her mind and returns," Miss Murdock breathed and passed on through the door that Jeannie held open for her. She observed Lady Lydia making her way down the hallway in the opposite direction of the stairs as she went to make ready for her visitor in whatever way she seemed to deem necessary, and Miss Murdock would not have spared her another thought except she chanced to notice that when Lady Lydia turned into her bedchamber it was on the opposite side of the hallway from Miss Murdock's room.

And that struck Miss Murdock as very odd indeed, enough for her to pause before going down the hallway, for her own bedroom looked over the mew, and she could not see how Lady Lydia would have thus been aware of the carriage parked in it last night when her own room faced the other direction.

"Jeannie, was that Lady Lydia's bedchamber that she turned into?" she asked her maid.

Jeannie glanced down the hallway, but of course Lady Lydia was already out of view, but she did say, "If you mean the third door down on the right, ma'am, I believe that to be her bedchamber."

Miss Murdock smiled with distraction at this confirmation that Lady Lydia had indeed gone into her own bedchamber. "Thank you, Jeannie. I was merely curious," and she turned to go below without any further delay.

"Ah, there you are, Miss Murdock," the Dowager Duchess said when Ashton opened the door for her to enter the sitting salon. "I was just telling Lady Frobisher that I hoped I was not interrupting you taking a rest, for you only arrived the night before last and are still feeling a little tired from your journey."

Miss Murdock curtsied before that lady, said, "I am very pleased to meet you, Lady Frobisher," and then replied to the duchess, "I was endur. . . er, enjoying a *tête-à-tête* with Lady Larrimer, ma'am, and she has said she will be down momentarily to join us."

"Oh," the Duchess said, sounding less than pleased at the thought of her daughter-in-law joining them. "But have a seat, Miss Murdock. Lady Frobisher was very surprised to learn I had a visitor to launch for the season this year."

"Indeed, I was," Lady Frobisher agreed. "And I am very charmed to meet you."

"Thank you, Lady Frobisher," Miss Murdock acknowledged.

"And I shall be seeing you again this evening," Lady Frobisher went on to tell her, "for the Duchess tells me you shall be attending tonight and that it is to be your first time in Almacks."

"Yes. It is my first time in London, so every thing is quite new, and a little overwhelming, I dare say."

Lady Frobisher smiled at this confession, and appeared to take some pride in the fact that she must seem very *urban* indeed to this rural miss. "I find it very entertaining to see ourselves through someone's eyes who is uninitiated, Miss Murdock, for I fear that the wonder of it all has escaped me many years ago."

"Oh, surely it could not be so many years ago," Miss Murdock told her, twinkling, "for you scarce look as though you had your coming out yourself but recently."

Lady Frobisher laughed with delight. "Oh, but she is a flatterer, Dowager Larrimer!" she said.

"I am learning very quickly," Miss Murdock explained.

"And you shall make out splendidly, I am sure," Lady Frobisher agreed. She turned to glance at the Duchess with a raised eyebrow. "I can see just what you had been saying, Dowager, and I have only spoken but a scarce few words with her."

"Then you can understand, I hope, my urgency on the matter I was speaking of with you?"

Lady Frobisher nodded her head in understanding. "Yes. I believe I do." She turned to Miss Murdock and told her as though enlightening her in some manner, "I am the head of the ladies who organize the events at Almacks, Miss Murdock."

"Oh! I see," Miss Murdock said with what she deemed to be the proper amount of awe in her voice. "I am sure it must be an incredible amount of work."

"And indeed it is," Lady Frobisher said. "For you must have an *inexhaustible* knowledge of all the families of the peerage, and know who is properly respectable and who is somewhat lacking. The assemblies at Almacks have been built on the tradition of respectability, Miss Murdock," she lectured with sternness. "And we in charge of the assemblies are trusted by everyone to insure that when our young people mingle, that there is none of bad influence among them, and that anyone they meet in our assembly room is a desirable match in marriage. It is a great responsibility and I take it *very* seriously."

"I see," Miss Murdock said, but she had a great desire to laugh, for it all seemed very pompous and pretentious to her.

"So you may rest assured," Lady Frobisher continued, "that if we perhaps were to allow someone access that had been denied access before, it is *only* because we have great hopes that he is at last reforming, and it is our duty as Christians to afford him an opportunity to redeem himself in the eyes of society."

"But of course," Miss Murdock said, wondering how this particular wrinkle managed to make its way into the conversation.

Lady Frobisher nodded at her in approval, as though she had given precisely the answer she had been looking for. "I just do not want it to be even *hinted* at that we ladies of the board had somehow been swayed by the *rank* of any particular person."

"Certainly not," Miss Murdock agreed. "For I can see that you take your position quite sincerely and it would be an injustice indeed for any one to think you could be swayed to a decision by anything but a person's character."

"Exactly," Lady Frobisher agreed and gave the Dowager, who had been sitting and listening to this exchange with a great deal of amusement on her face, another approving nod. "I must say that your Miss Murdock is a most *sensible* girl!"

Miss Murdock, who could see no sense in any of this conversation, merely said, "Thank you."

The Dowager told Lady Frobisher, "As I had said, Lady Frobisher."

Lady Frobisher glanced at the clock, said, "Well, my hour is up, Duchess St. James. If I can be of any other assistance, you know you only need to call upon me."

The Duchess told her, "You are doing me a great service already, Lady Frobisher."

"Well," that Lady said as she rose from her seat. "Allowances must be made, I have always said. Although I must tell you, had it been anyone but you to ask, well, the outcome may have been different."

"I understand," the Dowager agreed. "And I do not blame you in the least."

"And begging your pardon," Lady Frobisher added, "but I always knew this day would come. For no one can do the 'proper' without Almacks to help guide the way!"

"And I am certainly aware of it," the Duchess returned. "And I hope the wedding present I have made out for your daughter expresses my thanks adequately."

Lady Frobisher paused at that, her eyes losing a great deal of their self-important gleam. "It does, indeed, Duchess St. James. So please, do not even mention your gratitude further."

"Of course not," the Duchess agreed. "For I would not want it to be thought that I had suddenly shown your daughter some sort of favoritism when we both know I have been very fond of her since she was born. So perhaps we should keep it our little secret or I shall have people I do not know as well as I know you suddenly sending me invitations for weddings when I am but on nodding acquaintance with them."

Lady Frobisher was all smiles again. "I'm sure that would be best, Dowager, for I would not want any one less scrupulous than I to take advantage of your generosity."

"Oh, a horrid thought."

"Yes. Most horrid."

"Good day, Lady Frobisher."

"And good day to you, Dowager, Miss Murdock."

Lady Frobisher took her leave and the Duchess sat back and smiled.

"Oh, my," Lady Lydia exclaimed from the door, "Did I miss our caller, then?"

"I'm afraid you have, Lydia," the Duchess told her. "But nevermind, for you shall see her tonight at Almacks of course, along with many others. I have no doubt it will be a horrendous crush."

"Oh, I certainly hope so," Lady Lydia returned. "Aren't you looking forward to it, Miss Murdock?" she asked breathlessly.

Miss Murdock smiled to be agreeable. "I'm sure it shall be very interesting," she offered. She was all the more disconcerted when the Duchess laughed gaily.

By the time Tyler perceived and set out upon St. James' trail, it was late afternoon. The finer weather of that morning had clouded over and it looked to be only a brief time before cold rain would fall from the sky. Tyler could think of several better places to be than riding out of London toward a horse market.

In all likelihood, even if he found his employer, it was a fruitless endeavor, for he was quite certain that even as he rode, Miss Murdock must already be feeling the consequences of her escapade with the duke the night before. At this thought, Tyler spit a determined stream of tobacco juice from his mouth and shook his head. He muttered beneath his breath, as he had frequently since he had begun his search for his employer over two hours before. "Can't credit it, can't credit it, can't credit it," he said. "For him to be so bloody *careless*--" He cursed a little with worry, added to himself, "And now I can't bloody find him when he should be well aware that it be important I know where he is, and when I do get wind of where he is, he's off purchasing another bloody horse."

As if to punctuate his dark displeasure with his lordship, the rain that had been threatening began to fall. No kind drizzle this, but an outpouring of great drenching drops that forced Tyler to halt his horse and tug his cap down more tightly on his head and lift the collar of his coat as high as he could coax it. Then with an even grimmer expression, he kicked his unhappy horse forward on down the road.

He had just come into sight of the market place, which was in an open field and was fast breaking up with the sudden onslaught of rain, when he saw the familiar figure of his lordship just leaving. Beside him rode Ryan Tempton, as Tyler had expected, having gained his first insight of where the duke had gone that day by following a hunch and inquiring at the Tempton residence when calling at the duke's home had been of no help.

Ryan had on lead a flashy black filly, her coat shining in the rain like so much crude oil, and St. James for his part was leading a horse behind his mount that was possibly the poorest specimen of an equine that Tyler had ever seen. The groom pulled his horse to a stop, as they were headed for him at any rate, and merely sat there observing the elegant duke and his lamentable purchase: a sway backed, heavy headed, small horse just slightly larger than a pony, more appropriately called a cob.

By sitting there and observing, he became aware that although his lordship and young Mister Tempton appeared to be having conversation between them, that St. James nonetheless was turning every so often in his saddle, his mind obviously only half attending whatever Ryan was saying to him, as his intent eyes took in his surroundings behind him. And when he turned back to face forward, his eyes scoped far up ahead of him and even from the distance between them, Tyler caught a chill as their gold depths settled on him with a snap and his lordship (who unlike Ryan had been holding both the reins *and* the lead in one hand, leaving the other hand free) pressed his hand to the inside of his *open* coat (unusual in this weather) and half-drew a pistol before he recognized the groom.

Tyler, who out of surprise had spat his entire cud of tobacco from his mouth in preparation to calling out, saw at once that this simple act may have saved him, for his lordship evidently recognized his particular habit. He waited no longer, but kicked his horse forward, and trotted down to meet them.

"Mighty nervous, milord," he said as way of greeting even as Ryan exclaimed surprise at his unexpected appearance.

"A tad," St. James replied. "Take this horse, will you, Tyler," and he passed the lead over to his groom, leaving him more control of his own mount. He did not button his coat, but the pistol he had half drawn was again out of sight.

Ryan, oblivious to his lordship's strange actions, asked, "Whatever brings you here, Tyler? And however did you find us?"

As way of answer, Tyler opened the pocket flap of his coat and pulled from it a handkerchief, handed it to St. James, whose gold eyes left off their restless circling for a moment to appraise it. "Bloody Hell!" he exclaimed as all the possible implications must have ran through his mind. He shoved it without ceremony into his own coat pocket, turned to Ryan. "Let's try to get out of this rain, shall we, Ryan," and with no further warning of his intent, kicked his horse into a gallop.

Ryan and Tyler urged their horses along after him, the black filly seeming to merely lope along, but the smallish cob of a horse that Tyler now led with its awkward head and heavy, swaying body did nothing but labor and slow them down. Still, they made good time, and Tyler was as satisfied as he could possibly be in the situation.

They rode through the rain for an hour, the drenching downpour not slackening and neither did their horses. As they entered the West End of London, St. James slowed his horse and said to Ryan, "I'll be going straight to my home, Ryan, if you should care to join us."

Ryan, drenched and all the excitement he had felt at riding out with the infamous duke quite squashed with the weather and the rather mundane way in which their day had turned out after all (for the duke had remained most disappointingly calm and tractable throughout their excursion), said with some relief that he really should head home as he was still to go to Almacks that evening.

St. James nodded once, took the lead from Ryan's hand, told him, "Well, I shall see you there then, I expect," and rode off with his groom, leaving Ryan to ride on to his own residence.

Fifteen minutes later, the duke and Tyler rode into the stables, where their horses' bodies began to steam, and they each dismounted. Two undergrooms came running up, as Tyler had enjoyed the position of headgroom now for many years, and they took the four horses, two on leads and two under saddle, from Tyler and his lordship. "Come into the house with me, Tyler," St. James bade, "for I shall have to talk to you while I change, for it is getting late."

"Aye," Tyler responded. But his hand went with longing for his chewing tobacco only to leave it alone.

St. James, with a little grin, said, "By all means, indulge yourself. Only spit in the fireplace is all I ask."

"Aye. Thank you, milord," Tyler said with a note of relief in his voice.

St. James turned and together they strode out of the stable and into a back entrance of the house reserved for servants, startling a good deal of the kitchen staff into sharp curtsies as they went through. St. James went first to his study, with Tyler companionably at his side, for they worked together as more than employer and servant. St. James ruffled through the mail on his desk that had arrived that day by either post or by messenger, found a smallish envelope that he had apparently been looking for, and opened it for a brief look inside. "Thank you, grand-mother," he murmured. "Knew I could count on you." Then he dropped the envelope back into the pile and they left the study as quickly as they had entered it.

They trotted up the stairs, panting a little, and Tyler said between his breaths, "Your hand was rather quick t'your pistol today."

St. James glanced at him. "So it was," he agreed between his own gasps. They reached the second floor hallway, and he continued a little more quietly, "You caught that did you? Ryan did not! I'm afraid that boy is feeling a great deal disillusioned, for he was quite certain I would be about some sort of trouble that would entertain him."

"You very nearly were, from t'looks of it," Tyler countered. "I'd have not noticed it meself except I had stopped t'watch you. Quite a bit shocked at that sorry piece of horseflesh you were leading. Do not tell me you *purchased* it?"

St. James was delayed in answering for as they entered his rooms, Effington appeared in the door behind them, and he nodded at his valet before saying, "I did. I believe my new messenger boy should have a horse. By the by, Effington, send that boy up to me, would you?"

Effington drew himself up. He was already most unhappy to see a *groom* in his lordship's rooms and now his employer's request seemed designed, as usual, for no other reason than to deprive the valet of his rightful duties. "Do not think you are going to send me on some unim-portant task just so you may change your clothing yourself, milord!" he warned.

But St. James was in no mood for their ongoing game today. "Go," he said. "Or you may resign on the spot as you have so often threatened, Almacks or no Almacks tonight!"

Effington seemed to be in a true struggle over this ultimatum, but in the end his lordship's use of the word 'Almacks' bore down his outrage and with haughty deference, he sniffed and said, "Certainly, milord."

As soon as the door closed behind him, St. James pulled his two pis-tols from beneath his dripping coat, laid them on the table and then be-gan tearing off his wet clothes. He paused long enough to dig the handkerchief from his pocket before dropping his sodden coat to the floor. He tossed the handkerchief to Tyler. "Who found it?" he asked.

"Earl Larrimer."

St. James paused in unbuttoning his shirt. "Could have been worse," he said. Then he let out a steam of curses. "What in hell was I thinking!"

"I'm afraid it *was* worse, milord," Tyler told him and caught the towel that St. James picked up from beside his wash basin and tossed to him. He proceeded to dry his neck as he spoke. "Lady Larrimer was there t'see it found, which had a convenience about it that I could scarce cred-it t'bein' accidental. And Miss Murdock was there t'catch the full shock of what looked t'be a great deal of outrage on yer aunt's part. I fear that with it takin' me so long t'find you today, that poor Miss Murdock has likely already been grilled."

"*Damnation!*" St. James peeled off his breeches, undid the laces of his shorts in sharp, preoccupied movements and dropped them as well. He turned and took his dressing robe down from the hook where it hung and shrugged into it. Then he ran both hands through his wet, dark hair and tied the belt of his robe about him. He turned back to Tyler. "If I show up now without knowing what Miss Murdock has said, I may very well only make it worse."

"I'd say t'is a distinct possibility, milord. If you had been more available. . . ."

"You needn't tell me. I could have arrived and perhaps made some excuse for it being there that would mollify my aunt. As it is, there is no telling what excuse Miss Murdock has made, and if I should contradict her, it will make her out to be a liar."

"I don't think she'd baldly lie about it, milord," Tyler observed.

St. James' gold eyes focused on him. "Quite," he said sounding a good deal grimmer than he had the moment before. "Mayhaps she has at least been evasive. If my aunt has somehow contrived to get confirmation of her suspicions from Miss Murdock, I fear that she will use it if for no other reason than to further blacken my name and to hell with Miss Murdock."

"I fear t'same," Tyler said. "Otherwise I'd not been ridin' about in t'rain in search of you."

"I can not credit I was so careless!" St. James admitted with sudden, savage anger. "I am never careless. And if I am being careless about something like that, what else am I being careless about? Damn it, Tyler, this whole plan is turning into one bloody fiasco."

"Be that as it may, milord, but what I want t'know is what did you get wind of t'make you so ready with yer piece today? You were ridin' with one hand free even 'fore you saw me."

St. James, who had begun pacing the room with his thoughts, whirled, his robe fluttering about him. "I was being watched today, Tyler. I could feel it from the time I left the Tempton's with Ryan. And I've come to the conclusion that it must be by more than one person, for I could not catch the same face twice! And do you know," he added, "that my begging off last night was because I had been summoned to Buckingham Palace, and the Queen wished to congratulate me on my upcoming nuptials to Miss Murdock?"

Tyler's old salt and pepper eyebrows rose a great degree.

"Yes," St. James confirmed. "And she offered herself the observation that if she is able to keep track of my activities, others are equally as able. So I do not think I am suffering a sudden case of the nerves. I believe I am just enjoying a heightened awareness."

"What's t'cob for, milord?" Tyler asked.

"Steven, as I said."

And as if cued by his name, there was a tap on the door, and Effington escorted that young man in. One glance by the valet at his lordship undressed and in his robe caused Effington to say, "Milord!" But St. James waved a hand at him.

"You may stay, Tyler," St. James said as his groom made a motion to leave. "And you also, Effington, for if I am to make it to Almacks at a decent time tonight, you had better start your dreadful ministrations." Without pause, he turned to Steven. "By the by, Steven, have you still your clothing that you arrived in yesterday?"

"Aye, m'lord, though I much prefer me new ones I must say."

"And so you may keep your new ones. But I have a little job for you to do tonight, and it might be better if you did not look like one of my servants. Are you willing? I doubt if it will be dangerous, but I still must ask you to use caution and a degree of common sense."

"Am I to rouse Miss Murdock from her window again tonight?" he asked with eagerness.

"No, not tonight, you wretched lad, and you should not bandy such information about, although Effington here is the only one that was ignorant of that young lady's name and he, fortunately, is endlessly discreet," St. James ended, his voice a little mocking.

Effington gave him a withering look and as his own form of snide retaliation asked, "Was it she who did the slapping, milord?"

"Just go about your business, Effington, and nevermind," his lordship retorted. "If you are sure you wish to help, Steven, this is what I wish for you to do."

And for the next hour, Effington worked as efficiently as he could at dressing the duke, who could not remain still as he hashed through plans and thoughts, putting forth different summations and conclusions only to discard them as Tyler, sometimes Steven, and even Effington brought up a differing point of view that either disproved one theory or seemed to point to another. He seemed very much like a war lord, but in fact his only council was a groom who, smelling rather damply of the stables, spat tobacco into the fire, an eager street urchin who seemed more excited than cautious, and a valet who was trying to listen, advise and ready his lordship with growing frustration.

At the end of this hour, Effington pronounced himself done with a great deal of pride and, frankly, relief. "Ah, you look as they used to speak of you when you were 'the catch of the decade'," he murmured. "Except, of course, for Miss Murdock's palm print upon your face."

And St. James was diverted enough by this announcement to ask his valet, "Good God! Do not tell me that old nonsense is what prevailed upon you to come and work for me?"

"Indeed, milord," Effington admitted. "It swayed me quite completely, for I knew if anyone were to be able to help you to your former standing, it was I!"

"And how very disappointed you must have been to find I have no desire whatsoever to reach those lofty and unsought heights again," St. James observed. But as he stood at the end of his words, the deep wine red of his velvet coat and matching tight knee breeches with wisteria colored silk cravat and stockings, his gold buckled shoes, his dark hair brushed back from his pale brow and tied in a ponytail with a matching wine colored ribbon, seemed to prove his own words wrong.

But for once, Effington had mercy upon his employer and did not point this out to him.

Tyler, rather less concerned with any delicate feelings his lordship may have, guffawed without restraint.

His lordship's gold eyes caressed over him in amused tolerance. "Hush, Tyler. If I am to go to Almacks, I must be willing to put on the required show of a man hopelessly and rather foolishly in love."

Steven caught all of their attention by saying with awe in his voice, "Coo! I think you look like t'king of the world, m'lord," which caused St. James' smile to fade into faintness.

With sudden brusqueness, he directed Tyler to ready his carriage for the evening while he went below stairs to dine. "You do not wish me to return to the Duchess's home?" Tyler asked.

"No. For Miss Murdock will be at Almacks tonight at any rate." The duke picked up his two pistols, handed them to Tyler. "And I need someone I can trust to handle these."

Tyler took them without comment, but Effington, who had watched this exchange, said, "I hardly think you will need those at Almacks, milord. T'is not one of your gaming hells, you know," and he sniffed.

But his lordship paid him not the slightest heed, only turned to Steven and asked, "And you understand what you are to be about tonight?"

"Aye, m'lord."

"And you'll have a care?"

"Aye," Steven answered, his face sober.

"Very well, then." He turned to go below, leaving the others to disperse as they would behind him.

Upon reaching the ground floor of his home, St. James met with Applegate, informed him that he would like his dinner served in his study. "Yes, milord," Applegate acknowledged. "And may I say you look very fine tonight, milord."

"Bah!" St. James answered and he went down the wide hallway to his study, closed the door behind him and went to his desk. There he flipped through the envelopes that he had pawed through earlier. Most of them appeared to be the run-of-the-mill invitations and correspondence. One of these he scrutinized a little more sharply, as the handwriting on it seemed to bespeak of someone mostly uneducated and hence was unusual, and he lay it aside. Then as he reached the bottom of the pile, he found a larger envelope with no postage that indicated it had been brought by messenger. He lifted it and tapped it into the palm of his other hand. Then he set it with the other envelope that had struck his interest at the fore of his desk.

He went to the sideboard, poured himself a comfortable brandy in a large glass, and then seated himself at his desk, turned the wick up on his reading lamp, took a sip of his drink, and proceeded to open the large envelope first.

There was a brief cover letter, unsigned, but he had anticipated that. It simply read: *Materials as discussed. More to follow. Would be very interested in any thoughts you have. I will have a man call on you in a few days.*

St. James took a deep drink, flipped the cover letter over and began reading hand writing that was as familiar to him as a long forgotten song:

From the hand of Duke of St. James, William Desmond Larrimer
At the request of Her Royal Highness, Queen Victoria
On Behalf of the Crown.

Subject: China's seizure of East India Company Opium
Date: November 29, 1839

And the date was like a slap to St. James' face, for it was a month to the day before his parents had been killed.

Your Royal Highness,

I trust that you are in good health.
I have no final conclusions on the present situation here in China. I will remain here until the week before Christmas to continue my investigation, but thus far this is what I have discovered:
As you already are aware, our East India Company has been trading opium from India with China, mostly through the Canton sea ports, for manufactured goods and tea, which we then ship to England and trade with other countries. In 1836, the Chinese government banned this trade, designated Opium as an illegal commodity and have been trying to stem any flow of this product into their country.
This has been a mostly futile effort as I am afraid our traders have quite blatantly disregarded their laws, have bribed the Cantonese officials, and illegal smuggling has been nearly as profitable to them as legal trading had been in previous years, if not more profitable as they are no longer paying tariffs on any of the product they are importing, and no longer paying taxes on any of the products they are exporting.
In March of this year a new Imperial Commissioner of Canton was appointed, Lin Tse-hsuuml. He has made it his mission to expose and remove the corrupt officials that have made this illegal smuggling so pro-

liferate. He has taken action against Chinese merchants dealing in opium and destroyed all stores of it on land.

This has led up to the seizure of our English merchant vessels earlier this month, that necessitated my being here at your request.

I understand of course that there are many other matters on the table to be considered beside this one product, but I am very much afraid after being here for a fortnight, that whether we go to war or not will hinge most decidedly on the opium problem.

It is the one point of contention that the Chinese will not be swayed on, and unfortunately, as the East India Company relies immensely upon the sale of this product to China, they are quite immovable upon voluntarily withdrawing from the trading of opium with China.

I well understand their position. They have an obligation to their investors (of which I am one, which I only mention, because in light of my tentative conclusions, which are below, you may find it interesting to know this), and without this lucrative trade, they will go from being a very rich company to a very poor one. Possibly a ruined one.

I fear the estimates of loss already sustained that have been given you have been misleadingly conservative. I deem it well into millions of £'s.

Treaty talks are going poorly and I understand, even here, that there are rumors that the Crown will not tolerate this action taken by the Chinese Imperial government for long unless some encouraging progress is made that these matters will be settled reasonably quickly. I fear from my meetings with the diplomats here that this seems unlikely. I trust you have reached the same conclusion from their reports to you.

At this point, I can well imagine the pressure being brought to bear on you and the Prime Minister from those who have much at stake, as I myself have much at stake. I well understand also, that although the opium is the focal point, that China's action to refuse any trade at all with our sovereign until there is a treaty in place is putting other commodities at stake also. I am sure it is being pointed out to you quite strongly that if we go to war, we may be able to improve our trading position on these other necessary commodities as well.

But the fact is, and I offer this to you respectfully, that our previous trading agreements with China were not onerous to our sovereign regarding other commodities, so contrary to what may be being presented to you by others, please keep in mind that their main concern is the loss they are taking on the opium, despite this other argument.

So what you must ask yourself now, I humbly recommend, is whether you are willing to, in fact, go to war for this single commodity, which is very valuable to be sure, and necessary from a medical standpoint, but which has a grievous paradox to it also, which I have seen firsthand here in China in a way that had never been brought home to me in England, even on the meanest streets of London.

I shall try very hard to explain my observations in the simplest, most straight-forward manner, but as they are, frankly, perplexing to me, I do not know how well I will achieve my endeavor of relaying my thoughts to you.

Opium seems to be a scourge on this land. I had noticed first upon my--

"Your dinner, milord, as you had requested."

St. James glanced up from reading, his eyes taking a moment to focus. "Very well, Applegate. Thank you." He indicated that Applegate should place it on a corner of his desk.

"I knocked, milord, but I fear you did not hear me."

"That is quite all right, Applegate."

"Anything else, milord?"

St. James shook his head. "No. Thank you. Wait. Refill my glass and then nothing else."

Applegate took the empty glass, went to the sideboard and refilled it. "Do not forget that you are scheduled to leave in less than an hour, milord."

St. James nodded as he rubbed a finger over his upper lip, his eyes preoccupied. "Remind me again at the appointed time, Applegate." And then as Applegate left the room, closing the door behind him, he ignored his plate and returned to his reading.

. . .I had noticed first upon my arrival a strange lackadaisicalness of the people. From small children to old men. I observed people sleeping on sidewalks at mid day, appearing unwashed and underfed. When they are awake, they move about as though they are in a trance and are unable to comprehend anything to any degree. Of course, I can not understand their language, but I have noticed a distinct lack of purpose or continuity to their speech when they are speaking. At first, God forgive me, I supposed it to be some sort of cultural lacking on their part.

As I moved further inland and away from the seaport towns, I noticed that more of the people appeared to be industrious and intelligent, although there was still a marked percentage of them that spent their days in this otherworldly state. Upon returning to the seaboard, I spent a great deal of time on the docks and spoke at length with some of our British sailors, a rough group to be sure, but very informative. They told me that it is the 'Opium Dens' that are causing the results of what I had observed, and that they are common throughout the country of China as far as they could discern, but most noticeably around the seaports as that is where the Opium is most prolific.

I expressed my astonishment that people should be taking a drug intended for medicinal purposes when they have no need of it, thinking, I suppose, about such dreaded draughts as cod-liver oil and the such. I was enlightened that Opium has long been used as a means of pleasure in China, and as I could see for myself, the results are damnedable.

I shall try to sum up briefly what I have learned: As some people (And I am sure you have had your acquaintances with such, as have I) can not merely drink but one or two drinks but are seemingly compelled to drink to a degree of intoxication in which they cannot even function, so are these that use this Opium. Only, I am given to understand, it has a potency in which anyone smoking it (for they use pipes to smoke it), even once, is compelled to spend his time doing nothing but procuring more and more. Many die, though whether it is from some toxic side effect with the continued use or merely from the starvation and neglect of their bodies I have been unable to determine.

Of course, many may point out to you, and perhaps you are thinking the same yourself, it could be some sort of character deficiency innate to the Chinese, but I was promptly disabused of this notion when I observed a great deal of our own British sailors enslaved by this drug also. Most damnedable of all, I had opportunity to observe some of our own sailors of the Royal Navy being felled by this same Opium. It is not beyond my imagination to realize that although this drug has been illegal for some time in our country (and you will of course note the paradox there: we do not wish it to be in our country, but we are perfectly happy to profit from it being traded to another country) that of a certainty, there is still an illegal trade of it to England, and that our country is dreadfully susceptible to this same dreaded scourge.

In short, this may be a commodity that, although very useful and promising when used correctly, may be better left in short supply. I would suggest that we for once look to the human factor in this debate, and although we will lose much in the way of profits, I feel that if all opium trade were immediately and voluntarily discontinued, that not only would the other points of disagreement preventing us from reaching treaty with China be rapidly overcome, but that we would also be insuring that we do not leave ourselves open to a similar crisis on our own shores.

By thus avoiding war, we would save the unnecessary loss of life that war always entails, and we would also likely protect good English people from a grave and seemingly insidious menace to their health and I am afraid even their morals.

The example I have seen here in China is frightening, and in truth, I can not fault their position. If the British Empire were to develop a similar fate, the loss of productivity alone in our country, if one does not care to study on the other negative factors, could be enough to rob us of our place as a leading nation in the new world of industry. I am afraid it would make our gin problem seem quite incidental in comparison.

As I had mentioned before, I have as much at stake as anyone in term of profits if we should lose this trade. I mention this so that if I have not adequately conveyed my feeling of horror over the possible consequences of going to war with China over a commodity that is currently savaging their population, and that by winning it, we may very well jeopardize more in our future than we are to gain in the present, that you may perhaps gain some understanding when I say that I would take my losses with no regret if you should decide to bypass pursuing this to the degree of going to war.

Let it be noted also, that I will not change my investments. For although if I had known what exactly I were investing in, I would not have bought into these holdings (as I feel probably a great many other investors would feel the same), I will not have it said that I anticipated any decision on your part and protected myself unfairly.

I do realize the position my recommendation would put you in, and that it is a vastly unpopular notion to allow one of our major companies to fail for what most will deem a failure on our foreign policy. I can only humbly suggest that you consider my observations in the decisions that you and your counsel come to.

I remain sincerely and loyally at your service.

St. James sat for several long moments stunned and deliberating. He shuffled through the remaining reports in the envelope, determined that there were two more yet to be read, but for now, he thought he had quite enough to study upon just in what had been written in the first one.

"If your recommendations were made known," St. James murmured to himself, "then I am sure you made your share of enemies overnight."

For as his father had pointed out in his missive to a young and somewhat uncertain, at that point, Queen Victoria, there was a great deal of money at stake. And Dante's father's advice had been to throw profits to the wind and for people to possibly lose their initial investment also. Including his own.

But would someone have been enraged and threatened by bankruptcy enough to kill not only Dante's father, but his mother and her unborn child as well? And Dante if he had been in that coach as he was supposed to have been?

Also, St. James tapped his thumb on the report in front of him, these papers were highly confidential, from his father's pen to the Queen's eyes. Who else had gained knowledge of what his father had been recommending the Queen to do? Who had discovered that the Queen had at least seriously considered it, for if she had not been swayed by his father's arguments, then his arguments would have not been a threat. Had there been, possibly still was, a mole in the Queen's trusted inner circle? One who had been threatened by the loss of his fortune, or had he been a tool for someone else?

St. James picked up his glass, saw that during his reading he had finished the second drink as efficiently as he had finished the first. His plate of dinner, quite cold, sat untouched by his side, but he did not feel like eating. Instead, in a rare show of hopelessness, he laid his head in his arms on his father's report and thought now that he was making some progress, that he may in fact be unequal to the task after all of a-venging his parents' deaths.

He did not have the luxury of lying there long, for there was a tap on the door, and raising his head from off his wine velvet sleeves he called, "Enter."

Applegate opened the door. "Milord, it is time for you to be leaving."

"Thank you, Applegate," but he did not move to get up as Applegate withdrew. He unlocked his top drawer, moved his father's reports into it and locked it again, but his mind was very far away as he did so. It had turned not to what had been written, but to the picture he had gained of his father. His memory of that man was not dim, for he had very clear and haunting memories of him, if rather few, for it had seemed that he rarely saw him as he was always on one assignment or another for the crown.

The picture he had gained of his father suggested someone not at all hard or cynical but someone earnest, dedicated and trustworthy. A man more concerned about human suffering than riches. A man untouched by dark thoughts and dark deeds.

And perhaps that hurt the most, because St. James had a glimpse of what he may have been, was meant to have become, if he had not been twisted at the young age of ten by a need to avenge.

His father had been the epitome of respectability. Not only a lord but a gentleman. If he were to know St. James as he had grown to be, he would have held him and his actions in abhorrence.

His father had never fought a duel, for he would not have been in company of anyone that would offend or be easily or ridiculously offend-ed. He would not have ever played in a gaming hell worse than Whites or Boodles, and infrequently at those. He would have never walked the gin streets of London in search of assassins, and more rewarding in the way of information, women of assassins. He would not have set out to seduce young females of quality who were willing to bring him docu-ments from their fathers' desks, unread and unaware. He would have never become involved with his peers' wives and opened dusty closet doors of their minds, asking questions of their husbands' business affairs that their husbands would have been shocked to know they even knew about.

And his father would have never proposed to elope with a girl he did not know or care for with the hopes of impregnating her and then springing her on society as only his fiancé with the grave possibility that he would not even be alive when the child was born to take care of either of them in any way but monetary.

And although Miss Murdock would have been protected by his name when after his death, his barrister would have produced the marriage certificate, her life would still have been a living hell.

He snapped from his inactivity. He rose from his seat, delayed long enough to go again to the sideboard, pour another brandy and downed it. His resolve, which had seemed wavering there for those few minutes as he examined all that his father had been, all that he should have been, returned to a strength that made him dizzy.

He could not change what had happened, he had accepted that fact long ago, and he reminded himself of it now.

Mayhaps his father would have held him in abhorrence if he were to be acquainted with him now. But if his father had walked with the dead as St. James for so long had, his father would not have fallen so easily at the whim of another and St. James would have been afforded the luxury of believing his world was safe.

He intended that luxury for his son, and damn it, he intended it for his soon to be wife. And if it meant being as he was, then that was the way he would be.

But of course, he had known that for many years now.

Only with the death of another could he in turn live. If it meant sacrificing his life in the effort, he did not feel that it was an unfair trade. As long as his objective was met.

"I have let her delay long enough," he mused. "Mayhaps, too long." He turned on his heel and strode from the room, a good deal of his anticipation for a pleasant evening provoking Miss Murdock drained from him. He had wasted too much time indulging his affection for her and he reminded himself that affection had no place in his plans.

By fair means or foul, he had to get her down the marriage aisle.

The longer he delayed, the more likely he would not be alive to see the nuptials.

And at odds with all that he had just read was still the gut instinct that his foe could tolerate him being alive, but would not tolerate his producing an heir. If it were so very important to his enemy that he did not produce an heir, then it was equally important to St. James that he should, and with some haste.

He went from the room, very aware of the lateness of the hour. And Miss Murdock was waiting.

Inside the drawer, trapped between the reports, was the other, smaller envelope that St. James had set aside for his perusal that evening. But with three drinks, no dinner, and a great deal on his mind, he had forgotten its existence.

Chapter Sixteen

"You look enchanting, Lizzie," Andrew told her. Ashton had just closed the door of the drawing room behind her and she smiled up at Earl Larrimer as she came across the room

"I do not believe you, you know, but I still appreciate the sentiment."

"No, I am quite serious. The pale yellow of that gown brings out just how refreshingly different you are. You make everyone I know seem too tall and too pale."

She blushed, still only half attending him, for she was so full of trepidation she was nearly sick with it. "Yes, but in all their powdered paleness, they appear so cool, where as I am afraid I merely look as I am: flustered, and I fear, a little sweaty."

He laughed the easy, boyish laugh that came so easily to him and that was infectious to anyone that heard it. "You do *not* look sweaty," he reassured her. "At most, just pleasantly glowing. Dewy fresh."

She smiled at his description which made her sound, she thought, like some manner of fruit. "I will ask your opinion again when we reach the assembly rooms and I am quite drenched with nervousness."

"Whatever do you have to be nervous about?" he asked. "You realize that all the others being launched are several years younger than yourself, so you are sure to look gratifyingly self-possessed compared to them."

"Oh, you are reassuring me immensely by reminding me that I am an aging spinster," she teased. He gave her a half-humorous, half-hurt look that she seemed to be forever rebuffing his admiration for her, and she continued with more seriousness. "But I am afraid *they* have the advantage on me as *they* are fresh out of dancing class, and I, well the only tutor I had was my father," she admitted.

"Really?" Andrew asked, quite diverted at this revelation. "You never had a proper dance instructor?"

"No, not at all," Miss Murdock responded, thinking there had been no money to even have a maid, let alone tutors. But of course, Andrew had no clear understanding of this. She had the sudden vision of him being in place of St. James on that ill-fated night when the duke had arrived. Andrew following her to the kitchens. *Good God, Miss Murdock, where are all your servants?* He could not realize yet that there would be times when one merely did what needed to be done, for there was nothing else for it. "But I must say that for as portly as my father is, and, of course before his gout was quite as bad as it is, he was exceptionally light on his feet. I only fear that the dances he taught me are now so outdated that they will be useless."

"Have you at least learned to waltz, Lizzie? For it is very popular, you know, although Almacks in all its 'wisdom' will only allow one per assembly."

Miss Murdock looked more relieved than crestfallen to have her fears of inadequacy confirmed. "No, I have not, for my father says such a dance was not at all allowed when he was a young man."

And Andrew with undeniable enthusiasm, said, "Well, then I must teach you immediately." Before she could demur, he caught her hand, held it out from them in the correct position and quite took her breath away by wrapping an arm around her waist and pulling her to the proper distance from him.

"But there is no music," Miss Murdock hedged with desperation.

"I shall hum," Andrew told her grandly.

He did begin to hum, and Miss Murdock laughed, and he went slowly at first until she caught the steps. He interrupted his impromptu music to tell her, "Hand on my shoulder, Miss Murdock, and three quarter time! One, two, three. One, two, three. Splendid! Now we shall speed up a bit, shall we?"

He swooped her in ever widening circles about the room until the large hoop of her buttermilk ball gown swayed about her like a bell being tolled. Despite herself she was enchanted, her face flushing as his humming became more exuberant and he swirled her ever faster, she clinging to his shoulder and he holding to her waist. Lizzie was laughing and breathless, and he was laughing and humming between his laughs, his face delighted.

Then in the midst of all this lightness, he dropped his hand from holding hers and released her waist also, so that, surprised and dizzy, she nearly fell. Andrew cupped her face in both his hands and kissed her with quick warmth.

She did not reject him, perhaps a little too stunned to even gather her wits. He was a handsome young man and reminded her most painfully of his cousin, but where St. James' mere kisses upon her wrist had induced her to slap him, when Andrew released her, she only had a sudden, lamentable fit of the giggles.

Which perhaps was not the reaction Andrew had been looking for.

"That is not at all kind, Lizzie," he admonished her, frowning in real perplexity. "Has no one told you that when a man makes improper advances toward you, you are to promptly swoon from the thrill and danger of it?"

"Oh," she managed through her giggles, which had redoubled at his chastisement, and said, "I have come up lacking again!"

"Well, since you have, you may as well tell me what is so funny. I was quite serious you know, for you are the grandest, if I may also say the damnedest, female I ever met."

"Oh, now you are getting cross," she said. "I am sorry," but she continued to laugh. She put a hand on his shoulder. "It is only that I did not realize you were so thorough. You have taught me the art of flattery, waltzing, and now kissing. I am only afraid of what you will next deem necessary for me to learn."

"That is not at all in the spirit that I meant it, Lizzie, as I believe you know perfectly well," he told her, and she could see that she was trying him sorely, for although he was by nature amiable, even he had his limits to being a good sport.

"Yes, Andrew," she told him, growing sober, "but I think it is best if that is the spirit in which I accept it, for it would not do otherwise, you know."

"I do not know that at all," he persisted, a little petulant.

"Oh, do not be upset, for I was having such a lovely time before this," she begged. "It is only that I care very much for you as things are and I do not wish to change them and have everything end in a great deal of unpleasantness."

"Ah," he said, brightening, "you have forgotten that I intend to be the epitome of respectability to redeem the Larrimer name that my cousin has so inadvertently besmirched, not that I blame him in any way. So do not get it in your head that I am merely dallying with you."

Miss Murdock, with rashness, but with no other inspiration at hand to soothe him and at the same time discourage his behavior, told him, "I did not think you would, Andrew. It is rather myself that I am afraid of, for I fear you quite turned my head, and I do not wish to take advantage of what I am sure are honorable intentions, only to hurt you in the end. For although I find your company very exhilarating, I can not foresee my heart becoming involved and it would not do for me to pretend more than a passion for you in order to only gain my own ends."

"Lizzie," he said quite a bit shocked. "Are you saying you are dangerously close to considering a *liaison* with me?"

"It would be indelicate of me to confirm that, Andrew," she said with a great deal of primness.

"Of course," he said with wonder, then pressed, "But I fail to see how you could consider that particular situation and not consider, well, a more honorable solution?"

"I fear that my very attraction to you makes me afraid of considering anything so drastic! For how am I to know that I am not being blinded by a fleeting feeling of ardor that may unexpectedly pass, as it may for you?" she added gently. "Then each of us would be left with regrets. I beg that you do not repeat your behavior, for I may be tempted to take the low road rather than the high, and then where would I be?"

"You are so right, Lizzie," Andrew said, his voice contrite. "Whatever was I thinking to put such temptation before you?"

"Indeed, I forgive you," Miss Murdock said. "As long as you are aware that you are putting my mortal soul in danger of toppling to the depths of self-indulgence by your actions and you must promise to never so entice me again."

"Certainly I will promise!" Andrew said with conviction. "And as usual you are showing your good common sense, for if you are to reach a point where you may wish to consider my suit, then it must be because of those gentler emotions and not from the wildness of your nearly un-controllable desires."

Miss Murdock, trying not to show how very amused she was at his self-gratifying statement, only said, "I am glad you understand me so completely."

There was a brief understanding look between them, and then they were interrupted by Andrew's mother saying, "Oh, there you both are! It is nearly time to leave for Almacks, you know."

Lizzie, reminded of the evening before her, lost all her feelings of sat-isfaction that she had managed to put off Andrew from any amorous actions toward her while also boosting his feelings of manly prowess rather than doing them some grievous harm, turned to Lady Lydia with a pasty smile plastered to her lips and said, "Oh, yes, of course."

Lady Lydia gave her such a warm smile that it nearly dazzled her with its brilliance. "You look lovely, tonight, Miss Murdock. I could not ask for a more rewarding young lady to launch. I think you will make some happy suitor's mother feel very lucky to have you some day as her daughter-in-law," she said, her face bright.

And Miss Murdock wondered just how long Lady Lydia had been standing in the door, after all.

Almacks was a crush when they arrived at ten o'clock. It was the first assembly of the Big Season, that social period when most members of the peerage take up residence in London to spend the winter months, with only a break to return to their country estates at Christmas time for a brief few weeks. And although the Season would continue when every-one again returned to London, by then the weather would have worsen-ed, and with Christmas over, everyone would be a little weary of the endless socializing and so after Christmas, it was no longer considered the Big Season, but merely the Season. Then of course, there was the Little Season, in summer, but as those of importance would spend their summer enjoying their country estates, it was of not much consequence. Although there were those who could not tolerate being so long in the country, viewing it as boring rather than relaxing, and they in turn re-turned to London early and so the Little Season had its place also. But everyone agreed that nothing matched the Big Season.

The Larrimer party made their way into the assembly room, which Miss Murdock, upon taking in her surroundings, found rather disappoint-ing. It was as large and open as a barn, and had not much in the way of adornment. She soon realized that the adornments were left to the guests to provide, for the amount of jewelry, and the luxuriant range of colors of silk and velvet and lace were breathtaking against the plain backdrop of their setting.

Andrew escorted them through the crush, all of his cheerful attention taken up with making sure the Dowager Duchess on his arm was not tripped up by the pushing and jostling of the high-heeled crowd. She seemed to be enjoying herself, nodding to the left and to the right to old acquaintances of hers, who, from what Miss Murdock could tell, seemed somewhat surprised by her attendance. She and Lady Lydia followed behind the Duchess and Andrew, and she was in positive dread that she would somehow be separated from them and would be left among this tight throng of people on her own.

The faces about her were laughing and smiling, some had not seen each other since the Season of last year apparently, and there was much catching up to do, and yet, it seemed to Lizzie, they were always glancing about, and as their bright eyes chanced to settle on one of the debutantes to be launched this season, there would be a quick fluttering of fans over their faces as they identified each and passed on any *on dits* they may know.

If this were not intimidating enough, there were the men, presumably many of which were 'hanging out for a wife'. They barely spoke to each other at all, but stood in little groups in their elegant clothing as though they were at a polo match, and it appeared that any conversation they had was only asides as they pointed out something (or in this case, someone) of interest to them. Although there were many that were young and handsome (and many that were young and mayhaps not so handsome), there were a good many that, to Miss Murdock's surprise, appeared rather old. As she was trying to puzzle out why men apparently well past this stage of their lives should still be so avidly 'scanning the market', so to speak, Lady Lydia whispered enlightenment in her ear.

"Widowers, Miss Murdock. And I beg you, do not dismiss them out of hand for being old, as they are *quite* well set in the pocket, if you know what I mean."

Miss Murdock, distracted by one of this set of men raising a quizzing glass to study her (which, to her immense relief, he dropped a disappointed second later), returned to Lady Lydia that she would certainly bear this in mind.

"Do," Lady Lydia encouraged her, and slanted a beguiling smile upon the discussed gaggle of hopefuls, and Miss Murdock remembered that of course, Lady Lydia's husband, St. James' uncle, had died nearly a year ago. Lady Lydia would be out of mourning very soon.

Andrew at last found a path for them toward one of the walls where there were lined many chairs and a few settees, and luckily, he found one of the latter and settled the Duchess down upon it. Lady Lydia dived upon the other cushion of it, complaining bitterly but happily that her new shoes were killing her feet. Miss Murdock, who had observed that Lady Lydia was not only fond of squeezing herself into stays that were too tight, but she also seemed fond of squeezing her feet into shoes that were too small, made a commiserate sound in her throat. Feeling conspicuous, as she was the only one of their party standing (Andrew had abandoned them, saying something of getting them all refreshment from the tables, but as she could see that he had only gone a few feet before being waylaid by first male friends and then interested, flirtatious females, it was doubtful that they would see him again for some time) she turned and settled herself in awkward, and, yes, dowdy position on the arm of the settee. It was not as good as sitting properly, but as she was not very tall at any rate, it gave her the satisfaction of feeling somewhat hidden behind the wall of people before her that seemed to fill the room in a solid mass from end to end and side to side. However there would be room to dance when the music started, Miss Murdock had no idea.

"It is a *frightful* crush!" the Dowager Duchess just beside and a little below her said. "I can not remember ever seeing it so crowded. And look there, Lydia. Is that not Bertram Tempton?"

Lady Lydia squinted through the moving crowd. "Why, yes. Yes, it is," she agreed, a little amazed. "I always believed him to be one of those who was devoted to Whites rather than to Almacks."

"Indeed, yes," the Dowager returned.

Miss Murdock leaned in a little to ask, "Whites?" for she had recognized Lord Tempton also and it was rather nice to know *someone* in the crowd other than whom she had come with.

"Gaming Hell," the Duchess explained.

Miss Murdock digested this, then perplexed by another question, asked, "But if he does not ever come to Almacks either, why was he not denied vouchers as St. James has been?"

The Duchess looked at her a little surprised. "Whoever told you that St. James had been denied vouchers?"

"My maid," Miss Murdock said with a guilty flush, for she was certain there must be some protocol about gossiping with the servants, or at least *admitting* to gossiping with the servants.

The duchess harrumphed and gave her a stern look, but she did answer her question. "No scandals laid at Bertram's door, my child. And I am sure they have searched quite diligently for some wrongdoing on his part, but although he always seems to be on the scene whenever St. James is up to one of his tricks, it is always generally agreed that it would have been much worse had Tempton not been there."

"Oh," Miss Murdock said.

"They would dearly love to deny him vouchers also, I am sure," the Duchess continued. "But they can not, for then it would obviously be because they felt snubbed. And never would it do for them to admit that anyone dares to snub them."

Lady Lydia said in a thoughtful voice, "Most odd that he should be here." She paused a moment, glancing around the room. "Now that I am noticing, there are a great deal of faces here that I would have never expected to see. It seems as though Whites must be suffering an extreme lack of attendance tonight. And Boodles, also, I daresay."

"Boodles?" Miss Murdock asked.

"Another Gaming Hell," the Duchess replied. "You are right, Lydia. For there is Marquis Engleson. And over there is Viscount Brookline."

Lady Lydia pointed out several other discoveries and Miss Murdock looked around trying to catch glimpses of those being nodded at in rapid succession. She saw that a great many others in the crowd of what she could only suppose were the 'regulars' were chatting with animation amongst themselves and seemed to be nodding to one person and another and exclaiming also.

"Do you suppose," Lady Lydia asked, "that there is an *incomparable* to be launched tonight?"

"I could not say, of course, Lydia," the Duchess returned with impatience, "but it seems obvious that rumor of someone's being here tonight has lured a great many more people than would come otherwise."

"Well, it *must* be an exceptionally beautiful debutante," Lady Lydia insisted, "for so many of the jaded set to show up."

"Oh, I do not know," the Duchess disagreed, "for I saw the same thing happen nearly thirty years ago when Earl Abormaril was pursuing his future wife. He had been a rake until well into his forties, and when he was at last taken with a young lass half his age, the betting at Whites as to whether she could reel him in was stupendous." As an afterthought, she added, "So I was told at any rate."

Miss Murdock, with the sudden insight that in all probability, the Duchess had someone placing her money down for her at that establishment, gave a small chuckle. "And did you win, ma'am?" she asked when the Duchess looked at her.

The Duchess grinned. "Oh, yes. You may be certain of that. But it was quite an entertaining affair, at any rate, and as so many of the jaded set had money riding on the outcome, they showed up at the functions just as they are tonight to decide for themselves the odds." She added a little musingly, "I never thought I would see such a ridiculous Season repeated, for it was most outlandish."

"Well, if it is happening again, I can only say that I shall be just a little bit sorry not to see it," Miss Murdock said with honesty, for she was finding it quite enjoyable to sit and be an onlooker at this great throng of boisterous people and hearing what the Duchess and Lady Lydia were making of it all.

Then Andrew was back, and as he had balanced two small cups in one hand and a third in the other, it was evident that he had been about procuring them all refreshment despite how it may have looked to the contrary. "You will never guess the rumor I have heard, nor credit it, I dare say!" he exclaimed without preamble as he handed out the cups, but before he could go on there was a sudden disturbance in the assembly room, starting, it appeared, at the entrance, and he turned (as did, it seemed, everyone else present) to observe this, and never did enlighten them as to the rumor he had heard.

Miss Murdock heard a sudden growing whisper run through the crowd, jumping impossible distances so that those in the back of the room appeared to hear before those in the middle. It encompassed everyone in just a brief few seconds, and those who had not heard it began to see for themselves what the whispering was about, until they too said it with amazed anticipation. Disjointed words and phrases came to Lizzie's ears: *Impossible. . . . Virtually barred, I had heard. . . . And Egads! his face. . . . They say he. . . . That can not be what I think it is. . . .Really, I had not heard. . . . Slapped. . . . The nerve to show up looking like that. . . . Is she here tonight. . . . Scandalous. . . . They will have no choice but to bar him now. . . . No one decent. . . . Can you credit it. . . . Well, I certainly shan't let my daughter dance with him. . . . Ruinous. . . . Such a shame he is the way he is for his worth, you know. . . . Waste. . . . Once 'the catch of the decade', now look at him. . . . Obscene. . . . Even he should know. . . . Simply unacceptable. . . .*

Miss Murdock heard these rustlings about her in an ever increasing wave. She saw the crowd break back as someone, who was not overly tall, strode through them. There was a great deal of back clapping of this gentleman, and as though all had been waiting for something to begin some great, and somehow not quite decent, revelry, the crowd took on a new element that was a little frightening.

To her dismay, there seemed to be a sudden turning of heads, a searching throughout the large expanse of the ball room, and then first one set of eyes found the Duchess and then settled upon Miss Murdock. And then another set of eyes, and then another, and then there were whisperings of *there. . . there. . . that must be she. . . . Nonsense. . . . Can't be. . . .* But all the same a path opened like magic between she and he who had strode through the door and had charged the room, and even before the last few people fell back, she knew with dread in her heart that it would be St. James.

And she sat like a dowd on the arm of the settee, her punch tipping precariously in its cup, feeling her world fall from beneath her feet.

Andrew popped in front of her, his face a comical (if she had been in the proper frame of mind to appreciate it) mask of disconcertedness and he said, "Lizzie. . .?" and then even he fell back, and as she was certain that his retreat was motivated by the look on her own face, it caused her some alarm for she could not even guess what expression she must be displaying.

Then she saw St. James. The path that had opened for him was narrow, and it closed in behind him as he passed. It changed some, a little to the left, then a little to the right, as someone would be jostled out by those who were shoving to see from behind, but it never closed. And the fact that he was barely taller than most of the women, and certainly shorter than most of the men, made it all seem a joke, like a court jester snagging the crown of a King and wearing it for His Highness's entertainment, swaggering and ridiculous.

But St. James did not swagger and he was not ridiculous. If anything, he seemed to find the crowd and its actions ridiculous, as if the jester was suddenly revealed as true royalty, and the crowd as so many imposters. But perhaps only Miss Murdock, and the Duchess surely, were able to read that snapping, mocking disdain in his eyes as he walked toward them.

Miss Murdock, despite her complete feeling of being *floored* by an unseen, unexpected blow had a brief small thought run through her mind. *Something has changed. Oh, Lord. Something has changed.* And then she had no more time for any thoughts for her attention was caught by the bright red, swollen palm print on his cheek, and her own cheeks began to burn as though in sympathy.

He reached them, his coiled tenseness covered in resplendent red velvet with Wisteria lace at sleeves and neck, and stockings of the same color. His gold eyes dwelt with intentness on Miss Murdock and she made some effort to school her features, cool them, remembered Andrew's description of her being 'dewy fresh' and had to bite her lip to keep from letting loose with a nervous laugh that she was sure in the sudden hush of the room would have come out sounding brayingly hysterical.

Everyone quieted, waiting for the action that would stamp the tone of the rest of the evening (and very possibly the remainder of the Season). If St. James did something outrageous, if etiquette was breached any further than it already had been by his merely striding in with that mark upon his face that branded him for all to see that although he was a lord, he was surely no gentleman, then it would seem that the very foundation of Almacks would be rocked and toppled and all decorum lost. Mayhaps, some of them were eager to be released from those constraints.

St. James tore his eyes from Miss Murdock, shifted, bent down, kissed his grandmother on her cheek. "Thank you," he whispered.

In a high, loud, fluting voice, the duchess answered, "*Humph*! Took you long enough to get here!"

And the people gathered that night found an unexpected satisfaction in this display of devotion by grandson to grandmother, and her two pronged remark seemed to say to all of them that St. James, at last, *had* gotten there. And if he was a little marked upon his arrival, they suddenly did not care, for he was a Duke, after all.

The musicians which had delayed playing at all this fuss, read the mood of the crowd and struck up playing. As fast as Miss Murdock and St. James had been at the mercy of the scrutiny of the crowd, they were now ignored, and only then did St. James return his gaze to her and say, "Miss Murdock, you are looking very well tonight."

"Was it worth it, milord?" she asked in a strained undertone. "To come and provoke me once again?"

He cocked his head slightly to the side. "We shall see," he answered and held out his arm to her. "Shall we dance?"

She shook her head, feeling as though she were paralyzed on the arm of the settee, and that if she rose the sudden oblivion everyone seemed to be holding them to would stop and they would again be devoured by the crowd's eyes.

"Come, Miss Murdock," St. James coaxed. "There is no point in my coming here at all and suffering through that if you refuse to dance with me."

"It was your choice, milord, to subject yourself to that. I, on the other hand, had no choice at all."

She moved her hand as she spoke, handing her glass to Andrew, who stood exuding malevolence at her side, for fear that she would spill it in her agitation. Before she could replace her hand into her lap, St. James took it in his own and tucked it into the crook of his arm. "If we are to argue, let us go onto the dance floor to do it, for we will in fact have more privacy there than standing here elbow to elbow with this crowd."

She saw the sense in that, for they were playing a country dance, one she was familiar with and where each had a partner, and they would not be split up as they may be in a different dance. "Very well, milord," she agreed, and rose from the arm of the settee.

As soon as she stood up, she was aware it was a mistake. There was no longer the obvious staring they had been subject to, but the furtive, speculating glances were in their own way as bad. She clung to St. James' arm, shaking a little, and to her alarm, he did not lead her to the edge of the dancers but in amongst them until they were at the very middle of the floor. Then he took her hand in one of his, and her elbow in his other, and they began moving.

He was silent, which Miss Murdock was grateful for, since she was concentrating on the steps, and then when she seemed to have it smoothly and looked up into his face from her diminutive height, she saw that he was smiling. "We have it now, yes, Miss Murdock?"

"I--I think so," she answered, a little embarrassed. "It has been a long time since I have danced, and never," she chanced looking around, "in a setting such as this."

"It has been a very long while since I have danced also, Miss Murdock," he reminded her.

"Oh, yes, of course!" she exclaimed. "For I am given to understand that you have never come to Almacks before."

"So you see, we are both suffering equally."

"I fear you are suffering much more, milord, for I do not have such a topic for conversation upon my cheek," she pointed out.

"Oh, do not start, Miss Murdock," he grimaced. "For I have heard quite enough about it already today."

"Have you, indeed?"

"Indeed."

She became serious. "I am sorry. In retrospect, I fear I overreacted." Which she felt was true, for if she hadn't felt compelled to slap Andrew after his kiss this evening, she could not guess what had come over her to induce her to slap St. James for what was in reality a far less serious offense.

He lifted an amused brow. "Are you, Miss Murdock? If I were to repeat my performance, I would be safe from any further blows? Perhaps I should try my luck now before you change your mind."

"I do not find that funny, milord," she warned, and changed the subject. "How is it you were able to come tonight, at any rate? I had it on good account that you could not obtain vouchers."

"Really? And from whom did you hear that bit of scandalous gossip?"

"My lady's maid, milord."

His lips quirked but he did not question what discussion she had been having about himself with her lady's maid. "Well, she was correct. You may thank my grandmother for helping to subject you to my presence this evening."

"Oh!" she exclaimed. It all became clear to her now. The Duchess's cackling over her missive from St. James this morning and the unexpected caller, Lady Frobisher. "Oh dear," she said, a little shocked. "Now that I think upon it, I dare say when one of the Ladies of the board visited today, that your grandmother bought her off!"

St. James gave a startled, loud laugh, drawing a good deal of attention. "I should not have put it past her," he said, still chuckling. Then seeing her haunted look, he asked, "What is it?"

"It is just that--all these people!" She shook her head in exasperation. "You did not have to do this to me, milord!" she accused him.

"Look at me, Miss Murdock. No, not my neck or my chest or whatever it is you are studying upon. Look at my eyes."

She did with reluctance, found that they steadied her, like a horse shying away from a jump and hearing its rider calling with calm authority that it was to take it, and then finding that it could. "I shall get you through this, Miss Murdock, if you only focus on me and do not begin to look at all the others. We are alone and there is no one else here. See, I hold your hand, and we hold each other's elbows, and we make a little circle with just you and I. They are outside of it, and they can not breach it if you do not look at them."

She held onto his eyes with her own. As if to remind herself as well as him, she said, "I trusted you. And I fear very much that what you have done to me this evening was catch me in some well-laid trap, which I can find no purpose for, but a trap all the same. Those are not the actions of a trustworthy man, milord. Does that not concern you?"

"Miss Murdock?"

"Yes?"

"Must you always ask questions that I can not immediately answer?"

"Oh," she said and felt deflated, for she had been expecting, just a little bit, that he would have some ready explanation that would reassure her that she *could* trust him.

The music ended, and they dropped their arms from each other and stood for a moment on the floor. St. James brought his finger to rub across his lip. Miss Murdock said in a subdued voice, "You had better escort me back to your grandmother now, milord."

The chords of a waltz struck up. "No, Miss Murdock. I think we have your question to answer," he replied, and for the second time that evening, her hand was taken, held out to the correct position, and a man's arm settled around her waist. She remembered Andrew's instruction, placed her hand upon St. James' shoulder, and it seemed as though her hand was heated by a low burning flame. His arm around her waist was searing fire, and when they moved out into the dance, she glanced up into his eyes and saw to her utter consternation that he had hooded them against her, leaving only part of their expression to be seen and covering the other half.

Something has changed.

"Did I tell you, Miss Murdock, that your hair is very becoming in that mode?"

"No, I--I don't think you did," she answered. His body, fluid and taut, controlled their steps, their rhythm.

"I suppose I was remiss and did not tell you that your skin warms my eyes when I look upon your neck, your shoulders. . . and elsewhere?"

She faltered in her dancing, the low swoop of her neckline embarrassing her when before she had been satisfied that it was in fact, quite modest.

"Ah, it warms my eyes all the more when you flush rosily as you are doing now." He brought his half-hooded eyes again to her face, her own rounded eyes. "And as I told you once before, you have very fine eyes and they appear all the finer when you blush, for you look so suddenly exposed. You enjoy hiding, do you not, Miss Murdock--" He leaned his head toward hers, drawing back his lids and the full impact of his golden stare impaled her brown ones. "Lizzie. . ." He drew out her name into a teasing taste on his tongue. His nostrils flared and she realized that he had drawn her inexorably closer to him in the moves of the waltz, until they were not quite touching, but she could feel his heat radiating from his body like so many small, damning flames.

With an effort, she put more distance between them, and even that was bittersweet, for his arm slid around her waist with maddening friction so that she wanted to embrace him and flee from him all at once. "Do not make me slap your face again here in Almacks, milord," she warned him in a frightened, hushed voice.

"But that would answer so much speculation," he returned. "For I am sure everyone is dying to know whose palm print it is upon my cheek and if it could, in fact, be from the young lady now dancing in my arms. Shall we satisfy their curiosity? I think we shall."

The blood came roaring into her ears, and her feet deserted her, leaving her standing still, facing him. That they were utterly conspicuous, she had no doubt. The music went on and the other dancers moved in circles around them. And she was certain he was going to kiss her, for reasons known only to himself, and she was equally certain she would slap him, for her hand was jerking in his own for release and she was unable to control her response any more than she had been able to control her heart's quick thumping and the weak, warm flush of her body that evidenced just how very damnedably enmeshed she was in the spell he had laid so thickly, adroitly and bloody *quickly* upon her.

But St. James surprised her by taking not a step forward, but a step backward. He was laughing softly at her dumbfounded (and she feared, disappointed) look, and he swept her hand, fingers spread, to the side of his face, laying it in the prior branding of her palm in a mock slap that showed everyone the perfect match her hand was to his mark. The dancers about them stuttered to a stop and the musician's playing died in mid chord.

Miss Murdock, with high color, stood in the center of this attention. St. James caressed her palm across his cheek and even in all her chagrin, she was aware of the pale, burning skin of it, how her fingers with a mind of their own twitched into a caress, causing his eyebrow to raise a degree higher in his forehead. Then he slid her palm down to his mouth, and she understood where the other had been for show, this was for her alone, and he kissed the palm of her hand with an intensity that made her for the first time in her life, feel as if she would faint.

And all she was aware of as everything swam in her eyes was St. James' low, delighted laughter.

Then Andrew was there, and she was not sure how it came about, still being nearly insensible upon her feet. St. James was gone and she was in Andrew's arms as they had been in the salon just a few hours ago, and he was whispering with desperation in her ear, "Hand on my shoulder. One, two, three! One, two, three!" Her feet moved and her eyes cleared and little by little she realized that Andrew had saved her. The musicians struck up again and the other dancers began to dance and everything went from chaos to a veneer of normalcy. "Where is he?" she asked in a numb voice.

"He is gone, Lizzie. He has gone."

"You have tutored me well, Andrew," she choked. "When a man makes improper advances you told me I was to swoon from the thrill and danger of it."

"Just dance, Lizzie. Just dance."

She did, and although she did not immediately understand the importance of it, she came to realize that if she had left the floor after St. James' display and not danced with Andrew, there was no one in society that would not have snubbed her and branded her a fallen woman.

As it was, she was dangerously close.

Chapter Seventeen

"What now?" she asked Andrew, for she was well aware that the dance could not go on forever. Nor did she wish it to, for she wanted nothing better than to go curl in a ball somewhere and cry her eyes out.

"I do not know," he told her, worried. "I can not possibly dance two dances in a row with you after his little show. I can only think that I lead you off the floor with as little fuss as possible and we leave immediately. Damn him! Why would he do such a thing to you? He has effectively ruined all your chances with any other suitor, for it will be thought that you are used--Nevermind!"

"Goods," she ended tonelessly. "I expect that was his intention all a-long."

Andrew gave her a sharp glance and she saw that he had a deal more maturity in his eyes than she had witnessed before. "For whatever bloody purpose?" he demanded.

"Oh, nevermind, Andrew, for I can no longer even guess myself," she answered with weariness.

The music ended and he took her arm and as judiciously as possible led her from the floor, but they were not even to the edge when Ryan Tempton stepped to in front of them. "Miss Murdock," he asked with a sober smile. "May I have this dance?"

Miss Murdock did not even have a chance to answer for Andrew exclaimed in a relieved whisper, "Good man, Tempton! Take her," and she was passed from the one to the other in short order and headed out onto the floor again.

"Oh, Ryan," she began, dispensing with formalities as soon as the music started. "You should not have put your reputation at risk by danc-ing with me. Bad enough that Andrew--"

"Not at all, Miss Murdock," he returned with a warm grin on his raw-boned face. "I intend that we have such a good time out here that everyone will be rushing to dance with you to see what all the fuss is about."

She laughed in surprise, admiring his unorthodox approach. "I fear that I shall not be much help, for I am not enjoying myself in the least!"

"That is only because you have not had the proper partner, but I am here now and so that problem is remedied," he told her with mock lofti-ness.

"Is it as bad as I fear?" she asked.

"It is merely all in how you look upon it," he told her with attempted lightness. "If you act as though you were deeply affected, then it shall be every bit as bad as you fear and worse, but if you can endeavor to act as though St. James were only being his usual naughty self, and that you put no weight on his actions, then they will have nothing to believe but that he were merely misbehaving again. Which will hardly shock anyone. So, please, Miss Murdock, try to laugh and look carefree, and I am sure between Earl Larrimer and myself, and one or two others, we can get you out of this nearly intact."

Miss Murdock did laugh, because he managed to make it all seem somehow ridiculous. "I should not even care, because I plan on leaving at the end of the week. It is just more shock than anything, that he could truly be so bad!"

"I'm afraid I suffered the same shock on the night of your unfortunate meeting with him. But I am beginning to think there is usually a method to his madness. Although, I confess, I do think very badly of this night's piece of work. But I also happen to know that what he was about earlier today directly benefits you, so I have that to measure with also."

"Really? What?"

"No, no. I am sure he means it as a surprise so I will not tell. Only let me assure you that I think, knowing what little I do of you, that you shall enjoy it very much."

"Well," Miss Murdock said with returning spirit, "I was certainly surprised this evening and I can assure you that it was not at all to my liking! So forgive me if I look forward to this further surprise with some trepidation."

He laughed and she was moved to join him and this time it was not quite so forced, and she realized that it all was as easy as he had said, for although a great many people were still watching her, they were now shaking their heads as if to say to themselves, *that St. James! Up to his old tricks. No wonder she had obviously already slapped him once before. Good for her.*

She pondered this then frowned with worry. "Oh, dear, Mister Tempton, but I believe for every notch I go up in their eyes, he goes down three."

"Not at all, for if he is showing interest in you and you are clearly not allowing him leeway, then they have nothing to believe but that good shall prevail and he will in the end do the proper and propose. I am proud to say, Miss Murdock, that I believe you are fast being hailed as a 'rake-reformer'!"

"Good God!" she exclaimed, almost losing her step, but he guided her on without incident. "And he planned it all, I am sure. That bloody fool!"

He twinkled down at her. "I suspect the same, Miss Murdock, for he seemed to me today rather taken with his notion of marrying you."

"Well, I am not at all taken with the notion of marrying him," she returned. "And as you are aware that he wishes to marry me for no other reason than--than to obtain my horse, then I think you can well understand why," she said.

"I can not believe he would be going to all this trouble for a horse, Miss Murdock."

"Well," she said, dropping her eyes from his in sudden guilt, "he is!" And now I am lying for him, she thought. He treats me shabbily in front of several hundred people, and I am lying for him. Lord help her, whatever next?

"No, no. I don't believe that. St. James seems to hold you in a respect that he reserves for few people."

"And he has a fine way of showing it!"

"Nevertheless," Ryan coaxed, "I am sure he saw in you something from the first that the rest of us are just beginning to discover."

"Yes," Miss Murdock returned, angry at St. James, herself, and the whole mess, "he says I have a way of asking questions that he can not answer, and then he goes on to answer them in a way which then makes me wish I had not asked!" And she blushed hotly, and shoved ruthlessly the image out of her mind of--Oh, damn it! She had to think of something else!

"Really?" Ryan asked, a great deal diverted. "That is a very odd basis for a marriage: to be forever playing games with each other."

"Well, he is a very odd man," Miss Murdock returned, and was amazed that her voice had taken on a defensive quality. First I attack him, but if anyone else does, I turn right around and defend him. She glanced up at Ryan's laughing face. "Oh, do not point it out to me, for I have already seen it," she said. "I can not wait for this night to be over."

"Forgive me if I can not agree," Ryan teased. "For I can not remember when I have had such a jolly time at Almacks or a better time dancing with a female. T'is almost better than Whites!" he confided.

Their dance came to an end and Ryan went to take her once again from the floor, headed very much in the direction of Lord Tempton, his brother, so that he could be convinced to come to Miss Murdock's aid also, but he did not reach him for they were stopped and she was asked to dance by a nice looking young man whom she had not even made acquaintance with before.

Her suspicion that Andrew had been busy enlisting another man to aid her in her hour of need was laid to rest when she asked her surprised partner upon taking the dance floor with him, "And how were you prevailed upon to rescue me from being ruined, Mister Thomas?"

Choking back an incredulous laugh, he answered, "They could not have prevailed upon me to *not* come and dance with you, Miss Murdock, for I wish to see for myself what all the hullabaloo is about!"

From there they struck up an excellent conversation, and Miss Murdock, distracted by his banter, found to her surprise that she was having a very good time and, to her gratitude, her partner told her that he was having a most unexpected good time also. "It is usually frightfully dull, Miss Murdock, and we all have you to thank for livening it up. And the Duke, of course," he dared to add.

"Oh, he is just being as he usually is," she said with a great deal of feigned unconcern. "And you must not put too much weight upon it for I am sure he will be here the next time making some other poor girl the object of everyone's attention. At least until the ladies of the board have had enough of his antics and revoke his vouchers from him again!"

"That, Miss Murdock, will be a sad day indeed! I have not the pleasure of his acquaintance, but from his reputation, I had no idea he had such a spirit of fun! Rather naughty, yes, but I can see that he must know you well enough that he was confident you would see the humor in it and so no harm done."

Miss Murdock agreed.

She was most gratified when yet another man asked for her hand for dancing, and from that point on she did not see any of the party she had come with until Andrew managed to catch her for a final dance. "I have been trying for an hour to step back in!" he told her with a pleased grin. "I think we have managed it."

"Thank you, Andrew," she told him. "It really was not necessary, for I am leaving soon at any rate, but I would have so hated walking from the floor dejected and humiliated. Did he leave me there?"

"No. I--I'm afraid I busted in, for I very much feared what he would dare to do next. But he was not at all upset and only nodded to me and asked if I could handle it. Then he turned his back and left directly. I don't even think he spoke to grandmother again. The place was positively roaring with speculation."

"I thought all that roaring was the blood in my ears," she admitted.

"Thank God you were still lucid enough to dance!" he told her, fretting. "I just do not remember St. James ever being so, well, *cruel*."

"It was cruel, wasn't it?"

He didn't answer her and she was grateful. They were both silent for a moment, and then she asked, "Did I look as close to fainting as I felt?"

"No. Just very stunned."

"He may not have realized--" and she stopped, biting her lip.

Andrew comforted her. "I am sure he did not!" He swallowed and continued in a low voice, "And thank you, Lizzie, for telling me all that nonsense in the salon this evening."

"Oh," she said, feeling foolish. "I--oh, dear."

He gave a sudden laugh, his old self. "I knew all along. You were doing it just a tad too brown, you know!" With that he swung her into an exuberant circle that had everyone that remained (for quite a few had left with the lateness of the hour) once again staring at Miss Murdock. But she only laughed and did not care.

She would not find out until some time later that if the crowd in Almacks had not been roaring with speculation, as Andrew had said, that they all would have heard the gun shot that was fired from outside shortly after St. James made his exit.

If St. James felt any satisfaction with the predicament he had placed Miss Murdock in, he did not show it. His face was unconcerned as he nodded to Bertie, who, he would wager, he had to thank for the fine crowd attracted as witnesses tonight, and several other familiar faces as he made his way through the crowd at Almacks. He would have liked to turn, even once, to see if Andrew were indeed handling it, but an air of carelessness better suited his purposes.

When he reached the wide double doors, he pushed his shoulder against them hard, and went out into the cold of the night. There he paused, leaned for a single moment against one of the cool, white pillars that stood on either side of the entrance with his arm stretched above him and his head resting on it. But he did not close his eyes. He stared out into the darkness that was beyond the twin torches that lit the steps below him. After a moment, he dug out his pocket watch with his other hand, opened it, glanced at it, and then returned it. Not a bad piece of work for under thirty minutes.

Tyler would not be expecting him to be out so soon.

He moved from his uncharacteristically weary stance and as he walked on down the steps, there was nothing left in his demeanor to suggest that he had been affected at all.

He turned right and started down the long line of coaches facing him, most of them abandoned for now as the coachmen had left their posts to pop in to nearby pubs, secure in the knowledge that their employers would be preoccupied for some time to come. The light from the intermittent street lamps flickered across his face and his fine wine coat made a very nice target from the darkness surrounding him.

St. James heard a loud *crack!* and felt pain in the side of his chest and arm, as though stung by hornets, and was knocked off balance from the force of it. He let himself fall, but controlled it to the degree that he landed between the two coaches he had been passing, and he rolled into a crouch, his hand flying to beneath his coat for a pistol that was not there. The horses he had disturbed by his sudden dive beneath their noses tossed their heads and backed up a few steps, and then as they must have smelled blood coming from him, neighed loudly.

"Damnation!" St. James whispered to them. "Put out a bloody billet why don't you two nags?" but his left hand moved to soothe them as he peered into the alley that lay beyond. He winced at the movement, but he did not look down to see how badly he was injured.

He moved along the off-side of the horses and into the shadow of the coach they were harnessed to, then to the back corner of it. He crouched and using the wheel as cover, glanced into the dark mouth of the mew that ran between the building that housed Almacks and its neighbor to the left of it. A conveyance came at great speed toward him from down the street, and he crouched down lower into the shadow and turned his head to see if this were some new peril. But it was Tyler, driving his horses hard with one hand and resting one of his lordship's pistols on his knee with the other. St. James jumped to the side of the horses as they came up beside him, grabbed the near one's bridle, and slowed it to a stop beside the coach he was using as cover.

And very nearly got shot for his troubles by a nervous Tyler.

That man, made a bit more nervous by the fact that he had nearly shot who he had been coming to aid, jumped down and St. James gave him a crooked grin, his eyes bright and hard, but he said nothing. He held out his hand which Tyler filled. "The other?" Tyler whispered, but St. James shook his head. Then he darted from behind the coach, leaving Tyler behind, and back onto the sidewalk to the corner of Almacks, the pistol held loose but ready at his side as he half crouched against the brick of the wall and glanced into the blackness of the mew that ran along the side of the building. Utter darkness met his eyes. Without any apparent hesitation, he slid around the corner and made his way into the deepest of shadows. There he crouched for a moment, letting his eyes adjust to this new lack of light even as they were in constant motion. His piercing gaze pounced upon and marked several obstacles. A low row of barrels that had not yet been stored. A wagon resting empty and unhitched to one side, leaving but a narrow pathway around it in the narrowness between the two buildings. And in direct line across from him another barrel sitting upright and alone at the corner of the opposite building. St. James moved toward it, paused as he noticed the roll marks in the dirt of the alley. Then at the barrel itself, scuff marks where someone had righted it, and footprints throughout it all, all alike, indicating but one person. He knelt behind the barrel, saw that someone had a clear view of the sidewalk he had just been strolling down, and as he did so, he smelled freshly discharged gunpowder coming from the wood. He lifted a hand, ran it along the edge of the barrel's top, brought it up to peer at it. Then he cursed for his hand was covered with his own blood.

But he had no time for that now.

A fresh flurry of horsehooves came not from the street but from the dark mew at his back, and he sank down into shadow once again, lifted his pistol and trained it on the narrow space between the abandoned wagon and the brick side of the building. A small horse came through it with a smallish figure on its back. St. James waited until the hard riding horseman was nearly upon him before rising, spooking the horse into nearly unseating its rider.

"M'lord!" Steven gasped as he controlled the cob purchased for him that day. "He's headed east toward the river."

"Riding?"

"On foot!"

St. James grasped the lad and pulled him down from the skittish horse. "Well done! Find Tyler. Tell him to drive the carriage as you have said." With a single leap, he jumped into the ratty saddle that they had tacked the sad little horse with. He winced as his chest gave a fresh reminder of his injury, and then he turned the cob and headed it back through the small gap of the mew. He cantered through the main thoroughfare on the other end of the alley, rode south on it for a few yards and then turned into another shadowy mew that pointed toward the river. The cob was no Behemoth, nor even a Gold-Leaf-Lying-in-the-Sun, but with his assailant still presumably upon foot, St. James expected to come across him quickly. Especially when he would have taken little notice to the dirty urchin of a boy riding a sorry nag of a horse who had come across him. He should have no knowledge that he had been spotted, his direction noted, and that his intended victim was fast riding him down.

It was not until a third alley that St. James caught site of his quarry. He was running, but did not seem panicked in any way, indicating that he must believe himself safely away. Whether he was confident that he had done the duke enough grievous harm to insure his death, St. James could not guess, but his mouth tightened into furious grimace as he thought that if he did not find out soon precisely what his injury was, the man may very well have achieved his objective.

At the sound of horse hooves bearing down upon him with alarming quickness, the man turned. In the dim light, St. James saw a great deal of fearful astonishment on his face as he must have recognized that red velvet coat. But then he had no chance for any other expression or words, for St. James kicked the cob, commanding without question his supreme effort, which the cob gave to him as if a wolf had snapped at his heels. St. James with unrelenting direction on his reins ran the cob into the man, and over him.

There was a cry of fear and then pain. The cob squealed and managed a little leap to avoid the man fallen beneath him. St. James abandoned the saddle, landed awkwardly, turned swiftly, and as the man rolled groaning onto his back his first sight was of two gold buckled shoes, one on either side of his head. The mouth of a pistol barrel pointed down at his face.

The cob skittered around in a small circle at the loss of its rider, nickered and then stood trembling. The man stared up and St. James stared down. A large drop of blood ran down the barrel of the gun, hesitated, and then dripped onto the man's forehead. It ran down his temple and into his ear.

"Your weapon?" St. James asked. "Where is it?"

The man blinked. There was not much light but St. James could see that he was older than himself and extremely dirty. His hair was graying and his face was a great deal scarred. One eyelid kept twitching, but whether that was from some old injury or an indication of his distress at the situation he was in, St. James could not have said. Neither did he care. The assailant licked his lips and after a false start managed to say, "'Neath me coat."

The coat, so many rags, lay open for want of quite a few buttons and a butt of a pistol was just discernible at the man's waist. "Remove it," St. James commanded, "slowly and carefully and hand it to me."

The man's hand did not seem to want to work. It shook as it moved with infinite caution to his waistband beneath his coat. "Inch it out," St. James told him.

The man inched it out, his eyes locked with the duke's, the pistol St. James held a great exclamation point between their gazes. "Take it by the barrel," St. James instructed.

The man's hand fumbled, grabbed the barrel. With slow caution he brought the gun, a two barreled affair, in a stiff-armed arc up to in front of St. James' waist. St. James reached out and took it with his free right hand. Then St. James cocked the second hammer on it and pointed it down into the man's face.

The man looked up into the two pistol barrels trained on him. "I--It is all a mistake. . . milord!" he panicked.

"A very grave mistake on your part," St. James agreed.

"T'wasn't me that tried to kill you."

"I have in my hand your pistol with one chamber already empty. From the amount of powder I feel on it, I would say it has been fired within the past few minutes."

"What--what do you want me to do?" the man asked in desperation.

St. James moved back two steps, both guns still pointed on the man. "Get up!"

The man rolled, sat up, his eyes never leaving the duke nor his weapons. "Aye. I know when I'm beat," he said.

"Stand up," St. James commanded, and he stepped back again, but this time he reeled and it was only the wall behind him that saved him from falling. "Slowly."

The man stood up as slowly as he sat up the moment before. "I am not your enemy, milord," he persuaded. "I have no desire to see you dead. I am only a poor man trying to feed my children."

"Good. Then you have no care if I discover who has put you about this business."

"I--I do not know who is behind this."

St. James leaned hard against the wall and although the pistol he had taken from the man that was in his right hand was aimed at his assailant steadily, the left one was shaking. "How were you contacted?"

The man was silent, and St. James prodded him by saying, "I am growing rather tired from my loss of blood and as I have already squeezed the trigger and the only thing that keeps a bullet from entering your heart is my thumb on the hammer, I should not take overlong about this."

"By the same way as before, milord," the man strangled out.

"Before?"

"Aye, when it was t'other duke, the duke before you, out in Lincolnshire."

St. James' eyes flared into unholy fire. "You were involved in that?"

"I didn't mean to be, milord!" the man babbled. "I thought it to only be a robbery. I had kids to feed then, too, you know."

"You must have a great many children," St. James observed. "How were you contacted then? How were you contacted now?"

But the man seemed more intent upon pleading his case than providing information. "Never did I do it again, 'tween then and this day. That night turned me right off of t'business, milord. But then I gets this message sayin' if I's wished to keep that in t'past, I had best get t'one that shoulda been done that night and wasn't in t'coach. What was I t'do, I ask you?"

"Who sent you the message? Talk, man--"

But St. James' words were cut off by the sudden sound of carriage wheels and horses' hooves coming at a high speed into the mouth of the mew. St. James held his weapons on his quarry, but his attention shifted at this new distraction, and the man took the only chance he was likely to get.

He jumped to the side, snagged the cob that had stayed near, and put the smallish horse between he and St. James and with a yell, threatened it into a run with him beside it. St. James lurched from the wall, staggered as he did so.

The carriage horses were reined in at the sight of the fleeing man and the cob running toward them. St. James saw that it was Tyler at the reins, standing and pulling his pistol. Steven was up beside him. Before anyone could divine his intention or call out, the boy stood and dived forward off the carriage and onto the half crouched, running man. "Damn ya, lad!" Tyler shouted down into the darkness. The man and the boy struggled in the shadow of the carriage and it could not be seen who was who or even what was happening.

The cob reacted badly to the flying figure that had half landed on him before taking down the assailant. He reared back, startling the carriage horses. The carriage lurched forward. St. James found himself on one side of it and Steven and the man on the other. "Damn it, damn it, *damn it!*" He reeled to the head of the horses that Tyler reined in, steadying himself by leaning against the near one's neck. His hands held both pistols, thumbs still on the hammers of each. Blood stained the chest and side of his coat, and his left arm was drenched with it.

Tyler was making desperate attempt to control the horses, and at the same time trying to aim the pistol left in his care at the man, but he did not dare squeeze off a shot for fear of hitting Steven. The noise was chaotic and echoed against the walls of the buildings on either side of them. Nervous whickering, St. James cursing, Tyler damning the horses and Steven in equal measure, and the panting and scuffling from the man and the boy mixed with their cries of determination and pain.

"*Damnation!*" St. James said as the carriage horse he leaned upon spooked and half reared in the shafts. At the same time he glimpsed the two shadowed figures rolling on the ground and the cob giving an ill-

tempered kick that went over their heads by inches. The cob's kick landed on the near carriage horse's hindquarters and it squealed and jumped
forward. St. James was knocked to the ground. He fought the blackness
in his vision. His left hand, now beyond endurance, loosed the hammer
and his dueling pistol went off with what a *boom* that echoed endlessly
in the narrow mew. Then he lost the gun and he had no time to wonder
if he had shot himself, someone else, or if the bullet had only bit into the
ground. He rolled as the horses, now out of their minds with fear, bolted
forward. Tyler had ducked instinctively at the sound of the shot and now
he was nearly toppled from the driver's seat. St. James rolled again and
was just missed by the front carriage wheel. He clawed at the ground
with his fast weakening left hand, his right still holding the confiscated
gun, his one remaining weapon. By some miracle, his thumb still held
the hammer at the ready.

Tyler succeeded in controlling the horses but the carriage moving up
had removed the shadow that had been over the struggling boy and
man. St. James could now see them both in the light of the moon. Steven was on the bottom, which did not surprise St. James as his attacker
was older, heavier and much wiser in the ways of combat. St. James
clawed himself along with his weak and bloody left hand, his body
squirming until whatever wound he had in his chest screamed agony in
an endless piercing. His right hand stretched before him on the ground,
holding his pistol as he searched for a chance to shoot.

The man arched his back bringing his head from where it had been
close to the boy's neck. He managed to pull something from some secret
hiding place upon his person. The sudden flash of a knife gleamed
sharply in the moonlight.

Then three things happened at once. St. James would forever be uncertain of what happened first, second and last.

There was a startled cry that St. James supposed to be fear as Steven must have seen the blade of the knife (but which he would later
damningly come to understand was a sound of shock). Then Steven said
a single, bewildered word, "Da?"

At the same precise time, St. James heard the man say, "God, no,
Steven! Say t'isn't you, la--"

And at the same precise time, St. James loosed his thumb on the
hammer of the man's own pistol. The man's body jerked back in mid cry
before the crack of the shot was even heard. What St. James would always remember most was that brief, eternal silence between the man's
words cutting off and the final boom of the gun, like thunder following
lightening that has already struck.

St. James' gold eyes widened in sudden agony that had nothing to do
with his own injury. The man was half knocked, half slumped off of Steven and lay with his face up to the full light of the moon.

Steven cried out in a voice filled with abhorrence and pain and the
shock of tragic loss, "Me God, but t'was me own father! Me own Da!"

And St. James lay his face down on his outstretched arm that still held the smoking gun and shuddered.

Tyler's hands pulled at him, but he never raised his head, just motioned with the gun in his hand in Steven's direction in silent order that Tyler attend to him.

"Lad," Tyler said over that boy's incoherent speech that consisted of no understanding at this point. "Lad!" Tyler said more sharply. "I need your assistance, lad! Can you manage?" and something in Tyler's voice broke through to him for he became silent except for the heaving breathing in his chest.

Tyler went on with force. "We have to get his lordship into the coach and away from here. He is bleeding badly."

"Me father," Steven said. "Me da."

"I know, son. But your father put a bullet into St. James there and if we do not attend to him he is going to die also. Do you understand?" He picked up the knife and shoved it beneath Steven's eyes. "Do you see that, Steven. He thought this man were gonna kill ya. He didn't know it was your Da. *Neither did you*," he added a little brutally.

Steven was only gasping.

"Do you want to see his lordship *die*, lad?" Tyler asked.

"No."

"Then you have to help me! Can you do it, boy?"

Steven nodded, and a second later, they were rolling St. James over and struggling to sit him upright. They put their shoulders under his arms, forced him to his feet. He groaned once as his left arm was pulled around Steven's shoulders, and then he was oblivious.

"He's out of it," Tyler said as they shoved him into the carriage. "Tie that cob to the back, boy, and then drive, do ya hear?"

"What about me father?"

"Later, son. Haven't time now, do you ken? We'll come back, I promise, but first we have t'get his lordship taken care of or we'll have two bodies t'deal with 'stead a one!"

Steven went to slam shut the carriage door, but Tyler forestalled him. "Hand me that knife," he said and Steven bent over the body of his fallen father, took the knife that was at his side, large tears streaming down his face and gave it to Tyler as he had been bid. "Fine lad!" Tyler spared. "God help ya, but you're a good and brave one. Now on with it, son!"

And so saying he left the conveying of he and the duke home to a distraught thirteen year old boy, but he could see nothing for it. If he did not do something now, St. James was sure to die from loss of blood. He closed the carriage door behind him with a slam, bent over the unconscious man with the knife and slit his clothes from his chest and his sleeve from his arm with quick precision. There was so much blood that it took him a moment to locate the injuries. The bullet had grazed along one of St. James' ribs just above his heart, entered the underside of his upper arm and exited out the other side. "God a might! If he'd been turned another hair toward the man, he woulda been plugged proper for all," Tyler muttered.

He tried stopping the bleeding with the coat he had cut off, but velvet is not a very good packing for a wound. "Damn it! Can't make a tourniquet, have nothin' to stuff in there--" and then hit with inspiration, he pulled out his bag of chaw, opened it, and pulled out great handfuls and packed it into his lordship's chest.

Only when he saw that this appeared to be working did he become conscious of anything else. With a start he realized that the coach had not yet begun to move. "Hell and Damnation!" He kicked open the door and flung himself out. Nothing but silence and darkness met him in the alley. The cob was gone and Steven was no where to be seen. The boy's father lay staring sightlessly up at the glow of the moon.

Tyler, who had just begun feeling as though he had some control of the situation, slammed the door behind him in near despair, took the last bit of tobacco that was left in his bag, put it in his cheek, flung the bag to the ground and climbed hastily onto the driver's seat. He slapped the reins onto the horses, yelled at them, no longer even caring of the noise for if the shots being fired hadn't brought anyone then he doubted a common, "Yah!" to the horses was going to. He drove hell for leather to the duke's home on what seemed to be the longest ride of his life.

It was an hour later when St. James returned to consciousness. He recognized the familiar surroundings of his bedchamber. The fire was built up and threw flickering light out to join what came from the lamps on the tables at either side of the head of his bed. Effington was bent over him, examining his side and Tyler was holding a third lamp over his chest.

"Steven?" St. James' asked, but they did not even hear his weak question, for they were bickering in low voices to each other.

"How could you pack his wound with tobacco!" Effington asked with distaste.

"I hadn't nothin' else, man," Tyler returned. "I suppose if you'd been there, you would have had something a good deal more dainty t'place in him, like that ridiculous night cap a yourn for instance!"

"I would have never been there," Effington pointed out in a strait-laced voice. He looked incongruous leaning over his lordship with the point of his night cap dangling down and his sleeping gown making him appear as some ghost. "Well," he conceded at last, "it did *slow* the bleeding." Then he added, "I could weep, for look at his splendid clothes."

"You will have to burn them," Tyler informed him, "as soon as we manage to get the rest off 'im."

St. James, becoming a little more lucid as Tyler set down the lamp and they proceeded to jar him about in attempt to get him out of his clothes, said, "T'is why. . . I insist upon plain clothing. . . no great loss when faced with this. . . predicament."

Effington frowned down at him, "There you are, milord. I hope you can anticipate that I will be writing yet another letter of resignation over this night's work! But not until we get you safely out of danger for I daren't leave you to Tyler's hands."

A ghost of a smile flickered across St. James' lips, but he only asked, "Where. . . is the boy?"

Tyler and Effington exchanged glances. Tyler went to the sideboard, selected a bottle of whiskey as Effington pulled off the last of his lordship's bloody clothing. Tyler came toward St. James with the bottle. "Need t'get some of this in you, milord. Wasn't expectin' you to come 'round."

St. James raised a shaky right hand, took the bottle of whiskey from his groom, but before drinking it, he asked again, "What has become of the lad?"

Tyler went to the fireplace. St. James turned his gold eyes to Effington, but the valet was preoccupied by saying to himself, "Basin of water and linens. Shan't be a moment," and he left the room.

"Tyler!" St. James demanded, his voice a croak. "Do not tell me. . . that first bullet hit Steven?"

"No, milord," Tyler hastened to say. He pulled a red hot poker from the fireplace, nodded in satisfaction before placing it back. "Now drink t'whiskey, milord, for I'll be at ye as soon as Effington comes back."

St. James, with a curse, swung the bottle to his lips and drank as much as he could manage in as short a time possible. He broke off for air and gasped, "How bad, Tyler?"

"Grazed your rib and went through the underside of your arm. If you had been facing him by another inch, he would have drilled it right through your heart."

St. James had no time to ponder on this for Effington returned to the room, linens slung over his shoulder, a basin of clean water in his hands which he set down upon the table. He picked up the lamp that Tyler had left on the sideboard. "What do I do now?" he asked Tyler.

"Put down that lamp," Tyler told him. "And you'd better move the one on that side of t'bed outta reach of him," and he moved the one near him as he spoke, "so he don't flail about and catch t'whole house afire. Then hold him down and smother him with a pillow if you have to, for we can't have him screaming and waking t'household up."

St. James took another determined gulp from the bottle and then Effington was there, taking it from him. He was grinning as he did so.

"Damn you. . . Effington." St. James glared and struggled to sit up.

Effington shoved him easily down again. "Now, now, milord," he said with more satisfaction than sympathy. "Take your medicine like a good boy and let it be a lesson to you."

"I'm. . . going to. . . bloody--" St. James spat out.

Effington clapped a hand over his patient's mouth. He raised his sleeping gown up so that he could put his knee on St. James' shoulder. Tyler laughed at the valet's skinny, white leg holding milord down, but he did not delay. With methodical quickness he dug into the duke's wound, pulling out tobacco as best as he could.

St. James jerked with enough force to knock his valet's night cap from his head as he had his hands full keeping his employer as still as possible. There was a great deal of noise coming from his clamped mouth and his eyes spat fire and hate and damnation upon their souls.

Then Tyler got up from his knees, sweating, and fetched the poker.

"There's still a great deal of tobacco in there," Effington panted.

"It'll burn," Tyler reassured him. Then added, "Oh, Lordy, but it will burn. Be ready!" He set the poker into the wound.

St. James spasmed, his body going rigid. Tyler scrambled to sit on his legs while still holding the iron. Effington gagged and choked, his face turning green, and then, mercifully, St. James blacked out.

Chapter Eighteen
Thursday Morning

Miss Murdock sat up in bed and stared with disbelief at the window. Oh, he wouldn't, *couldn't* be so bold as to think she would come to him again tonight. Not after his display at Almacks!

But the tapping came again, and where it had been gentle the night before, it was more insistent this night, and she hurried out of bed and put on her robe. As she had no doubt who it would be, she paused to light her lamp and went to the window. With exasperation, she pulled back the drapes, shoved up the sash, and whispered without preamble, "You may tell his lordship that *nothing* he could say could induce me to come--" but she stopped as she got a closer look at Steven's face.

"He's not down there, miss," he whimpered. His teeth were chattering but Lizzie had sudden certainty it was not from the cold.

"Come in, Steven. My God, what has happened?" She assisted him into the room, the flame in the lamp jumping from the draft of the open window and making shadows move along the wall. He stood shivering in the middle of the floor looking quite lost. "Oh, what ever are you doing out at this hour of the night alone?" she exclaimed. She took him by the shoulders, led him to the chaise lounge and sat him down upon it. Then she gathered a blanket from her own bed and wrapped it around his narrow shoulders. "No wonder you are so cold," she soothed, "for you are all wet." And she drew her hands back and catching sight of them in the light from the lamp let out a little exclamation of horror. "Blood! My God, Steven, are you hurt?" She knelt so that her face was below his and looked up into his miserable eyes. "You must show me where you are hurt, for you are bleeding, Steven!"

"T'is not my blood," he mumbled.

Miss Murdock made a conscious effort not to panic. "Whose blood is it, Steven?"

"Me--me father's. And St. James'," and he cried in a great burst of confusion as well as grief, and she held him in her arms and comforted him as best she could. All the time her heart hammered and she could only think, and then refuse to think, that St. James was dead. Oh, God, he was dead.

"Steven," she said. "Can you tell me what has happened? Can you at least tell me if St. James is alive? Has he been badly injured?" and she tried to keep her voice even for she feared that if she indicated just how frantic she was that she would frighten him to such a degree that she would never get any answers from him.

"He was alive the last I saw, but I do not know if he shall live," Steven sniffled. "But me father, me da--he's dead," and his tears intensified in proportion to the knot growing in Miss Murdock's stomach.

"Where is he now?" Miss Murdock asked in desperation.

"Lying in the middle of an alley for someone to find in the morning," Steven sobbed.

Miss Murdock gave a sound of pure horror. "No! Do not tell me that you left St. James to bleed to death in the middle of an alley?"

But he shook his head. "No, miss. Tyler was taking milord home. Me father, he's the one lying dead in the mew."

"Oh, thank--" but Miss Murdock had the presence of mind to leave that exclamation unfinished. Instead she asked, "Can you sit here by yourself for just one moment? I will return directly, I assure you. You won't leave, will you?" she asked in sudden panic.

"No. I have no place t'go, for I don't know how I am t'tell me mother," he told her.

"Oh, Lord help us," Miss Murdock breathed, then she was up from her crouch in front of him and hurrying to the door without even pausing for slippers. She opened the door, went into the hall and ran down it in her bare feet. She stopped in front of the door she knew to be Andrew's and tapped on it, biting her lip in fear that she would awaken anyone else. He did not answer, and with a little burst of impatience, she turned the knob and entered.

From the hallway, she thought she heard the soft click of another door's closing, but she was in no mood to debate within herself whether it was in fact what she had heard. Instead, she went to Andrew's bed and felt up by his pillow until she found his head, and then patted down a few inches to his shoulder, which was bare, and she gave it a fierce shake. "Andrew," she hissed. "Andrew, do wake up!"

He sat up in his bed, nearly hitting her with the top of his head. "What? Who's there?" he asked more loudly than she would have liked.

"Shh! It's Lizzie."

"Lizzie!"

There were so many things she could have read into his voice that she did not even want to begin. "Yes. I fear your cousin has been injured in some way. Possibly," and she swallowed, "possibly grievously."

"St. James?" he asked. He swung his legs over the side of the bed. She was grateful for the darkness in the room, for she had no way of knowing in what manner he slept and had no desire to find out now. She stepped back from the bed. "When did this happen!" he demanded.

"I--I don't know. Tonight, obviously. Oh, Andrew, you must ride 'round immediately to see what has happened!"

"I intend to," he said with a new grimness in his voice. Then he frightened her completely by saying, "I should have been with him!"

"No!" she begged, but he was already pushing her to the door.

"Out," he said.

And she understood that of course he wished to get dressed. "Send me word, Andrew, as quickly as you can."

"I will," he promised and shoved her out of his room. She ran back to her own rooms, breathless and pale with apprehension, but slowed before entering, not wishing to burst in on Steven and upset him any more than he already was. She slipped through the door, and was relieved to find him still upon the chaise lounge, slumped on his side along the length of it, his feet hanging down.

"Steven?" she whispered after shutting the door and he had not stirred. She had the sudden thought that he had been injured after all and that in all his grief, he had not noticed it, but when she went to him, she saw that he was sleeping, his eyes darkly circled and his young face sagging.

"Oh, Steven," she murmured. She removed his shoes, which were very worn, and tucked his feet up onto the lounge and pulled the blanket further around him. His pants were ragged, she noticed, and she remembered that he had been dressed much smarter the night before, so she found this dress of his rather odd. But her mind was so filled that it was not working at all. She pulled the chair in her room up to the open window to wait and sat staring out at the moon, her mind skittering around nervous edges.

Presently, she heard the sound of a horse's nicker through her opened window, and then the fast beat of hooves that were pulled to a sharp halt. Andrew's muttered curse floated up to her. "What the devil!"

Miss Murdock rose from her seat, shoved her head out the window and looked below just in time to catch Andrew's eye as he looked up. He had caught the reins of a cob, a beastly looking thing that was as ugly as it was small. Even from this distance she could see the dark stains of blood soaked into the worn saddle leather, and the dark sheen of it smeared upon the horse's flanks. On impulse, she said, "Wait! I'm coming also!"

"Lizzie!" he hissed. "I haven't time!"

"Well, you can't leave that horse there at any rate," she argued. "It'll be much quicker if you wait just one moment!" and she ducked her head back inside, forestalling any further argument. But then she faced another problem, for to get into her riding habit would be time consuming and pointless at any rate as the horse below had no sidesaddle. Then she glanced down at Steven still sleeping deeply.

A very few minutes later, she let herself out the front door as she had the night before and Andrew, having evidently anticipated her way of exit, was there waiting. "Hurry!" he ordered, not at all happy to be taking her along, and full of questions as to what a strange horse was doing below her window at any rate.

She had pulled on a cloak, and stuffed a wadded bundle partway down her sleeve so that her arm stuck out from her side, but as he started to slide down to assist her in mounting, she forestalled him by jumping into the saddle and landing astride. Her cloak floated to settle around her. Andrew raised his eyebrows a good deal at this maneuver, and she pulled her cloak back to reveal a pair of tattered breeches tucked into her fashionable riding boots.

"Where--?"

"Oh, Andrew, not now!" she exclaimed, and put her heels to the horse, which lumbered into as fast a pace as it could manage after its long and tiring night.

Andrew caught her in an instant, his temperamental colt overtaking the older cob with ease, and he held his gloved hand out to restrain Miss Murdock's reins. "Slowly," he cautioned. "We need not draw attention to ourselves. Not with you along, at any rate," he added, "for if it had just been myself, I could have adequately covered."

Lizzie agreed, a little contrite, and kept her horse to a trot, which was not an uncommon gate in Town. Her hood had fallen back and she brought it up once again over her head, wishing that it was anything but mint green in color. "You are right, of course, Andrew. I fully appreciate that no respectable female should be out this time of the night, and a-lone with a man."

"And wearing men's breeches and riding astride," he finished sounding irritated. Miss Murdock found that riding more slowly was not at all to her liking, for not only was she anxious to get to St. James, it also gave Andrew opportunity to begin asking questions. "You may also like to tell me how it came about that you had a horse beneath your window." He glanced over at her, his blue eyes in his otherwise similar to the duke's face annoyed. "And where you got those breeches, also! They certainly are not a pair of mine, which is the only logical explanation I could come up with."

"Well," Miss Murdock replied with impatience, "it should be obvious that there is someone visiting in my room."

Andrew pulled his mount up short. "The devil there is!"

"A boy, Andrew," Miss Murdock explained. "St. James' messenger boy."

He relaxed somewhat. "And that is how you are aware that St. James has been injured," he said, kicking his horse again into a trot. Miss Murdock coaxed the cob back into keeping pace, for it had stopped of its own accord when his horse had.

"Yes. But he is quite overwrought and I could not get more out of him than that his lordship was badly injured, and his own father is even now lying dead in some alley. I can only surmise that his father must have been employed by St. James in some capacity also, and was killed trying to aid his lordship."

Andrew let out a curse. "But you have no idea what came about. . .?"

Lizzie shook her head.

Andrew, with a sudden thought, struck his forehead lightly with his gloved hand. "The boy. Is he still in your room?"

"Yes. But he is sleeping soundly on the chaise lounge. All the same, we shall have to figure out what to do with him when we return, for it will not do for Jeannie to come in with my chocolate in the morning and find him there."

"I should say not," Andrew agreed. "Boy or no, there would be more questions than we would ever manage to answer! Turn left here, Lizzie, and it is just up the street."

Lizzie only nodded, too tense now to even speak. She feared finding St. James on his death bed and Andrew's questions had at least enabled her to squash them back some, but now she was trembling.

Andrew slowed his horse to a walk and Miss Murdock did the same. "We'll go to the stables first, for we shall have to put the horses up at any rate," he whispered as they turned into the narrow mew to the side of a very large and imposing home. "Mayhaps Tyler will be there, and will have some knowledge of what is going on."

"Of course!" Miss Murdock said, suddenly heartened.

"Otherwise," Andrew worried, "I am not sure how we will ever gain admittance without disturbing the household."

"It is very quiet," Miss Murdock observed, having expected to see some sort of frantic activity, and a doctor's carriage outside the home. The mew ended in front of the stables' entrance, and to both of their surprise, the doors were open and St. James' carriage stood half in and half out of the entrance, his black horses still harnessed, but there was no one about to be seen at all.

Earl Larrimer dismounted and Lizzie, after a brief second of feeling a great deal of queasiness in her stomach at this somehow foreboding sight, followed suit. They led their mounts single file along the side of the carriage, for it blocked the most of the doorway and there was only just enough room for them to be able to get the horses through. Andrew paused beside the door of it. "Look," he said and pointed to the ground. There was a trail of blood coming from the now closed door and puddled half on the cobblestones of the drive and half soaked in where it lay on the floorboards of the stables.

Then he took his horse on through and Lizzie followed him. They found an empty stall for each, and only loosened the girths of the saddles and removed the bits from their mouths before closing them into their confines. In the next stall, a fine, coal black filly stuck her head over the door, her ears twitching forward as she observed what had wakened her.

Miss Murdock spared her a pat, no more able to walk past a fine horse without petting it than a doting parent could go past their child without ruffling its hair. "You are a fine lass, are you not?" she said, then dropped her hand as Andrew came out of the stall. They went back to the carriage, and Andrew opened the door. Together they peered in. One leather seat was covered with a dark, still sticky wet, stain. The rug on the floor was soaked with blood, and somehow most alarming to Lizzie was a bloody hand print half smeared on the side window.

Andrew closed the door. "This carriage will have to be cleaned," he said. "And before morning."

"Oh, Andrew," she said, her voice quavering. "That is too much blood!"

"C'mon. Let us see if we can gain entrance somehow."

They went first to the back servants' entrance, as it was closest, and it seemed only perfunctory to try it, though they each had their doubts that it could be so easy. But Andrew tried the handle and to each of their amazement, it swung readily in. Then they looked down, saw the trail of blood over the doorstep, and it was apparent that whoever had brought St. James in had had his hands just a bit too full to be able to be throwing home the bolts.

"Where now?" Miss Murdock whispered as Andrew closed the door behind them and they hurried as quietly as possible through the kitchens. "They wouldn't attempt to haul him up the stairs, would they?"

But just then, they came upon the back servants stairs and there was a trail of blood going up them and disappearing around the abrupt twist they made halfway up. And from above them, they heard the soft, furtive sounds of a scrub brush being used with hasty diligence. The dim, very dim glow of a lamp shone forth from above. Andrew took her arm and they moved together, squeaking a step here and there, and when they went around the twist, they observed Tyler on his knees, a low burning lamp by his side. His shirt was covered with blood, his cap off and his gray hair mussed considerably, with a great deal of red streaks in it. He was working hard and fast with the brush while at the same time trying to do it as silently as possible, and it was obvious from the degree of red in his bucket of water that he had been at it for some time.

They had only a second to observe all this, for he looked up, nearly overturning his bucket, and his hand did a little dance toward his waist as someone who were used to keeping some weapon in his belt would do. Then his eyes narrowed and his brows rose, and from his knees, he exclaimed in a whisper, "Bloody Hell, Miss Murdock, is that you and Earl Larrimer?"

"Yes. Do not be alarmed," she said in hushed tones back. "I would ask if his lordship were injured as we had heard, but I believe it is rather evident that he has been."

He looked at Andrew. "Take her out of here, Earl. His lordship will kill us all if he finds she is even aware of this state of affairs, let alone here in the midst of it."

"He's alive then?" Andrew asked.

"For now," Tyler returned and began again to scrub as though if he managed to clean the blood up, then it would magically return to his lordship's body. "Now you know. You better go. I'll send word 'round as soon as I can."

Miss Murdock was very disturbed, for she noticed that Tyler had not even asked how they knew of St. James' injury to begin with. It indicated just how very distracted he was, and hence, how bad off the duke must be. "No, I'm not leaving," she said. "For I can not see how you are going to get along handling this yourself."

"I've Effington to help. We'll manage," Tyler returned, but there was a great deal of doubt in his voice.

"Take me to St. James," she asked and placed a hand on his shoulder.

His relenting was brusque. "All right Miss, I haven't time to be arguin' with you, but you'll see he is unconscious and therefore yer trip wasted. All t'same, if you'll leave after seeing him, then see him you shall."

"Thank you, Tyler," she said.

He got up from his knees and she realized that he was getting too old for these shenanigans. He seemed to realize it also, for he looked very tired. Then he led them into the hallway and to his lordship's rooms where he tapped on the door. A furtive voice said, "Tyler?" and then they heard the click of a key turning in the lock as Tyler whispered to the affirmative.

The door opened with caution and a very tall, thin man in a long sleeping gown, smeared with blood, and a crumpled night cap upon his head said, "I nearly have all the clothing burned as you said, and--oh, heaven! Who are these people?"

"T'duke's cousin, Earl Larrimer, and Miss Murdock," Tyler answered. "It's all right, Effington, let 'em in."

Effington said, "Ah, the slapper," and he grinned a little, but his face was concerned and his smile died quickly.

"Yes," Miss Murdock replied ruefully. "I fear it is I."

Effington opened the door wider and admitted them into milord's bedchamber. The clock began to strike the hour, three strokes, and then settled into ticking again. The fireplace crackled and an unpleasant smell came from it, a mixture of fabric and blood. A pair of scissors were set on a table, and the remnant of what had been a red wine velvet jacket was on the floor. It was a dark, unsettling color, not at all as Lizzie remembered it being just a few hours ago.

St. James lay in the large four poster bed, his eyes closed, his face and torso as white as the linens that were wrapped around his shallowly breathing chest. The sheet of his bed was pulled to just above his hips, and Miss Murdock saw that his skin was papery thin and dry. He had been sponged, but there was still a great deal of stiff, dried blood in the dark hair that lay in a brief pattern down his belly. His face was still welted from her hand, but instead of being red, it was now a washed out purple. Most alarming, she could see that blood had spread through his bandage, the source of it seeming to come from just over his heart. And his left arm was also wrapped.

She moved toward him, removed her cloak and the bundle she had kept stuffed in the upper part of her sleeve, laid them both aside. She had tucked her billowy night costume into the breeches she wore, and now she lacked only an eyepatch to complete the illusion of a rather small pirate. She was not at all aware of how ridiculous she looked, only reached two fingers to his lordship's throat, found the pulse that was there and was not reassured by the erratic faintness of it. His neck was very hot and her fingers burned.

"What happened?" Andrew asked Tyler.

"An assailant plugged him from the alley beside Almacks," Tyler explained. Lizzie flinched at the fact that she had been so close by and so oblivious.

"Is that where Steven's father lies?" Andrew asked.

Tyler's tired eyes shifted and he didn't answer. Miss Murdock filled the silence by saying, "This is not right. I fear he needs a doctor."

Effington said in a doleful voice, "As I had pointed out, miss, an hour ago."

But Tyler gave an adamant shake of his head. "No, miss. We can't do that to him."

She turned her anxious brown eyes to him. "We can't let him die either! He's still bleeding. He's running a temperature which has me quite baffled for surely he can not have the infection already and I fear that he is fast dehydrating also."

"De-what?" Tyler asked.

"Not enough fluid in his body," Miss Murdock tried to explain. "He needs to drink and with his being unconscious, I do not know how we can endeavor to get anything into him."

"Well, that should not be the problem," Tyler told her with relief in his voice, "for I saw to it myself that he had quite a bit of whiskey before I soddered him."

Miss Murdock gave him a very strange look, the same look she gave her father before launching into an acerbic attack at some utterly foolish, irresponsible, lamebrained, idiotic action of his that had managed to set her back two steps for every one she had worked so hard to go forward. But she reminded herself that he had done what he thought was best, and indeed, in the older school of thought that he was a product of, had been accepted as the proper action to take. So she drew in a breath, said with a great deal of control, "I see that you took every necessary precaution, but I still think he should see a doctor."

"Can't do it, miss," Tyler said reverting to a certain obstinacy that his lordship had seen many times but that Miss Murdock had not yet encountered. "He'd rather die than risk having whatever enemy is out there find out that he is laid up and helpless, a sitting duck. And there's other factors involved too. He'll not have no doctor and I won't go against his wishes."

Andrew broke in. "You seem to know uncommonly much about this sort of thing, Lizzie. I mean, dehydration. I'd never heard such a word."

"I do have a knack at vetting," she admitted, "but surely you must see this is far, far different." But as they only stared at her, she said, "You do see that, don't you?" Then she sighed, for she could see very well that they did not. She sank into the chair at St. James' bedside and put her forehead in her hand for a long moment, chewing on her lip. It was madness to even consider it. He was not a horse or a cow or a pig for heaven's sake. But she could not just leave him as he was either. "All right," she said less than graciously when she looked up to the three men that had unconsciously put her in charge. "This is what I should need, and this is what we should do."

She stood up again, but her hand fluttered down to rest on St. James' brow. "Tyler, you know the stables best. I'm supposing you have supplies there for minor veterinary incidents."

"Oh! Aye," he nodded. He picked up his cap from where at some point it had been tossed onto a chair and placed it on his head.

"Bring me up some clean needles and suturing thread. Also an antiseptic agent, Borax if you have it."

"Yer gonna stitch him then?" he asked.

"Yes. I fear with his wound being constantly aggravated by the breathing movements of his chest that your method, a very good method usually, mind you, is not holding."

Tyler nodded but he looked worried again. "I've the carriage t'see to first, miss, if you think he will be all right in t'meanwhile."

"No. There's no sense cleaning out the carriage until you and Andrew go and retrieve the body of Steven's father from the mew. I can not think that his lordship would wish to abandon that man who gave his life helping him to lay there until someone finds him in the morning. It will be a miracle if no one has stumbled upon him already," she added, then shook off this horrible thought. "So gather what I need and then Andrew will accompany you to fetch the. . . ," and she stumbled a little here, as she realized just what she was discussing, "the corpse. You shall have to wake an undertaker and assure him that he will be settled with upon the morrow, and that he will receive extra for his discretion."

Tyler looked at her, his eyes unreadable, but he only said, "As you say, miss," causing Effington to shift and fumble for the scissors. Andrew glanced at the groom, but Tyler shook his head at him in warning.

Miss Murdock did not notice, for she turned to Effington to continue. "That leaves you to clean up the mess on the stairs and anywhere else in the house that there is blood," she said to Effington.

"Yes, miss," that man said without inflection.

"But first I will need a great deal of clean linens, and fresh water. You may go ahead, if you would please, and fetch those now. I will finish what--what you are currently occupied with."

"Yes, miss," Effington said, dropping his work and giving her an approving glance. "I would be happy to, miss."

Miss Murdock moved from his lordship, looking incongruous in the worn, tattered breeches and fashionable, new riding boots, and tucked in, long sleeved night gown. She settled on the arm of the chair Effington had just abandoned and picked up the scissors and bloody jacket.

"Andrew," she continued as Effington left the room. "Don't forget that after you have taken care of--of Steven's father, that you will have to somehow get him out of my bedroom at your grandmother's and bring him back here, I suppose. And then, I am sorry to say, you will need to help Tyler clean the carriage."

"And you are not going to be back in your bed in time to avoid detection at this rate," he told her.

"And neither are you," she countered, looking up, and for the first time she saw just how stunned the two remaining men were at all her firmly sure orders, and she blushed. "So we had better come up with some idea to explain why it is we are not there."

But Andrew was not happy about this suggestion. "You are going home, Lizzie. Whatever needs to be done, we can handle it. If you are found missing, that will be bad enough! If you are discovered to be here--!"

"Oh, I do not care!" she cried. "He has done his best to ruin me at any rate and it is not as if I had any notion of actually securing a husband, God forbid. If I am discovered, then I will merely return home, which I was going to do at the end of the week at any rate."

"Lizzie--!"

"There you go, miss," Tyler interrupted. "You merely need say you got sick of t'duke's antics and have run home. A letter will do the trick. Write it up and t'Earl here can place it in your room when he fetches t'lad."

Miss Murdock nodded approval but Andrew rounded on the groom. "You are going to encourage her--!"

"T'wasn't I that brought her here," Tyler reminded him.

"Oh, bloody hell! Write the note, Lizzie, and you had better add that I am escorting you, so they will not set up a manhunt for fear you are going by yourself. It'll explain my absence, also, by-the-by."

"You see," Miss Murdock said, her heart thumping a little unevenly. "It is all very simple. Now you had both better go, for we have a great deal to accomplish and only a few hours to do it in."

They did go, and she noted that Tyler's face had lightened and was now set with purpose rather than worry. She finished cutting the cloth, fed the last of it into the flames, then, hoping that Effington would knock before entering, stripped off the ridiculous breeches she had been wearing, threw the sleeping costume off over her head, and unrolled the bundle she had brought with her. It was the brown dress she had been wearing when arriving in London, for she had not wanted to crinkle anything just bought for her by rolling it up as she had. As it appeared she was going to get a good deal messy also, she was happy with her choice.

She was into it in under two seconds, buttoned it, and took a second to examine her feelings of being in her old attire and acting as the old Lizzie would, calm, capable and a little insistent. It felt very good, indeed, for she feared that for the past four days that so much had been happening that she had nearly lost track of who she was. But with the old dress on and her hair quite down (which at that thought, she took a brief second to quickly wrap it into the bun she had always worn, and lacking any pins, tied one of his lordship's hair ribbons around it to hold it in place that she found on his dresser), she felt a great relief.

Effington did tap lightly on the door, and when she opened it to him, dressed except for her boots, she surmised he must have done it with his foot, for his hands were filled with a fresh basin of water and over his shoulder were as many linens as he must have been able to lay hands on. "Oh, dear," Miss Murdock said. "Whatever will the housekeeper think tomorrow?"

"Linens day is not until Monday, miss. We shall have to contrive to replace them by then. Though I am sure she will notice."

"Well, it can't be helped," Miss Murdock replied and took the water from him and carried it to the table by his lordship. Effington closed the door, handed her the linens.

"Anything else, miss?" he asked. He also had changed into more serviceable clothing and had rolled his sleeves up like a man ready to tackle a difficult job.

"Just the floors, as I had said. I will help you if I finish in here before you return."

He left, and Miss Murdock had to wonder how many times the door could be opened and closed before someone inadvertently banged it in their haste.

As she was still unable to begin on St. James until Tyler returned, she went to the small secretary in the corner of St. James' room and finding a piece of paper and pen and ink, sat down in the dainty chair and tried to word her letter. It ended sounding blunt and hurried, which she was sorry for, thinking of how upset the Duchess would be, but she simply could not put any more time into it than she had to spare.

Dearest Lady Lenora,

I find that upon reflection over your grandson's behavior at Almacks this evening, that I can not bear to be in London knowing what a spectacle I have become. Hence, I am returning home this very night, for I do not wish to argue with you and upset us both more than we both already are (I am sure). Please forgive me. I will explain more adequately as soon as I possibly can.

Earl Larrimer has kindly offered to escort me. Please do not blame him, for I insisted and he was afraid that if he did not accompany me that I would set out on my own. Which I of a certainty would have.

I express my most heart felt affection and appreciation for you, and hope you can find it in your heart to forgive me someday.

Yours sincerely
Miss Sara Elizabeth Murdock

Tyler returned even as she was writing the Dowager's name on the envelope. "You have them then?" she asked.

"Aye, miss. Everything I could lay me hands on that I thought may be of help," he said and placed a wicker basket full of supplies on the chair next to the bed.

"Thank you," she said. "You are incredible, Tyler," and to her amazement, he looked a good deal embarrassed. She handed him the letter in its envelope, reminded him to make sure that Andrew took it into the house and left it in her bedroom when he went to get Steven out, and then he was gone leaving Miss Murdock alone with the unconscious duke of St. James.

She delayed for a deliberate moment, going through the basket Tyler had brought in, taking inventory and pulling out those items she felt she should need, and a few others just in case. She lined up these items on a folded white cloth on a small table that she pulled up to join the one already at the head of the bed that held the fresh water and the lamp, which she turned up to its brightest. She had three different needles and she made a small solution of Borax and water in his lordship's empty (and thanks to Effington, spotlessly clean) shaving cup and soaked the needles in it as she unwound the suture thread and cut it off three different times. Then she pulled the needles out one at a time and secured the thread to each and laid them in line so that she could get to them with the least amount of fuss or effort. She put the open tin of Borax powder beside them. Then, taking a deep breath, she picked up the sharp scissors she had also laid out and turned to the unawares St. James.

Tyler met with Earl Larrimer in the stables, his hand going to his breast pocket for his bag of chaw only to come out empty again. "Damn it," he muttered. Then looking at Andrew, he asked, "Ready?"

"Yes. I got the horse blankets as you said and disposed of the rug also. No need hauling that around when it can only add to the mess."

"Aye. Good thinking, milord. You're learnin' fast." Tyler climbed up onto the driver's seat, and Earl Larrimer surprised him by joining him. "Sure you don't want to ride below where yer less likely to be seen?"

"Not until we've finished and get it cleaned out," Andrew answered with distaste.

Tyler laughed, backed the horses, which were relieved to be moving after standing for so long. He sobered as he turned the carriage skillfully around until it faced in the proper direction. "I think someone's gonna have to ride below, because near as I can tell, we're gonna have to change the plan slightly and pick up t'lad first. If we wait 'til we get this business finished, may be too late."

"I agree," Andrew said. "I can't like him being alone in Miss Murdock's room. What if he awakes and finds her not there? But I hate to have him with us while we fetch his father's body. Do you think we would have time to bring him back here, first?"

Tyler considered as he drove, glancing at the low hanging moon. Then he shook his head. "Nay. Might do him some good at any rate to see that his father isn't just going to rot there but is being properly taken care of." He added in a mutter, "More than he deserved at any rate."

Andrew gave him a sharp glance. "It's not quite the way Miss Murdock pieced it together then?"

"No, milord," Tyler shook his head, his face grim. "Not at all. And damningly, I have discovered that St. James' pistol has been left behind as well, and that we must locate it also."

Andrew, who was well aware that his cousin owned an extremely rare and fine pair of dueling pistols, and that, quite understandably, they were well known, fully understood the implications of this last remark. "Whatever shall Miss Murdock say if she discovers this?" he wondered a-loud.

Tyler nodded. "Know it isn't going to be me to tell her that Steven's father lying dead in the mew is from St. James' hand," he said with conviction. "Neither do I think his lordship will be pleased to learn that his would be assassin is getting a proper burial courtesy of milord's pocket-book!"

"Is Steven aware of how his father died?" Andrew asked, troubled.

"Aye. T'lad was there," Tyler answered. "And you can see what a great mess this all is!" As they were now a small distance from his lordship's home, Tyler laid the reins on the horses' backs, and they moved out into a fast, long reaching trot as they headed for the Dowager Duchess' home in the surrounding night.

At this pace, they reached the Dowager's residence in short time, and Tyler was soon slowing the horses down to approach the house more quietly. He and Andrew each scanned the windows but found no indication of anyone being up or about, at least not until they turned the corner into the mew, and then Miss Murdock's light was on in her room. But as Andrew expected that she had forgotten to blow it out, dangerous, but understandable in the circumstances, he was not alarmed by it.

Tyler stopped the horses as soon as the back of the carriage was out of sight from the street, and Andrew jumped down. "I'll move as quickly as I can manage," he told the groom in a hushed voice, and then he was running to the front of the house, where the door should still be unlocked, but if it were not, he had the proper keys as it was not unusual for him to be out late at night.

As Tyler kept the restless horses, who no doubt had had about e-nough for one night, calm, he noted that Miss Murdock's window was still open also. He hoped Andrew would think to close it. He took a brief second to reflect that when St. James had been here just twenty-four hours ago, they could not have fathomed how quickly everything was to change for the worse.

Then Andrew's dark head was hanging out the window, drawing his attention once again. "He's not here!" he hissed down.

Tyler had the sudden gut feeling that everything had just turned a good deal more worse than he had first thought. "Mayhaps we'll find him in the mew, with his father," he returned. Then added, "We haven't time at any rate, the moon is falling and dawn can't be far!"

Andrew nodded in understanding and his head moved back inside the window, which, to Tyler's relief, he remembered to close. Then the lamp was extinguished, leaving that window black, and Tyler backed the horses and the carriage out of the mew and onto the street, facing in the direction that would take them toward the Thames and the mew.

Earl Larrimer came out of the house a brief second later and wasted no time in joining the groom. "I can't like it," he said with vehemence.

"Did you leave t'letter?" Tyler asked.

"Yes, damn it. I did. But this business with, what is his name, Steven? I can't like it."

"If he's gone, he's gone," Tyler said, trying to calm his own uneasy feelings. "We haven't time to spare searching for him and we daren't wake the house doing so at any rate. He's probably gone home to his mother."

But Andrew said, "Without any breeches on?"

Chapter Nineteen

Her hand stilled upon the white cloth of his bandage and the scissors in her other hand dropped to her side. He was vulnerable, and she had not ever thought to see him like that. His eyelids were closed, and the fluctuating emotions of his gold eyes were hidden from her. That sharp, dancing contradiction in them that bespoke of endlessly seeking thoughts, like twin candle flames that flickered and burned and gorged themselves on the very wax that kept them alive, until they burned the wax completely down and gutted out, a victim of their own brightness.

It was not the thoughts she should be thinking. A moment ago, she had been ready to embark on her task, but that was before her hand had fallen on his bandaged chest, and her eyes had roamed enough to notice the puckering of scars in his pale skin. It was not the first time he had been injured. It was not the first time he had been vulnerable.

She wondered if he had always survived on nothing but the rough ministrations of a crusty old groom whose methods dated back to Waterloo. And she shuddered.

Who was she to think that her attempts would be any better? And she bowed her head and fought back a sudden urge to shed tears.

There was nothing for it but to press on. In the pressing on, she was aware that everything she had fought against had come about on its own accord anyway. Had she not foreseen just this situation? Had she not dreaded loving him, and watching him die?

Oh, yes, she did love him, and she acknowledged this to herself as she stood with one hand upon his shallowly breathing, bandaged chest and her head bent in tears. Foolish and impossible as it was to love someone in the space of four days. Four days? If she would be honest with herself, she had loved him that first night when he had been so drunk that he walked her hallway with his shoulder propped against the wall, and stopped and turned and given her that crooked grin that made her stomach do a sudden lurch and her own smile freeze on her face.

Lizzie the caregiver, the rational part of her mind admonished her. And my, haven't you picked a project for yourself this time.

But she had tried to retreat from his needs! Had tried to explain that the picture he presented of her entertaining herself with all his money while he fought a struggle for his life and his future was not how it would be, *could* be, with her. She could not have stopped herself from caring for him any more than she could have passed by a bird with an injured wing, and the only sanctuary for her would have been to purposefully take a different path. A path where she could not see his needs, or his hurt.

But of course, he had not understood this. Or, if she were to be honest, and by God, she was being honest right now, wasn't she? Was fairly slapping herself in the face with the truth. If she were to be honest, she had never boldly explained it to him, had shrank from it, a complete coward.

Milord, the simple truth is that if I come with you, you will break my heart. Either you will die, and I will have to witness it, or you will prevail and suffer through a marriage with me that you would have never desired under normal circumstances and that you will regret for the remainder of your life. So, you see, your plan is really quite impossible.

And he had been so full of dismayed wonder at her using the word sacrifice!

She was becoming angry now, but at least with anger, she could do what had to be done. It steadied her. She swiped at the salty tears in her eyes, brought up the scissors and began snipping through the bandages.

The very sound of the scissors cutting through the threads of the linen made her calm. It was a sound she had heard often, and she began to have that feeling of confidence that she was able to do something and to do it well, and if it were an uncommon talent and one no where near ladylike, her penchant for healing, she still took a great deal of satisfaction in it.

She pulled gently on the fabric, took a sponge and squeezed water beneath it where it was pasted to him by drying blood. Her anger and her distress were rushed away in a wave of concentration. From habit, she began to speak, of nothing and everything, for she was too used to having to soothe a frightened animal as she worked.

Her voice took on that quality she had used when Leaf had been in the fence, a sort of soft teasing that it should be in such a mess that reassured by its light tone that someone with more sense could and would get it out.

Do you know that Tyler and I decided you should be Lord Habitual Ill-Humor, Dante? Indeed, we agreed upon it quite totally.

The cloth was loosening, a little at a time, but it still must be pulling painfully at his skin. He groaned but did not stir.

It gave me a great deal of satisfaction to see the look upon your face when I threw your flask into the ditch. I knew quite a bit about you just from that, Dante. I knew you were not given to temper tantrums, although I am sure many would argue with me, for if you were to be given to them, you would have had one then.

Her voice went on, soft and soothing, and if St. James could weave a spell with his eyes and his mouth on her wrist or her palm, Lizzie could weave a spell with her voice.

You gave me your gloves, do you remember? I felt like boxing your ears for that. It frightened me that you could so easily shoulder the complete responsibility of another person's life, clear down to whether her fingers were cold. It frightened me because it showed me just how very, very serious you were.

Then the wound of his chest was exposed and she did not like what she saw. The blood was not clotting properly, despite Tyler's rough cauterization of the vessels, and she sniffed in a most undignified manner at it, pausing for that instant in her talking, but then her voice began again after that small break.

You promised to listen to my concerns once we reached the inn, and you did, although I am sure you would have rather told me to be quiet and do as you said without question. I've noticed that Tyler and the Tempton brothers do so. That frightened me also, that they should take your word as law, then I came to see they merely trusted you a great deal.

Tobacco? Whyever should she smell tobacco? Oh, Heavens, do not tell her that Tyler packed his wound with tobacco! But even as she thought this, there was a revealing wisp of it that had fallen inside the bandage. No wonder he was not clotting properly, he had absorbed whatever it was that brought Tyler so much pleasure.

I do not know what to do about this, Dante, except to disinfect it and stitch you up the best I know how and hope that as you make new blood you dilute whatever it is in the tobacco that is thinning it.

You did listen to my concerns, and I respected you for that. Then you told me to be quiet so you could think, and I thought that would be nothing but a ploy before you flatly refused to change your intentions. But you were thinking, and if you did not change your intentions, you amended them to the degree that, although I was not happy, I had hope that you were not totally without heart.

She took the Borax powder and dusted the gaping hollow of skin. It was a good three inches long and all the meat of him in the middle of it was quite gone as though a plow had furrowed through, and she could see the white bone of his rib beneath. The skin around it showed the brutality of Tyler's ministrations and she shuddered to think of the pain St. James had endured.

But I could not fathom why you were so determined to do as you had said, to marry me when you did not know me, when I could see upon my first glimpse of you that there were surely many that would desire to be your wife. And we spoke of motive, and I did not like how easily you read how I thought my life would be. Had it been so obvious? But you did not ridicule my intentions, even though after you had spoken them, they seemed somehow very sad.

If only there were something to keep this blood away from where she worked! She was sopping it up every minute it seemed and it was slowing her down. She took up her first needle and suturing thread.

You did not want to tell me your story. You did not want me to know your motives, and I guess even then, I knew that if I heard it, something was going to change quite profoundly between us, for you do not have the look about you of one who oft tells his woes.

Funny how the most unacceptable actions can be made understandable when one knows what prompts them. But I do not condone it, Dante, never will. You should have let it go a long time ago and tried to rise above it. Living life as you should and being happy, even if you die unexpectedly and young, is better than this battle you have been engaged in for the most of your life. You may die anyway and not have lived at all. But of course, I should know that you accepted that risk, perhaps with rancor but accepting it all the same, wanting what should have been yours by right and nothing less.

Her stitches were uniform and even, each knotting and snipping was swift, a feat that always amazed her in retrospect and brought her a good deal of teasing from her father. "If you can sew up some foal as neat as that, whyever can't you sew a new dress, Lizzie, my love?" She could only think that it was the degree of concentration she fell into when something she loved was hurt. She did not care two pins about a new dress.

But the price you pay, I fear it is too much. You will never get back these years of hate and searching. And I am very much afraid of what you will be left to live with if you should prevail. I worry for you, Dante. I worry a great deal. And I do not know how to stop you or turn you. You may as well be Leaf heading for that fence, for there is nothing for it but for me to hang on and await that crash, for you will not accept any pulling on the reins.

The fact that you were scandalized at my wearing breeches, that I found so very amusing, considering what I had heard of you. But in looking back I have to wonder if it were not even then that I gained your attention. Oh, not in that way, for that would be silly, although you seem to find it amusing to try to convince me that--well nevermind! All I am saying is that your mind must have already been analyzing what sort of woman would wear breeches, and unfortunately for me, I surmise you judged one that was not easily shocked. And since your proposal was very shocking indeed, I must conclude that this were an asset in your eyes.

And that is where I get so very upset with you, for you were only pondering if I would be adequate for your purposes. You never consider, Dante, what you are fully asking of others. Or no, maybe that is not true. Maybe you do consider it and in your arrogance you think that you shall be able to make it up to them in some manner when all this is over. But will you be able to atone for Tyler never taking a wife? Oh, you do not like to see it, but I very much suspect that if he had not felt impelled to aid your cause and keep you safe that he would have married long ago. Or I may be doing you an injustice. He was there to see your parents' bodies, after all, and he may have his own feelings of wanting to see vengeance done.

But your grandmother hurts. I am sure she could get over her own long-standing grief if she could see you happy. But you will not desist, nor will you even pretend that you have to her, for you will not lie, will you, Dante, even to comfort an old woman that you love?

She tied off the last of the thick, black thread from the first needle, cut the needle free, laid it aside and picked up the second needle.

And Andrew. Oh dear! Andrew. He wants to further your cause, and if you fail then he will surely fail also for although I think a great deal of him he is not as you are. But we have talked about him once, and you were very angry with me, and I am afraid it only made you all the more determined rather than discouraging you.

You take on too much, Dante. You are only one man. You are not to blame for living when your parents died. How often do you think that you were meant to be in that coach? How often do you tell yourself that the only reason you were divinely spared was to seek vengeance?

His muscles tensed, alerting her, just, before he moved. Then his right hand was clawing at his side where she worked and she was hard pressed to keep him from undoing her work. "Milord!" His eyes opened, but there was such a feverish gleam in them she did not even think he knew where he was. She rose from where she had been on her knees and leaned over him, catching a glancing blow to her side as she did so. She caught his flailing right hand and at the same time she spoke with soothing sternness. "St. James. St. James! Lie still, you are safe."

But he was swearing and fighting her holding his hand as though in the midst of some battle, and his injured left arm contracted in effort to aid him in gaining release from her. "Dante!"

His eyes cleared, settled on her in fretful fever, and he stilled.

"You're in your own bedchamber," she went on, her voice now quiet. "Quite safe. But you *must* lie still for you have lost a great deal of blood and I am endeavoring to stitch up your wound."

For answer he groaned, and his hand jerked in hers, not flailing now, but making a determined effort to go to his chest and his injury. She hung onto it in desperation. "No, no, milord. You cannot be pawing a-bout at it. I know it must hurt--"

"Damn. . . right!" he forced out and bit his teeth down hard together in closed eyed effort to control his groans. She watched him, worried. Oh, if only he had stayed out for just a little longer! Then his eyes snapped open and blazed at her. "What. . . are *you*. . . doing here? No . . . place for you. . . to be!"

"Do you want a doctor?"

"No!"

"Then I am the best you are going to get. At least I am not packing you full of tobacco and burning you with an iron."

He gave such a grimace that she nearly smiled. "Do not remind. . . me of that. Damn. . . Tyler!"

"He did what he thought was best, milord, and managed to keep you from bleeding to death before I got here, but I really must finish for I am only half done, you know, and I can not delay any longer."

"Whiskey. . . first."

"No, St. James. Only water for now," and she loosed his hand from hers, which he had been holding with enough pressure to make her wince. "Which I will fetch if you promise to not be tearing at yourself."

"Wretched. . . lass! Probably. . . thrown. . . all out the window." Then he cursed again, a broken stream of profanity that had her ears burning, but she understood that it was either that or a less masculine expression of pain, which he would not show. Silly fool. All the same, it was probably better, for screaming would bring somebody, and she understood that St. James did not want anyone to know of his injury. How he was to maintain that secret, she had no idea.

She poured the water from the pitcher that Effington kept fresh in his room and returned to the bed with the glass. She placed her hand beneath his head, lifted him enough to put the glass to his mouth and was at least relieved at the momentary lapse in his cursing as he sipped. "More," she told him, and he was in so much pain that he obeyed without argument, which made her smile slightly.

When he finished, she set the glass aside. "I have to finish, milord. And I fear it is going to be painful."

"I shall. . . endeavor. . . to manage. Just. . . get on. . . with it."

She settled herself back on her knees, began where she had left off and she had to admit that he did not even twitch when the needle pushed through the brutalized flaps of his skin.

"Talk. . . Lizzie," he muttered through clenched teeth. "You. . . were talking. . . before, weren't you?"

She blushed, but kept her eyes on her work. "Yes, milord. What do you wish me to talk about?"

"Tell me what. . . happened at Almacks. Did Andrew. . . manage?"

Her hand steadied. "Yes. Quite admirably, I should say, as I was quite stupid at that point. It was a most unforgivable display, milord."

A faint smile slanted his compressed lips.

Her hands began to find their rhythm again. "But then you planned it that way, did you not? You had every intention of ruining me so that I would agree to walk shamefacedly to the alter with you. Shame on you, milord."

"As we are under. . . the most intimate of. . . circumstances presently," he fought to get out with a hint of his usual teasing, "you must. . . call me. . . Dante."

"Hush! You are no sight to see at the moment, so do not try to make more of this than it is. And as I was saying, *Dante*, what you did was quite cruel." She glanced up at him, his profile but a foot away from her own concentrating face, but his eyes were closed and his brow was knotted in an effort to remain in control, and, she suspected, to not slip again into unconsciousness. "I see you do not deny it," she said. "But I did not think you would. Nor do I expect you will apologize, for you are quite without shame, but that does not surprise me either. But as I said, your cousin came leaping to the rescue, and Ryan Temp- (and her voice took on that whimsical teasing quality again as she fell quite completely into her work)

ton also. And as Ryan said that I must make a great show of thinking nothing of it myself, I managed to laugh and appear to have a very good time and then there were many young men asking for my hand in dancing, and I did have a good time. And it was all very strange for although you had the damnedest of intentions, it ended having just the opposite effect as you expected, or at least what I think you expected, for I did have to wonder if even this result was as you wanted it. But the degree of convolution your mind must work at to anticipate that reaction and already know of how you could use it to your advantage is so intimidating to me that I refuse to even delve into it. So we shall settle that you, for once, misjudged. I confess, it gives me more pleasure at any rate to believe that you are not infallible in your reasoning. In conclusion, I fear, milord--Dante, that you accomplished nothing, except to blacken your own reputation as usual.

Your grandmother was furious at your behavior, and I would wager very much regrets the money she paid to Lady Frobisher to entice your voucher out of her. Lady Frobisher, I noticed, was explaining quite earnestly to some other ladies present that I can only think were the other members of the board. I hope her daughter's wedding gift was worth it. It all entertained me very much, I confess.

But your grandmother did not dare say anything on the ride home, only sat immovable in the carriage, for your aunt Lydia of course was spouting off in a way that made me want to reach across and shake her and tell her to be quiet for your grandmother's sake if not for yours. Or mine either, for it was not at all comfortable to listen to it. Oddly enough, she managed to make me out to be some sort of heroine who had withstood the very fires of hell and come out unscathed. She really does not see anything good in you at all, you know, milord--Dante. Which upsets me, I admit, for she was there at the time of your tragedy and you would think she could understand at least some of what you do.

But she is a great feather-brain, so I should not be surprised that it all completely escapes her. Nothing is to interrupt the sacredness of the conventions. I do not know how she was before your uncle died, but I believe that she unhealthily dotes on Andrew, remarkable that he has not been adversely effected! and I am sure she is always so angry with you because she is afraid that Society will punish Andrew to some degree over it. Not that Andrew would care if they did. But she cares very much.

She paused as she tied off the last of the thread from her second needle, cut the needle from it and chanced a glance up before reaching for the third. She was sure he had slipped back into unconsciousness, but his eyes flickered open at her brief silence, and she took the third needle and began stitching again and fell back into speaking her thoughts with little arrangement or design, just offering that soothing quality of her voice.

So everyone was a great deal out of sorts by the time we reached your grandmother's house, for your aunt had stirred it all back up most lamentably. I retired, and even though I thought I would be unable to sleep, I did almost immediately until I heard Steven tapping on--

"Steven!"

Miss Murdock's fingers faltered and she had to think what she had just been saying for she had been only partially aware of it, the greater part of her mind on sewing his lordship back together. "Yes. Steven." Then her voice rose, for he was struggling to sit up. "What are you doing!" But he neither heeded nor answered her. "You must lie still, milord, for I am not done yet!" She rose from her knees once again and bent over him.

He fell back from his half-rise, panting. She was nearly in tears at the thought of her stitches tearing. "Oh, can't you lie still! I assure you Steven is as well as can be expected."

His eyes closed again, and his face was so pale that she feared he had really done it and would be unconscious again in short order, which at this moment, she would not necessarily look upon as something bad. "Where?" he ground out, and the word turned into a groan, which he bit off between his teeth.

"In my bedchamber at your grandmother's," and as his eyes snapped open again at this pronouncement, she hurried to soothe him as best she could. "He is *sleeping*, milord, and no one knows of his presence, and even now Tyler and Andrew are about getting him out and bringing him here." She did not add that they were also about removing Steven's father's body from the mew, for she did not know if St. James were aware of that loss of life and she would not upset him further.

His panting subsided and he half raised his head again. "Damn it! I am. . . too bloody weak!"

"Yes, milord," she told him. "And you will only get weaker instead of stronger if you do not let me finish!"

"You should. . . not be here."

"Yes, yes, milord. And I will go as soon as I am done," she soothed, although she had no intention of leaving. "So please lie still and I will finish in short order, I promise you."

"Tell me what. . . Steven said."

"While I work. I will tell you all I know while I work."

He did lie still, but his eyes did not shut as before but were dark and brooding. Lizzie knelt and picked up the needle once again, settled herself to resume her work. Her hands were shaking, and so there was a moment when she did nothing but try to calm herself. She expected him to be impatient, but a glance at him showed he was so preoccupied with his thoughts that she was loathe to interrupt him when she did begin to speak. "He came to my window, as he had the night before. And he had--had blood on him and was very upset."

His face was immobile and even his pain seemed to be set aside to the immediacy of his contemplation. She was not even sure he were listening to her, but at her hesitation, for she was trying to think ahead and, yes, edit her tale for she did not wish to upset him any further than he already was, he prompted her.

"Go on."

"So I--I brought him in the window and asked him what had happened and he. . . he said you were injured and here."

"Is. . . that all?"

"He fell asleep very quickly, milord--Dante. He was overwrought and exhausted." Which was not the same as answering him yes or no, but would have to do for she did not wish to outright lie to him. Although she had always been a staunch believer that lying by omission was only one step below lying outright.

"Did he tell. . . you his father. . . is dead?"

Her hand trembled, for his tone was too flat, too emotionless, and she had the first foreboding that there was something terribly, terribly wrong with the scene she had in her mind of what had happened. She forced the needle through, for she was on the very last stitch, and some part of her commanded that she finish what had to be done before she answered him, before he again spoke. She tied off the last stitch, snipped the thread from the needle, and then said in a small whisper, "Yes." Then she lifted her head to find his eyes were no longer focused on his inner mind but on her.

"Did he tell. . . you. . . how his father died?"

And sudden bile rose in Miss Murdock's throat and her eyes became large and pleading in her face. *Don't tell me! But you are already telling me, aren't you. Your eyes! My God, do not look at me with eyes like that.* She couldn't speak but only slowly shook her head.

But he did not look down, did not spare her the bright gleam of his gold gaze that beaconed out and impaled her. And she *could* not look down, could not deny him that access to her, even when she knew it was about to cause her an unspeakable pain.

"I. . . killed him."

Still she held his gaze. But he seemed to shrink in her eyes, for her vision began to encompass not just his eyes, but his pale, pain-harshened face, the white pillow he lay upon with his mat of dark hair the only border between white linen and white face. The bed posts reached high above him and the bed stretched out long beneath him. The room itself shrank until she saw the flickering flames of the lamps, the secretary in one corner and one of three, high, wide highboys in the other corner. The sideboard with all of his many bottles and decanters of various liquors. The fireplace still putting out fumes of burned blood and velvet. The various dressers and tables, and even though it was to her back, she was aware of the door, and yet in the center of all of this were his two gold eyes, his expression unfathomable to her, mayhaps unfathomable to himself.

And then she closed her eyes and all she could see was Steven's face. His young, much too young, shocked, bewildered and grieving face. *Whose blood is it, Steven? Me father's. . . and St. James'.* Victim's and Victor's mingled together in some unholy alliance. One dead, one nearly dead. And all for what? For *what?* For something that happened twenty-three years ago and could never be righted! No matter how many people died.

And when she at last spoke, opening her eyes, she had only a feeling of coldness. "How does vengeance feel, milord? Will you look at the scar when you heal, thanks to my stitches, and feel satisfaction?"

He held her eyes steady, but he did not defend himself, and somewhere in her brain, she knew this could not be right. He was lying there, injured. He had been attacked, hadn't he? Why wasn't he pointing this out to her? She *needed* it pointed out to her. Needed something to counteract Steven's face in her mind's eye. "And what of when you look at Steven now, without a father. Is that going to bring you pleasure?"

And she could not stem the cold fury that poured from her. *He* should be stemming it. She *needed* him to stem it. She needed for him to at least *flinch*, to feel *something*. But despite her brutal words, he only lay there, injured, weak, pale and helpless, and took it.

"Oh, damn it! Why don't you say something?" and she broke, ashamed of her words, and at the same time, ashamed to be crying over him, St. James, when all she could see was Steven's face. "Why don't you tell me you had no choice! Why don't you tell me you didn't know it was Steven's father!" He still didn't answer her, and she wanted to pound on his chest, wanted to rip at her hair, wanted to claw those eyes out of his face. "Oh, damn it! *Did* you have any choice? *Did* you know it was Steven's father?"

Slowly, very slowly, he shook his head, but the knot between his eyes grew, and his mouth took on a shape that a man who is about to amputate his own leg would take on. And he said a single word that terrified her, "But--"

"No! No buts! You didn't know and that is the end of it! Do you hear me, Dante! That is the end of it!" And sobbing and wild, she put her hand to his lips to keep him from speaking whatever damning words were in his mind. His right hand came up to her hand, and his eyes took on a sudden weary resignation that made him seem all the more helpless. He kissed her palm with his blood on it, pulled her hand away from his lips and held it in his hand. "For. . . now. I haven't. . . the strength."

He gave a weak tug at her hand and Lizzie collapsed more than sat on the bed, crying. She was aware that he had just done something for her, something he had never done for anyone else, but she refused to acknowledge it, for to acknowledge it would be to acknowledge those unspoken words that she did not want to hear. *But*--!

His arm fell to his side, and her hand in his fell with it, so that she was stretched across his bare torso. His eyes closed, and although his breathing was still shallow, it seemed more even and she dared to lay her head upon his chest feeling near to despair.

She lay like that for a long time, him sleeping and she worrying. Then his chest moved and he spoke. And his words told her that he had not been sleeping at all even though every law of nature demanded that he should be, but had been burrowed inside his own psyche. "Jesus, what. . . have you done to me? In four. . . short days. What. . . have you done to me?"

And Lizzie, in a man's bedchamber, lying across his nude chest, and shedding tears, heard the same question echoing in her heart.

He was silent after that and Lizzie, still resting her head on his chest, was certain that he slept, but she could not sleep, despite how very exhausted she was. At some point she began to realize a sudden change in the house. She heard no noise, the night was still thick and dark against the glass, but there was that elusive quality that comes just before dawn that makes itself known more by instinct than by senses, and she raised her head.

Oh, God, it was nearly morning! She glanced at the clock, ticking and impassive upon the fireplace mantel. Where were Andrew and Tyler with Steven? It could not be long before the house began to stir.

With her worry she moved from the bed. She checked his stitches, very much exposed, but they had held and she went to the wash basin, poured cold water into it, splashed her face until she was certain there were no tear tracks left. She neatened her hair, straightened her dress, and feeling a deal better, selected fresh linens and began the tedious job of wrapping his lordship's chest. It took some maneuvering, for if he were not unconscious, he was at least deeply asleep, and so was of no help. She lifted one side of his torso as much as she could, slid the bulk of the folded sheet beneath him, then ran around the bed to lift his other side and snagged the sheet through. She did this as many times as necessary, pulling it snug each time, and then pinned it off.

She still had his arm to look at, but although there was blood on its bandage, it did not seem to be spreading, indicating that it had stopped bleeding, so instead, she left the room and went into the darkened house in search of Effington. She found he had progressed all the way to the servants entrance, where he even now had the door open as he scrubbed smears from the door frame. He glanced up a little startled at her appearance, but only asked upon seeing it was her, "Have you finished then?"

Miss Murdock nodded. "Yes, although I still need to look at his arm. Can I help? It will be dawn soon."

"No, Miss. If I am discovered, I will think up some excuse for my activity and any blood I may have not cleaned yet. If you are discovered--"

"Yes. You're quite right of course," Lizzie said. "Have Andrew and Tyler arrived?"

"No, Miss," he admitted. "But you had better go up all the same. I will be sending Earl Larrimer up as soon as he arrives and assisting Tyler with the carriage, for it will not do to have speculation on what the duke's cousin is doing in his lordship's stables so very early in the morning."

"Yes, thank you, Effington. St. James is very lucky to have you."

There was a moment when Effington stopped his scrubbing completely as though weighing her words. "Yes, Miss, but I certainly did not think it would be for my skills as a scullery maid," he said resentfully, and she smiled.

Miss Murdock returned to his lordship's chambers, and although she hated to disturb him, she set about cutting the bandages from his upper left arm. She need not have feared, for he seemed beyond waking for now, and even her gentle maneuvering of his arm and close examination of the flesh wound there brought nothing but a little catch in his breathing.

She was satisfied that he would not need stitches, and settled with dusting the wound with Borax powder and rewrapping it. With the finish of that job, she was left feeling at loose ends. And the first blush of dawn could be seen outside the windows.

She moved the table she had pushed over back to where she had found it, replaced all the supplies that Tyler had brought up into the wicker basket, wrapped the bloody, used bandages in a ball to be disposed of later and took an inventory of the remaining linens Effington had brought in. The basins of stained water needed poured out and washed, but she didn't dare leave St. James' rooms again to do so, settled with combining what was left of the water into one and stacking the now empty one beneath it.

Throughout all this busy work she was aware that with the coming of dawn, her decision to stay was irrevocable. There could be no sudden change of heart and sneaking back to her room at Dante's grandmother's home.

With a last lingering look at St. James, she went through the connecting door into his sitting room, and spying his chaise lounge, settled onto it. She was tired in every bone of her body and her last thought before drifting off into sleep was that she had not had a full night's rest since he had first banged on her door in the wee hours of the morning.

Chapter Twenty

"Damn it all to Hell and back!" St. James' voice pierced through the crack of the connecting door and into Miss Murdock's sleeping mind. "When did this arrive, Effington!"

Effington's voice, an unflappable, if rather tired, drone: "In the morning's post, milord. I delayed on bringing it up as you were sleeping and I could not see disturbing you."

Miss Murdock, trying to make some sense of why she should be hearing a conversation between St. James and his valet in the room next to her bedchamber, opened her eyes. It was not her bedchamber, she realized, it was, in fact, St. James' sitting room and she was lying on his chaise lounge. She sat up, her head groggy, and took in her surroundings, noticing that she was in her old, worn, brown dress, and that it had a good deal of dried blood smeared across it.

Then of course, she remember it all: Steven, St. James' injury, the furtive activities of (this morning?) earlier.

She looked out the window, saw that it was a rainy, dreary day and quite impossible to tell whether it was morning or evening or whether she had slept one hour or ten.

"Whatever is going on now, St. James?" a third voice asked. It did not belong to Tyler or Andrew, she was sure, and she could not place it, although it did sound familiar. "I've never known you to be so indisposed by drink that you were still in bed at this hour of the day. I was quite surprised to have your man bring me up here."

"It's not from drink. I was shot last night," but even through the crack of the connecting door, Miss Murdock heard the preoccupation in St. James' voice, and recalling his oaths that had wakened her, she wondered what, oh *what*, possibly more could have gone wrong!

"The devil you were! When did this happen?"

"Last night obviously," St. James answered. "But hush, Bertie. Look at this handwriting. Why does it look familiar to me?"

Miss Murdock, relaxing somewhat with St. James' visitor being identified as Lord Tempton, quietly stood, stretched, smoothed her rumpled brown dress into some semblance of order, and then took an interest in a covered tray she spied upon one table, complete with coffee (now cold), napkin and silver. Evidently some considerate soul, probably Effington, had brought it some time while she was sleeping.

She went to it, lifted the lid. She did not like to be eavesdropping, but she could not latch the door for fear of alerting Bertie to her presence. Leaving the sitting room by the door to the hall was out of the question. So, she decided, she would try to keep herself quietly occupied and let their words only become a background noise, and pay as little attention to them as possible.

All the same, when Effington spoke, she was aware of it, and when St. James answered, she found herself guilty of attending.

"I beg pardon, milord," Effington offered, "but I seem to recall you receiving an envelope yesterday with the address written in the same, rather uneducated fist."

"Blast it, Effington, but you are right!" St. James swore.

Miss Murdock imagined Effington was not surprised in the least to discover that he was correct.

Bertie's voice interrupted, "This is serious, St. James. Whoever wrote this letter is telling you quite plainly to watch your back."

"Yes. And if I had read the one sent yesterday, I may have been more prepared, damn it! It's the second time I've been careless, and I do so hate to be caught out. Bad enough yesterday that Miss Murdock was made extremely uncomfortable for my mistake. . . ."

"But somewhat worse this time, milord, when it nearly cost you your life," Effington finished.

"Quite," St. James agreed. "Run down to my study. The other letter must still be on my desk, and I will be very interested in what it has to say."

Miss Murdock heard the bedroom's hall door opening and then closing. She had given up on eating, but she sipped at the cold coffee gratefully and watched the rain coming down the window pane and wondered if the mysterious letters that St. James was discussing were good or bad. If someone had seen fit to warn him of his danger, then certainly they must be good, mustn't they?

She was in no position to judge, only knew that for someone who had always been calm and sensible that she had a bad case of the nerves now. That he could sit in there only cursing his carelessness, she found annoying, for she felt like screaming in vexation. Why hadn't he read this other letter yesterday? And what further danger was he in that this second letter should arrive today? Oh, damn it, she wanted to march in there and snatch the letter for herself and read it.

"Well, St. James, you had better tell me the whole of it," Bertie was saying. "Were you confronted?"

"Hmm? Oh, the shooting. No. He shot at me from the dark mouth of the mew to the side of Almacks. I can scarce believe no one was aware of it."

"Outside *Almacks!*" Bertie cried. "I've no need to tell you--extremely bad *ton* that, old boy, to have the effrontery to be shot outside Almacks." St. James laughed and Bertie joined him before pointing out, "I fear if it is discovered your voucher will be revoked again."

"Yes, and a great pity, that, for I understand from Miss Murdock that my grandmother was reduced to 'buying off' one of the board members to regain my welcome status."

Bertie laughed with glee. "She did not! Oh, she is a card, Dante. I have often said if I could find a woman as your grandmother must have been in her day, I would marry with no regrets."

"Quite," St. James returned in a musing voice.

"But as to why no one heard the shot, must tell you, the place was in a stir. In fact," Bertie added, "I would not be surprised if your assailant were not someone seeking to protect Miss Murdock from you after your display. She proved to be quite popular, you know, after you left. And you should well know also that if she were not in London under only your family's protection, you most certainly would have been called out after your behavior of last night. Not at all the thing, St. James," he concluded, "to be responsible for protecting the girl and perversely also the one she needs protecting from."

"You manage to make me feel more of an ogre than I already am convinced I must be to do that to that poor child. But I've reached a point where I can not turn back, and Miss Murdock is still being aggravatingly reluctant to accept my suit."

"Do you really think it matters?" Bertie asked. "I understand that you have managed to stir someone, clearly, from their complacency of your being alive. But as last night was your first public display of interest in Miss Murdock, I can not see how they would have had time to observe it, digest it, feel threatened by it, for Lord knows what reason, and be in position to then do you some harm as you walked out the door of the place!"

"Obviously, they were somehow already aware of it," St. James replied. "And as the man who shot me last night was a hired assassin, they had been aware of it long enough to make some very thorough plans for my demise. And now, equally as obvious with the delivery of this letter, someone else has become aware of these plans and is trying to warn me. For what purpose, though, is what is bothering me," he added in a baffled voice. "I can not help but think that even this is some sort of trap. You notice it asks I come alone?"

"Then they could not know that you were even now laid up in bed, wounded," Bertie pointed out. "So they can not be all that intimate with whoever is laying these plans."

"Ah, but they can not know for sure if I have been wounded or not, since their assassin never made it back to them, can they?" St. James asked.

"You mean--?"

"Of course. You did not think that I would take *kindly* to getting shot, did you? Quite ruined my best red velvet suit, of which Effington, I am sure, is heartbroken. Where *is* he, by-the-by? He should have been back by now."

"Any clue to the identity of the bastard?"

"Yes. I know his identity. And he is quite dead."

"I hope you had enough sense to ask him a few questions and did not merely kill him outright in a blind rage."

A bitter laugh. "No. Circumstances went rather beyond my control, with Steven, my messenger lad, wrestling with the man on the ground in the dark. He nearly got stabbed for his trouble. I saw the knife flash and I had a final clear shot, though damned if I know how I hit him, for I was nearly unconscious at that point, and lying on the ground myself."

Miss Murdock, in the midst of hearing this speech, choked on her coffee and had a hard time of it to keep from making a great deal of noise. She put her napkin over her mouth and for a moment her eyes were very large from the effort.

"Which is a damnedable thing," St. James continued, "for I had gained from him that he was involved with the murder of my parents--"

And Miss Murdock's eyes grew larger and she rose from her chair and went to the corner of the room, choking mightily now and doing everything in her power to stifle it.

"--and was contacted apparently by the same person for both jobs."

"To be so goddamned close!" Bertie exclaimed. "What confounded luck. Of course you would have killed him at any rate, I imagine, after hearing that, but it would have been nice to gain some knowledge of who your true enemy is."

Before St. James could reply, Miss Murdock heard his lordship's bedroom door from the hallway open and then close, and Effington said, "I can not find it, milord, and I fairly tore your study apart looking for it."

"Damn it," St. James said. There was a long silence after that, when Bertie and Effington seemed to be waiting for his next move, and he was evidently busy pondering it.

Miss Murdock, with no distraction, heard only two things in her mind: St. James telling her *but* early that morning and Bertie's off hand summation that St. James would have killed the man at any rate! But that man had been Steven's father! Surely, if St. James had been aware of that and had had any choice, surely he would not have—!

"Then I have no choice but to go to this assignation I have been invited to," St. James' voice broke into her thoughts, and she whirled from the corner and stared at the door between them, her mouth gaping and her brows drawn together in great consternation.

"You can not be serious, St. James," Bertie told him. "It is for tonight, and frankly, you look like hell! I can't imagine you leaving your bed, let alone your house."

"I was going to have to be about tonight, at any rate, Bertie, for I already have another pressing matter to take care of. And as Tyler and Andrew are busy looking for my errant messenger boy, I can not ask either of them to do it for me."

Miss Murdock, who expected Steven to be even now somewhere on the premises, and Tyler and Andrew enjoying rest from their activities (as she, now feeling guilty, had) was shocked that he had somehow turned missing, and she walked over to the door and stood in the shadow beyond the slight crack to listen more closely.

Bertie sounded a good deal puzzled. "*What* are you talking about?" he asked. "Errant messenger boy? Tyler and *Andrew* searching for him? You must be delirious, St. James, for the object of my visiting you today was to tell you that Earl Larrimer and Miss Murdock eloped last night!"

Miss Murdock, standing just beyond their sight, let out such an exclamation that had St. James not been speaking at the same time, she would have surely been heard.

"What fool tale is this?" he demanded.

"I tell you, St. James! Ryan went over this morning to invite Miss Murdock for a ride in the park, and the house was in an uproar. He had it from Lady Lydia herself that Miss Murdock and your cousin had snuck off together in the middle of the night and she could put no other connotation upon it than that they were eloping!"

St. James began to laugh and, as Bertie must have been looking at him very strangely at this odd reaction, he managed to say, "But Bertie, Miss Murdock is even now sleeping in my sitting room."

"The devil she is!" Bertie sputtered. "Have you lost your mind, St. James?"

But Miss Murdock, perceiving that St. James had no worry in allowing Bertie into his confidence of her presence, and ashamed of herself for eavesdropping, reached for the door handle and swung the door back and took a timid step into the room. "I fear it is true, Bertie," she said, a great deal embarrassed. "For I was the one that stitched St. James up last night."

And Lord Tempton turned his portly figure around in his chair and gaped at her.

Miss Murdock looked past him to St. James, who was propped up on several pillows in his bed.

Effington had managed to shave him and wash him, tie his hair back and wrap him into a dressing gown. Except for the pallid paleness of his face, and the rather rigid way he was sitting, one would not even know that he were injured.

And if her initial reaction was a bit of self-congratulations that she had attended him so well, she should naturally be forgiven, for he had not been the easiest of patients to work upon. "Miss Murdock," his lips twitched in a great deal of amusement at sight of her standing shame-faced in the door. "You are looking very well today."

"Oh, botheration!" she said, annoyed with him already. "Do not try to divert me with your foolishness, milord, for I very well know I look the contrary. What is this of Steven missing? And if you think you are going anywhere this night, you are quite mistaken!"

But St. James was laughing. "Shame, shame, Miss Murdock, for listening at key-holes."

"The door was not latched," she said in weak defense, "and I could hardly burst in here and tell you I had awakened when I did not know if you could fully trust Bertie. Sorry, Lord Tempton, I am not implying that you can not be trusted," she hastened to add.

"Indeed!" Bertie reassured her. "If you *had* burst in, I am sure I would have had an apoplexy, so I am most grateful. I thought I was beyond being shocked at St. James' activities, but I did not dream of this in my wildest imaginings."

"Neither did I," St. James said with perfect dryness and Miss Murdock flushed, because of course, for once, he had had nothing to do with her being so improper, and it had, in fact, been her idea.

"Steven?" she asked, refusing to allow herself to be distracted. Effington pulled a chair forward for her, and she gave him a grateful look as she sat, but then her eyes returned to the duke.

St. James delayed in answering her by saying to his valet instead, "Effington, see if you can not rattle up a change of clothes for Miss Murdock. Something dark, mind you, and suitable for riding. And a cloak that will not draw attention to her either."

Effington left to do this, and Miss Murdock had a second's wondering wherever he should find these items, and to whence she should be riding, but then she turned her attention back to St. James and he answered her with quiet concern. "I do not know, Miss Murdock. Andrew and Tyler are even now searching, and have orders not to return without him. I gather that he was not in your room when they returned to fetch him."

Bertie said, "I shan't ask what your messenger boy was doing in Miss Murdock's room, by the by."

"I would be grateful if you did not!" St. James returned. "But what is this business of Miss Murdock and Andrew's elopement?" he asked. "For that is what interests me greatly. Surely, Miss Murdock, you and Andrew did not intentionally lead my aunt to believe you had eloped?"

"Certainly not!" Miss Murdock said, very much affronted. "Though on retrospect, I should have guessed that she would leap to such a ridiculous conclusion. We left a note in my room saying that I was quite disgusted with your behavior last night," and she paused, letting that sink in, which he infuriated her by only grinning, "and that I was returning to my father. Andrew, of course worried about my safety, was accompanying me, after trying valiantly to change my mind, to no avail."

"Well, that all seems very simple," Bertie admitted. "Ryan did say that Lady Lydia had told him that there was a note left indicating they were going to Miss Murdock's home, but she was certain it was only a red herring and that the true destination had been Gretna Green."

"Oh, for Heaven's sake!" Miss Murdock exclaimed, very much irritated by Lady Lydia's penchant for the dramatic. "I only hope that she is not busy spreading this ludicrous tale to anyone else she comes into contact with today."

St. James seemed to be pondering this same possibility and with more than the mild annoyance that Miss Murdock felt if the frown between his brows were any indication. "That confounded, foolish woman. She may very well have put such an iron in the spokes--! But what else am I to believe? For Ryan can scarcely be designated as an intimate of hers, and she saw fit to tell him--"

But Bertie's exclamation interrupted the rest of his thought. "Ryan, yes! Egads, St. James, but he rode out just before noon with his destination being Miss Murdock's home. He hoped to find Earl Larrimer and Miss Murdock there and warn them of what Lady Lydia had concluded. It was he who suggested that I should let you know for he feared very much that you would cause trouble and did not want you going after them yourself, telling me to assure you he had it all well in hand."

"And when he arrives there, and finds no Andrew and no Miss Murdock, he will assume the worst. Damn it!"

"Not to mention--my father!" Miss Murdock added, beginning to feel upset. "Oh, Lord," she fretted. "Whatever will he think? I leave supposedly engaged to one man and elope less than a week later with his cousin. Oh, I shall die!"

St. James glanced at her with compassion. "Indeed, Miss Murdock, I hate to point this out to you, but your father will not be the only one in a state of outraged shock at this apparent activity on your part." He lay his head back on the top of the pillows and looked at the ceiling. "I can not *fathom* what Tyler and Andrew were thinking of to involve you."

"It was Steven that involved me, milord, and I ran quite roughshod over Andrew and Tyler's objections, so do not blame them. And if I had not, I remind you, you would be in a good deal worse shape than you are now."

He raised his head to give her a brief grin and said, "I know that very well, Miss Murdock! But it does not change the fact that you are in an incredible jam, far worse than I ever intended by my little show at Almacks. And in the same fell stroke, my aunt has managed to remove all the pressure that I had been placing on my adversary, for they will scarcely believe that I am about to propose to you when you have apparently already eloped with my cousin!"

"Oh my! I had not thought of that!" she admitted. And if she had thought his tactics deplorable, she could still very well understand his frustration at having his plans wrecked by a feather-headed gossip.

He swore and said, "Well, there is nothing for it, Miss Murdock. I already knew I must get you out of my rooms tonight, for I can not hide you here forever, however titillating it may be for me to try," he added.

She flushed. "Hush, milord! I haven't time for your games now."

"Neither do I, Miss Murdock, which I very much regret," he told her. "The only thing that had been worrying me was where to then stash you." He turned his eyes to Lord Tempton. "Bertie, are you up to smuggling a smallish female from my rooms tonight?"

"Of a certainty, St. James. Must admit though, never expected to be smuggling one *out*!"

To which St. James gave him a quelling look.

"You intend for me to return home, then?" Miss Murdock asked, trying to catch up with St. James' mind and think of where he would logically wish her to be.

"Precisely. You are very quick, Miss Murdock," he said with a pleased smile. "If you are where you stated you intended to be, and of course, neither Andrew nor Ryan will dispute the fact that you were not there all along, it will dispel some of Lady Lydia's tale-mongering. Assuming we can either catch Ryan at your home or intercept him on his return to London. I only pray he does not get it in his head to chase your phantoms all the way to Gretna Green.

"But I fear," he continued, looking at her with a good deal of concern on his face that warned her she was not going to like what he was about to add, "that in the end, it is not going to do very much good at all, for it will be surmised that you had attempted to elope and that one or the other of you turned coward and that you are now merely trying to cover your tracks."

"Then I can see no reason for me to even return there," she answered. "As if my reputation is any reason to begin with."

He gave her a very odd, somewhat exasperated look. "Miss Murdock," he reminded her, "I seem to recall several conversations with you in which you did nothing but demand to be returned home immediately."

"Oh, do not throw that up in my face, milord," she told him with impatience, much to Bertie's amusement. "For I was trying to keep from becoming involved with. . . all of this! Now, it is just a little too late for such squeamishness, obviously."

"And if you had just done as I asked, you wretched lass, you would have been entirely oblivious and unmoved by. . . *all of this*," and he paused, "and instead would be enjoying a very luxurious lifestyle without a care in the world."

"Be that as it may," she countered, her words becoming fast and desperate, "being oblivious and unmoved is now an impossibility, as it was very much an impossibility when you offered me your ridiculous proposal, I may add, and what we face now behooves me to be in London. I can *not* go to Chestershire when we have no idea what has become of Steven and when you have some wild plan of going out on an assignation tonight that may very well end in your assassination!"

"By God!" Bertie interrupted. "I wager even you could not say all of that three times very quickly, St. James."

"Oh, do shut up, Bertie," St. James said, but his eyes did not leave Miss Murdock's as they seemed to be locked in some contest of wills.

Then St. James began to speak, and where Miss Murdock's words had been very fast, his were slow and succinct. "This rumor that you have eloped with my cousin needs to be dispelled, and if *you* have no care for your reputation, I do."

"After that display last night, milord! I doubt it."

"That *display* was to show the extent of my total besottedness in regards to you, Miss Murdock, and was to lead up quite nicely to our announced engagement--"

"Which I have *not* agreed to, and can not *foresee* myself agreeing to--"

"*Even* if you do not, it would hardly be as damning to you as your perceived elopement, and more damningly, an elopement that has gone awry." And he paused before adding in a dangerous tone, "Unless you and my cousin decide at some point to continue that particular charade indefinitely, which for my cousin's sake, I would heartily advise you against doing so."

She had no quick response to this, only sat back in her chair feeling a good deal out of breath.

"Now," he said, "you may rest assured that we will find Steven, and as for this meeting I have been invited to, I will be better prepared than I was last night."

But she was close to tears and could not resist interrupting again to say, "With stitches not even twenty-four hours old, milord? And alone?"

He sighed wearily at that, earning a sympathetic look from Bertie, before continuing with a beleaguered air, "All of which is of no concern of yours, Miss Murdock, as I have tried to point out to you repeatedly."

"And I have tried to point out to *you*, milord, that if you see fit to involve me, then you will suffer the consequences of my involvement."

"I never intended you to be involved to this degree, you aggravating child, and Bertie, do me a kindness and pour me a drink, for I swear I am ready to strangle her."

"Milord!" Miss Murdock fumed. "You have no call to be drinking with those stitches in your chest."

"Certainly, I do, Miss Murdock, for I shall tear them out, I am sure, if I lay hands on you, which I am tempted to do. Bertie, damn it! Are you going to listen to me or to her?"

Bertie still appeared to be hesitating, and St. James tore his gold eyes away from where they had been challenging Miss Murdock and pinned them upon his old friend. "Really, St. James," that man cried in defense. "You *are* bedridden and she is not."

"But *she*," St. James explained with a great deal of condescension, "does not have a pistol beneath her pillow."

"Ah," Bertie said. "I quite see your point." He lumbered up from his seat and went to the sideboard. "I only hope that you are willing to defend me as quickly as you are willing to threaten me, for I have every expectation of her throwing herself at my throat."

And indeed, Miss Murdock was glowering at him most intimidatingly. "You are a coward to let him frighten you, Bertie, you know," she told that man without mercy. "If you would but not fetch it for him, he would be cured by the time he were able to reach it himself."

"Tut, Miss Murdock! St. James without his drink is like a baby without his sugar-tit. And whoever wishes to hear all that crying?" he asked, and he poured into not just one glass but two, and handed one to St. James and kept the other for himself. Before drinking, his twinkling blue eyes met hers and he asked with perfect gentlemanliness, "Care to join us, Miss Murdock?"

"Indeed, I do not!" she told him. But she shook her head a little in exasperation and only ended by saying, "You are both quite abominable, you know."

St. James drank from his glass with every appearance of relief, and then setting the remainder of it aside, said more calmly, "Now, Miss Murdock, you must see that it is quite impossible for you to remain, so please do not continue to argue with me."

"But my letter states quite clearly from the start that I was going no where but my father's!" Miss Murdock pointed out. "When Andrew appears and reassures Lady Lydia that I am there, whether I am or not, surely she will tell everyone else as well that she was mistaken, and it should not matter."

"It *will* matter, I fear, Miss Murdock," St. James took pains to explain to her. "For once a scandal is begun, it takes on a life of its own and nothing will kill it."

"St. James knows of what he is speaking of, Miss Murdock," Bertie interjected with what he believed to be a reassuring tone.

"Yes. I do," St. James agreed, unperturbed. "And I should know also, that if one wishes to dispel it, there is nothing better than starting a countering rumor that is, although more respectable, also equally as stimulating."

Miss Murdock was not following him at all now. She only understood that where he had been adamant in preventing her from going home before, he was now as adamant that she should leave. She grasped the smooth wood of her chair's arms and turned her head to each gentleman as they discussed her problem as if it were no more, now, than the rising and falling of the price of grain.

"You have an idea, St. James?" Bertie asked.

"I do. However, it will not be one to Miss Murdock's liking."

And she tightened her grip on the chair arms.

St. James looked at her, "We shall have to post the banns, Miss Murdock."

"Banns?" she asked, her voice faint.

"Your engagement to me. It will have to be announced in tomorrow's papers."

"Oh, no, milord!" she demurred and rose from her chair. She turned her back to him, then whirled to face him again. "I thought I made it clear! I would sooner have it said I *had* eloped with Andrew than that I was to marry you!"

Bertie made an exclamation, but in her sudden terror, she could not grasp what he had said.

St. James took his glass again and sipped from it, but his gold eyes never left hers over its rim. She could almost see the great wheels of his mind spinning behind those two blazing eyes, and she began to realize that she was in for the real battle and that the skirmish over whether she was to return home or not had just been the calling to arms. "As bad as all that, Miss Murdock?" he asked.

She waved a hand in agitation even as she felt her face flushing. "Unfair!" she cried. "You can not mean to make me list my reasons when you must be perfectly aware of them by now. I am sure I made it blatantly clear to you by my actions this morning!"

A sudden, startled movement by Lord Tempton brought her attention to him. He was standing up from his chair, and to her amazement, his face was very red. "*Ahem*," he coughed. "I shall just wait in the other room!"

Miss Murdock, with a sinking feeling, realized that her words had been quite suggestive. "Oh, sit down!" she snapped at the hapless Bertie. "He was barely conscious, let alone capable of. . .oh, *nevermind*!"

St. James was laughing. "Yes, yes," he agreed between his chuckles, "for do you think, Bertie, that I would have survived any display of impropriety without receiving another blow to the cheek? Despite my already grievous condition?"

"Oh, stop it!" she cried, and broke into very unladylike tears. "Can you not see," she snuffled into her hand, "that you are provoking me again?"

"Indeed, I do see it," he told her, his voice tender. "And if you can forgive me for not fetching you a handkerchief, you will find one in my top wardrobe drawer."

Bertie, who never had sat down, got this item for Miss Murdock before she could move for it, and then let himself out the bedroom door to go, Miss Murdock could only assume, to wait below in St. James' study.

"Come sit with me, Lizzie," St. James persuaded once the door was again closed, "and tell me all of your concerns, and we shall endeavor to come up with something that you can accept."

"No, no," she continued to cry. "For I well know what tactics you will choose, and you can not understand--" and she was beside herself with tears and worry, "that what I do is for the best for both of us! Why can you not see it? Why must you insist upon making me wish and want when it can only make me more afraid than I already am? And if the worst does *not* happen then we will be sentenced to making each other perfectly miserable for the remainder of our lives."

He threw back the sheet that covered him. His robe fell open to bare his bandaged chest, and he swung his legs around to get out of the bed.

His face paled with the effort, but it was so set with determination, that she knew he would sooner pass out than admit that he could not get up from that bed.

She paled herself to see him risking the stitches she had sewn into him. "Oh, stop it! You are going to *kill* me with worry. How can you torment me this way?" and she went to him, where he remained on the side of the bed, robe open revealing his laced shorts beneath, his head bowed, his right hand clutching his bandage wrapped chest, but his teeth clenched in readiness to continue his effort. "Jesus, Mary and Joseph, I will sit with you, if you will only remain in that bed!"

He raised his head enough to give her a grim smile. "Swearing like a sailor again, Lizzie?"

"You provoke me into it, milord, for even my father could not agitate me to this degree." Then she knelt in front of him. "Please, I promise I will listen to you if you only stay in your bed and rest."

He moved his right hand from where it had been holding his chest, laid it along her cheek and his fingers curved to feel the line of her jaw. "You intoxicate me, Lizzie," he murmured.

"No," she said, and lowered her eyes. With desperation, she raised her hand to his, where it warmed her face and his fingers caressed beneath the angle of her jaw. He caught her hand in his, held it and began lying back on the bed, his eyes half hooded in twin gold flames, and pulled her with him.

"Come to me, Lizzie."

Lizzie, in an attempt to keep from falling on him, placed her free hand on the white bandage of his chest, and to her horror she realized that she was in nearly the same position she had been in at the inn, when she had attempted to button his shirt and straighten his cravat. The skirt of her dress was again between his spread legs. She was again leaning with precariousness over him, one of her hands already on his chest. In a motion of either mocking her, or reminding her, or of claiming some promise previously made, he placed her other hand on his chest also and pinned it. His other hand moved up and he held both of her palms captive above his thumping heart. Again she was aware of the movement of his breathing. And the lids of his eyes drew back and his nostrils quivered at her nearness.

Then he buckled both of her trembling arms and she landed with a thump on his chest, her small body laid out along his own. He gave a small groan and she could not discern if it were from his stitches being aggravated or from another reason entirely.

As a cat thrown into water seems to leap out as soon as its feet hit only the surface, she fought to get up. But he wrapped his right arm about her, and his legs, and held her there.

Miss Murdock, shocked and panicking at his most improper actions, raised her head and shoulders and glared down at him.

"As bad as all that, Miss Murdock?" he asked her with teasing lightness, and then his hand moved and she stiffened more in her difficult position. But he only ran it up her back, her neck, and to the ribbon in her hair, and he untied the knot of it with the same adeptness he had shown her once before when he had pinned her hair up.

"Dante," she choked. A tear dripped from her face and landed on one harsh plain of his pale cheek.

"Shh. Do not argue with me now, Lizzie, for can you not see, can you not *feel*, that I am too busy to talk?"

She closed her eyes, unable to meet the tender depths of his own, and she felt the dark warmth of his body beneath hers, as hard and tightly strained as she had always sensed it would be. He shifted her, his grip loosening, so that her hips turned until she lay on her side atop him. He pressed her skirted legs up to rest in a bent position along his thighs. Finally, he slipped her head to rest on his shoulder and he turned his head and studied her eyes that had opened wide throughout all this sure maneuvering.

She was more comfortable and less threatened, lying more like a baby than a lover in his arms, even though the most of her body still lay, in fact, upon his. With a little faint but profound sigh, she moved her hand to take his.

He was quiet for a long time and only his right hand moved, coming up to rub through her hair, caressing the back of her head again and again in a slow ritual of comfort that made her heart slow from where it had been quickly beating to a slow tempo that made her feel sluggish in his arms as one on the verge of deep sleep or death.

When he finally spoke, his voice husky, she heard him as someone who has been hypnotized hears the voice of he who cast the spell. "Don't ever be afraid to come to me, Lizzie."

And without any thought at all, she said, "I won't be."

"Tell me your concerns, Lizzie, and we shall endeavor to come up with something that you can accept."

And she smiled a little through her tears that she feared were dampening his chest even through his bandages. "You know my concerns, Dante. There is nothing I can accept that will alleviate them."

"Can you accept that it is too late for me to walk away from this?" he asked her. "Can you accept that if I live then I am yours, and if we are not married already, I will pursue you until we are?"

"No," she whispered. "It can not be so. You've only known me for four days. And what is poignant and new to me is only," and she swallowed, "diverting to you."

His hand continued its movements through her hair, working through the strands in an endless combing over his fingers.

"Diverting," he mused, and his voice questioned, pried into his own soul. "No." And he shifted, kissed the tip of her nose. "Enchanting, I think is a better word. You are enchanting and I am enchanted. I lay in this bed with you and I wish to ravish you, and make your skin glow as bright as your cheeks. I could easily grow drunk on you, for you are like wine in my blood, fine, dark and full. And I curse all the blackness around me that keeps me from courting you and wooing you as you should be, and which, I think, I would enjoy very much," and he smiled but his eyes seemed in equal measure sad and divine. "And yet, if it were not for all of this, would I have ever known you, Lizzie? And would I have ever loved you as I do?"

His mouth met hers on the end of his words, his lips caressing across hers in faint greeting and she trembled. His lips came again, caressing across in the opposite direction, and she turned her head in following. And he returned his lips to her, and as hers were openly seeking his, he settled his mouth upon her lips at last with finality, and what Miss Murdock had thought had been love before she realized had only been the vague thunder one hears before an oncoming storm.

His mouth was in constant and almost violent motion. It left her lips and widened until he scraped his teeth gently but urgently along her jaw. He moved down her neck and kissed up the point of her chin. His hand tightened in her hair, until he had a knot of it around his fist, and when his body moved so that she was slipped to the bed and he rose over her and onto his elbows, she could not have told when it happened or if she even noticed it. She only knew that her arms wrapped about his neck, as someone clinging to life. And he spoke, hurried, thick murmurings of satisfaction and frustration that were muffled against her skin, in her hair and her neck. And when he reached her ear, she understood what he was saying, "Marry me, Lizzie. Tell me you'll marry me. For if I can not have you soon, God help me but I may as well die."

With an effort, he pulled back and his gold eyes were above her, demanding answer, demanding she accede, and she did by nodding once, her eyes very large and hart-like. For an instant, he looked pained, as though she were a hart, and he had just pierced her with his oft too often deadly aim. And mayhaps he had a sudden picture of Steven saying 'Da' and his thumb dropping on the hammer, and that brief, eternal silence between the man's words cutting off, *God, no, Steven! Say t'isn't you, la--* and the final deathly boom of the gun, like thunder following lightning that had already struck.

Then he lowered his head until his mouth found once again her trusting one and any thoughts or memories were swept into oblivion.

By the time Effington tapped on the door Miss Murdock felt as possessed as any woman ever had in a man's bed, and he had never, in fact, done more than kiss her. Dante, with a curse, raised his head enough to call out in a thick voice, "Another minute, Effington, blast you!"

"No, milord. Pardon me, milord, but you've been in there," and he coughed, "long enough. Lord Tempton bade me to tell you that he is still waiting. Perhaps you need some help with your attire?"

St. James stared down at Miss Murdock, and he shook his head as if to clear it. "Mayhaps, you are right, Effington. I seem to have lost track of the time. You may go tell Lord Tempton that he may come up and I will speak to him while, yes, you dress me." Then more softly, he said, "Miss Murdock, if you think we are adequately finished for now?"

She blushed furiously, pushed up so that she was sitting next to him. "As I have agreed to marry you, then you have achieved your objective, milord, so I can not see any point in--"

"But I have not met my *entire* objective," he teased. "Ah, I can see you are becoming angry. But unless you wish Effington and Tempton to see you here in my bed, I suggest that you save your ire and tiptoe to the sitting room."

"I should box your ears for you are insufferable."

"But if you do that, Miss Murdock, everyone will see that I have been taking liberties with you again," and he raised his brow. Then he took her hand, kissed the back of it. "Go, Lizzie, before they burst in here and you are left to feel embarrassed, for if either one makes a snide remark to you, I shall have to call him out, and then whatever will I do without my valet or Bertie's keen intellect?"

And she did go, for she realized that he would kill for her (for was that not what St. James was about? Killing for those he loved?) and her heart stopped rather coldly in her chest. She managed to softly close the connecting door behind her and then she heard the outer door opening a mere second later and St. James said with a tone of laziness, "You needn't look so scandalized. I had merely lost track of the time, you know."

And Miss Murdock, who had been standing numb for that brief few seconds, stumbled over to the chaise lounge and collapsed not upon it, but on the floor beside it. She rested her elbows on the seat of it and her head in her hands, and dwelled on the fact that St. James professed to love her and had indeed convinced her with a great deal of skill that he did.

She gave a soft laugh and then her hands dropped from supporting her face and she cried into the seat of the lounge, her hands clawing at the fabric as she made an effort to restrain her great, gulping, heart-wrenching sobs, for she would rather die than have him hear her crying for no other reason than that he loved her and she was terrified.

Strangely enough, when her sobs subsided to some degree, and the silence in the next room told her that Effington must have in fact dressed St. James and helped him below so that he and Bertie could discuss whatever plans St. James had in mind now while she had been in the midst of her fit, she thought of Lady Lydia.

She certainly was not dense, as Miss Murdock had discovered once before. She had proclaimed it her duty to help Miss Murdock elude the improper attentions of St. James, and spreading the rumor that Miss Murdock and her son had eloped must have seemed the perfect way to go about it.

But at the dreadful blow to Andrew's reputation? No. Miss Murdock could not believe that Lady Lydia would warrant any crisis serious enough to sacrifice her son, not for Miss Murdock's virtue or anything else.

So, in the end, Miss Murdock concluded, she must be a great featherbrain, after all, and all that had come about had only been because of Lady Lydia's foolishness and not from any cunning plan to save Miss Murdock from a Fate Worse than Death.

Chapter Twenty-one

At some point, Miss Murdock's mind and indeed, probably her heart, just refused to dwell on all the horrible possibilities that her active imagination could create for it any longer, and with her head still bowed on her arms, she dozed there resting on the damp seat of the chaise lounge.

She awoke with a start sometime later, but she was not disoriented as she had been before for it felt as though she had not slept at all, but had spent the entire time running. She was certain that St. James had been in her dreams but whether she had been running toward him or away from him, she could not be certain. In some manner, it seemed she had been doing both things at the same time, which only showed how curious dreams could be, for that was quite impossible.

She got up from the floor, her knees stiff for the room had grown chilly and the fire in the fireplace had burned low. Her first instinct was to go to the connecting door. Opening it, she noted that the room was indeed empty, and in all honesty, she felt nothing but relief, for she felt if she had to face St. James again at this minute, or even Bertie or Effington, that it would be the final straw and it would kill her.

She noticed a pile of clothing in the chair, and another tray of food had been left for her. The curtains were drawn closed and the fire was not as low as the one in the sitting room, showing that someone had attended to it recently. She investigated the food, ate so mindlessly that after it was gone, she was not even sure what she had eaten. She stared at her plate, saw that it had been something with gravy, and the empty bowl beside it seemed to indicate some manner of soup, but there was not even any lingering taste in her mouth to give her a clue. Her mouth was only dry.

The fire crackled and the shadows of it danced across the walls, the furniture and the now neatly made bed. And if she did not know any better, she could believe that nothing had happened to St. James the night before, for there was nothing out of place to indicate otherwise. Except for her own presence, of course.

She sighed and rose from where she had sat at the secretary to dine and again noticed the clothing in the chair. The amount of material that was neatly folded seemed to indicate something other than a man's attire, and she went to it, saw that it was, indeed, a splendid riding habit. It was black, as Effington had followed St. James' direction on procuring something dark, but it was also a very fine, gleaming silk which made her smile for the first time since she had awakened. And although it would not really suit her coloring, it did suit her mood.

Folded beneath it was a lacy chemise, clean stockings and garters, a bustle (as a crinoline was not appropriate for a riding habit), a split slip and to her consternation, stays. "Oh, good heavens," she said to herself, "and whoever did Effington think was going to tie them?" And with the realization of who would probably be most happy to do that task for her, she hurried and took the pile of clothing into the sitting room, returned to pour water from the pitcher and into the basin, located his lordship's soap and towel, and then retreated once again through the connecting door and closed it with firmness behind her.

She disrobed, bathed as best she could in the cold water (which was quite a shock from the pleasant hip baths she had enjoyed at the Dowager's but since she was returning home at any rate, she may as well get used to it again) and dressed. Then she returned to his lordship's warmer bedchamber, found her riding boots she had worn the night before stowed in the bottom of the wardrobe with a mass array of St. James' boots, and put those on as well. The stays she had of course left out of her ensemble and for lack of anything better to do with them, stuffed them into one of St. James' drawers. The clothing she had taken off she wrapped in a pillow case from off his bed, which she trusted that Effington could replace. She put this and her mint green cloak in the wardrobe where they would be out of sight but where Effington would find them if she by chance forgot to tell him they were there before she departed. Then she brushed out her hair, knotted it into its normal bun and secured it with another ribbon from the handy supply on milord's dresser and at last dared to look at herself in the mirror.

Her eyes were more solemn than what they normally were and the black silk of her habit made her appear as if she were in mourning. She did have to admit that Effington had sized her with incredible accuracy, for the clothing was a perfect fit and she had to wonder where he had procured the items she wore, for they looked as if they could be new. And as she was unusually short and her shape accordingly slighter, it could not have been easy to stumble across something that was as though tailored for her.

Her face was rather washed out, as though all of the night-time activity she had been involved in since meeting St. James had managed to fade her sun-browned skin, but other than that and a slight puffiness under her eyes from all the crying she had done that day, she did not look too terrible and even dared to admit that in fact, she looked rather handsome in a modest way.

She was surprised out of this minute self-examination by the clock striking the hour, and as she counted the tolls, she turned with incredulity when it reached eight and continued to chime nine, and fastened her eyes on the face of it just in time to see that it read ten of the clock and the tenth hour was struck also as though to alleviate any doubt in her mind. "Oh, it can not be that late!" she worried to herself. "Or is it still morning? Oh, I am so confused!" And she went to the window, where the drapes remained drawn, and pulling them back saw that it was night, and still sullenly raining.

She wondered where St. James was, was very much afraid that without her to stop him, he had gone out into that cold and rainy night with his wounds far from healed and his strength far from back, to meet whoever had written the letters asking for a meeting at some odd hour of the night and requesting that he come alone.

But he could not be so stupid as to go alone? Surely if it were this late already, Tyler and Andrew were back and they would have found Steven, so they could have gone with him. Or Bertie. Or, maybe, but more doubtful, Effington. But surely, he did not really go alone?

As if in answer to her questions, there was a light, perfunctory tap on the door, and then as whoever it was did not seem to be expecting that she were awake or even in the room, it opened. And she turned in time to catch Effington's surprised expression at seeing that she was, indeed, awake and present. He closed the door before either of them spoke. "You found your dinner, Miss, and your clothing, I am glad to see," and he did look pleased.

"Yes. Thank you, Effington. Where ever did you obtain such a fine habit on so short of notice?" Then she could have bitten off her tongue, for she was not all that certain she really wished to know.

But his words relieved her of the sudden thought that St. James, *being* St. James, perhaps had an endless supply of women's clothing tucked away in some odd corner of the house for just these occasions. "I took the liberty of looking at your clothing bills in milord's study that were to be sent on to his barrister for payment," Effington explained with some pride at his own resourcefulness. "Then I merely went to the same shop that you had patroned and had a word with the shopkeeper. It took a bit of delicacy, but I managed it with my usual discretion and as she seemed to remember you quite fondly, she was very happy to be of assistance to you. I, of course, suggested the silk, for although his lordship suggested dark (and I very much thought black would be far better than brown for you, don't you agree?), I could see no reason why it could not be *flamboyantly* dark and she agreed quite readily with me, which shows she has impeccable taste.

"As she already had your measurements and a good deal of notes on what should suit you, and as she was assured that every expeditiousness on her part would of course be amply rewarded, it turned out to be not at all difficult," he finished and his somber face radiated self-satisfaction.

Miss Murdock, wondering what embellishments he must have dreamed up to convince Dora of the *Mystique Boutique* that there was nothing at all odd with a young Miss needing not only a riding habit on short notice, but the accompanying intimate apparel, only said, "You are uncommonly canny, Effington! Has Tyler and Andrew returned with Steven?"

His face lost its smugness and his voice turned grave, "Earl Larrimer and Tyler have returned, Miss, but they were unable to locate the lad."

"Oh, that is terrible, Effington! And I am sure they are feeling very disheartened after searching for so very long. Were they able to discover anything at all?"

But he shook his head, dashing her slim hopes. "Nothing, Miss. And they are indeed very concerned. As is his lordship."

"Of course, he would be," Miss Murdock agreed, her words faint. Then with a fragile flush, she asked, "And his lordship? Is he. . . ?"

"He's gone, Miss," Effington told her with sympathy.

And she turned from him so that he would not see the expression on her face.

"I imagine he did not. . . delay. . . for he had to attain a certain. . . mind set for his night's activities. . . and I am sure he did not wish for you to see him in that manner." He hesitated before adding in a low voice, "And I fear he can not afford the distraction tonight."

"Did he go alone?" she asked, and turned so that she looked at him over one half-defensive, half-vulnerable shoulder, but her eyes were very steady, if somewhat solemn.

"To my knowledge, yes, Miss."

"Damnation!" she said, sounding as bad as Effington's employer. "Why did he not take Tyler or Andrew? Or Bertie even, though Lord knows he would be, I fear, of poor help."

And if Effington were a bit taken aback by her sudden vehemence, he made no indication of it, only said, "They are quite done in, Miss, and he would not expect them to be in such a. . . such a situation when they were not fully capable of defending themselves, if that unlikely need were to arise."

"But it is fine for *him* to go out there in less than a capable condition!" she exclaimed with wrath. "Oh, I do not mean to bluster at you, Effington, for I well know no one can do anything to stop him. It is just so blasted senseless of him. But Bertie?"

"Lord Tempton will be up shortly to escort you out Miss, for St. James expressly told him that he was not to delay beyond midnight, but that he wanted to be assured that you were safely away by that hour at the latest."

And Miss Murdock's reply was bitter. "In case he is shot again, or even killed."

Effington, damningly, did not contradict her.

It was only half an hour before Bertie came in to the room. As most of the household had retired, there was not much worry of their being seen as long as they were quiet in their departure, which rather relieved Lizzie's mind, for she had half feared she would be expected to make some awkward escape from the bedchamber window. Effington, understandably even for his preciseness, had forgotten to procure her a dark colored cloak, but he remedied this by taking one of St. James' coats and draping it about her small shoulders. And if it were somewhat heavy, it was also snug, and smelled of *him*, which comforted her.

She said her goodbyes to Effington, who touched her very much by telling her he would look forward to the happy day when she would be the lady of the house, and if they both had their doubts that it would ever come about, neither dared express them.

Then Bertie offered her his arm, and though he may seem for the most part rather ineffectual, he did display now an underlying core of steady nerves, and she found herself counting on him a great deal, when before she was afraid that she would have to be the strong one. And although she had experience with that role, on this night, knowing that St. James may even now be confronting his nemesis, she was just as happy to be weak.

They didn't speak until they had left the house, and then she only made a small exclamation to see the fine, coal black filly she had admired the night before side-saddled in readiness for her.

Bertie whispered, "St. James bade me to tell you she is yours, Miss Murdock, whatever comes out of all of this, for he expressly purchased her for you yesterday. He says he knows she's no Gold Leaf, but he hopes that she will do adequately until such time as you are at Morningside and are able to be reunited with your horse."

"Oh, she will do splendidly," Miss Murdock breathed. "And he should not have been worried about a mount for me when he has so many other matters on his mind."

"Well, that is St. James, Miss Murdock. Forever unpredictable," he told her, and if he sounded a little off-hand, his next words showed her that he was not nearly as flighty as she had first assumed that he was. "And as I can see from the look on your face that you are predicting that he will come to harm tonight, just remember that he will surely come out unscathed just to be contrary."

And she gave a sudden laugh, finding a degree of comfort in his words that she had been unable to produce for herself. "Is that how you bear it, Bertie?"

"But, of course!" he laughed with her. "However, there is a rather nasty flip side to that coin."

"Meaning that when you least expect there to be trouble with him, that is when you need to be the most on your guard?"

"Alas. But for tonight we shall not dwell on that little unpleasantness," and his blue eyes twinkled at her in the darkness of the courtyard between house and stables. "If you are ready to mount, Miss Murdock?" and he threw her into the saddle and mounted his own horse with less difficulty than she would have guessed from the size of his girth.

The filly danced beneath her, and she had her hands full for a moment in controlling her mount, but somehow, that natural activity, and the fresh coldness of the damp air after the previous rain helped to clear her mind. Or perhaps it had been Bertie's words, also. But whatever the reason, she now felt as though she had spent the last hour sleepwalking for her mind had been so numb, but now she began to feel quite calm and purposeful.

Bertie, unaware of any change in Miss Murdock's bearing, started out, and she allowed him to keep them to a walk until they left the mew along side the house and also a short distance down the main street. But then as he turned them down a side street, she only continued until they were out of sight of the main road, and then brought her horse to an abrupt stop.

Bertie, with some surprise, halted his horse and looked back at her. "Is something amiss, Miss Murdock?" he asked.

And she had to bite back a grin, for she could see that he was looking pained already, as though he had not expected the task set for him to be so easy and was not all *that* surprised when it now seemed that it may not be. "It is just that we are going in the wrong direction, you know," she told him.

He frowned at her with annoyance. "No, no, Miss Murdock, I assure you, it may not be the same way we arrived, but we are headed for the North Road and Chestershire."

"Indeed, I am aware of that," Miss Murdock agreed, "but it is not at all the direction I wish to go in."

He turned his horse and came back so that they were facing each other on their mounts. "Now, Miss Murdock, you are trying to get me into a great deal of trouble, I can see! Now, mind, St. James told me he had settled all with you, and I have even already visited the paper's office so that the banns shall be in tomorrow. And although I know that you are not happy about any of this, I assure you, that he really does have your best interests at heart--"

"Of course he does," she agreed, and Lord Tempton looked a little bewildered at this ready admission, when he had seen for himself her complete reluctance earlier that afternoon. "But although I agreed to the banns being posted, I really do not recall expressly agreeing to returning to my home. Now, we are headed in the wrong direction, so we must turn our horses back, at this point, and onto the main road. And if you wish to avoid the main road, then we must take a side street headed not northeast, but south and west."

And he gaped at her, but as she only remained calm, he resorted to a rather pitiful pleading. "Now, Miss Murdock," he whined, "you can not be suggesting that I take you to where his meeting is taking place?"

And Miss Murdock had the sudden insight that if this *were* where she wished to go, she could in fact induce him to take her, despite his fear of displeasing St. James, and his own common sense on the lack of this being in any way recommendable. This amused her a great deal, and rather than hold it against him, it merely made her understand why St. James put such a high value on Bertie's friendship, for there was nothing, in fact, that he would not do when asked of him, even if he felt it most unadvisable. And she felt sympathy for him as well, for she could only imagine the many scrapes that St. James had led him with reluctance into.

But that was not what she had in mind at all. "No," she said, her voice decisive. "For if we did not manage to muck up whatever plans he has made, and perhaps get him killed in the bargain, he would murder both of us, I am sure. And although I have come to understand that he allows me a great deal of leeway, even I should not care to push him to that degree."

Bertie looked somewhat relieved at these words. "Well, thank God, Miss Murdock, that you are indeed going to be sensible upon that point! Now if you will only see your way clear to understand that we must--"

But she interrupted him with a little laugh. "Indeed, not, Bertie! For if I am sensible enough to see that my presence is unwanted and unneeded for his activities tonight, I am also sensible enough to see that there is absolutely *nothing* I can do from Chestershire to aid him, whereas if I am here, there is at least one thing I can see to, or hope, at any rate, to see to. And that is finding Steven."

Bertie gave an emphatic shake of his head. "That is hardly better, Miss Murdock! For if you think St. James will take a charitable view of my allowing you to wander the streets of London at night, then you are quite mistaken!"

"I am hoping that will not be necessary, and if you would but bear with me for one moment, I shall endeavor to explain."

And Bertie, with a great sigh of resignation, said, "I am sure you shall, Miss Murdock."

At about the same time as Bertie was fast losing his battle to Miss Murdock, St. James was but a half mile from them riding not south and west as Miss Murdock wished to go, but south and east, toward the heart of London. His horse was walking, and he was taking a route of side streets and mews, and he was quite alone as Miss Murdock had feared.

Contrarily, St. James found a good deal of satisfaction in this circumstance, and relief. Having company on a night such as this when his business was nefarious would have been nothing but a distraction and a nuisance. His greatest nightmare was not of his own death, but the loss of a friend on his behalf. And it had frittered through his mind on more than one occasion that in some sort of chaotic misfortune, he may end by killing someone there to help him by mistake.

No. It had been no great hardship for him to decline offers of assistance that night. And although Tyler had taken the desistance of his help without complaint but with a great deal of disapproval, Andrew on the other hand had been more inclined to argue, and St. James had been forced to be blunt in saying that tired as Andrew was he would be of no use to him, and more than likely, a hindrance, perhaps even a peril.

Andrew had at last accepted this argument, but with a quantity of cursing that he should have wasted his energies looking for a messenger boy who by all appearances did not wish to be found at any rate, when he would have been of more use to St. James that evening if he had but conserved his energy. St. James had told him with sharpness that as he had shot that boy's father the night before, he felt rather responsible for him, and hence the searching had been as necessary, in fact to his mind, more necessary, than having his cousin acting as a nanny for him.

"And do not forget, Andrew, that I have managed up to this point without your well-meaning assistance, and you will forgive me if I am confident that I can manage tonight without it also. I have a rather more daunting task for you on the morrow at any rate."

Andrew had been rather intrigued at this notion. "Indeed? Only tell me what it is you wish me to do, St. James, for you must know by now that I am your man!"

"You will need to convince your rather misguided mother that you have not eloped with Miss Murdock."

And as Andrew had been a good deal shocked by this statement, St. James proceeded to explain Lady Lydia's assumption and the problems that it would produce. The first consequence of which was Ryan's well-meaning but ill-advised flight after the presumed eloping couple who had in fact, never left London.

And through out all of this interview in St. James' study, with Tyler, Earl Larrimer, Lord Tempton and Effington, Dante had paced with unsteadiness about the room, flexing his left arm in a constant testing of how much pressure and movement it could take so that he would be aware to a certainty to what degree he could count upon it.

"And grandmother?" Andrew asked, anxious. "She must be out of her mind with worry."

"More likely with vexation," St. James returned, "for I do not think she would swallow such a tale out of hand. Especially when it is Aunt Lydia who has surmised it. No insult intended against your mother, Andrew," he added.

"You needn't tell me that she has the most damnedably insane notions at times," Andrew replied. "But they are at least usually harmless. For something to possess her to take this idea into her head, and then apparently speak of it without compunction to who ever happened to be on hand, is even more irresponsible of her than normal. And I needn't tell you, that for her to be in any way damaging *my* snowy white reputation nearly boggles my mind, for she has always held it as near holy to be respectable! It is quite, quite unlike her."

He sounded a great deal bewildered as well as tired, and St. James had spared him a wry grin. "Do not fret, Andrew. I have already had Bertie post the banns of my and Miss Murdock's engagement and they should be in the morning's paper. That will certainly throw some doubt on the story your mother has told. And the females, I imagine, will look upon you as very dangerous indeed to have tried eloping with your cousin's fiancé."

"Yes," Bertie agreed as Andrew expressed surprise that St. James had in fact, offered for Miss Murdock. "None of them will feel safe in your presence, and so they shall find being in your presence all that more desirable."

The clock on the mantel had then struck ten times, interrupting their laughter and Andrew's demands for explanation, for he had not thought that St. James had progressed to a point where he desired engagement (and especially to a female he had only met some four days before!).

But St. James had not enlightened him in the least, the tolling of the clock seeming to drive all but the most immediate matters from his mind. He nodded at Effington, his face losing its brief look of diversion and he now appeared very grim indeed.

Effington left the room. St. James reminded Bertie, "No later than midnight, Bertie, mind you. Earlier if she is ready before. Tyler will have the horses in readiness for you."

"I understand, St. James. Needn't badger me."

But St. James was busy taking down a second weapon from where it hung, an intimidating decoration, amongst many others on the wall. There was still no sign of his missing dueling pistol, and he regretted very much not having it, but he only selected another to take the place of the one that was lost. He checked it with expertise before lying it with his remaining dueling pistol upon his desk. Then, with a little difficulty, he shrugged into his great coat that Effington had before brought down to him, and secured his pistols into his waist band beneath it. He tested his left cross draw, wincing as he did so, but nodded with resignation if not satisfaction. He was capable with it, although lamentably slower than normal.

Andrew interrupted all of this activity by asking once again, "But what about grandmother, St. James? You know as well as I that she will positively grill me!"

"She'll see the banns. Stick with your story. Miss Murdock is safely at her home in Chestershire, which by the time you speak to grandmother, such will be the truth. You needn't add that her arrival there was delayed by a full twenty-four hours. I know you dislike misleading her, but it will only upset her further if she is aware of any of this, and as, I believe, her main concern is whether I am to marry the chit or not, she will be mollified."

Then without further delay, he made a little motion of goodbye and turned to the door to take his leave. His eyes were bright beneath their half closed lids and there was a strange half-smile upon his features that rather than comforting any of those that were left, only made them feel a good deal more concerned. Then he was gone, the door clicking behind him, and in that second they perhaps all understood how completely content he was to be, in fact, alone. It made them all feel quite useless.

Now he directed his horse onto a little used path into Hyde Park, and was swallowed into the night as he left the street lamps behind. He rode a little off the trail, his mount's feet slipping in the wet grass. But the rain had stopped and all that was left was an increasing fog spreading upon the ground. He found this ideal, for it muffled the sound of his horse's movements.

The dark irises of his gold eyes enlarged as his glance probed about. He remained beneath a row of trees, his horse moving with unhurried ease, until he came at last to near the center of the empty park and a large monument rose out of the darkness twenty yards in front of him. Instead of going to it, he dismounted beneath the cover of the trees, scanned the area, then turned his horse into the shadows and secured it to a low branch. He took the bit from its mouth, which would slow him if he needed to be off quickly, but he did not wish it snorting or nickering either, and the best way he knew to keep it occupied was to allow it enough rein for it to access the still plentiful grass.

Its soft biting off of those blades was its only sound as he turned and left it there, and an occasional muted stomp of one of its feet.

St. James judged it to be eleven of the clock, and as his letter had stated the hour of midnight for the meeting, he was in fact an hour early. He moved in a wide circle around the monument, keeping to tree and shrub, pausing often to listen, searching for any sign of another horse or person. At last, satisfied that he was, as of now, alone, he settled in to watch the south side of the monument, as he had been instructed for the meeting to take place there, to see who might arrive.

The longer he waited, the more he was convinced that the writer of the letter was rather inexperienced in intrigue, otherwise, St. James expected, they would have been there early as well, and waiting under cover for milord to appear, rather than the other way around. But it was near the appointed hour of midnight before he saw any sign of movement.

The fog across the monument from him stirred first, a little announcement that was as significant as it was silent. He rose from his half crouch and leaned his back against the tree. His right hand went to beneath his open coat, but it remained there, relaxed, on the butt of one gun, and he was still.

Then from the fog, he saw the sudden appearance of a figure. Swirling, faded gray cloak mixed with the mystical grayness of the fog, so it seemed that the person was born from the fog rather than walking out of it. Beneath the knee length of the cloak was a colorless ankle length of skirt, damp at the hem, and it confirmed to him his rather startling conclusion that his letter writer was female.

She came to just in front of the monument, pushed back the hood of her cloak away from her face and turned in a complete circle upon one heel. Her face was ghostly white in the dark, and he had only one quick glimpse of rather large and frightened gray eyes before she was turned with her back to him, staring into the muted white wall of dark in the opposite direction.

He stepped forward, his attention divested into every direction at once, but it appeared as if she had come in fact alone, and he was but a few feet from her when she whirled with a little gasp and faced him.

Her clothing was clean but oft mended. Her hair was braided into a long, somewhat thin plait that hung over one shoulder. Her face was lined and very thin and her body was frail. She had a haggardness about her that bespoke of struggle and work and premature aging and it was easy for him to believe that she had indeed written the letter, for she did not look well educated. And when she spoke, although she strove for a certain dignity, her whispered speech confirmed it.

"Yer t'duke?" she asked, her voice breathless.

And St. James with narrowed eyes, nodded.

"Of St. James?" she asked, as if she were expecting any number of Dukes to be lollygagging about Hyde Park at midnight.

"Of St. James," he reassured her.

She stood clutching and unclutching at the folds of her cloak, which, he noticed, had only a single pin holding it together and no buttons at all. Her eyes seemed familiar to him, and his mind dug with unrelenting quickness as to where he should have seen her before, and if he had seen her before, why it was that her face was not recognizable. "Please," he began, indicating a bench a little distance from the monument and beneath the shadowy overhang of a tree. "Won't you be seated?"

She glanced at him, uncertain, and he added, "I have come alone as you asked. If I am willing to trust you to that degree, surely you will trust me to sit upon a bench with you without harming you."

And she gave a nervous smile, revealing stained and spaced teeth in her fleshless face. "Aye, milord," she said, "and it's havin' me on, you are, for even if that were what I were 'fraid of, I well know that you are promised to another."

He stiffened at her easy revelation of this knowledge, thinking that for an engagement that had yet to be announced, a precious many seemed to know of it already, but he only said, "Then you should rest easy. Come, let us be more comfortable, and you may tell me all that you wish to tell me." He led her to the bench. She seated herself without fuss, but her back was very straight and stiff. He did not sit himself, but paced about the bench in reflective vigil. She watched him with wariness. His gold eyes flickered over to her and he said, "You may begin. What brings you here? I will not ask your name unless you wish to reveal it."

She hugged her cape closer and seemed more relieved than otherwise when his eyes left her to again probe about the silent, fog filled darkness of the night. "Nay, milord. I willn't tell ya me name, for I very much fear what'd happen if it were found out I t'was here. With you."

"No one else knows of this meeting, then?"

She shook her head, and he had to glance again at her to see this response. "Do you know me in some manner?" he asked. "You spoke in your letter of warning me. Why do you risk yourself to contact me, to come here?"

She swallowed. "T'is not for you, milord, forgive me, but for--for another."

He turned at her words, moved along the bench until he leaned over the back of it. "Tell me. Do not hesitate. I have no care that it is for another. Simply tell me what you know and that you wish me to know."

Her humble composure failed her under the intent gaze of his eyes. "I can not tell you more than to be on your guard. For I know there to be several that are. . . hired t'do you in, milord. All t'same as did yer parents in before you those many years ago."

She paused and then her eyes closed and she raised both hands to her face to muffle her own sudden outpouring of words. "And I'm afraid! Not just for you but one of these men has changed in these twenty-three years! I do not 'spect you t'understand, or even t'care," she cried, "but I wouldn't be here if t'weren't for him. I tried. I begged. I told him, t'is in the past, and t'let it lie there and t'was not his concern anymore. If you had some enemy, t'was not for him t'be involved again! Not after all these years. Not after all the strugglin' we done to be right and tight and honest when we see's those dishonest livin' easier."

And St. James asked, "It is your man you are afraid for?"

And she dropped her hands to look at him with great woebegone eyes. "Aye, milord," she whimpered. "I know you cans't think of him but badly after what he was involved in those years ago, but he changed, milord. He become a straight and true man and I never thought I'd see him to turn back, 'til he got's the message three days ago. And I couldn'st understand *why* they should be back at him to get him to go their way after so many years. Then I came to understand, t'was the *same* job! After all these years, t'was the same job.

"And Gawd help me, I was gonna stay outta it, cause he flat told me not to interfere, nor to pry, but let him be about his business and not worry, and then I realized you t'were the same duke that--" and she clamped her mouth closed, putting the back of one hand to it and began to sob with her eyes closed and her shoulders shaking.

St. James bowed his head, his arms crossed along the back of the bench, and then with half intuition, half deduction, he filled in the missing words. "Steven, your son, is working for me."

The woman cried harder, but she nodded her head. "Gawd! But now ya know it! And he bein' so proud in his new finery, and tellin' me tales of what a soft touch you are, not at all likes the way ever'one hears of ya. And here to find out, his own Da is bein' sent ta kill ya--! Oh, Gawd forgive me, but I could'na bare it. And now I haven't seen me man for one full round the clock, nor Steven neither, and I am afraid!"

St. James let out a rather sharp curse that made her cower, as though he were about to beat her, and he moved around the bench to sit next to her. He dug beneath his coat, pulled out one of his endless supply of hanky's, made a brief, bitter, mental note to himself that this time, no matter how abused the garment became, to *not* throw it with disregard on the ground, and pulled her hand down from her face far enough for him to wipe her tears.

At the same time he asked her, "Did your man not know that Steven was working for me?"

And she shook her head. "Nay. For he'd have been most angry and told me to make him stop. But the first day me lad met you, he brought me home a crown, and milord, forgive me, but we need'dit sorely! And he tol' me t'was honest come by. And I had no idea as of yet, 'bout. . . 'bout the rest."

"I can quite understand," he soothed. "And you have not seen Steven since before last night?"

She shook her head again, but she seemed a deal calmer, and he pressed the handkerchief into her shaking hand, for he very much feared she was going to need it again in another minute. But although he was honest, he had never said that he was not ruthless, so he set out to get as many answers from her as possible before telling her that he had killed her husband the night before, seeing as how that revelation may be inclined to make her somewhat uncooperative.

"Tell me what you know," he pleaded. "I have had men searching for Steven, for I am worried for him also, and I promise you that we will find him, but it will help if you tell me what you know. How many other men involved besides your husband? Do you know who hired them?"

She gave a helpless shrug. "If they are all t'same as afore then there are four others. For there were five the night of t'murders. But I don't know who or why. I doubts that even me man knows of t'at. Me man was only told t'was to be a robbery of some rich muckety-muck an' his wife. An easy mark as they was travelin' at night with only a driver and a footman 'n' a lad. He was told they could keep whate'er jewelry and money they's got but that there'd be a leather case, not a luggage case, but t'kind the swells keep their impo'tant doc'ments 'n' t'like in. They was t'get it as well, and take it t'whoever had hired 'em.

"My husband, he didna know about no murder'n 'til t'shots were gettin' fired. Said he hadn't seen no trouble, but all t'sudden two of t'men he was with was shootin' and then he knew everythin' was gone in a bad way, and that if t'were ever known he'd been there, it'd be the hangman's noose for him for sure. He said he hadn't hired on for no murderin', m'lord. And he wanted nothin' t'do with the jewel's they took offen that poor woman. He wasn't even sure who it were 'til all the papers was screamin' 'bloody murder' of t'duke and duchess of St. James."

And she choked to a halt, perhaps realizing anew that it was the victims' son that she was confiding to.

And St. James muttered, "And so perhaps the one man that could have in fact helped me, I have already killed," and his eyes raised to meet hers.

She shuddered once, as though a cold wind had swept down her back, and what emotion she could be feeling to realize that she were looking into the eyes of the man that had killed her husband was unreadable to him. Then she seemed to break, so that he had a sudden sense of every bone in her body splintering inside of her, and her thin back bent forward as she hugged her face into her knees and cried without any withholding of herself or her grief.

St. James, in a torment, gathered her thin and hopeless body to him, so that she cried into his lap, and he could not tell her any of the circumstances, for not only would it only upset her more to find that her son had nearly been killed by his own father, and then had witnessed his father's death, he could not in truth defend his killing of her husband.

For as Bertie had said, of course he would have killed him at any rate.

And St. James swallowed that knowledge with dread, for he well remembered the raging blackness that had coursed through his veins at the discovery that the man had been there the night of his parents' murders, and he very much feared that even had an angel of God stood before him and pleaded the man's case, that he could not have turned back the fury inside him that had sought to bring that man down.

So he did not speak of his own injury, nor the true manner in which her husband had died, for to do so would be unjust in leading her to believe that had circumstances been different, her husband would have been spared. Instead all he could say above her weeping head was, "He is even now being made ready for burial. I can give you the address so that you may see him, and you may tell me where you wish him to lie."

And she nodded, raised her head as far as his chest. "I can not blame you, m'lord," she choked. "For I well know what his intent was, but I hope you will not blame me if I wish--" and her voice cracked, "if I wish it were he here this minute and your burial being discussed."

Then she drew back from him, wiping at her eyes. "He oft said t'was a nightmare of his, that t'wicked duke twould one day find him out. He oft said, too," and she shook her head in weary hopelessness, "that he could'na blame ya, for t'were as much 'is fault as t'anyone's that you were the way you t'were."

St. James felt a sudden surging of anger at these words, and he grabbed one of her small, claw-like hands, forcing her to look at him. "No. It was not his fault. It's whoever put him up to this, and misled him twenty-three years ago into being in on a crime that was much worse than they led him to believe. You have to help me find this person, as much for his revenge as for my own."

And she blinked, her grief overridden by the force of the dreadful savageness of his voice. And perhaps she had the sudden insight that he believed he had wronged her and her family, and that he very much disliked that feeling.

Realizing that he had her complete attention, he asked her, "How did he get the message? Where did he go? Who did he see? Or did someone come to him?"

And she answered him with sudden certainty. "Red's Pub. On t'banks of t'Thames' pool where t'dockworkers drink. He went tharn Tuesday eve, and when he returned, I ken somethin' diff'rent 'bout him then. It was a bad diff'rence, like he aged ten years in that couple hours. Someone approached him there about it then, I'm sure of it."

St. James nodded, said, "I owe you a great deal. And now you are a widow, and since I am the one that made you so, you are my responsibility. If I give you an address, can you go there tomorrow afternoon?"

She nodded, a little hesitant, and he pulled back the flap of his great coat. If she saw the handles of the two pistols sticking up from his waistband, she did not flinch, just followed his movement of digging into his coat pocket with rather dead eyes, and he pulled out a small notepad and a lead pencil. He wrote down the address, folded it and handed it to her. "Now, will you be all right going home? Do you need me to take you?"

But she shook her head. "Nay. Nay, m'lord," and she sniffled. "T'wouldn't do for me to be seen. . . . As I said, there are t'others, m'-lord. At least four, I s'pect." And with sudden fury, she added, "An' I hope's you get 'em. I hope's you get every one of 'em, and who's behind 'em, for they killed me husband just as sure as you did, m'lord. I don't ask that you do anythin' for me, other than find me son, and kill the bastards."

And St. James with a great deal of steadiness, told her, "You will have both. And more. I promise you," and he hesitated.

"Lucy Crockner, m'lord."

He nodded, repeated, "I promise you, Mrs. Crockner, that it shall be as I said, or I will die in the trying."

And then he moved from the bench before she could make any reply and disappeared into the surrounding fog and she was left quite alone.

He made his way to his horse, still grazing, and slipped the bit back into its mouth, unloosed the reins and mounted. Then he circled around and watched as Steven's mother rose from the bench, looked around with the back of her hand to her thin cheek, and then walked the same path by which she had arrived. And like a ghost, he followed along behind her for a full hour as she headed east, met up with the northern loop of the Thames and continued down the mean streets of the waterfront until she at last turned aside and into a small shanty of a house along a long row of many such houses. The sudden glow of a lamp told him that she had arrived in her own home and appeared to be in fact safe.

It was only then that he allowed himself to think of all that she had said, a particular point of interest her words that the assassins involved that night had been instructed to retrieve a case of paperwork from the coach for whomever had hired them. He turned his horse and went down the waterfront street. It was dirty and dark and stank of garbage and more than just horse urine and droppings, as well as the sultry smell of the river. It was a very rough section of town and it had its share of ribald laughter floating out from unsavory pubs. There were numerous drunks on the street and their glazed eyes watched him ride by as though he were some strange apparition produced by their gin soaked minds.

He studied each door that looked as though it led into a bar as he passed, but there were virtually no placards to show what establishment was what, and he could not discern if any of them were 'Red's Pub', or if in fact, he were even in the correct neighborhood. But he could not think that the man he had killed the night before would have frequented an establishment very far from his own home, and as his wife had not hesitated on naming the Pub it indicated to him that he was a regular at the place.

As he seemed to be making no progress, he at last directed his horse along a street away from the river. But instead of going, yet, back to his own home, he made his way once again to Hyde park by a circumspect route, and once there, he again dismounted and took the time to do what he would have done earlier if he had not been otherwise occupied on ensuring his informant's safe return to her home. He crept around in a similar circle as he had done upon first arriving for the mysterious meeting, again searching for any sign of someone else's presence. And he was not surprised when he found a set of footprints in the grass and the mud that were not his previously made ones. They led up to a little grouping of shrubbery within sight of where he and Lucy Crockner had sat upon the bench and talked. He judged it to be within earshot distance as well, and he was very disturbed to think that they had been overheard, but he dared not discount it.

The one thing that did surprise him was the fact that the footprints were less than man-sized, indicating yet another woman watching them, or possibly. . . a lad. St. James' eyes glimmered out into the dark and he had a very strong feeling that his sought-for messenger boy had been very close at hand indeed.

Chapter Twenty-two

At about the same time as St. James was waiting in the fog of Hyde Park for his informant to appear, his cousin, Earl Andrew Larrimer, arrived home at the Dowager Duchess's house.

He headed first toward the drawing room for a nightcap and with the expectation that his mother and grandmother should still be up and would be there. As he walked toward the room, he tried to prepare himself mentally for the interview with his grandmother. He had debated on waiting until morning, but with the lateness of the hour, he had hopes that if she were still awake, that she would be tired, and hence a little less sharp than usual.

And, he had decided, the quicker it was made known that he had returned, the more obvious it would be to them that a disreputable trip to Gretna Green and back was quite beyond the time span that he had been gone. Indeed, he had every intention of riding through the park in the morning, for as most people he were likely to meet there had seen both he and Miss Murdock at Almacks only the night before, even they would see that it would be quite impossible to make the trip all the way to the Scotland border and return less than twenty-four hours later.

That was all very easily taken care of. And his mother, he expected, as he hesitated at the door, would be as easily chastised for her silly indiscretion. But his grandmother was quite another story, and it was in anticipation of seeing that inquisitive and not to be denied old lady that had him going over the points of his story a final time with a fine-toothed comb in search of any loose particle that may trip him up.

Feeling at last prepared, he turned the knob and entered the drawing room, was surprised to see the room empty and Ashton not in attendance. With a little shrug, he went to the sideboard, found the customary tray of evening snacks and glasses already removed. He checked his pocket watch a little perplexed; it was not overly late, for he and his mother at least. The Duchess did on occasion turn in earlier.

A discreet cough came from the door, and he turned to find Ashton, his grandmother's butler, looking at him with some surprise and a little reproach. "Milord," he said, "I apologize, but we were not aware that you had returned."

"Indeed, *I* apologize, Ashton. It is only that I should think my mother would still be up. Although it *is* close to grandmother's normal hour."

Ashton cleared his throat, a habit most unlike him, and said with a strained voice, "I fear your grandmother left early this afternoon. For Chestershire."

Andrew looked heavenward for a brief, muted curse of a second and then asked Ashton, "Indeed? Is my mother, perhaps, still in residence, or has she seen it necessary to make a sudden sojourn also?"

"She's asked for a late tray in her room, milord," Ashton told him, and then coughed again. "I imagine she will be most. . . surprised to see you."

"Thank you, Ashton," Andrew said, and without further delay, left the room to go above stairs and tap upon his mother's sitting room door. She bade entrance and he opened the door to find her sitting in her dressing gown upon the chaise lounge. The early edition of the next morning's London paper was raised in her hands and she was staring with such intensity at it that she did not look up as he entered, and he had a moment to see that she was not only intent upon reading it, but that her face had such a stark look of open fury that he was taken aback by it. "Mother?" he asked.

At his voice, she dropped the paper to her lap. Her blue eyes, so much like his own, flew to his face. "Andrew! For heaven's sake, what ever are you doing here?" and she seemed beyond startled, she somehow seemed culpable to something.

"What ever are you reading to make you look as though you had murder in your eye?" he asked in mild question. Then glancing and seeing that the paper was open to the social pages, he said, "Oh. Is St. James' announcement in there already, then?"

"Indeed, it is!" she huffed. And for emphasis, she knocked the paper onto the floor in a pout. "And I could scarce believe it when I happen to know that you eloped with Miss Murdock just last night!"

And it all became clear to him. His mother had developed an unexpected affection for Miss Murdock, and her silly conclusion had only been so much wishful thinking upon her part that the two of them had made a match of it. He smiled with indulgence down upon her as he stepped further into the room and closed the door behind him. "Oh, darling mother," he said, and she glanced up at him with hurt in her eyes. "Did you really wish that I should marry her that badly then?"

As though he had touched the very center of her ache, she began to cry, and he knelt to comfort her as she said between her delicate sobs, "Oh, I am such a foolish mother, Andrew. I thought that you had developed a *tendress* for the girl. I *did* see you kissing her in the drawing room, you know, so it is not all my fault!" she added in her defense.

"Oh, I am so sorry, mama. That was just a bit of foolish fancy on my part and really did not. . . did not mean anything." And he swallowed as he rubbed her back to soothe her. "But I never dreamed you would jump to such a conclusion. Oh, my poor dear. No wonder you thought we had eloped."

But instead of comforting her, his words only seemed to make her cry the harder. "Oh, but I wish you *had* married her," she choked out.

"Of course, you do, darling. But I really do have plenty of time, and there will be other young females that will catch my eye--"

"No. No," she choked. She drew her head back enough to let him see her watery eyes. "You don't understand. St. James is going to ruin her!"

"Ruin--! Why, no, mama, it's right there in the paper, you see. You were just looking at it. He's posted the banns and--"

But she would not listen. "I fear he already *has* ruined her, oh that poor, sweet child!" she wailed. "For do you know that he came and drove her in a hired carriage in the middle of the night? And if that is not enough to ruin her, I do not know what is!"

And Andrew, despite himself, was a little intrigued by this notion. "Surely you are mistaken," he said.

"Indeed, I am not! For I saw him with my own eyes, returning her here in the dead of night, and her in nothing but her sleeping costume with a cloak thrown over it. Did you not wonder *when* he received that slap on his face, if it were from her, as he made it clear in Almacks that it certainly was?"

He was feeling just a little bit flummoxed, for he had not even thought of the fact that to his knowledge, Miss Murdock had never (up until last night at least) spent two minutes alone with his cousin, let alone been driving about with him in the middle of the night. A little less surely, he said, "But it little matters, mama. The banns are posted and--"

"Yes. Yes. *Posted*. But no date set! He will cry off and he will ruin her. I know he shall, for there is no reason for him to marry her now that he has so obviously already Had His Way With Her!"

"Mother!" Andrew said a great deal shocked. "I am sure that St. James, even *being* St. James, would take into consid--"

But his mother would not be mollified in the least, but began to shake her head. "Oh, it just goes to show how very *young* you still are. And you laugh at me behind my back for being so careful of your reputation, but I have *seen* how these things work. He will no more marry her than the next man now that he has compromised her, for why should he? And as bad as that may seem for me to believe it, I would rather believe that than to believe that he really *is* going to marry her for a far more terrible--" and she stopped and bit her lip and her eyes were wide, and blue, and terrified.

"What, mother?" Andrew asked her with growing alarm. "What are you afraid of? What reason could he have to marry her that terrifies you as it does?"

"Oh," she cried. "Do not make me tell you for it is probably only a very foolish and I dare say paranoid notion upon my part," and she hesitated. The way she looked up at Andrew with such helplessness made him realize that his mother was getting up in years, and that he was of age that he should be taking responsibility for all of her troubles instead of having her hiding them from him as if he were still a mere, helpless boy.

"Tell me, mother," he demanded. "Whatever it is, you must simply tell me, and I will tell you if you have reason to fear."

"It is just, oh, I am so ashamed to tell you this. Ashamed of your own father, *my* husband. Ashamed of St. James. Ashamed of myself for thinking. . . . But, oh, the possibility is there, and what else am I to think if he suddenly is to marry in such an odd manner?"

"*What?*" Andrew asked again in growing annoyance. "Whatever are you talking about?"

And his mother gave a brave sniff, choked out, "Your father's will!" and she managed to point to the top drawer of her small writing desk in the corner before collapsing into uncontrollable tears.

Andrew, feeling a good deal exasperated, but at the same time very concerned, jumped to his feet and went to the top drawer of the desk. He pulled it open, ruffled through the stationary and found a legal looking document that proclaimed it to be a copy of the last will and testament of his father, Earl Mortimer Larrimer. He flipped the pages, scanning, searching for something that would explain his mother's puzzling, bizarre behavior, and his eyes settled at last on a part of a paragraph, reading: . . .*Until the date of son's marriage, and after date of Duke of St. James, Dante William Larrimer's marriage, all these assets will be in the possession and control of said Duke, and will be retained by said Duke in the event of premature death of son, Andrew.*

He looked at it in shock for a moment, and then let out an incredulous little laugh. "Rot, mother," he pronounced. "Is this what has you beside yourself?" and he pointed to the paragraph he had come across.

Her eyes searched his before glancing at the page of the will he held out for her. "Yes," she said, but her voice quavered a little. "You think I am just over-reacting?"

"Of course, you are," he told her. "It is not uncommon to have an older male relative hold the estate in trust for an heir. My father held St. James', did he not? I trust St. James to handle it adequately until such time that I marry or he deems me of enough experience to handle my own affairs."

"Oh," she said and gave a watery smile. "I suppose I was just letting my imagination run away with me."

And he knelt by her again, and half laughing asked her, "Did you suppose that St. James would bandy a pistol at me from beneath the cover of dark in order to kill me for my inheritance?" But even as he said the words, he realized that it *was* very odd that the will had been written in such a way as to seem to encourage such foul play in someone of less moral character than St. James. But he smiled for the sake of his mother, for of course, he had implicit trust in St. James.

But his mother said with worry in her voice, "I have never wished to upset you, Andrew, but I *do* have my doubts about the manner in which your father died."

"It was a simple accident," he reassured her. "A hunting accident."

"Your father was always most careful. And I always thought it very strange that the same shotgun he had used for years and devotedly oiled and cleaned should suddenly become defective and back-fire on him."

"It *is* very strange," Andrew agreed, "but these things do happen at times. And St. James was not even in the area at the time."

"But, still," she insisted, weeping, "it is possible that he sabotaged it in some manner, and then went away with the knowledge that Morty would die the very next time--"

"Oh, mother!" he exclaimed. "You are being *quite* ridiculous. For whatever reason would he do such a thing?"

"Why," she said, looking at him as if he were missing the entire point, "for your inheritance. Then there would only be you between he and it!"

"Mother," he told her with strained patience. "He doesn't need it! Why he could probably buy us out several times over."

"No, he couldn't," she said and he looked at her with incredulity. "For I know for a fact that when I--your father invested quite heavily in the East India Company Stocks, that his own father judged it too risky, for it was before the war with China, you know. He already had, oh, perhaps ten percent of the company as did I--your father and I, also. But then your father decided to take the risk and where other people were getting nervous and dumping their holdings in the company, for there were rumors of, oh! I don't know. Something unsavory about the company. But your father bought it all up quite cheaply, and now your inheritance, among other holdings, is nearly thirty percent of the company. And St. James still owns only ten because his father was too conservative. And now of course, with the new treaties that came from the war, each share is worth a fortune, and quite difficult to come by. So you see, Andrew, just with those stocks alone, you own more than he does with his entire holdings."

And Andrew's jaw dropped and hung for a long, astonished moment.

After a minute, he managed to collect himself enough to mutter, "It is still just so much rot, mother!"

But there was just that niggling of doubt in his voice and Lady Lydia was satisfied that she had made him see that perhaps he did have reason to fear, and she was not just being a foolish old woman after all.

"And he does run through it as though it were *water,*" she pointed out.

Andrew glanced at her, but now his eyes were preoccupied. "He is still hardly a pauper, mother!"

But even so, an hour later when he stopped back in her rooms (for her lady's maid was now attending her, brushing out her hair before the vanity) he was not dressed for turning in for the night, but more substantially, as though he intended to be gone on a journey. "I'll be using the carriage, mother, I hope that will not inconvenience you to any great degree."

"No, of course not," she said as she watched the progress of her hair in the mirror, "for I can have a hired one brought around with no difficulty, and it *is* your carriage." But then she pouted and met his eyes in the mirror. "But, Andrew, where are you going? You have only just returned

and with your grandmother gone to Chestershire, I shall be here all a-
lone."

"Chestershire also, mother."

"You just *came* from there!"

And he flushed a little, but only said, "There is something I was remiss in not speaking with Miss Murdock about." Then, as his mother
turned in her seat to look at him straight on, interrupting her lady's
maid's work, he added, "Nothing that you need concern yourself with for
now, mother, I assure you. Now, I must run, and do not fret, for I shall
be back in several days to escort you to any balls or dinners we are invited to," he coaxed her. And she smiled and was happy.

At about the same time as Earl Larrimer was bidding goodbye to his
mother, Ryan Tempton arrived at Squire Murdock's home. He had considered staying at the inn five miles away, had decided that he would
instead journey to the manor and see if the Squire, being a widower and
thus perhaps used to keeping odd hours, was still awake.

He turned onto the overgrown lane and rode his weary horse to the
end of the drive, and saw with satisfaction that there were still lamps lit
on the lower level of the house.

He tied his horse off at the hitching ring in the drive, making sure it
could reach the trough of water that was there, and then with still a
great deal of youthful energy, bounded up the well-swept steps to the
door of the house. The wide stone of the stoop, even in the dim gleam
of the moon, was swept also, and he thought that rather odd when he
had been under the impression from the Squire's speech at the inn that
fateful night not even a week ago that they did not have much in the
way of servants. And as Miss Murdock had, of course, been in London,
he could not quite wrap his mind around the vision of the Squire out
sweeping the porch in her absence.

The door knocker was well polished also, he noticed, as he let it fall
with a bang.

After a second knocking, the door swung open, and he was faced not
with a surly and rather unkempt Squire Murdock as he had been expecting, but by a neatly dressed woman of indeterminate middle years with a
crisp apron tied around her middle. Her hair, a shiny mass of coppery
waves with a pronounced streak of white through it, was pinned with
precision and twisted into a serviceable topknot on the crown of her
head, and her rather rotund figure stood formidable in the door, causing
him to take a startled step backward. Then he caught himself, asked,
"Mrs. Herriot?"

She looked him over with critical eyes, holding the lamp up higher to
better see his face that was a good distance above her own, and then
the soft wrinkles of her cheeks fanned back into a wide and radiant
smile. "Why if it isn't Mister Tempton!" she said. "What a most pleasant
surprise. You must come in, of course, and I will tell the Squire that you

are here, although I dare say he was not expecting you, for he made no mention of it to me."

And thus bade, he followed her into the house. There he stood for a moment, blinking, for if he had pictured the inside of the house at all, it had not been this vision of prim and immaculate neatness. There was not a cobweb to be seen anywhere, nor a speck of dust, and the chimneys of the chandelier, not much of a chandelier, but a chandelier all the same, in the hallway positively sparkled, with not a hint of built up soot or ash to betray use without regular cleaning.

The hardwood floor beneath his feet was polished to a high degree, as was the banister that wound up the steep flight of stairs. And although the home still showed its age, and a rather pronounced pitching of walls, floors and ceilings, it seemed to be in the midst of some remarkable transformation that promised that in but another five or six days, it could be a very respectable home indeed. "How ever did you come to be here, Mrs. Herriot?" he asked her somewhat mystified. "For I had not realized that you had left Morningside."

"Why, I was asked to provide a few house maids from his lordship's manor until more permanent arrangements could be made here, and I thought I should just come along to see that all was being done right and tight." And her voice dropped to a whisper, "T'is rumored that milord is to be married at last!" and she could not have seemed happier than if it were own son's nuptials that were expected to be announced.

And Ryan frowned. "St. James set all this up then?"

Mrs. Herriot nodded as she led him into the parlor and returned the lamp to the table she had taken it from. "Aye, indeed! The roof is under repair, the stables are being restored, and a proper gardener has been retained to tear out the vegetables and plant something more suitable for gentry to have on display. The pigs and the chickens have been carted to market and those awful sheds will be, of course, destroyed. I should not tell you, I know, but the place was in the most lamentable condition, but, well," and her face wreathed into endless smiles, "it little matters, does it? What matters is that his lordship has fallen at last and I cannot wait to see what lovely creature has finally done the trick. I daresay, she must be the most beautiful of girls!"

"Indeed," Ryan said, a little numb. "She is certainly not in the common way." But somehow, seeing all this activity set to action on St. James' bequest filled him with a great deal of unease. The banns hadn't even been posted, for heaven's sake, and if it should get out that the duke was spending what Ryan could only surmise to be an incredible amount of blunt on Miss Murdock's behalf--! Well, the situation could be read in quite a negative manner.

"I'll just let the Squire know you are here," Mrs. Herriot told him. "He is settled in for a little late snack in the kitchens," and she made a little moue of distaste, "which I can not convince him is unnecessary as the dining room is now perfectly habitable," but she smiled and ended with, "but I shall have him brought around soon enough, I dare say, although he has been fighting me, and indeed, all the maids and workers, tooth and nail since I arrived. Quite a card, he is! And such a temper! I daresay his lordship's proposed fiancé has a gentler nature that must surely come from her dear, sweet, departed mother."

And Ryan stared at her feeling a great deal disconcerted, for if he hadn't seen Miss Murdock angry (other than the brief display at the Dowager's house upon their arrival in London), he *had* seen the results of her anger on St. James' cheek, and he had to wonder, just a little bit, what Mrs. Herriot would make of Miss Murdock's gentle nature if she were to become aware that Miss Murdock had clobbered the duke most effectively. "Quite," he said, his voice a little weak.

Mrs. Herriot held her hand out for his coat, and he removed it in distracted motions and she took it from him. "Just make yourself comfortable," she told him, and then she scurried off in search of Squire Murdock.

And Ryan was left with the sinking feeling that evidently Mrs. Herriot had not made Miss Murdock's acquaintance, and hence, Miss Murdock was not here.

He had no time to know what to make of this discovery, for the hall floor boards creaked in protesting, and then the Squire lumbered through the door. And if the house had improved in its condition, the Squire had not.

He wore a worn dressing gown in need of washing. One leg, bared from mid-calf down to his slipper, was swelled beyond even its usual obesity, and as he lurched upon it the pain it caused him was obvious. He held in one puffy hand a bottle of rum, and there were stains down the front of him to show he had been drinking at it for some time. His thick thatch of gray hair was mussed and matted, and looked as though it had not had a comb through it for several days. To complete this impression of someone who has been on an extended drinking binge, when he spoke, his words were slurred and pugnacious.

"You!" he said, hurting Ryan's ears. "You're t'lad that was here the night that son of a fiend ran off with me daughter!"

Mrs. Herriot, who stood in the door frame, cringed with distress. She glanced at Ryan, looking a deal embarrassed, and Ryan could well understand her chagrin that the Duke of St. James had picked a lass with a roaring drunk as a father. He smiled in sympathy to her from around the massive bulk of the Squire, and she dared to hiss, "My apologies, Mister Tempton, but he utterly refuses--"

But her words were cut off as the Squire swung around and bawled at her. "Get on with ye, you pesky hen! How many times am I to tell ya your presence is not needed and not welcome?"

And with a little squeak, Mrs. Herriot fled from the door frame and quite disappeared.

This little by-play between the Squire and the housekeeper at least shifted the Squire's apparent ire to that unfortunate lady and as he turned back to Ryan, he did not continue to rail at him, but instead collapsed onto the sofa (which Ryan judged to be recently upholstered) and muttered of high-handed females bursting into his home and refusing to leave even when he threatened to bodily throw them out. "Who are you again?" he asked Ryan in the midst of his dire diatribe. "I rem'ber *who* you are, just what was yer *bloody* name, I mean?"

And Ryan coughed, plastered a polite smile on his face and said, "Mister Ryan Tempton, Squire. I was here to see your filly run with my brother, Lord Tempton and Milord Duke of St.--"

"Aye! I rem'ber! That son of a heathen! What's become of me daughter, Mister Ryan?"

"Tempton. Mister Tempton."

"Yes, Tempton," and the Squire waved the bottle of rum before him in a drunken ark. "Whate'er. Where's me Lizzie? For I tell ya, I've traveled e'ery day to the inn, five miles t'is. Five miles in the rain most morns or afternoons or eve's or whene'er I man'ge t'get there. But five miles in the rain most, uh, covered that, I think, but where was I? Traveled to the inn, and I looks for the banns," and he nodded his head and put a sage finger up to tap upon his forehead, nearly stabbing one eye as he was about it, "for the banns, mind ya! And does ya think I finds any?" and his head was back very far and his eyes opened very wide and Ryan swallowed for answer and the Squire boomed, "No, be God, I sure as bloody *do not!* Now what says ya to that, Mister Ryan!"

Ryan, who had not the least idea what to say to that, and as to the question of where Lizzie was, could not even answer it with any certainty, only fumbled for an answer that would not put the Squire into even more of a rage.

But the Squire did not even heed his hesitancy. Instead he lurched to his feet. "Here!" he bellowed. "I'll show 'em to ya, if'n ya don't believes me." And he swayed about the room, looking on first one table and then another, and then looked beneath the sofa and the chairs, of which Ryan politely lifted his feet when the Squire stumbled over to his, and it was when he was tearing the cushions from the sofa that the Squire began to curse. "Blasted, bloody Mrs. Hooligan with her incessant tidy'n up'n all. Man can't even have a bloody newspaper 'round for more than a single day!"

"Herriot," Ryan corrected for want of something better to say.

"What's that?" the Squire demanded.

"The housekeeper. Her name is Mrs. Herriot, I'm sure."

The Squire waved his bottle of rum again. "Whate'er." He sat down with a force onto the now disarrayed cushions of the sofa and his blustering left him with the sitting. He took a long, unsteady pull from the mouth of the bottle, fixed Ryan with his drunken and rather bewildered eyes and said with sad finality, "Me thinks the duke has ruined me lass.

That's what me thinks. And all this--" and he waved his arm about to indicate the changes being made in his home, "is the buy off. That and a hundred quid a month." Then his eyes closed, the bottle listed in his hand, and in but a moment he was snoring, his chin resting in the thick folds of his neck.

Ryan cocked his head, looked at the Squire with some amazement at this rapid nodding off. Then he frowned, for a hundred pounds a month did seem too generous to be legitimate. Add to that the cost of repairs and refurbishing. . . .

He was interrupted in his thoughts by Mrs. Herriot peeking around the door frame, and her face once again wreathed into smiles when she saw that the Squire was asleep. "Now then," she said, "I've taken the liberty of bringing you a spot of tea and I have made up an extra room for you so you should be quite comfortable, and asked the groom to take care of your horse." She bustled into the room, ignoring the Squire's fitful snores, and held a saucer and cup out to him, which he took.

"Thank you, Mrs. Herriot," he told her with pleasure.

Mrs. Herriot beamed at him and said, "Yes, she must be quite a lass to have his lordship not only overlooking the behavior of her father, but being quite generous toward him also. And before any announcements have even been made," she confided to him.

And Ryan felt a sick twisting in his stomach that perhaps, just perhaps, he had not been doing St. James a service by coming here, but had nearly mangled up a very neat job on his part of managing to shirk off his responsibility toward Miss Murdock.

For how better to dally with a young lady and then sweep the whole affair beneath the rug than to persuade a rather impressionable younger man to elope with her?

And he would have admired this trick quite completely, chalking it off as another sign of St. James' infinite resourcefulness, if it had been played upon any other young female besides Miss Murdock.

"What's yer name, lad?" the bald bartender asked. He leaned one massive forearm along the smooth, worn surface of what passed as a bar in Red's Pub.

The bar was, in fact, nothing more than an old barn door, cut in half, and then laid end to end across four saw horses along the length of the narrow room. The dim room was crowded, even at half past two in the morning, and the smell of gin and sweaty men attracted a steady swarm of flies in the windows that were blocked with nothing but gaping oil cloth. The flies were sluggish from the cold and the wet and the foggy night air, but there were a great deal of them all the same, and if they flew somewhat slower, they also buzzed somewhat louder.

There was no proper door entering the pub, but only clapped together boards, which seemed more nuisance than otherwise as it was constantly being yanked open as tired men made their way in, and others, drunk, made their way out. Below the rumble of rising and dying voices, the cold murmur of the Thames was heard, and the creaking of dock ropes as they held their barges in discipline.

"Steven. Steven Crockner," Steven said and he stared at the bald man with his gray eyes. "Me dad was on a job for Red. Tell 'im that."

The bartender frowned, said beneath his breath, "Shut up about that business here in the front room, lad. Wait here." He turned and pushed his way down the narrow space between bar and barrels and Steven was left standing only shoulder high between the press of men.

They looked at him, curious, and he looked with insolence back at them. It was a look that he had not had but for perhaps twenty-four hours, and it was not one that he was aware that he had now, but it was there all the same. Mayhaps milordship's pistol beneath his coat had something to do with it. But the men only ignored him, and he stood amongst them and watch as they drank.

Then the large, bald man was back in front of him, and he poked a finger across the bar and into Steven's narrow chest. "Yer wanted in t'back," he growled. And Steven looked up at him and in a voice un-recognizable to himself, said, "Coo, mister. Don't e'er be pokin' me in the chest again, do ya ken?"

And the men hooted in laughter at this remark, but the bartender, seeing something in the eyes of the boy that he did not like, did remove his finger. "Sure, m'lad," he said with an exaggerated chuckle. "Fer if ya be a 'man' of Red's, I t'wouldn't want to be steppin' over to yer wrong side." And the laughter increased as the bartender threw his hands in the air for dramatic effect.

But Steven didn't smile, he just nodded and said, "You'd be wise t'remember it."

"Oh ho," the bartender exclaimed. "I'd be *wise* to rem'ber it, he says. And where'd a dirty scrap of a lad such as you get such fancy talk, I wonder? Mayhaps t'same place ye got those fancy breeches, for if t'rest of ya is a ragtag bit, those are some mighty fine bloomers!"

And the press of men roared and glanced at the pants that were be-low Steven's unbuttoned coat. They *were* a fine quality of thread, and a deal too large for him, but he had remedied this by cutting the hems to the proper lengths and belting the waist of it about him with twine.

Steven didn't answer, but his eyes moved around the men that sur-rounded him, laughing until tears streamed down their faces and clap-ping each other on the back. "Be wise!" they mimicked. "Oh, hoity-toity, but you'd be wise! for I be here in me fancy muckety-muck breeches!"

And he marked all their faces, one by one, and it was something in his demeanor, the way he did not flush with embarrassment at their laughter, nor even seemed to notice it over much, but just marked them with intentness, that they subsided and settled back to leaning upon the bar, their shoulders hunched. The bartender said, "Ah, get on with ya, lad," and he made a motion again to a door at the end of the room, a proper door this time, and Steven turned and went to it. And he was very aware of all those men's eyes upon him as he went.

He opened the door without knocking, stepped inside and closed it behind him. A man was seated there with very blue eyes and a very red face. His hair was reddish blonde. He was older than Steve's Da had been and his physique showed his age, being rather bowed at the shoulders and thick at the waist line. But it was easy to see that at one time he had been quite fit, and if he were not taller than average, he had once been fairly powerful. Now, he looked flabby, all that one-time muscle gone soft. But he didn't seem concerned about it, and the pistol sitting on his desk, a very odd pistol that Steven had never seen the like of before, made it clear that he had long since given up his fists as his weapon of choice.

"Yeah? What'cha want, lad?" he asked and he smoked something that Steven had never seen before either. It was a long pipe with a small bowl on the end, and the smoke coming from it had a strange, sweet smell that made his stomach ill.

"Me name's Steven. Crockner. Me Da was on a job for you."

"Don't know nothin' bout dat, lad," the man said.

"Yer Red, aren't ya?"

The man nodded. The motion of his head was exaggerated, as though he were nodding from sleep rather than in agreement. He drew the pipe from his mouth, and that motion was slow, languid also. Steven had the sudden thought that he could probably pull his pistol and shoot him where he sat before the man could get one of those slow moving hands to the gun that sat on the table.

"I was told t'talk to Red. And you say that's you," Steven told him.

"Yeah? And who by?"

And Steven said, "Me dead father."

Red started, the lazy look leaving his eyes, and he pointed with the long stem of his pipe to the chair that Steven had thus far ignored. "Sit, lad, and tell me about yer Da."

Steven spurned the seat. "Me Da's dead by the man you sent him to kill. T'Duke of St. James. I want to know when and where the next hit is, an' I want t'be in on it. An' I want the money he was to get fer doin' it when I'm done, so's I can support me mother."

Red stared at him. "Yer on fire for ven'gence, are ye now, lad?"

Steven nodded, his gray eyes unflinching. "Aye. I am 'n' all."

"An' now ya think yer man enuff t'settle t'score with t'bloke? After ya seen yer own Da couldna do it?"

"Aye," Steven said again.

"Well, I'd like t'see that 'n' all," Red chuckled. "Ya got a weapon or was ya plannin on starin him t'death with those mean eyes of yourn?"

For answer, Steven pulled the most of the long dueling pistol from beneath his coat, let it linger there for a brief second, and then pushed it back beneath his waist band again.

Red's eyebrows went up. "From t'looks a that, not the first time you been on a job," he said, and Steven only smiled. Red looked him up and down, his eyes narrowing. "From t'looks of t'gun 'n' those breeches, I'd wager you've killed yourself some swell," and he glanced into Steven's face.

But Steven only held to his cold and silent smile.

Red smiled, waved a lazy hand. "Come back t'morrow night then, same time. Ya can keep yer trap shut, well 'nuff, an' ya got the proper nerve t'do it. More than yer Da had, any rate. There'll be some men waitin' fer ya outside."

And Steven said, "I wants t'same share me father was t'get. Ye tell yer other men not t'be tryin' to cheat me 'cause I'm just a lad. Or I'll be taken theirs from them and sharin' with no one."

Red shook his head. "I'll tell 'em, lad. But don't be thinkin' that they'll take kindly t'that kinda talk. Likely slit yer throat fer ya." He sat back, lit up his pipe and drew in a great lungful of creamy smoke. "Not that I care two bits, one way or t'other. Understand that, lad. Ye hire on with me, ye take care of yer own skin."

And Steven said, "I ken that. I can do that."

"Tomorrow night, then. We'll see what yer made of, right 'nuff." And his laugh was a sudden loud boom in Steven's ears as the boy turned and left.

He made it through the crush of men, but they paid him no mind now, only kept to their drinks and their loud conversations, and he pushed through the rickety door of the pub entrance. He walked down the shadowy street, and with each step he took, he began to shake, and finally, he darted into a mew, not unlike the one his father had died in, and his shaking, empty stomach spasmed. But he could throw nothing up, for he had not eaten in the past twenty-four hours.

He wiped his mouth with the back of his hand, and set off once again in the night, not headed for his home, for he could not yet face his mother, but headed for the Dowager Duchess's house.

Chapter Twenty-three
Friday Morning

It was well after three in the morning when St. James arrived back to his London home. He rode into the stables and dismounted, and as there were no grooms up at this late hour, he saw to unsaddling his mount (an awkward undertaking as his stitches limited his movement and he was forced to do the most of the work with but his right hand, arm and shoulder) and leading it to its stall.

He walked with weariness from the stables, bypassed the servants entrance and went along the garden path to the side of the house and the French doors that were there. He rubbed at his aching chest as he did so and was deep in thought.

Expecting the doors to be locked when he reached them, he was fumbling in yet another inner pocket of his coat for his keys when it unexpectedly opened. Effington peered out from the doorway. "Is that you, milord?" he asked.

"Damn it, yes, Effington." St. James glanced at him with annoyance. "Why in the devil are you still up?"

"I should think the answer would be obvious, milord," Effington sniffed ed as he closed the door behind the duke.

St. James walked through the drawing room and into the hallway, going toward his study. Effington dogged him, hesitated at the door as St. James struggled from his coat and handed it to the valet, and continued to his desk. "Are you not turning in now, milord?" Effington asked.

"No. And pour me a drink."

Effington laid the coat upon the back of a chair and followed this instruction.

St. James unlocked the top drawer of his desk, pulled out the file of correspondence between his father and a young Queen Victoria. He didn't sit then, after laying it on top of the desk, but instead strode with agitation about the room, not trusting himself to study it properly when his mind was being distracted by another matter.

Effington held out his drink to him and St. James took it in passing, but even in sipping it, he did not stop pacing, but went to and fro and back and forth, and all the while his left hand held the goblet, his right hand massaged the painful left side of his chest.

"Your wound is bothering you," Effington observed.

"Hmm," St. James glanced his way. "Yes. Damn it."

"You met with this letter writer tonight, milord?" Effington persisted.

"Yes." St. James turned, paced back. He stopped and stared into the fireplace and unwilling to further endure his preoccupation, asked in a guarded voice, "Miss Murdock?"

Effington sighed. "Gone as you had ordered, milord. With no apparent misadventure."

St. James nodded, sipped from his glass. "Her demeanor?" he questioned, unable to help himself and very much resenting the fact that he could not.

Effington paused in picking up his lordship's coat once again as though giving his answer some thought. Then he said, "I should say that she was 'defiantly vulnerable'."

And St. James gave an unexpected, short laugh. "Defiantly vulnerable," he mused. "Yes. I should say that is what I would have expected from my Miss Murdock. No tears. Not then at any rate." He turned from the fireplace. "Thank you, Effington. You may go now."

"My pleasure, milord," Effington said. "And may I add my congratulations, also, milord."

St. James glanced at him but seemed far from pleased. "Yes," he said after a moment. "I suppose I should be congratulated," and his voice was quietly derisive, "for I have managed to overcome her objections in the end, so I must be a very bright fellow, indeed."

Effington gathered the coat to him and went with less than his normal dignity to the door, but he had not closed it entirely before the duke gave out a sudden, violent curse. St. James clinked decanter on glass as he refilled his drink.

He drank half of it in an instant, quelled his sudden impulse to slam the glass into the fireplace and instead take the entire bottle. He stood, the glass in his tight grip until at last he forced himself to go over and seat himself at his desk.

He took another few moments clearing his mind with a will, then turned his attention to the papers in front of him. He was further delayed once, when upon turning from the first letter that he had previously read to the next, he found in between these two sheaves of paper an envelope, the one that he had sent Effington to find the afternoon before. He opened it, skimmed it, laid it aside with a quiet wondering of how much grief could have been saved if he had only read it before going to Almacks that night.

Then he turned his attention to reading the haunting, half-remembered song of his father's handwriting, and it was not until another hour later that he at last turned the final page. Even then, he only got up to refresh his glass, and then sat again at his desk, his fingers caressing with gentleness the words his father had written nearly a quarter of a century ago as he stared pondering into the low burning flames of the fireplace.

Then he picked up a pen, dabbed it into a bottle of ink, and on a fresh piece of paper began to write:

Question: How close was Queen Victoria to heeding my father's advice? Tentative Conclusion: Very close. Ask Queen, if possible.

Question: What documents could he have been carrying with him the night he was killed that someone felt that they could not afford having the Queen receive? What information did my father know that it necessitated him to be forever silenced? Why my mother (and presumably myself) also? *Tentative Conclusions: Documents contained (possibly) misrepresentations by the East India Company of the exact nature of the primary product they were trading from India to China--its uses--its addictive nature--the fact that it was mostly being consumed by the Chinese population as some drugging, numbing pleasure device (i.e. alcohol when used to extremes but apparently from my father's writings much worse) and not being used for any legitimate or legal purpose. Possibly this product was even minimalized in their accountings of their trade. It was illegal trade, after all, and they probably inflated profits from other legitimate trade to cover the opium profits. How many investors would have bulked if they had true knowledge of product and true nature of the illegality of the trading that was going on? If investors pulled out, would company have gone bankrupt? Did documents contain evidence of fraud?*

My father wrote of other trade agreements being jeopardized, but although England stood to suffer if trade with China was lost, the East India Trading Company would have been ruined, along with all of its investors. Along with my own father if his holdings in company were significant.

Did my father have evidence of this fraud? Was it that evidence that was in the case the night of murders and was thus imperative that it not reach Queen Victoria, nor that my father remain alive to expose the extent of the Company's activities?

Or, if no outright evidence of fraud, did 'enemy' fear that my father would 'dump' his East India Company Holdings and that, combined with general unease over prewar situation, would cause a mass 'dumping' on the Exchange?

Need to investigate how much stock my father owned at the time. Was amount significant enough to change the market if he dumped?

Had he foreseen own murder? Did 'enemy' anticipate that he had left verbal instructions with my mother to dump stocks if he died unexpectedly, and worse, to publicly expose fraud? Could 'enemy' be sure this would not happen if she were left alive? Did 'enemy' have some indication that my father had confided in her? Letters? Messages? Overheard conversations?

Tentative Conclusion: Agent of East India Company, or Another large investor in said Company.

Fact: If someone involved with Company, they would almost certainly have to be in a social circle of my parents and have some insight into their relationship for them to believe my mother had intimate knowledge of my father's work (if, in fact, they feared my mother had knowledge). Unlikely an agent would be in that circle. Leaves only another large investor.

Note: As I, myself, doubt she had intimate knowledge, this could indicate that an extremely nervous 'enemy' were only guessing that they need kill her also, and all of this could be just so much rot.

St. James held the pen poised for another moment after that last sentence. So much rot. But if he *were* in fact puzzling through to a motive, then he could find no reason in it why his death would be desirable. And as his chest was aching, he knew very well that there had to be a motive for his death as well somewhere in this puzzle.

He rubbed a finger across his upper lip as he thought, his face a scowl of concentration (for it is not pleasant to try and figure out why someone is bent upon taking your life, and indeed, has already killed both of your parents) and his gold eyes were very dark in his pale face.

His inheritance had been held in trust for him by his uncle Mortimer, and he had not received it until he had reached his majority, and even then, that had been at his uncle's discretion. He would have had no decision making ability, even if, at the tender age of ten, he had been inclined to make a decision. Any worry that he would 'dump' East India Company stock was ridiculous. And if the 'enemy' mayhaps feared that his father had confided in his mother, they would not likely think that he had been irresponsible enough to also confide in his ten year old son.

Just maybe, the fact that he had not been in the coach that night had been insignificant. Perhaps, even the fact that his mother had been in the coach was insignificant. Perhaps, after all, his father had been the only target, and Dante had lived because he had an unexpected case of the croup, and his mother had died because she had been too bored to remain the few days until his grandmother had been returning to London.

But if this were true, why, *again*, the recent attempt on his life? Why did it *now* matter to someone that he should die?

No. If it mattered now, it had to have mattered then also.

But if he *had* been an intended target those twenty-three years ago, why had he been allowed to live undisturbed until now?

Nothing seemed to make sense, and he could not discount the fact that Miss Murdock's arrival on the scene seemed to be the defining factor that had induced someone to take action against him. To believe it were coincidental seemed to go contrary to what was quite obvious. For some unknown reason, he was not a threat as long as he were not married. Whether it was as Tyler had always claimed, and no one expected him to live to a ripe old age with his wild ways in any event, and now his sudden apparent interest indicated that he would settle down and perhaps live beyond what someone desired, or whether it were some other factor, he did not know.

He had acted on nothing but a hunch when he had orchestrated an interest in Miss Murdock, and his gut feeling told him that he had to dog that hunch to the end.

He started a new page.

My interest in Miss Murdock is disturbing to someone. Know from Steven's father that same assassins were hired, and confirmed again by Steven's mother, hence, logical they have been hired by same 'enemy' that hired them to kill father (parents?)

Why should my planned marriage be a threat?

Motive One:

Most logical, most oft thought and most oft discarded notion: matters of inheritance.

List of why this motive does not withstand scrutiny in the briefest, starkest terms: Only one standing to profit at time of my father's death (presuming I was meant to be in carriage and would also be killed): uncle Morty. Who is now dead, and hence could not be now reinstigating assassins to 'finish t'job' as Steven's mother so succinctly put it.

Only one standing to profit today upon my death is Andrew, who was not even born upon night of my parents' deaths.

Motive of inheritance thus discarded.

Motive Two:

Investor in East India Company fearing ruination.

Now bent on murdering me because he is afraid that I am digging about in that nasty old graveyard and that he will be discovered. Question: Why not act sooner? Possible Reason One: I was able to move about with enough subtlety that he did not realize what I was truly up to. Or Possible Reason Two: He was aware of what I was doing, but I was not close enough to make him nervous and now I have in some indefinable way gotten closer. Or Possible Reason Three: He was aware that Queen was considering me for my father's vacant post, and was intimate enough with her to understand that if I should marry, she would take it as a sign that I had left my evil ways behind and was ready to accept the responsibility of that post. With taking of said post, information will be made available to me that will point to him.

If third possible reason: I was not meant to be in coach, my mother's murder was pure circumstance, and threat to my life now is only a result of what I may discover through my own investigating and promised access to Queen's files. If I had not appeared to take a notion to marrying, I would not have been a threat, for I would not have access to Crown records.

Conclusion: A member of the Queen's own inner circle.

He set down his pen and sat back in his chair. There was still a swallow of brandy left in his glass, and he finished it before murmuring to himself, "And I am fairly certain she suspects the same. She must think I am being exceedingly slow." And he smiled. "But I am getting there, Your Highness, so I hope I am not disappointing you too mightily."

The clock distracted him by striking the half hour, and he glanced at it and saw that it was half past four. He wondered how Miss Murdock was getting along. They should be nearly half way to her home. And despite his extreme tiredness, he had a sudden wish to do nothing else but saddle a horse and ride hard after her and run her down, and to go somewhere with her where there was none of this or any other but just the two of them.

Nothing to put shadows of worry beneath her eyes, and nothing to distract him from the pure pleasantness of her serenity. And he thought of her hands stitching his wound back together, and the low, teasing, soothing note of her voice as she spoke, a mere voicing of thoughts and observances that were both artless and probing.

But he only got up from his desk, refilled his glass, shaking loose the subtle but maddening call of Miss Murdock before his mind could dwell on the further activity in his bedchamber that had nothing to do with stitches or even talking. He returned to his desk and focused his mind instead on the tasks that would need to be done that day.

He would need to go to his barrister and instruct him to dig back and ascertain how much stock his father had held in the East India Company at the time of his death. If possible, he needed him to also discover who had significant holdings in that company in the same period of time. If what he suspected were true, he should find a large share holder who was also an intimate of the Queen, probably holding a high position in the running of her affairs.

He would need to send someone to meet with Steven's mother, Lucy Crockner, at the undertaker's address he had given her (and praise God, Miss Murdock in her mistaken notions had seen fit to direct Tyler and Andrew to take that fallen man to an undertaker! For wouldn't he have felt even more like scum if he had told Lucy Crockner her husband were rotting in a mew?) and to find out what, if anything, was in Dante's power to be of assistance to her.

He debated for a moment on who he should send, decided that Tyler would make her the most comfortable, for all of his brusqueness, he was gentle enough, and he had no fine airs to put her ill-at-ease. Although he imagined Tyler would be most unhappy about being assigned to what he would call a fit of folly sentimentalism on St. James' part (He were gonna kill you, weren't he? Damn near did. If he got's a bawlin' widow now and a heartsick son, really 'tis none of your concern). But he would go all the same, he always did, and if he spat his chewing tobacco with more force than necessary, and aimed with insolence toward his lordship's boots upon hearing his orders, St. James was certainly not going to take him to task over it.

After these items were taken care of, he would have to closet himself with Tyler and decide how one or the other or both of them were to find 'Red's Pub' and enter it without being marked for what they were: a duke of the realm and his groom.

He made several notes to himself, wrote a short, rather cryptic note to Queen Victoria to be delivered to her promised man in the event he should show up while St. James was out. It read simply: *With the utmost respect, I question the security and confidentiality of your correspondence. Please advise if this notion should be disregarded, and accept my apologies if it should be so. Your humble servant, St. J.* If he had made some inaccurate assumptions, he imagined this note would bring down upon his head a rather severe reprimand from the Queen herself (and who could blame her, as he was rather impertinently questioning her ability to keep her affairs private?), but if he were correct and she suspected the same, it would let her know that he had sniffed upon a trail that may interest her. And if her security had been breached, was possibly still being breached, he was quite certain she would be very interested indeed.

He sat back in his chair again, his eyes very heavy with tiredness, and gave himself over to letting his thoughts roam from the pointed avenues they had been on for the past few hours to where ever they would, and it should not be surprising that they settled onto the memory of a rather disheveled Miss Murdock lying beneath him in his bed as their thought of choice.

But then he must have dozed, for the clock was suddenly striking five strokes and there came tapping on his study door.

"Enter," St. James called with weariness.

And Applegate, his butler, entered to announce that the morning paper had arrived. He came across the room to hand his employer the paper, and stood for a moment nearby as St. James opened it with purpose to the social page. There, as Bertie had seen to it, was his announcement of engagement to Miss Sara Elizabeth Murdock, daughter of Squire Edward Murdock, of Chestershire. He studied it before laying it aside, and with the reading felt at last that his night's work was finished.

"Send a tray up to my room, would you Applegate, for I think I shall turn in for an hour or two."

"Certainly, milord," Applegate replied and as he left, St. James opened the top drawer of his desk, replaced his father's letters, the letter from Steven's mother that had been misplaced and not found until it was quite useless, and his notes to himself, and locked them away. The note he had written for the Queen he placed in an envelope and took the time to put his seal upon it, so she should know if it had been disturbed, and he pocketed it to give to Effington. Then with a final glance at the newspaper in front of him, he withdrew his letter opener, used the sharp point of it to cut out around the brief banns of his engagement, folded it. He took out his pocket watch, opened the back of the casing that was there for no other reason, that he had ever been able to discern, but for just such romantic little items and placed the clipping inside.

He left his study and climbed the stairs to where Effington would once again have the dubious honor of undressing him and putting him to bed as though he were some overgrown baby. And if St. James were less than happy about this circumstance, he also admitted he was too tired and in enough pain from his abused stitches that he was in no condition this morning to tweak his valet by denying him his rightful duties.

At about the same time as St. James was being met by Effington at his door as he returned home, Bertie, Lord Tempton, was crouched in some shrubbery and exclaiming in a whisper to Miss Murdock beside him. "Now where in the blazes, I wonder, could he be going at this hour of the night?"

It was Andrew's coach passing by them that caused his wonderment. They were hidden in the landscaping beside the mew, the second time that they had been forced into undignified retreat during their now hours long vigil, and ironically, it had been Andrew's movements both times. The first when he had returned from his cousin's townhouse to his grandmother's home. Miss Murdock had thought to hail him then, but she could not see having him waiting out in the cold and the dark with them when there was no guarantee that their endeavor would bear fruit. And as he had ridden in on his mount, and she had seen his face, he had also looked exhausted. It caused her to wonder all the more that he should be leaving again now, instead of getting some much deserved rest. It explained the carriage, at any rate, for he must plan to sleep on the road. But all the same, what was so urgent that he should be leaving now at all?

"Are you certain that it is Andrew's carriage?" she asked. Her teeth were clenched with cold, despite her wearing St. James' heavy coat, and her legs had gone quite numb.

"Yes. It must be Earl Larrimer for the Dowager has her own coach and I can't imagine Lady Lydia being about this late." Bertie's voice was thoughtful as well as perplexed and Lizzie turned to look at him.

In sudden fear, she asked, "Oh, Bertie! You don't think that St. James has been--?"

He placed a hand on her arm. "No. And be quiet. Someone is approaching."

She quieted, fretting. Bertie continued in a low voice even as his eyes remained focused on the mouth of the mew. "It is not St. James Andrew is going to. He would have had to get word and no one has ridden in, for we would have seen them."

"Yes. Of course." Miss Murdock said, relieved. Then, as she too studied the entrance to the mew, said, "Someone *is* there. But I can not tell if it is Steven."

"Nor can I as of yet. Stay still until we know for certain."

The figure at the mouth of the mew hesitated. He was as slight as Steven, but this figure's stance was different. The shoulders sagged, suggesting someone older, and his head was down, in sharp contrast to the audacious adolescent that Miss Murdock had come to know. The figure started forward, his arms clutched about his thin body in an attempt to warm himself, and Miss Murdock wished that he would raise his head so that the street lamp at the corner might catch his features.

Bertie's hand was still on her arm, steadying her, but when the slight figure stopped just below her bedchamber window, looking up, and made as if to make his climb once again, her doubts vanished. It was Steven.

She pulled from Lord Tempton's grasp, stumbled forward, heart beating fast, and called to him. Even then she was afraid he would flee. "Steven! It's Miss Murdock. We have been awaiting you."

He whirled at her hushed voice, located her in the darkness. In unexpected fervor he ran forward and threw himself into her arms. A great hiccupping sob escaped him.

Miss Murdock held him anchored to her, feeling his shoulders shake, and soothed him as best she could. Lord Tempton arrived out of the bushes beside her and she gave him a grateful look over Steven's head that he had allowed her to test her theory that Steven may return to her window a third night in search of her and of comfort.

"We have been so worried for you," she told the crying boy. "I should have never left you alone."

He sniffled into the shoulder of St. James' coat that she wore. "You left me t'go t'him," he said, and she could not tell whether he was accusing her or merely stating a fact.

She pulled back from him so that she could see his face, but she held his shoulders so that he could not bolt. "Yes, I did, Steven, for he was in a very bad way."

He put a child's dirty hand to his face, gave a harsh wipe down across it in a gesture of a full-grown man very much ashamed of his tears. "Coo, I know's it, Miss. And if he had died, t'woulda been me fault, for I left him when they needed me. I been too shamed t'go to me ma, an' tell her I seen me da die, and was t'reason St. James killed him. An' too shamed t'go to St. James, for 'bandonin' him when he were 'bout to die."

"Oh," Miss Murdock exclaimed. "You can not feel that way, Steven! For you were doing your very best to help his lordship and had no way of knowing that your father was involved in this! And St. James has been very grieved to learn that it was your father, and beside himself with worry for you. And what of your mother? She does not know what happened to your father, and now does not know what has happened to you either, and she must be sick with the worry and her fears. Oh, Steven, now that you are here, we must let everyone know that you are safe, and indeed, I am so glad that you are."

Steven blinked and she hugged him to her again, but he did not cry any longer, only told her on her shoulder, "Me mother knows now, Miss, that me da is dead and that St. James killed 'im."

"How do you know that, Steven?" Miss Murdock asked with surprise.

"I seen 'im meet with her tonight. He told her 'n all."

And Miss Murdock let out an exclamation as she held the boy back away from her again, but before she could question him further, Lord Tempton laid his hand upon her shoulder and told her, "We can't just stand here and talk, Miss Murdock. You two are already making enough noise to bring the whole household down upon our ears!"

She said, "Yes, of course you are right, Bertie. But whatever shall we do with him now that we have him?" And when her eyes met Lord Tempton's over Steven's head, she realized that they were in a fix indeed. She could not possibly go to St. James' home and force his already strained valet into hiding her in milord's bedchambers once again. It had been a small miracle that she had not been discovered before, and she could not think that particular ruse would work for any further length of time. Neither, she admitted, was she looking forward to the certain wrath of her new fiancé when he found that she and Lord Tempton had gone contrary to his orders.

The expression in Bertie's eyes seemed to confirm her fear on that point.

"You can't stay here at the Duchess's, Miss Murdock," he told her, as though having already discarded the idea of her going to St. James out of hand as complete and thorough lunacy.

"And well I know it, since I am supposed to be at my father's and would have a good deal of explaining to do as to where I have been for the past twenty-four hours if neither there nor here."

"I'd take you to my home, but--"

She made a little motion with one hand, releasing Steven's patient shoulder as she did so. "No. No, of course not. The last thing we need to do is involve another household and risk another score of servants discovering me. That is hardly any better than going to St. James."

"I could take you to your home in Chestershire," Bertie said with a brightening look. "St. James need never know that you weren't there quite as promptly as he expected."

"But whatever shall we do with Steven?" Miss Murdock countered. "I can not haul him up there with me and leave his poor mother to continue worrying about him. Let alone St. James."

"S'cuse me, Miss," Steven interrupted. "But I'd go see me mother first, that is, if you'd and m'lord Tempton would go with me," he added, looking a little self-conscious.

Miss Murdock looked at Bertie, and Bertie looked at her. "Well," he said, trying to fumble his way through to a conclusion. "That'd take care of one worry."

"And I could send a note 'round to St. James," she added. "And although it seems cowardly to not tell him to his face that we didn't do as he asked, it mayhaps would be better. And surely he can not be too angry when he has discovered that we found Steven, or rather, Steven found us," she amended, for if he had not come to her that night, they obviously would not have had a clue where to look for him, "and that we will be shortly headed for where I was to be to begin with."

Lord Tempton grasped on to this idea with enthusiasm. "Just the thing," he said. "A note. You are very sensible, Miss Murdock. By the time I have to see him again, he should have enough other things occupying his mind that I should get nothing more than a mild dressing down."

Miss Murdock laughed at this obvious attempt to elude St. James' ire on Bertie's part, but as she was feeling rather relieved herself to not have to immediately face him, she could not blame him. "Steven," she said. "You seem to have hit upon a solution to our problem. I only hope that we can help you as well as you think we should with facing your mother." Then she added, her voice more sober, "I think she will understand, so do not fear."

Steven gave a glum nod. Bertie said, "Well, we should gather the horses and set off then."

Steven said, "Coo, m'lord, don't think ya should take t'horses. There be no place t'stable them, and if'n ya leave them on t'street, they'll be stoled 'fore we ever reach t'door."

And that was the first inkling that Miss Murdock got that Steven's home was perhaps not a place that St. James would be happy to see her or Bertie visiting, but as she could see no other option, and indeed, she did want to help Steven, and be assistance to his poor mother, who must be in a state of shock at this point to have learned that her husband had been killed, she only said, "We shall walk, then, Steven, if you think that is best."

"Aye, miss. Have no fear, though. For I know's the best and safest way to get there." He opened his coat as he spoke and said, "I have milord's pistol, also."

"Good God!" Bertie exclaimed. "Never tell me you've had that since last night?"

"Aye," Steven nodded. "For I first thought I'd kill St. James himself with it, but then I come t'realize, he'd never shot me father if it hadn't been for him thinkin' me da was 'bout t'stab me. So t'was my fault and not his."

Miss Murdock did not say anything to that, and Bertie was silent also. But they again met each other's eyes over Steven's head, and Bertie's gaze dropped away, and Miss Murdock's gaze was very troubled.

And so they set out, in the cold and the dark and the foggy night, and Miss Murdock was grateful that her new riding boots had low heels, but they were stiff with their newness, and they chaffed at her ankles. Bertie looked to be making out rather less as well, as he was not used to any more exertion than he deemed absolutely necessary, and they had not gone far before he began to voice some regrets.

Steven walked ahead, and it was clear that he was familiar with the city, especially those routes that were less traveled, and he did not seem the least put out by the dark or the fog. Miss Murdock recalled his saying that he had been on less honorable jobs than waking a female in her bedchamber, and from his sure navigation, she was now certain that he had not been exaggerating.

But he seemed if not in light spirits, at least a great deal calmer, and as she had the suspicion that it had very much to do with her accompanying him, she blithely tuned out Bertie's low-voiced mutterings of complaint.

As they progressed, their surroundings deteriorated. Miss Murdock was not familiar with London, of course, and she had no more than a basic sense of direction, but something about the steady dampening smell of the air led her to believe that they must be approaching the Thames.

Bertie's rather vague complaints turned more explicit. "Not a good neighborhood, Miss Murdock, to be in, not even in the day, let alone, middle of the night."

And Miss Murdock frowned, for she could well see that this was so, for the buildings they passed were derelict, and the rats rustled around with enough boldness that she nearly had to kick one from beneath her booted feet. "Well, we should not possibly meet anyone that would know us, then, should we, Bertie," she pointed out. "For if we were on a more fashionable street, however would we explain my being about in the night with only you for protection?"

"I have t'duke's gun, Miss," Steven reminded her from a pace ahead of them.

"Indeed, yes," she replied. "And a comfort it is to me to know that I have a messenger boy with a weapon as well as Mr. Tempton for protection." She said it lightly enough that Steven should not be offended, but she was certain that Bertie should pick up on her point at any rate. She continued, "So you see, Bertie, although I feel very safe, I am afraid that if we were to meet someone we knew, that the propriety of all this should mayhaps escape them. I think Steven is doing a splendid job of making sure that does not happen by this route."

"I just hope he does not expect us to take to the bloody roofs next," Bertie muttered. And this did cause Miss Murdock to laugh, the picture in her mind of the foppish Lord Tempton clambering up a drain pipe or some other accessory to the rooftops causing her quite a bit of amusement. But Bertie, a little more loudly, asked, "Are we headed for the waterfront then, lad?"

And Steven said, "Aye. Down by t'pool."

"The pool!" Bertie gave soft exclamation with horror in his voice.

"What is the pool?" Miss Murdock asked, and lifted her skirts to jump over some ancient garbage that lay across her way.

"Where the locks hold the waters for the ships to dock, Miss Murdock. And if you can not know what an unsavory part of town it is, then let me present you with a picture of scores of rough, muscle-hewed dockworkers, dirty and sweaty and smelling of gin, whose idea of a night's entertainment is to drink each other into the gutters and to have knife fights where the winner is the one who has lost the least amount of parts of his anatomy."

"Oh," Miss Murdock said, then, "I am sure they can not all be so bad. And it will be dawn soon. They will have gone home to their families by now, I am sure."

But Steven answered before Bertie could argue further. "Nay, miss. For it is a right gin row down here. But ne'er fear, for we are only a mew away from me house, 'n' 'though we mays not avoid 'em's that drink entirely, we should only run into a couple of 'em back here with their pieces of comfort for t'night, 'n' they'll pay us no mind. Bein' busy 'n' all."

And Miss Murdock said, "Pieces of comfort?"

"Never you mind, Miss Murdock!" Bertie hastened to say. He added to Steven, "Is there not some other route?"

"Coo, no," Steven returned looking over his shoulder at Lord Tempton as though he were daft. "For if they'rn't busy with that 'n' all, then they'll be the ones that are still lookin', 'n' if they see the Miss there, they'll be swarmin' 'round us like she were a week's worth of wages. For she's clean y'know, 'n' they t'aint used to seein' one that t'aint needin' a dip in t'Thames to freshen' her up some."

Miss Murdock, perceiving at last what they were discussing, said to Bertie, "I assure you, I would rather take a route where I do not have a gaggle of dockworkers chasing after me because I am 'clean'. Let Steven continue in what way he thinks best."

And Bertie only sighed, muttered that if St. James ever discovered any of this night's piece of work that he would probably not even have the decency of calling Bertie out, but would kill him on the spot.

Miss Murdock gave a soft laugh. "I begin to see why St. James thinks so much of you, Bertie, for although you are reluctant and let it be known you have your doubts, you do not argue in the least!"

And Bertie said in a doleful voice, "I shall only lose in the end at any rate, and it all goes so much quicker if I merely complain along the way."

But Steven drew to a stop in front of them, and he turned his gray eyes to them in warning and they fell silent. "We live down this row, miss," he whispered, "but we'll have to go quiet and cautious like, for the street frontin' t'river is just there at t'end also. They'll be some few of t'men 'bout, but what e'er happens or ya see, don't scream. For they'll come runnin' then, 'n' it t'won't be for t'helpin' ye."

And Miss Murdock pulled the turned-up collar of St. James' dark coat a little closer about her face and nodded as she did so. "I understand," she whispered back. "Thank you, Steven."

Bertie took her arm, and if he had been complaining before, now he only seemed resigned to the task ahead of him. He put his other hand beneath his unbuttoned coat, which surprised Miss Murdock very much, but then, of course, St. James would have never tolerated Lord Tempton if he had not thought he were prepared in a pinch.

Then Steven moved out again, and they turned on to the narrow street that he had indicated. The houses were (and Miss Murdock could think of no other word in her mind) unfit. There was no walk way, and the small, clapboard shacks' doors opened directly onto the street, so that one only would step over the flooding, stenching gutter and into the front room, or possibly, the only room, from the smallness of them.

The smell had been building as they walked, but now it seemed more pronounced, each division of its compound identifiable. First and foremost, the smell of human excrement. And there was a rot to the smell also, as though death came here in many forms, large and small. From rat and cat to stray dogs and used up horses. And to man also, from gangrenous injuries or premature failings brought on by drink and damp or from his fellow sufferer.

And as they walked, huddled together, there were forms, deep in the shadows, and if Miss Murdock did not wish to look at them, she was not going to *not* look at them, for now, she felt, was a time when delicacy of sensibility could very well get one killed. For if she did not look to discern for certain that it was only desperate activity between man and woman, then she could not discount the fact that it may be a danger of which she should be aware.

And as she walked, she had the sudden wondering if Andrew had thought to include this little street upon her tour of London? Or if he were even aware of it and others like it.

She thought of St. James. She would swear that he knew of them, and that in fact, he had moved through them, and she wondered if he had ever been touched by the desolate hopelessness of these people in these streets of the night, doing acts that were meant to bring hope but using them only to assuage despair. And rather than being shocked, she was only moved to feeling very, very helpless.

And if her mind somehow connected the two, acts of hope reduced to assuaging despair and St. James, she did not yet understand it. She only knew that it was the same helplessness she had felt when she had cried, clawing at his chaise lounge.

Chapter Twenty-four

He awoke with a start, but he lay very still, and did not even open his eyes. There had been a disturbing element in his dreams. And although his first instinct, perhaps his first honed survival skill, was to not linger between sleep and wakefulness, but to be alert in an instance, to open his eyes, scan, assess and act if necessary, he for once, this *one* time, fought this instinct and lay grasping at his dream.

Some rich muckety-muck an' his wife.

He puzzled over this sudden invasion of Lucy Crockner's voice into the wisps of his dream. His dream had nothing to do with her and what she had told him, had it? No, he was certain that it had not, for his father had been in it and his uncle Morty, and they had been searching for someone. Yes, searching for their killer (*their* killer? Uncle Morty had died in an accident). And his only concession to wakefulness was the frown that turned down his lips, but he still did not open his eyes, but remained suspended between sleep and wake.

Not their killer. No, they had not been searching for their killer, but for his father's--No. Searching for Dante's killer. They had been searching for who had killed the son of one and the nephew of the other.

An' his wife. . . 'n' a lad.

His gold eyes snapped open, and St. James rolled and sat up in the bed. He stared without seeing for a moment, only the picture of his own thoughts before him, and then in a cold rage he pulled himself from the bed, far from rested, and asked himself with harshness, "How could I be so bloody, God damned *blind*?" Then through a zig-zagging of thought process that bore him around a countless score of other issues, he added, "And damn it, I have not protected her in the least! But have only added fuel to the fire by putting that confounded announcement in the paper."

He went to the door in only his shorts, tightening the laces with hard yanks and tying them as he went, and upon opening the door, bellowed into the activity of his house, "Effington! Damn it, Effington, I have need of you! Now!"

Then he turned, went to his wardrobe and pulled from it his normal attire of plain riding breeches and simple shirt with only lace at the cravat and cuffs.

"Milord?" Effington asked from behind him, and for once there was not the usual affront in his voice that was there when he felt as if he were being ill-used.

St. James raised a brow at this unexpected ease of disposition, but only said, "Have you that missive I gave to you earlier?"

"The one for a messenger of the Queen?"

"Yes." St. James pulled on his breeches, his chest twinging in protest at his rapid activity.

Effington watched him without bemoaning his lordship's lack of help-lessness. He pulled the sealed envelope from the inside pocket of his starched uniform. "I have it, of course."

"Very good," St. James replied, and he took the envelope from Effing-ton and tore it across. He walked over to the fireplace and threw it into the flames.

Effington observed this activity, and then seeing that his lordship had every intention of continuing with putting on his shirt, advised him, "You need a shave, milord."

"Haven't time, Effington."

"I assure you I can shave you in the little amount of time that you can explain to me what I am to tell the Queen's man when he arrives."

And St. James threw down his shirt, struggled into his high, gleaming leather boots instead, stamped his feet into them and said as he did so, "You've got two minutes, and you shall have to endeavor to do it while I compose a new message."

Effington poured water into the basin. "And one also for your grand-mother, as I am sure she is worried?" he asked.

"Yes. Damn it. One to my grandmother as I am sure she is worried."

Effington gathered towel, basin and razor as he followed his employer who went bare-chested to the secretary in his room. "If you can wait just one second, milord, I will get the shaving cup."

But St. James was pawing through his stationery. "No, I'll do without, Effington, for I have little care if it is not close or if you nick me. Just do not do me fatal injury is all I ask," and he opened a bottle of ink, dipped his pen and began writing.

And if Effington had a difficult time of it shaving his lordship, especial-ly along his throat, as St. James only tilted his head first in one direction and then the other, and would not at any time forgo his writing to give his valet more access, he did not complain, but only did the job with as much efficiency as he could muster.

St. James muttered as he paused in thought. "I no longer know who I can trust, damn it! Years of eliminating possible culprits and I am back at the beginning, where every face could be a murderer."

Effington said, "And you trust me with a razor to your throat, milord?"

"Yes. God damn it! I trust you with a razor to my throat. Now do be quiet for you are distracting me."

"And I am sure you can trust Miss Murdock," Effington continued de-spite orders to the contrary.

And St. James gave him a lethal look from his heavy gold eyes. "Yes. I am sure that I may. Unfortunately," he continued, going back to his writings, "I very much fear she should not have trusted me. *Damn* it!"

"And Lord Tempton?"

"If Bertie were going to kill me, he has had his chances."

"And Tyler?"

"With my life," St. James returned. But he appeared to be gaining a degree of lesser agitation and Effington persisted.

"Your grandmother?"

St. James hesitated in his writing. Then said, "Too old and too vulnerable. Too without knowledge of my actions and my suspicions, of which I am at fault. I can not trust her to not make a decision that although well-meaning, may be all the same fatal. And I worry all the more for I fear that if she gets wind of this, she will act rather than trust me to finish it."

Effington struggled to follow his lordship's movements without cutting him. "Young Mister Tempton?" he asked.

"No," St. James returned. "Too young, too impetuous, too impressionable."

"Earl Larrimer?"

And St. James paused again in brief and searching thought. "No. Too ruled by emotion," and then in a scouring undertone, "as I am myself at this late date. Damn it, Effington! Finish! And when you are done, pack me a bag, for I will be leaving in short order to fetch Miss Murdock." He put a sudden weary hand to his eyes, frustrating Effington's efforts all the more. "And whatever I am to do with her, I do not know!"

"Milord, you will have to remove your hand."

St. James moved his hand and read over his missives, then addressed the envelopes for them and folded them inside.

Effington put the razor aside, picked up a towel. St. James took the towel from him, gave his face and neck two swift swipes as he rose from his chair, and then flung the towel onto the chair he had just vacated.

"I will not be back up," he told his valet. "So, if you would, take my bag down to the stables. I will be taking the curricle and you may deposit my bag there." St. James put on his shirt as he spoke, buttoned his cuffs and flipped the lace down over his pale wrists. "Go, man," he said, his voice softer as Effington seemed to be hesitating, torn between packing a bag as asked and his natural instinct to do up the buttons of milord's shirt and to tie the lace of his cravat.

Effington stirred into action and as he hurried to the wardrobe he observed St. James tucking his unmatched pistols into his waistband. "Luck to you, milord," he said.

And St. James replied with bitterness, "And I shall need it, Effington, for I have been very stupid about this, chasing a phantom culprit and a complicated motive when it has all been quite simple and clear from the very beginning."

With those words, he gathered his great coat and put it on. And the tight wrap of his fresh bandages that Effington had changed earlier that morning constricted him to a degree. But as he moved his left hand in a quick motion of testing his ability to the butt of one hidden gun, he was satisfied that he could draw it with effectiveness and would probably tear out no more than one or two stitches in the true effort.

Then he gathered up the two sealed envelopes, entrusted one to Effington, and the other he placed in his pocket. He left the bedchamber and if the thought crossed his mind that at this point, he had no idea how he was to do what had to be done, and still endeavor to walk back through that portal, he did not entertain it.

He only knew that first and foremost, he must fetch Miss Murdock and the rest of it would have to come to him as he went along.

And he was quite unawares that Effington's singular thought was that St. James, for once, had not started his day with a drink.

"Tyler?" St. James called into the dimness of the stables once he had entered. As he had expected, Tyler had found chores needing done to the fore of the stable and his answer was immediate.

"Aye, milord." He appeared out of a stall but a brief ways down the center aisle. "It's barely ten but I figured you'd be 'long shortly at any rate."

"I've slept too damned long as it is," St. James said and Tyler narrowed his eyes at the tone of his lordship's voice.

"You've found somethin' then?" he asked.

"Something that has been in front of my face for far too long. And which has been pointed out to me twice in as many days. And still I was too blind to pick up on it!"

Tyler spat with force into the gutter. "You'll have to 'splain it to me then, milord, for I haven't t'clue."

St. James moved forward with purpose. "We'll talk while tacking up, for I have need of you to go to my grandmother's and give her this," and he handed Tyler the envelope he had brought down with him.

Tyler pocketed it. "Aye."

"And you shall need to speak with her also, and tell her that you need a bag made up for Miss Murdock with several changes of clothing and whatever items her lady's maid deems necessary, but it must be done quietly and without fuss."

"And her lady's maid also?" Tyler asked.

"No."

"Damn it, milord! Your grandmother will not have it. You 'spect me to persuade her to readyin' Miss Murdock for some unknown journey, undoubtedly with you, and not have her lady's maid present?"

St. James turned upon his groom and his words came out as nearly a snarl, "I have little care how you accomplish it, Tyler! I don't care if you allow that the maid is coming and then you pitch her in the gutter along your route of return. Just see that you have the bag and no maid!"

Tyler shifted his cud of tobacco. "Aye."

St. James strode further down the aisle then opened the stall door there. He paused as he caught the horse inside. Tyler moved to gather saddle and St. James had the horse out of the stall when he returned. Tyler tossed him the bridle and began the saddling. And they each moved as though they had worked together in this manner many times before. "After you complete that little duty," St. James continued, "I will need you to go to the same under-taker that you took Steven's father to. You'll be meeting with his mother there."

Tyler said, "Bloody hell, I will! When and how did she come to be in to this mess? Is Steven with her?"

St. James paused in his bridling of the horse, and it lipped his shoulder softly. "I do not know where Steven is. As of last night, neither did she."

Tyler looked at him with disbelief but his hands never paused in the sure working of saddle straps. "She be t'letter writer, then?"

"Yes. And I spent a damned uncomfortable time with her, for it is not at all pleasant to tell someone that is worried about their husband that they need not worry any longer for he is dead. And that I killed him."

"Bloody goddamned mess," Tyler muttered and brought down the stirrup iron as he finished his task. "Shoulda ne'er told her, milord! Any information ye got from her can only be suspect now, for I dare say she'd dearly love to see ye in difficulty."

St. James examined this remark, his eyes brooding, then he said, "I think not. T'is a long story and I won't go into it now. And the damning revelation is one that I had already had told to me, by her husband before he died."

"That bein'?" Tyler asked. He mounted and leaned from the saddle.

"They were told before hand that there would be three occupants riding in the coach that night."

Tyler looked at him in momentary incomprehension, then his face tightened and his eyes became very hard. "No one t'would have known that, milord, except for someone inside Morningside."

St. James nodded, said with a cold twist to his mouth, "You are so right, Tyler. For if it had been someone outside the household, they could not have anticipated anything but my father traveling alone, as he was expected to be traveling lightly and quickly and through the night. Only someone at Morningside could have known that my mother would not be put off and was returning with him and that they were taking their son as well."

"Do you know who--?"

"I have a very good idea." St. James stepped back from the horse. "If you return before I, wait for me. I will be taking the curricle and going for a brief visit to my barrister's, for there is something else I need to investigate and if it is as I suspect, then it is the final nail in the coffin. All I need figure out then is how to go about it, and damn it, there are all sorts of complications upon that head." And his frown was deep and dark. Tyler held in his mount and with concern watched him, and St. James finished by saying, "And all sorts of complications upon what to do with Miss Murdock." He raised his eyes with sudden savageness and added, "for I fear that she is no longer an innocent bystander in this and that she will be a target as well."

Tyler nodded, said with sudden grave understanding, "The hanky's what did it then?"

"Yes. One damned, careless mistake on my part, and it has turned all of this totally upside down. I have no need to tell you, Tyler, that I had planned to elope with her immediately and secretly, get her with child if God had been willing and then hide all of this circumstance by launching her and courting her. In that manner she would have been perfectly safe. If I had died, I'd still have an heir and both of them would have lived very comfortably indeed with her in control of my estates. At the same time, I would have been putting pressure on who I wished to put pressure upon without any fear of endangering her, for they would have thought her no more than my betrothed."

"I'd figured that was what went on in your mind," Tyler said.

"Now," St. James said with an embittered, tight smile, "I fear that I have *not* married her, and that my little indiscretion with her that night in the carriage will lead someone to believe that possibly God may have blessed us at any rate. And I ask you, Tyler, if you were to stand to gain by my death, would you leave her alive long enough for me to marry her and make a possibly coming babe a legitimate heir?"

"Yer dealin' with someone who has gone to great lengths already," Tyler agreed. "Much easier to be rid of t'one afore t'marriage an take no chances, than to wait 'til after and it be born and then need to be rid of two!"

And St. James said with uncompromising fury in his voice, "After all, my mother was with child at the time of her death. So I should say the precedent is there." He stepped back from the side of Tyler's mount. "Go," he said. "We waste time."

Tyler put his heels to his horse and trotted from the stables. St. James turned and bellowed into the depths of the stables. "Groom!" A younger one came half-running from far down the aisle. St. James moved toward him. He stopped outside the two stalls that held his bays, told the undergroom, "I'll be needing my curricle, lad, without delay. Get someone to help you, for if I am not out of this stables in five minutes, I shall flay you and your co-hort."

"Aye, m'lord," the younger groom tugged his cap and was off running again. And as he had not been employed there long, but had oft heard tales of the duke's foul and frightening temper, he could now quite believe it.

It was not a very great deal of time later that St. James strode into C. Edmund Bickerstaff's office.

"Milord Duke," the Barrister rose in surprise from behind his desk.

"And good morning to you, Charles," St. James returned. "No, thank you, I shan't take up more than ten minutes of your time," he added as Bickerstaff motioned for him to take a seat.

"I knew it," the Barrister replied a little piqued. "You now wish me to reverse everything that I have changed in regards to your will."

And St. James was diverted enough from his problems to give a thin smile. "Not in the least, Charles. So put your mind at ease. You have completed all of that, have you not?"

"Only needs that certificate of marriage, milord."

"I will get it to you if I have to crawl the length of England on my hands and knees," St. James told him and if he noticed the sudden surprised and somewhat gleeful lift of the Barrister's eyebrows to imagine any man, let alone the infamously immoral Duke of St. James, going to such lengths to secure a female's hand in marriage, St. James only ignored it. "What I need from you now, Charles, rather promptly, is to know what holdings are in my uncle's estate."

And Charles frowned, for to have someone show such blatant interest in what they stood to inherit upon the death of another was frightfully crass.

But St. James only ignored this look also, and prompted him by saying, "I would think you would have a listing of his assets along with his will, would you not?"

"Yes. Of course. Standard procedure."

"Then simply look, man," St. James bade. "As I said, I will not tie you up for more than ten minutes. East India Company holdings is what I am interested in, if that should help."

Barrister Bickerstaff, understanding, of course, that St. James' reference to not tying him up for more than ten minutes was in fact an advisory that it had better not take him longer than ten minutes to find the required information, only said with disapproval, "I shall endeavor to see what I can find, milord. Please have a seat and I will have it momentarily."

And St. James gave a maddening smile and said, "I shall remain standing, thank you."

Bickerstaff moved to where he kept the further documents dealing with Mortimer Larrimer's will and began digging through the protracted amount of paperwork that listed properties, jewelry, personal assets, trusts, etc, etc, until he reached a five page long listing of holdings on the Exchange.

St. James had indeed remained standing, and had disconcertingly begun to pace, rubbing his upper lip with one finger, when the Barrister was no more than a minute into his search, and the Barrister may be forgiven if he felt that the duke were breathing down his neck in impatience. He was on the third page of the holdings before he was able to say with triumph, "Yes. Here, milord. A *thirty* percent share in the company," and despite himself he sounded a little awed.

St. James stilled, and somehow his stillness was more disturbing to the Barrister than his pacing. And then he turned and when his gold eyes fixed upon the old man, the Barrister backed up a pace from where he had been standing beside the cabinet.

"Do you have a date," St. James asked with lethal quiet, "as to when those stocks were obtained?"

And Bickerstaff glanced down at the paperwork to show that he was very certain, and said, "No, milord. They do not have the date of obtainment, only the holdings upon his death."

St. James, frustrated, began pacing again. "*Damn* it! I shall have to go to my uncle's solicitor and I can not waste the bloody *time!*"

Bickerstaff cleared his throat. "If you don't mind me observing, milord," and St. James fixed his attention back upon him with a speed that nearly made him stutter his next words, "but East India Company Stocks have rarely been traded since the end of the war with China. They are far too valuable, you know. I would hazard to guess that for your uncle to have had such a large share that he would have had to have purchased them before the war, when they were being sold quite indiscriminately and, indeed, cheaply."

St. James gave him a profound look of understanding and Bickerstaff, thus emboldened, added, "And I do not know if this makes any difference to you, milord, but I notice that this holding is listed on the sheet that contains those assets that were brought into the marriage by your aunt."

St. James threw him off stride then by dropping into the seat that he had before refused, and placing one elegant hand over his pale face. Bickerstaff observed this odd behavior for the full minute that it lasted. Then St. James removed his hand, and his face was calm and immobile, his lids half drawn in secretive revelation, and he only said, "Thank you, Charles," and rose and walked from that bewildered man's office. At the door he stopped, turned, added one last note, "About my cousin's inheritance. You may direct that upon the instance of my marriage to Miss Murdock and it comes into my control, that it be immediately released to him. I see no reason to wait until he is older, or until he is married. And I," and his words were bruising in their contemptuousness, "have no use for it."

Then he was gone, and Bickerstaff numbly wrote this direction into his notes, the Duke's behavior beyond all comprehension to him.

St. James mounted his curricle and sat upon the high seat for only a brief second before turning the horses about. His mind was very full, but even as he wished to do nothing so much as to find somewhere to pace and think in quiet, he knew that he could not take the time to delay and ponder his discoveries now.

His eyes searched out around him, as much in a searching of Steven (for it had been here that he had first met the lad, and could that really be but three days ago?) as much as to be aware of anyone following or threatening.

The urgency he had felt upon awaking had intensified, and he decided now that as the undertaker of Steven's father was not far, and that Lucy Crockner and Tyler may even now be meeting, that he would go in that direction rather than back to his own home to possibly cool his heels while waiting for his groom to appear.

The address of the undertaker was not a savory one. But as people in better neighborhood's did not normally die anonymously and have need of their body being stored anywhere but the parlors of their own homes, it was not surprising. Tyler had merely found the nearest one, and so it was but a short distance from the mean streets of the waterfront of the Thames.

St. James found the proper number, and the building itself was but a long, low-slung, crumbling brick that held the dampness and even had he not known of what went on within its walls, it would have reminded St. James of decay.

Then a cheeky voice was saying from at the head of his horses, "Hold yer horses, m'lord, for tuppence," and St. James brought his attention from the building and down to the somber eyed lad below him. There was an attempt at a smile across his dirty face, but St. James could see that it was very strained, and that he was quite unsure of himself and of the welcome, or lack of it, he was afraid he would receive.

And St. James, with eyes glowing, replied, "And I'll give you a crown if you run a message for me." He swung down from the curricle and turned to catch Steven by the shoulder. "Thank God you are well, lad, for I have been eaten alive with what may have become of you."

Steven swallowed under the intensity of St. James gaze. "I'm sorry," he managed to choke out, but he did not shame himself by crying as he had with Miss Murdock. "'Been a right confusin' time for me, m'lord."

"I very well know it," St. James returned. "It was your mother that found you then?"

Steven shook his head. "No, m'lord, but Miss Murdock, and she were good 'nough to help me face me mother, for I don't know which I was more shamed to see, you or her."

St. James' fingers tightened on the lad's shoulder. "Miss Murdock!" he asked. "How can that be, Steven, when as of only twelve hours ago, she was set out for Chestershire?"

"Nay, m'lord. She and Lord Tempton waited at the Dowager's home for me, for Miss Murdock, she said she was made sure I would return, and 'deed I did, just as she s'pected. She said she weren't going t'let me down 'gain, for she felt most sore bad leavin' me there by meself t'other night. But, course, I know she had t'go t'you for you were in a bad way. An' I'm glad she did, for I didn't wish t'see you die, milord, e'en if I did 'bandon you when you most needed me."

"Hush," St. James told him with mock sharpness. "For you were but a lad, and now I think you are fast becoming a man, so it is your actions now that I shall judge you on and not your actions of before."

And Steven swelled with sudden pride, and St. James knew that he had been desperate for reassurance that he had not done badly. Indeed, St. James believed he had done very well, for somehow he had managed to work through all the complicated circumstances and arrive at some conclusion that allowed him to forgive the duke even after the duke killed his father. And he did not seem shamed either by his father's actions, as though understanding that his father had made a very fatal mistake, but that Steven were alive to learn from it at any rate.

He had worked all of this out for himself in his thirteen year old mind, had matured to a great degree over night, and now, had come to St. James in renewed friendship.

So despite St. James' great concern for Miss Murdock, he could not deny the boy his words of respect, but he did go on to ask just on their heels, "And where, by-the-by, is Miss Murdock now, Steven?"

"At me house," Steven said with some pride. "For she was not afeared at all to go there in the wee hours of this morning, and all to make sure that me mother should understand that t'was not me fault that me father died."

St. James took his hand from the boy's shoulder, for he was afraid that he would clutch him to the degree that the lad would be bruised to the bone. He fought the stream of obscenities that threatened to come from his mouth at their rash stupidity. He wanted to travel at once to Steven's home (and God knows he knew exactly the situation of that home, as he had just seen it the night before) and murder Bertie for taking her there. And God help Bertie if that man had not stayed with her. And, finally, he thought he would throttle his serene Lizzie until she for once would think of herself instead of everyone but herself.

He struggled for a full minute with his rage, turning to the side and adjusting an harness strap so that Steven could not be aware of how furious he was with all of them. When he could control his voice and his emotions, he only said, "Well, at least you have saved me a trip to Chestershire, lad, and I know where she is, at any rate. Now, let us settle with this man in here. I take it your mother is not coming and that she sent you in her place?"

"Aye, m'lord. She thought you may be happy to see me, and Miss Murdock, she was sure of it." And Steven looked guilty of being remiss, and added, "Oh, coo, Miss Murdock sent ye a note also, that I was to give to you!"

Steven pulled a note from what appeared to be a very fine pair of breeches rather worse the wear now from a ruthless shearing of cuffs and a dirty rope about their middle. Not to mention they were now extremely in need of a wash.

St. James unfolded it and as he read it, he could almost hear that soothing, teasing quality of Lizzie's voice as she had spoken to him when he had been in much pain and very weak from loss of blood and she had been endeavoring to stitch him back together again.

Milord St. James--Dante,

I know you will be angry to find that we did not go directly to my home as you had wished. And I apologize most heartily. I am only glad to say that my venture proved successful and that Steven is well and accounted for, as I am sure you are very, very relieved to see for yourself.

Bertie and I will be setting off this evening as soon as it is dark enough for us to once again move about hopefully undetected. And do not come down upon him too hard, Dante, for I quite insisted, and I have found that dear quality in him that I dare say you admire him for, which is that he is perfectly pliable even when he is most heartily overwhelmed with misgivings. No wonder you have managed to drag him, protesting all the while, I am sure, through so many of your scrapes.

And I have found him to be quite steady of nerve when the occasion demands it, so was most happily surprised and appreciative. But I should have known you would have no use for someone totally ineffectual, and that his comical helplessness is but a great masquerade to protect him from more people taking advantage of him as I so shamelessly did last night.

And do not blame Steven, either, for I was most happy to assist him, and not only for his sake but for mine, for I learned from Steven and Mrs. Crockner that it had been she you met with last night, and thus you were quite safe. For I was worried to the point of obsession and would not have rested easy in Chestershire at any rate.

I know of course, that you are far from finished, and far from leaving it be. I will be content to be where you wish me to be now that I have taken care of this distraction, so do not feel compelled to come and upbraid me now, for I am sure you will do an adequate job upon our next meeting.

Know all that I dare not say. Not even to myself.

Lizzie.

And he stood for a long moment, letting her voice wash through him, and wondered how she could think he could read such a letter and not rush to her side? That even if he did not fear for her safety, he would have dropped everything he was about and gone to her and once again drew her into his arms and kissed her until her silly, sensible ideas all melted into nothing but so much soft caring that she could hold even the harsh, unyielding vengeance that flowed in him and soothe it into serene acceptance.

With a sudden despair, he wadded the letter and went to dash it to the ground. But he could not, could *not* throw those words away, any more than he had been able to leave their announced nuptials to be tossed with the paper. And so he only shoved the letter into his pocket and realized that he had not noticed as he had been reading that Tyler had arrived.

It pointed out damningly the completeness of his distraction.

Tyler, with brutality, said, "Aye, milord, and I could have shot you and you would have not known you were dead 'til you reached t'end of your letter."

St. James, for once, could find nothing to say to this, and he only flashed his groom a warning look.

Steven pointed out, "But I was here, keepin' watch, so he were safe enough."

"Indeed, lad," Tyler encouraged, "and damned lucky of it too, I dare say." He dismounted and put a large hand on that youth's shoulder, but his next words were aimed again at St. James. "You can be angry with me if you wish, milord, but you're as sick with her as I've ever seen 'em come." He turned to unfasten a small bag that was tied to his saddle, and he threw it into the curricle to join the one Effington had sent down. "And now's a damned bad time t'be entertainin' an affection for t'young lady."

"T'is not your concern, Tyler," St. James told him, his voice dangerous.

"Aye. I'll shut up," the groom agreed. "But you best be aware of it and get control, milord, or t'only letters you'll be reading will be from six feet under, studyin' yer head stone." And with force he spat tobacco to within an inch of milord's boots and added, "Her's too."

"Enough!" St. James told him. "What took you so bloody long? For I expected you to be here before me."

"I saw the filly of course. Which I gather now comes as no surprise t'you, but I spent a deal of time tryin' t'determine why Miss's filly should be there and where she was. No one knew, of which I was relieved as well as concerned."

"You did not have the ill-conceived notion to set up a hue and cry did you?" St. James asked.

But Tyler shook his head. "No. Only asked Bedrow, and advised him not t'mention that the horses were there unexpectedly and t'say nothin' of it if someone were t'ask other than that you had sent over two of yours that you suddenly found yourself short of room for. Then," he continued, "I come to find your grandmother not in residence."

"Damn it, Tyler, you can not be serious!"

"Oh, 'deed, I am, milord. I've never seen anythin' going as badly as this seems t'be. She's gone to Chestershire."

St. James pondered this, then said, "Little matters. I should have expected she would do such a thing. And I'd rather she not be in her home here now at any rate. Lady Lydia did not accompany her, did she?"

"No."

"I did not think she would. Did you speak to Andrew then?"

But Tyler shook his head again. "No, for damned if he has not gone to Chestershire also, and in his carriage of all things, rather than on horseback."

And St. James, taken aback, rubbed his lip at this point and admitted, "*That* surprises me and I do not know what to make of it as of yet." Then he glanced up, a little bemused. "So how did you get the bloody bag?"

"Ashton is sympathetic t'our cause. And he'll not say anything t'any-one of it."

"Ah. Very good. Steven, has your mother told you where your father is to be buried?"

"Aye, m'lord. And she asked that I extend her thanks, our thanks t'ye, for she said t'is quite decent of you an' all."

"Well, she will be able to thank me in person, however little I may deserve it, for we will wrap this business up and then, Steven, we will be going to your home. That is, if you would be so kind as to invite us?"

Steven nodded, "Coo, m'lord. Be right honored to have ye. 'N' I'm glad to have time to talk to ye at any rate, for I've a meetin' at Red's Pub t'night."

St. James closed his eyes for an instance for he felt if he had one more piece of unexpected news he would crack, and when he opened them again he could do nothing but meet Tyler's eyes over Steven's head, and although he had not had chance to tell Tyler that part of the tale, evidently his own expression was enough to tell the groom that this was a significant announcement, and that St. James was not sure what to make of it.

"Lord help ye, St. James, but if you don't look as though you just swallow'd a whole cud of chaw. What's in t'works? And where is Miss Murdock?"

"Miss Murdock is sitting no more than around the corner, I would lief wager, from the very men that would kill her, and Steven here, has man-aged to make sure that they have been delayed from following her be-lieved movements to Chestershire. And although they may not yet be aware that she is in their midst, they are very much gathered nigh about her. And this could be a very fortuitous circumstance, or a very bad one." He turned to Steven, told him with earnestness, "We must finish very quickly, lad, and make haste to your home. And you must think of some route to get us there that we will not be seen."

"Coo, milord, in broad day? It willn't be easy."

"Well, think upon it, shall you, while we take care of this business in here," and with that, he and Steven at last went through the doors of the undertaking establishment, and Tyler remained with the horses and the conveyance.

Chapter Twenty-five

"I dearly wish," Bertie complained, "that we could be away from here now, for despite what you may think, I know that ten to one he will come here if for no other reason than to dress me down."

The shanty that he and Miss Murdock were visiting had no panes of glass in the two small windows that looked out onto the narrow street, and so it had not much in the way of privacy, and Lord Tempton, despite the grievance in his tone, kept his voice quiet.

He was seated at the table that with its two chairs was the sole furniture in the room, and he had pulled from his coat pocket a deck of cards, much to Miss Murdock's amusement, and had been playing solitaire for the past two hours since Steven's departure.

Miss Murdock, also aware of the open windows, but rather less concerned, as she expected that the noise being made by Mrs. Crockner's other two young children would drown out her words before they could reach beyond the small house, replied from where she sat across from him, "Oh, Bertie, surely not! I am certain he has far too many other matters on his mind to come down here for no other reason than to scold us. And I explained, did I not, that I wrote that we would be going on to Chestershire at night fall? That must have mollified him to some degree."

One of Mrs. Crockner's children, the seven year old, was playing with nothing more than a string as he sat on the rough floor before the stove, which he occupied himself with by making differing and complicated designs between his spread fingers. This is naturally a quiet endeavor, but he made up for this deficiency in his entertainment by singing a rather bawdy tune that Miss Murdock was making a valiant effort to not follow the words of too closely. The three year old sat upon her lap and was crying despite her every effort to distract him. She spoke to him now at the end of her words to Lord Tempton, "See the pretty cards? See Uncle Bertie playing with the pretty cards?"

And Bertie snorted at his new title and only said, "Do you care to wager upon it, Miss Murdock? And by the by, do you perchance play poker?"

"No, I do not," she returned. "And I would not expose young children to such even if I did." Which seemed a rather lame expostulation to direct at him when she considered the song the elder one was singing.

"Well, I still say we should leave now and take our chances. Only stands to reason that the drunks have to sleep sometime, and the more decent of them should be down on the docks at any rate. Can't see the necessity of waiting until night fall."

Lord Tempton, she suspected, was urging an earlier departure in order to escape the noisy children as much as any fear he may have of St. James' displeasure. "I shan't leave at least until Steven is returned," she reminded him. "For I wish to know if St. James is taking any action to help this family as Lucy had said he offered, for I swear if he knew of their conditions he would not tolerate their being here this long."

"You can hardly expect Steven to explain to him all of this, Miss Murdock," Bertie advised, "for it is something that is unbelievable unless seen for oneself."

And Miss Murdock had to concede that he may be right upon that head. She never would have dreamed that any one could live in such squalor and survive. It was no wonder that Lucy looked as though she were fifty when Miss Murdock had gained from her that she was but thirty-nine.

That exhausted female, after urging from Miss Murdock, had retired to the only other room of the small house, a long narrow space that held one proper bed and two straw filled mattresses upon the floor behind the large stove that acted as fireplace and cooking appliance. The room Miss Murdock and Bertie sat in now was hardly larger, and the light was dim, for although, as noted, there were two windows, the lack of panes in them had induced Steven's mother to cover them with worn canvas, and the only sun that came through was muted. It did have the advantage of keeping out the cold air, and at least a portion of the smell. But the home was still cold and drafty, and Miss Murdock had not even taken off St. James' coat, but remained huddled in it.

The children seemed warmly enough covered, but their clothing was a hodge podging of layers of too large over too small, and though oft mended, there were many thin, bare spots of material that threatened to be yet another hole.

The rooms were clean but lacked any adornment or comfort. Miss Murdock had sent Steven for supplies, after procuring funds from Lord Tempton, for there had been no food in the house at all, and she had spent much of her morning with cooking and feeding the grief-stricken household. She was very tired indeed, despite sleeping the day before, but it had been no hardship for her to persuade Lucy to get some much needed rest, as she was exhausted from her excursion to meet with St. James the night before, and Lizzie did not fancy sleeping on any of the beds at any rate.

Now, she managed to shush the child on her lap and the other's singing petered off to a hum, and Bertie observed, "I am sure St. James shall do something, for I would wager these are company owned houses, and as her husband is no longer alive and hence no longer an employee, then they will be evicted."

Miss Murdock looked at him with dismay. "They would throw out a widow and three orphaned children?"

"I'm not all that familiar with how they operate, but the houses are for the workers, I am sure. It will be none of their concern other than that she no longer has a man working for them."

Miss Murdock took a dispirited look around. "I would only say they were doing her a favor except that I am well aware she could not possibly have any place better to go. If St. James is too preoccupied to do anything immediately, Bertie, you shall have to."

He winced a little. "Miss Murdock," he begged, "I am sure I can make some arrangements, but I hope you are not suggesting--?"

"Indeed I am, Lord Tempton," she replied. "When we leave, they must come with us, for I can not tolerate the thought that they be here another night, and she worrying of where they are to go when they are unceremoniously tossed out."

"But whatever am *I* to do with them?" Bertie asked with desperation. "Needn't tell you, *I* did not kill the poor woman's husband."

And Miss Murdock flashed him a disapproving look from her brown eyes. "That is a poor way to get out of your obligation, Bertie. For I am certain that St. James had no choice, and the very manner in which Mrs. Crockner is unwilling to bear a grudge against him only proves me right, along with the story that Steven told of how it all came about."

"But walking out of here with a woman and two small children? When you know very well how dicey it was last night coming in! It's not seemly they should see what we saw, what *you* should not have been seeing."

"Well, it will be a great deal more unseemly if they are living in the street rather than merely walking through it a final time, will it not?" she asked him. "No, Bertie, they must go and that must be the end of it. At least there should be no luggage. My only concern is what we shall do with them after we have them out of here," she worried.

But Bertie left off playing his cards and his eyes, which had remained on his game throughout all this conversation, now glanced up. Miss Murdock watched him, trying to discern what had disturbed him, for other than the boy on her lap babbling, she had heard nothing.

"Do you smell smoke?" Bertie asked. She stiffened, sniffed. There *was* a smoky smell to the air.

"Yes. Yes, I think I do." She turned to check the stove, but there seemed nothing amiss there. Then she had no further time to wonder for there was a muffled sound of something falling, as though on the roof, and they both looked up. "I don't see anything," she said with quiet hopefulness.

"Neither do I," Bertie said. "But the smell seems to be stronger."

There was a snapping sound from nearer the far wall, and as they both looked in that direction, a hot ash floated with whimsy to the floor. Then there was another snap, and another ash, and even as they watched this, they noted with sudden horror that the roof appeared to be burning.

"Good God! The bloody place is on fire!" Lord Tempton rose from his seat. But even in his urgency, he had the presence of mind to slide his cards into a deck and pocket them.

"I'll get the children, you wake Mrs. Crockner!" Miss Murdock exclaimed, rising also. She clutched the one child in her arms and hurried to the other in front of the stove.

"Most improper for *me* to wake her," Bertie advised, and Miss Murdock turned to exclaim that this was certainly not a time to worry about decorum, when she saw that his merry eyes were twinkling even as he moved to the back room.

And she almost laughed, for it was apparent to her that Bertie thoroughly enjoyed whatever scrape he was dragged into. But although they should have plenty of time to leave the shanty without fear for their lives, she was much too nervous to find anything thrilling about their predicament. She took the seven year old by the hand and Bertie returned with a frightened Mrs. Crockner. He nodded to Lizzie and said, "Out the door then," and taking Mrs. Crockner's arm, and Lizzie behind him with the two children, he pulled the door open.

There was a sudden sharp thud and a splintering of wood. A report of gunfire came to their ears, and it was very close, and with amazement, they looked at the door, saw the bullet hole drilled through it, and of one accord, they all fell back into the small house, and Bertie slammed the door. "Get down on the floor! Mrs. Crockner, is there another way out?" he asked.

But she only shook her head. "No, m'lord! An' we're trapped in here 'n' all with me two young babies!"

Lizzie met Bertie's eyes and she saw that the merriment had left them. The three year old began to cry and the older one said, "Ma, it's burnin', ma! Why canst we go out?"

Miss Murdock soothed him as best she could. "We'll go out, we just have to wait a minute," and she looked with helplessness to Bertie but he was already crawling along the floor to a window with his pistol drawn. He rose high enough to peer from it, but as he drew back the canvas to better see, there was another splintering of wood and a loud crack, and he ducked back down with a curse.

"We shall have to try to break through the back wall," he explained, but at the rate that the flames were fast consuming the wood the place was made of, Miss Murdock could well understand the sudden doubt in his voice.

St. James learned from Steven that he knew of no better route to his home than the one he had taken Lord Tempton and Miss Murdock along in the wee hours of that morning. They were in his curricle, St. James driving and Steven up behind where Tyler normally would stand, and Tyler rode astride upon his mount. They were near the pool's neighborhood (as Steven's father had naturally been returning to that area the night of his attempt on milord's life, and hence, the undertaker Tyler had found as handiest was not all that far) with the imposing new London Bridge to be seen over the rooftops ahead of them. St. James scanned his memory of the street Lucy had led him to the night before and asked Steven, "There are the houses to one side of the street and warehouses to the other, are there not?"

To which Steven nodded affirmative and added an "Aye," with the realization that St. James from his position in front of him could not see his answer. "T'is between two warehouses that we'll come out into our street. But 'twill be some hundred feet or so from me own doorstep."

"You will have to let me know, Steven, when we are drawing close to this mew, for I did not come in this way last night and am unfamiliar with it."

"Last night?" Steven asked.

"Yes, of course." St. James gave him an impatient look from his gold eyes. "You do not think that I allowed your mother to go home without any protection, do you?"

And if Steven had any lingering doubt that he were somehow betraying his father by renewing his friendship with St. James, his lordship's words of concern for his mother erased them.

"Coo, then you'd best slow now, m'lord. For we'll be but t'length of t'warehouse from t'end of that mew when we next turn up here."

St. James slowed the curricle, and Tyler, who had been forced to follow behind because of the narrowness of the side street, did likewise. When they arrived close to the mew that ran at a counterpoint to it, St. James stopped the curricle, said to Steven, "Jump down, lad, and peep about and see if there is any one about, and if there is a door to the warehouse upon this side. Large enough for a curricle to fit through, mind you."

Steven did as he was asked, feeling a great deal trusted, and St. James was a little surprised when after just a brief second of glancing down the mew from the corner, the lad drew his head back as though seeing something to alarm him. St. James waited for no further explanation, as Steven seemed bent upon looking again with even more caution, but jumped down from the curricle with a significant look to Tyler, who was trapped behind the curricle and could do nothing but wait at any rate. Then he joined Steven at the corner, and ducking down so that he was pressed against the boy's legs, moved his own head to where he could get a take on the situation.

He had expected a few children to mayhaps be playing in the mew, as it was afternoon by now, and although cold, it was clear. That in itself would have been a challenge, for they would undoubtedly be moved to some kind of excitement when seeing a curricle driven down an alley that did not see such sights on just any given day. But although such a situation would have been less than perfect, he felt that he still would have enough time to gather Miss Murdock from the house and be off again with her before any one of significance had a chance to investigate what was happening.

As it was, there were no children, to his relief. But there was a man at the far end, where the mew ended and Steven's street cut across the mouth of it, and even as St. James spied him, the man was turned and looking back along the mew, and in his hand he held a gun, which was

His brief hope that no one was in residence was squelched as the door to the shanty burst opened and he saw Bertie and Mrs. Crockner and Lizzie behind and God help him, two children. The man on the ground behind him could not have torched the house, there hadn't been time. He must have been waiting as another set it aflame. Without further thought, St. James aimed and fired and plowed a bullet into the door but a few inches from Bertie's face and saw with satisfaction that they all fell back into the house with great panic and slammed the door.

An angry voice called from the other side of the warehouse from him, "Too damned soon, ya bloody idjit! I'd had a clean shot if you'd just waited but another second!"

"What the hell are you doing!" Tyler asked, his mildness gone and his own weapons drawn. St. James whirled, was amazed to see Steven had drawn a pistol also, and he recognized it as his own even in the distraction.

"Here, lad, I'll take that," he told the boy and Steven looked disappointed as he handed it over, but brightened when St. James handed him a replacement in the form of the one he had just fired. "Load it!" Then he hastened to explain to Tyler. "They'll burn them out, and shoot Miss Murdock when she walks from the door. I've managed to give them fair warning not to come out, but we have got to do something now, or they'll only die inside!"

"They wouldna have shot the children!" Tyler protested. "You coulda let her take her chances and at least seen that the rest of them lived!"

"I haven't time to argue about this now, goddamn it! We get them all out, or they all die, but I'll not see her sacrificed, do you understand me?" St. James roared. "Now boost me up onto this roof, for I estimate we have less than two minutes before the house caves in and they're all done for."

With that he secured his two pistols, one drawn, one taken back from Steven (and if he had a moment of renewed confidence that he at least had his most prized and, to his way of thinking, most accurate weapons back as a set in his possession again, he had no time to consider it) which with the pistol he had taken from the man bound on the ground replacing the one he had given to Steven meant he now had three in his waist band, and he jumped at the wall of the warehouse and managed to get the fingers of his left hand over the edge of the slate roof of the low slung building. His right hand slipped, and he felt a piercing of pain in his chest and knew that at least half of Lizzie's stitches had just broken open. Then Tyler was beneath him, shoving him up by the ass, and St. James kicked off from Tyler's shoulders and was up on the roof. He had a clear sight of the house and it was burning furiously, smoke pouring out from it in great cloudy plumes. The street below was filling with women and children as they poured out from neighboring houses, for the fire would no doubt spread in just a moment's time to its close neighbors. But the milling crowd proved no deterrent in keeping any one from shooting again for another shot rang out from just on the further side of the warehouse.

St. James scrambled up the pitch of the roof to the top and he filled both hands with weapons as he went. He tripped going over the peak and was hard pressed to control his fall. He landed hard on his knees, sprawled face down arrowing down the slant of it, nearly lost one pistol but managed to retain it, his chest screaming pain, and he skidded with more luck than precision to just to the edge of the roof, where he clawed to a stop before falling off the further side. He looked down, his right hand pointing his pistol in that direction and was just in time to see a startled, grizzled face look up with surprised shock into the barrel of his gun.

And Dante released the hammer and blew that man's face from his head.

The man flung back, his own weapon going off as he had held it at the ready to shoot the occupants of the burning house.

St. James rolled around, slid from the roof and landed awkwardly on the ground, catching himself hard with one elbow as he still had a pistol in either hand. He rose, pocketed the one he had just fired and took the third from his waist band. He ran from the corner of the warehouse to the burning home. A bullet skidded just below one of his flying heels, and he gritted his teeth, for he had suspected there would be more than the two now neutralized, but he dared not try for another when he had no clear idea where they may be and no further time to waste looking.

He only hoped that with no help from their accomplices, that those left were not skilled enough shots and had not enough ready weapons to do the job themselves.

Then he was at the door, and he slammed his shoulder into it without slowing, and it flung open with a bang and he landed into the midst of the small room sliding on his side and with both pistols pointed out the open door in case a third aggressor should be so bold as to follow him.

And Bertie said, coughs punctuating his words from the swirling smoke in the room, "Damn it, St. James! I nearly shot you!"

The heat was intolerable, and Bertie had to shout to even make these words heard for the noise of the clapboards burning above their heads was an endless din, and there was a great bawling from a child. "Lizzie!" St. James bellowed, and she was there beside him, crawling on her hands and knees. He pulled himself around, put his feet beneath him and into a crouch. "Hang onto my coat, and stay close, do you understand?"

"What about the others?"

"Bertie, wait as long as you can after we leave, do you hear me? As long as you possibly can! Then get them out through the front door!"

"No worry," Bertie replied. "Go!"

"No!" Miss Murdock protested. "I won't be so cowardly as to leave them in here! Damn it, Dante--!"

St. James, with one fluid motion, turned his gun to the interior of the room, aimed it at the first face that was discernible in the smoke, a young lad of a boy about seven years old, and told Miss Murdock in a ruthless, furious voice, "You'll come now, or I'll relieve you of the cause of your reluctance immediately!"

"Bastard!" But her hands found his coat, and without further delay, he moved forward with her behind him, and kept his body between her and where he had judged the shots to be coming from.

The street was a melee of people, but even so another shot was fired, and the people fled, screaming, in either direction, and he and Miss Murdock were left quite alone to run toward the mew and Tyler. St. James held his two pistols at the ready, but he saw Tyler leaning from the corner of the warehouse, and that man's gun went off, spooking back whomever he had caught sight of who had been shooting at them. Then Steven was there beside Tyler and he had loosed Tyler's mount from the back of the curricle, and with a slap on its flank, sent it toward them. St. James cursed, thrust one of his guns at Miss Murdock, who had the presence of mind to take it, and he grabbed one rein as the horse went to go by, turned it, and then he had it between the shooters and he and Miss Murdock, and in this manner, they made it to the mouth of the mew.

She was furious and frightened, and as soon as they made cover she turned with a great deal of agitation, and he was forced to yell, "Tyler! Get her, or the little fool will go back!" for he still had a gun in one hand and the horse he dared not let go of in the other, as it was so spooked he would never get it back.

And Miss Murdock turned with sudden ferocity and lifted the gun that he had handed her and pointed it at him. "Damn you! St. James. Would you let them die then for my sake!" she asked him.

Tyler grabbed the gun from her hand and St. James secured his pistol back into his waist band, and he snagged her arm and pulled her forward. "Up!" he told her, and threw her with roughness into the saddle, grabbed his other still loaded pistol from Tyler. "Tyler, stay and see that all goes well with them. Use the curricle once they're out! Cover us as long as you can from here!" and then he thrust his foot into the iron, swung onto the horse behind Lizzie even as he shouted at it, so that it was startled and running before he even made his way into the portion of saddle he could find behind Lizzie's disarrayed riding habit.

She picked up the reins, but as she went to draw in the mount, still furious at his abandoning his friend and a woman with two small children to the flames, he goaded her, "Go, damn it! They will come out all right, for those that are shooting will be after us, not them." He filled his hands once again with his pistols, and she, still with no clear understanding of his reasoning, at least perceived that it was not his intention to see Bertie or Steven's family die, loosed the reins and urged the horse forward with its double load.

Then Dante brought his knees to rest over Lizzie's stockinged legs, for her habit was not made for riding astride and had pulled up far higher than was decent. Before she could protest or question, he was speaking into her ear, "Turn right, here, Lizzie, and that's the last I am going to be able to tell you, for I fear I am going to be busy. Have you ever ridden a mount that took leg signals?"

"Yes. Of course," she answered, for she knew he referred to a horse that could be directed into turning by pressure of one knee or the other rather than by reining.

"Then you are going to pretend to be that horse, my dear. If you feel pressure from one of my knees or the other, rein in that direction and keep reining until I let the pressure up. Can you do that?"

"Yes."

"Good lass." He said nothing more but turned as far as he could in his position behind her to see what may be occurring to their rear. And he was not surprised to see two riders now following. Even from a distance he could see that one had a very red face, and reddish blonde hair, and that his eyes seemed very blue, and from Steven's description to him when questioned about his meeting of the night before in Red's pub, he gathered this must be Red himself.

The other was the one remaining assassin hired through Red, he surmised, and that left one assassin, besides Steven's father, dead, and the other trussed and in the warehouse. Which meant that unless Red had hired more, they were all accounted for and Bertie should have no problem getting the Crockner's from their home, merely leaving through the door as they should have been able to from the beginning, without anyone shooting at them.

No. Only he and Miss Murdock had any worry at this point.

Even as he thought this, Red's hired man pointed his pistol at him and fired, and the bullet skimmed past and ricocheted from the brick of the building to the side of them. He felt Lizzie flinch, and he could feel her legs shaking, and he pressed his left knee against hers with insistent pressure and was relieved to see that she still had enough nerve to rein the horse in that direction. And as he did not let up pressure, she kept it turning, until they were going in a small, sharp circle back onto their foe. Still he kept pressure on her knee, not wanting her to be a target instead of himself, and he aimed and fired from over her shoulder as the horse charged back in direct line at their pursuers. He could not tell if he had done any damage, but it did have the effect of making their pursuers drop back with abruptness and he could hear their loud cursing even from this distance. Then the horse was turned in completion of its tight-haunched circle, and Miss Murdock needed no instruction to urge it again into as quick a pace as it could possibly go.

"Where?" she panted.

"Can you find the North road from here?"

"I--I think so!"

"Find it, and put as many buildings as you can between ourselves and them as you do so, for I have but one bullet at the ready until I am able to reload."

She directed the horse around a corner of a building and they came out into a market, and if it were not Piccadilly, it was still fashionable enough for her to cringe wondering if they should be recognized, but it did have the advantage of many wagons and carts and conveyances, and she threaded them through as adeptly as she could, screening their route from their pursuers, and all the while, she was aware of Dante at her back, reloading powder and ball into his spent pistols.

And that is how, Miss Murdock thought, one came to have a reputation for being a rake. For in all their powdered and protected existence, few of the peerage would view their antics as anything but a bit of scandalous misbehavior on their part.

Then Dante turned once again, scanning behind them, and he secured his pistols, leaned up against her back and his hands came around her to take the reins. "I think that has done it for now," he said, "and perhaps we should get off this stage before any one further recognizes us. I am afraid, Miss Murdock, that your reputation will be quite ruined after this little escapade."

"Oh, it no longer even matters," she exclaimed, close to tears as he directed them down another mew and they left the raucous cries for fish and fruit behind. "I assume that we are just supposed to die in a respectable manner rather than do what is necessary to save our own lives!"

"Why yes, Miss Murdock," he replied with dry amusement. "You understand precisely." And then he pressed his lips to the back of her neck that he found through her half undone hair before adding, "But do not fret too much, for this is all going to be finished very shortly."

And rather than filling her with relief, his words only made her all the more frightened.

"You know then?" she asked over the drum of the horse's hooves. His arms tightened about her as he reined down yet another street, followed it for a short distance and threaded into another mew that was taking them north and east.

"Yes," he told her. "I have been a great fool, and I have put you in danger because of my foolishness, and the only thing that keeps me from turning this horse back now and taking care of the two knaves in pursuit of us is the fact that you are with me."

"So you are taking me to Chestershire after all," she perceived.

And he hesitated, filling her with even more unease before saying, "Yes. After a brief but necessary trip to Gretna Green, my dear."

And she stiffened and flushed with sudden anger, nearly as much anger as she had felt when he had pointed a gun at a seven year old in order to gain his way with her, and she could only say, "Damn you, Dante! Damn you!"

But he said nothing to regain her trust, and she realized that perhaps there was nothing he *could* say to regain her trust. And his silent admissions were damning.

The longer the silence stretched between them, the more irrevocable it seemed his actions were. Her thoughts shut down, and for hours she was only aware of the horse moving beneath her, slowed to a trot and laboring now, and of St. James' hard body pressed up against her back; the strength in his elegant, pale hands as they controlled their mount, and the arms that were wrapped about her. His breath enveloped her hair and her neck, and every so often, as though he could not stop himself, he leaned his head against hers and smelled her hair, or whispered his lips along the lobe of her ear.

And she fought the tears that threatened to come from her eyes, first in frustration and anger and then as she realized that they had in fact left London well behind and were traveling the North road, and that he had, if not relaxed, at least seemed to have lost some of that dreadful, tightly wound tautness, she cried in hopelessness.

And instead of upbraiding her for crying when they may still be in danger and he could not afford the distraction, he only said, "Go ahead, Lizzie, for I know you have held off as long as you could." He directed the horse into a deserted lane off from the main road and after following it for a small ways he dismounted from behind her and pulled her down into his arms. She buried her face into the tight steel of his chest and sought comfort from the very person that made her in need of comforting.

But she only allowed herself that gruesome weakness for a bare moment, and then she rejected him.

"Oh, no, Dante," she told him through her tears as she pushed back from him. "Do not think that I will allow you to maneuver me in that manner any longer. For you use the very love I have for you as a weapon against myself, and love should not be that way."

And his face closed to her in his hurt as it had not for a long time (but she had only known him for five days so how long could it really be? Half of eternity, maybe. And how does one halve eternity?) and his eyes shuttered down to heavy half masts, and he turned from her. And she realized that they had traveled much further than she had thought for most of the day had gone, and it was in fact that bloody sky time of dusk when the day died and the darkness enveloped it.

His profile was bathed in this dimming, winter, crimson light, and now that his eyes were from beneath her scrutiny, he raised his lids to watch the sunset, and they glistened very gold in the soft bath of that day's death, and she had a sudden certainty that he would not be alive to see another ending of a day, and that he was watching his last twilight.

To the very core of her being, she did not know whether to be mad with anticipated grief, or to be turned loose with bittersweet relief. And she only felt a numbness that she could not shake off, as though with his coming death, she could already feel herself dying. She wavered there as she watched him. Wavered between going to him and sacrificing herself to the full long pain and the full short bliss that he offered her, or of cutting him off from her in a last desperate bid of saving what she had left of herself, before he encompassed her so completely that she would never remember who she had been without him.

But at that moment he turned to her, the full, steady divineness of his gold eyes beaconing out to her and he gave a small, twisted, bitter smile, and said with quiet finality, "But, Miss Murdock, you promised to marry me."

Thus the sacrifice was made, not by her but by him.

But she would not understand this for a time. She only understood at that moment that she hated him.

"I beg that you release me from that promise made, sir, as it was made under duress," she told him, and how many minutes had passed since his reminding of her, she did not know, only knew that they stood in the lane and the sun was quite gone and there was only a dim lingering of its spirit to the west of them and that the air had grown colder.

"No," he said without reasoning or arguing or any sign of being moved. He did not even take affront at her using the word duress as though he had beat her into submission rather than poured his heart out to her. He only added, "I expect Bertie or Tyler to be along before too very much longer with fresh horses, if they are thinking at the speed of which I think they are capable. I will not tolerate any desertion on your part, Miss Murdock, when those mounts arrive."

And Miss Murdock let out a small, cold laugh. "Indeed, you need have no worry on that head. Your only worry, milord, is in how you shall react when you at last put me in front of a minister in Scotland and he asks if 'I do' and there is only a great, damning silence for answer."

But he would not be provoked into arguing.

"Stand warned," she told him. "For I will not change my mind."

But he still said nothing, and his silence frightened her and she drew the coat she wore (*his* coat) about her more tightly over the now rumpled silk of her riding habit that he had purchased for her.

And he at last acknowledged her words only by taking her own words from the day before and misquoting them, "I have tried to point out to you, Miss Murdock, that if you see fit to become involved with me, then you will suffer the consequences of your involvement." Then he added ever so softly to the end of them his own words, "As do I."

He turned and loosened the girth on the saddle and removed the bit from his horse's mouth, and she was given to understand that such was his faith in Tyler and Bertie, that they would move no further that night until one or the other of them arrived.

As he saw her standing there, looking forlorn, he removed the saddle, tossed it to the ground, and pulled the saddle pad from the horse also and threw it on the ground a few feet from her. "Sit, Lizzie, if you do not mind a sweaty saddle pad, for it may be some time and it is better than sitting directly on the cold ground."

And she did sit, not minding in the least a sweaty saddle pad, but very much comforting herself in the warm odor of horse that came from it. But he did not sit, nor did he pace, he only walked a small ways toward the road, leaned against the trunk of an ancient tree, and with his back to her waited for the arrival of one or the other or both of his trusted friends.

"You do not think," she asked as a way to distract herself, "that we will not be overtaken by those--those men?"

"No," he said, and turned to look at her in the darkness. "For they will have in all probability gone to my home expecting us to run there in some foolish belief that we would be safe. But if they are willing to shoot at me from outside Almacks, they will not hesitate upon shooting at us at my own home."

"Oh," she said.

"But I do not expect it to take them long to perceive where we are headed. Or for them to be turned in that direction by someone who will certainly anticipate it upon hearing that you were not in Chestershire but apparently with me all along."

"Oh," she said again. Then almost against her will, "You are very certain who has been behind all of this, then?"

"Yes. As certain as I can be without having a smoking gun in their hand."

"Will you tell me--tell me who it is?"

And he smiled with gentleness down upon her from across the small space that separated them. The horse had begun grazing and the only sound was its teeth ripping off the grass and the murmurings of the night about them. "No, Lizzie."

Being unable to help herself, she asked, "You would have shot Steven's father at any rate, would you not have?"

His answer was almost calm. "Yes."

"Even knowing it was his father?"

The briefest of hesitations, and then, "Yes."

By rights, she should have left it go at that, for he gave no indication that she should pursue it or that he was holding anything back, but she persisted. "If you knew of him then what you know now, would you have still shot him?"

And he rubbed his upper lip for a time before answering her. He came to where she sat and knelt and met her solemn brown eyes with his gold ones and told her, "No, Lizzie, I would not have, but that is much like asking Lucifer if he would have still reached for heaven if he had known then what he knows now. Some actions can not be made better on retrospect. Don't look for any righteousness in me, for there simply is none."

"But you are honest," she countered, desperate.

And he gave a soft laugh. "Yes, Lizzie. For only someone ashamed of their actions will seek to cover them with lies. Does that not tell you something?"

She closed her eyes, hiding from him. "And Steven's brother?" she choked. "Would you have shot him and the others?"

"Do not ask me questions that I can not answer, Lizzie, as I have reminded you before."

But at least he had not answered her a flat yes. Nor no.

He took her hand then and raised it to his lips. "Let me just say that there is only one pure thing I have ever done, and that is to love you. And the very presumptuousness of my loving you, I am afraid, has made it impure. Do you understand, Lizzie?"

But she shook her head, and opened her eyes to look at him. "It didn't have to be like this," she said. "For I--" but she could not go on, could only lean into his ready arms and hold him with desperation. And he gathered her into him, opening his great coat and wrapping it about her and hiding her within it, within him, and as she wept, his gold eyes did not close but remained open and aware of all that went on about him, and of the pain that was inside of him.

But he did not kiss her, even after her crying subsided and she snuggled down within his coat against him like some furtive and insidious restorative in his blood. For he was afraid that if he kissed her she would go from half hating him as she did, to loving him beyond recall and he would not do that to her. For it was perhaps better in the hours that came that she did hate him, for he could not do what had to be done if he feared that his death would destroy her. And if he lived, she was as like to abhor him by the time he was finished at any rate.

So they sat in that manner for what could have been hours or could have been only minutes, and then he heard his horse's head lift, and it nickered, and there was a soft answering nicker from the lane, and he moved his hand and revealed the pistol that had lain in his grasp all along.

But it was only Bertie, looking tired and out of sorts and with two fresh mounts in tow behind him.

He pulled up a few feet from where St. James sat upon the ground with Miss Murdock huddled in his arms. "Thought I'd find you here," Bertie said.

"Thought you would come," St. James returned. Miss Murdock pulled her head from where she had been half dozing curled against his chest. With his old teasing note, he asked her, "If you are quite rested now, my dear?"

She blushed to be caught in such a position by Lord Tempton, but only moved to get up, and he opened his coat and she slid from him, and he rose and helped her to rise also. He asked Bertie, "Tyler?"

"He's taking the Crockner's to his cottage at Morningside for the time being. He'll swing around from there and come across at Chestershire and follow you to Gretna Green," Bertie replied and dismounted. "Miss Murdock, I am happy to see you came out unscathed."

"And you also, Bertie," she replied with enough normalcy to her voice to surprise herself. "Everyone is unharmed then?"

"Yes. For St. James was correct and when they saw their targets fleeing, they turned all of their attention to you and our getting out was an insignificant matter to them at that point. I fear much of that entire street will burn before they are able to extinguish the fire."

"The rogue tied in the warehouse?" St. James asked.

Bertie shook his head. "Tyler saw to him. He knew nothing you did not already know and he will no longer be a worry."

"I did not think he would," St. James replied, "but the one that has hired them, this Red, we will need him alive, for although I am certain who is behind this, I would prefer to have someone that may be able to confirm my deductions."

Miss Murdock was looking pained, for she had no idea of any man in any warehouse, and she could only conclude from Bertie's words that he had met a similar fate as Steven's father, and she began to feel like a conspirator to murder rather than mere fliers from harm.

St. James asked, "Any sign of being followed?"

"Can't say for certain, St. James. I went as circumspectly as I could and saw no one, but there is no telling. I wouldn't tarry long here, at any rate."

"I do not intend to. Are you riding on with us?"

"Of course."

"Then we will set off now, and should reach the border by tomorrow afternoon."

Miss Murdock saw fit to interrupt at this point. "We shall reach Chestershire by early morning, milord."

"Stubborn lass! You should know, Miss Murdock, that I cannot accommodate your reluctance any longer."

"You shall have to, milord," she returned, "for I have come to discover that your stitches have been ripped open, and although I will tolerate you going without treatment for another few hours, I will not tolerate you going without treatment longer."

He pondered this, then said, "I do not think it will matter much in the final outcome, Miss Murdock."

But Bertie reminded him, "Tyler will be swinging past there at any rate, St. James. You may as well allow Miss Murdock to stitch you once again and then set out when we have an extra person to help with any difficulty along the way. And although I know very well that you can go without sleep like some manner of vampire, I, and I am certain, Miss Murdock, can not."

And St. James gave a twisted smile of amusement at this reminder. "You are right, of course, Bertie, for I can not have Miss Murdock falling asleep on me on the wedding night."

"Oh, do shut up, St. James!" she told him, irritated that he could still make her blush hotly with only a careless sentence.

St. James turned to her and snugged her coat closer about her. "Are we ready then, Miss Murdock?" he asked, and although she was given to understand that he was only asking if she were ready to mount and set off, she had the sudden feeling that by answering to the affirmative, she was answering some other question in his mind.

"Oh, botheration," she said. "Fighting you is like fighting a maelstrom."

And he gave her an amused look at her abrupt exasperation with him. "But, Miss Murdock, you are winning," he told her in glib response, "for I have not had a drink this entire day." He took her arm, led her over to her mount, which turned out to be the black filly that she and Lord Tempton had left at the Dowager's the night before, and she noted that Lord Tempton's mount was his own horse of the night before also.

"Oh, that is good!" she exclaimed. "For I have been waiting for five days now to catch you when you were completely sober, so that I may adequately voice my grievances!"

And he threw her up onto her horse and grinned up at her. "Then by all means, Lizzie. Tell me your concerns and I will endeavor to come up with a solution that you may live with."

Chapter Twenty-six
Saturday Morning

She awoke in the dark for no real reason, that she could discern, other than that at her age one does not sleep well. The room was unfamiliar and that came as a shock, for she had not slept in any rooms but the townhouse in London and Morningside in Lincolnshire for well over the past quarter century. And of course, one inn in between, but even they always had a particular room reserved for her, and it seemed almost a part of home now at any rate.

And she sighed in the early morning hour as she remembered that she was in Chestershire, at the home of Squire Murdock (a *Squire*, God help her) and that Miss Murdock had not been there as she was supposed to be.

And she had her concerns. Oh, indeed, she had her concerns.

The Dowager Duchess lay in her bed, with her faded eyes staring into the dark and her frail hands holding the coverlet up close beneath her chin, like a small child who thinks it has seen a ghost, or a very old woman facing demons in the night.

What was her grandson about? And surely he meant that child no harm. Did he? But where was Miss Murdock?

Everything she had encountered since arriving had unsettled her to the core.

She had arrived at noon as she had spent the night in an inn and her traveling had been slow. Mrs. Herriot, her own housekeeper from Morningside, had been there to greet her, and that had come as a great surprise. And that lady had seemed nearly frantic and a great deal relieved to see the Dowager. The housekeeper spoke in disjointed sentences of a drunken Squire and the unexpected arrival of Ryan Tempton the night before, who had, most regretfully, begun drinking with the Squire upon arising that morning. And that they were both even now in the parlor drinking without compunction.

And although Mrs. Herriot did not say so specifically, the Duchess was given to understand that there was a great deal of dire and foreboding talk about her grandson and his intentions, or lack of them, toward Miss Murdock. "But now that you are here," Mrs. Herriot had beamed, "I am sure that you will be able to tell the Squire exactly where his daughter is, for neither of them seem to know, and reassure him that of course your grandson means to marry her."

And so the Dowager had been apprised of the mood of the house and the fact that Miss Murdock, of whom *she* was responsible for, was not where she was supposed to be, upon the very moment that she had been helped from her coach. And she had leaned on her cane and the forebodings had washed over her in heavy waves. She could not believe that Dante had intended this circumstance. It was too damning. Something had gone wrong.

But she grasped tighter the gold handle of her cane, allowed Mrs. Herriot to assist her up the steps and into the house, and so forewarned, prepared herself to defend her grandson until such time that he could give adequate enlightenment to every one on what was happening.

And defend him she had been forced to do. For Squire Murdock was of the mind that the repairs and the generous allowance he was receiving was a buy off for him to cause no trouble. And young Ryan Tempton was of the opinion that St. James had induced Andrew to elope with Miss Murdock, just as Lady Lydia had told him, so that the duke would not be forced to live up to his responsibility.

"Do not be ridiculous, Squire," she had told that man with tartness at his accusation. "For I would certainly not be here if I thought that your daughter were merely one of his lightskirts! And as for you, young Ryan Tempton, you should not be such a boob as to believe any thing my daughter-in-law has to say."

And so she bullied them into a semblance of patience, for she did not doubt that St. James would send word or that Miss Murdock would appear, and that there would be adequate explanation.

But then Andrew had shown up that evening.

Oddly enough, he had ridden in his carriage. His double team of horses were blown, and his driver and footman were tired, but none looked as bad as he upon alighting. And when *he* found that Miss Murdock was not in residence, he looked a good deal worse. And as it had been Andrew that had left with Miss Murdock the night of her disappearance, and even *he* had no idea where she was, it only served to bow the old Dowager's back further. He refused to speak of where he had last seen the Miss in question or what their business had been, but he swore that his cousin had better have a *very* good explanation for misleading him into thinking that Miss Murdock had been on her way home to her father.

And the Dowager had been too flattened by this latest development to even argue further. For with Andrew's angry disillusionment, the Squire and Ryan's simmering discontent of course boiled back up. She had left them then, to their drinking and their growing dissatisfaction, and only retired to her bed at that point, with very different worries on her mind.

Something had gone badly wrong, she was certain of it.

Now, hours later and the house in silence, the Dowager lay in the dark and thought back over these events and she was old and frail and feeling very helpless. She worried that St. James was into something so deep and so dangerous that even she would not be able to help him. And that in some manner or another, Miss Murdock had become enmeshed in it also.

So it was that she was still awake when she heard the sound of horses' hooves on the lane outside her window, and her faded eyes widened, and she struggled to sit up in the bed.

She had brought Soren with her, that poor lady, for she was nearly as old as her employer, and Jeannie also, for she had expected Miss Murdock to be in need of her lady's maid as well as a good deal of Miss Murdock's clothing. But she called to no one, only looked at her watch upon the night stand and saw that it was after four in the morning.

She took her cane from where it leaned, put her trembling legs upon the floor, and struggled to her feet, something she had not done without assistance for several years, and then stumbled the few feet to the window, caught herself on the sill of it, and peered down between the drapes and into the drive below.

And there was St. James, as recognizable to her as her own husband had been so many years ago, for they were very much alike in stature and build as well as in eye-color and temperament. He slid from his saddle, his great coat opened, and he raised a hand to Miss Murdock who sat with primness upon her sidesaddle in what appeared to be a man's coat, and with black silk falling from beneath it in the form of a riding habit that the Duchess did not recall being one of their purchases (for hadn't they agreed on red velvet?)

With considerable relief she saw a third rider, and from the size of his girth, and the shock of red hair gleaming in the moonlight, she recognized him as that faithful partner in the nefarious deeds of her grandson: Bertram Tempton.

"Thank the Lord," she whispered to herself. And then more techtily, "But why they must insist on dragging that poor child around in the middle of the night, I will never know. I could cane him for this!" And she knew that her old heart could not take any more uncertainty, and that whatever Dante thought he was protecting her from could not be as bad as worrying over all the possibilities. She would get it from him in some manner if it were the last thing she did.

But St. James was handing his reins over to Bertie, and Miss Murdock's reins over also, and there was an extra horse, unmounted, and she saw that Lord Tempton was receiving the dubious honor of riding to the stables with these three horses on lead and rousing a groom. Then Dante took hold of Miss Murdock's elbow and escorted her to the steps and the old Dowager lost sight of them.

She remained where she stood for another moment, and then struggled to turn and stumbled back to collapse in the bed, and although there had been nothing to upset her or to exalt her in that little show, there had been something about the way that St. James had taken Miss Murdock's arm that had the old Dowager's heart hammering in her chest.

She was desperate to go below, to demand explanation, and to observe the two of them together, to settle in her mind once and for all what was between them, but she did not think she could manage the steps alone, and she was so loathe to have someone help her. But as she half sat, half lay, debating, she heard quiet footsteps come in tandem up the stairs, and then soft treading in the hallway, and then the door next to her own room opened and closed with softness.

Surely they had not both entered the same bedchamber?

But then Miss Murdock's muffled voice came to her from the other side of the wall: "I can not believe you had the temerity to order staff hired and improvements made! Bad enough I am in to you for the expense of my coming out, but this is beyond all bounds of decency."

"And so is my being in your bedchamber, Lizzie," Dante's amused voice came to his grandmother. "But I do not see you throwing a fit over that."

"Oh, do shut up, for you are trying my patience again, as you are so wont to do. I had not known you for more than two minutes before I wanted to box your ears over your highhanded manner," she admonished him. And then, shocking the Duchess, "Well, do not just stand there but you shall have to remove your coat and your shirt."

"You have what you need on hand?" he asked, causing the Duchess to raise her eyebrows at this odd question.

"Yes. For I keep a supply in my room for household use. So please just hurry so I can get this done before the house awakes and finds you in my bedchamber. I can not believe that in my own home, of all places, that I have to worry about a gaggle of gossiping servants! My father must be beside himself."

"You were worried of who should take care of him. I was just seeing that he were taken care of."

"You presume too much. Oh, here, let me get those buttons, for frankly you are making a mess of it!"

"Damn it! My arm has gone numb, you impatient lass."

"And it is no wonder, for although you have lost no where near the blood you did two nights ago, you have been bleeding steadily for hours now. You should have never been out of bed, Dante, and you very well know it."

And the Duchess, perceiving that there was nothing untoward going on in the other room, struggled to her feet with renewed vigor, and picking up her cane, shuffled to the door, for even she could make it the short distance down the hallway to the next room, and she did so, heart pounding but refusing to be denied. If Dante were injured she would have the how and wherefore of it, and if he were helpless beneath the ministrations of Miss Murdock, it meant that he could not avoid her easily.

She reached the bedchamber door in time to hear Miss Murdock saying, "This will hurt, as I am sure you remember, but I will be as gentle as I can." Then the Dowager opened the door, and the sight that met her eyes made her face redden.

Dante lay naked from the waist up, half propped on pillows on the bed, one arm stretched above his head in more relaxed languor than was seemly for a sick room. Miss Murdock knelt beside him and as she tied off a strand of thick, black suturing thread to a needle, his hand caressed down her face in such a tender and intimate gesture that the Dowager nearly retreated. But at her entrance, Miss Murdock looked up, her solemn eyes startled and big, and her face flushed rosily, and St. James made a quick movement with his other hand and a pistol appeared from beneath the propped pillow behind his head and was pointed with disconcerting swiftness at the Dowager.

And that old lady, recovering quickly, only said, "Rather difficult to make love to a female with a pistol in one hand, Dante," and for the first time in her life, she saw St. James blush.

Miss Murdock bowed her head and said in a small voice, "You had better come in and close the door, ma'am, or I'm certain the rest of the household will be in here as well."

The old Dowager did as was suggested, and settled into a chair across from Miss Murdock with her grandson between them.

"What the devil are you doing up at this time of the night?" St. James asked, and then added, "ouch," as Miss Murdock ran her needle through him with perhaps more force than was necessary.

"Lying awake worrying," the Duchess told him, her hands crossed over the head of her cane. "As I am sure you realize is quite my normal occupation when it comes to regards to you, but quite a new experience for me to also have to worry about Miss Murdock," she chided.

"I am sorry, grandmother. It was not my intention for you to worry at all. I should have guessed that you would come traipsing off here after her."

"But of course," she returned, taking some satisfaction from the pained look upon St. James' face as Miss Murdock continued her stitching. "For I did not believe for an instant that she had eloped with Andrew. I *did* expect her to be where her letter placed her, however."

"Things went rather awry," St. James said with what the duchess could only deem a good deal of understatement considering that he was even now having his chest stitched.

The Duchess was silent for a moment, and St. James only lay frowning in concentration to not voice his pain. The old lady said, "You had better tell me why Miss Murdock has need to sew up your chest, St. James, and I will not be put off for I gather that you have reopened a prior injury."

He sighed. "I was shot, grandmother, if you must know. Two nights ago, leaving Almacks."

"Little wonder," she replied, hiding her shock, "after the disgraceful show you put on with this young lady."

"A means to an end. Leave it at that."

But she would not be put off. "You know that you shall have to marry her, of course, for you can not *not* marry her after that public and scandalous display. Not to mention the fact that she has been missing for two nights and has apparently been in your company."

"I have every intention of marrying her," St. James replied with impatience. "And if Andrew has arrived here as I expect, I am only surprised that he did not tell you of the banns posted in the paper."

"No," the Duchess said in some surprise. "He did not apprise me of that development."

St. James said to Lizzie, "Excuse me, my dear, while I get my pocket watch," and she drew back and allowed him time to remove that item, and then began stitching again as he handed it to his grandmother. "In the back clasp, grandmother."

She opened it with her old, arthritic hands and the folded announcement fluttered down into her lap. And she did not know which held more significance for her, the announcement itself, or the fact that it had been in the back of his watch for safekeeping, and she felt as though she had been in some long and grueling race and that at last the finish line were in sight.

But she only unfolded it, scanned it and said, "Well, that is very good, St. James. I am relieved to see that you are living up to at least one of your responsibilities."

"Do not say it as though I have done something that forces me to marry her," he advised his grandmother, "for she has not been compromised in any way."

"And I did not intimate that she had been," his grandmother replied as she returned the watch and the announcement to him. "So you needn't look at me in that manner. Now you had better tell me the whole of what is going on, for I tell you, Dante, if you do not, you are going to kill me with the worry over all the possibilities."

"I can not, grandmother. Do not ask."

"Hold still, Dante," Miss Murdock interrupted.

"I am not stupid," the Duchess cried. "For I have known what you have been about for years! If you have suspicion of who robbed me of my son and my daughter-in-law and my unborn grandchild, I have the right to know."

But he only sighed and shook his head. "I will not see your heart broken further," he told her in a tone that brooked no argument.

"Poppycock, Dante! For it can be no one close to us for I have studied the possibilities as closely, I dare say, as you have."

But damningly he made no answer.

"Can it?" she asked with sudden dread in her heart.

"Leave it be, grandmother, for ignorance is your ally in this matter." He closed his eyes, the frown growing between their dark winged brows, and she knew she would gain nothing more from him.

"Andrew was not even born," she reminded him.

"It is not him. That is all I am going to say, so do not ask me further," and his eyes snapped open and he stared at her with finality. "Enough, grandmother," he told her. "I do not intend that you ever know, although in the end you may have your suspicions. Just rest assured that it will be taken care of and that you may spend the remainder of your days knowing that it is done."

"I have as much right to know as you do," she challenged him.

"You also have the right to some peace. I will not compromise that peace by telling you. Leave it be."

"Damn you, St. James. You have always been too stubborn for your own good."

"I do not deny it."

"Do you wish me to grill Miss Murdock?" she threatened.

"You will only waste your time for she does not know. Damn it, I need a drink!"

"I am almost done, milord, so never mind about a drink now," Miss Murdock told him.

"Wretched lass," but he said no more and the only sound was of her scissors snipping through the final thread after she knotted it off.

Then she got up and procured clean linens from above the wardrobe, and St. James moved to sit on the edge of the bed and raised his arms so that she could wrap his chest, and the Dowager watched this activity with her eyes stinging, and she swiped at them feeling very much an interloper.

St. James took up his shirt, and the Dowager told him, "It is all bloody you know, Dante. Have you nothing else to wear?"

"No. But Tyler should be here in the morning with the curricle, and I have a bag in it so that I may change then." He looked preoccupied as he struggled into the discussed garment. As though coming to some decision, his eyes snapped to full attention upon the dowager. "Grandmother, would it be too much trouble for Miss Murdock to share your room with you tonight?"

"Actually," the old lady said with some acridness, "I think I would be relieved to have Miss Murdock in my room for the remainder of the night."

St. James, of course, understood her instantly. "Posh," he said, amused. "If I were bent on ruining her, your presence would hardly deter me."

"I do not think that is funny, milord," Miss Murdock chastised.

"Nor do I!" the Duchess exclaimed, but her lips twitched. "For that is the most wicked thing I have ever heard you say."

"Be that as it may, I will not leave her to sleep unprotected tonight, and it would be rather better if you were in presence in case it is discovered that I am in the bedchamber also."

"You don't mean to sleep in there with us!" The Dowager asked.

"Yes. I mean to do so. But do not look so scandalized, for Miss Murdock is far too tired for me to take any advantage even if you were not present, and I am hardly in better condition."

But Miss Murdock interrupted before the Dowager could argue further. "You can not think that they would come into my home!"

"I do not think they will, Lizzie," he told her with quiet reassurance, "but you must know by now that I will not take any risk where your safety is concerned."

But she seemed a great deal pained and his words hardly reassured her. "What if they see fit to try burning us out again?"

"There are only two left," he told her. "I do not think they will be so bold, for there are far too many people in residence, and even they must see that they would be swarmed, if not by people leaving the house, then by the grooms in the stable."

And the Dowager cried in sudden fear and exclamation, "What ever has been going on? Do not mean to tell me that you have managed to put Miss Murdock in danger as well!"

St. James sighed. "Yes, grandmother, I have. Through my own blindness and stupidity and one damned, wayward handkerchief, I find that Miss Murdock has been made a target also, and if not quite as satisfactory as my own death, hers is still greatly desired, for my enemy can not take any chance that we marry."

And the Duchess felt very much like that child hiding beneath the bedclothes again. "Who does this?" she demanded. "Who dares to threaten not only my grandson, but his betrothed? How long are you going to be forced to delay this marriage because of this fiend that dares to interfere in our lives once again?"

But St. James went to his grandmother and crouched in front of her. "I will not answer your first question, but as for the marriage being delayed, I expect that Miss Murdock and I will be celebrating that very occasion by tonight just across the Scottish border."

The Dowager, stunned, looked to Miss Murdock for guidance, and was just in time to see an equally stunned look on that young lady's face. "Miss Murdock?" the old lady asked. "You were unaware of this circumstance?"

But Miss Murdock did not even appear to hear her, but stood motionless in the middle of the room, her and St. James' coats that she had picked up clutched to her chest, and her face was paled with more than tiredness as though she were in shock.

At her lack of response, St. James turned his head to observe her also, and slowly her eyes sought his, wide and frightened and filled with sick dismay. "The *handkerchief?*"

The Duchess felt St. James' start of astonishment through his hand upon her arm, and his face darkened, and his only answer was a stream of soft curses that ended with, "God damn it, Lizzie, you will put that notion out of your head immediately."

But with his cursing she regained her composure, although she was still very pale, and she only said with calm faintness, "I nearly had it, you know, that very day in the mew. Something so clear and obvious that only its very evilness made it seem impossible--"

"Shut up," St. James snapped and it acted like a slap to her face.

Miss Murdock with a flinch quieted. "Of course. I apologize."

In unison Miss Murdock and St. James looked to his grandmother, but she did not notice, for her own eyes had narrowed in thought.

St. James asked Lizzie, "Does she know of the handkerchief?"

"No. For I expressly made sure that she did not." But Miss Murdock's voice was worried all the same.

St. James did not answer, only kissed his grandmother's hand and held it to his cheek for a moment until the concentration left her face and she looked at him. "It is not your concern any longer, grandmother," he told her, "and you should not worry about it, for you will know nothing until it is over, and should not know anything then if I can help it."

The papery lines about her mouth went back into a tight smile. "And, tsk, St. James. What are you afraid of an old lady such as myself doing at any rate?"

St. James had no answer for that and he only helped her from her chair and the three of them went to the old lady's room next door. There was the bed and two chairs, but no chaise lounge for Miss Murdock to sleep upon and the Dowager told her that she must sleep in bed with her, if she did not mind the slumbering ravings of an old woman at any rate, and Miss Murdock fretted that she was sure she would only make the Dowager uncomfortable, but in the end, the bed was large enough for two, and they both lay down.

The Dowager did not sleep but lay upon her side and watched her grandson draw up a chair before the window. He did not sit for a time, but paced along the floor behind it. The Duchess heard Miss Murdock's breathing turn deeper as she slept. She saw Dante finally sit in the chair, draw a pistol into one hand and place his booted feet upon the sill. At last, he appeared to doze, but even so his eyes opened with regular frequency to evaluate any small noise he may have heard that had escaped the Dowager completely.

But she herself slept no more that night, and her mind spun in her head, and although she could not be sure, she had her suspicions.

When dawn came, St. James turned his head as movement came from the bed behind him. He met his grandmother's faded eyes in the fresh glow of the not yet seen but rising sun. And if he looked tired, she looked nearly as tired.

But she only bade in a hushed voice, "Help me to the other room, Dante, and send Soren to me."

And he rose to do as she bid. Once in the hallway, she asked, "Your man has not arrived as you anticipated?"

"No, damn it, he has not," St. James answered. "I will give him but another hour before we go on without him." He gave his grandmother a rueful smile. "You did not rest well, grandmother," he chided her.

"I never do at any rate, Dante, so do not blame yourself and Miss Murdock. And you had better get a clean shirt from Andrew as your clothing has not arrived, for if you walk about looking like that, you may as well put out a billet proclaiming your injury. Does Andrew know of it, by the by?"

"Yes. For of course, he was with Miss Murdock when she came to nurse me. Which was a damnedable circumstance I could have never foreseen, but then there has been much about this I have failed to foresee."

But she only patted his arm. "You have done well, Dante, and your only job now is to marry the lass and see that she remain safe a little while longer."

"Yes," he answered. "And this will be over on the morrow, I expect, and she will be safe after that whether I am here to see to it or not."

The Dowager frowned, but she did not argue, and he left her in Miss Murdock's former bedchamber and returned to the hallway. Before closing the door, he asked, "Which room is Andrew in?"

"The Squire's. Across the hall."

He nodded. "I shall have Soren in to you directly, grandmother, so do not become impatient and attempt to dress yourself."

"Humph! As if I have not already been the most patient of people," she replied. "Get on with you, Dante, for the hour only grows later."

He went to the Squire's room, was not surprised to find that man not in residence as he remembered Lizzie saying that he rarely came above stairs because of his gout. Andrew was sleeping in the old bed, the blankets tossed in disarray about him as though he had spent a restless night. St. James found his clothing set neatly out, as Andrew did not have the deplorable habit of treating his attire as though it were some unforgivable nuisance to be tolerated as his cousin did.

St. James pawed through a surprising variety of shirts for someone on a short journey, and had selected the plainest and least adorned of the lot when Andrew spoke from the bed. "Bloody hell, St. James, but you've managed to rumple the whole lot of them!"

St. James turned to the bed as Andrew sat up. "I apologize, Andrew, I did not wish to disturb you, nor to have you in a state over your clothing," he told the younger man with a grin.

"When the hell did you blow in? And where is Miss Murdock?"

St. James removed his bloody shirt. "About three hours ago and Miss Murdock is currently sleeping in our grandmother's room."

"Have you been shot again?" Andrew asked as St. James tossed his ruined shirt into the lit fireplace as though it were so much old newsprint.

"No. Only tore the stitches of Miss Murdock's previous endeavors, of which she has been kind enough to sew me up once again."

"Well, I hope you know," Andrew continued with indignation, "that we have all been in a state wondering where she was and what should have become of her! We had decided that we would travel to London today to demand explanation from you!"

"You should have very well known that I would have her with me," St. James countered, "and that I would not let any harm befall her."

"No," Andrew replied, petulant, "for how was I to know that, when you assured me she would be here in Chestershire, a little late perhaps, but here all the same."

"And so she now is," St. James said, buttoning his pilfered shirt. "And get dressed, Andrew, for I can not waste time and if you wish to know the story you shall have to ask your questions while I fetch grandmother's lady's maid, for she is waiting, you know."

"Hell and Damnation upon your soul, St. James, for you are the most aggravating of cousins!" Andrew threw back his covers and stood entirely naked from the bed. "I need not tell you that you have a good deal of explaining to do and not only to me but to the Squire, who is convinced you have ruined his daughter and are buying him off with this display of improvement in his home, and to Ryan also, who is livid that you should have in any way besmirched Miss Murdock's name further."

But St. James, diverted by Andrew's complete lack of clothing when sleeping, only said, "My God! But how do you get away with it, for my own valet is in horrors that I sleep in only my shorts!"

Andrew blushed at these laughing words, snagged some clothing to don. "I would not have expected you of all people to bring me to task over the way I sleep!" he grumbled. "And Miss Murdock, by the by, gave me quite a fright the night she came in to wake me to tell me of your injury. I only thank God that I do not sleep with my curtains open and the moon shining in as you have said on occasion that you do."

"Well, you really should wear at least shorts, you know, Andrew, although even they are a great bother. For one night you may have a visitor bent on doing you harm and it is hard to concentrate upon defending yourself when you are mindful that if you should fire a shot, the whole household will be down upon your head and you shall be standing there in all your glory. Or worse, dead upon the floor with not even a stitch of clothing on."

Andrew turned thoughtful at this advice and admitted, "Had not considered that, I confess. But I can see where it could be a distraction."

St. James went to the door, Andrew's plain white lawn shirt drooping overlarge at the shoulders, but even this careless look made him seem only somehow more dangerous. "I shall see you below for coffee for I dare not make grandmother wait any longer than necessary or she shall be banging her cane and we will not get even a moment to talk quietly before every one else is up and about."

Even as he spoke these words, there was a loud banging from the closed door across from them that reverberated through the floor and throughout the house. "Damn it!" St. James muttered and left the room.

He met Mrs. Herriot in the hallway, looking a little less crisp than was her norm. She curtsied her large figure and her face was a creasing of rapturous smiles. "Oh, milord! You have arrived at last! And is your Miss Murdock here also?"

"Yes, Mrs. Herriot, and Lord Tempton is with us also. Will you fetch Soren for grandmother? And send her to Miss Murdock's old bedchamber, as she has gone in there so that she may be dressed without disturbing my betrothed?"

"Oh, yes, milord! It is true then that you have become engaged?" and he would have been pleasantly distracted by her joyous response if he had not so much upon his mind.

"Indeed, yes, Mrs. Herriot, but I must go below--"

The door down the hallway opened and Miss Murdock appeared from the bedchamber, and since she had slept in her riding habit she was looking very deplorable indeed. St. James cut off his words at sight of her and stood grinning in the hallway, and Mrs. Herriot, perceiving the expression on his face, turned with a great deal of anticipated delight to see at last what young Miss could put such a look of devotion upon his lordship's face.

And the smile froze upon her face for the sight that met her eyes was so far from what she had been expecting that she nearly burst into frustrated tears. The young Miss that turned to her was of small stature and inconsequential figure. Her hair was a mass of tangles that she was even now trying to distractedly arrange. Her face was much too tanned and her eyes were of no particular shade of brown, but were rather solemn and a great deal dulled by fatigue (and, Mrs. Herriot noted with something akin to horror, bloodshot!), and she did not have any laudable feature that Mrs. Herriot could determine but was frankly, quite plain.

And the Duke just behind her, rather than being put *off* by this lamentable picture, only said, "You are looking very well this morning, Miss Murdock," in a teasing voice that for some reason made Mrs. Herriot's comfortably round face blush.

"And I am certain that I do not," Miss Murdock said with tired annoyance, "and I can not understand why you insist upon saying I do when I dare say you have not seen me at my best for even one moment since we have met."

"But you were looking very fine at Almacks," he replied.

"Do not remind me of that, milord, or you shall have me angry at you already this morning, for I need not tell you that I am still most unhappy with your behavior of that night." Then she turned her attention to the housekeeper that stood rather stunned between them. "I am sorry, for I can only guess what you must be thinking to find me in such a pitiful state and arguing with milord at this early hour of the morning."

And Mrs. Herriot, touched somehow by this tired sincerity, clucked and said, "And I am sure that you are quite done in, Miss, and should return immediately to your bed and allow your lady's maid to bring up chocolate to you! I am Mrs. Herriot, by the way, and you--you are Miss Murdock?" and there was such question in her voice that milord behind her burst out laughing, causing Miss Murdock to give him a quelling glare.

"Yes," that Miss reassured the housekeeper. "I know that everyone is always most disappointed in me, of which I can hardly blame them, but I am Miss Murdock."

"Shame, Lizzie," St. James teased, "for you will put even me to the blush at such a self-deprecating speech, when I am sure Mrs. Herriot will agree with me that you are quite the loveliest thing she has ever seen, even with your hair a mess and your clothing looking as though you had slept in them."

"Oh, botheration!" Miss Murdock returned. "I can see that you are looking nearly fresh this morning after only a few hours sleep, and so, as usual, are looking much finer than I. And for someone who has claimed to never knowingly lie, I have found that you do so on an appallingly regular basis when it comes to my appearance."

"Not at all," St. James denied and added as his grandmother's cane could be heard banging again from behind the closed bedchamber door, "Mrs. Herriot, if you would fetch Soren?"

"Of course," Mrs. Herriot said, jumping slightly, for she had been standing somewhat dazed in betwixt them and she bobbed a curtsy to Miss Murdock. "Pleased to meet you, Miss," and she bustled down the hallway.

St. James said, "Come here, Lizzie, and let me fix your hair, for frankly you are making a mess of it."

He straightened and pinned her hair and when his finger smoothed down the vein in her neck, Lizzie leaned back against him and sighed. "I shall feel better, I wager, after I have had a cup of coffee."

Downstairs, they checked in on her father, who was sleeping upon the sofa in the parlor. The sound of hurried footsteps on the stairs forewarned them of Andrew, who came into the parlor, dressed and shaved.

Miss Murdock gave an exclamation of surprise, went to him and gave him a brief hug beneath St. James' bemused gold eyes. "Andrew! What ever are you doing here?"

And unaccountably he colored. "I came to make sure that you and Bertie had arrived safely, and found when I got here that you had not arrived at all."

"Well we are here now," she told him. "And Bertie, also, but he must have found a room above stairs, for I have not seen him yet this morning and he must still be sleeping. And I did not mean to cause worry but I was very concerned about Steven, you know, and could not in all conscious come to Chestershire when he was still unaccounted for."

"*That* is what delayed you then," and he gave St. James such a look of accusation that Lizzie was taken aback with it.

"Why, yes, of course. What else would I have been doing?" she asked a little puzzled.

"We were not sure," Andrew returned, "but I fear that between your father and Ryan, and yes, I admit, myself, we had jumped to some rather damning conclusions."

"Oh, you did not!" and she gave a peal of laughter. "For I assure you, we have been much too busy for any such nonsense as the three of you have dreamed up."

"I do not find it such a ridiculous notion," Andrew huffed, "when one considers that St. James has done nothing but try to ruin you from the beginning. Even my mother told me that she caught the two of you riding in a coach in the midst of the night, of which *I* was quite unawares." And he looked hurt as well as angry.

But St. James interrupted at this point. "Indeed, Andrew? And she has put in your head the notion that I have compromised Miss Murdock?"

Andrew reddened. "She did not 'put it in my head', she merely observed that it was most unseemly and if one were to draw conclusions, what other conclusion was there to draw. And then when you consider your showing up at Almack's with that damned handprint upon your face," he added with growing anger, "which you made blatantly clear to everyone that Miss Murdock had placed it there, and it seems to me that my mother's take on the situation has not been inaccurate."

"Go carefully, Andrew," St. James warned, "for you are very close to crossing the line. You may call into question my character all you wish, but I advise you most heartily against questioning Miss Murdock's virtue."

"If her virtue is in question, you have no one to blame but yourself!" Andrew exclaimed with heat.

But Miss Murdock stepped between them. "Enough!" she cried. "For I have not even yet had a cup of coffee this morning and I can not take this sudden bickering between the two of you. Andrew," her brown eyes flashed, "whatever has come over you, for I would have sworn that you knew your cousin well enough to know that he would in no way harm me?"

"I no longer know what to believe," Andrew replied with as much confusion as wrath.

He glanced at St. James half in challenge, half searching for reassurance, but St. James only regarded him with a steady reflective look.

Before anything else could be said, the Squire's snoring stopped with a snort. The three of them turned to him as he opened his eyes, and his gaze fell first on Lizzie, who was standing closest to him. His eyes widened and he sat ponderously up and held a hand to her, which she took, and he drew her down to sit next to him on the sofa. He was dirty and sweaty and smelled of too much drinking and not enough bathing, but she did not care, only hugged him and hid her face in his shoulder, very near tears.

"Oh, father. I have been so worried for you. And now I find that you have been pestered nearly to death with all of St. James' servants."

"'Deed, I have been," the Squire pronounced. "And I should have hunted him down for only that even if he had not abused you terribly as I am convinced he has."

But Lizzie drew back at his words and wiped at her eyes. "Oh, that is all so much rot, you know, father, for the banns are in the paper and he does in fact mean to marry me, however much I may beg him not to."

"What is this?" the Squire asked, and he raised his eyes to St. James. "I have checked the papers daily and have seen no sign of banns, miduke, so you have best not assured my Lizzie that they are in when I am afraid you are but misleading her to gain your own purposes."

And St. James, with a weary gesture, pulled his watch once again from his pocket and muttered as he did so from between clenched teeth, "I did not think that a simple gesture on my part would prove to be so necessary." He opened the back of the watch and tossed the folded paper to the Squire. "Here, damn it! For it was in yesterday's paper and I would wager it has not made it to this area until this morning."

The Squire unfolded the paper, scanned it and handed it back. "It had best not be a trick, miduke, for I had already made up my mind to demand satisfaction and damn you and your attempts at buying me off!"

"Jesus, God in Heaven," St. James said, losing patience. "I swear I shall marry her if I have to ride through hell to accomplish it, however much everyone seems to doubt and disbelieve it. I had no other intention from the beginning, and I have no other intention now! So you may all be hanged, for all I care. I have not the time to stand here and argue with you any further. Make of it what you will and be damned." He turned and strode from the room and they heard the front door slam behind him.

"Damn right you will!" the Squire cried in belated triumph. Then he turned to Lizzie at his side with a pleased smile on his face as though he had accomplished a great deal. "There!" he told her. "I told you I should get you married."

She disappointed him with her lack of gratitude. "Oh, do shut up, father, for I have not forgiven you for getting me into this mess to begin with!" and she rose from the settee.

"And where are you going, lass?" her father asked. "For you look like hell and you can not blame me for thinking the worst when he brings you home in that condition! And I'll not have you traipsing off with him again until we have had a discussion and have set a proper date. Even then, I think he should leave you here until the wedding day, for I still do not trust the bugger!"

"I am only going to make coffee," she returned from the door. "For my head is fairly splitting with all this shouting."

But her father only cried after her, "There's a cook for that now, ye know, ya damned, bloody, daft girl, and a maid to bring it in!"

"I do not--" she began, but Ryan came bounding down the stairs toward her, hastily dressed and a pistol in either hand.

"Where is he?" he demanded.

And Miss Murdock only said in an aggravated voice, "If you mean St. James, and I expect you mean no other, I believe he has gone to the stables."

Ryan pushed past her and slammed out the door. She leaned over the banister and shouted up the stairs, "Lord Tempton! Bertie! You had better come down for your brother is about to be killed!"

"On my way!" Bertie called, and he came to the head of the stairs, puffing as he tucked in his shirt. "No fear, Miss Murdock, I shall handle it!" and then he too shoved out the door. But he was not alone, for the Squire, still in his soiled robe and with only a pair of boots shoved upon his swollen feet, and Andrew, rather better turned out, jounced against each other in their haste to catch the front door before it slammed and were outside upon Bertie's heels.

Miss Murdock watched all this activity with weary detachment, was a-bout to turn again to the kitchens when the banging of a cane above her forestalled her once again, and she looked up to see the Dowager, with Soren to one side of her, and Mrs. Herriot to the other, following as quickly as she was able.

Miss Murdock watched their descent with exasperation, and when they reached the bottom and the Duchess glanced at her with some surprise to see her standing waiting for her, Miss Murdock merely said, "You take cream in your coffee, do you not, ma'am?"

"Why, yes, child. Yes, I do," that old lady answered.

"Then if you will make yourself comfortable in the parlor, I shall return momentarily with a tray," and Miss Murdock turned to go toward the kitchens as had been her initial intent upon first getting up that morning.

"Oh, Bloody Hell, What Now!" St. James said as he turned from conferring with one of several grooms in the rapidly improving stables. "Yes, young Ryan? Can I be of service to you?"

Ryan stumbled to a stop in front of him, panting, secured his pistols and removed his riding gloves from his pocket, and with as much force as he could muster, slapped St. James across the face.

Bertie appeared in the door behind Ryan, saw the red glow of St. James' cheek and the lethal coldness in his eyes and exclaimed to no one in particular, "Now he's done it! St. James--"

But St. James snapped, "Name your second! I should have known I would not get out of here before something like this occurred."

"Bertie," Ryan pronounced.

"Not at all, lad," that man interrupted with indignation, "for I have always been St. James' second!"

Ryan turned on him, incredulous. "You are my *brother*, I need not remind you!"

"Yes. But *he* is right, and you, my boy, are wrong."

For the briefest of seconds it looked as though the whole sorry affair would end there, with Ryan looking helpless to find his way around this sudden roadblock and St. James only fuming at this further waste of time. But then Andrew, who had arrived in the midst of this with the Squire not far behind, spoke up. "I will be your second, Ryan, for if your brother can side with him, I can certainly side with you, for I believe you to be right, and he wrong."

St. James clicked his teeth once in furious regret. "Let's get on with it then. Squire, you may as well ride out in a cart to pick up the remains of who falls."

At this off-hand summation of the consequences, Ryan's face blanched, but he was well and truly offended over what he believed the ruination of Miss Murdock and he would not back down.

"The training track, do you think, St. James?" Bertie asked. "For then the shots will not be heard at the house. Or at least, not loudly."

"No. I haven't the time. We'll have our go in the lane." He drew one of his dueling pistols from his coat, handed it to Bertie, and then withdrew the unmatched third gun also so that he was left with but one pistol.

Ryan, observing this, relieved himself of his extra pistol, perceiving that the proper etiquette was one shot to you and be damned if you missed. Andrew took it a little nervously. St. James proceeded to check the load in his chosen weapon, and Ryan followed his lead, but he was so worked up at this point that he would have hardly noticed if his pistol had been empty instead of previously loaded.

The Squire hurried away and was heard bawling for a cart to be hitched to a horse, and St. James, with a single assessing look at his challenger, only said, "If you are ready, young Ryan?"

Ryan nodded, his face tight as he held himself together. He followed the smaller man from the stables as St. James strode from the entrance and the four of them headed to the lane.

"Count them off, Bertie," St. James bade.

"Ten or twenty?" that man asked.

"Ryan? Your choice. Ten paces or twenty?"

"Uh, twenty. If that's all right with you?"

"It's your show, Ryan, by all means, you choose," St. James told him with impatience. "And don't be overlong about it."

"Twenty then," Ryan said with renewed fury. "And damn you."

But St. James only said to Bertie, "You heard him, Bertie. That straight section there beyond that tree should be adequate."

And they strode in unison, the two older men, the two younger men, to beyond the curve in the drive. "You have handkerchiefs?" Bertie asked St. James.

St. James pulled two out, handed one to Lord Tempton, who dropped it without fuss on to the road. "You will stand there, Ryan," Bertie explained. Then he strode up the lane, keeping his paces even as he counted off twenty. St. James followed behind and supplied him the other handkerchief, which Bertie dropped in the road at the end of his count.

St. James took his mark without looking back and stood facing away from Ryan.

Ryan, perceiving that they were to wait with their backs turned, and somehow unnerved that St. James had not even bothered to look back and appraise the distance between them, turned hastily around. "What do I do now?" he asked Andrew to his side.

Andrew, as nervous as Ryan, said, "Devil if I know! Haven't you done this before?"

"No! He's your cousin. Haven't you ever been with him when he's done this?" Ryan asked with anxiety.

"No! And why ever did you call him out? Damned if I would not have had my first go with someone else!"

But Bertie yelled to Andrew and Ryan did not have a chance to answer but jumped a little at the unexpected bellow of his brother's voice. "Earl Larrimer! On the count of three. Which you will start the count, I will continue it, and you will end it, at which point they will turn and fire. And you had better step back a bit, by the by, for that is a damned bad place to be standing!"

And Andrew, flushing, stepped back several yards from young Ryan Tempton, leaving that man to feel very much alone. "Luck to you!" he exclaimed.

Twenty paces away, St. James was studying the field to one side of them and the woods to the other. "Damned bad timing, this," he told Bertie.

"I know it, St. James. I had no idea what he was up to until, as you saw, it was too late. Guess he took your previous lesson a little too to heart!"

From behind him, St. James heard Andrew shout out, "One!"

"Ready?" Bertie asked in an undertone.

"Yes. And try not to look so concerned, I shall try mightily not to kill him outright."

"I'd appreciate it," Bertie said and then shouted, "Two!" and stepped back from the line of fire.

Upon the heels of this second count, Andrew shouted again, but damningly, he did not say 'three' but instead exclaimed in sudden outrage, "Those are my bloody pants, damn it!"

Ryan whirled at Andrew's words and he saw that St. James turned also, although St. James' demeanor was of one pushed well beyond endurance with someone else's folly. But before Ryan could fully appreciate the lack of intent upon his opponent's face, or the fact that he had not raised his pistol, Ryan had already fired.

The gunpowder from his pistol stung his nostrils, and that combined with the recoil of the gun nearly made him drop his weapon. Andrew screamed beside him, "Bloody Hell, Ryan! I did not say three, damn it!"

"Oh," Ryan said foolishly. "I say, is he all right?"

Andrew peered through the dissipating smoke, said through clenched teeth, "No, by God, he isn't for he is doubled over and clutching his stomach!"

"Oh, God! Gut shot!" Ryan said with horror. They both broke from their frozen, shocked stances and ran down the lane, expecting St. James to drop to his knees as they neared him and to lie dying in horrible pain upon the lane.

But as they drew closer, their running slowed, and they were both more angered than relieved to find that although he was doubled over and clutching his stomach, he had not been shot, but was laughing until the tears streamed down his face, and that Bertie was laughing as hard, and had picked up the handkerchief that had been at St. James' feet and was wiping his face with the dusty folds of it.

"I had wondered," St. James gasped as he tried to recover himself, "where Steven had gotten those breeches!"

And Andrew, recalling what had distracted him to the degree that he had miscounted, looked to where he had caught sight of that lad, who had moved closer at this turn of events, and exclaimed hotly, "Yes, by God! The little heathen has stolen my pants, and they were quite the best pair I owned! And look at what he has done to them, for not only are they dirty beyond cleaning, they are sheared off and will never fit again."

Steven, with wide gray eyes, said, "Aye, I'm sorry, m'lord, but I awoke without me own, and never have I been able t'ken what happened to 'em."

Ryan turned with fury on Andrew. "You nearly made me kill him, damn you, for you could not even keep your mind upon the count. And I would have been a murderer, thanks to you!"

"I say!" Andrew defended himself. "T'is up to you to wait until the count of three! Don't blame me if you were so nervous that you jumped the count!"

St. James, still laughing, but at last able to stand erect, asked, "Care for another go, Ryan?"

"No, by God, I don't!" Ryan said with ill-grace. "For I have had quite enough, with you and my own brother laughing your fool heads off at me!"

"Very well, Ryan," St. James agreed, trying to curb his amusement. "Let us just chalk it up as another lesson learned, shall we, and no hard feelings? For if you had only asked, you would have learned that Miss Murdock is quite unharmed and that the banns of our engagement were posted in yesterday's newspaper."

"Oh," Ryan said. "But I was only following your advice!"

"I generally recommend that you apprise yourself of all the facts before you go off in a dudgeon, but I must have missed that point," St. James explained.

But Steven interrupted. "Pardon, m'lord, but I've come to fetch you, for Tyler lies an hour back on t'road, an' I don't know how long he will last without help."

"Damn it!" St. James said, his amusement gone and all his attention now on the boy. "How bad, Steven?"

"Don't think too bad, m'lord, but he's in pain, and bleedin' an' unable to ride further."

St. James closed his eyes for one second. Then they snapped open and he said, "Is your horse blown, lad?"

"Aye. I rode 'im 'til he was on his knees an' left 'im a mile back."

"To the stables, then," St. James said and turned in that direction. Bertie followed and, after a second's hesitation, Andrew and Ryan hurried to catch up. They met the Squire a dozen yards up the lane with the cart and horse. "Very good," St. James nodded. "Steven, can you drive it?"

"Aye. Think I can."

"Then up you go, lad, and Squire, you'd best get down."

"We're going with you," Ryan told him.

"No. You're not," and he turned long enough to pierce them both with his gold eyes. "You're to remain here and make sure that no harm comes to Miss Murdock. You, also, Bertie, for after this display out here, I think they are as likely to shoot each other as they are any attacker and will need someone to show them the ropes."

"You're going alone then?" Bertie asked.

"Yes. Steven will get Tyler with the cart, and I will take care of these two remaining threats before they cause more trouble, damn them!" They reached the stables and St. James continued, "Ryan, which is your horse, for mine is in no condition after being ridden hard all night."

Ryan sped down the aisle until he located his horse, St. James upon his heels. When they reached the proper stall, St. James threw open the door. "Fetch the tack, Ryan," and if he were cursing the fact that he had not Tyler with him who knew his every move, nearly, before he made it, he made no indication of it, only went about his business with a tired and singular purpose.

Chapter Twenty-seven

Whereas Milord Duke of St. James found a great deal of amusement in the shot fired from Ryan's pistol, Miss Murdock, sitting in the parlor with the duke's staid grandmother, found it rather less so.

She had not fetched the coffee, as had been her intention, being shooed from that task by a scandalized Mrs. Herriot. Miss Murdock, disgusted, returned to the parlor, and although she had a good deal of faith in Bertie to not allow a tragedy, without the looked for preoccupation of preparing the morning beverage, she was very concerned, indeed.

She went to the settee, across from the Dowager in her chair, who looked a good deal strained also, and they made no conversation, as it was useless to think of entertaining each other until they were assured that all had been handled without anyone befalling harm.

Presently, Mrs. Herriot came in with the coffee tray, loaded with a tall silver urn surrounded by several silver cups, which Miss Murdock had never before seen in her life. It was not her father's, by any means, and she had to wonder what ever in heaven else St. James' energetic and purposeful housekeeper had changed in her absence. It was no wonder Miss Murdock's father had looked fagged to death.

She poured and although she was preoccupied with worry and doubt, it was not evident as she completed this task with her normal somber grace and handed a cup over to the duchess, who took it with a shaking hand, which could have been from old age, or could have been from agitation.

"I am not used to knowing of any of this sort until it is quite finished," the duchess lamented, and Miss Murdock spared her a sympathetic look.

"I am sure we worry for no reason, ma'am," she comforted. "For St. James has far too much on his mind to allow himself to be drawn into anything so ridiculous, and of course, Bertie shall not let any harm befall his brother."

"You sound very certain that it will not be St. James that comes to harm," the Duchess said with equal measures of relief and irritation.

"Which is hardly more of a comfort, for I do not wish to see Ryan come to harm either. Oh, men are such bloody fools!"

"Indeed they are, Miss Murdock," the Duchess agreed. "And I am afraid that my grandson is the biggest fool of them all."

But before Miss Murdock could say anything in return, a pistol was fired from near at hand and she nearly dropped her coffee cup, stunned that they could, in fact, be so stupid! Her brown eyes flew to the Dowager's startled, faded ones, and then Miss Murdock sprang from her seat and slammed her cup down upon the table. "Well, it is done now, damn him! I shall kill him if he is not already lying dead!" But her own words bore home to her the very possibility that Ryan may have prevailed rather than the duke, and as much as she had tried to remain detached, she knew herself helpless to be so.

"Excuse me, ma'am," she said and rushed from the room, not even aware of the Duchess struggling to arise from her own seat.

She did not have to search, upon coming outside, to find them, for they were immediately in her line of vision, but a short ways down the lane, and her first sight was of a small cloud of smoke drifting above Ryan and Andrew's heads, who seemed to be in some earnest and heated discussion.

The fact that Ryan was still standing filled her with dread.

Then she looked beyond them and her worst fear was brought to the fore as she saw St. James doubled over and clutching his stomach.

She picked up her skirts and flew down the steps, hot tears stinging her eyes. Ryan and Andrew turned toward St. James also and, as if her own action had spurred them, ran toward the duke, who oddly enough, had not yet fallen to the ground.

And Miss Murdock had but reached the head of the lane, where the wide drive in front of the house narrowed, when she saw St. James straighten as Andrew and Ryan reached him. She had one clear look at his face before he was blocked from her sight by the two taller young men.

She stopped running and stood motionless, for she saw that he was not injured, but was overcome with laughter to a near helpless degree.

She stood there for several minutes, her heart booming in her chest from her fright, and she called herself a fool. A bigger fool than the Dowager thought her grandson. A bigger fool, even, than she had been to ride from her home with him five mornings ago, to go to him in the night in his carriage, to go to him again and tend to his wounds, to go with him yet again when rushing from flames and from bullets, and then instead of cutting him off from her when she had a final chance, had contrarily crawled into his open arms, his open coat, and fused herself to his bleeding chest and rested and took comfort in him.

It all rushed home to her as she stood there for those few minutes, St. James immersed in mirth, and she immersed in terror. The one final thing he asked of her was nearly insignificant to all that she had already willingly given.

She was a fool to have thought that there would be some point of no return that she would recognize and heed and turn back before passing. She had passed it already, and she was not sure at which action taken it had been. It may have been the first, when she had cooked him a meal instead of giving him only coffee as he had asked, or perhaps not until the last, when he admitted to having every intention of killing Steven's father, and had threatened a seven year old boy, and she had not held him in abhorrence even then.

Perhaps for that second, she understood him completely.

He laughed at his own pain and his own misery. He was moved to an uncommon degree by the sufferings of others, but his own he disregarded as some old handicap that he had grown used to, had learned to not only bear it, but use it to some sick and twisted advantage. He killed without qualm, for he accepted his own death without qualm, and perhaps even with relief, for only then would grief, succored and nurtured, be at last laid to rest.

The very thing he sought to destroy another with destroyed him also. And he called it justice. He called it vengeance.

Miss Murdock called it abomination.

The fact that she knew herself to be willing to die for him, she took as madness and iniquity, but she could not help herself, and neither would she fight it any longer. If he came to her at that moment and plunged a knife into his own heart, she would follow him without hesitation.

The small group of men that she stared at without seeing came into sudden activity, speeding toward the stables. She waited for St. James to look up, to see her there, to perhaps come to her, but he did not even glance in her direction and there was no longer any amusement in his face, nor those of the others.

Her father came into the lane from the back road to the stables, she noticed, and he rode in a cart, his dressing gown looking incongruous, and St. James paused to speak to him. And Miss Murdock noticed at last that Steven was there in the midst of the men, and somehow she knew that this could not be good, for Tyler and the curricle were no where to be seen.

As if drawn by her thoughts of him, Steven's gray eyes flashed over to her, finding a path through the restless movements of Ryan, Bertie and Andrew. St. James continued to the stables, the others following, and Miss Murdock's father was climbing from the cart, but Steven, alone, came toward Miss Murdock.

"What is the matter, Steven?" she asked as he came up to her.

"T'is Tyler, Miss! We was set upon on t'road, by the same two as had it in fer you an' t'duke, Tyler 'spects. He got wounded in 'is leg and t'horse he were ridin' went down. He rode with me for a ways, but then he couldn't hang on any further an' sent me on ahead to warn m'lord they was as like headed here sooner if not later."

"And St. James is even now going to him?" she asked, but she knew that of course he would.

"Aye. T'is what he is 'bout now. I'm to take t'cart to fetch Tyler in, an' m'lord, he says he'll see that I'm undisturbed to go 'bout me business."

"You will be careful, Steven, won't you?"

"Aye. Coo, miss! Wouldn't miss it, I wouldn't! For t'was a grand sight watchin' 'im get you from me 'ouse yesterday!"

"And you are getting more of an education than is necessarily good for you," she told him. "But nevermind, for I would wager that milord trusts you more than Ryan or Andrew at any rate, and I doubt that he will take Bertie, for of course, he will ask him to stay here to keep me safe. Silly fool."

"Aye, miss. T'is what I gathered," Steven agreed. "But I had a message to give to t'duchess from Tyler, if she be up," he added.

Surprised, Miss Murdock said, "Why I will give it to her if you do not wish to delay."

And Steven looked very uncomfortable and only said, "Sorry, miss, but Tyler, he tolds me not t'give it t'anyone but t'duchess, not even m'lord himself. So's I better give it t'her meself."

"Well, of course, then," Miss Murdock agreed. "She is right through the door and on your left if she remains where I last saw her. Go on now, for I shall be going to the stables for a word with St. James before he leaves out of here without even a goodbye, which I would wager is his intention."

Steven pulled at the lock of his hair and hurried past, and Miss Murdock turned to go to the stables. And she did not know if she were about to kill St. James or mayhaps save him, she only knew what had to be said and what had to be done.

There was a great deal of activity once she reached the stables, but for the most part it appeared to be useless. Only St. James was going about anything with an appearance of purpose, leading a horse that Miss Murdock was unfamiliar with from a stall partway down the aisle.

Bertie and Andrew conferred in hushed tones with each other. Ryan walked with quick and flustered strides up the aisle with a saddle in his hands, its girth straps dragging so that he was nearly tripping on them causing Miss Murdock to wonder if that young man had ever even saddled his own horse.

A young groom ran toward milord, but his hands were empty and he appeared to not have the least idea what was expected of him.

At the same time, St. James said, "Damn it, Ryan, I need a bridle also!"

And Miss Murdock with perfect calmness went to fetch that item as Ryan awkwardly handed the saddle to the groom just arriving. The stirrup irons dangled, as well as the straps, and St. James stepped forward while still holding the horse's halter and with impatience flipped up one iron and one strap so the groom could place the saddle on the horse. He glanced up, perceiving Miss Murdock's presence and he hesitated in whatever dire curse he seemed about to utter.

Ryan turned, nearly ran into Miss Murdock as she came forward with the bridle. "Miss Murdock!" he exclaimed. "You should not be here now, for you will only get in the way, you know!"

But she only stepped around him and handed the bridle to St. James. He gave her a searching look that showed he was uneasy with her presence, but she only said, "Milord, if you think you and the groom have your mount well in hand, I should like to send Ryan to fetch for a doctor so that he may be here upon your and Tyler's return."

His hands did not falter from forcing the horse's mouth open and placing in the bit of the bridle. "If it shall make you content to remain here, Miss Murdock, then I will agree. For I do not wish you to get some wild notion in your head that you are going to follow along with your needle and thread in order to run triage at the scene."

"That is not my intention in the least," she told him and he gave her a lauding look from his gold eyes despite his involvement in readying to go.

"You heard her, Ryan. Fetch the nearest doctor and have him waiting. I am sure the Squire can instruct you upon where that good man can be found."

"I take it that you intend to go alone, milord, with only Steven to drive the cart?" Miss Murdock asked.

"Yes. And I will brook no argument upon that point either, Miss Murdock. Steven should be quite safe, as I intend to have whatever business needs being done finished before he should arrive. One way or the other."

"Of course," she agreed, and this time his hands stopped and he frowned at her.

"Unusually compliant, Miss Murdock. I find that foreboding rather than comforting."

"I have every intention of meeting your wishes, milord, so indeed, you *should* find that comforting. I will not follow along behind you, nor will I argue and insist that you should take Bertie or anyone else with you. Nor do I have any doubt that you would die sooner than see Steven come to harm. I only ask that when you are finished here, that you meet me outside for a private word before leaving." Only the small shaking in her voice warned him that there was something else going on in her mind that he was not going to like.

"Very well, Miss Murdock. But be advised that if I had any choice, I would not be delaying my plans for tonight so drastically, and hence I can not accommodate any of your wishes at this time that may run contrary to my going."

"Indeed, I did not expect that you could." She turned from him before he could say anything further, but she was very aware of his gold eyes on her back, frowning and concerned.

She stopped to speak to Lord Tempton before passing from the stables. "Bertie, as I take it you are to remain with me, I wish you to direct that Andrew's carriage be made ready as soon as possible, if you please."

"Now, Miss Murdock," he sputtered. "He'll not have you trailing him, as you should very well know!"

"Which is not my intention in the least--"

"And he'll not have you disappear--"

But she interrupted. "Tsk, Bertie, complain along the way, remember? For you shall only lose at any rate and it goes so much quicker than otherwise."

He gave her a reluctant grin, his blue eyes twinkling. "You are as bad as he, Miss Murdock, when it comes to getting your own way."

"And I shall be a great deal worse before I am through, but that will be for him to find out and so you must not worry upon that head. Now, I shall be outside, so you may go ahead, if you would, please."

"Do you not wish me to wait until he leaves?" he asked in a conspiratory whisper.

"Oh, no. For whatever would be the point if he were not aware of it?"

Bertie chuckled, bowed in her direction. "You have my respect, Miss Murdock, for you are certainly much braver than I!" But as if proving his own words wrong, he shouted the length of the stables. "Groom here! I'll need Earl Larrimer's carriage brought up!"

St. James' head snapped around at this sudden order from Bertie, and Andrew turned from where he had been watching his cousin in some impatience as he had clearly desired to be of help and had not yet seen a chance to be. But Miss Murdock only turned and walked out.

She made her way to the far corner of the outside of the stables. There was a small grove of fruit trees here, their branches mostly bare now, but low hanging and dense, and she waited here for St. James to come out of the stables.

Her waiting was short, and when he arrived out, leading his horse, she could see from his face that he was thunderously angry. He caught sight of her, came to her and they both retreated around the corner of the stables and out of sight of any others. "I haven't time for this now, you wretched lass," he began. "I will have explanation, but can tell you even now that you can disabuse yourself of whatever idea that you have."

"But I am not asking permission, milord, I am merely apprising you of my plans so that you may make whatever necessary adjustments to your own."

"Go on," he said.

She had a sudden thought that perhaps *this* was the point of no return, and that she had not passed it after all.

As it was, she only duly noted the sign, chalked it off on her inner map as met and passed, and plunged ahead. "I will only be traveling to Gretna Green to await you, milord."

And his face relaxed as though in relief. "I should have guessed, you misguided lass," he told her. "And although I appreciate the sentiment to a degree that I am certain you can not even be aware, it is quite unnecessary." His gold eyes searched hers for understanding, and when she did not change expression, he continued in a low voice, as though perhaps she needed explanation, of which, of course, she did not.

"I have let you down at every turn, Lizzie. But I have, at least, come to understand that my notion of protecting you with my name and my title is of no comfort to you, and perhaps, at least, I can find some satisfaction that if I can only make it through to day, that if we marry then, it will be because of your own desire, and not because I have induced you by one unsavory action after another.

"For you must understand that if I die, you will be again safe. And if I live, it will only be because this is all at last at a finish, and so you shall be safe also. But either way, a trip to the border now is either too late or too soon, but not needed in any way at this time," he ended softly.

But she still did not change expression, only waited for him to finish.

He frowned at her lack of response. "I'm sorry, Lizzie, if that inadequately expresses my sentiment for you, but you must understand that I have been in the midst of pushing you as far from my mind as I am able. I can not go into this with any desire to live, or I shall die as surely as if I put a gun to my own head."

At last she spoke, her voice flat. "No. You would have no care if you lived if it were only your life at stake, would you?" But there was no question in her voice.

His expression darkened and his eyes rekindled. "Do not question my methods, Lizzie. It is not easy to kill and if I am not equally willing to chance all that I have, I will hesitate at expecting the same from another, no matter what the motivation. Even that second's hesitation can be damning."

"Well, milord," she replied, "since you insist upon speaking as though you were at a gaming table, I am just going to up the ante on you a small bit. I am going to Gretna Green as I have said, being absolutely aware of your saying that it is not necessary. Bertie will accompany me so that you have no fear for my safety or distraction in what you must do. And I will await there for you, forever if it is necessary, until you either arrive to marry me, or send word that you are alive and well but have decided you do not wish to marry me after all, of which, I would not blame you, especially after what I am about to add."

"You are exhausting me again, Miss Murdock," he warned, his voice rough. "I do not blame you for seeing to it that I fulfill the promise I made to your father, especially after all that I have put you through, but it irks me considerably for you to think that you have to in some manner induce me to do so! If I live, I shall marry you, and if you can not believe that, perhaps you can believe this!" He snagged her with the hand that was not holding his horse's reins, and pulled her against him. His eyes bored into hers for a brief second, but before he could lower his mouth to hers, she stopped him.

"No. Not until you have heard what I have to say."

His eyes flared and snapped and he did not release her from him, but neither did he kiss her, and his lips twisted with grimness. "I haven't the time for this, Miss Murdock," he told her. "You are doing your damnedest to ruin my resolve and as I tell you I shall go at any rate, I see no purpose in it other than you must wish to see Tyler and Steven killed as well as myself!"

"Then I will take responsibility for those deaths," she told him brashly. "As well as the others that you, I am sure, will kill, including your *Aunt*, which I am sure will kill Andrew, and possibly your grandmother!"

"Damn you," he said, his voice harsh. "Do you think I can leave it be now, you little fool! Do you think I can go and bring Steven's father back to life and tell him it was all a mistake, and that I am sorry but since it is my *aunt* that did this dreadful deed that I quite changed my mind and shall merely lie down and allow her to kill me and you! Is *that* what you think?"

"Oh, but you *would* lie down and die, wouldn't you!" she accused, her voice ravaged. "For although you hate her with a passion for what she has already done, still does, you would in the end decide that if it kept Andrew happy, and your grandmother at peace, that you would merely allow yourself to be sacrificed!"

"God *damn* you!"

But she continued even though she knew she had pushed him to the edge and quite beyond it and that he was beside himself with fury. "But you will not now, because of me. Because they threatened me, and you can not be certain that if you die promptly and courteously that there will *still* not be some element that has escaped you to make you think I should still be in danger. That your aunt will fear that the marriage did somehow secretly take place, and that I even now carry a legitimate heir. Is that not right, Dante? Can you, *dare* you deny it?"

But he gave her no answer, only held her roughly, his eyes blazing.

"So this is how it shall be. I will go as I have said. I will wait. And if I get word that you have not survived, I will follow you in death with no regrets! No regrets and no hesitation! Do you understand me, Dante! If you don't wish to marry me after this, I will not blame you! If you despise me after this, I will not blame you! But unless you wish to see me dead as well, you had better get through this alive. Tyler and Steven be damned. Andrew be damned. Your grandmother be damned. For I have become as you, and I would sacrifice *anyone* to protect you. And since I can not rely on any one to protect you to the degree that I know you are capable of protecting, then I can only make sure that you do what ever is necessary without any thought on your part of whether your life is worth it. For it is worth it to me and I will bear the guilt of seeing the others die, for I well know that if it were up to you and it came to the ultimate choice, you would choose your own death before allowing any one else to be hurt."

With an incomprehensible roar, he pushed her from him, hard, and she fell back upon the ground. But she did not flinch or even blink her eyes, but only raised herself on her elbows and stared at him from behind her brownness.

He turned from her, his back rigid, his hands on both butts of his pistols as his initial response was always his weapons, and then without looking back, he caught the reins of his horse and went to mount it. But before he put his foot in the stirrup, he paused, his taut shoulders bunching beneath the cloth of his coat, and then with ferocity he flung himself away from the side of his horse and leaped at her where she still lay upon the ground, raised only on her elbows.

He dropped to his knees and straddled her, and she had no idea if his intention were to love her or kill her. He stretched his body down the length of hers so that her elbows collapsed and she lay beneath him.

His hand went to her face, held her jaw, and he looked at her very deeply and exposed for one second and then his mouth was on hers with no gentleness or consideration if he hurt her but only filled with desperate need. She wrapped her fingers in his dark hair and pulled him closer and the kiss lasted for far too short a time.

Then he pulled his head back, and he told her with curtness, "We play in hard earnest now, Lizzie, for I am past the recall and you have pushed me there. You had better be in Gretna Green as you say, for the next time I have you beneath me, it will not end with a kiss. Up!" And he stood and yanked her with urgency to her feet.

He released her, mounted quickly, reined his horse in a swift circle, turning his head so that his eyes did not leave hers but for a second, then he kicked his mount and its hooves tore up the sod as he pushed it into hard canter around the corner of the stables and he was gone from her sight.

Lizzie put a dazed hand to her lips, but she did not cry.

"Mrs. Herriot!" the duchess yelled and banged her cane. "Damn--! Soren!" But there was no response, which annoyed the old dowager, for they had surely heard the shot as well and should know that she would be wanting up from her chair.

She heard the front entrance door open. "Miss Murdock!" she cried with relief. But it was not Miss Murdock. A dirty lad peeped around the door frame at her, her only impression of him besides dirtiness: two large gray eyes. "Lad! You shall do! Come in, come in."

The boy came in, wiping his nose on his sleeve as he did so, a filthy habit, and the duchess was tetching a little at this sight. "Yer t'duchess, ma'am?" he asked her.

"Indeed I am and you will help me up from my chair so that I may see what has become of my grandson," the old lady said as she once again leaned forward and attempted to rise, but the legs that had obeyed her in the middle of the night refused her this morning.

"St. James, ma'am?" the boy asked and then went on without waiting for confirmation. "'E's fine. An' t'other one, too, t'tall gent with t'red hair."

"Young Mister Tempton," the dowager supplied, but she leaned back again in her chair, her face very pale and her child-like chest breathing hard and closed her eyes. "And t'is milord to you, lad, as far as the duke is concerned."

"Aye, m'lady," the lad agreed. "I's forget's sometimes, I do, but he hasn't boxed me ears yet t'over it."

"You are acquainted with my grandson then?" the duchess asked, her eyes opening and filling with interest as she thought of ways to grill the boy in front of her.

"Aye," he said. "But Tyler, he warned me 'bout you. Said I was t'de-liver 'is message and get out right quick. An' stay outta reach o' your cane, too!"

The dowager gave a low chuckle. "A message from Tyler? Well, lets have it, lad!" and she held out her hand.

Her other hand, however, had not left her cane, and Steven, seeing this, bethought himself to take no chances, and he pulled out the folded missive with its atrocious hand-printing upon it, and threw it to her from several cautious feet away. It landed in her lap, and as he saw that his mission was fulfilled, he bolted for the door, a stream of curses ringing in his ears at his neat escape.

"--bloody, insolent, young ruffian, beggar boy," the duchess finished, but her hands were unfolding the note, and there was an unconscious prayer in her mind that for once, just one time, Tyler would have put St. James' wishes aside and perhaps done something out of duty to her, his original employer.

She read the missive slowly. Indeed, she could not have read it quickly, for deciphering it was a challenge in itself. But at last she had the whole of it, and she read it through again, and her thin lips tighten-ed, and the wrinkled flesh of her face sagged and her doll-like body stiff-ened.

Milady Duchess of St. James, it read a good deal unevenly.

I've been plugged on t'road to London, gone to take care of t'piece of the business that I can't rightly reckon St. James can have t'stomach for. The one behind the foul deed is none other than yer daughter-in-law, Lady Lydia Larrimer! I don't entirely know how milord arrived at this conclusion, but what I knows of it is damnin'. I stand on it as correct at any rate. After twenty-three years of searchin' I can't hardly see where he'd be wrong at this late date.

I won't be makin' me appointment, I don't think.

I 'spect ye know what he'll be about. Too many good people have died already fer him t'let it go.

I leave this knowledge in yer hands, which I know to be capable.
Tyler

She closed the heavy, creased lids of her eyes, and remembered the old adage that one should be careful of what one prayed for, for one might have it answered.

But she allowed this weakness for but one moment, and then she banged her cane again, and this time, as the news had spread that no one had come to harm with the pistol shot heard, Soren arrived by her side in an instant. The dowager bade her, "Pack, please, Soren, for we shall be going home now."

"Yes, milady."

"And send someone to the stables to have my coach made ready and to fetch my grandson."

"Milord Duke, milady?"

"No. Earl Larrimer."

St. James caught sight of Steven driving the cart before they had reached the end of the lane. He pulled his horse to a sharp halt beside the lad. "I'll have some answers, Steven," he began. "Was Tyler or was Tyler not driving the curricle?"

Steven, looking guilty, allowed that there had been a slight change of plans.

"And will I find that man on the road between here and Morningside, or am I to be looking for him somewhere along the route to London?" St. James asked.

Steven hung his head, unable to meet those gold, damning eyes. "'Twixt here and t'junction, m'lord. But only 'cause we doubled back from t'main road to London and shot across this way t'warns ye when's we run's into trouble."

St. James was very still, even his horse seemed leery of moving and he did not curse nor rage. He only snapped out another question. "Is it possible you lost them at the junction?"

"Tyler, 'e said 'e thought we 'ad. For t'time bein' at least. But won't take overlong for them t'get to yer manor and find ye not there, and then they'll sure to come here. That's what Tyler said, m'lord."

St. James paused further, calculating the distance, the time, time wasted by Steven having to walk the last mile, time with--! Damn it! He spurred his horse, then yanked back on the reins so that it jumped forward and then slid to a halt again, and he turned in the saddle, asked harshly, "You have the gun I gave you, Steven? And extra loads?"

"Aye, m'lord," Steven said with more enthusiasm. "For Tyler, he said I may need it!"

St. James nodded. "Very likely you shall. Remember that Red's seen you and by now he knows you were meaning to cross him. He'll kill you out of spite if he gets the chance."

"I ken, m'lord," Steven said a good deal more somberly.

St. James turned his horse back to the cart, knowing that he was wasting still more precious time, but he had to say it. "You can't count on me, Steven, do you understand?" he asked. "It's going to be every man for himself. If you're not up to it, turn back now."

And Steven looked stunned, but his eyes did not flicker, and St. James had no doubt that he was making an informed decision (for had not St. James seen to just that particular tutelage by in fact killing that boy's father?) and Steven only said, "I'm going, m'lord, for I know that Tyler needs me."

And St. James spared a nod at this. "He does, indeed, Steven. He does indeed."

And then at last, he spurred his horse forward with a great unleashing of power.

He judged that it would be a very close thing, whether he would reach Tyler first, or whether Red and his hired man would find Tyler before him as they made their way toward the Squire's home. If the luck were really against him, they had found Tyler already, finished him off if he were not already dead, and could be waiting for him now around most any bend in the road.

The horse that Steven had ridden to exhaustion had wandered quite a bit now that it had no rider on its back, and St. James did not see it until nearly two miles from the Squire's property. It startled him when he came across it, for the sun had become obscured behind fast moving and dark clouds, and it was becoming overcast and muted, so that he caught sight of it abruptly.

He passed it by, but the unpleasant shock it gave him, combined with his thoughts of his foe being closer than he may anticipate led him to fill both hands with his pistols, so that he rode with the reins cupped between palms and butts, which could at times be as much a hindrance as an advantage. But for coming across someone heading toward him that was perhaps not as well prepared, it could be quite handy, if he did not shoot his own horse in the head in his haste to fire while his target was still reaching for his own weapon.

It was less than a gentlemanly approach to combat, but St. James was not feeling particularly gentlemanly.

It was not yet an hour before noon, but the sky continued to darken, and when the road led into a copse of woods, it was shadowy and dark. But St. James only put his heels to the horse he rode with all the more vigor, for he did not fancy Tyler lying out in the coming rain as well as being injured and mayhaps having unsought for company.

And it was in this little copse, as the sky brewed with clouds above the naked branches of the thickly growing trees and there were the beginnings of vague flashes of lightning, that he came around a bend in the road and met the very men he had prepared for but had not really expected.

His fingers moved in simple and automatic reflex to both triggers, and he raised his pistols for a clear shot over his horse's head. But his brain screamed warning and he jerked his horse to a halt and did not fire.

There were three men on the two horses. One red-faced and blue-eyed on one mount and two men up on the other mount. The man in front was covered with blood, his hands were tied and only the rider up behind him held him in the saddle.

And it was Tyler, bound and unconscious.

As quickly as St. James recognized Red and Tyler, Red recognized St. James. He reached across the narrow space between the horses and tipped Tyler to in front of him. All three horses were now halted and danced with nervousness within only a few feet from each other. St. James, finding himself hindered by his unorthodox handling of both weapons and reins simultaneously, did some frantic working to keep his horse under control. Red's hired man, exposed to St. James' aim now that Tyler was half tipped in front of Red, dug with haste for his own weapon.

For a moment only curses were heard. St. James cursed at his horse. The hired gunman cursed his employer for leaving him naked to the duke's gun while covering *his* own ass admirably. And Red cursed as he struggled to control his own horse, keeping it close to his co-hort's as Tyler's legs were still on that man's mount, and at the same time trying to bring his own weapon to bear on St. James.

The hired assassin next to Red succeeded in drawing his gun, as he had the least amount of confusion going on and had made full use of it. St. James straightened his mount, drew a quick bead on the accomplice and snapped a shot. That man toppled from the saddle. The horses squealed and spooked. Red was delayed in his own aiming as his horse danced to the side and Tyler's legs were left to dangle. St. James well knew that his groom was not light, but the muscles in Red's body that Steven had marked off as flab were not entirely gone to waste, and he managed to pull Tyler more fully in front of him on his own horse.

Then he and the duke faced each other, Red using Tyler as a shield. There was a brief silence that was nearly loud after the chaos of before and Dante heard the wind picking up in the trees above them.

His one loaded gun was aimed at Red, but although Dante was an uncommonly good shot, he dared not try anything of such precision from the back of a nervous horse and where if he were off by but a hair, he would splatter Tyler's brains instead of Red's.

Red damningly had his gun on St. James. And St. James had no such protection as a hostage in front of him.

"When you shoot me, are you going to let him go?" St. James asked.

"T'won't make no difference. He's 'bout dead already," Red pointed out.

"Are you sure of that?" St. James asked. "For if he's going to live, there'll be someone along shortly to doctor him. If he's going to live that long, you may as well let him go and let him have his chance."

"Sure," Red said. "If it'll make ye happy. Never want it said old Red didn't try to accommodate a man's dyin' wish. Don't think it'll matter at any rate. Plugged good and proper through t'leg there, ye can see fer yerself, and without no tight wrappin' he been bleedin' right an' proper. Did me heart good to know I hadn't missed."

St. James' horse sidled in unrest and his hand and unfired gun wavered with the motion.

"May as well jus' drop it, now, duke," Red advised. "For if ye be hopin' that I'll fire and by some miracle miss, or only wing ye, and ye'll get off a shot while I'm fetchin' another gun out, you'd do yerself a care to look at t'piece I'm holdin'."

St. James recognized it. "Samuel Colt pistol."

Red grinned, or at least the part of his face that St. James could see behind Tyler's unconscious head grinned. "Aye! Six shots, duke, and right quick. If'n I miss ye on t'first one, I got five more to yer one!"

"And you are but the first of a new era, I can see," St. James said. "For I had not thought they were common any where but to the officers of the war going on in America. But my groom there, you'll let him go then?"

"I said I would, did'n I?"

"Even though you think he'll just die at any rate?" St. James asked. "You're certain he's going to die?"

"Well, duke, I ain't no doctor, and I'd lay odds he's gonna live longer than you," and Red chuckled, "and certainly longer than my man you done already plugged, but in t'end, I don't figure he'll ever wake from--"

But his words were cut off as St. James snapped his pistol into line and fired with near carelessness. He could not be sure if he hit Tyler, but if he had, it did not deflected the shot to any great degree, for the side of Red's face that had been peeping from behind his hostage exploded outward. Even as he fell, his arm did not slacken from his grip on the groom but pulled that man to the ground with him, like a constrictor or a python that even though its head has been cut from it, still coils about its prey.

St. James sat astride his horse and reloaded his pistols, and he nudged his horse around in a slow circle and glanced piercingly into the woods on either side of him. The wind blew the trees in hard earnest, and it was very dim except for when lightening lit up the copse, and that was even worse for it ruined his vision for a small length of time after each flashing. A faint groan came from on the ground beside the two riderless horses that nuzzled each other as though in consolation.

St. James moved his mount around the horses, pointed his pistol down at the back of Red's head, but he was quite certain that man was dead, and the other he had shot as well, and so he stowed his pistol, dismounted and pried the dead man's arm from around Tyler. He had resigned himself to the fact that he had killed his groom as well as his man and his hands shook as he rolled Tyler over.

There was a monstrous amount of blood on his face and St. James took out one of his fast dwindling supply of hankies and with tenderness wiped the blood from him. It was not all Red's either, he saw, for his bullet had creased Tyler's cheek before finding its final target, and although it would not have been fatal, he could not quite reconcile himself to the fact that he had nearly murdered his groom. And the last thing Tyler needed was to be losing more blood.

He unbound Tyler's swollen wrists. "Tyler?"

Another groan, but the old, familiar eyes twitched open. "Aye," Tyler murmured. "Was tryin'. . .t'play. . . 'possum. . . . Waitin'. . . on a. . . chance t'help. . . . Just too. . . damn. . . weak t'do. . . anythin'."

"I'm afraid I shot you as well as him," St. James told him softly.

"Aye. . . . Felt. . . it. Killed. . . 'im?"

"Yes."

"Did. . . good. . . lad," and his hand twitched as though it wanted to pat St. James, and St. James took it and held it tight.

"Stay with me awhile, Tyler. Steven is coming with the cart and it should not be overlong." He dug in his coat pocket for another handkerchief with his other hand and tried to stem the bleeding from Tyler's leg, but it was up near the hip, the bone shattered. "Miss Murdock has already sent Ryan for a doctor, and we will cart you there in quick time and they'll sew you up right again."

"Don't. . . doubt. . . it," Tyler agreed.

There was a dreadful boom of thunder and the skies that had been threatening let loose with a great deal of fury, and the rain spattered down into the groom's face. Dante struggled from his coat, only removing his hand from Tyler's when he could immediately reclasp it with the other, and he lay the coat over the groom. He held Tyler's hand beneath the coat, the rain soaking his dark hair and pouring into his eyes.

He did not know how long he remained in that manner, but he did not stir or look up until there was the sound of horse hooves. He glanced up and saw a cart with a very wet Steven in the flash of the lightning.

Steven pulled up in that same flash, for the scene before him was something from a nightmare. Two bodies dead in the muddy, rain splattering road, pink rivers of diluted blood running from them. Three horses huddled in nervous resignation beneath the trees, their empty saddles shedding water. And St. James in only his shirt sleeves with the white fabric plastered to him, hunched and shivering over a third form lying beneath his coat.

Steven knelt beside St. James. "Are you all right, m'lord?"

"Yes, Steven."

"An' Tyler?"

"Dead, Steven. Can you find your way to Morningside again?"

"Aye. But Miss Murdock's closer."

"But we have no need for her to be seeing this, do we, Steven? And Morningside is where he would wish to lie at any rate."

And together they loaded Tyler into the cart.

The Squire had thrown in some horse blankets to carry a fallen dueler back to the stables and they rolled Tyler in these and St. James took back his coat for he could not afford for the powder in his pistols to become any more soaked than they undoubtedly already were.

He caught the three horses that had remained huddled together, trying to find shelter beneath the bare branches of the trees. He tied the two that belonged to Red and his man behind the cart. "Go on, Steven. I take it that Tyler has put your mother in his cottage there?"

"Aye," Steven said, his face blank.

"Stay home with her awhile lad, will you?"

"Aye," Steven said again. He clapped the reins on the cart horse's wet back and it moved out at a doleful walk, a dead man in the back and two horses with empty saddles to the rear.

And St. James stood and watched it go as the thunder rolled about and the lightning exclaimed through the sky and the rain poured relentlessly down. And he reminded himself that it was but noon of this dark day.

Chapter Twenty-eight

"Damn it, Lizzie, what is the meaning of this?" Andrew asked.

She had hesitated before again making appearance from around the corner of the stables, and she was grateful that she had taken the time to compose herself for instead of being able to go directly to her rooms and change out of her battered black silk riding habit (that she had now, when she thought of it, spent thirty-eight grueling hours in) she found Andrew looking imperiously around for her from in front of the stables' entrance.

"Which 'this' are we speaking of?" she asked with tiredness, for in her state of mind it seemed there were a great deal of 'this's' that made no sense and which she could not have stated the meaning of even after a hundred years' rest and thought.

He frowned at her, annoyed. "You look like hell, Lizzie, and I swear I could kill my cousin, for I am sure the condition you are in is directly his fault, if that is what you mean. But leave that be for now. Why is my carriage being made ready?"

And she sighed, for she was in no mood to argue with him over this point, but as it was his carriage, she supposed that he had some right to know. "I'm leaving here and I would as lief have a carriage to ride in so that I may get some sleep," she answered. "That is, of course, if you do not mind my use of it?"

"Of course I do not! And I shall travel with you, for I have no wish to be here either if you are not to be here."

But before she could make answer to this, and really, she was rather relieved, a footman from the house interrupted them with a discreet cough. "Milord Larrimer, there is word from the Duchess that she would like your audience."

"Yes, yes. I will be with her in just one moment," Andrew waved him away. "Now, Lizzie--"

"Oh, not now, Andrew," she pleaded. "For I want nothing so much as to go in the house and to bathe and change and make ready. Go see your grandmother, by all means, and then I will discuss this with you."

He looked at her with frowning intensity and relented with a muttered oath. "Well, I shall at least walk with you to the house as we are both going there at any rate," he told her, and he took her elbow and together they went toward the old and rapidly metamorphosing manor.

Even now, she was aware of activity upon its roof as slaters' were replacing those slabs that were cracked or broken. There was a wiry chimney sweep and he was black with soot as he moved from one chimney to the next. The fact that there *was* a footman to bear messages from house to stable seemed surreal.

As usual, St. James had covered every contingency. She had no doubt that even were he to die without their marrying that he had made arrangements that she and her father would be taken care of, and as he would have had to have done this maneuvering quite early on, the thought made her furious with him.

At least she had thrown one circumstance at him that he had not foreseen and had not been prepared for. The fact that he had not doubted that she was serious or had tried to sway her from her stated intention only showed that he understood her completely. But then, mayhaps he had from the beginning, when he had not asked where her servants were.

One only did what must be done.

"You will be staying with grandmother again?" Andrew asked her, interrupting her thoughts.

"Pardon? No," she answered, distracted. "I'll be going to Scotland, of course, otherwise I would not be going anywhere."

But Andrew stopped in mid-stride and his hand upon her arm kept her from continuing also. They were at the foot of the six flagstone steps to the entrance, and she recalled that but five days ago, St. James' hand had been upon her arm, propelling her up those same stairs to get reassurance from her father that he was not abducting her against that man's wishes.

And it seemed very long ago.

"Damn it, Lizzie! You can not mean to be going to *Gretna Green*?"

"Yes. I am. I have. . . promised. . . St. James that I shall be there waiting for him when he is at a finish with this. . . business."

But Andrew looked very troubled. "I know he has posted the banns, but what ever is the rush? It is very odd, Lizzie, that there be such immediacy about your nuptials."

And unaccountably she blushed. "It is at my insistence, I assure you." But her words only made his expression darker.

"Damn him!" he swore. "And he had the nerve to act affronted when I suggested that--Nevermind!" His blue eyes latched onto hers with an intensity that frightened her. "Lizzie, I'm asking you if you desire this marriage? For if you do not, if you have reservations of any kind, then you must marry me instead. Immediately."

He dropped to one knee on the dirt and stone of the drive before the house, and he moved his hand down her arm to clutch at her hand. "Go to Gretna Green with *me*, Lizzie! I understand that you may be in some manner of condition as to make you reluctant to join with me in matrimony, but I assure you that there would never be a word of reproach from my lips or any indication that I thought any child from you were any other but my own!"

And she opened her lips in astonishment, a warm flush sweeping across her features. "Andrew, I assure you--!"

"I *know* that it is too early for you to be anything but frightened at that possible circumstance perhaps being reality, but I know my own mind, Lizzie, and I swear that if the worst were to be true, I would not in any way hold it against you, or the child, but would raise it as my own!"

"My *God*! Andrew! Do you think St. James is as entirely without scruple as that!"

He hesitated, but when he spoke again his voice was low and savage. "Yes, damn it! For I have opened my eyes fully at last. Lizzie, I do not expect you to understand this, but there is more reason for him to marry you speedily than what you are aware! For once he has married, Lizzie, he has control of my estate, and indeed, if I were to die, he would not only control it, but would own it."

Miss Murdock's mouth closed from her prior astonishment, and her eyes snapped in return. "So it has come to this?" she asked him with rancor. "She has seen fit to set her own son upon him, is willing to sacrifice even you, whom presumably she has done all for, for the sake of saving herself!"

He flushed, not understanding her words in the least, but understanding the loathing in her tone.

"And so you offer to marry me because of your deep, abiding love for me, Andrew? Or do you offer to spite St. James and keep him from his obviously evil intention of stealing your inheritance?"

He stuttered there on his knee in front of her, the white fury evident in her face and making him feel very low, "I--I assure you, Lizzie! If it were anyone but you, I would not interfere, but would wait and take on the coward as a gentleman would--"

But he didn't finish his words, for Miss Murdock, in an rage, slapped him hard in the face. He sat back on his heels, stunned.

"When I think of what he had made up his mind to do for your sake and then hear you talk in this manner, it makes me sick! *Sick*, do you hear me, Andrew! And I do not expect you to understand, and probably you will end up hating him at any rate, if he lives, but at least I can have no regrets in fully unleashing him.

"And although I have no knowledge of how your inheritance has been set up, I can assure you without reservation that you need have no *fear*," and her lip curled, "that he shall try to steal it from you in any manner what-so-ever.

"And if you take that little integer from your equation, what do you have left, Andrew? Have you been set upon him to save your own inheritance, or have you been set upon him to gain his?" She turned from him, leaving him stunned and upon one knee in the drive, and she did not look back but slammed through the door of the house, fearing she had said too much.

One had fallen and St. James watched him driven away with only the rain as a dirge to his passing. And although with the deaths of Red and his hired man his immediate danger was at an end, he knew that in reality the worst had only begun.

At least he could ride on to London without fear for Miss Murdock's safety. Or for Tyler's any longer.

. . . I'll relieve you of the cause of your reluctance. . . .

"I did not murder him," St. James whispered. "I did not murder him." But as he remained in the pouring rain, dripping and blowing from the tree branches overhead to splatter with first large drops then small, he knew in his heart he would not have chanced that shot except for Lizzie's ultimatum. That Tyler had been dying would have made no difference. As long as there had been breath in that man's body, he would have not risked taking away his next. Even if St. James had to die to ensure it.

Until today.

And today had been the day that it mattered. Not all of the thirty-three years before it.

Thirty three years of the man's constant presence. The man who taught him to ride as a child, and warned him over his headstrong ways. Who spanked his butt when warnings were not heeded. Who was there when a ten year old boy came to understand that his hopes of seeing his parents, of knowing his father, could not be pinned upon tomorrow any longer. For there were no more tomorrows.

And a man that will spank a child's butt has some care for that child. Dante's father had never done such, preferring to wait until Dante was grown to become acquainted with him then. Wanting to know that child as a man, but taking no responsibility for the man he would become.

But Tyler had stepped in for Tyler had seen the need. And where Dante first resented his interference, after his parents' deaths, he resented him no longer.

And it was an odd and awkward relationship, where the surrogate father called the adopted son 'milord', but the very strangeness of it suited them, and Dante could not even remember a serious falling out between the two of them, for so masterful of a mentor had Tyler been that he well understood to guide with a light rein, and only check when it was needed.

St. James told himself that his shot at Red made no difference, that the creasing of Tyler's cheek was not the cause of his death, but he found no comfort in it.

For he had been weighing. . . .

You're certain he's going to die?

. . . and the scales, his life or Tyler's, had tipped even, and St. James knew if it had been Tyler holding the pistol, and St. James fighting for life that Tyler would have dropped his gun and died.

But that level balance had been disrupted. For Lizzie had fallen onto the scales. Now it had been two lives for the one, and any mathematician would have sided with him, he was sure, and even Tyler would have said, Aye, t'is only right.

St. James could have left it at that. Except. . . .

You coulda let her take her chances and at least seen that t'rest of them lived.

What would that same mathematician had said to that? Dante wondered. What would he have said when there had been four lives to Miss Murdock's, two of them children, and St. James had ignored that monstrous imbalance?

No. He had not killed Tyler. Not technically. But in his heart, he felt very much that he had.

Steven and the cart were long out of sight, but the storm about him did not abate but intensified. The lightning left off playing tag with the clouds and began seeking more interesting targets upon the ground. It was one of these abrupt flashes, boom, acrid smell in the air from close by that finally shook St. James from his melancholy.

And as though the lightning had struck him instead of being near him, he realized he was alive.

For someone that has walked among the dead for twenty-three years, it was a very strange feeling indeed.

He looked down at the two corpses that yet lay in the road in the turbulent dimness of the storm. And he felt as though he glowed in contrast, a product of the lightning, a St. Elmo's fire burning in the middle of that forsaken copse.

Before him lay death, by his hand. Beyond him lay death, despite his hand. And yet he stood, alive. His hand went to the stitches sewn into his chest. Half old, half new. What delicate thread to keep in life and fend off death. He thought of Lizzie. What delicate emotion and yet the power of it.

If one wished to quit drinking, one threw the flask away.

If one wished to live, one lived.

In the pouring rain he moved. Like a ghoul he dragged the body of his first victim from the road to the ditch. He turned to Red, rolled that man over and felt through his pockets. There was a long, small bowled pipe in one. And a small, wax lined brown bag that contained what appeared to be opium.

Perhaps the scales tipped more in his favor. If Red had lived, what abominable business of his would have lived with him? Mayhaps his death made no difference at all in that direction. But, mayhaps it did.

It hit him hard for a moment. Had it even been a question of his life or Tyler's? Or had it been a question of Red's? Perhaps evil being taken from the world is larger than the question of which soldier falls in the battle to bring it down.

Vengeance is Mine, saith the Lord.

St. James had thought for twenty-three years that it had been his.

And he trembled, humbled. He had delayed so long in snapping off that last shot. How much blood had Tyler lost while he had hesitated, weighing the risks?

There had been a chance for life for him, a chance for life for Lizzie, and even a chance for life for Tyler. And a chance to be rid of a solid chunk of evil in the same instance.

And he had *hesitated*. The man had killed his father, his mother, his unborn sibling. He had Tyler struggling for life, held hostage and St. James at gunpoint, and Dante had stood there weighing the odds, the risks, the consequences.

. . . I'll relieve you of the cause of your reluctance. . . .

St. James dug through the wet, difficult fabric of the man's pockets. He found several notebooks and he pocketed these. He dug further, found several scraps of paper, pocketed these. Dug once again, found a folded bank draft. This he opened instead of pocketing it unread. It was written out for fifteen thousand pounds on the account of the estate of Earl Mortimer Larrimer (deceased) with Lady Lydia Larrimer signing as trustee.

And he found this very rich, for it showed how Lady Lydia had managed to convey her urgency to these men. If they did not stop the wedding with his death, or Miss Murdock's if he were unfairly uncooperative, the very draft, the fortune, they held was worthless, for Andrew's inheritance would no longer be beneath her control, and no funds could be withdrawn on the authority of her name. And of course, she was shrewd enough to put a stop on that cheque's payment until the deed was done.

What a clever little mind the feather-headed widow of his uncle had.

What a spiteful little revenge Red himself had orchestrated, damning her if he should die on his mission.

And although Dante had not doubted his conclusions, he still sucked in a heavy breath at this indisputable revelation now held in his hands.

But he felt no elation as he glanced up from the draft, for the job a-head of him was a most unsavory task and he did not relish it or its results in the least.

He knew a great weariness. Except for a brief, uneasy doze that morning, he had been up for twenty-six or twenty-seven hours. Dragging Red's body was agony, and he was panting when he finished, but at least the storm began to abate, and the rain that fell became soft, and the dimness began to lighten and the lightning was again content to re-main between the clouds and to no longer menace the trees around.

He did not bury the two men fallen, only made a mental note to him-self that he would need stop at the inn and send for a constable and in-form him of where the bodies lay and that he had been set upon by highwaymen in the copse. At last he moved toward his horse that had been working its way along the green blades of the sparse grass to the side of the road. He gathered its reins, pulled himself into the saddle and turned his mount toward the junction of the North road and the inn that stood there at the crossroads, of which he had, five nights ago, declared that the daughter of Squire Murdock would do for his purposes.

He rode his horse slowly, content to let it set its own pace as he dwelt on vengeance no longer, but on justice. And he now saw that justice was a far more difficult task. For justice encompassed doing the correct thing for everyone involved and not merely assuaging grief.

What a childish brat he had been to consider sacrificing himself. Either the sword of vengeance impaled to the hilt or he would have none of it at all.

And Jesus Christ! Lizzie.

She had seen the stupidity, the utter willfulness of it and still she followed him.

He turned his horse around on the road. The inn would have to wait. London would have to wait. Aunt Lydia would have one further day of gnawing her guts out wondering if she had succeeded or were about to lose all.

Lizzie could not wait. Her vow must be made void and he must explain why he no longer needed her to spur him toward life rather than death. Her serenity and acceptance had at last touched something in him and made it quiver into life on its own, and as a patient no longer needs resuscuscitated, he no longer needed her frantic ministrations.

He no longer needed her very badly. But he wanted her infinitely.

His horse entered the dimness of the copse again, and he urged it to a trot, not really worried, for he realized that she had not left her home as of yet for Andrew's carriage would have come in this direction. All the same, he understood the full enormity of her statement, and he could not relax until she rescinded it.

St. James nudged his horse into a canter. He passed the bodies of Red and his employed assassin to the side of the road. He passed around the bend and the edge of the copse was in front of him. The brighter light of the surrounding fields was startling in contrast and he wondered how long it had been since he had noticed whether the sun were shining or if the sky were blue.

But his attention was diverted as a rider galloped hard down the road toward him. He slowed his own mount to study what was what, and recognized the horse being ridden as Miss Murdock's black filly. And the rider was Andrew.

St. James halted his horse there on the edge of the copse and Andrew pulled the filly back to a trot at sight of him, and then to a walk. As he drew closer, Dante called to him, "What has happened?"

"Nothing to you, I see," Andrew replied as he drew the filly to a halt but a few feet from his cousin and St. James did not like the angry sneer that was evident in his voice.

"Ah. I am sorry to disappoint you, Andrew, if you had been expecting me to courteously die." He studied the younger man, then continued, "I had not realized that my death were somehow desirable to you. It had not appeared to be so three nights back."

Andrew's jaw tightened and he ground his teeth. "I should have let you bleed to death than help you if I had known of all your treachery then, St. James."

"Indeed?" St. James asked. "And that hand print upon your face is a part of my treachery?" His voice dropped to a dangerous tone. "What ever did you do to induce that reaction, I wonder, Andrew. And I must ask you if it is, indeed, from my fiancé, for I confess myself ignorant of any other female on hand for you to receive it from, unless, of course, you have developed a *tendress* for Mrs. Herriot."

"I should not be surprised that you would immediately jump to some filthy conclusion, cousin," Andrew told him with derision. "But I assure you, I received it for no other reason than that I proposed to her. Which I daresay is not how you received yours when it was your turn."

"And so that is what has you so out of temper. You have been, rather roundly I should say, refused."

"Damn you!" Andrew sputtered. "No, damn it, it is not why I am out of temper. I am out of temper because I have found you out! You have been maneuvering about behind my back for no other purpose but to steal my inheritance." And perhaps he himself did not know if he believed this, but it was more soothing to his ego to think that St. James had compromised Lizzie, and for no other reason than to force her into marriage, and all, of course, so that St. James could kill him and gain his inheritance (which, he had been assured, was much larger than St. James' own holdings. So maybe there was just a bit of puffed up pride as well, a blind assumption that of course, another would desire what he was lucky enough to have).

But St. James disconcerted him by laughing. "*That* is what you believe?" he asked, but his eyes were scornful. "As if I could even *want* your inheritance, let alone spend years scheming up some murderous plot to get it. You had better go back and rethink your position, Andrew," he told him with near pity, "for you will find that upon the instance of mine and Miss Murdock's marriage that it shall be released to you."

But Andrew only felt affront that St. James put no significance upon his coming fortune. "Oh, you would like me to believe that, wouldn't you?"

St. James had been reining his horse to go around the younger man in disgust but Andrew's words made him halt his mount.

Now they were quite close to each other, and St. James turned in his saddle to face his cousin. "I am sorry, Andrew, I did not quite catch that."

"I said," Andrew repeated, "I am sure you would like me to believe that."

"And are you indicating in some manner that I am not to be believed?" St. James asked, his tone deadly quiet.

Andrew hesitated, perhaps reaching his own point of no return, but his anger and his hurt was such that he stiffened suddenly, white showing about his lips. "I'm saying that you compromised Miss Murdock to force her into wedding you. I'm saying that you have no other intention in marrying her than to gain control of my estate. I'm saying that you in all likelihood murdered my father and that you in all likelihood intend to murder me!" He thrust his chin up, daring St. James to pull his glove and initiate the challenge. St. James stared at him with blazing eyes but made no move and Andrew went further to say, "And in case it has escaped your notice, I am also calling you a liar!"

St. James balanced upon the edge of a precipice. He was nearly overcome with fury, but he reminded himself with urgency that these ideas did not spring from this lad's head of their own accord. And to the forefront of his mind was Lizzie and her vow. For the first time in his life he was terrified of dying, and he closed his eyes with a groan of frustration.

He opened his eyes, looked at Andrew and attempted to answer the charges against him in the order that he could recall them. "I did not murder your father. I reiterate that I do not want your inheritance and that if you were to drop dead the day I married and it were in my control, I would give it to the Sisters of an Irish orphanage before I took a penny of it. I have not compromised Miss Murdock but intend to marry her for no other reason than that I love her deeply and I daresay she loves--"

Andrew, with a snarl of anger, slapped him full across the face without even removing his glove to do the challenge in the proper manner.

St. James was rocked back in his saddle, for Andrew was taller and bulkier, and even the flat of his hand bore a deal of strength. But St. James, even as he rocked back, kicked his stirrup iron from his foot and swung his leg over the saddle pommel and his horse's neck. As he recovered from the blow he was clear to throw himself at the younger man and he did so with ferocity and the force of it bore them both from the black filly's back and onto the ground.

He had once told Effington that he had never been so short as to be unable to thrash someone that was annoying him, and he now set about proving those words correct. He landed on top of Andrew, both of them grunting at the impact. The filly danced to the side. Andrew's foot was still caught in the stirrup and he was dragged by the filly, St. James on top of him, until he managed to kick it free.

"Twisted your foot, did you?" St. James asked, panting, as he looked down into Andrew's face that had flinched. But then St. James flung his opened coat from his shoulders and powered his right fist into Andrew's jaw.

Andrew's head snapped back and his teeth clicked with the impact. He put one hand up and pushed St. James up by the throat and struggled to free his other hand, which was caught beneath St. James' knee. St. James gave a vicious chop to the inside of Andrew's arm. Andrew's elbow doubled and he gave a gasp of pain, releasing St.

James' neck. At the same time he freed his other hand and brought it up in a punch to St. James' face.

St. James smashed his forehead into Andrew's nose and there was a sudden spraying of blood. Andrew clutched at St. James' chest, trying to thrust the smaller man from him despite the exploding pain in his head. But St. James would not be loosened. He knew that if Andrew managed to get atop him, he would lose his advantage over the heavier man.

Andrew clawed at his cousin's chest. St. James' shirt ripped and it enraged Andrew all the more as he remembered that it was *his* shirt the other man wore. The blood from his nose went into his mouth and gagged him, and in the struggling his head tilted back and it ran into his eyes as well. His satisfaction upon provoking St. James into a realm where Andrew should have been able to master him was fast leaving him, for his cousin seemed bent upon beating him as though he were the lowest of curs.

St. James was furious beyond reason. He would have never taken half the abuse that Andrew had flung at him in the way of accusations from any other man at any other time. If Andrew thought that St. James was only dangerous when he had weapons in his hands, he was fast finding himself wrong. But all the same, St. James was exhausted, his left arm was weak, and Andrew's clawing at his chest sent waves of pain up from his stitches.

If he were beating Andrew like a dog, it wasn't only because he thought the younger man needed it most badly, but because he was certain if he didn't knock Andrew unconscious soon, he wasn't going to control the battle much longer.

St. James pistoned his right fist down in as rapid of a succession of blows as he could manage while still keeping Andrew from rolling to atop him. Andrew's clawing on his chest changed. And St. James read his cousin's mind as clearly as if Andrew had spoken his intention aloud.

St. James' linen bandage half-rolled, half-ripped from his chest and he flung one more desperate punch. It landed a second too late, for Andrew dug all four fingers into the wound over St James' rib and ripped his stitches asunder.

St. James' head flung back, his hair, sticky from Andrew's blood and wet from the prior rain, plastered itself to his pale forehead. Andrew, dazed from that last, forceful punch to his head, watched St. James fall back, his torn white shirt staining with blood, spreading like high tide coming in on the shore.

The older man cursed and Andrew struggled to sit up. He was stopped in his motion by the sudden appearance of a pistol in St. James' hand.

"Jesus Christ, St. James!" Andrew said through the blood in his mouth. His hand trembled as he wiped it across his face, trying to clear his vision. "You're not going to shoot me?"

"You would doubt that I would after all your crystal clear revelations about my character?" St. James asked, his other hand clutched to his bleeding chest.

"I--uh--Good God! I didn't think I was really correct, you know," Andrew said nervously.

"I will take that as a retraction then, thank you," St. James said in cold fury. "Now you will forgive me if I still do not put away my weapon as I still do not quite trust you with my life, you dirty son of a bitch. I'm taking the filly back to Miss Murdock and you had better pray upon your life that I don't pass out and die before I reach her." Which was an uncommonly bizarre statement for St. James, for quite obviously, if he were to die, then Andrew would probably not be fearing for his life.

But Andrew only nodded, for he had never seen his cousin so beside himself with rage. And as St. James kept the pistol leveled with remarkable steadiness upon him for all his pain and exhausted, weakened condition, Andrew made no attempt to help him even as that man stumbled to his feet, gathered his coat and placed it across his shoulders and then reached for the reins of the filly.

"You're leaving me Ryan's horse?" Andrew asked, anxious. "For I did twist my ankle, you know."

"Yes, goddamn it! I'm leaving you the horse," St. James returned. Then he turned the filly, placed his arm holding the pistol across her neck and aimed down at Andrew and struggled into the saddle. "Don't follow me, Andrew, or I swear I shall kill you." He hesitated a panting moment and then fumbled into his coat pocket for something, pulled out a folded slip of paper and dropped it on the road between the filly's black silk legs and Andrew's sprawled out ones. "Make a trip to London and do something with your mother, for after you read that, I am sure you will understand that I will not wish to see her planted in grandmother's house upon my return. Or anywhere on English soil for that matter." He turned the horse with a sudden jerk on the reins, kicked it into a furious gallop, and listing in the saddle with pain and fatigue, his coat sliding to reveal his blood soaked shirt, headed for Lizzie.

Andrew watched him go with sudden doubt that St. James would make it. Which seemed incredible, for his cousin always came through everything, no matter how impossible the odds seemed.

But with one angry, jealous act on Andrew's part, he realized he may indeed have killed his cousin. It suddenly seemed very cowardly to him, what he had done. It had not been a life or death struggle. If St. James had really meant to kill him, he would have shot him immediately and not bothered fighting with him in the mud of the road at all.

The paper that St. James had flung down lay in the mud of that road. Andrew struggled to his feet, wincing as he did so, his ankle swelling in his boot. His face throbbed but at least his nose had clotted. He hobbled to the paper, bent and picked it up, unfolding it as he did so.

It was a bank draft, written on an account held in trust for him. And his mother's signature was at the bottom. But the payee was puzzling and the amount was shocking enough to make him draw in a deep breath. Why ever would his mother have written out such a stupendous amount? And without even speaking to him about it! It were not as if he were two years old and could have no input on how his inheritance were being spent, for God's sake.

And how ever had St. James come across it?

Andrew looked up, but St. James and the black filly were gone. He turned, found Ryan's horse that his cousin had been riding near at hand, snagged the reins with one agonizing step. He mounted with difficulty and it took him some few minutes, but when he was at last in the saddle, he turned his horse not toward the junction and the road that would take him to London, but back to follow on the heels of St. James.

Chapter Twenty-nine

Miss Murdock went above stairs to bathe and to change. And when her lady's maid, Jeannie, appeared, Miss Murdock told her that she wished no assistance but preferred to be alone and that poor young lady was left to only go and lament her troubles to Mrs. Herriot.

Mrs. Herriot was of course scandalized over this lack of consideration on Miss Murdock's part of her soon to be role in life and she determined she must go above stairs and straighten that young Miss out at once, except that the imperious banging of the Duchess's cane sounded from in the parlor. With a sigh, she turned in to that old lady instead, telling Jeannie that she must go back above stairs and pound upon the door until the young Miss had seen reason and admitted her.

So while Mrs. Herriot was hearing a loud, long and irate tirade by the Duchess on the gall of her grandson, Earl Larrimer, in ignoring her summons, Miss Murdock was being treated to the devious tactics of Jeannie to be allowed admittance in to her room, which varied from the before recommended poundings to desperate pleading.

Miss Murdock looked at the window, wondering if she could escape, swore beneath her breath that she would choke Mrs. Herriot, and applauded her father for surviving without shooting himself. Then she capitulated less than gracefully, flung the door open beneath Jeannie's knuckles and bade her to come in already and to stop that infernal banging and pleading, for she was giving her the headache.

Mrs. Herriot, who by this point was coming up the stairs on one side of the Duchess, with a summoned Soren upon the Dowager's other side, was just in time to hear this loud summation, and any lingering hopes she had maintained of milord's fiancé having a gentle nature were quite squashed.

Miss Murdock slammed the door behind Jeannie as she entered the room. "No. You may not help me bathe or to dress, for I am perfectly capable and can do it much faster without you. But you may pack a valise for me, as I have been given to understand that the Dowager saw fit to bring a good many of my clothing with her from London."

"You are leaving then, Miss?" Jeannie dared to ask, for the easygoing and easily guided Miss that she had become accustomed to in London was not in the least evident.

"Indeed, I am. For I could scarce call this home any longer even if circumstances were different. It is a wonder my father has not choked me for bringing all this down upon his head. Although it was his folly that brought it on, so perhaps I should be grateful to see him made so uncomfortable. No. No stays, Jeannie, for I shall be damned if I am going to be laced to the point where I can barely breathe."

In the room next door, the Duchess was bidding Soren that she be made ready to leave also, and that her luggage be light as the rest could follow later. And if Soren bethought this very strange of her employer to be traveling without her multitude of baggage she was wise enough to not question it.

Miss Murdock bathed and washed her hair, which Jeannie rinsed for her and Miss Murdock did not upbraid her, as that, at least, was quicker when having someone helping. Then she dressed in a powder blue traveling dress, allowed Jeannie to put her hair up in something called a French twist, that Jeannie assured her was just beginning to become all the rage, and which in its severity, suited her.

She forwent her bonnet, as Jeannie did not have it at hand and would be forced to search through the still largely unpacked luggage, and she hurried from the room and down the stairs.

If Lizzie's eyes were still somewhat bloodshot, and her face still paler than was normal for her, Mrs. Herriot upon coming across her at the bottom of the stairs was still brought up short at this somewhat remarkable transformation of milord's fiancé. "Why, Miss, you are not so very bad after all!" she exclaimed with happy pleasure.

But Miss Murdock only waved an irritated hand at her. "Oh, bother. As if I care a whit one way or the other. Has Lord Larrimer's coach been brought around yet?" and she opened the entrance door to see for herself. "And I shall need a cloak, Mrs. Herriot, if you do not mind running above stairs and getting one from Jeannie." For Jeannie was still digging frantically in search of a matching cloak, not heeding advice from Lizzie that she did not care if it matched or not.

But even as Lizzie said this, Jeannie bounded down the stairs with the discussed garment in her hands, and as it was powder blue also, she held it up with triumph. Outside the open door, Bertie came to the foot of the flagstone steps, the Squire at his side, still in his dirty robe and boots. They moved slowly, for it had stormed (a circumstance that Miss Murdock had not even particularly noticed) and although it had quit raining there was still a good deal of damp in the air, and her father's gout had not taken kindly to this spurt of bad weather.

Andrew's carriage was waiting, and Lizzie saw this with relief. Although she imagined she would spend many grueling hours of worry in it, and still more hours across the border waiting, she still had an urgent feeling of haste. The fact that St. James would in all likelihood, if he survived, be many hours behind her could not dispel this feeling. For she well realized that there would be Tyler to attend to, and St. James would not leave him until he was certain that he could be made well and comfortable. And there would be the business of the two assassins. And finally the business with his aunt that would necessitate him traveling to London, quite the opposite direction of Miss Murdock, and the actual confrontation, and then of course a great deal of distance to be covered in coming back. Somewhere in there, he would have to sleep also.

She reasoned this all out, but still had this dreadful feeling of hurry, hurry, and she refused to study upon this compulsion, for she very much feared her true reason was that she was afraid if she did not leave soon, she would have word of his death, and would not even have the hours of hope that the traveling and waiting would afford her.

And if she were normally not so cowardly as to not want to face up to bad news immediately, she was feeling a good deal cowardly now and wished to delay that possible news as long as possible.

Bertie glanced up at sight of her in the door. "They are ready, Miss Murdock, as you can see. If you can but give me a few spare minutes, I will gather a few of my items and be with you."

"Of course," she agreed, but had no chance to expound, for her father, perceiving Bertie's words and Lizzie's intent, interrupted her.

"What is this, lass? You do not mean to say that you are leaving a-gain? Not when you have only just arrived and that infernal scoundrel of a fiancé of yours. . . has. . . ridden--" his words trailed and then broke off as he turned with distraction, as did Bertie, and they were part way up the steps and had a clear view of the lane, and it was the sound of horse's hooves, galloping unchecked toward them, that had drawn their attention.

Lizzie saw over the top of the waiting carriage that a horse ran with abandon toward them. She recognized it as her black filly, and before she could wonder who had saddled her and taken her out, she saw that the figure in the saddle listed far down, one arm hugging the filly's bobbing neck as a last resort before falling.

And as illogical as it was that he had ridden out on one horse and was returning on another, Miss Murdock was certain it was St. James!

"Egad!" her father exclaimed. "Someone check that horse, for I am certain it is running wild and he is not even conscious to control it!"

But before any of them could decide how this feat was to be done, or make a move to try and do so, another horse they had not even noticed spurted forward from behind the filly. Its rider worked it hard with pumping legs, risking his own life for if he did not catch the filly and pull both mounts to a halt, he would soon be past a point of being able to rein in his own mount from this great speed, and they would both crash into the parked coach.

His horse shied in desperation, having more sense than the young filly that was only aware of the awkward and frightening position of her rider hanging on her neck. Lizzie now recognized Andrew on the second horse, but more from his build than his countenance, which was blood-ied and swollen and bruised.

Andrew gave a loud curse, reined his mount into line again, kicked it hard in its barrel in command for it to make up the ground it had lost with its swerving. Then he leaned from his saddle, made a last desperate snag at the filly's loose reins, and dragged back on them and his own mount's in a manner that surely bloodied both horses' mouths.

There was a great spraying up of mud from beneath eight braced hooves. The carriage jolted forward in a delayed reaction from the groom that had sat atop watching all of this with stunned awe, and then there was a sudden squealing, shrill neighing from the black filly and an answering call of panic from Andrew's horse as their front legs somehow intertwined and both horses went down sliding in the mud. St. James was thrown into the midst of this jumble, sliding limp with the two heavy, flailing bodies of the horses. Andrew tried abandoning his saddle as he felt his horse going down, but his already twisted ankle caught beneath his horse before he could free it, and there was a great yell from his throat as he was dragged, the full weight of his horse on his already injured leg.

This whole melee slid for an eternity beneath Miss Murdock's horrified eyes. And although she had accepted that St. James may die, she had never in her wildest imaginings thought that she would be on hand to see it.

"Jesus," Bertie said as the two horses and the two men came to a stop, finally, just below the party standing upon the stairs. For a brief second no one moved, not the horses, the two men in their midst, nor any of that horrified group that was just above, looking down on them.

Then all snapped from their immobility at the same instance. The horses struggled, whickering nervously and with pain. Andrew gave a long grunt and said, "Get my bloody cousin out of this mess, damn it!" Miss Murdock, the Squire, Bertie, Mrs. Herriot and Jeannie all leaped down the stairs. And from inside the house they heard from above stairs and through the open door, the imperious banging of the Duchess's cane as she shrilled for someone to attend her and to bring her below stairs immediately.

"Mrs. Herriot!" Bertie commanded. "Be so good as to take care of that!" And Mrs. Herriot, rather pale at the sickening mess before them, was most relieved to be sent away.

"Miss Murdock, can you keep your filly from rising yet until I see what is what? And Squire, the other horse?"

"Yes, of course," Miss Murdock agreed and went to the filly's head, her face very white, and the Squire, despite his gout, moved quickly.

"Where is St. James?" Miss Murdock asked trying to keep calm but fearing she sounded frantic.

"I can not tell as of yet, for all this blasted mud!"

"Here!" Andrew called. "By God, he is just peeking out from beneath my mount's nose! Get him up off of him! But careful, for God's sake!"

"Oh, Bertie, has Ryan come with the doctor as of yet?" Miss Murdock pleaded.

"No. Damn it! Groom! Squire, hold him for he is trying to flail about!"
"The horse? He's not moving!"

"No, damn it! St. James! By God, he is still alive!"

Miss Murdock grabbed the groom's arm as he hurried to be of assistance and bade him to hold the filly in her place, and then she crawled through the mud around her filly's stretched out head and over to in front of the other horse. "Dante! Lie still," she ordered. "Until we get this horse from you!" He had come around despite everything, and had managed to maneuver one hand free, and she saw that he still held his pistol, mud plugging the barrel, and fearing that in some pain filled delirium he would try to fire it off and it would explode and kill him the rest of the way, she took the time to pull it from him and fling it away.

She prayed his other hand did not hold one as well for she could not even see where his other hand was. Only one shoulder and his head was visible and the rest of him disappeared beneath the mud and Andrew's mount.

His eyes flickered open in his muddy face and she leaned further over him, the top of her head pushing against the neck of Andrew's mount so that he should see her. He focused on her and grimaced as he tried to speak and she leaned closer still.

"Rescind. . ." he gasped, "your. . . vow!"

"No!" she cried.

"Rescind! You've. . . followed far. . . enough. Don't. . . need you. . . to follow. . . me to. . . hell. . . also!"

And she was crying and her hand went to his muddy hair but she was afraid to move him or jar him and so could only touch him through its filth. "No."

He gasped harder, and she was afraid he was gasping his last, but he still choked out, his voice faint and, with all the frantic speaking about them, nearly indiscernible, but she strained to hear him. "Lizzie. . . I. . . want. . . to. . . live. No longer. . . need. . . you. . . to prop. . . me. . . up. Stubborn. . . lass!" He moved his hand that she had robbed of his pistol and grasped her hand resting near his throat. He squeezed it hard with the waning strength of his body. "Rescind. . . damn you! I. . . shall. . . fight. I. . . will. . . not. . . give in! Rescind. . . just in. . . case. Rescind!"

His eyes would not close and she realized he was wasting himself on these efforts and with a complete capitulation to his will she said, "I rescind! I rescind! Just live, damn you! Just live! Or even though I shall live I shall still be in hell! Without even you to comfort me!"

He gave a slight nod, and his eyes closed and his hand slackened in hers and the other voices about her came again into her awareness.

Andrew clawed his way free. He lost his boot in the process, it still being beneath the horse, but the mud was such that his foot had sank into it instead of being trapped against hard ground and this circumstance gave Lizzie some hope that St. James may be as lucky.

A groom supported Andrew as his stockinged foot rested with gingerness just touching the ground, and Andrew barked orders almost as fast as Bertie. "Go! Go, damn it! For he's losing blood like a sieve also!"

"Back, now, Miss Murdock!" Bertie told her, and she freed her hand from St. James' now still one and hurried aside. Her father rose from where he knelt, his hands firm on the horse's halter as he directed its head up and helped it to rise. "Grab him and pull him, ye bloody useless footman!"

Then Ryan appeared, and another man that Miss Murdock recognized as the doctor he had been sent to fetch. And Ryan rushed in beside the half-risen, trembling horse that the others were endeavoring to keep from rising further and stepping on the man beneath it, and at the same time trying to keep it from collapsing again upon St. James. Ryan grabbed St. James' shoulders and tugged him out with a mighty pull and the horse sank back to the ground and Miss Murdock saw with horror that one of its forelegs was broken and she had not even noticed.

Then the doctor knelt over St. James. He checked his pulse and his voice was clipped as he bade that the duke be carried into the house and a bed, that water be fetched, and by God what was this hole in the man's chest, for he did not rightly get that from this mishap, and the ripped stitches fluttering from it were proof he was right.

But Lizzie was only numb and beside herself, and she swallowed the fact that she did not have to hold herself together because for once, St. James had someone a great deal more able than herself to care for him. She was not even aware that she was crying hysterically until she heard the Dowager from the door to the house above her bidding Mrs. Herriot to come down and fetch her from that sorry scene. And if the Dowager's voice was choked at the sight of her grandson, possibly even now dead, being carried into the house by Ryan and Bertie, Lizzie barely understood it.

She only knew that Mrs. Herriot came down to her and gathered her into her great bosom, and then helped her up the stone stairs and into the house, St. James carried ahead of her.

They placed him in the Squire's bedroom. Several maids scurried past Miss Murdock with large basins of steaming water, and she realized that she really was not needed in any way. She made no argument when Mrs. Herriot took her to her own room, but only collapsed on to the bed.

But she only lay there for a brief moment before she sprang up again, because where before the thought that St. James had someone more able than herself to care for him had brought her comfort, now it brought a great dread to her heart. For how else had he survived his prior misfortune except for his team of odd and mis-matched care-takers: the groom, the valet, the lad and Miss Murdock?

And Tyler was not there. Nor was Steven. And Effington was many miles away in London. Only Miss Murdock remained and she feared leaving St. James in the care of another.

But Mrs. Herriot would have none of it, and between she and Jeannie, they nearly sat on Miss Murdock to keep her in the bed and they pled with her that there was nothing more she could do and that it was out of her hands now. And Miss Murdock understood at that point that it very much was out of her hands. She had done everything in her power and if Dante died now she could in no way prevent it.

She remained in the bed crying, aware of the door across the hall from her room opening and closing repeatedly with urgency and the low voices of the doctor and Bertie, he of the steady nerves, coming from the other side of it.

The hours ticked on and Jeannie returned at some point and convinced her that she should bathe and change again as she was quite muddy, and Miss Murdock agreed that of course she should. But even through this she was aware of every activity she could possibly be aware of going on across the hallway.

Somewhere in her consciousness she was also aware of the sounds from outside and below her window: the voices of Andrew apologizing to Ryan for the ruination of his horse, and Ryan's reply back that he should think nothing of it before summarily pulling his pistol and shooting that poor beast. The duchess's coach when it was brought around and after that the dowager when she was helped into her coach. And she heard the sounds in the room next door when Mrs. Herriot tended to Andrew's ankle and his various other scrapes and bruises, some from the accident, some not, and then she was aware of his leaving also.

She was aware of all these noises but she paid them no mind except to be irritated by them, for they at times rose to drown out the small sounds of furtive and frantic activity from behind the closed door across the hall.

More hours went by and she went from pacing and wringing her hands to again lying on the bed but still the door remained closed, not even opening and closing to admit or relieve someone from the room as before. And she lay very still and finally half slept and St. James galloped dead through her dreams and he said, *come to me, Lizzie*. She awoke, startled, standing by her bed and it was many, *many* hours later, for the house was still and it was dark outside, and she was given to understand that it was sometime in the night. But Bertie was before her, holding a dim lamp and looking tired and not relieved in the least, but he only said, "He asks for you."

And the door opened to her and she went through.

He lay, face tight and white, in her father's shabby bed. There was a cut with ten stitches just below one cheek bone. The bed sheet was pulled to his waist and his pale chest was again wrapped with bandages, but there were far more than he had needed before and they extended down the length of his rib cage and she understood by these bandages that some of his ribs were broken. She prayed that he had not punctured his lungs or any other vital organs.

The doctor looked up at her entrance, his face grave and tired and bloody, and as she looked to him for guidance, he nodded and said in a low voice, "Miss Murdock. I will give you but a minute with him and then

I am going to give him a dose of laudanum so that he may again rest without pain." He wiped his hands on a wet cloth and then dropped it back into a red-clouded basin of water. Taking off his spectacles, he went from the room and it wasn't until the door closed behind him that Lizzie moved toward the bed.

She sat upon it and took one of St. James' scraped hands in both of hers, held it up to her cheek. His eyes did not open, but his tight set mouth twitched in an attempt at a smile, and she knew by this that he was aware she was there.

Her calmness returned. He was not dead. He had promised to fight and she knew the power of his will and took comfort in it. She began to speak as she had once before when he had lain helpless and weak and she had sought to comfort him. Her words were choked and unsteady at first, but they became more even and softly lilting when his hand squeezed hers and she knew that he heard.

Do you remember the story of King David and Bathsheba, Dante? And her husband Uriah? I am sure that you do, although I dare say it has been some time since you have read your Bible. But I am not going to say what you have done is wrong, or that it was right. I am only going to say that perhaps it was not the will of God that you followed.

But David, he was as you have been. What he did he knew was not right and not pleasing in the sight of the Lord, but he seemed helpless to stop himself once he had seen the beautiful Bathsheba, and he took her, even though he knew her to be a wife of another, and got her with child. And her husband, Uriah, who was a soldier, he ordered sent to the part of the war they were waging where the fighting was heaviest and there were a great many deaths. And Uriah was killed, all so that David could marry Bathsheba and claim the child he had put into her womb.

And God was not pleased, Dante. No, He was not pleased at all.

And because God was not pleased, when the child was born, it died. And although David repented and prayed mightily that it should not be made to pay for his sin, he accepted this as his punishment.

And Bathsheba conceived of another child and this child survived. And do you know what this child's name was, Dante? I am sure that you do, but I shall remind you because it pleases me to speak of it. It was Solomon, the wise king.

And so you see, Dante, God can take our own willfulness and use it to His advantage, even when we think we are going quite contrary to Him. And if He can accomplish so much when we are going against Him, think of how much He can accomplish when we are working with Him. And I think He must have great plans for you and your willfulness. I think that He has known for many years exactly how He shall use you and your unorthodox self-education in the ways of fury and vengeance, and that from your prior sins will be born wisdom if you will now, finally, only learn to accept His will in the stead of your own.

And I do not know if He will mete out punishment, or if He sees you lying here now and considers the tally paid fully. I only beg that you live not only for me but for yourself and to fulfill whatever tasks He may now set before you.

He squeezed her hand and she leaned to lay her cheek next to his. He turned his head in closed eyes searching and she followed his direction and moved her mouth to touch his lips.

Even that light touch sent a shiver up her back and when she went to withdraw, he moved his mouth in silent demand for further contact and she obeyed. She trembled as his hand tightened in hers and her mouth locked fully with his. His shallow breathing deepened as he pulled great lungfuls of air from her own body and into his. And she nurtured him with her mouth and felt him drawing strength from her as though she were some manner of restorative unique only to him. And if she felt drained simultaneously, she did not count it as cost but as profit. Her head swam as she closed her eyes and she shook at the urgency of his mouth on hers. And he ravished her mouth as though he would devour her in total as an antidote to his pain.

There was a discreet tap on the door, and with an effort she let off from his mouth. His eyes opened at this interruption but he only sighed as he looked upon her and then his eyes closed again and she was certain that he slept.

The door opened and she turned her head, afraid that she was flushed as well as dizzy and the doctor and Bertie entered the room. Bertie came to her and Lizzie arose and he took her in his arms. "Are you all right, Miss Murdock?" he asked. "For he will kill me, you know, if he comes through this to find that I have let you die from exhaustion and worry."

And she gave a soft laugh but did not answer as she was not certain if she were all right or not.

The doctor observed, "He has gained some color in his cheeks at least. That is a good sign. And he seems to be sleeping well enough that I will hold off on the laudanum."

And it was at that point that Miss Murdock was certain he would live. And whether it was God's will or St. James' will or her own will, she could not be sure, but suspected that it was all three of theirs, and who would dare to try and go against that combination?

Chapter Thirty

The dowager traveled late into the night and as it was the first time she had done so in many years, her driver and her footman found much to comment upon this circumstance. And much to be unhappy about, as they were not getting younger either and quite resented the fact that they were not afforded the luxury of a break for the night but were forced to gallivant toward London as though they were half their ages and of less than half their wits.

But the duchess tolerated no bellyaching, and she told them that the horses were to be changed out as needed and that they were to continue without delay to her London home. She, however, slept as well as she were ever able to sleep, despite the jouncing of the coach. And if she knew herself to be very weak in her old age, she only reassured herself that this would all soon be over and that she could rest a great deal longer, and no doubt better, then.

Her thoughts churned with leaving her grandson. She worried about him and only the thought of Miss Murdock being there consoled her. He had looked very bad when she left, and she knew not if he were to live or die, but she knew where her duty lay and his accident and Andrew's lesser misfortune allowed her to attend that duty without interference from either of those two men.

She was set upon keeping St. James, if he survived, from killing Lydia, as she was sure was his intent. And Andrew must not then seek to kill his cousin, as she was sure would be his intent. And which would fall in that circumstance, she did not know, but it was an unacceptable conclusion with either result and she knew herself capable of preventing it. But it meant that she must reach London before either of them were able. If indeed, St. James were ever able.

So she traveled through the night and she slept as she went, resolved to see this through to the end and to give both of her grandsons a clear future with both of them alive and hopefully upon speaking terms. That one or the other or both should despise her for interfering, she thought of not at all. It did not particularly concern her.

It was in the wee hours of the morning when she arrived and it was with weariness that she allowed herself to be helped from the coach at the front of her London home. She looked up at it, thinking of how many times over the years she had been dropped here. First as a blushing bride and now sixty years later as an old widow. And all the years in between seemed but a blink of an eye. The raising of two sons. The death of her husband, the deaths of her son and daughter-in-law and that unborn grandchild. The raising of Dante when she was getting beyond the age of controlling one of his temperament. The death of Morty.

And she remembered that foreboding she had felt when she had read a letter from St. James informing her of a Miss Murdock being sent to her, and although she held a great deal of affection for that young Miss, she also now understood that foreboding. But she was not afraid any longer. No, she was not afraid now that she understood all of it clearly.

For she had faint suspicions for many years. The suspicions had seemed such madness that she refused to entertain them. But the letter in her reticule from Tyler now confirmed them and she did not doubt her grandson of his conclusions.

She was certain that Dante had tread carefully, that he had been absolutely sure, or he would not have voiced the thought. All the same, she had to be certain also, and she fingered the head of her gold handled cane as she stood there at the foot of the steps to her own door and looked up at the mute, black windows above her.

She had to be absolutely sure.

The old lady nodded and the driver and the footman that patiently supported her moved now and helped her up the stairs. They unlocked the front door and helped her inside and she bade that she be seated on the upholstered bench that stood along one wall and that they fetch Ashton from his bed, please, and they did so.

And she reflected not at all as she waited, but only sat with head bowed and her fingers working the top of her cane and studied the parquet flooring that rested beneath her old and twisted feet shod in her comfortable, old lady shoes.

Ashton came and she dismissed the footman and the carriage driver and then looked up to him. She gave a faint smile and took his old arm he held down to her.

"To bed, milady?"

"Not yet, Ashton. I fear that we must wake Lady Lydia."

"As you wish." He helped her to her feet and together, the old Duchess and the old butler struggled up the stairs in the silence of the house.

"This is a bad piece of business, Ashton. Are you up for it?"

"Yes, milady."

They reached the top of the stairs and shuffled down the hallway, through Lady Lydia's sitting room to her bedchamber door.

"Shall I knock?" Ashton asked.

"I think not. Merely throw open the door and let us see how the snake sleeps in its nest while its poison works upon its victims far off."

Ashton turned the knob and opened the door inward, and the Dowager saw that Lady Lydia did not sleep, but by the light of a single lamp was packing her baggage.

She turned as she must have heard their near silent entering, or perhaps it was just the sudden admittance of fresh air that alerted her, a small flickering of the flame in the lamp. She looked frightened in that instance, her blue eyes widening, but when she saw it was the old lady and the old man, her look turned contemptuous.

She turned her head in an effort to hide this expression. "Lady Lenora, I had not realized that you had returned. Did my being up somehow disturb you?"

"I find much about you disturbing, Lydia," the Dowager said. "What are you doing?"

With only her night clothing and a robe on and without her stays, Lydia appeared neither as delicate nor as helpless as she normally did. "I was packing a few of my things," she answered. "I find that I am getting arthritis, which should not surprise me, although I do so hate getting old, and I was rather thinking of traveling to Bath on the morrow to find some relief in the waters. As I could not sleep, I was going ahead and packing a little. That is all."

The duchess leaned upon her cane and Ashton almost as equally bowed held to her arm to support her. Her faded eyes studied her daughter-in-law as she moved about the room. The innocent, vapid eyes that she had always marked off to a lacking of intelligence. The vain silkiness of her bedclothes and robe. She may be up in the middle of the night, but she had found time for a faint hint of rouge, a slight blush across the lips and a little light rice powder to fill in the coming wrinkles on her face. Ah, but her face and her form had once been her greatest asset and she was loathe to admit that perhaps their value had decreased to a degree, even at this late date. "You lie so glibly, Lydia," the duchess commented. "Tell me, do you think of these stories before hand or are you able to come up with them truly on the spur of a moment?"

And Lydia flushed but her eyes, which had been exuding innocence and warmth turned more pointed. "I resent that very much, Lenora."

"And I resent the deaths of my son and daughter-in-law and unborn grandchild very much. And I daresay Morty also."

Lydia stopped her packing, standing in stunned silence. The old Dowager almost believed that St. James was wrong (please, Lord, let him be wrong!) after all. But then Lydia laughed with a sudden unpleasant shrillness and it cut off awkwardly at the end. "I do not know whether to laugh or to cry to have you make such a mad accusation, Lenora," she choked. "I can see you would rather believe any thing than believe that your darling St. James could be behind any of this. For it was he that killed Morty. I am certain of it."

The duchess straightened from her bowed and weary stance. "I should have expected that you would fight, would do as much damage as you could with your lies rather than accept that you have lost at last," she said to her daughter-in-law. "I suppose you will next have me believe that at the age of ten he planned the death of his own parents."

"And I should say he may have!" Lydia insisted and she was shaking. "For he has always been evil, even at that age. It is only that he looks like your late husband that you refuse to see anything bad in him, despite how many times he has flaunted it in your very face!"

"I do not doubt that in your mind you do find him somehow at fault," the duchess agreed. "Tell me, Lydia. Tell me of my grandson's guilt. Convince me of how he has been behind the all of this even from the age of ten."

But Lydia, whose intention had been just that, perversely changed her mind. For to be invited to do so seemed somehow not promising. She turned from the Duchess, and with desperation began again to pack in the low light of the lamp. "You will not draw me into this debate, for I am quite above it," she warned. "I have no doubt that he has gone to you with some tale that makes me seem somehow at fault, for he has always hated me, you know."

"Why would he hate you, Lydia?" the dowager asked, and she motioned at last for a chair and Ashton brought one, so that she sat, but she somehow contrived for the door to be directly at her back.

Lydia halted in her packing as she saw the Duchess blocked her way of exit and the lines in her face seemed heavier, and the weight she had put on in her middle age seemed more cumbersome, and not at all the graceful woman she normally was. She went to her dresser and pulled open a drawer and retrieved a handkerchief to dab at her eyes. "You have me so upset already," she told her mother-in-law. "To even suggest--!"

"Why would my grandson hate you, Lydia? I truly wish to know."

"Because I know what he is," Lydia said without looking at her. "I am not blind as you seem to be and as Andrew seems to be. I have known what he is since he was born, for he is like his father you know. Evil."

"Indeed?" The dowager raised her silver brows. "And how was his father evil, Lydia, for I confess it quite escaped my notice that I had somehow raised the spawn of the devil."

"Oh, of course you would not see it!" Lydia turned to look at the Dowager. "He was always the shining apple of your eye, was he not? The glorious Duke of St. James. A true gentleman everyone called him. But they knew nothing of how he really was. Nothing! I knew, though. I knew more than any one! He was deceitful, dishonorable and adulterous. The only difference between he and St. James is that your grandson has not even the decency to try and hide what he is, but flaunts it for all to see and for all to be embarrassed by."

She hesitated, her blue eyes clouding with inward thought, or perhaps memories. "He had his scruples," she murmured, "but only when it was convenient to him. And when he first put those scruples aside, I thought, in all my foolishness, that it was because he loved me beyond even decency."

The Dowager's old heart trembled as one's heart would when seeing the first ashes waft up from a volcano, knowing there was no where to run or hide from the eruption that would come. But still she nudged the woman in front of her with her words, and even she did not know if it were loathing in her voice or sympathy, compassion or condemnation.

She only knew she had to be certain. "Lydia. You must tell me the all of it, do you understand, Lydia? Now is the time for you to tell all."

"Confession. Yes, yes. Confession," Lydia whispered. "And I admit that I am grateful that it is you I am speaking to, for I always feared that St. James would only kill me and would never allow me to tell. . ." and she looked into the flame of the lamp, "why. . . . That he would have it all worked out in his mind already. All the obvious reasons, all of them making his father seem entirely victim and myself entirely," and she swallowed, "at fault."

The Dowager asked, "You spoke of William being adulterous. I was not aware of that circumstance, Lydia. Are you sure?"

"Of course I am sure!" Lydia snapped. Her blue eyes went from the lamp to the Duchess. "Why do you think there were ten long years between his first child and the coming of his second? Because his own wife would not even share his bed. *She* knew he was having an affair. She knew that he was in love with some one else and she was not willing to compete, of which I do not blame her. She only stepped aside and a-mused herself. She was my friend before she was my sister-in-law and it quite tore me apart."

Ashton shifted and the Duchess was grateful he was there, for her heart was pounding and her head was pounding and her blood was pounding in her ears.

Lydia continued, "And you blamed her all those ten long years, think-ing to yourself that there was something wrong with her for her not to conceive again and give you more precious grandchildren. And all along, it was my fault. For I told her, you know. I told her that her husband was unfaithful to her."

"I did not blame her," the dowager returned, her frail voice weak and small. "He traveled a great deal. I understood that their time together may have been curtailed to such a degree that another pregnancy on her part was made difficult."

"Yes," Lydia intoned. "He traveled a great deal, but it was not always on his business for the crown. He was with his mistress. He was with me." The tears ran down her face, but she neither snuffled nor bawled nor made any notice of them, and it was quite, quite unlike the Lydia the duchess knew, who always made a great show of her distress and was most annoying about it. The drops only ran, collecting rice powder in their path and leaving two naked streaks on her cheeks.

The Duchess, feeling faint and overwhelmed, only said, "I had no idea, Lydia. I had no idea at all."

"I have wanted to tell you for years," Lydia replied. "But I knew how you would react. You would blame me. You would blame me for his adultery. You would blame me for telling her and preventing her becom-ing with child again. And I admit that I put my own happiness first. For in retrospect, I know I should not have told her. But I convinced myself that it was my duty to her as her friend to tell her. And of course, I did not tell her it was me that her husband was being indiscreet with. But I know I meant her harm all the same, for I told her just days after St. James was born." And Lydia gave a wistful smile. "That is how I know that I meant her harm, for I could not have picked a more vulnerable time for her, you see. But at the time, I convinced myself that I was doing it for her."

Her eyes met the Duchess's stare again, and they were a little startled, as though she had forgotten and remembered her presence simultaneously. "Do you see what love can do, Lenora? Drive you to where you would stab your own friend in the back for you wish to have what they have?"

The Duchess swallowed and said, "I know very well what love can do, Lydia. I have seen it bring about great good, and I have seen it bring about great evil. And all of it in the name of love."

Lydia made no answer and the dowager asked, "What did it bring you to do, Lydia?"

But Lydia only smiled. "No, Lenora. That bit of melancholy recollection is all you shall get. There will be no further revelations tonight. You have only caught me out on a weak moment, I confess, for the lamplight in the early morning hour will do that to anyone." She wiped her eyes with the handkerchief again. "I may have been a fool for love, but I assure you I never killed your son over such. Nor his wife. For she was my friend, as I had said."

The duchess was perplexed and all that feeling she had of holding her breath went from her, and she was left to sit and stare at her daughter-in-law in bafflement.

Lydia seemed oblivious to her, or of the conversation they had just had. She rose and began packing again. The duchess watched her and tried to understand what was missing. *Was* St. James correct? Or had he made a gross mistake? If only he had confided in her. If only he had told her of what evidence he had. Surely it was not just some indication that Lydia had an affair with his father? St. James could not have based his presumption upon only that!

Lydia again wiped her face, and the Duchess realized that she was still quietly crying, even as she packed.

And something about the handkerchief in Lydia's hand tugged at her memory.

Something so clear and obvious that only its very evilness made it seem impossible--

Into the quiet movements of Lydia's packing, the Dowager spoke. "Yes. I've no doubt you loved my son, Lydia. But was that before or after you had already made your plans? Was your love for him the start of your schemes, or was it an unforeseen consequence?"

Lydia turned with such abrupt fury in her face that only then did the Dowager realize that Lydia had been playing upon her emotions with her tale as only the most masterful of liars were able to do. And if she had not been sitting down, she would have collapsed. But all the same, she held her eyes steady upon her daughter-in-law. "It was the title you craved for your own son! For although we did not yet know you were with child, you did!"

Lydia gave her a look of incredulity and the Dowager nearly thought she was mistaken again!

Then Lydia laughed, and it was not the gentle, pleasantly honed laugh of an *incomparable*, but a bitter, razor sharp one full of contempt and scorn. "And I have always been the one thought of as the *fool*," she exclaimed. "Oh yes! I know you all think I am stupid! I've put up with the exasperated looks for years! 'Oh, I know she can be insufferable at times but I do not think she has the wit to know better'," she mimicked. "Dull Lydia. Dim Lydia. Vain Lydia. All she ever had was her looks and we must indulge her. Fools. The title was only the icing on the cake and the death of your precious grandson would have only been a very nice bonus!"

The Dowager panted as if she had just made this speech instead of Lydia. "*Why?*" she demanded and banged her cane. "Tell me why!"

"Why?" Lydia asked. "Ask your grandson, Lenora! Ask *him* why! Vengeance! Vengeance is why! Why else do you think I am packing? Why else do you think that I fear him? Because I *know* what lengths he will go to in seeking vengeance. I know what lengths *I* went to!"

Lydia was beyond caution in her contempt. It sizzled from her in molten words. "Your son betrayed me three times, Lenora. Three times!

"I was but sixteen when he seduced me. Does that shock you? Yes, my first season in London. I was the *incomparable* of the season and he was already married to Margaret, two years older than I. And I had met him of course, before this through her, for as I said, we *were* friends. But that had been the year before, and he had been blind to any but his new wife. But then I came to London to seek my own husband, and of course, Margaret being as she was, they were at every party, every function. And by the end of my first season, I was ruined, by him. And what did he have to lose, I ask you? *Nothing*. And I had everything to lose, for how could I marry when I was compromised? Everyone thought I was biding my time until the next year, waiting for a better catch. And the men swarmed around me and I wanted no one but him!

"And he did love me. It was not his fault that he had already married before I had my coming out. It was not his fault that he was a rare man that was not satisfied with the fact that I was an incomparable, but sought me out because he discovered that I was keenly intelligent also. He was not only unfaithful to Margaret with me in body, he was unfaithful to her in his mind and his wit, in our discussions of politics and religion, finance and history.

"And then Morty came home from University. And of course, he was as all the rest. He thought I was beautiful, but he had no further interest in me than that. Had no interest in my mind or what I thought or how I felt. But still, even then, I saw that it may one day become necessary. . . So where I put off the others, I allowed him to court me. But I hemmed and hawed, for I had been lucky for years by then. Dante had been born, of course, but I forgave William his birth, for Margaret was already pregnant when our affair began. But there were no other children and I knew it was because William was with me only and not his wife. But I feared that I would become with child as well, so I kept Morty where I wanted him, for years, the fool!

"And then it paid off. For I found myself, of course, with child. William's child. And how better to legitimize that babe than to marry William's own brother! He would have the proper last name and of course he would look like a Larrimer, for he *was* a Larrimer, and as there was but one heir between my child and William's title, my child's *rightful* title, it was a promising circumstance. But still, you see, I was content to leave well enough alone. Content to know that if something happened naturally my child would inherit and if he did not, well, he was still an Earl.

"And so I allowed Morty to compromise me, for I could not have him questioning the father of the child, and I was very frightened that he would not marry me then, but he only pushed up the wedding date and told everyone that we had courted for four years and that he would tolerate no further delay. And as I was nearly twenty-six, I am sure my family was only relieved rather than scandalized.

"So you see, I had given ten years of my life to William already. I was with his child. I had compromised myself with his own brother and schemed in great detail to insure his child's future. And how am I repaid for this? A month after our wedding, much too early for me to be able to decently announce that I am expecting, William's own wife stands up at the Christmas dinner table and announces that *she* is with child!"

Lydia paused, breathing hard. "I do not even know why I am telling you this," she said. "Except that I have wanted to throw your son's behavior in your face for years! The man of great scruples set his scruples aside long enough to ruin a debutante! That was sin number one, Lenora, and I forgave him for it. For he was in agony. I admit he was in agony also, all those years. But still, well, we shall get to that part in a moment. You will see how fully he betrayed me! How he was willing to forgo his scruples when it suited his wants, but not when it suited mine.

"Can you guess what sin number two was, Lenora? No? I can see you are quite speechless! I can see that you think I am mad. Sin number two was his adultery. Not to Margaret, for he had no care for her after all these years other than fondness and guilt. No. He was adulterous to *me*! He got her with child again after he had sworn to me time and again that they had not shared a bed since the first row they had after St. James was born.

"And not only had he betrayed me in this manner, I came to understand in my rage that he had also managed to shuffle back my own coming child, *our* child, another step from his rightful title and his rightful inheritance!

"And even this, I would have been willing to forgive. Even after this I was so blinded with love for him that I would have continued as we had been!

"But there was one more betrayal. And it came damningly upon the heels of that Christmas dinner. That very same evening we met in secret. He had shared a great deal with me about his work, and why should he not have for I fully understood it, every nuance of it. And I knew why he had been in China. I knew that the East India Company was lobbying for war so that they could continue to sell their precious opium. I had already bought every holding in that company that I could lay my hands on and people were dumping them right and left as the rumors flew of the company going bankrupt if action were not taken. I had done this already, you see, and urged him to do the same.

"But that night he advised me to buy no more and would not tell me more than that. But I pried. And I was ruthless, for the hurt of his wife's pregnancy was sore upon me, and I knew that I could see to my son's future beyond anything William would have for his other children if only this one gamble could be made to pay off, and I sensed in him that he would do something that would jeopardize it. And I went to his study when I could gain no more from him and I pried into his attaché and found the notes he had written to Queen Victoria herself.

"And there was the third betrayal. He knew how many shares I had bought in the company, but his precious scruples were such that he would see even me ruined before advise her against his conscience!

"It was very simple after that. I sent a note by messenger to the foreman of the East India Company shipping docks, who was in charge of the warehouses and all the dockworkers, suspecting that they were nervous for their jobs. And I hit upon a great bit of luck, for that man in charge of the docks was also, I later found, dealing a great deal of opium on the black market, and he feared having his supply dry up. He was very interested when he received my note saying that I knew of a way to remove a roadblock preventing the war between Britain and China.

"I set it up. I anticipated the moves. I *knew* William would go immediately upon a summons from the Queen. I *knew* Margaret would jump at the chance to escape Morningside and go back to her shallow partying and that Dante would plead in his pitiful way to be allowed to accompany them.

"The men were in place. The coach was brought around. In one act, I could ensure my holdings would be beyond value, my coming child would get his rightful inheritance, and William, well, William would pay for all of his perfidy."

Lydia stopped, steadying herself. "So you see how it came about Lenora? It was not me but the three sins. The three sins of your son.

"It was not so bad that there should be three deaths to atone for them. And perhaps that is why St. James was allowed to escape, because then I would have not been even, but ahead. William, Margaret, and her unborn child. Three for three. And what I did was not so very wrong, for even had St. James died, it would still have been William's own son that would inherit. Andrew was born the son of a Duke, not an Earl.

"For twenty-three years I have lived with the consequences of my vengeance, Lenora. For twenty-three years I have lived with the specter of St. James digging about, seeking his own vengeance, and knowing that if he were not stopped that the trail would someday lead to me. And I do owe him now, for you were correct and I did kill Morty, for he was very close indeed, and I find that his will was made out in such a way as to confirm my suspicion, for did you know that he has stripped me of everything upon St. James' marriage? Oh, yes. So you see, even if I feel a little contrite, even if I feel that I may in fact deserve to die for what I have done, I can not let him have control of all that I worked so hard for if Andrew should die and the estate still be in St. James' control. I sacrificed too much to allow St. James to own it. And he is as bad, worse than his father. For he does not even have the decency to hide his sins, but flaunts them for all to see.

"He simply can not marry. I would have tolerated his being alive otherwise. I was certain he would die before Andrew, for look at the way he has lived, and I was content to wait. But you will not be too surprised to learn, I am sure, that with Miss Murdock's appearance on the scene that it has been necessary to take action once again. Even as we speak, I have assassins that may now be killing your precious grandson.

"And then who will stop me? You? Your aging butler? I think not. For I am leaving and you will not find me and soon you will both die, for you are very old. And then Andrew will heed my every wish. He will be the Duke of St. James and I--"

But the Dowager attempted to stand at the words of St. James mayhaps even now being killed, and the specter of him lying helpless and injured, perhaps even now *dead* overcame her completely. Ashton, despite being numb with the horror of Lydia's revelations, automatically took the dowager's arm and helped her to rise. And even as the old lady rose, she turned the cane in her hand so that the heavy gold head of it raised high in the air. As Lydia spit out her final words of scheming, unable even now to see more than a minor hitch in her plans at being forced into exile, the dowager swung the cane with her weak but determined arm.

Lydia gave a squeak as, too late, she saw the blow coming. She jerked her arms up to deflect the blow, but it whistled down before she could defend herself and the heavy gold head of the cane caught her between the eyes.

She went down hard, a large round dent where the bridge of her nose had been, and she squirmed on the floor, her face a mass of running blood. Ashton released the Duchess's arm in horror as he realized what had been done and he backed quickly away.

But the dowager remained standing as she had patiently waited for twenty-three years and she was not about to allow her legs to keep her from her task now. Panting but determined, she whistled the gold head of her cane down on Lydia again. And a third time. And gasping, and clutching her chest, she brought it down a fourth time. Then she collapsed to the floor beside her daughter-in-law and her own throat gurgled, loud, raspy and prophetic, joining the gagging coming from Lydia. The two of them together rattled their last breaths, Lydia with her skull smashed in and the Duchess with an attack of her old heart. Ashton looked on helplessly and wondered however he was to explain this mess and his old heart felt close to an apoplexy itself.

He turned to the door, wanting first a steadying cup of tea and time to desperately think. And the door was opened, the chair that the dowager had risen from (with *his* help, God forgive him!) was pushed from in front of it and Ashton looked up and met the frozen eyes of Earl Larrimer.

They stared at each other for a long moment, both of them heavily breathing and immobile in their stances, and then Ashton cleared his throat and said, "I thought a cup of tea might be what was needed at this moment, milord, until I can quite get my wits back."

Andrew nodded his head like a puppet, said in a dull voice, "Better put a large dose of whiskey in them, Ashton. I tell you what. You get the tea and I shall get the whiskey." Ashton left the room and Andrew closed the door behind them, but whereas Ashton continued down to the kitchens, Andrew remained leaning against the door, his eyes closed and every limb shaking for many minutes.

Then he pulled himself from the door, hobbled on his injured leg below stairs and to the drawing room. There he selected a fine decanter of liquor, removed the crystal stopper and took a deep drink.

Ashton shuffled in a moment later with a tea tray which he set down with a nervous rattle of his age-spotted hands. Andrew added whiskey to both cups and they drank until both cups were empty. Then they each poured another and added more whiskey, and only when these cups were finished did Andrew speak.

"Dreadful tragedy, Ashton. I take it an intruder managed to break into the house and murder my mother."

"Indeed, sir. I am sure if we look closely enough we shall find a window has been broken."

"And of course, my poor grandmother, brought by the screams of my mother, found her dead already and had an attack upon the sight of her dear daughter-in-law lying there with her face quite bludgeoned in," Andrew went on with gruesome steadiness.

"And I daresay it was the coal shovel the intruder used."

"Yes. Yes. The coal shovel. And of course the only reason the cane is bloody is that it fell into the midst of things when my grandmother died."

"Indeed. And we shall have to have a look around to see what this murderer stole, for undoubtedly it was a robbery gone awry," Ashton added in gloomy intone

"Without doubt. My poor mother must have wakened to find him there in her room. Bold bugger. I am most certain he must have stolen her rings from her very fingers. Most particularly her wedding bands," Andrew ended on a bitter note.

"Yes. I am certain that I saw those missing already," Ashton agreed. "Sad, sad business this, Earl Larrimer."

"Yes. Well, tragedy happens to even the most deserving of persons, don't you agree. But, by God, Ashton, I do not know if I can bear it. I knew already, you know," Andrew broke. "For St. James gave me the proof, although it took me the most of the journey from Chestershire to here to understand the full import of it, and bade me to get her from the country, of which is why I am here. It all could have been taken care of so neatly, and although I daresay I would have hated her, I would not have hated her enough to see her dead, for she was my *mother*. And grandmother, too. Oh, God, not grandmother."

Ashton met those hellish blue eyes for an instance before saying, "Family is like one body, milord, and when the left hand slashes the right, the whole of it will bleed together."

Andrew forwent the tea, poured straight whiskey into his cup. "I need to ask you one thing, Ashton, that I am not certain I heard correctly."

"As you wish, milord."

"Am I correct in gathering that St. James is not my cousin but my half brother?"

Ashton hesitated for only a brief second before saying, "Indeed, sir, it is how I understood it. You heard a deal of the conversation that pre-ceded--what it preceded?"

"Yes. I am not proud to say that I arrived home and was determined to gain a few answers from my mother as well, never dreaming that grandmother had any clue. I heard voices when I arrived at her bed-chamber door, and I admit that I hesitated intentionally for grandmother had managed to tap her quite completely it would seem." And he gave a shudder. "God forgive me, I did not try to open the door until I was giv-en to understand that grandmother had hit her with that bloody cane and only then discovered that grandmother had her chair against the door. I take it that you were not even aware of my trying to gain en-trance in the midst of--of all of that."

"Forgive me, milord, but it quite escaped my notice."

"Well, we shall try to forget all that we have seen this night, shall we? As soon as we have broken a window, which shall not be easy as the glass must come into the room and not go out, and we must dispose of a bit of jewelry while we are at it." He put his swollen and bruised face into his hands for a brief, weary second. "I swear I have done nothing but attend to dead bodies since I dared to become involved in my brother's business. If he has done this for twenty-three years, I do not know how he has survived."

"But it is all at an end now, milord," Ashton reminded him, and he too tipped straight whiskey into his cup as he spoke. "If, indeed, you can let it rest as finished and will not blame him for this tragedy."

"Blame him! No, I can not blame him. I resent that he could not let it lie, but I wager I would have done the same. And in the end, he gave me to understand that he would allow me to get her out safely before he could kill her. I just came too late, damn it. I just came too late. For both of them. And if this is killing me, I dare say it will kill him as well. If he is not already dead. Jesus." With those words he at last wept and Ashton let himself out, having a clear idea of what needed done and leaving Andrew alone with his grieving.

But Andrew did not remain that way long, for he knew he had not the luxury. It would not be as simple as he and Ashton had discussed. His mother had been packing and everything must be unpacked and restowed before dawn so that no one would think anything but that she had been sleeping as on any other night. The fact that the murder had been so silent, just a single squeak from her before she died, he could only thank God. And also for the fact that every employee in the place was closer to death than to life when they slept.

And with that thought he realized that most every one of them would now take tenure, and as he had every intention of living in his father's (and oh, God, he could not even call him his father any longer!) house, he saw no reason why this house should not be closed after the funerals and remain closed until St. James decided what was to be done with it.

And the fact that the man that lay struggling for his life in Chestershire, may even now be dead because of him, was his brother? To that, Andrew only poured another drink and downed it with desperation. Then he rose and went above stairs to help Ashton with their morbid mission.

Andrew may have thought it was luck or mere chance that he found Effington awake and below stairs when he went to St. James' establishment just before dawn a few hours later, but it was neither, for Effington, as had become his habit, was prowling around on the half expectation that his employer would arrive and be in need of his services.

So when Earl Larrimer rode up, Effington heard his mount's hooves and peeked through the front window just in time to see that man going around the corner to the mew and the stables in the back.

Effington pulled his robe tighter about his sleeping gown and hurried to the back of the house and out the servant's entrance in his slippers. And he was glad that he did, for it was obvious that Earl Larrimer was not only very tired, and somewhat battered, but also half-drunk. And when he dismounted, it appeared that he had some debilitating injury to his leg.

Effington hurried forward, the cold morning air biting his thin cheeks and the point of his night cap jouncing, and propped a shoulder beneath the earl's arm just as that man reeled as his less than stable leg took the shock of his weight.

"Here, milord!" Effington said. "I will see to your horse if you will only allow me to get you into the house. And do not curse so loudly, unless you wish for the house to awake."

Andrew's blue eyes focused on him. "Effington, by God! Well, Lord knows I can use your help." He allowed Effington to help him into the house and on into St. James' study where there was a sofa and Effington settled him upon it.

"I will be back directly," Effington advised, but Andrew forestalled him.

"Be a good man and pour me a drink before you go, Effington, for I need one badly."

"I dare say you have had more than one already!" Effington said.

"I have, and I am in dire need of another. As you shall be, I wager, after I tell you about this night's work."

And Effington, already certain that Earl Larrimer's appearance was not caused by anything good, only sighed and poured the drink, handed it to him, and then went on to see to what needed done. As usual.

It was later in the morning when the shocking and horrible news of the Dowager Duchess dying in the night, along with her daughter-in-law, one from an attack of the heart, one from foul murder, spread from the servants of one household to the other. Effington was dressed and had his bags packed. He placed them in the wardrobe of his bedchamber on the third floor of the house, and then went out from his room as though just joining the household for the day.

Applegate met him as soon as he reached the second floor. "Effington!" the butler said. "You will not believe the most startling, horrendous and tragic news that has just come to us." And the distraught butler imparted the dreadful tidings and Effington imitated shock, leaning hard against the newel post. Then, as the butler trailed off and Effington made choking back grief noises in his throat, he suddenly flung his head up. "Heavens, Applegate! And Earl Larrimer himself arrived here just last night!"

"No!" Applegate said. "He did not!"

"Indeed, he did!" Effington insisted. "For he himself brought tidings of the duke being in a rather bad riding accident, of which Earl Larrimer was also involved. Why he even now lies above in his lordship's chamber as I thought it was easier to put him there than to disturb any of the maids, for it was late, and he was so done in that he was nearly dropping with exhaustion and I could not see him going any further in that condition, for he had ridden clear from Chestershire, you see."

And so Andrew's whereabouts were carefully established. Not that they thought there to be any trouble upon that head, but if it were suspected that Andrew had been in his grandmother's house at the time of the incident, some bright soul was sure to wonder how it was that his grandmother had heard his mother's screams when Andrew, who was much younger and had much better hearing, had not. All the servants' quarters were either on the third or fourth floors, and as they were all nearly as old as their employer had been, there should be no cause for wonderment as to why they had not heard.

Applegate's face paled at this additional news. "Milord has been in an accident also?" he asked with dreadful disbelief. "Is he to be all right?"

And although Effington understood from Andrew that St. James' condition was in grave question indeed, he knew his fellow employees well enough to know that if he were to state this on top of the news they had just received, that it would send the entire household into a panic. Although St. James' grandmother's servants were ready for tenure at any rate, St. James' servants, for the most part, were not. So Effington bypassed this question and rammed home the more important issue (at this moment, anyway) of Andrew's whereabouts. "Do you not see, Applegate?" he told that man in impatient and dire tones. "Earl Larrimer does not even yet know of his own mother and grandmother's deaths!"

And Applegate paled and stammered, "Oh, my! Oh, yes!" He gathered himself, added in a whisper, "One of us shall have to tell him!"

Effington drew himself up as a man would who is resigned to doing a very difficult duty. "I shall do it, Applegate. Never fear."

Applegate said, "You are a good man, Effington. A very good man!" He wiped a tear from his eye and turned to go below. Effington turned to go to milord's bedchamber.

And Applegate reported in the kitchens of what was even then going on above stairs, that Earl Larrimer had arrived last night and was there even now, and that Effington was about the heartbreaking task of breaking the news to that poor lad, who had just had a riding accident with milord duke on the yesterday also.

There was a good deal of exclaiming, and they all pondered and sympathized with how the handsome and likable Earl must even now be reacting, and by the time the rest of the staff of St. James' home were alerted to this circumstance, and a groom volunteered to ride over and alert the Duchess's home to this circumstance, the story was that milord Larrimer was very distraught indeed with the tidings.

And no one dwelled upon the fact that none of them had witnessed this distraught state, for of course, it was understood that was how he would be.

Effington, back in St. James' chambers where Andrew had managed to sleep a few fretful hours, was the only one to observe Andrew's dark head raise from where he was sitting in only his shorts on the side of his cousin's/brother's bed, and ask in a flat voice, "It is done then?"

Effington nodded and said, "It is done."

Ashton's job was more difficult. He was normally the first to arise so other than changing his clothes he only went to the kitchens to wait, and as was his habit, he made a cup of tea and sat at the servant's table and read the newspaper that had been delivered. He had done this every morning for thirty-five years, always folding it neatly again so that the Dowager would have no inkling that someone had been reading *her* paper, although he suspected she knew perfectly well that he did.

But this morning, he opened it and stared blankly at it and counted the minutes until what appeared to be a normal morning would become quite macabre. He glanced at the clock, saw he still had some time, and the only concession he made to his nervousness was to go and fetch some whiskey in his tea. By the time anyone would perhaps notice it upon his breath, the household would be aroar and no one would think it odd that he had needed a steadying dose.

And it did steady him, and he even began to read, a little, and when the first scream came from upstairs, by Lady Lydia's lady's maid, he calculated, he had distracted himself to the point that it came as a shock and he jumped.

He downed the last of his spiked tea, rinsed his cup, and turned to head up stairs and begin the ordeal of looking shocked, horrified, and mystified, but at the same time observant enough to point out a broken window and jewelry missing.

By the time he reached the hallway, the entire second floor seemed to be crowded with every servant employed, from the kitchen potscrubber to Andrew's valet with a lot of maids in between, and every one of them was screaming and crying and clutching their old chests.

Ashton strode in amongst them, for he was at the very top of the hierarchy and it was his place to take charge and make semblance. And so he observed with a pale face the scene of the double tragedy, and then he directed with a shaky but authoritive voice for Scotland Yard to be sent for and an undertaker to be sent for, and for someone to be sent to Chestershire, for to his knowledge Earl Larrimer and Milord Duke were still sojourning there.

Then he closed the door on the scene and the distressed crowd dispersed and he went down to fortify himself with another furtive drink before the men from Scotland Yard should arrive.

They of course went over the scene. But there was nothing very surprising about any of it. There was a broken window with the glass inside on the floor as it should be when someone has broken it from outside. There was the small but heavy coal shovel taken from the fireplace and lying quite bloody beside Lady Lydia. There was the poor, old and fragile Dowager where she must have come to her daughter-in-law's aid, but of course, for her to have made that journey in her weakened condition, it was no wonder that Lady Lydia was already dead and the villain gone by the time she arrived. And no wonder she suffered a fatal attack of the heart and died at the sight that met her eyes.

Yes, it was all very sad. But it accounted for why Lady Lydia's rings were gone from her very fingers and the Dowager still retained hers. For if she had come in while the villain was still there, then surely he would have taken her jewelry also. So he must have been quite gone. The men took an inventory of the room with the help of a trembling but brave Ashton and a trembling and not-so-brave lady's maid, and discovered more jewelry missing.

They said they should like to talk to Earl Larrimer. Ashton told them that he was out of town but would of course be informed and if they would need to speak to him when he arrived?

But no. If they should discover anything else, they would speak to him then, but as it all seemed a very clear, if tragic, case of a burglary gone awry, they could not see disturbing him when he would be busy with making arrangements for his mother's interment. "And the Duke?" they asked. "Will he be making arrangements for the Dowager or will the Earl be doing that also?"

And Ashton replied that he imagined the Duke would take care of his grandmother, but that he would probably arrive when the Earl did, as they were both in Chestershire where milord duke's new fiancé resided.

So Scotland Yard's men were satisfied that no one who was to inherit was connected with the crime scene and they wished all their cases were opened and closed so neatly. Of course, it was a shame about the jewels, for they would probably never be found, for they very seldom were in cases such as these.

They took their leave just as the undertaker and his assistants were coming in and the undertaker asked if there would be some delay. But the Scotland Yard men told him that, no, they were quite finished.

The undertaker began the task of readying the bodies and setting up viewing in the drawing room for both ladies (although he suggested Lady Lydia's coffin remain closed) in their caskets half buried in great troughs of ice. There would be black curtaining to hide this circumstance, for no one, especially the peerage, wished to be reminded that their loved ones, without the ice, would very quickly become odorous. Even as it was, by the time both ladies were taken to their crypts the room would need fumigated.

Although the servants of both households had the 'true' story, it was still agreed upon that they owed the old Dowager and both her grandsons their loyalty, and by the time the newspaper men came knocking on doors, the story had been changed slightly.

Lady Lydia had indeed died by the hand of a murderous burglar, but she died of a single stab wound (for bludgeoning was just too disturbing). The Dowager, that poor, frail lady, died of an attack upon hearing the news, for that seemed more decent than stating she had been found lying in a pool of Lady Lydia's blood.

And as Scotland Yard's standard response when dealing with a crime that involved anyone in the peerage, let alone a Dowager Duchess, was a firm 'no comment', there was no one to dispute these facts. When the story was made ready for print in the next day's newspaper, it was this still tragic but much sanitized version that was reported. It reminded no one of a day twenty-three years before when the then Duke of St. James and his wife's deaths had been screamed on the front page with every horrible detail put down for their perusal.

Indeed, only a few of the older members of society even recalled it, and they only said that it seemed as though the Larrimer family had certainly had its share of tragedies.

Chapter Thirty-one

There are times, Dante was later to reflect, when not being in complete control of one's senses, or thoughts or coherent reasoning was a blessing. For acceptance arrived at in small degrees is easier to swallow than trying to bolt a great bit of it back at once.

And so it was for him as he lay in the bed at Miss Murdock's home.

He was on intimate terms with his injuries, for the pain from each had its own character and its own torment and his minutes of awareness were punctuated by many hours of embattled sleep.

Lizzie was there every time he wakened, whether it was light or whether it was dark. Sometimes she was sitting, sometimes she was pacing the floor, and sometimes she was dozing, and sometimes she was attempting to feed him or to give him something to drink. But it was the small things that seeped into his consciousness and niggled at him while he slept.

Effington arrived at some point and St. James wakened to that man sponge bathing him and shaving him and otherwise treating him like a baby. He became aware that the noise of work on the house had stopped. And he came to realize that he no longer heard servants scurrying about during the day, or grooms calling to each other from outside. He had not heard his grandmother's cane for two days. He had not heard Andrew's voice for as long. Bertie and Ryan were still in residence, but he only caught their voices on occasion, and their hushed tones unsettled him.

He watched a fine layer of dust collect on furniture and become more pronounced. A spider in its web in the corner failed to appear to repair its web and the web tore in more places and the dust settled on it also, and in short time it turned into a cobweb.

All these small things he observed in his brief periods of wakefulness and he was equally comforted and alarmed by them. For it is peaceful watching the dust settle at times onto furniture and cobwebs. No great activity to stir it up, no great push to clean it away, but to allow it repose for a brief time undisturbed.

But it was alarming as well, as though all those dedicated to clearing the dust and cobwebs had been drawn away by some greater mission. He appreciated the peace he was left to, but he also wondered what greater mess needed seeing to.

And Lizzie's face upon each of his awakenings did not reassure him. Her eyes were swollen as though the only time she did *not* cry were the brief instances when he was awake and aware of her, and she was aware that he was aware of her.

And in this manner, he came to know that there was something very wrong.

But also in this manner he filed through all the possibilities in his sleeping mind, one at a time and in various combinations, until he covered every conceivable tragedy of one or more that he cared for.

And as a man who speculates on what he would do if his left hand were cut off, or mayhaps his right, or what if both, or possibly a leg, or his other leg, or both, or all of his limbs, how he would survive, so he speculated on the losses that were possible. And each time he only told himself with grim determination that as long as he had his heart he could live.

And of course, Lizzie was there, so he knew that it was not his heart that was lost.

This time he awakened and his eyes came open without him having to force the lids up. He was still on close terms with his pains but they were not as jealous of his attention as before, and he saw the sun was shining in the windows and Lizzie herself dusted the furniture in the room. The cobweb was gone.

He watched her, his gold eyes taking in that serene economy of movement, the flutter of hummingbird wings in mid-flight. And when he spoke, his voice was cracked and harsh, and it hurt his chest to speak, but he only said, "Tell me your concerns, Lizzie, and I will endeavor to come up with a solution you may live with."

She whirled at his words, a bit of dust on one cheek, and he saw again that her eyes were red and swollen, but she came to sit with him and buried her head in his shoulder.

"I was beginning to fear that you would never fully come back," she said, her voice muffled in his neck. He moved his chin in a gesture of holding her.

"Tsk. I was very tired, you know."

"I know." She raised her head. "As I have been as well, for it has been the most hellish week."

"As bad as all that, Lizzie?" he asked.

Her hesitation confirmed his observances even before she spoke. "Indeed, it is worse than you know. I do not even wish to tell you, but I do not know how I can not."

With some hope of easing her burden, he told her, "I know that Tyler is dead, if you fear that I was unaware."

She swallowed and nodded. "Ryan rode out in search of him and found--well, the constable was contacted and Ryan went on to Morningside and found Steven there. Steven told him of what he knew. Which was not much, but was enough for us to know that you were aware of. . . that circumstance."

"Then it is something more?" he asked, but already knew that it must be.

She nodded again and had trouble forming the words. "Dante. . . your aunt is dead. And your grandmother has died as well." She was already crying, and he knew she had cried all of her own tears already and that it were his that she shed for him.

"So it was grandmother's death that took all the servants from the house."

"Yes. For they all wished to go and pay their respects. Mrs. Herriot was going to stay, but I insisted that she go also as you were out of danger and I convinced her that between Bertie and myself and Effington, that we could care for you quite adequately. And of course the doctor comes around daily also. Dante, I am so sorry to have to tell you this immediately upon your wakening and when you are lying here in pain already--"

"Hush," he told her, "for you very well know I should have had to strangle you if you had delayed in telling me, for I would not have had you worrying that I should break into many pieces if someone but let slip with the wrong word in my hearing."

"I realized that, of course," she said. "But it does not make it any easier and I can really tell you nothing more. I gather from Effington that there was some sort of altercation between your grandmother and Lydia and that your grandmother died of a heart attack."

"Well, thank God for that," St. James said. "For I very much feared at first that Lydia had managed to kill her. And although you can imagine my distress at knowing she has died, I could not have born it if that woman had laid a hand on her." He paused for a moment, reflecting. "I had sent Andrew to do something with her."

Lizzie sat back, startled. "You sent Andrew to do something with his mother?"

"Yes, Lizzie. I said you were winning when I went an entire day without a drink, so I do not know why you are so surprised. But you must tell me what happened for I am growing tired again, you know, and I do not know how long I can be awake. Did Andrew go, or was he as injured as I was in that monstrous piece of work that ended with a horse atop me for once instead of me atop it as it should be?"

"I do not know how you can make light of it, for you have more stitches in you than hairs upon your head, I would wager," Lizzie told him with irritation. "And you have three cracked ribs and a torn muscle in your leg, which I dare say is because your foot did not properly leave the iron, and the doctor says you will most likely have a limp for the rest of your life even after it heals. Not to mention a very nasty scar across your cheek."

"Ah. Bertie will only say that my true colors are showing. But Andrew? I believe he must at least have a twisted ankle?"

"Indeed he did. And I will not ask how you would know of that, or indeed how his face came to look so frightful even before that accident. Just as I will not ask how your stitches came to be torn out so completely again, of which his knowledge that you were bleeding like a sieve as well as your obviously poor condition upon your riding in leads me to believe that did not happen in the accident either."

"And you, Miss Murdock," he teased her gently, "are finally learning not to ask questions I can not easily answer."

"I am learning, milord, not to ask questions that I do not think I will like the answer to," she rebuked. "So do not think I am merely acceding to your wishes on that head."

"But of course not," he agreed. "But Andrew? Is he at least alive, for it seems that everyone else has died in this fiasco," and as much as he tried to prevent it, his words were bitter.

"Yes. Effington said he will be delayed for a few days as he is seeing to the arrangements," Lizzie told him, bowing her head. "And St. James, please, do not feel as though it is all your fault for if you recall--"

"Hush, Lizzie, for you are exhausting me and I did not wish to spend all my time awake hashing through this now. Lean forward, lass, for I swear I am so damn weak I can not even raise my arms."

And she did, trembling, and he grinned a little that she should be so timid even when he was as helpless as a baby. He raised his head a degree and met her lips and with only the power of his mouth on hers he drew her with him when he again lay back.

Her lips were as he remembered, as shy on his mouth as a humming-bird plundering nectar from a morning-glory and all the dark and brooding thoughts that he still had to ponder were pushed back in his urgency to delve into that serene center of her. The tiredness washed over him and he gave a soft groan of frustration that he could not embrace her and roll her beneath him and turn all of her body into blushing rose to match her face.

Then the sleep washed over him once again and in his sleep he swallowed his acceptance a little further and his grief settled gently instead of churning with bitterness in his heart.

Again he wakened and the sun was no longer slanted but beamed down from full and high in the sky. The room was bright but there was no longer direct beams through the windows and so he understood it was early afternoon.

Effington was in the room and St. James watched as that man bent frowning over a pair of milord's boots. He knocked the caked mud and blood onto newspaper upon the floor and brushed them one at a time with earnest and energetic swipes.

St. James smiled at this picture of intense battle being fought between man and mud but he only asked, "Whatever day is it, Effington?"

Effington, with a little jolt of his thin shoulders, raised his doleful head in surprise, but answered with unerring precision, "Tuesday. Of the first of December, milord. And the year is 1863 if you are in ignorance of that also."

"Very funny, Effington. Fetch me--" and St. James nearly said 'a drink' for old habits did die hard but he amended his words, "something to eat. For I can not see how you expect me to regain my strength when you seem to be intent upon starving me."

Effington set aside the boots and advising milord that he would be but a moment, went from the room to secure this request.

St. James, left alone, began taking full stock of his injuries. The original wound in his chest was again sewed, and although it was wrapped and covered he had the suspicion that Andrew's abrupt tearing of it had necessitated more stitches than it had originally needed.

His wrapped ribs made his breaths tight and shallow but did not seem to impend his movement to any great degree. And although he had a great deal of various cuts, some stitched, some not, and a greater deal of bruises, he didn't believe there was anything that would vitally restrict his movement other than the torn muscle in the calf of his right leg. And weakness, of course.

He did not like being confined to his bed. He understood that the peace about the house would not last. The funerals would take place. The servants would return. The work begun on the house would continue when the workers that had left in respect for the grief of the household returned.

And Andrew, he expected, would arrive not too many days after the completion of the duties that interring loved ones involved. It irked St. James that he could not help his cousin with these tasks but that Andrew was forced to bear all of this himself.

It was not supposed to have ended in this manner. Not with Steven without a father. Not with Tyler dead, and his grandmother dead, and Andrew in grief over his mother also.

No. He did not like feeling helpless. He did not like being bedridden. And he had a sense of urgency, as though there was something that still must be done before the servants again arrived and Andrew again arrived.

And he did not doubt that Andrew would come. St. James may have been without strength and unable to control the black filly on that dreadful charge up the lane, but he had not been unconscious. He knew of Andrew's relentless riding of his own horse in attempting to prevent St. James from further difficulty.

He understood that between ripping his cousin's stitches and attempting to save his cousin's life, Andrew had reached a point in his own acceptance. He may not have understood the full significance of what he was accepting, but he must have at least conceded all was not as his mother had presented.

And so St. James had no doubt that Andrew would return. And he feared he would spend a good deal of his energy defending his own actions that had resulted in the deaths of Tyler and Lydia and grandmother. How he was to manage defending the undefendable, he did not know.

It wearied him even thinking upon it. It seemed that instead of lying in bed and watching the peace of the house shorten in time and then disappear into a maelstrom of violent emotion in just a day or two hence, that there was something that must be done in this small interim.

And he pondered this as he lay in the silence of the room.

Effington returned with a tray, set it aside, helped St. James to sit up. St. James cursed his weakness, but managed to feed himself. As he ate his thoughts deepened and by the time he was finished and Effington took the tray again, St. James' eyes were dark with his recondite deliberations.

He dozed again and upon awaking later, asked, "When are the interments, Effington, do you know?"

Effington was going through Andrew's clothes that he had left in the room in his haste to again reach London. "I believe they were scheduled for yesterday, milord. This robe should do adequately if you should wish me to help you into it," he added, "for although I had made arrangements for your own clothing to be sent down when I left London night before last, they have not yet arrived."

"That will do, Effington. And I should also wish a wash and a shave. And a cane. The Squire, I imagine, should have one or more about to aid him when his gout is at its worse."

Effington looked a little startled at this request, but only said, "Very well, milord. I shall see to it, of course."

"And how is Miss Murdock, for I have not seen her since this morning?" St. James asked.

"She is well, milord, and has been sleeping since being in your room earlier. It is the first real sleep she has achieved since your accident so I have not disturbed her."

"No. I am glad you have not. I should like a very large dinner, Effington, for I plan on gorging myself to an unusual degree."

"It would be well if you did," the valet agreed. "For I need not point out that you shall regain your strength all the faster if you will for once eat appropriately."

"Well, let us become busy on these minor details, Effington, and then I am going to have several more tasks for you to see to a little later. But we shall discuss those while you are shaving me, shall we?"

A few hours later Effington fetched Bertie and Ryan at milord's request. St. James was bathed and shaved and sitting up in his bed in Andrew's robe, and the two men walking through the door with a great deal of pained concern on their faces drew up short at sight of him.

"How does he do that?" Ryan exclaimed upon inspecting the duke, who although looking worse the wear was remarkably alert and recovered for someone who had been near senseless just that morning.

"Damn you, St. James!" Bertie said with irritation. "You never fail to make me feel like a fool for spending my precious time worrying about your sorry life."

St. James, amused at these sayings, only said, "As I believe my betrothed is still sleeping and I do not wish to disturb her, perhaps you would be so kind as to close the door."

"Of course," Bertie said, and did so. "Needn't tell you, St. James, that you have put that chit through more than her share of grief this past ten days."

St. James frowned, the stitched cut on his cheek pulling down to make him look more ferocious in his displeasure than even what he normally appeared. "No, you needn't tell me that in the least, Bertie, for I am well aware of it. Which brings us to the little request that I have for you two gentlemen for this evening."

"Of course, St. James," Ryan said from where he stood at the foot of the bed as his brother seated himself in the chair. "You should know by now that we shall be of whatever assistance to you that we possibly can!"

"Well it is not so very big a thing," St. James chided. "It is just that I have come to understand that the servants have left to go to the funeral of my grandmother and I dare say that Miss Murdock has taken it upon herself to do at least some of the preparing of meals in their absence."

And both Bertie and Ryan looked guilty. "Well, St. James," Bertie began, "we did endeavor to fix our own, you know, but damned if I could get that bloody stove to work as it should. A monstrous piece of equipment, that!"

"And *I* certainly tried to put together a few edible dishes, but I am afraid that it is not as easily done as I had always assumed," Ryan added.

But St. James raised a scraped hand to cut them both short. "I am not blaming you. I can well guess that Miss Murdock saw to it with some relief, preferring it very much to having Mrs. Herriot here fagging her to death. I am merely saying that since I am no longer on my death bed and she has at last been able to find some rest for herself that we do not interrupt it this evening but that perhaps you would care to take the Squire and travel to the inn for your meal."

"Why, yes, of course. Should be happy to," Bertie agreed, but his eyes twinkled and he controlled a grin as St. James gave him a look of warning.

Ryan, oblivious to any deeper intent, said, "Jolly good, St. James. Can not think why we did not hit upon it ourselves. We shall enjoy a nicely prepared meal and Miss Murdock shall get her well deserved rest." He gave St. James an earnest look. "You are surprisingly considerate, St. James."

St. James chuckled but did not disabuse him of his summation. "And I can not see why you need hurry back. I dare say it has been a most trying time for the two of you and the Squire also. By all means, enjoy a hand or two of cards. Bertie," he continued, "I am sure the Squire would welcome a few drinks and a release from his worries for a night."

"Indeed, St. James," Bertie said. "I am quite certain that we all should. I don't imagine we would be back much before dawn, if even then. May be better to just stay the night and allow Miss Murdock time to adequately recover."

"You understand me completely, Bertie."

An hour later, Effington returned to St. James' bedchamber. "Is there anything further I can get for you, milord, before my leaving?" he asked.

"No, Effington, thank you." St. James sat propped against his pillows. His robe was opened showing the white of his bandages, and his hands fingered the cane in his hands. "Just see to the arrangements I have asked you to see to and I should see you in the morning, I expect."

"Of course you realize that if I should run into no difficulty I could well return late tonight?" Effington warned.

St. James glanced up, his eyes dark and preoccupied. He focused on his valet long enough to say, "But that would be very unwise, would it not, Effington?"

And Effington conceded to say, "I dare say it may be, milord." But it was clear that he was less than happy with his employer once again as he dared to sniff with disapproval upon the end of his words.

"Just see to what I have asked you to see to, Effington, and there should be no need for your scandalized expression."

"Yes, milord," Effington returned. "I only hope that you know what you are about."

"It is the only thing of which I am certain that I know what I am about."

Effington left the bedchamber and a short time later St. James heard his cousin's coach driven along the lane as St. James had instructed Effington to use it upon his mission, that man not being inclined to riding a mount.

Within an hour he heard Ryan, Bertie and the Squire setting off for the inn. The house was silent about him and the night darkened upon the windows with the setting of the sun.

Everything was neatly in place. Now if he could only manage to get from this damned bed.

Miss Murdock lay in nothing but her chemise upon the coverlet of the bed. Night had fallen and the fire in her chamber had burned low as there were no servants in residence to build it back up, and she shivered with the chill.

She had intended on lying down for only a moment, and had removed her dress to avoid wrinkling it. But now, she saw, she had slept very long and she sat up in a panic. How could she abandon St. James in his hour of need? Then she recalled that as of that morning he had been awake and coherent for the first time since the accident and she sighed with relief.

A noise came from the hall, a thumping and a curse. The voice was nearly unrecognizable to her for surely it could not be St. James, bed-bound across the hall. She curled her legs beneath her and sat straighter on the bed, her hair mussed and down her back. She tried matching the voice to the other members of the house. The very proper Effington would not bang about in such a manner or use a word as foul as this one had been. And the voice was strained and did not fit Ryan nor Bertie, nor her father either.

But surely it could not be St. James? He could not be making that much noise from his bedchamber and she should not be hearing his curse as clearly as that.

The noise repeated itself but this time there was no curse or any sound of human voice at all and she became afraid. The house was too silent other than this disturbing activity in the hallway. It had the silence of abandonment and she was filled with an unreasonable dread that she was alone with whatever was out in the hallway.

A heavy weight thumped against the door, and this time, beyond reason, she was certain that it *was* St. James. But that thought reassured her not at all for she could only imagine what terrible circumstance made him determined to be out of bed and had given him the strength of will to accomplish it.

The door flung open, its abruptness adding to her fright. The form standing in the dim light frightened her completely. It was St. James, but his eyes were ferocious, his face drawn into a half grimace and the stitches upon his cheek stood out in harsh contrast to his pale face.

He was gasping, leaning hard against the door, a cane in one hand and his other hand upon the door knob. His robe was undone and half hung from one shoulder. He seemed but a mass of bandages and stit-ches and dark colored bruises. His dark hair was disheveled, his brows knotted tight in pain and effort and his eyes pried with determination deep into the dimness of the room.

His gaze lighted upon her and in a single flash of incoherent thought Lizzie had a vision of someone who has clawed their way from a grave standing before her.

But then he said in a tight, strained, panting, but still somewhat teas-ing voice, "You are looking very well tonight, Miss Murdock."

As she remembered that she wore nothing but her chemise, she blushed quite furiously. "Jesus, Mary and Joseph, St. James, whatever are you doing out of bed? Can you never leave be tormenting me for even a moment?"

But he only lay his head against the door frame, catching his breath, and she realized that the ferocity of his expression was a symptom of his whole-willed effort to obtain that brief port on his journey.

Lizzie scooted from the bed, snagged her robe and slid into it with a good deal of anxiety and turned to go to him. He halted her with his words before she could reach him. "No, Lizzie. Stay where you are for but another moment."

She stopped, perplexed. He gathered himself with an effort, controlled his breathing so that his voice was steadier and continued. "I have no intention of returning to my room if that is where you think you were going to hurriedly aid me back to."

His eyes in the pain-harshened features of his face met hers and she trembled, understanding his intent. And she stood, uncertain, in the center of the room.

He nodded as though by reading only her expression he knew that she had digested all that he had not spoken. "I can see that I am quite terrifying you already," he chided.

"I am not terrified," she said. "I am only--only--Oh, damn you, St. James! I do not know what I am. I only know that you are in no condition. And neither am I, I dare say."

His lips quirked as with his resting there against the door frame he was able to leave go his dreadful concentration for a moment. "I admit it is not quite how I had foreseen it, but I dare say we shall manage adequately."

Lizzie's face flamed at even the brief picture this brought to mind. "Hush!" she said. "I swear you must be delirious to even consider it." But she bowed her head for she could not meet the amused tenderness in his eyes without it blinding her beyond reason.

"I really do not think it can wait, Lizzie," he continued and his voice was very gentle. "And although I know that must shock you to a great degree, I must point out that I am very much afraid that as early as tomorrow or the next day at the latest this now peaceful house is going to be swarmed once again. And although it would irk me considerably to wait until we were married, I would wait if it were only that. But I am also afraid that my attention is going to be taken considerably up with dealing with my cousin when he arrives. And I've no doubt that you shall be doing as much as possible to prop him up also until he gets through this.

"And I am equally certain that if we delay until this circumstance is behind us that there will be yet another circumstance that will necessitate another delay and so on and so forth. For I am beginning to believe, Lizzie dear, that life is no easier to deal with than death.

"And if you are afraid that God will be frowning quite displeased from His throne, I can only point out that Effington is about making the arrangements and getting the proper paperwork so that our waiting period may begin even as we speak and so that we shall marry as soon as possible at any rate. Sooner, I believe, than I would manage a journey to Gretna Green in my condition, otherwise, we would be on our way there even now. And of course," he added, self-mocking, "I am certain that God is fully aware that he is not working with a saint here at any rate."

"St. James!"

But he only grinned a little. "Hush, Lizzie, and let me finish, shall you, dear, and then, I promise you, I shall allow you to have the last word."

It occurred to her that for the moment, propriety ruled, and he would not cross her door frame unless she allowed it. That realization made her tremble all the more.

"That is not to say that I do not fully know of what I ask of you." His voice changed from caressing indulgence to intense imparting, and she nearly flinched, but her brown eyes were no longer dropped from him but were held steady by his as he spoke. "For I well understand that even the best of intentions is not a guarantee that something will not happen that will prevent me from wedding you in as speedy a manner as I can arrange. After a week in my company, I am sure that you are equally aware of that possibility.

"The consequences could in fact be damning for you," he warned. "And although you have said you have no care that I have tried ruining you, I think you will find that the appearance of being ruined and the actuality of it are far different."

And she did flinch at that, but took a step toward him.

"No, Lizzie. Let me finish!" he told her, his voice rough. "For once you allow me through this door, I will no longer be taking into consideration any of these things. I have cleared the house of everyone. There is no one here but ourselves. For you must know I would not come to you if there were any chance of our being interrupted or your being embarrassed or shamed. But there will be suspicions, Lizzie, for they are bright and I am certain that there will be little signs on the morrow that we will be helpless to stop that will show that neither of us spent the night gently sleeping. You must be prepared for that also. Although we are to be shortly married, I am sure it will be remembered. Your father, particularly--"

But she swept forward and although she only stopped and stood in front of him, looking at him, her presence there was enough for him to cut short his words with a little groan and a click of his teeth.

He stared down at her and she stared up. Still he did not reach for her although his eyes blazed with a fire that seemed to scald her. She swallowed in effort to make her voice steady and then she only said, "Yes."

With that single word he placed his hand upon her shoulder and leaning upon his cane in his other hand, he moved into the room. He turned slightly, and his weight was heavy upon her shoulder for that second, and he caught the door with the tip of his cane and swung it closed behind him with he and Lizzie upon one side of it, and the rest of the world upon the other.

With the closing of that door, he seemed in no hurry at all, only leaned upon his cane once again, took his hand from her shoulder and moved it to cup her chin. "Come to me, Lizzie," he told her. "For tonight is our moment of brief, eternal silence between the lightning's striking and the rolling of the thunder. There will be no distraction for me tonight and my attention will be upon you fully. For this one night we shall live in a cottage surrounded by gardens and there will be no other consideration except for how we care for each other."

Chapter Thirty-two

It was a difficult interview with Andrew when he arrived, but St. James had not foreseen it as any but such. For some truths are so difficult to accept that one searches with eagerness for lies if only to console oneself. Although Andrew had matured to a degree that he recognized this tendency, it still seemed they had to go over many points repeatedly for the full import to settle long enough to be digested.

Even with the most of his mother's confessions still fresh in his mind, his grief over her death and his grandmother's was enough to induce him to make certain accusations. Accusations that St. James had sent grandmother in his stead. Accusations that St. James had been blinded by rage and furious vendetta and had never had any intention other than murdering Andrew's mother outright.

Of which St. James replied, "Indeed, you are correct, Andrew. Up until the moment I gave you the draft made out on your account held in trust by her, I had every intention of stomping her into a lifeless mass upon the floor. For I dare say that shooting her would not have satisfied me in the least."

And if this brutal summary made Andrew blanche and become sickened with disgust, reminding him of how his mother had died, it also held such a ring of unsuppressed truth that he knew St. James' further answers were equally as honest.

It was not a matter for a single afternoon, nor even a single day, nor week, nor as St. James reflected, even a single lifetime. But Andrew did not leave the Squire's home for many days, and his willingness to be there said much about that young man's character.

Miss Murdock did not interfere with these meetings, which began in the Squire's bedchamber and as the week progressed moved to the parlor and then to slow walks outside in the cold air. December was advancing as was Christmas. As was the twenty-fourth anniversary of the deaths of William Desmond Larrimer and his wife and their unborn child.

But Miss Murdock only left St. James to his business and she went about her own. Mrs. Herriot returned as did Jeannie and the other staff. Miss Murdock tolerated the cook and she kept on one maid and Jeannie, but she convinced Mrs. Herriot to return to Morningside and ensure that it was made ready, for the duke would be returning there for the holidays.

And as Mrs. Herriot was not quite bold enough to ask Miss Murdock if she would be returning with him, Miss Murdock left that unasked question equally unanswered.

For the most part, Lizzie managed to keep the house in some degree of peace.

She did not ask St. James of his conversations with Andrew, but she came to understand that Andrew had learned much more of the true circumstances of St. James' parents' deaths than St. James had ever fathomed, and many evenings St. James spent alone, only silently brooding in his room.

He came to her no more in the night, and she knew that he would not. It was one thing for those other members of the household to have their suspicions, it was quite another to risk actual detection, and she knew he would not do that to her. But she was satisfied that what he had sought she had supplied and throughout all these long days of reckoning, it seemed to be sustaining him in a way that she did not understand.

Only on occasion when he came out of his deep preoccupations did he flash her a look from his gold eyes that was intense with remembered pleasure and bright with anticipated renewal did she then falter in whatever she may be doing and only stand blushing beneath his gaze.

But for now, it was very much as he had foreseen and they were both taken up with the task of helping Andrew find some semblance of order in a world that had been torn apart, very much as St. James' had been at the age of ten.

But there came a day when further discussion would reveal no more truths, and that the dust must again settle and on that day, Andrew ordered his coach made ready, for it had remained at the Squire's after Effington's use of it and return.

And Andrew dressed for leaving and when he was ready he went down the hall to St. James' bedroom and knocked upon the door. Effington opened it and St. James looked up from where he was reading the Bible in a chair near the window. His stitches had been cut from his cheek, but the scar was thick and shiny with newness, and Andrew still flinched each time he looked at it. St. James' words came back to him, for he had said with a strange twist to his mouth when conversation had turned to what could be called nothing so much as a 'conversation piece' that he considered it very much his 'Tyler scar'.

And although Andrew could not fathom why St. James should determine it as such, he had observed that his normal habit of rubbing his upper lip with the tip of his finger when deep in thought had metamorphosed into a rubbing of this shiny scar upon his cheek instead.

St. James looked at him now and something about the expression in Andrew's face caused the tip of his finger to rub with thoughtfulness up that scar. "Leave us, Effington, and see if Miss Murdock is in need of assistance, as I still do not like how drastically she has reduced the staff of the house."

And Effington only bowed out and closed the door behind Andrew.

Andrew, at a loss for words at this abrupt setting of mood in the room, turned and paced a little. And he almost stopped when he realized how much his action mirrored the habit of the man that sat across the bedchamber from him. But he continued, for he did find it a good means to pace thoughts that were running so quickly through his head that he feared he would lose the full significance of them in their rapidity.

And it was frightening to think at such speed that he felt that he would reach a conclusion without having a clear idea of what avenues he had used to attain it. And indeed, he found that he was at the conclusion and that in his pacing he was thinking backward, finding the roads that had led him there and going over them and testing them for soundness and his thinking was only verification for what he had already come to know as true.

And it was disquieting to him to think that whenever his brother had paced and Andrew had thought it was in effort to reach a decision, St. James had in reality already made his decision and had only been back-testing it in his mind with dreadful and calculating determination to make sure that it was the absolute soundest decision he could make.

For a twenty-three year old young man the questioning of his own impetuousness was a new experience for him. And St. James, he guessed with bitterness, had been doing such since he was ten.

With this thought he turned and spoke to the waiting man who had observed all this pacing in silence, only rubbing his scar.

"There is something I have held back from you, St. James," Andrew began.

"Indeed?" St. James said. "And I gather now that you think it may be of some importance to me."

"Yes," Andrew returned. "As it is, I might add, important to me. I have not told you for, frankly, I was not certain how I felt about this little wrinkle myself."

"And you have come to some kind of terms with this as yet untold revelation?" St. James asked and Andrew could see that despite himself, the duke was very puzzled.

"You are my half-brother, St. James. It seems that the affair I spoke of that my mother had with your father in fact produced me."

St. James looked at him for a long moment and his only indication that he understood what Andrew had said was a slight cocking of his head. And Andrew felt his face redden a little at this response, or lack of it. "Really, St. James, I did not expect transports of joy from you, and I understand that you will probably in no way know how you feel about such a circumstance since I myself am only now coming to terms with it--"

But St. James cut him off with a tender word, a small smile playing about his lips. "Whist, Andrew. I am only in my mind bewailing the fact that my favorite pony has been dead for some years."

Andrew did not quite understand what his words meant, but he understood that when St. James rose from his chair with the help of his cane and turned to the window for a moment that it was so Andrew could not see the extent of emotion upon his face. Then St. James' voice came to him, low and once again in control. "And as you have held this knowledge for a time when I have not, perhaps you can guide me by telling me how you yourself feel about this circumstance."

Andrew went forward and his hand fell upon St. James' shoulder and his voice was not as in control as his brother's so that it came out sounding choked. "I am, myself, feeling very blessed to find that I have a brother. If you yourself think that there may come a day when you in fact would wish to call me--"

But he didn't continue for St. James turned and of mutual accord they embraced each other and they were both a little relieved that there was no one in the room to see the two remaining Larrimers clapping each other on the back and surreptitiously wiping at damp eyes.

They pulled apart after a brief minute and retreated self-consciously from each other. Andrew began pacing again and St. James returned to his chair, his damaged leg stretched before him, giving him an indolent demeanor even when he did not intend it.

"Damn, St. James," Andrew said when he felt as though his voice were normal again. "I wish I had told you that before, for I feel as though I have just awakened from some manner of nightmare."

"You told me when it was the proper time, Andrew," St. James told him. "For there were too many questions in your mind and I dare say part of you realized that we would never truly be brothers unless we ourselves acknowledged it and you were cautious of that state of affairs."

"You are right of course. And indeed, the last few days I have had some fear that you should balk at acknowledging it yourself."

"Never," St. James said with sureness. "For you have been a lot less misguided than I have been."

Andrew let out a bitter laugh and paused in his pacing to throw his brother a fierce look. "I have been misguided my entire life it turns out, St. James. I never knew who my father was for twenty-three years--"

But again he stopped for St. James' face became pained and the frown between his eyes appeared as startling as a storm cloud out of blue skies. He glanced up at Andrew's abrupt halt in speech. "Neither, apparently, have I known who my father was for twenty-three years, either, Andrew. But that will have to wait." And he smiled again as he focused on his brother across from him. "You can not leave now, you know, Andrew, for I am getting married this evening and I would not have my own brother miss it."

Andrew, taken a bit off stride by this announcement, said faintly, "To Miss Murdock of course." And then, feeling very slow indeed, he accused, "You had put it off because of my being here."

"Yes. I did, Andrew. We both agreed that we would not rub our happiness in your face when you needed us. And quite frankly, I feared it would take something from our happiness when we would surely feel that you were perfectly miserable while we were saying our 'I do's'."

"Devil take you, St. James," Andrew growled. "I know that you may have your doubts, but I really do not begrudge your marrying her at all.

I have come to realize that she would have beaten me into submission within a week if she had accepted my proposal."

St. James gave a rude laugh. "And I assure you, it was not with any thought that you would be jealous that we held off on the ceremony. I was merely indicating that we realized that you have been in a great deal of grief and that happy weddings are not necessarily a welcome sight when one is feeling that low."

"Well you have been feeling as low yourself," Andrew pointed out. "Oh, you have done an admirable job of being strong so that I could fall apart like some ninny, but I assure you, I have not been unaware of the effort it has cost you, and indeed I can not properly convey how much in your debt I am."

"Do not speak of debt, Andrew," St. James warned, "for we will open up that whole discussion again, as to who should pay and why. Let us just say that I did it with no hardship and would do it again even if I had never learned you were my brother. And I admit that I bent the rules slightly and availed myself of some sustenance for I foresaw that none of this would be easy. But that is a private matter and I shall not go into it. Just let it rest that I have not been as entirely miserable as I should have rightfully been or as you have been."

Andrew gave him an odd look, but St. James only added, "Stay for the wedding, Andrew, if you feel up to it, for I should like very much for you to be there."

"How did you know I was leaving today?" Andrew asked, a little suspicious. "For I did not even realize it myself until I rose from my bed this morning."

And St. James colored in what Andrew almost would have termed as a blush, but of course that was quite impossible, St. James *being* St. James. "I confess, I have had a minister on hand for days now. Ever since the waiting period was fulfilled."

For some reason, which he could not explain, Andrew found this very funny. It felt good to laugh and at the end of his laughter, he wiped his eyes on his sleeve and said, "Then of course I shall stay, and you shall get married for I can not see that poor minister having to cool his heels awaiting your whim any longer."

St. James sat for a long time after his brother left the room. And if he felt a good deal of quiet amazement as though he were a child again and was discovering many things that adults took for granted, he still had knowledge that there were one or two things that must be seen to. There was Steven and his family. He had kept tabs through a messenger sent to Morningside and knew that they were still residing there in Tyler's cottage. He had not had much time to consider further from there, and he knew himself well enough to know that he would not be spending the remainder of the day, his wedding day, or tonight considering it either. So he settled with reminding himself that he would need to think about that at first light tomorrow, and indeed, he doubted that Miss Murdock would throw a fit if they forwent their honeymoon and traveled straight to Morningside at any rate.

But the other detail, although he could not take care of it entirely, could at least be partially seen to even then, and so thinking that, he got up from the chair, moved with his cane to a desk in the corner of the Squire's room and found the necessary items to write a letter. This he composed with no joy but with enough detail to allow Queen Victoria to understand that although her fears had not been unfounded and there had been a leak in her security, that it had been in fact his own father, who was obviously no longer discussing the crown's policies with anyone.

It was not a pleasant letter to write but he was at least able to inform her that he would be forwarding some materials to her that she may find interesting and that may lead to the breaking up of a significant opium ring. He closed it by reiterating that he would still gladly be at her service if she still deemed it desirable that he should be and that he was now available to take up these said duties at her convenience.

He had no more than finished this missive and sealed it when Effington came in and informed him that the minister would be there in an hour and that perhaps milord would care to begin dressing?

"And what abominable outfit do you have in mind for me tonight?" St. James asked.

"Well, milord," Effington began and he rubbed his hands together as he spoke, "as I have had some knowledge, of course, of your coming nuptials, being as it was I that made all the arrangements, I have of course had time to collect and put together a rather stunning attire for you tonight."

"Your glee is not reassuring me in the least, Effington."

"Of course you have my deepest sympathies for making you apprehensive, milord," Effington told him. "But be that as it may," and he walked to the wardrobe and opened it in his precise way and with a flourish removed the costume that he had spent a deal of time considering before settling upon as the proper attire for milord Duke of St. James' wedding ceremony.

And St. James blinked once, in an unusual display of dumbfoundedness. "That?" he asked. "Effington, you selected that?"

"Why, yes, milord. Do you not care for it?"

But St. James only laughed for in Effington's hands was a new shirt, plainly white with the only adornment being lace at cuffs and cravat and a pair of tanned breeches.

"Of course, milord," Effington explained as though he could not believe the perfect sense of it had escaped his employer, "for one can not know when one may be faced with a predicament which will necessitate the removal of your clothing, and it would be so much waste if perhaps in haste a very fine outfit should become torn. Of course, I am hoping that you shall not somehow become injured and *bleed* upon them as well as ripping them--"

But St. James waved his hand as he tried to control his laughter, and he choked out, "Very well, Effington. I quite see your point. And as usual, your choice of clothing is beyond reproach. I only ask that if Miss Murdock should question your choice that you do not place before her the reasons you are currently placing in front of me!"

"Indeed, I would not, milord," Effington replied, affronted. "For I am much too discreet."

"Indeed, Effington, that you have proven to be. You may go now, and see that my betrothed has all that she needs."

"Milord. You do not wish me to help with your attire?"

"I believe I can manage adequately, Effington, as I have all these years before."

Effington restrained his urge to argue, only nodded. But before he turned to leave, he added, "Congratulations, milord."

St. James turned to him at his words. "Thank you, Effington. You shall be there as a witness, of course."

"Thank you, milord. I would be honored."

With that he left the room, and St. James stood for a brief moment in the silence. Then he busied himself with readying, for Lizzie was waiting.

Finite.